# KNITORIOUS MURDER MYSTERIES BOOKS 10-12

*A Knitorious Murder Mysteries Collection*

## REAGAN DAVIS

# COPYRIGHT

ISBN: 978-1-990228-39-1 (ebook)

ISBN: 978-1-990228-38-4 (print)

# CONTENTS

## IN STITCHNESS AND IN HEALTH

## BAIT & STITCH

## MURDER IT SEAMS

# In Stitchness
## and in
# Health

# REAGAN DAVIS

# COPYRIGHT

ISBN: 978-1-990228-08-7 (ebook)

ISBN: 978-1-990228-09-4 (paperback)

ISBN: 978-1-990228-32-2 (hardcover)

ISBN: 978-1-990228-33-9 (large print paperback)

# FOREWORD

Dear Reader,

Despite several layers of editing and proofreading, occasionally a typo or grammar mistake is so stubborn that it manages to thwart my editing efforts and camouflage itself amongst the words in the book.

If you encounter one of these obstinate typos or errors in this book, please let me know by contacting me at Hello@ReaganDavis.com.

Hopefully, together we can exterminate the annoying pests.

Thank you!
Reagan Davis

# CHAPTER 1

THURSDAY, December 16th

There's a low-key hum of restless energy running through Harmony Lake. It vibrates through me the same way an approaching train does moments before it's visible from the station platform.

On the outside, Harmony Lake is a life-sized snow globe—a cozy, postcard-worthy winter wonderland. But on the inside, we're on the brink of chaos. Next week, hundreds of A-list celebrities will descend on our sweet, snowy town. Hundreds of paparazzi from around the world will follow them, for what the media has dubbed, *The Celebrity Wedding of the Century.*

World-famous actor Jules Janssen and her equally famous and beautiful fiancé have chosen Harmony Lake as the venue for their much-anticipated Christmas Eve wedding. They've booked every hotel, motel, vacation rental, and bed-and-breakfast in town for the comfort of their VIP guests, and to prevent the parasitic paparazzi from finding local accommodation. They want to get married in peace. The love-struck couple wants a private, intimate affair with only several hundred of their nearest and dearest.

"Are you going to ask for autographs?" April asks, gazing into the distance and daydreaming about the celebrities who will venture into her bakery, Artsy Tartsy.

April is my best friend. We've known each other since I moved to Harmony Lake almost twenty years ago. We met at a mummy-and-me playgroup when our daughters were babies.

"I haven't thought about it," I reply.

"T says it's tacky to ask for autographs." April crosses her arms in front of her chest and huffs. "Like T wouldn't ask for an autograph if Oprah walked into our bakery. Or George Clooney," she adds under her breath.

T is April's wife. Her full name is Tamara, but everyone calls her T. She's Artsy Tartsy's talented pastry chef, and she's less star-struck than April, which isn't saying much. Most people are less star-struck than April. She's the most dedicated celebrity-watcher I know.

"It's too quiet," I comment. "I miss the pre-Christmas hustle and bustle. It's peaceful without any tourists, but it's also kind of eerie."

Harmony Lake is a tourist town. City escapees flock to our lake in the summer and our mountains in the winter. This should be one of the busiest weeks of the year, but without tourists, my yarn store, Knitorious, is dead. Local knitters have already purchased the yarn and supplies they need for Christmas knitting, and now they're nestled snugly at home, knitting as fast as they can to beat the Christmas Eve deadline.

"Enjoy the quiet while you can. It'll be plenty busy this weekend when the celebrities arrive!" April rubs her hands in front of her. "Imagine the rich and famous wandering in and out of Knitorious, asking you knitting questions and touching everything." Her blue eyes are bright, and her voice is giddy, like a kid on Christmas morning.

"Easy for you to say," I say. "Artsy Tartsy is so busy baking for the wedding that you had to hire a second pastry chef to help. And everybody loves dessert, so the bakery will have lots of customers. I doubt our famous visitors will be as hungry for yarn and knitting supplies as for T's delicious desserts." I sigh. "This wedding will be a media circus. I can't wait until Harmony Lake goes back to normal."

"Knitorious has benefitted from the wedding too," April reminds me. "You said your online sales are way up over last December."

"They are," I admit. "And I'm grateful, but I still miss the in-person customers."

Online business is booming, thanks to the publicity from Jules Janssen's upcoming nuptials. Online orders are through the roof, and Knitorious is trending toward having our best December in history. But I still miss the tourists. Other local businesses, like Artsy Tartsy, are busy preparing for the wedding. It's unfortunate for me that Jules Janssen's star-studded celebration doesn't require yarn or needlework supplies.

The tourists bring a certain energy with them, though, and that energy is part of what makes Harmony Lake feel like home. We need the tourists, and they need us.

"Speaking of weddings," April says, crossing her arms in front of her chest and tilting her head so her long blonde ponytail swings like a pendulum. "Have you set a date yet?" She arches her eyebrows. "You've put off picking a date every month since you and Eric got engaged. What's the hold up?"

"We're working on it," I reply, trying not to smirk.

This might be another reason I don't share everyone's

collective enthusiasm for Jules Janssen's wedding. It's a constant reminder that *I* need to plan a wedding.

I love Eric, and I can't wait to marry him, but I'm not looking forward to planning the wedding. We've both been married before, and we've both done the big-wedding thing. Just thinking about all the planning, decisions, and details that are necessary to pull off even a simple wedding makes me want to elope. But eloping isn't an option, we already discussed it. We'd never stop hearing about it from our friends and family, and to be honest, I can't imagine getting married without them. We want everyone we love to be there. Since it's unlikely the universe will send us a Christmas miracle disguised as a fully planned wedding with all the details pre-arranged, I'll have to do it. And I will. Right after Christmas, I swear.

"What aren't you telling me?" April asks. "I know that smirk, Megnifico. You have a secret."

April likes to come up with nicknames that are based on my actual name, Megan. Today I'm Megnifico.

"We're getting married at the end of May," I admit, then point to April and give her a stern look. "Don't tell anyone. Nothing has been confirmed yet."

"May is nice," April contemplates, staring off into the distance. "Warm weather and long days."

"Hannah will be home for the summer," I add. "Harmony lake will be between tourist seasons, and it will give our families enough time to make travel arrangements."

Hannah is my daughter. She's in her third year of university in Toronto, but right now she's home for Christmas.

"Good morning, my dears," Connie sings, drowning out the jingle of the bell over the door. "This is from Eleanor Bigg." She drops a yellow paper gift bag on the counter on her way to the backroom to hang up her coat. "Scrap yarn for the yarn drive," she croons, her sing-song voice growing fainter as she gets closer to the back room.

"Thank you!" I call after her.

Startled by Connie's arrival, my dog, Sophie, jolts awake from her nap, jumps off the sofa in the cozy sitting area, and gives her short, corgi body a good shake. Then she trots after Connie toward the backroom.

"That reminds me," April says, nodding toward the paper bag on the counter. "I have some scrap yarn to donate too. How long are you collecting it?"

"Until the end of the month."

The local charity knitting guild is collecting yarn. They're accepting donations of scrap yarn for an upcoming, top-secret, yarn bombing project.

Yarn bombing is to knitters and crocheters what graffiti is to street artists. But instead of spray paint or chalk, knitters and crocheters create colourful displays in yarn. They adorn lamp posts, bike racks, stop signs, statues, and anything else that stays put, with colourful knitted and crocheted fabric.

"I told Mrs. Bigg we would remember to enter her name in the draw," Connie announces upon her and Sophie's return from the backroom.

"Got it."

I write Mrs. Bigg's name on a ballot and poke it into the slot on top of the ballot box.

Knitorious is the collection hub for the yarn donation drive. To encourage donations, we're entering the donors into a draw to win a Knitorious gift card.

"Oooh, wait until you see the gorgeous scarf Mrs. Bigg is working on," Connie adds. "She was binding it off when I ran into her at the library. It's such a lovely yarn. She bought it when she and Mr. Bigg were on vacation last month. The scarf is for her son, and she's making him

9

a matching hat." Connie picks up the paper bag from the counter and opens it. "Maybe she put some of the left-over yarn in here," she says, shaking the bag and peering inside.

She raises her reading glasses, dangling around her neck like a necklace, to her eyes. "It's the loveliest shade of cerulean blue with beige tweed flecks. And so soft. It's a merino-camel hair blend." She folds the bag shut, reseals the decorative tape, and abandons it on the counter. "There's none in here." She smiles, tucking a chunk of her sleek, silver, chin-length bob behind her ear.

Connie is one of the most beautiful, sophisticated women I know. I hope when I'm seventy years young, I age with just some of Connie's grace and style.

I take the paper bag to the back of the store and drop it in the donation box with the rest of the donated yarn, making a mental note to sort it by weight before the charity knitters pick it up at the end of the month.

"Megan and I were just discussing weddings," April declares, encouraging Connie to join her in peer-pres-suring me to set the wedding wheels in motion. "What do you think about a May wedding, Connie?"

I asked April to keep quiet about our May wedding, but that vow of silence doesn't apply to Connie, and April knows it. April and Connie aren't just my friends. They're family. We're a non-traditional family of choice.

"A May wedding will be lovely," Connie says, smiling from ear to ear and bringing her hands together in front of her chin. "A spring wedding! I can't wait!"

Connie and April were the first friends I made in Harmony Lake eighteen years ago. Connie is my mother-friend. She calls me her daughter-friend. My ex-husband and I moved here when Hannah was a baby. He was a workaholic, I was a new mum, and I was grieving because my mum passed away just before we moved here. I was lonely and overwhelmed. I grief-knitted, during Hannah's naps and after her bedtime, until I ran out of yarn. Connie and I met when I pushed Hannah's stroller into Knitorious to replenish my yarn stash. Connie took Hannah and me under her wing and filled the mother and grandmother-shaped holes in our hearts. We became fast friends, and soon we were family. When Hannah was older, Connie hired me to work part-time at Knitorious, and when she retired a couple of years ago, I took over the store. Now, I own Knitorious, and Connie works here part-time.

"Have you booked a venue?" Connie asks.

"We'd like something informal," I explain, hoping they don't realize that when I say *informal,* I mean simple and easy to plan. "We're thinking we might book the pub or have an outdoor barbecue."

Their blank stares speak volumes. Connie and April are unimpressed. Even Sophie's glare is heavy with disappointment. They're looking forward to a bigger, more formal wedding with all the traditions and trimmings.

"The pub won't be big enough to hold everyone," Connie says, shaking her head and tucking a few more strands of sleek, silver hair behind her ear.

"And where would you have the barbecue?" April asks. "What if it rains? You'll need multiple, massive tents."

"April is right, my dear," Connie agrees. "You can't have hundreds of people huddled under a few tiny tents."

"Hundreds?" I ask, wondering if I even *know* hundreds of people.

"Who *won't* you invite, my dear?"

I open my mouth to answer, but I can't. Connie's right. Everyone in town will want to come, and Eric and I will want them there. It never occurred to me that, in a town as small as Harmony Lake, our wedding would be a public event. This is a hazard of living in a friendly, tight-knit community—hundreds of people love us and want to share in our special day.

Still speechless, I'm saved by the literal bell when the door swings open.

# CHAPTER 2

"MEGAN MARTEL?" the courier asks, eyeing all three of us.

April and Connie point at me.

"That's me," I say.

"Sign here."

He hands me the stylus, and I sign the screen.

"Can I leave it on the counter?" he asks, dropping the box on the counter without waiting for a reply.

He squats down to greet Sophie, rubbing her between the ears. He reaches into his pocket and looks up at me. I nod. He pulls out a dog treat and gives it to Sophie.

"Thank you," I say, smiling.

"Have a nice day." He smiles, stands up, then looks down at Sophie. "See you later, Sophie."

He leaves.

It's amazing that a courier who has made deliveries to Knitorious for years can be on a first name basis with my dog, yet when faced with three completely different-looking women, has to ask which one is me.

"Is that your dress?" April asks.

I nod.

"The one you ordered for the police gala next month?" Connie asks.

I nod again.

Eric and I are attending a police gala next month. It's a black-tie event, and we'll have to spend a night in the city. It's an award ceremony and fundraising event. Eric will receive an award for his perfect, murder-solving record.

"I love this dress," I say, running my hand along the taped seam of the box. "I fell in love with it the second I saw it. But the boutique only had my size in *Blood Rush Red*. They special-ordered it for me in *Midnight Rendezvous*."

I pluck the letter opener from the mug of pens next to the cash register, slice the packing tape, and fold back the box flaps. A sticker bearing the boutique's logo seals the blush-coloured tissue paper that envelops my dream dress. However, excitement turns to disappointment when I tear the sticker, part the tissue paper, and find myself staring at the wrong dress. I exhale a long, loud breath.

"What is it, my dear?" Connie asks, setting her knitting on the table and standing up.

"They sent me the wrong dress," I reply, pouting and lifting the white dress out of the box. "This isn't *Midnight Rendezvous*." I trap the dangling tag between my thumb and forefinger and read it aloud. "*Wife of the party*." My shoulders slump. "What a lame name for a colour."

"It's a beautiful dress," April says.

"I'm sure the store can fix it," Connie suggests. "The gala isn't until next month. There's lots of time to exchange it for *Midnight Rendezvous*."

I sigh and lower the dress back into the box.

"The universe doesn't make mistakes, Megpie," April

counsels. "Maybe instead of the dress you *want*, the universe sent you the dress you *need*."

"Why would I need a white dress for a black-tie function?" I ask.

"Everything happens for a reason." April shrugs. "Only the universe knows why."

"The universe can have whatever reasons it wants, but I don't have to agree."

"Try it on," urges Connie. "I'd like to see it on you. Even if it is *Wife of the Party* instead of *Midnight Rendezvous.*"

With no more coaxing, I retreat to the washroom to try on the dress.

"It's gorgeous!" I mutter to myself, looking in the full-length mirror on the washroom door.

Shades of white and off-white rarely flatter my pale skin, but somehow, this dress compliments my fair complexion. I take the hair tie from my wrist and grip it between my teeth. I twist my long, brown curls into a messy bun, ignoring the few rebellious tendrils that fall around my face. This dress definitely requires an updo. And neutral eye makeup on my hazel eyes. But a bold lipstick. Red. Yes! Cranberry or Holly. *Sigh.* "I wish I could get away with wearing a white dress to a black-tie event." *Sigh.*

"It's beautiful," April says when I emerge from the washroom.

"Breathtaking, my dear."

"Now that you're wearing it, it's more ivory than pure white," April observes. "The colour is gorgeous on you."

"I like it too."

I turn to show off the back of the dress.

The form-fitting bodice has an open back and a wide boat neck with short cap sleeves. A tea-length, full skirt flows out from the bottom of the fitted bodice. I swing my hips, and the skirt billows around my legs. This dress fits like it was custom made for me.

"It would be a lovely wedding dress," Connie points out.

I hate to dampen her enthusiasm, but this dress is too formal for the casual wedding Eric and I envision.

"We don't know for sure when or where we're getting married," I remind her. "If I didn't wear it as a wedding dress, when would I ever wear such a white, expensive dress?"

Disappointed to send it back to the store, I take off the dress, lovingly refold it, lay it in the box, and reseal it.

"*HMMMPH!*" I huff after I end the call. "The store won't pay the shipping cost to return the dress. And I won't pay the shipping cost because it would be much less expensive to make the two-and-a-half-hour round trip and return the thing myself."

"But it's their fault. They sent you the wrong dress," April sympathizes.

"I know, but they made an exception by shipping it to me. They only offer in-store pickup. The store manager made an exception because I live far away. They won't pay to ship it twice." I shrug. "I understand their position. I just don't like it. The manager said I have thirty days to return it. I'll go after the holidays to avoid the Christmas rush."

"What will you wear to the gala?" Connie asks.

"I'll shop for something else when I return the dress, otherwise I have a few options in my closet. It was this specific dress." I tap on the box. "I fell in love with it."

The bell over the door jingles, and Sophie springs to attention, ready to greet the newcomer.

"Hey, handsome! I thought you had a big meeting this morning with Jules Janssen's security team?"

Eric kisses me on the forehead and hands me a to-go cup from Latte Da.

"They cancelled." He shrugs.

"Again? Did they reschedule?" I ask. "The VIPs fly in tomorrow."

"They didn't reschedule." He sits in one of the over-stuffed chairs with a sigh. "Fine with me. They asked for the meeting."

Sophie jumps up and nestles into his lap, and he scratches her neck.

Eric is the chief of the Harmony Lake Police Department. Jules Janssen's security team has been harassing him to meet with them about the security arrangements for the wedding. They want to coordinate efforts to protect the wedding guests and manage the unwanted media people. This is the third time they've cancelled, but it's the first time they haven't rescheduled.

While Eric talks to Connie and April, I crack the lid on my gingerbread latte and savour the moment when the warmth of the first sip touches my soul.

"Is that the dress you ordered for the gala?" Eric asks, nodding at the box on the counter.

"It's the dress I'm returning to the store."

"Where's the dress for the gala?"

"Either at the mall or in my closet."

Eric furrows his brow. His brown eyes and handsome face cloud with confusion. But before I can elaborate, the bell jingles again. The only place busier than Knitorious today is Santa's workshop.

"Hi, Amber!" I smile.

Amber Windermere is Jules Janssen's executive project planner. Amber says it's a fancy title for an event planner. She's been staying in Harmony Lake since

October, overseeing the seemingly endless wedding details.

"Hi, Megan." Amber smiles. "Hi, everyone." She smiles and waves at everyone in the cozy sitting area.

Amber is young—I'd guess mid-twenties—and ambitious. I've only known her for a couple of months, but she's career-focused and determined to make this wedding an enormous success. According to Amber, if this wedding goes off without a hitch, it will launch her career to a whole new level. When I asked how she landed such a high-profile gig, Amber told me Jules requested her because she was so pleased with a previous party Amber organized for her.

"I have a donation for the yarn drive," Amber explains, reaching into her bag. "It looks like I'll be leaving town sooner than expected, and I won't be needing this yarn."

I've been teaching Amber how to knit. Event planning is stressful—especially when the entire world is watching—and she was looking for a hobby to help her relax. We knit together a few times each week. Amber is a brilliant student. She mastered the knit and purl stitches right away, and her stitches are remarkably consistent for someone who swears she's never picked up knitting needles before we met.

"Are you sure?" I ask. "You're doing so well. Maybe if your next wedding is stressful, you'll want to pick up the needles again."

"That's sweet of you to say, Megan," Amber says. "But you're the only person I know who knits. After I leave Harmony Lake, I won't have a knitting guru to help me."

I'm about to offer to video chat with Amber when she needs knitting help, and recommend several good

YouTube channels for new knitters, but Connie speaks first.

"Why are you leaving town, Amber? Is everything all right? Is there a problem at home?"

"Nothing like that...." Amber says, flashing Connie a wide, bright, reassuring smile.

Amber opens her mouth to continue speaking, but doesn't get the chance because our local florist Phillip rushes in. His eyes search the store with determined urgency until his focus lands on Amber.

"Is it true?" Phillip demands, glaring at her. "Is it true that Jules Janssen cancelled her wedding? She and her huge guest list aren't coming to Harmony Lake?"

The wheeze from our collective gasp could rival a giant air mattress with a leak.

# CHAPTER 3

"IT'S TRUE," Amber confirms, her cleft chin quivering, her large brown eyes glassy with moisture. "They cancelled the wedding. Seb and I are leaving town in the next couple of days."

Seb Gillespie, assistant project manager, is Amber's assistant. This is the first event they've worked on together, and since their arrival in Harmony Lake, we've watched their professional relationship blossom into a romantic one. Everyone in town was rooting for them to get together. Now we're cheering them on from the sidelines for a happily ever after.

"Where will you go?" April asks.

Amber's shrug bounces the brown hair resting on her shoulders.

"I'm not sure yet. We'll go home to our families, then after the holidays the company will give us our next assignments."

"At least you'll get to spend the holidays with your family," I say, hoping to cheer her up.

"I know," Amber replies. "But this wedding would have elevated me to celebrity-wedding-planner status."

She shrugs and forces her face into a sad smile. "Oh, well."

"Why did they cancel the wedding?" Connie asks. "Did they break up?"

Amber unlocks her phone and swipes the screen a few times, then reads a press release that Jules and her husband—yes, *husband*—will release in a few hours.

According to the brief statement, Jules and her new husband tied the knot at his Italian vineyard a few hours ago. The wedding was a surprise to guests, who believed they were attending a dinner party before boarding a fleet of private jets to take them to the couple's rumoured destination wedding in Harmony Lake.

Well played, Jules, well played. She got the intimate, paparazzi-free wedding she wanted.

"Brilliant," April says. "Every paparazzi on the planet is here, waiting for the happy couple and their superstar guest list to arrive tomorrow. She beat them at their own game."

I dare not say it out loud and further upset Amber, but I wonder if Jules ever intended to get married here? Did Jules and her husband plan this elaborate wedding as a distraction, so they could get married in peace on the other side of the Atlantic?

"Anyway, Megan, I want to donate my leftover yarn and give you a gift to thank you for welcoming me to Harmony Lake and teaching me to knit."

Amber hands me a gold gift bag with gold tissue paper sticking out of the top.

"You didn't have to do that," I gush. "I've loved our time knitting together." I reach into the bag, push past the tissue paper, and pull out a book. "A wedding planner! Thank you, Amber." I give her a hug, then browse through the book.

"I made a few notes for you." Amber reaches over

and flips the book to a few specific pages. "A few professional tips and tricks to help you and Eric plan your wedding."

"That's great, Amber, thank you!" Eric says, jumping to his feet and taking the book from me so he can leaf through it.

"Yes!" Connie concurs, looking at the pages over his shoulder. "This might encourage you two to get the matrimonial ball rolling."

"Don't look at me," Eric says to Connie. "I've been trying to get the ball rolling for months."

It's true. Eric is eager to say *I do.* I'm eager too. But as much as he says he wants to take part in every aspect of planning the wedding, I can't help but think I'll end up responsible for the bulk of the to-do list.

"What does this mean for the local businesses that were involved with the wedding?" I ask no one in particular, changing the subject.

"Jules Janssen's wedding was going to be the highlight of my florist career. My legacy!" Phillip declares, waving his hands with a double flourish. "And my friend, Rose, is on her way to Harmony Lake as we speak to help me." His face flushes, and he swallows hard, fanning himself with one hand while gripping the counter with the other. "Do you know how many poinsettias it takes to make a flower wall?" His breaths are shallow and fast. "Do you?" he demands, eyes bulging. "Over two thousand!" He fans himself again. "What am I supposed to do with thousands of poinsettias?" He tries to catch his breath. "Not to mention the thousands of flowers for the centerpieces, the urns to line the aisle, the boutonnieres, the bouquets... oh my..."

Connie wraps an arm around Phillip's waist and guides him to the closest chair.

"Breathe, Phillip." She shushes him in soothing tones, lowers him into the chair, and rubs his back in big circles. "There, there. It'll be all right."

Phillip puts his head between his knees and inhales deep, audible breaths while Connie comforts him.

"This will disappoint T and Trevor," April says. "You wouldn't believe how much butter and sugar we have for all the wedding baking."

"Because of the non-disclosure agreements everyone signed, preventing them from disclosing that they provided any goods or services for the wedding, you're not losing bragging rights for your contribution," Amber says. "But everyone we hired for the wedding has a pay or play clause in their contract. Everyone gets paid regardless of whether the wedding happens."

"Thank goodness Adam convinced us to negotiate that clause into the contracts!" Phillip pipes in.

Adam Martel, my ex-husband, is Harmony Lake's mayor and resident lawyer. He's an excellent attorney, and like Phillip, I'm relieved he gave our local business owners sound advice when they negotiated their contracts for the celebrity wedding.

"At least no one will suffer financially," April says, "but I'm bummed that our streets and businesses won't be full of A-list celebrities."

"This will disappoint the entire town," Connie adds. "Everyone has been looking forward to it for months. This is the biggest event in Harmony Lake history. First, we lost the tourists, then we lost the wedding we were looking forward to. Everyone who has worked hard to make this event the *Celebrity Wedding of the Century* won't get to show off their hard work."

She put my exact feelings into words!

"Hear, hear!" Phillip agrees.

A phone chimes, and Eric puts down the wedding planner and pulls his phone from his pocket.

"It's official," Eric confirms. "Jules Janssen's security team says the wedding is off. They won't need to consult with HLPD regarding security."

"You two should take it," Phillip says, pointing back and forth from me to Eric.

Appearing to have recovered from the shock, Phillip is sitting upright with his head now at the top of his body where it belongs.

"Take what?" I ask.

"The wedding."

"The wedding?"

"Yes. You and Eric should get married instead of Jules and the Italian Stallion."

"It's perfect!" April blurts out. "Think about it"—she takes my arms and looks down at me—"the work is done. Everything is planned and paid for. If no one gets married, everyone's hard work and preparation will go to waste. If you get married, the town still gets the big wedding they're looking forward to, you won't have to plan a wedding, and the businesses of Harmony Lake can enjoy the fruits of our labour."

"April's right, babe," Eric says. Of course, he thinks it's a great idea. Why am I surprised? "With no tourists, work is slow for both of us, and Hannah's here for the holidays. It's kind of perfect."

"We talked about a small, casual wedding, remember?" I remind him gently. "Not the biggest, most formal event Harmony Lake has ever hosted."

I look at Amber, hoping for support, but she's engrossed in her phone, oblivious to the conversation around her as her thumbs move at warp speed across the keyboard.

"A turnkey wedding just fell into our laps," he says, amazed. "We just have to show up."

"It doesn't feel right to hijack someone else's wedding," I insist. "And we don't have the same wedding budget as Jules Janssen and her billionaire, vintner husband."

"You won't need their budget," Amber chimes in. "I'm texting with Jules now. She *loves* the idea! Jules wants to give you and Eric the wedding as a gift. She says she owes you for clearing her name last time she was in town?" Amber shrugs, shaking her head. "Whatever that means."

It means, last time Jules Janssen visited Harmony Lake she got tangled up in a murder investigation. Eric and I helped eliminate her as a suspect. I'm impressed she remembers us. She must meet so many people.

"How about this?" Eric takes my hands and looks at me. Gazing back into his brown eyes and beautiful, chiseled face, I tell the butterflies in my belly to settle down for a minute so I can focus on his words. "We'll donate our wedding budget to a worthy cause, and we'll ask our guests to make donations instead of giving us wedding gifts."

It's hard to argue with him, especially when I'm close enough to be intoxicated by his smell and feel the warmth radiating off him. I'm convinced he knows he distracts me in the best way possible and uses it to his advantage.

"Jules *loves* that idea!" Amber says, still staring at her phone as her thumbs fly across the keyboard. "She says, *No pressure, but my non-profit organization could benefit a lot of people with your wedding funds.*"

Amber must type at talking speed. With fingers that nimble, no wonder she picked up knitting so fast.

"The wedding is next week," I say to Eric, ignoring

Amber's comment. "It's short notice for our families to rearrange their lives and make travel plans. We don't have rings. I don't even have a dress."

"Yes, you do," April interjects, glaring at the dress box with a smug I-told-you-so expression on her face. "The universe doesn't make mistakes, Megawatt, remember? A courier delivered your wedding dress this morning."

Oh my God! She's right.

"Who are you texting?" I ask Eric, distracted and typing on his phone.

"Our families."

Why do I feel like this is a done deal? My phone dings, and I pick it up off the counter, sighing as I unlock the screen to a text from Jules Janssen.

*Jules: Hi Megan. Congratulations to you and Eric! Please accept the wedding as a gift from us to you. Without you, I'd be stitched up for murder right now instead of boarding a plane for my honeymoon. We hope you and Eric will be as happy as us. XX.*

"My parents can make it. Your dad and Zoe are changing their Christmas travel plans as we speak, and your sister says she can't wait! My brothers and their families will be here."

He swipes his phone screen a few times and starts typing again.

"Now, who are you texting?" I ask.

"No one," he replies without looking up from his phone. "I'm looking for honeymoon ideas." He shoots me a smug grin.

"Where?"

I stretch my neck and try to read his phone screen.

"It's a secret."

He winks, tilting his phone away from me.

"I guess we're getting married next week," I declare, smiling.

April, Connie, Amber, and Phillip cheer.

"Congratulations, my dear!" Connie pulls me into a tight hug.

"I can't wait!" I say, grinning.

"Your wedding will be perfect!" Connie insists. "You'll see, this next week will fly by, and it'll be the happiest, least stressful week of your life!"

# CHAPTER 4

FASTER THAN THE babysitter's boyfriend when a car pulls up, word of the cancelled *Wedding of the Century* spreads through Harmony Lake, disappointing the locals who are caught up in the wedding fever that has swept our town.

However, the town's emotional rollercoaster rises again when word spreads that the wedding will go on with a substitute bride and groom and a less-famous guest list.

Instead of disappointment that no movie stars will stroll up and down Water Street this Christmas season, everyone is thrilled about attending the festivities first-hand rather than reading secondhand accounts online. Or so they tell Eric and me when they congratulate us.

Someone—most likely Sheamus, the publican—orga-nized an impromptu pre-wedding celebration at the local pub, The Irish Embassy.

Eric and I arrive at the packed pub and join our jovial family, friends, and neighbours, laughing and enjoying each other's company.

The town's energy has shifted. The undercurrent of

jittery anticipation of the last several weeks has reverted to the relaxed friendliness that I'm used to.

"Megan! Woo hoo! Megan!"

I scan the pub, searching for the source of my name, and Mrs. Bigg's waving arm catches my attention.

"Hi, Mrs. Bigg." I wave to her and her family as I make my way through the crowd toward their booth.

"Congratulations, Megan!" Mrs. Bigg says with a wide grin.

"Thank you," I say, smiling.

"Where's the groom-to-be?" Without missing a stitch on the hat she's knitting, she cranes her neck, combing the crowd behind me for Eric.

"He's somewhere near the bar. People keep buying him drinks, and he keeps accepting," I reply. "I hope the Bigg family will join us next week."

"Mr. Bigg and I wouldn't miss it for all the yarn in the world," she says with a chuckle, nodding at Mr. Bigg, who raises his glass with a smile and is perhaps a tad tipsy. "But Doyle has to work, I'm afraid."

"Oh?" I ask, then look at Doyle, sitting in the booth next to his mother. "You're working on Christmas Eve?"

"I'm catering a huge wedding," he shouts over the din of the crowd, then shoots me a sly grin.

"Right! I forgot." I laugh and bring my palm to my forehead. "You were the head chef for the celebrity wedding."

"Now I'm the head chef for *your* wedding," he reminds me.

"We're glad you're catering our wedding," I say. "It means so much to us that everything about the ceremony and reception is local. It's more special than anything we could have planned."

He asks if Eric and I can stop by the venue for a tasting. Doyle and I pull out our phones, check our calendars, and agree on a convenient time.

"That's a lovely hat, Mrs. Bigg," I say before I leave the booth. "Is this the yarn Connie told me about earlier?"

"Yes," Mrs. Bigg replies, pausing her hands mid-stitch and handing me the hat-in-progress. I pet the soft, squishy cerulean blue yarn and admire the stitches. "I finished the scarf this morning"—she gestures to the scarf draped around Doyle's neck—"and I hope to finish the hat tomorrow."

"The yarn is beautiful," I compliment, handing back her knitting project.

Mrs. Bigg tells me the story of how she found the yarn in a small yarn store when she and Mr. Bigg were skiing in Vermont. She offers to give me the yarn tag if I'm interested in stocking it at Knitorious. I take her up on it, but she can't find the tag in her knitting bag, so she offers to drop it off at the store tomorrow or Saturday.

"I'm not working tomorrow, but you can leave it with Marla," I say. "Have a good evening."

I walk away from the booth and glance at Eric. He's leaning against the bar, laughing, and drinking with his friends. He's happier and more relaxed than I've ever seen him, but that could be because he's slightly drunk. Eric doesn't drink to excess. In fact, I don't recall ever seeing him intoxicated. He has more will power than the average human and prefers to stay in complete control of his faculties at all times. It's nice to see him let go a little and give his superhuman willpower a well-deserved evening off.

I take a small sip of my Diet Coke. Tonight, I'll be the clear-headed one and take a turn as our designated driver.

"Seb Gillespie is enjoying the pre-wedding shindig

more than the bride and groom," April whispers in my ear, then jerks her head toward Seb, who's propped up on a bar stool at the opposite end of the bar from Eric. Seb's carefully cultivated, messy-on-top hairstyle is messier than usual. His bedroom eyes which, according to my daughter, make the younger women of Harmony Lake weak in the knees, are more closed than open, and his gaze is dreamy and vacant. Blissfully oblivious is the term that comes to mind.

"Seb is at that threshold where if he stops now, he *might* feel OK tomorrow, but if he keeps going, he'll regret it until the day after tomorrow," I say, only half joking. "What option do you think he'll choose?"

"He won't stop," April replies. "He's committed. And I doubt he realizes how drunk he is."

"I agree with you."

We giggle.

"Can I get either of you a drink?" Trevor Chipperfield asks on his way to the bar.

Trevor is April and T's friend. He's a pastry chef and owns a bakery in another town. He arrived in Harmony Lake yesterday. T recruited him to help bake for the wedding.

"No thanks," April and I say in unison.

"Listen, Megan, can you and Eric swing by Artsy Tartsy tomorrow? We'd like to talk to you about the cake."

"Umm... sure." I pull out my phone and open the calendar. "I'm not available until the evening, though."

"That's perfect. Gives us a chance to sketch out a few ideas. T and I want to make the cake less Jules-ish and more Megan-ish." He chuckles.

We input the appointment in our respective calendars, then Trevor continues to the bar. As he turns to walk away, Seb lets out a loud, drunken laugh. Trevor shakes his head, flashing Seb a brief, contemptuous sneer.

"What's that about?" I ask April. "Is there a problem between Trevor and Seb?"

"Trevor lit up like a Christmas tree when he heard Seb was leaving town early," April says into my ear. "He's sad that the rich and famous won't be eating his pastries, but he's thrilled not to spend another week in the same town as Seb Gillespie."

"Why? What happened between them?"

"They had worked a wedding together a couple of years ago, and it didn't go well. Seb told Trevor the client changed the colour scheme and wanted big, last-minute changes to the wedding cake. Trevor worked all night to make the client's changes. Except the client didn't request any changes, and when they saw their altered cake, the bride burst into tears. And there wasn't enough time to fix it."

"Why did Seb tell Trevor to change the cake if the client didn't want the changes?"

"Seb made a mistake. He mixed up two clients. A different client wanted to change their cake, but Seb gave the instructions to the wrong pastry chef."

"So, Seb had two distressed brides," I conclude. "One whose cake was changed when it *shouldn't* have been, and one whose cake wasn't changed when it *should* have been." I shrug. "It was an honest mistake, and it happened two years ago. Why is Trevor still angry?"

"The situation got ugly. Seb refused to accept responsibility for the error. He insisted he never told Trevor to alter the cake. The couple threatened to sue Trevor for ruining their wedding. He ended up giving them the altered cake for free, and his reputation took a big hit."

I remind myself there are two sides to every story and wonder how Seb would describe the situation. I peer through the crowd in his direction, and he's so inebriated that Amber is holding his arm and using her body weight to keep him from falling off the bar stool.

"I'll be right back," I whisper in April's ear, pulling on the neckline of my wool tunic to release some pent-up heat and fan myself with the fabric. "It's warm. I need some fresh air."

"Do you want me to come?"

"No. You stay and enjoy yourself. I'll be right back."

I thread my way through the crowd and step into the chilly December evening. The cold air on my exposed skin is a relief, and my first deep breath is refreshing. But it's below zero out here, and I left my coat inside. In a couple of minutes, the chill will catch up to me, and I'll long for the warmth of the crowded pub.

"Hey, Meg, are you OK?"

"Fine," I assure Adam as he follows me outside. "I just need some fresh air. It's warm in there, and I'm wearing this heavy... thing." I gesture to my hand-knit, worsted-weight, cabled tunic and tights.

Adam and I met when I was eighteen and got married when I was twenty. I fell pregnant with Hannah a few months later. Over the years, we grew apart. I immersed myself in motherhood and the community, and Adam immersed himself in becoming a senior partner at a large law firm. Apathy crept into our relationship without us realizing until it was too late. Next thing we knew, the only common interest we had was Hannah.

After unsuccessful attempts to reconnect, we decided it would be best for our family to end our marriage. We still love each other, but not as husband and wife. We've worked hard to redefine our relationship and build a friendship. We're not a couple anymore, but we're Hannah's parents, and we'll always be family. After the split, Adam left the large law firm and opened a practice in Harmony Lake. He's been the mayor for almost a year. We spend more time together in divorce than we did in marriage.

"Listen, if you're feeling overwhelmed about the wedding, it's understandable. I mean, it came out of nowhere. On Sunday, you told me you guys hadn't even set a date, and now you're getting married in a week?"

"It was a shock," I agree. "But it feels right, and I'm happy, Adam. Really, really happy."

"So is your fiancé," Adam observes. "He's had a big, goofy grin plastered on his face all night."

We laugh.

Adam isn't being nasty; he and Eric are friends. Close friends. They golf together, watch sports together, and work out together. Yes, it was weird at first. For me, anyway. But it works for our non-traditional family.

"But seriously, Meg, you deserve to be happy. Eric is a great guy, and if you're happy, I'm happy for you. But no matter what, I'm here for you. Eric is my friend, but you're my family. I'll always have your back."

His blue eyes are full of sincerity and a hint of nostalgia.

"Thank you," I say, standing on my tippy toes to hug him. "Your support means a lot. This won't change anything between us. We'll always be close. You, Hannah, and I will always be Team Martel.

"Except you'll be a Sloane," he mutters, referring to Eric's last name.

I pull away from our hug and lower myself to my natural height. Adam is tall, and I am short. He's the same height as Eric. Hugging the men in my life requires a good deal of stretching on my part and stooping on theirs.

As soon as we pull apart, I miss his warmth, and the icy breeze coming off the lake chills me to the bone. I shiver and cross my arms in front of me, rubbing my shoulders.

"You know who might be happier about this wedding than you and Eric combined?" Adam asks, taking off his sports jacket and draping it over my shoulders.

"Connie?" I ask, gathering the jacket around me like a cocoon.

"Even happier than Connie."

"Our daughter?"

"She might be the happiest maid of honour on earth."

"It's her first time in a wedding," I remind him.

"She's been texting me photos of dresses all day. Asking my opinion about the colour or the style. I know nothing about dresses!"

We discuss Hannah, her joy about being maid of honour, and our shopping trip to the city tomorrow. Adam offers to stop by Knitorious and help Marla. I thank him and assure him Eric is on Knitorious-duty tomorrow.

Though he denies it, I can tell Adam is getting cold without his jacket. I suggest we head back inside, slide his jacket off my shoulders, and return it to him.

Adam reaches for the pub door, but before he grabs it, the door opens. He catches the handle and holds it open while a woman I don't recognize strides through. She's a few years younger than me and has long, straight, shiny dark hair. She's beautiful in a refined, classic way. Her designer coat, thick belt, and designer stiletto heels complete her polished look. Seeming not to notice us standing next to the door, she strides onto the sidewalk, then stops, and glances left and right. Adam and I watch her pivot left and sashay into the darkness, the clicking of her heels on the sidewalk growing fainter with each stride.

"Do you know her?" I ask.

"Never seen her before."

Adam reaches for the door again, but the double doors swing open, and Seb Gillespie staggers onto the sidewalk. He's well past the drunk threshold. He's smashed. Plastered. Bombed. Whatever word applies to someone who could be on the verge of alcohol poisoning.

Seb staggers right, left, then right again. Confusion and intoxication cloud his face and probably his judgement. He slurs something, but I can't understand what he's saying.

"Rawsieeee?" he moans. "Rowwwwshh? Rowshie Pettle!"

"What's he saying?" I ask.

"No idea." Adam shakes his head. "I'm not fluent in drunk."

"I think he's looking for that woman," I theorize. "He looks like he's searching for someone."

"He looks hammered," Adam says.

From inside one of Seb's pockets, his cell phone rings and vibrates.

Suddenly, Seb picks up speed and staggers right at us. We jump apart when he lunges himself between Adam and me like we aren't here. Adam grabs Seb's elbow, preventing him from stumbling off the curb and into the street. I hold the door while Adam commandeers Seb and steers him inside the pub. Seb's phone stops ringing, then starts again.

"There you are!" says an exasperated Amber.

Amber helps Adam pour Seb into a booth. She slides in next to him, and he leans on her to prop himself up.

"You've had enough to drink. You're cut off!" Amber tells her drunken boyfriend.

"Yes, he is," Sheamus says, his Irish accent thick with authority. Sheamus looks at Adam and me. "We didn't overserve him. The fella's only had two drinks in my pub, I swear." He gestures toward Seb, the empty pint glasses in his hand clanging against each other. "He must've started before he got here." He looks at Amber again. "I'll get yer lad some coffee."

Sheamus turns and disappears into the crowd.

"I was only in the washroom for a minute," Amber says, looking at me. "When I got back, he was gone. He's the fastest drunk person I know." She chuckles. "Sheamus is right. Seb only had a few drinks. He must've started before we got here. The wedding cancellation must have upset him more than I thought. This is his first big event since he joined the company. It's the biggest event either of us has ever planned. I guess he drank to numb his feelings." She tries to lean Seb against the back of the booth. "This is so embarrassing."

Seb's phone rings again.

"Someone's trying hard to get in touch with him," Adam says.

"I don't think he's fit to talk to anyone," Amber responds.

"Why don't I help you take him home," I offer. "I'm sober. I'll help you get him settled in the hotel room."

"I'll go with you," Adam adds. "He's heavier than he looks."

"Thanks, but we'll be fine," Amber says. "I can take care of him. This isn't my first time babysitting Seb after he drank too much. I've had nothing to drink, and I'm parked right outside. After he has some coffee, I'll take him back to the hotel."

"Are you sure?" Adam asks, unconvinced. "I don't mind."

"I'm positive."

Amber smiles, and her body slumps under Seb's weight when he falls against her.

"Let us know if you change your mind," I say.

We say good night, and Adam and I wish Amber good luck. Seb's cell phone rings again as I walk toward Eric at the bar.

Adam nudges me and jerks his head behind him, toward Seb and Amber.

"I don't have a good feeling about this, Meg."

## CHAPTER 5

FRIDAY, December 17th

"This makes it real, babe," Eric says, waving the envelope as I pull into the parking lot behind Knitorious. "A week from today, we'll be Mr. and Mrs. Sloane."

He leans across the console and kisses me.

"I can't wait," I say. "Marrying you is the best Christmas gift ever."

After we took Sophie for her morning walk and dropped her off at Knitorious, Eric and I went to Harmony Lake Town Hall and got our marriage license. We were waiting at the door when the town clerk unlocked it. Eric hasn't loosened his grip on the envelope since she handed it to him. Every few minutes, he opens it, slides out the sheet of paper, looks at it, grins, then slides it back into the envelope.

"Are you taking it to work with you?" I ask, nodding at the envelope.

"No," he says, rolling his eyes like it's a dumb question. "I thought I'd put it in the cash register until after work. For safekeeping."

"Won't it be safe in your desk drawer? In your office?

At the super-secure police station?" I tease, enjoying how distracted he is.

"It didn't occur to me."

We get out of the car and lock it. I plop my bag on the hood of the car and rummage around inside, searching for my store keys to unlock the back door. I'm eager to get inside and cross the marriage license off our wedding to-do list.

Eric squints when the morning sun peeks out from behind the clouds.

"How's your head?" I ask. "Did the ibuprofen help your hangover?"

"It's not a hangover."

Eric lowers his sunglasses from the top of his head and covers his eyes. He's paler than normal. He rubs his temples and swallows.

"If it's not a hangover, maybe you're sick, honey." I touch his forehead with the back of my hand, pretending to check for a fever. "I hope it's not serious. The flu can last for three weeks. Can we even get married if you have the flu?"

"I don't have the flu."

He removes my hand from his forehead and kisses it.

"If it's not a hangover or the flu, what is it?"

I'm determined to hear him admit he's hungover.

"Fine," he concedes, dropping his chin. "I feel a little rough this morning. It might be a *tiny* hangover. I just need some coffee. And water. And more coffee. And maybe a nap."

"Found them." I hold up my store keys.

He hugs me.

"The sore head is worth it," Eric says. "We had fun last night."

"If *you* feel rough this morning, I can't imagine how Seb Gillespie feels."

"Was he drunk?" Eric asks.

"You didn't notice?" I ask. "He was a mess."

Eric shrugs and shakes his head.

"I was busy enjoying myself. Seb wasn't on my radar last night."

Eric is so observant; I'm surprised he didn't notice Seb's drunken shenanigans. But I'm glad he relaxed and turned off cop-mode for an entire evening.

We take our time walking across the parking lot toward the back door.

"Your passport is up to date, right?" Eric asks.

"Yes." I squeeze his waist. "Are you asking because our honeymoon is in another country?"

"It's a surprise."

Eric booked our honeymoon yesterday but won't tell me where we're going, despite my attempts to needle it out of him. I even tried to convince drunk-Eric to give me a clue about the destination, but with no luck. So far, he'll only tell me our departure and return dates.

"How am I supposed to pack if you won't tell me where we're going?"

"You won't need clothes."

"That's presumptuous, Chief Sloane!" I tease, giving his chest a playful slap.

"That's not what I meant." Eric chuckles, blushing and rubbing the back of his neck with his free hand. "We'll be lounging on a beach all day. Pack swimsuits and whatever you would wear to dinner on a summer night."

Pushing the key into the lock, I spy something in my peripheral vision. Turning toward it, I lift my sunglasses and squint. Crumpled clothes? A bunch of blankets? A pile of discarded rags? Whatever it is, it wasn't there yesterday when I left.

"What's that?" I ask.

41

"What?"

I pull the key out of the lock and use it to point to the lumpy mass leaning against the wall outside Wilde Flowers.

As we approach it, the mystery mound becomes more distinct. It's not clothes, blankets, or rags. It's a person. A man. His back is against the brick wall. His head droops down and to the side, and his legs are bent. In my mind's eye, I imagine he was standing against the wall and slid down.

Where did he come from? How long has he been here? Was he here when we dropped off Sophie earlier? If we hadn't parked out front to drop her off, would we have found him in time to save him?

Eric hands me our marriage certificate, pulls a rubber glove from his coat pocket, and puts it on. Then he squats next to the man and tries to lift his head.

"Frozen solid," Eric observes. "He's been here for hours."

I bend a few body parts and stretch others to look at the man's face without moving closer. The messy-on-top hair is my first clue, despite the fact that the tips are frozen into icicles.

"Seb? Seb Gillespie?"

"Looks like it," Eric confirms.

"Amber said she would take him home from the pub. She told Adam and me she would take care of him. Why is he here?"

"That's a good question, babe."

What happened after Adam and I walked away from Amber and Seb? Where is Amber? Is she OK? Is she looking for Seb? Does she know he's missing? Maybe he wandered away from the hotel. No, that wouldn't make sense. Seb and Amber are staying at one of the mountain resorts. A long walk to Knitorious, and Seb isn't dressed for the weather. I doubt he would have made it this far before freezing to death.

"He must have wandered away from the pub, passed out, and frozen to death," I speculate.

Eric is on the ground, his body and neck contorted so he can assess Seb's situation without disturbing the body or the surrounding area.

"Petechiae!"

"Gesundheit!"

"I didn't sneeze," Eric responds. "I was referring to the tiny red spots on Seb's eyes." He stands up and pulls his cell phone from his coat pocket. "Seb didn't freeze to death, babe."

"Those red spots... the petechiae... they're a sign of strangulation, right?" I ask.

Last week, I watched a British murder mystery, and the victim had those same red spots. Petechial hemorrhage, the British sleuth called it.

Eric nods, pulls off his glove, and unlocks his phone.

"Seb Gillespie was murdered."

# CHAPTER 6

A SHIVER RUNS along my spine, and I'm not sure if it's because of the frosty morning air, the dead body behind me, or both.

The cold is bearable because the brick building acts as a shield against the chilly wind coming off the lake.

Eric is on the phone. He's rallying his troops and setting Seb's murder investigation in motion.

I hit send on a group text to Hannah, Connie, April, and my sister, then put our marriage license under my arm, and slip my frigid fingers back inside my warm mitts. Burrowing my chilly hands into my parka pocket, I shudder again, and my teeth chatter as another shiver courses through me. I resist the urge to turn around and look at Seb. To confirm this is real. Part of my brain wants to convince me it's not and wants me to check that it's definitely Seb; he's definitely dead and definitely frozen. I'm trying to ignore that part of my brain.

"Go inside, babe," Eric says when he ends his call. "You'll catch your death out here."

I nod, relieved to put some distance between myself and the frozen corpse.

"Are you OK?" he asks, rubbing my shoulders and scanning me from head to toe. "Are you in shock or anything?"

"I'm fine," I assure him. "It's not like this is the first dead body I've stumbled across. Is there anything I can do?"

"There's nothing anyone can do," Eric replies. "I'll secure the scene until more police arrive, then I'll wait for the coroner. After that, I'll reconstruct the final hours of Seb's life which should lead me to who killed him, how they killed him, and why." His phone rings, and he looks at the screen, then back at me. "Promise you'll call me if you need anything?"

"Promise."

He kisses my forehead and answers the call.

On my way to the door, Phillip's flower-painted van pulls into our shared parking lot. Eric waves him down and runs in front of the van, forcing Phillip to stop before encroaching farther on the crime scene. His phone still to his ear, Eric signals for Phillip to put the van in park and turn it off.

Taking tentative steps, Phillip climbs down from the van. I lose sight of him when he walks around to the passenger side. The passenger door closes with a dull thud and seconds later, Phillip reappears with a woman. *The* woman. The elegant woman Adam and I saw leaving the pub last night. Who is she?

Eric is off the phone now. The upper half of his body is in the trunk of his car, collecting crime scene things and whistling the tune the seven dwarfs whistle on their way to work. He emerges with crime scene tape, a blanket, and evidence identification markers.

"What happened?" Phillip asks, approaching me with the mystery woman.

"We just got here," I reply. "And found him." I gesture at Seb's body behind me without looking.

Phillip and the mystery woman lean in to look without moving closer.

"I assure you, Rose, this never happens. Dead bodies in parking lots are not typical for Harmony Lake," Phillip assures his friend, whose name I now know is Rose. He looks at me. "Is that Seb Gillespie?"

I nod.

"He froze to death?"

I shrug. It's not my place to mention the petechiae, or that someone took Seb's life.

"We just got here," I repeat. "Eric is still assessing the situation."

"Seb was pretty drunk when I left the pub last night," Phillip remarks. "I guess he passed out and froze to death." Phillip shakes his head and clucks his tongue. "Such a shame."

Were Phillip and Rose at the pub together? I don't remember seeing them together. The first time I saw Rose, she was leaving the pub. Alone.

"What time did you leave last night?" I ask Phillip.

"Early," he confirms. "Just after you and Eric showed up."

I'm not surprised. Phillip isn't a late-night person. He often has to wake up in the middle of the night to receive floral deliveries, so he goes to bed early. Phillip is our next-door neighbour at home and work, and I can attest that he rarely ventures out past eight p.m.

"Hi, I'm Megan Martel," I say, extending a hand toward Phillip's companion.

She's fixated on Seb's body, and my introduction distracts her. I sometimes forget that most people aren't used to encountering dead bodies. I'm told most people live their entire lives without discovering a dead body. I envy those people.

"Rose Thorne," she replies in a cultured voice, shaking my hand with her long, slender, leather-gloved fingers.

She reminds me of a ballerina. She's refined, graceful, and composed. Her body is long, angular, and fluid.

"Rose is here to help me with the wedding flowers," Phillip explains. "She just got here. I wasn't expecting her until this afternoon, but she got an early start this morning, and here she is!"

"Harmony Lake is a long drive from where I live," Rose adds.

"You just arrived in town this morning?" I confirm.

"That's right," Rose replies, correcting her already perfect posture.

Why is she lying? I'd bet my life Rose Thorne is the woman Adam and I saw leaving the pub. She's even wearing the same gorgeous designer coat. Where was she between leaving the pub last night and landing on Phillip's doorstep this morning?

"I'm sorry your first impression of us includes a dead body," I say.

"I could have found him," Rose says, her eyes wide with distress. "This morning, I came to Wilde Flowers first, but Phillip wasn't here yet, so I drove to his house. Luckily, I parked on the street out front and tried the front door, instead of coming back here." She clutches the faux-fur trim on the wide lapel of her coat. Her gloved hand disappears into the lush faux-fur forest created when her faux fur cuff and lapel meet. "I would've been alone in a strange town with a dead body." She gestures to Seb's frozen, slumped frame on the ground a few feet away. "Poor man."

"I told Rose I'm always at work by now," Phillip says.

47

"But today is an exception because I was out late last night celebrating your pending nuptials."

"Yes, congratulations, by the way!" Rose says, smiling at me. "I look forward to helping Phillip with the flowers for your wedding. Less pressure and more fun than the flowers for Jules Janssen's wedding." She laughs.

Even her laugh sounds well-bred.

"Did you know Seb?" I ask, once again tilting my head toward the frozen corpse without looking at it.

"No." Rose shakes her head. "I've never seen him before. His name was Seb, you say?"

The tone of her question suggests I might be mistaken about his name.

"Sebastian Gillespie," I confirm.

"How would Rose know Seb?" Phillip asks. "She's only been in Harmony Lake for an hour."

"Amber always says event planning is a small world." I shrug. "It could be possible."

"Amber Windermere?" Rose asks.

"You know her?" Phillip asks, shocked.

"See?" I say, poking Phillip's ribs through his thick winter coat. "Small world."

"I know Amber. She's lovely. I once did the flowers for a wedding she planned."

Eric covers Seb with a blanket, then joins us. Phillip introduces him to Rose, then Eric asks us not to disclose Seb's identity until the police notify his next of kin.

"No one will hear it from me," Phillip promises.

"I won't," Rose responds.

"Me neither," I add.

"The parking lot and back doors to both stores are part of the crime scene and will be inaccessible until further notice," Eric advises.

"Crime scene?!" Phillip demands, shocked. "Seb Gillespie was murdered?"

"Until the coroner determines the cause of death, we have to treat it like a crime scene," Eric explains, answering Phillip's question without answering the question.

Eric asks Phillip to remove his van from the parking lot, or risk not being able to access it until the police release the crime scene. Phillip and Rose climb in the van and leave the parking lot.

"Shouldn't April have picked you up by now?" Eric asks, checking the time.

I had planned to go shopping with my bridal party today. They need dresses, and we all need shoes. I'd planned to be away from Harmony Lake all day. Marla would take care of Knitorious, and Eric would stop by to cover her breaks and tend to Sophie. But due to this morning's events, I've changed my plans.

"I'm not going shopping."

"Why not?" he asks, his forehead creased with worry lines. "We're getting married in a week, babe. You need shoes. The girls need dresses."

"I have to work." I shift my weight from foot to foot, trying to warm my cold feet. "You were covering Marla's breaks, but now there's a dead body in the parking lot, and you have to find a murderer. Also, I wasn't sure if I *could* leave. Don't I have to give a statement? I'm a witness."

Eric unzips his coat, slides our marriage license out from under my arm, and pulls me in. I wrap my arms around his waist and soak up his warmth.

"We found the body together, babe. You didn't see or experience anything I didn't. Go shopping. Someone else can help Marla, or she can close the store for lunch."

"They already left without me," I say. "Anyway, I might be more useful here. People will visit the store to ask about Seb. If we're lucky, someone who knows something about what happened to him might stop by. I can't hear rumours and ask questions if I'm not here."

"If that's what you want," Eric says, rubbing my back through my coat. "Thank you." He kisses my nose. "Your insight is always helpful."

Patrol cars pull up and block the entrance to the parking lot. I bundle Eric's scarf around his exposed neck and remind him to stay warm.

"I'll let you work," I say, stretching to kiss him goodbye.

"By the way," he calls after me. "Did you and Phillip talk about the flowers?"

"No. Were we supposed to?"

"At the pub last night, he said he needed to set up a time to meet with us. I offered to look at our calendar, but he said he'd arrange it with you."

"He didn't mention it," I say. "He was probably distracted by the dead body outside his back door. Did he say anything else?"

"Something about the bouquets and boutonnieres. And the rose situation? Do you know what that means?"

I shake my head.

Phillip will have to wait a few hours while I unravel my own Rose situation. Why did Rose Thorne lie about when she arrived in Harmony Lake? And where did she go when Adam and I watched her stride away from the pub?

# CHAPTER 7

THE HARMONY LAKE Rumour Mill is faster than high-speed internet.

People file into the store as soon as I unlock the door. They ask about the police activity in the parking lot and the rumour that someone died back there. I answer their questions honestly and disclose nothing that Eric might want to keep quiet.

"Yes, we found a body in the parking lot."

"It's closer to Wilde Flowers than Knitorious, but it's a shared parking lot, so the police cordoned off the whole thing."

"A man."

"It was hard to see his face."

"Seb Gillespie? Where did you hear that?"

"Eric says he's waiting for the coroner to determine the cause of death."

In between chatting with concerned and nosy neighbours in person, I also field phone calls and text messages from friends and neighbours with the same questions.

Looking for an excuse to witness the police activity in person, several people drop off their yarn donations, or come up with last minute donations, as an excuse to visit Knitorious. The donation bin and ballot box are on the brink of overflowing. At least a good cause will benefit from the chaos caused by Seb's death.

By late morning, most people are satisfied they have all the current information, and the volume and frequency of visits, calls, and texts dwindles. I'm able to make a few discreet inquiries about Phillip's fibbing florist friend, the current thorn—or should I say Thorne—in my side.

"Where's Marla?" Eric asks, closing the door behind him.

Sophie rushes over to greet him like they've been apart for three months instead of three hours.

"She went to Latte Da for coffee," I reply. "I told her to take her time. In fact, I might let her go home early because, aside from people asking about Seb, it's dead in here."

"Pardon the pun." Eric chuckles, taking off his green knitted toque.

He combs his fingers through his short, dark hair, smoothing it into place.

"Did the coroner show up?"

"He just left," Eric replies. "He'll gather as much evidence as he can, but he can't perform the autopsy until Seb thaws out."

"How long will that take?" I ask as images swirl inside my head of the coroner, thawing Seb in a human-sized microwave oven. Or a team of helpers holding hair dryers aimed at his frozen, dead body.

"A few days," Eric replies. "The body has to defrost slowly in a refrigerated room. If he thaws too fast, the parts that thaw first will start to decompose before the deep tissue thaws..."

"OK. I get it." I raise my hand to interrupt his graphic

description. "You won't have much information for a while."

Taking off his coat and getting comfortable in the cozy sitting area, Eric opens his notebook to a fresh page and readies his pen.

Having satisfied her role as unofficial greeter, Sophie resumes her morning nap on the dog bed in front of the display window.

"Can you tell me about your interaction with Seb last night? And whatever else you noticed?"

Starting from the moment April first pointed out that Seb was drunk, I tell Eric everything.

"Did you see Seb's phone? Did you see a name on the screen?" he asks when I finish my statement.

"I only heard it," I reply. "It was in his pocket, and he didn't seem to notice the incessant ringing and vibrating. Can you find out who was trying to reach him by checking the call history on his phone?"

"We haven't found his phone," Eric divulges. "It's not in any of his pockets, and it's not in the immediate area around his body."

"Do you think the killer took Seb's phone?"

"It's an option. But it sounds like he was pretty drunk. He could've dropped it or left it somewhere."

"Rose Thorne is the woman Adam and I saw. She left the pub when we were on the sidewalk. I'd bet all the yarn in Knitorious on it," I insist. "And I think Seb was looking for her when he staggered out after. I'm sure I heard him slur her name."

"You heard Seb Gillespie say Rose Thorne's name?"

"Not exactly," I admit. "I heard him slur something that sounded like her name." Eric seems unimpressed by my imitation of the slurred words Seb uttered on the sidewalk. "I think he was trying to say, *Rosie, Rose, Rose petal.* It didn't make sense last night, but now that I know her name, and considering he followed her outside the pub, I'm sure he was calling Rose and searching for her."

"We call that hearsay evidence," Eric says. "It's not admissible unless Seb himself can testify to what he said."

"But it's compelling evidence," I argue. "Rose was in Harmony Lake before Seb's murder. They were in the pub at the same time. He knew her name."

"Rose told you she didn't arrive in Harmony Lake until this morning."

"I know. But I'm telling you, honey. It was her. Adam saw her too. He might recognize her."

"It was dark, though, and you only saw her for a few seconds."

"Right. But I know what I saw." I walk over to the counter, tear a page from my planner, and return to the cozy sitting area. "Rose checked into the Hav-a-nap motel last night."

"How do you know?" he asks, narrowing his eyes. "And how did she get a room? Jules Janssen reserved every room in town."

I hand him the sheet of paper from my planner.

"I made a few calls," I confess. "The manager at the Hav-a-nap was helpful. We've known each other a long time. When Rose checked in, she told them she's working on the wedding flowers with Phillip. She told them she arrived early and didn't want to show up at Phillip's house unannounced the night before he was expecting her." I shrug. "They gave her a room."

"I'll get a copy of the receipt from the motel and question Rose Thorne." He taps his fingers on the arm of the chair. "Why would Rose lie about something so easy to verify? Half the town would have seen her at the pub last night. She was the only stranger in a crowd of locals. She would've stuck out like a sore thumb. Why not tell the truth?"

"Because she interacted with a dead guy hours before he died?" I theorize. "Maybe she's freaked out. She must not understand how small towns work and assumes no one noticed her in the crowded pub."

"You've already found a suspect." Eric's eyes beam with pride. "Just a sec," he says when his phone rings.

While the caller speaks, Eric listens, nodding and uttering occasional sounds of acknowledgment.

"Have someone else search the bushes again to make sure we missed nothing." More nodding accompanied by, "Uh-huh," then Eric advises the caller he'll be there soon and ends the call.

"What is it?" I ask.

"Good news. They found Seb's cellphone in the bushes behind the parking lot."

"Seb dropped his phone in the bushes?"

"Or the killer discarded it in the bushes. The phone is damaged. More damaged than an accidental fall in the snow would cause. I'll know more when I see it for myself." He rubs his chin, deep in contemplation.

"Maybe the killer damaged it and threw it in the bushes," I suggest.

"It's possible," Eric agrees, nodding. "There's no evidence Seb was in the bushes. No twigs or branches on him, no scratches. The snow around the bushes was undisturbed. No footprints or anything."

"I hope you find something on his phone that leads to his killer."

"Babe, I want to use the phone as a holdback. OK?" He looks at me for agreement.

"Of course," I say. "I won't tell anyone."

A holdback is evidence the police don't disclose to the public. Evidence only someone involved with the crime could know about. According to Eric, holdback evidence helps police verify a confession. If the confessor mentions the holdback, there's a good chance they're telling the truth. If the confessor doesn't mention the holdback, it's less likely they were there, and that they're lying. Because, also according to Eric, sometimes people confess to a crime they didn't commit. I can't imagine why, but he says it happens.

Seb's murder changes everything; solving it will require all of Eric's time and attention. It could take weeks to find the killer, especially if Seb needs several days to defrost before the coroner can perform the autopsy.

"Honey, maybe Seb's murder is a bad omen," I say, taking his hand. "Maybe we should rethink the wedding."

"Are you serious? Why would you say that? We..."

"You'll be working on this case twenty-four hours a day until it's solved," I say, interrupting his objection. "How will you get a wedding ring, get fitted for a tux, attend the rehearsal dinner? It's too much pressure."

"Uh-uh! No way," he insists, shaking his head. "I won't let this murder stop us from getting married next week. I won't let anything stop us. Babe, I've been trying to get you down the aisle since the day we met. I'll quit my job before I let this case interfere with our wedding."

"What if you don't solve Seb's murder before the wedding? The case will distract you. I know you. You won't be able to let it go. How will you relax and enjoy our top-secret honeymoon with Seb's unsolved murder nagging at you?"

"We will solve this case before we get married," Eric announces like it's a forgone conclusion.

He speaks with such conviction and carries himself

with so much confidence, that I wonder if there's something he hasn't told me.

"How can you be sure?"

"Because I have the best partner in the world," he replies, wrapping his hand around the side of my neck and stroking my cheek with his thumb. His eyes and face soften. "No one can outsmart us. We're Team Sloane. We haven't encountered a killer yet who can slip past us, and we never will."

I sigh.

"*Fine.* You're right."

How am I supposed to argue with him?

"About the best partner in the world? I know, I'm right."

He grins, knowing flattery will get him everywhere.

"You win. We'll solve Seb's murder and get married. All in the same week." I bite the inside of my cheek. "But if we don't…"

"We will," he interrupts. "And we'll make it look easy."

"Let's not get carried away."

Eric wraps his arm around my hip and slides me across the sofa toward him. I snuggle into him, and we cuddle until we're interrupted by the violent clamour of the bell when the door bursts open and slams into the wall.

"Is it true?" Amber demands.

Eric and I jump up and apart.

Sophie leaps up from her bed with a shrill bark.

"Is what true?" Eric asks.

The taut muscles around Amber's left eye twitch, and her grip on her cellphone is so tight, her knuckles are white, and her hand is shaking.

"Is it true that Seb froze to death in the parking lot?"

"Where did you hear that?" he asks.

I take Amber's arm and lead her to the sofa. Her hand isn't the only thing shaking; her entire body is shuddering. I can feel it through her coat. This isn't a shiver from the chilly weather. It's the distinct head-to-toe tremble of pent-up emotions threatening to explode any second.

We sit down in unison.

"Trevor told me," Amber replies. "I'm leaving town tomorrow, and I was visiting everyone today to say goodbye. I went to the bakery to thank Trevor for his hard work and tell him it was a pleasure working together, and he said someone texted him that Seb died. He said the police were at Knitorious because you and Megan found Seb's frozen body in the parking lot."

"It's true," Eric admits.

Amber bursts into tears, and Eric locks the door and turns the sign from OPEN to CLOSED. I make eye contact with him and using my gaze, direct him to the tissue box on the counter. Eric retrieves the box and places it on the table in front of Amber. Sobbing, she pulls a tissue from the box.

"It's my fault Seb died!"

# CHAPTER 8

"If I had kept my word and taken Seb back to the hotel, he'd still be alive," Amber wails.

"Why didn't you?" I ask, shocked by her admission.

It never occurred to me that Amber abandoned Seb at the pub. I assumed he sneaked away from her again, like he did when Adam and I found him on the sidewalk.

"We had a fight," Amber confesses. "I was angry and stormed out. I left him at the pub." She continues to weep. "I left him drunk and alone," she says between sobs.

"What did you fight about?" I ask, after giving her some time to absorb the shock and compose herself.

"Last night I found out I wasn't Seb's only girlfriend," she scoffs.

"What?" I ask. "Are you sure?"

"Positive." Amber nods and sniffles. "Seb's *real* girl-friend, the one he never told me about when he pursued me, texted him last night at the pub."

"His phone rang a lot when Adam and I wrangled him back inside," I admit. "Was it her?"

Amber nods again.

"His phone kept ringing and vibrating. I'd had enough. It didn't stop all night. But Seb wouldn't answer it, and to be honest, he wasn't in a fit state to talk to anyone. I worried it might be urgent. A family emergency or something. And if it wasn't urgent, I wanted to turn off the sound, so I wouldn't have to hear it anymore."

"Did you?" Eric asks. "Turn off the sound?"

"I held the phone up to his face to unlock the screen. There were dozens of texts from his girlfriend. She was worried because Seb was supposed to call her with his travel arrangements, but she hadn't heard from him. She was excited that he'd be home for Christmas but worried because he wasn't responding to her texts or calls."

"Maybe she isn't his girlfriend," I suggest. "Maybe she's a family member or friend?"

"She's his girlfriend," Amber insists with a sarcastic half-laugh. "I went through their text history. They've been together for over six months. Way longer than Seb and I were seeing each other."

"Oh, Amber! I'm sorry." I give her a tight squeeze, and she rests her head on my shoulder, her body heaving with silent sobs.

"What happened after you intercepted the texts from Seb's girlfriend?" Eric asks, bringing the conversation back to Seb's murder.

"I flipped out," Amber replies, sitting up straight and blowing her nose. "I was so... so... angry." She squeezes the used tissue and bangs her fist on her lap. "Embarrassed. Violated," she says through clenched teeth. "He lied to me. And to her. He lied on purpose. He knew what he was doing. Why would he do that? Why would he hurt me?"

Watching Amber escalate in an instant from sad to angry makes me wonder if Seb's lying and cheating made her angry enough to kill him. *Could* she kill him in a fit of rage? Seb was about fifty pounds heavier than Amber and at least four inches taller. If Seb fought back, she would have defensive wounds, wouldn't she? I don't see any marks or cuts. But she's wearing a coat. Mind you, she would have worn a coat last night too. It was freezing outside. Maybe Seb *couldn't* fight back. Maybe she strangled him after he had passed out drunk. Will the coroner be able to tell if Seb was conscious or unconscious when his killer strangled him? Amber is neither big nor small. She's average. Average height, weight, and body shape. Therefore, I assume she also possesses average strength. I'm also of average strength, and I doubt I'd be strong enough to strangle Seb. Unless anger gives us strength. Hell hath no fury like a woman scorned, and all that.

"I can't believe I let this happen again," she says, squeezing the used tissue until her fingernails dig into her palm.

"You didn't *let* it happen. If Seb was a two-timing liar, his actions reflect him, not you," I remind her, rubbing her shoulder.

"Again?" Eric asks. "What do you mean, it happened again? Has Seb done this to you before, Amber?"

"Not Seb," Amber clarifies. "My ex lied and cheated on me. I even found out the same way, by intercepting his text conversation with her. I thought I'd learned from that. I thought I knew better and would see it coming next time."

"It's not your fault you trusted him," I say.

Did Amber take Seb's phone with her when she stormed out of the pub, smash it, and discard it in the bushes? Reading the texts between Seb and his other girlfriend would have reminded Amber of reading similar texts on her ex's phone. Twice the rage. Maybe she smashed the phone to destroy the texts that destroyed her life.

"Did you confront Seb?" Eric asks.

"I tried, but have you ever had a serious conversation with a drunk person?" she asks. "It was impossible to get a sensible word out of him. I don't think he understood why I was upset, which just made me angrier and more frustrated. I couldn't stand to look at him another second, so I left. If I hadn't left him, Seb would still be alive, wouldn't he?"

She looks from Eric to me, searching for someone to validate or invalidate her fear.

"You left the pub without Seb?" Eric clarifies.

Amber nods, tears streaming down her face.

"At that moment, I didn't care what happened him. I just needed to get away."

"Did you talk to Seb after you left the pub?" I ask.

She shakes her head.

"I sent him a few nasty texts when I got back to my hotel room. I figured he'd see them when he sobered up and call me."

"Did he reply to the texts you sent?" Eric asks.

"No," Amber replies, plucking two fresh tissues from the box. "He never read them. They say delivered but not read. I didn't worry because I figured he was sleeping it off and just hadn't seen them yet." She looks at Eric with pleading, watery eyes. "It never occurred to me he could be dead. Seb often has a few drinks after work, but he always finds his way home."

"Amber, I need to ask you more questions and get a full statement. Would you mind accompanying me to the station?"

Nodding, Amber stands up and wipes her eyes. "Can I freshen up first?"

"Sure," Eric replies.

I remind Amber where the washroom is, and we

watch her disappear into the back room. Sophie follows her and sits by the washroom door.

"If Amber sent text messages to Seb's phone after she got back to her room, that must mean he still had his phone when she left the pub," I whisper.

"Or that's what she wants us to think," Eric responds in a whisper. "If Amber killed Seb, she's had all night to work on her story and tie up any loose ends. She could have sent those text messages to make it *look like* she left him alone at the pub. I need to question her further, then verify her story."

"Hello, Megan!" Mrs. Bigg's cheerful smile and upbeat demeanour contrast with the sombre mood of the town after Seb's murder. "Where's Marla? I was looking forward to a good natter with her."

"She just left for lunch."

Mrs. Bigg removes her gloves and places them on the counter. She bends down and greets Sophie with a scratch between the ears.

Unlike her name, Mrs. Bigg isn't very big at all. She's a petite woman with delicate features and a small frame. I'm not used to being the tallest person in a room, but next to Mrs. Bigg, I feel statuesque. She wears her silver-streaked, tight curls short and puffy. According to Marla, she does it because the puffiness adds some height.

"I'm surprised to see you here. I'd heard you were in the city today, shopping for bridesmaid dresses and such." Mrs. Bigg smiles.

Has Mrs. Bigg not heard about Seb Gillespie's sudden death?

"Change of plans," I say. "Eric was supposed to help at the store, but he had to work so I stayed behind."

"Yes, I heard about Seb," Mrs. Bigg makes a *tsk tsk* sound. "Dreadful situation. Imagine drinking yourself into such a stupor that you freeze to death in a parking lot. And so close to Christmas." She shakes her head. "Shame." She shakes her head again. "It's too bad his drunken foolishness ruined your plans."

I bite my lip to stop myself from telling her that Seb didn't freeze to death, and in the grand scheme of things, my plans don't rank at the same level of importance as a murder investigation.

"Are you looking for Marla?" I ask. "Would you like me to pass on a message?"

"I brought you that yarn tag we discussed last night." Mrs. Bigg reaches into her purse and pulls out a cardboard tag with the yarn dyer's name, website, and the information about the yarn.

"Thank you," I say, taking the tag from her and placing it in my planner. "I'll contact the dyer after Christmas."

"I also brought more yarn to donate to the yarn drive," Mrs. Bigg adds. "This yarn drive is the excuse I needed to clean out my yarn stash and get rid of all the partial skeins I kept for no reason." She forms her face into a sly side grin. "And maybe make room for new yarn." She giggles. "Please don't tell Mr. Bigg I said that." She giggles again and produces a yellow paper gift bag, larger but otherwise identical to the one she gave to Connie yesterday.

"You're the only knitter who gift wraps her donations," I tease, admiring the paper gift bag and decorative tape seal.

"Paper is much better for the environment than plastic," Mrs. Bigg justifies. "I never use plastic if I can avoid it."

"Would you like the gift bag back?" I ask. "So you can reuse it?"

"No need, Megan," Mrs. Bigg replies. "But if you'd like to reuse them, please go ahead. Maybe if we both use paper instead of plastic, it'll become trendy, and we can eradicate plastic bags from Harmony Lake." She laughs.

"I'm a lot of things, Mrs. Bigg, but a trendsetter isn't one of them," I quip, walking the bag to the back of the store and dropping it in the donation bin.

The donation bin is getting full. I should set aside some time to sort the yarn before the charity knitters pick it up.

"Would you like a cup of tea, Mrs. Bigg? I was going to sit and knit until Marla gets back, and I'd love some company."

"Thank you, Megan. I'd love a cup of tea." Mrs. Bigg takes off her coat and settles into the cozy sitting area with her knitting bag on her lap. Sophie lies at her feet, resting her head on her front paws.

I bring Mrs. Bigg a mug of tea, then pull a skein of sock yarn from a nearby shelf and get to work winding it into a ball.

"Gorgeous colour!" Mrs. Bigg says, gesturing to my yarn. "Such a sophisticated shade of red. What is it called?"

"It's tonal," I reply. "The dyer used several subtle shades of the same colour. Tonal yarns are her specialty. This one is, *Here We Go Round the Mulberry Bush*," I read from the paper band that was around the yarn.

"Socks?" Mrs. Bigg asks.

"Eric's wedding socks. Think I can finish them in less than a week?"

"Easy peasy." Mrs. Bigg winks. "I've seen how fast you knit."

I join Mrs. Bigg in the cozy sitting area and cast on the first toe-up sock.

As we knit, Mrs. Bigg asks about the wedding and how Eric and I came to be the replacement couple for Jules Janssen and her husband. I tell her the story about Jules offering us the wedding as a gift and remind her of the commotion we had in Harmony Lake last time Jules Janssen was in town.

"Well, I for one am grateful you and Eric are getting married. It would devastate my Doyle if the wedding was cancelled. You and Eric might not be Hollywood royalty, but you're Harmony Lake royalty. I told him, 'Doyle,' I said, 'you might not get to brag about catering a celebrity wedding attended by VIPs, but at least you'll still get to cater a large wedding with hundreds of guests.' His self-esteem will benefit from the success." She pauses her needles and flashes me a sad smile. "My Doyle hasn't had many wins lately."

"How is Doyle doing?" I ask. "Is he happy at his new job? It must be a big change from running his own business."

"Stitch by stitch, he's knitting his life back together," she replies with a heavy sigh, resuming her knitting. "He's doing better than when he moved home a few months ago."

"That's good," I say. "What was his event-planning company called again? It was a clever play on words. The name is on the tip of my tongue. What was it?"

"Bigg Bash," Mrs. Bigg replies, putting my brain out of its misery so it can stop searching and move on to other things.

"Bigg with two g's? Like your name. What a clever name for a party-planning business."

"They named the company after themselves," Mrs. Bigg explains. "Doyle was Bigg and his partner was Bash.

They were only in business for a year before his so-called business-partner-slash-best friend double-crossed him and took everything that ever mattered to my Doyle. He took the business and Doyle's fiancée. And she took everything else. She cleared out their apartment and their bank account."

"Was his partner a chef too?"

"No, Doyle was the chef. His partner managed everything else. My Doyle was the creative one, you see. Doyle's fiancée worked for them. She handled the menial, administrative tasks." She drops her knitting in her lap. "I think losing her was harder for Doyle than losing the business."

"Losing one would be bad enough, but losing both would be awful," I concur.

"Yes, it seems to be easier to get his professional life back on track than his personal life." ·

"Poor Doyle! I can't imagine losing my fiancée, my business-partner-slash-best-friend, and my business."

"Don't forget Lancelot!" Mrs. Bigg adds.

"Lancelot?"

"Doyle's cat. His fiancé took Lancelot when she left. Broke my Doyle's heart. He had Lancelot long before he met her. Doyle adopted Lancelot from a shelter when he was away at culinary school. She had no right to take him. Doyle said they bonded instantly when they locked eyes at the animal shelter."

I assume she means Doyle and Lancelot bonded instantly, not Doyle and his former fiancée.

"That's heartbreaking," I agree.

"Listen, Megan, do you know any young ladies you could introduce to my Doyle?" Mrs. Bigg asks. "Someone nice. An introduction might help bolster his confidence and encourage him to dip his toe in the dating pool again."

"I can't think of anyone off the top of my head," I reply. "But I'll let you know if someone comes to mind."

I doubt anyone will come to mind, and if they do, I'll keep it to myself. Matchmaking has never been one of my strengths, and I'd rather not deal with Mrs. Bigg's disappointment if my attempt to set up her Doyle didn't end happily ever after. Shakespeare might have been describing Eleanor Bigg when he wrote, *Though she be but little, she is fierce.*

# CHAPTER 9

MARLA'S TIMING IS PERFECT. She returns from lunch just as I answer a video call from my bridal party. They've found *the perfect dresses*, their words, not mine, and want my opinion before they purchase them.

I spend the rest of the afternoon shopping with them on video chat. Thanks to the miracle of modern technology, I'm able to help choose dresses, colours, shoes, and accessories from the comfort of my cozy, small-town yarn store. We end the call just before it's time to close the store.

Just as I'm about to lock the door and turn the sign from OPEN to CLOSED, Amber comes in carrying a cardboard box. I assume this means Eric has questioned and released her.

"I know you're about to close for the day, so I won't keep you," Amber says. "These have been in my car for weeks, and I won't need them anymore since Jules cancelled the wedding. I thought you might make use of them."

With a smile, she thrusts the box at me. It's about the size of a shoe box but heavier than a pair of shoes.

"Thank you," I say, taking the box from her.

She bends down and rubs Sophie, who mustered all her patience to sit like a good girl, while waiting for Amber to notice her.

The loose contents shuffle and shift when I take the box from her and set it on the counter.

"Access passes and lanyards," Amber says as I open it to reveal the contents.

Just like she said, the box contains dozens of laminated access passes with QR codes and blue nylon lanyards to attach them to.

"Who are they for?" I ask.

"They *were* for workers who needed to access the wedding venue," Amber explains. "An extra layer of security to keep the paparazzi away." She picks up a laminated access pass and points to the QR code. "Security scans this code to see who the pass belongs to and what areas of the venue they're allowed to access. If the pass matches the person wearing it, and they're trying to access a permitted area, security grants them access. If not, security either redirects them or escorts them off the premises." She smiles. "It's a pretty common security feature at VIP events."

"I see," I say, nodding. "I don't think we'll need security at our wedding."

Amber drops the access pass into the box, and I close the lid.

"Keep them just in case," she says with a shrug. "I don't have any use for them."

"Thanks," I say. "How are you? I've been thinking about you all day. You've been through a lot since last night."

We sit on the sofa, and Amber tells me that while she's still in shock and sad about Seb's death, she's also still angry that he lied and used her throughout their brief relationship.

"I know what Seb did to me isn't my fault, but you have to admit, Megan, I'm the common denominator. Why do I keep falling for guys who lie and cheat on me?"

"I don't know," I reply. "But you're right, it's not your fault. You don't deserve to be treated like that. No one does. Do you need anything? I have to meet with Trevor soon, but I'm free after that if you want company."

"It's nice of you to offer," Amber says. "But I'm exhausted. I was at the police station for hours, and today has been emotional. I just want to fall into bed and sleep."

"If you change your mind, you have my number."

"Thanks, Megan."

After a hug, Amber leaves and I send a text to Trevor to let him know I'm running a few minutes behind schedule. I hate to be late for anything. But Amber's visit was unexpected, and considering the ordeal she's going through, I didn't want to rush her or turn her away if she needed a friend.

Trevor replies that it's not a problem, and he was so focused on the batter he's making that he didn't even realize the time until he got my text.

I help Sophie put on her dog sweater and leash, then take her across the street to the waterfront park for a quick walk. The back door is still off limits, but I peek around the corner and check out the parking lot. Crime scene tape still blocks the entrance to the parking lot, the bushes, and the area where we found Seb's body. A lone, uniformed police officer in a patrol car is stationed at the scene, but the rest of the police officers, police cars, and Seb's body are gone. It almost looks like a murder didn't happen here less than twenty-four hours ago.

"I'll be back soon to take you home, OK, Soph?" I say, detaching her leash. "I'm going to see a man about a cake." I pull Sophie's sweater over her head, and she gives her corgi body a head-to-tail shake. "There's fresh water in your bowl, and here's your dinner." I place her food bowl on the floor next to her water bowl. "Be a good girl."

On the short walk to Artsy Tartsy, I debate texting Eric to remind him about our meeting with Trevor. Eric made it clear he wants to take part in every meeting and all errands associated with the wedding. But, realistically, solving Seb's murder will require all his time and attention. I don't want to overwhelm him with demands, so I decide to meet Trevor alone. If Eric hates the cake, we'll deal with it later.

"Hello?" The bakery is unlocked but empty. "Trevor?"

It's dark and the chairs are upside down on the tables.

"Hey, Megan!" Trevor's silhouette appears in the doorway to the kitchen, the light behind him obscuring his face.

"Are you alone?" I ask.

"Yeah," Trevor replies. "April is shopping in the city, and T took Zach to hockey practice. She'll be back soon."

Zach is April and Tamara's seventeen-year-old son.

Trevor flips the light switch, and his silhouette is filled in with familiar features, like his wide smile, short, black, curly beard, and shaved head.

First, he shows me the concept drawings of the wedding cake Jules and Amber commissioned him and T to make for the original wedding. It's gorgeous and impressive, but it's more elaborate than the cake Eric and I had in mind.

"It's beautiful," I say. "An edible work of art."

"But it doesn't scream *Eric and Megan*, does it?"

"It doesn't," I agree. "But it's still a beautiful work of art."

"T sketched out a few ideas she thought you and Eric might like." He flips the sketchbook over and opens the other side. "She knows you guys better than me, so she took the lead. This is what she came up with." He hands me the sketchbook and talks me through the drawings on the page.

"These sketches are perfect!" I exclaim. "This is the exact cake we imagined. It's amazing. I couldn't have described it in as much detail as T sketched it."

Our cake is simpler than the original but just as impressive.

"I'm glad you like it," Trevor chuckles.

"I love it," I say, pulling out my phone. "Do you mind if I photograph the sketches to show Eric? He couldn't make it tonight."

"Of course," Trevor replies, holding the sketchbook while I snap a few photos. "You're sure this is the cake you want?" he asks. "With less than a week until the wedding, you won't have another opportunity to change it."

"I'm certain," I assure him.

"One hundred percent?"

"Yes," I insist, smiling. "I know someone burned you once before when you changed a wedding cake, so if it makes you feel better, I don't mind putting it in writing."

"You heard about that?"

"April told me," I admit. "I understand why you were unhappy about working with Seb on the original wedding. You paid the price for his big mistake."

"The mistake wasn't the problem," Trevor explains. "It was how Seb handled the mistake that was the problem. He told the bride and groom that *I* made the mistake. He told them *I* changed the wrong client's cake by accident. The couple almost sued me. I had to make their cake for free *and* give them money to compensate for their pain and suffering. I lost jobs because Seb told everyone in the industry what happened and that it was my fault. He made me out to be incompetent. He destroyed my reputation. I thought my reputation and business would never recover. Dead or not, I'll never forgive Seb Gillespie for lying about me and almost destroying my career."

It's obvious Trevor is still angry two years later. Did two years of simmering anger boil over when he saw Seb again? Did Trevor see an opportunity to get revenge and kill Seb?

Just as I'm about to ask Trevor what time he left the pub, the bakery door opens.

# CHAPTER 10

"HEY, BABE." Eric smiles at me, then looks at Trevor. "I'm sorry I'm late." He extends his hand for Trevor to shake. "Work is crazy today. I went to Knitorious to drive Megan home, found Sophie alone, and remembered our appointment."

"No worries," Trevor says, shaking Eric's hand. "Let me show you the drawings."

Like he did with me, Trevor walks Eric through T's sketches. Eric agrees T sketched our dream cake.

By the end of the conversation, we decide on a classic white buttercream tiered cake with sprigs of seasonal greenery to match the winter foliage Phillip is including in the flowers. Trevor says he'll coordinate with Phillip and Rose about the greenery.

We thank Trevor for meeting with us after hours and changing the cake at the last minute, then we leave.

"I'm sorry I was late," Eric says on the walk to Knitorious.

"Don't worry about it. No one expects you to put aside a murder investigation to fuss over some cake details."

"It's not some cake. It's our cake," Eric says, taking my hand. "And I want to be involved in planning our wedding. We should do this together. I can juggle wedding planning and work."

"It worked out well that you were late," I tease. "Trevor and I had an enlightening conversation before you arrived."

"What did you find out?"

I tell Eric about Trevor and Seb's adversarial work history, and the grudge Trevor still carries two years later.

"I'll question Trevor," Eric says.

"Did you find anything useful on Seb's phone?"

"His phone isn't usable, babe. Someone destroyed it."

"How?" I ask.

"The damage suggests a heavy, blunt object. A rock, or brick, or something."

"That sounds like an act of anger."

"It does," Eric agrees. "I suspect the killer destroyed the phone and threw it in the bushes."

"Fingerprints?" I ask, hopeful.

"None. Not even Seb's. Either the killer wiped the phone, or sitting in the snow destroyed the fingerprints. But I found some interesting stuff in Seb's hotel room."

"Like what?"

"Seb's laptop was there, and he didn't use password protection. His laptop and his phone sync to each other. I could read his texts without waiting for forensics to recover them."

"Anything incriminating?"

"Nothing." He sighs. "His girlfriend tried to reach him all night before he died. He would've left town this morning. There was a plane ticket confirmation in his email."

"If Seb had avoided his killer for a few more hours, he would have gotten out of Harmony Lake alive," I say.

"Jules cancelling the wedding really upset him. There was an unfinished email to Amber's boss in his drafts folder. It read like a drunken tirade. He blamed Amber for the cancelled wedding."

"How could the bride and groom cancelling the wedding be Amber's fault?"

I stop outside Knitorious and retrieve my keys from my purse.

"According to Seb, Amber made one mistake after another with the wedding. He claimed she overlooked vital details, and Jules lost confidence that the event would go off without a hitch. He closed the email by suggesting the company fire Amber and promote him as her replacement."

"Wow," I say, unlocking the door. "That does not sound like the Amber Windermere I've gotten to know. Not at all."

Eric pushes the door open, and I walk inside first.

"Like I said, I suspect he drunk-typed it."

He squats to greet Sophie, pawing at our knees.

"What time did Seb draft the email?" I ask.

"The timestamp was before Seb went to the pub. He cleared out the mini bar in his room. I found the empty bottles in the trash. He drank the entire mini bar, babe."

"Sheamus swore he only served Seb a couple of drinks at the pub. Amber confirmed it. Sheamus speculated Seb started drinking before he went to the pub."

"Seb's hotel room supports Sheamus's theory," Eric says. "Seb was still sober when he texted his girlfriend about the wedding and told her he would text her after dinner with his travel plans. His texts were clear and concise. Then he replied to work emails. His emails were professional and made sense. He was sober, or sober enough to pass as sober. Then, he packed his belongings, except for a change of clothes. He was sober enough to fold his clothes and pack them neatly, so I suspect he wasn't very drunk yet. The alcohol impaired his faculties after he finished packing, and that's when he typed the email to Amber's boss. It reads like a drunk person would talk. It's full of run-on sentences, typos, and missing spaces between words."

"But he had the sense not to send it," I point out.

"Or he ran out of booze before he finished it," Eric counters. "I think he went to the pub intending to finish the email and send it when he returned to his room."

"Except Seb never returned to his room. His killer made sure of that."

Is it possible Seb told Amber about the malicious email he planned to send to her boss? If alcohol impaired his judgement, he could've blurted it out. Or if his phone had access to his work emails, Amber could've found the draft email when she found the texts between Seb and his other girlfriend. If Amber knew Seb was trying to get her fired, it would give her another motive to kill him. But Amber's a smart woman. She would have deleted the email if she'd found it; I'm sure of it.

"Aside from you and Adam, several locals saw Rose Thorne at the pub last night. She wasn't there long. According to one person, she locked eyes on Seb, had a few words with him, then marched out."

"I knew it was her. But why did she lie?" I wonder out loud.

"I questioned Rose, and she admits she arrived in Harmony Lake last night. She planned to split the drive over two days but drove straight through. Rose told me she lied about when she got here because she didn't want to admit it in front of Phillip. She said he would feel bad that she spent the night at a motel instead of at his house."

"She's right," I agree. "You know what Phillip is like.

He would have scolded her for wasting money on a motel."

"Rose said she went to the pub for a bite to eat, not expecting to crash an impromptu engagement party. She also didn't expect to run into Sebastian Gillespie. Though she knew him by another name."

"Rose knew him? When I asked her, she insisted she'd never seen him before. What name did she know him as?"

In one brief conversation, Rose Thorne lied to me twice. That I know about. She lied about when she showed up in Harmony Lake and about recognizing Seb Gillespie. People lie to protect their secrets. What secret is Rose Thorne protecting?

"Rose knew him as Doyle Bigg. That's why she asked you if you were sure his name was Seb."

"Doyle Bigg?!" I exclaim, dropping myself into the nearest chair. "Why would Seb Gillespie tell Rose he was Doyle Bigg? Seb and Doyle knew each other before Seb came to Harmony Lake?"

"They must have," Eric replies. "What are the chances Seb pulled the name, Doyle Bigg, out of thin air? It couldn't have been random."

I stand up, put Sophie's food dish in the dishwasher, and gather her sweater and leash.

"Amber says VIP event planning is a small world." I recall. "Did Rose tell you when she and Seb met?"

"They met at a bridal convention last spring," Eric replies. "They had a one-night-stand, and he gave her a fake name and phone number. Rose says she was shocked to see him last night and was even more shocked when someone called him Seb. She said he recognized her, and when Amber left him to go to the washroom, he tried to talk to Rose."

"What did he say?"

"Rose said she didn't understand his drunken rambling. She thinks he was apologizing, but she's not sure. She said he disgusted her, so she left. But I think you were right about Seb slurring *Rose Petal*. Rose said that's what Seb called her the night they hooked up."

"That part of her story corresponds to Adam and I watching Rose leave the pub with Seb following behind her, trying to get her attention." I shake my head, overwhelmed by all the revelations. "Seb must have considered himself quite a ladies' man. First, we find out he had a secret girlfriend, then we find out he gave his one-night stand a fake name so she couldn't contact him."

"He was a creep."

"A cruel one," I agree. "Maybe Rose was so angry when she saw Seb again that she killed him."

"Maybe," Eric says. "I can't confirm her alibi. She says she was alone in her room at the Hav-a-nap hotel when Seb died."

"You know what time Seb died?" I ask. "I thought you had to wait for him to thaw out."

"It's a rough guesstimate," Eric cautions. "More guess than estimate. The coroner estimates that Seb died between midnight and four a.m."

"That's a wide window."

"He'll narrow it down when Seb thaws out."

"Did the coroner agree with you about the cause of death?"

"Strangulation," Eric confirms, nodding. "There are burn marks on Seb's neck."

"Like from a fire?"

"Like from a *fibre*," Eric reveals. "The burn marks are a holdback." He looks at me, and I nod in acknowledgement. "The murder weapon was a rope or something similar. It would be a fibre strong enough to strangle a person without breaking."

"Like Nylon?" I ask.

"It's possible," Eric replies, narrowing his gaze. "Why would you suggest something as specific as nylon?" He narrows his gaze even further. "You know something."

"I suspect something," I clarify. "Wait here." I retrieve the box of access passes and lanyards that Amber gave me earlier and hand it to Eric. "They often make lanyards out of nylon."

He opens the box, then places it on the table behind him. He pulls a latex glove out of his coat pocket and puts it on. How many latex gloves are in there? There's always a latex glove in his pocket when he needs one. It's the cop-equivalent of a magician reaching into a pocket and pulling out a never-ending chain of colourful hand-kerchiefs.

"Where did you get these?" he asks, picking up a lanyard and inspecting it.

"Amber," I reply, then tell him about my visit with Amber earlier when she dropped off the box at Knitorious. "Nylon is one of the strongest man-made fibres on earth," I say. "The strongest natural fibre is silk, but nylon is just as strong."

"Why are you so knowledgeable about nylon?"

"Most of your hand knit socks contain nylon," I explain. "Yarn companies blend nylon and wool to increase the wearability and lifespan of the socks." He stares at me and blinks. "You don't wear holes in your socks as fast because of the nylon content. Silk is more expensive than nylon and, some argue, has less elasticity, so nylon is the most common fibre to blend with wool sock yarn."

"A lanyard could strangle a person without break-ing," Eric concludes.

"That's what I thought when you told me the murder weapon was a strong fibre," I agree. "But if Amber used a

REAGAN DAVIS

lanyard to strangle Seb, I doubt she put it back in the box. She's smart. She would've disposed of it elsewhere."

If Amber strangled Seb with a lanyard, why would she dispose of the rest of the lanyards by giving them to the investigator's fiancée? Is she arrogant enough to believe she committed the perfect crime, and we can't catch her?

"I'm glad we're on the same side, and you use your powers for good," Eric teases. "I'll ask forensics and the coroner if the burn marks on Seb's neck are consistent with a lanyard. If the answer is yes, we'll test every lanyard in the box for Seb's DNA."

"Are we ready to go?" I ask, turning off the lights and heading toward the door.

"Ready when you are," Eric says, tucking the box of lanyards under his arm and following me. "We found a single cat hair stuck to the burns on Seb's neck."

This piques my interest and stops me dead in my tracks.

"Are you suggesting a cat strangled Seb Gillespie? Are you searching for a feline felon?"

Eric chuckles.

"No, but *purr*haps the killer has a cat. Or they had contact with a cat before they killed Seb."

I groan and roll my eyes at his cat pun.

"That could be anyone in town." I open the door and step onto the sidewalk. "I swear Harmony Lake has more cats per capita than anywhere in the world. We love our cats. And dogs. And birds. And ferrets. And lizards. And whatever else we can domesticate."

"This cat is unique." Eric unlocks his phone and swipes the screen a few times, then turns it toward me. "The cat I'm searching for looks like this."

"Awww, pretty kitty!"

I take the phone and zoom in on the cat photo.

"It's a Chartreux," Eric explains, taking my keys and locking the door while I admire the cat photo. "An expensive, rare breed. Breeders often have long waiting lists of potential owners. It's probably registered with papers and everything."

"Such a beautiful blue-grey coat and copper eyes." I hand him his phone.

"Do you know if there are any Chartreux cats in Harmony Lake?" Eric asks.

"I don't," I reply. "But I'll keep my eyes and ears open."

Eric texts me the stock photo of the cat.

"I'm *paws*itive we'll find the cat," I joke.

"*Fur* sure, babe!"

# CHAPTER 11

Hannah is helping at Knitorious while she's home for Christmas. Between her, Connie, and Marla, I'm not needed at the store. So, Eric and I are on a mission to cross items off our wedding to-do list.

First, we visit the jeweler to arrange wedding rings.

"Are you *kitten* me, Eric?" The jeweler asks, trying without success not to laugh when Eric shows him the cat photo on his phone. "Is the cat a *purr*son of interest in Seb's murder?"

When he realizes Eric isn't laughing with him, and the cat really is part of Seb's murder investigation, the jeweler pulls himself together and tells Eric he's never seen a cat resembling a Chartreux in Harmony Lake.

Because the wedding is less than a week away, I suggest we get our rings inscribed *after* we get married. But Eric is adamant that we get them inscribed *before*. Otherwise, he says, his ring will never get inscribed because he's never taking it off.

The patient jeweler accommodates my husband-to-be

and tells us we can pick up the rings on December 22nd—less than forty-eight hours before the ceremony.

Next, we go to Wilde Flowers to discuss the rose situation. I expect Phillip will discuss the flowers while Eric and I nod and smile. Phillip has definite ideas, and with anything plant-related, I trust his judgement more than mine.

Phillip's reaction to the cat photo is just as flippant as the jeweler's.

"Is the cat a witness or suspect?" The corners of Phillip's mouth twitch, defying his serious tone and facial expression.

"Do you recognize the cat or not?" Eric holds the phone out so Phillip can look at the cat photo again.

"It's not *furr*miliar," Phillip replies, bursting into laughter as the last syllable passes his lips. We wait while he gets it out of his system. "What if the cat *claw*yers up? Can you still question it?"

He barely makes it through his sentence before once again erupting in another fit of laughter. "I'm on a roll today." He wipes tears from the outer corners of his eyes. "Too bad Rose isn't here. She'd love this." He composes himself and meets Eric's intense glare. Phillip clears his throat. "No, the cat isn't familiar. I've never seen a Chartreux in person."

With his cat query answered, Eric wanders to the other side of the store to visit Kevin.

Kevin is Phillip's chihuahua. They're a bonded pair. Kevin sits perched on his purple velvet cushion in the display window.

"Where is Rose?" I ask.

"She's running errands," Phillip replies. "One of those errands is dropping off some samples at the bakery. All the wedding elements will be cohesive and carefully cultivated."

I hope April is there when Rose goes to Artsy Tartsy. I can't wait to find out her first impression of Ms. Thorne.

"That's too bad," I say. "I was looking forward to seeing her again."

"I know sarcasm when I hear it, sweetie." He wags his index finger at me. "Sarcasm causes wrinkles!"

"That's not true. If it were, I would look like an apple doll."

"You're right."

"I'm right about sarcasm not causing wrinkles?"

"You're right, you would look like an apple doll," Phillip clarifies. "You are fluent in sarcasm like bilingual people are fluent in a second language."

This feels like a compliment, but I don't tell Phillip because I'm sure he didn't intend to flatter me.

"Did you send Rose to run errands to avoid me?" I ask.

Phillip hesitates before answering, tapping his fingers on the counter.

"She may have said that she was uncomfortable attending your appointment," he finally admits. "Sweetie, you and Rose got off on the wrong foot. Rose knows she didn't make a good first impression, and she's embarrassed about lying to you."

"She lied to you too," I point out. "About when she arrived in town and about recognizing Seb."

"Rose and I go way back. We talked it out, and I forgave her. She lied about when she arrived in Harmony Lake because she knew I would feel bad that she checked into a motel for the night instead of staying at my house. She didn't want to show up a day early and inconvenience me. Rose feels horrible for lying to both of us."

"Then why did she do it?"

"She was in an awkward position," Phillip says in defense of his friend. "She was in an unfamiliar town.

There was a dead, frozen body blocking our path. And she had just met you. It would be enough to overwhelm anyone. Rose was embarrassed. She didn't want to admit the frozen corpse was a notch on her bedpost who gave her a fake name. Rose panicked and said the first thing that came to her. She was afraid you would judge her and think she's a woman of loose morals. It's not her fault she's a bad liar."

"Of course, I wouldn't judge her. I wouldn't judge anyone's choices about what they do with their body or who they do it with."

"I know, sweetie, but Rose didn't."

"I don't want Rose to feel uncomfortable," I say. "I want her to feel welcome in Harmony Lake, and I want her to know we appreciate her helping with our flowers, even though we aren't the celebrity couple she agreed to help." I sigh. "Maybe Rose and I can start over, and you can introduce us again."

Phillip smiles. He's Rose's friend and mine. He shouldn't be stuck in the middle of... whatever this is. There's no point in discussing it further. Phillip loves his friend, and he'll defend her to his last breath. That's who he is. He'd do the same for me. While I'd never judge Rose for her interaction with Seb, I would judge her for lying. She lied to avoid being considered a woman of loose morals, but doesn't lying imply loose moral standards? Without going into detail, she could have just said she met Seb at a convention. She didn't have to tell such an extreme lie, she just had to omit a few personal details, and disclose them only to the police. Instead, she outright lied and made it appear as though she's hiding something.

"Now that we've cleared that up"—Phillip takes a deep breath and gestures for me to sit in his sitting room—"let's discuss the other rose situation."

The rose situation, as Phillip calls it, is Jules Janssen's ardent enthusiasm for iceberg roses. According to Phillip, she loves them. Amber told Phillip that Jules has rose gardens at each of her homes with dozens of iceberg rose bushes. They're her favourite flower, and the only flower she would allow him to use for her wedding. Phillip doesn't share Jules's passion for iceberg roses.

"You don't like iceberg roses?" Eric asks Phillip.

"Oh no! I love them! They're lovely in bridal bouquets and wedding arrangements, but so are other flowers."

Phillip explains that Jules's bouquet was a massive, cascading bouquet that almost reached the floor.

"But her dress was billowy and extravagant, so the large cascade bouquet worked for her."

"It won't work for me," I say. "My dress isn't as extravagant."

"Exactly," Phillip agrees. "Connie sent me a photo of your dress. It's beautiful. Simple and elegant. Here's what I think…"

This is the part where Phillip talks about flowers while Eric and I nod and smile. With pleasure. I have neither an interest nor an eye for floral arranging.

By the end of Phillips' lecture, I agree to a round bridal bouquet featuring snowdrops, Sophie roses,—in honour of Sophie and because they work with Phillip's overall vision—and white Dendrobium orchids. The bridal party will have smaller bouquets that are a cross between a round bouquet and a posy bouquet, featuring Sophie roses and spider mums. The boutonnieres will be Sophie roses. Details about the centre pieces and urns are kind of a blur, but he's making a huge poinsettia wall as a photo backdrop. It will be on wheels so we can use it outdoors and indoors.

We thank Phillip and leave, my head full of information about cakes, rings, and flowers.

"I've shown this cat photo to at least a dozen people today," Eric says with a huff, on the sidewalk outside Wilde Flowers. "No one recognized it, and everyone thought it was a joke. If the cat isn't local, where did the cat fur on Seb come from?"

"Maybe Seb brought it from home," I venture a guess. "Assuming he had a cat, maybe some of its fur stuck to his clothes and accompanied him to Harmony Lake."

"Seb didn't have any pets. We've combed through his belongings, and the surfaces in the hotel room. No animal fur. The only hair we've found so far belonged to Seb."

"Did you contact the animal shelter and ask if they've seen a Chartreux?"

"They've *never* had a Chartreux at the shelter. And the vet doesn't have any Chartreux patients." He inhales deeply. "It's like searching for the rarest cat in the world."

"Maybe the cat isn't from Harmony Lake," I suggest. "Maybe the murderer isn't local and brought the cat hair with them from wherever they came from."

"Are you suggesting someone slipped into town, killed Seb, then slinked back to wherever they came from?"

"It's possible, right?"

"Yes," Eric admits. "But it would make my job a lot harder."

"What about Seb's girlfriend?" I ask. "Not Amber, the other one."

"She's too far away. She's staying with her parents for the holidays, and she doesn't have a cat. Her alibi is solid, babe."

We're standing on the sidewalk between Knitorious and Wilde Flowers. I hide my hands inside my coat sleeves and squeeze my shoulders toward my ears to stay warm.

The muscles in his face are tense, and he gnaws his bottom lip, then takes a discreet glance at his watch. Every second Eric spends away from work increases his stress about the case.

"What's next?" Eric asks.

"Next?"

"The wedding. What's next on our to-do list."

"The menu," I reply. "We have a tasting with Doyle Bigg tonight."

"Should I pick you up at Knitorious or at home?"

He tucks a stray curl behind my ear and strokes my cheek with his thumb.

"The tasting is a waste of time," I say, leaning into his warm touch. "A formality. The menu is a done deal. Doyle has already ordered the food. Would you mind if April comes with me instead? I don't want to exclude you, but she hinted that she wants to go. You know she loves these things."

"Are you sure? Shouldn't we go together? I can be there…"

"It's fine." I smile, hoping April doesn't have plans tonight and wants to attend a food tasting with me.

# CHAPTER 12

"ALL I'M SAYING IS, with the name Rose Thorne, florist is an obvious career choice," April says on the drive to meet Doyle Bigg. "If that's even her real name," she adds under her breath.

"You think Rose Thorne isn't Rose Thorne?"

"It's a weird coincidence that she's a florist, and her first name is a flower, and her last name is a flower part."

April and I decide that if we ever change our names to match our jobs, she'll be Suzette Crêpes, and I'll be Purl Stitcher.

"T's maiden name is Showers. If you took her name when you got married, you would be April Showers," I point out. "Does that mean you would have to become a meteorologist or an umbrella designer?"

"Why do you think I didn't take T's name?" April giggles. "Can you imagine the teasing I'd get if my name was April Showers? Anyway, I would've been an awful meteorologist," she says with a groan. "I can't imagine a more boring job."

"What was your impression of Rose Thorne?"

April met Rose when Rose dropped off samples at Artsy Tartsy.

"Her surname suits her prickly personality."

"I sense you don't like her very much?" I ask, pulling into the parking lot and finding a spot close to the door.

"I don't have any feelings about her," April shrugs. "She was neither friendly nor unfriendly. But she was uptight and looked unimpressed. She wasn't interested in making small talk. She didn't give me much to base an opinion on."

"Rose comes across as standoffish," I agree. "I think her shyness combined with her elegant appearance creates a snobby impression."

"You always look for the good in people, Nutmeg. But some people aren't that complicated. Maybe Rose Thorne is the pretentious snob she appears to be."

"Maybe."

WHEN DOYLE BIGG GREETS US, the first thing I notice is his beard and heavily tattooed arms. The piercings in his septum and eyebrow are a close second, followed by the venom piercing on his tongue when he opens his mouth to speak. His beard is thick, short, and well groomed. His short sleeve, white, V-neck t-shirt displays a rippling terrain of muscled tattoos that cover both arms from the hem of his short sleeves, to his wrist on one hand, and his knuckles on the other. I wonder how many more tattoos are hiding under his shirt? Doyle's dirty blond hair is long on top with an undercut. He secures his long hair in a high bun while he works.

Doyle shows us to a table set with the flatware, stemware, linens, and dinnerware that we'll use at the reception.

April and I remove our coats and sit down. Doyle hands us printed menus, then disappears into the kitchen.

"Is it just me, or is Doyle Bigg kinda hot?" April whispers, using her menu to hide her mouth from the kitchen door.

"He's not hard to look at," I agree.

"He looks like a cover model for a motorcycle club romance novel."

"A what?"

"It's a genre of romance novels. The male main character belongs to a biker club."

"I didn't know you read motorcycle club romance novels," I say, amused and shocked.

April shrugs one shoulder, raising the corresponding eyebrow.

"I enjoy a varied selection of genres."

"Lend me one."

"I'll grab one for you when you drop me off. There's one in particular I think you'll love!"

We peruse the menu and marvel at the amount of food and number of courses:

- *Baby spinach salad with pine nuts, feta cheese, and citrus vinaigrette dressing.*
- *Roasted butternut squash soup topped with prosciutto crisps.*
- *Cornish hen stuffed with apple-cranberry rice stuffing, accompanied by roasted sweet potatoes and parsnips.*
- *Oven-roasted prime rib au jus with a medley of roasted baby potatoes, carrots, and Brussels sprouts.*

The list continues, but Doyle interrupts us before we finish reading it. His tattooed arms now covered by the long sleeves of his white chef's coat, Doyle places the first dish in front of us.

Doyle comes alive when explaining the inspiration behind each item on our plates. His anecdotes are educational, interesting, and witty.

His eyes and face light up as he deconstructs each item. He explains how the flavours and textures work together, how they contrast and complement one another. Doyle's enthusiasm for the menu, the flavour combinations, and food in general is contagious and adds to our experience and enjoyment of the food. He's attuned to our reactions and takes obvious pleasure in watching people enjoy his culinary creations.

Food is Doyle Bigg's happy place, and cooking is his natural environment.

As we sample one course after another, I'm struck by his calm, content demeanour. He's so relaxed and comfortable that I can't help but feel relaxed and comfortable. He has a gift for creating a welcoming, nurturing atmosphere. If Doyle Bigg had a restaurant, it would be full every night.

Several courses later, I'm stuffed.

"Thank goodness there's no more food. I don't think I could eat another bite." I nudge my plate away and chide myself for wearing jeans instead of something with an elasticized waist.

"No one will have room for wedding cake," April jokes.

Just when we think we're finished, and there's no more food to sample, Doyle emerges from the kitchen carrying two plates of eggplant parmesan and twice-baked parmesan green beans.

"The vegetarian option," he declares with a proud smile, setting a plate in front of each of us.

"At this rate, I won't fit into my wedding dress," I mutter.

Doyle chuckles.

"In that case, I won't make you taste the vegan or gluten-free options."

"There's more?" April asks, dropping her fork in defeat.

"There sure is," Doyle nods.

The more we eat, the slower our pace. We're eating slower than sloths and have hardly touched our food when Doyle finishes telling us about the dish.

The conversation turns from food to small talk. The weather, Christmas, and Seb's murder.

"I try not to think about it," Doyle says with a half-shrug. "I'm sure Eric will figure out who did it."

"Seb had a one-night stand with a woman and told her his name was Doyle Bigg," I say, watching for Doyle's reaction.

He laughs and rolls his eyes.

"Unbelievable," Doyle mumbles. "When?"

"Earlier this year. In the spring. At a convention."

Doyle nods. "I think I know which convention it was."

"You don't seem shocked," April says. "Did you already know?"

"No," Doyle says. "But nothing Seb did surprises me. He had a reputation for being sneaky and dishonest. People who worked with him warned people who hadn't to watch their backs. Have you talked to Trevor Chipperfield? Seb burned him real bad."

"But why would he use *your* name?" I ask. "He could've picked any name in the world. Why did Seb claim he was Doyle Bigg?"

"Who knows," Doyle replies. "If it was the convention I'm thinking of, I was there too. Maybe he picked up one of my business cards, and my name was the first one that came to mind, or he gave her my card and told her it was his? It was a networking event, so people handed out business cards all over the place."

"Were you at the convention representing your party-planning company, Bigg Bash?" I ask.

"Yeah." Doyle nods. "It was my last event before Bigg Bash..." He makes a blast sound and uses his hands to mimic an explosion.

"Did you and Seb know each other before you worked together on this wedding?" April asks.

"We've been in each other's orbit more than once," Doyle admits. "This industry is smaller than you think."

"Did you work closely with Seb on the wedding before he died?" I ask.

"Amber was my primary contact. Seb and I crossed paths once or twice, but Amber was the hands-on project manager. He came here once. He toured the venue and took photos. Amber came to talk to me, and Seb waited over there." Doyle points to another table in the tasting room. "I don't even think we made eye contact."

"Did you see Seb the night he died?" I ask.

"At the pub," Doyle recalls. "He was drunk. Very drunk. Amber was trying to get him to drink coffee, and I could tell she was getting frustrated. Before she walked out, she slammed his phone onto the table and yelled, *Drop dead, Seb!*"

Amber mentioned nothing to Eric or me about telling Seb to drop dead. If those were her last words to him, were they a self-fulfilling prophecy?

"What did Seb do when Amber told him to drop dead?" April asks.

"Nothing," Doyle replies. "He just sat there. He didn't appear concerned."

"This must have happened after T and I left," April says to me.

"Us too," I say.

"Did you hear their conversation?" April asks. "What were they talking about before Amber left the pub?"

"I don't know," Doyle admits. "I only heard her shout, *drop dead* because she raised her voice, and I was on my way back from the washroom, which took me right past their booth." He sighs and puts his hands on the table. "Look, I don't think Amber Windermere is a killer, but ask her where she was when Seb was murdered. Their argument at the pub wasn't her only motive."

"We know," April says. "Seb had a girlfriend and didn't tell her."

"He did?!" Doyle's eyes spring open as wide as I've ever seen them.

"That's not the motive you meant?" I ask.

"Amber had another motive," Doyle says. "Seb was trying to get her fired. I think he was trying to take her job."

"How do you know?" I ask.

"I heard Seb on the phone with someone at their head office. It was the day he checked out the venue. He thought Amber and I were in the kitchen discussing the menu, but Amber left to get something from her car. While she was gone, I heard Seb on the phone. He talked about mistakes Amber made. Seb claimed she was having trouble coping, forgot things, and overlooked important details. He told their head office the wedding was too complicated and too high profile for Amber to handle. He said she was buckling under the pressure. Then he told them not to worry because he was picking up the slack and fixing her mistakes."

97

This corroborates the unsent email Eric found on Seb's laptop.

"Did you tell Amber what you heard?" April asks.

Doyle nods. "I thought she had a right to know."

"*Was* Amber making mistakes?" I ask. "*Was* she buckling under the pressure?"

"Not from my perspective," Doyle replies. "Whenever I dealt with Amber, she had a handle on everything and was on top of every detail. She was in constant contact with her client and with us, the service providers." He shrugs. "To me, it looked like Amber did a great job."

This sounds eerily similar to Seb blaming Trevor Chipperfield for changing the wrong wedding cake. Lying to damage other people's reputations seems to have been one of Seb's superpowers.

"Did you see Seb after Amber left him at the pub?" I ask Doyle, bringing the conversation back to the night Seb died.

"We left a few minutes after Amber. Just before eleven p.m. My dad had to go home and take his medication. He takes it in the morning and at bedtime. I drove since my dad can't drive anymore because of his condition, and my mum wanted to enjoy a glass of wine. I drove us home and went to bed. Last time I saw Seb Gillespie, he was in the booth where Amber left him. The next time I heard his name was Friday morning when everyone said he froze to death behind your store."

Doyle clears the dishes from our table and takes them into the kitchen. He reappears wearing a grey, hooded sweatshirt instead of his chef's whites. He's carrying several takeout containers, which he piles on the table in front of me.

"For Eric," Doyle says. "I know he's busy with work, but he told me he was looking forward to the tasting. He mentioned it at Latte Da earlier."

"Thank you, Doyle. He'll appreciate this," I say. "Eric mentioned he bumped into you today."

"Did he show you the cat photo?" April asks.

"Yeah, he did," Doyle replies with a chuckle. "He showed it to everyone in the cafe." He looks at me. "I hope Eric finds the killer and Seb's murder doesn't cast a shadow over your wedding."

"Me too," I agree with a light sigh.

I'm not capable of a deep sigh because my belly is distended from all the food I just ate. Deep breaths aren't very deep right now.

Standing up to leave, we thank Doyle for the tasting. April tells him again how amazing the food was. I tell him how grateful I am that he's our caterer.

"I'll walk you to your car," Doyle offers.

"Thanks," I say. "We'll wait while you get your coat."

"This is my coat." He half-chuckles and tugs on the sleeve of his grey hoodie.

"It's freezing out. Will you be warm enough?" April asks.

"I'll be fine," he insists, adjusting his knitted toque. The same toque Mrs. Bigg was knitting at the pub on Thursday night and at Knitorious yesterday morning. "I started the car ten minutes ago to warm it up. I hate driving in a coat. It's so restrictive."

"Where's the lovely matching scarf your mum made for you?" I ask, admiring his hat.

"Dunno," Doyle replies, shrugging. "I lost it. I'd hoped I left it at the pub, but I went back on Friday, and it wasn't there."

We say goodbye in the parking lot. April and I wave to Doyle as he drives away in his warm car while we wait for my car to warm up. I always forget to use the remote starter to warm it up in the winter, despite having an app on my phone to remind me.

"Wow," April whispers. "What do you make of that?"

"I've spent a lot of time with Amber since she came to Harmony Lake. Sure, her job stressed her out sometimes, but she was on top of it. Like Doyle said, she did a great job. She has an impressive attention to detail. I saw it firsthand when she was learning to knit. She was careful and intentional with each stitch. And she's ambitious. She's committed to her job and proud of being one of the best VIP event planners in the industry. She sacrificed Christmas with her family for her job."

"I bet she'd get angry if someone threatened her career," April suggests.

"Or if they already had a girlfriend but didn't tell her."

"Angry enough to kill?"

# CHAPTER 13

S<small>UNDAY</small>, December 19th

"Good morning!"

I stand aside so Adam can come in.

"Morning, Meg!" We exchange a cheek kiss, and he hands me a shopping bag, scanning the house. "Where's Hannah?" He bends over to greet Sophie, who is licking snow off his boots.

"Shower."

Adam, Hannah, and I have brunch together every Sunday. It's a tradition we started when we separated. We alternate between his condo and my house, but Adam always cooks. Most Sundays, Adam and I eat together, and Hannah joins us by video chat from her dorm, but since she's home for the holidays, we get to have brunch with our daughter in person.

When Adam stands up, I'm struck by how tired he looks. Dark, puffy shadows hang beneath his blue eyes, and his salt-and pepper, which is always neat, looks like he brushed it with a pillow.

"Are you OK, Adam? You look haggard."

"Thanks, Meg," he says with a soft chuckle. "Work is crazy."

"Lawyer-work or mayor-work?"

"Mayor," he replies, kicking off his boots. "Did you know Harmony Lake Town Hall closes between Christmas and New Year's?"

"I didn't know that. I guess in all the years we've lived here, I've never needed to visit the town hall between Christmas and New Year's."

"We close at noon on Christmas Eve. We don't unlock the door again until the new year," he informs me. "But there's a ton of year-end stuff to finish by December thirty-first."

"And you're busy trying to get it all done before noon on Christmas Eve?" I surmise.

"Exactly."

"Anything I can do to help?"

"How?" Adam asks. "You're even busier than me. You're getting married in five days and leaving the country in a week."

"I am?!" I demand. "Where am I going? Did Eric tell you where he booked our honeymoon?"

Adam shakes his head. "You're flying. That's all he'll tell anyone. I assume since you're flying it's out of the country." He shrugs. "I asked him, Hannah asked, and April tried to convince him to tell her in case there's an emergency and we need to reach you guys."

"Did he tell her?"

"He said Sophie knows."

We look down at Sophie, who's sitting at our feet, wagging her stubby tail, and looking up at us because she heard her name.

"I doubt she'll tell me," I say with a sigh. "Sophie's a brilliant listener, but she doesn't say much."

Adam follows me to the kitchen, and I place his shopping bag on the counter.

"What are we having?" I ask, opening the bag to peek inside.

"I'm keeping it simple this week," he says, snatching the bag away before I see the contents. "Mushroom egg-white omelets with avocado toast."

"Yummy," I say, thankful Adam isn't making a huge breakfast. "I'm glad you're not making a big meal. I'm still full from the tasting last night."

"I'll ask the tailor to give Eric and me elasticized waistbands," he jokes.

"*You'll* ask the tailor?"

"Yeah," Adam says, getting a mixing bowl from the cabinet above the stove. "I'm taking Eric for a fitting today. I had to beg and plead with the tailor to take us. He didn't want to work the week before Christmas. And it'll cost a fortune to finish the alterations in time. Holiday rates, the tailor called it." He scoffs. "I call it opportunism," he adds under his breath.

"*You're* taking Eric to get suited for the wedding?"

"Of course I am," he says, digging through the cutlery drawer until he finds a whisk. "His brothers won't be here in time, and I can't let my husband-in-law get married in an ill-fitting suit."

He says it like he's preventing the biggest fashion faux pas of the season.

"Of course you can't," I agree, distracted by the weirdness of my previous husband and my future husband getting fitted for wedding suits together. "Wait. Husband-in-law?"

"When you and Eric get married, he'll be my husband-in-law."

I've never heard this term before. Is it new?

"Will you be his husband-in-law or his ex-husband-in-law?" I ask, trying to understand the rules of this new label.

"We decided we'll be husbands-in-law."

"We?"

"Me and Eric," Adam clarifies. "We came up with it together. It's our brainchild. Catchy, isn't it? We're hoping it'll become as common as the other in-law titles."

"So, if you remarry, your wife would be my wife-in-law?"

"You got it!" he agrees. "It'll be easier than introducing Eric as my ex-wife's husband, or him introducing me as his wife's ex-husband."

"Can't you just introduce him as your friend, Eric? And he can refer to you as his friend, Adam?" I ask.

He contemplates for a moment.

"Ours is better," he proclaims, unpacking the shopping bag. "We have a non-traditional modern family, Meg, and it's time to update the traditional titles to reflect that."

"I guess," I agree.

"Anyway, I'm meeting up with Eric after brunch, and we're going to the tailor together."

"Can I help with brunch?" I ask, changing the subject.

"No, I've got this. When Hannah's ready, she can set the table."

With brunch under control, I retreat to the family room where, prior to Adam's arrival, I was contemplating my shoe conundrum.

When the bridal party went shopping on Friday, they found shoes that match the wedding dress the universe sent me. Six pairs. All in my size, all beautiful, and all look fabulous with my dress. I've been handed an entire wedding on a metaphorical silver platter, with all the decisions and arrangements already made. The only decision I have is which shoes to wear, yet I'm paralyzed with indecision. Imagine the mess we'd have if I had to make all the decisions. I'm determined to decide today which shoes I'll get married in. I'll return the other five pairs when we get back from our honeymoon.

I slip on the first pair and walk to the full-length mirror in the hall. I twist and turn one foot, then the other, admiring the shoes. I repeat this ritual five more times without eliminating even one pair. My favourite pair is whichever pair I'm currently wearing. In round two of shoe-elimination, I'll try them on with the dress.

"Geez, my friends and daughter have spectacular taste in shoes!" I mutter to myself, then release a long, loud sigh.

"What's wrong?" Adam asks, appearing in the kitchen doorway, wiping his hands on my frilly mistletoe apron.

"Nothing." I sigh again, shaking my head. "I don't know what to do. I think I know what I want, then a second later, I second guess myself. It's dumb that I'm so indecisive." I roll my eyes and chuckle.

"Listen, Meg." Adam takes my hand. "If you're hesitant, don't do it. No one will think less of you for changing your mind. This happened so fast, and you were under a lot of pressure to agree. Eric will understand. He wouldn't want you to feel rushed. I've got your back. I'll help you tell people, or cancel stuff, or whatever. It's understandable to have doubts, Meg. Marriage is a huge step."

Marriage? He thinks I'm waffling about marrying Eric?

"I'm talking about the shoes." I point to the champagne-coloured, sparkling glitter stiletto pumps on my feet. "I have six perfect but different pairs and can only choose one." I squeeze his hand. "I am one hundred percent certain about marrying Eric. It's the shoes that are tripping me up." I stretch and kiss Adam's cheek. "Thank you. Your support and opinion mean so much. You are one of the most important people in my life. We'll always be family. No matter what, or who, happens."

"Hey, Dad!" Hannah chirps from the kitchen, where she's sizing up breakfast.

"Morning, Princess!" Adam gives my hand a quick squeeze, then bounds into the kitchen and envelops our daughter in a hug, crushing her damp curls.

Hannah is a remarkable combination of both of us. She inherited enough of Adam's height to make her a few inches taller than me. She inherited my hazel eyes, which I inherited from my father. Her smile is Adam's, as is her penchant for sarcastic humour. She inherited my observation skills and ability to trust her intuition, but she inherited Adam's intelligence and passion for social justice. Luckily, she inherited his complexion and tans instead of burns when she forgets to apply SPF. Hannah's dark brown hair is courtesy of Adam, but her unruly curls are mine, and I apologize to her for it on humid days.

I slip off the champagne-glitter stiletto pumps and nestle them inside the tissue-paper lined box while Hannah sets the table and teases Adam for wearing my way-too-small-for-him Christmas apron.

OVER BRUNCH, Hannah asks about the tasting and the menu for the reception. When I tell her Doyle Bigg is the head chef in charge of catering the event, she swoons over his bearded-tattooed aesthetic.

"He pulls off the look so well," Hannah gushes. "The hair, the beard, the tatts, and the piercings. It really works for him."

"It does," I agree. "Aunt April thinks so too."

"And Doyle is so chill," Hannah adds. "He gives off this inner-calm vibe, you know? Like those monks who meditate a lot and post insightful observations about kindness and stuff on Pinterest."

"You're right," I agree, putting down my fork. "I picked up on it last night. There's something mellow and peaceful about him. And it sounds weird, but I swear it created an ambience that made us enjoy the food more."

"How do you know Doyle Bigg is chill?" Adam asks Hannah. "And when were you close enough to him to feel his vibe?"

"Doyle visits the library a lot," Hannah replies. "He's an avid reader."

Hannah helps at the library and Knitorious when she's home from university.

"What does he like to read?" I ask.

"Lots of stuff," Hannah replies. "He spends a lot of time in the non-fiction section and borrows books about business and biographies about successful business people. He also likes fantasy fiction. The sci-fi kind." She shrugs. "And the occasional thriller or murder mystery."

"Wow, Princess! You know a lot about his reading habits. Are you this informed about everyone who visits the library or is Doyle Bigg special?" Adam teases.

"Daaaad!" Hannah swats his arm. "Staaaahp!" She giggles and rolls her eyes. "I have a boyfriend. I don't *like* Doyle Bigg. I just think he's cool. Anyway, he's old. Like at least thirty."

"Remember when thirty was old?" I ask Adam rhetorically.

"Speaking of the Biggs," Adam interjects. "I ran into Doyle's parents, Mr. and Mrs. Bigg, yesterday when I was Christmas shopping in Harmony Hills."

"Did you say hi?" I ask.

"Yes. Then I helped them load a huge cat scratching post into their hatchback."

"I didn't know Mr. and Mrs. Bigg had a cat," Hannah comments, cutting a piece of omelette with her fork.

"Me neither," I say, then take a sip of coffee.

"They don't," Adam confirms. "Doyle does. His name is Lancelot, and the Biggs call him their grand-cat."

"Mrs. Bigg told me Doyle's former fiancée took Lancelot when she left," I say.

"She did," Adam confirms, then swallows a mouthful of coffee. "But she moved in with her parents, and her mother is allergic to cats, so she sent Lancelot to live with Doyle last week. Mrs. Bigg says it's the best Christmas gift Doyle could have received. She said having Lancelot around has lifted Doyle's spirits."

What are the chances Lancelot is a Chartreux? Mrs. Bigg said Doyle adopted Lancelot from a shelter. Chartreux cats are expensive and rare, so it's unlikely someone abandoned one at a shelter. I make a mental note to send Eric a text about the cat anyway, just in case.

"Did the Biggs show you a photo of their grand-cat?" I ask. "Or describe what the cat looks like?"

"No," Adam replies. "And I wasn't about to encourage their oversharing by asking questions."

"Fair enough," Hannah agrees. "Did the Biggs say anything about Seb Gillespie's murder? It's the only thing anyone talks about at the library and Knitorious."

"They said they hope Eric gets the killer off the street before he and mum leave for their honeymoon."

"We all hope that," I agree.

Hannah's phone rings, and her face lights up like a house on Christmas Eve when her boyfriend's smiling face appears on the screen. She excuses herself to answer the call and floats out of the room, buoyed by love.

I make us a second cup of coffee, and Adam and I move to the family room.

"Remember when we found Seb outside the pub on Thursday night and helped him back inside, Meg?" He sinks into the corner of the sofa, providing a lap for Sophie to snuggle into.

I nod, sitting cross-legged at the other end of the sofa.

"I told you when we left him and Amber in the booth that I had a bad feeling about it. If I had insisted on helping Amber, maybe Seb would still be alive."

"This isn't your fault, Adam," I say. "Don't blame yourself. We offered to help, and Amber declined. You offered twice, and she declined twice. You couldn't force her to accept your help."

"But I should have insisted when I saw him outside again," Adam clarifies.

"You saw Seb again?" I ask. "After we left him with Amber?"

"When I left." Adam nods. "I was leaving the parking lot when Amber stomped out of the pub. Seb wasn't with her. She was alone. I had a gut feeling, you know? I knew something wasn't right."

I nod. "Did you notice anything about Amber? Where she went? What she did next?"

"She looked angry. Even her walk was angry. Her strides were wide and fast. She stomped past my car when I was waiting to turn onto Water Street. I think she was crying. She was wiping her eyes with her palms. After she passed in front of me, I turned onto Water Street, and when I was passing the pub, Seb stumbled outside. Again. It was like déjà vu." He chuckles. "I pulled over and watched him stagger back and forth like he was looking for someone. Amber, I assumed. I was about to get out of my car and escort him back inside the pub, but Trevor came outside, and he helped Seb."

"Trevor Chipperfield?" I ask. "April and T's pastry-chef friend?"

"That's him," Adam verifies. "Trevor took Seb by the shoulders and steered him toward the pub doors, so I drove away."

"Did you tell Eric about this?"

"Not yet. We keep missing each other. He's working all hours, and I've been trying to finish year-end mayoral tasks before the holidays. I'll talk to him on the drive to the tailor. Meg, If I had stopped and insisted on helping, Seb might still be here."

"This isn't your fault, Adam," I insist again, resting my hand on his. "The only person at fault is the person who killed Seb."

"I shouldn't have driven away until I saw Trevor take Seb inside the pub."

"You didn't see them go inside? You only saw Trevor guide Seb *toward* the pub?"

Adam nods. "I should've trusted my instincts. I knew something wasn't right."

"You didn't leave Seb alone, you left him with a capable adult in a public place. Amber gave us her word she would take care of Seb and take him back to his hotel room. There was nothing you could have done."

Why would Trevor help Seb? Trevor told me he hates Seb. Did Trevor take him back inside the pub, or did he take Seb to the parking lot behind Knitorious and strangle him?

# CHAPTER 14

MONDAY, December 20th

"Hey, stranger! Why are you here? I thought you were heading home for the holidays?"

"Eric asked me not to leave town yet." We shuffle forward in line, and Amber touches my smooth, straight hair, then gestures to my made-up face. "You're not usually this formal on a Monday morning."

"We—the bridal party—just had our hair and makeup consultation at Hairway to Heaven," I explain.

"Aren't they closed on Mondays?"

"They are," I confirm. "But Kelly is a close friend, and she opened for the consultation. Knitorious is closed on Mondays, so Connie and I could attend the consultation without worrying about the store."

Amber leans into me, her mouth close to my ear. I tilt my ear toward her, ready to hear whatever she's about to say.

"I think I'm a suspect, Megan. The police think I killed Seb," she whispers. The line inches forward again, and Amber stands upright. "I didn't," she says in her usual, conversational tone of voice.

We take two more steps forward, and the barista inter-rupts our conversation to take Amber's order. Amber pays, then continues to the end of the counter to wait for her apple cinnamon herbal tea. I order and pay for my gingerbread latte, then join Amber.

"Did the police say you're a suspect?" I whisper.

"They don't have to," she replies, shaking her head. "They keep questioning me. Asking the same questions over and over. It's obvious they think I'm lying. They're trying to fluster me, so I'll contradict myself."

The barista calls Amber's name and points to a to-go cup on the counter. Amber thanks him, takes the tea, and returns to my side.

"You can talk to a lawyer," I whisper. "A lawyer will set boundaries on your conversations with the police."

The barista calls my name. I pick up my latte and say thank you.

"I'm not guilty," Amber declares on the sidewalk outside Latte Da. "If I get a lawyer, the police will think I'm hiding something."

"Innocent or guilty, everyone has the right to legal advice."

Squinting because of the harsh sunlight reflecting off the snow, I lower my sunglasses to my eyes. It's too cold to stand still, so we choose a direction and stroll along Water Street.

"I know, but I don't want to look guilty. Just because Seb lied, and made me the other woman, doesn't mean I killed him. If I killed every guy who lied to me or cheated, all my ex-boyfriends would be dead."

"Woo hoo! Megan!"

Amber and I wave, smiling at Mr. and Mrs. Bigg as they walk toward us. From a distance, the size differential between Mr. and Mrs. Bigg makes them look like adult and child, not a middle-aged married couple. I wonder if that's how Eric and I appear when we walk together, since he's almost a foot taller than me.

"Hi, Mr. and Mrs. Bigg," I say as they approach.

We go through the requisite greetings and small talk about the weather, Christmas, and the unfortunate timing of Seb's murder.

"His poor mother," Mrs. Bigg says, shaking her head. "This won't be a merry Christmas for the Gillespie family." She turns her focus to me, and her demeanour becomes less sombre and more cheerful. "I'm glad I ran into you, Megan."

"What can I do for you?" I ask.

"Do you remember the lovely scarf and hat I made for my Doyle? The one I was working on at the pub last week? Well, my Doyle lost the scarf!"

"He mentioned it when I saw him on Saturday."

"We've searched everywhere and can't find it, so I'd like to make him another one. Do you know when you will contact the dyer about carrying her yarn at Knitorious? Do you think you could order three skeins for a new scarf? In the colour noted on the ball band? I'd contact her myself, but I doubt she'd put it in the mail until after the holidays anyway, so I may as well wait and get it from you."

"I'll contact her tomorrow," I say. "I heard Doyle has custody of Lancelot again. Congratulations."

"Thank you!" Mrs. Bigg smiles. "We're thrilled Lancelot is back where he belongs. Lucky for us, the cat-thief's mother has a dander allergy." She chuckles. "Well, we should skedaddle. Only five days until Christmas, and we still have loads to do!"

We say goodbye, and the Biggs go on their merry way. Then Amber and I continue along the sidewalk.

"Was Seb's lying and cheating the only motive you would have had to kill him?"

"What do you mean?" Amber asks.

"Someone suggested that Seb tried to sabotage your professional reputation and take your job."

"Is this *someone* named Doyle Bigg?" Amber asks.

Neither confirming nor denying, I give her a tight-lipped shrug.

"Doyle told me he overheard Seb talking to my boss," Amber admits. "He warned me about Seb's reputation for using people to further his own career."

"Did you confront Seb?" I ask, sipping my latte.

"No," Amber replies. "I refused to believe it. I thought Seb loved me. But my perspective changed when I found out he lied and used me to cheat on his girlfriend."

"Now you think Doyle was telling the truth?"

"I know he was," Amber replies. "My boss confirmed it." She stops to discard her tea bag in a compost bin. "I asked her. Luckily, I have an excellent reputation, a history of successful events, and a list of happy clients to offset Seb's lies."

"Did your boss confirm it before or after Seb's death?"

"After. Yesterday, when she phoned to check in and ask how I'm doing."

"Did you tell Seb to drop dead on Thursday night?" I ask, sipping my coffee, sad at realizing I've finished it already. I knew I shouldn't have ordered a small.

"Is every conversation in Harmony Lake overheard by someone else?" Amber asks, stopping and turning to look at me. "Does anyone in this town understand the concept of privacy?"

"We have degrees of privacy, but there's no such thing as absolute privacy," I explain. "In Harmony Lake, it's best to always assume someone is watching, listening, or both."

"I didn't tell Seb to drop dead," Amber says as we resume our slow meander. "I said, *I hope you drop dead.*"

She tips her cup and finishes her tea. "Considering subsequent events, I regret saying it because it makes me look guilty. I didn't kill him, but Seb got what he deserved. I know that makes me sound heartless and guilty, but Seb Gillespie was heartless and guilty. He used people. He treated people like they existed for him to manipulate."

While her assessment of Seb isn't wrong, I suspect Amber is currently in the *anger* stage of grief.

"Did you notice if he tried to follow you when you left the pub? Did he call after you?"

"I didn't look back," Amber responds. "I was too furious and devastated. I'd just discovered I was the other woman, and he'd lied to me since the day we met. The only thing I remember between walking away from Seb and walking into my hotel room is Trevor Chipperfield, stopping me on my way out of the pub. He asked if I was OK and offered to drive me home."

"Did you take him up on his offer?"

"No," she says, shaking her head. "I told him no thank you. Then I ran off because I was about to burst into tears."

"This is my stop," I say, coming to a halt in front of Artsy Tartsy. "I need to visit April."

I also need to visit Trevor. I think he knows more than he admits about Seb's last moments alive.

"HEY, MEGASTAR!" April beams at me with her made-up face and bouncy blowout.

"Why are you glammed up?" Trevor asks, emerging from the kitchen and looking at April and me. "Are you going somewhere?"

"We had a hair and make-up consultation for the wedding," April explains.

"Our hair will be up for the wedding," I add.

"But we didn't want to leave the salon with updos," April says.

"Right," Trevor says, nodding and wiping his hands on a towel hanging over his apron strings. "Are you looking for Eric?" he asks me. "If you are, he's not here."

"I didn't expect he would be," I say, confused.

"He didn't give me an exact time, but he's coming by to talk to me," Trevor explains.

"About what?" April asks.

"Seb, I assume." Trevor shrugs. "He asked me to meet him at the station, but we're baking the wedding favours today, then we have to work on the layers for the cake. There's also the sweets table…"

"So, Eric is coming here instead?" April assumes, interrupting Trevor's to-do list.

He nods.

"Where's T?" I ask.

"Picking up more butter," Trevor and April reply in stereo.

"Megan, did Eric tell you why he wants to talk to me?"

"No," I say. "He tries to leave his work at the office."

I'm fibbing. We talk about Eric's job all the time, but Trevor doesn't need to know that.

"He already showed me the cat picture. I told him I don't know any cats like that.

"Maybe he wants to ask you about Thursday night when you helped Seb on the sidewalk outside the pub," I casually suggest.

"You know about that?" Trevor asks.

"Someone told me." I shrug.

"I thought Harmony Lake didn't have security cameras," Trevor says with a chuckle.

"We don't," April confirms. "Who needs cameras when there are eyes and ears everywhere?"

"Amber and Seb had an argument or something," he says. "I was near the door when Amber left. Then, right after she left, Seb came looking for her. He was unsteady on his feet, swaying and touching everything and everyone around him to keep his balance."

"How do you know he was looking for Amber?" April asks.

"He slurred her name," Trevor replies. "At least, I think it was Amber's name. It was hard to hear him over the sound of his phone ringing."

"Did you see Seb's phone?" I ask. "Did he answer it or look at it when it rang?"

Trevor's confirmation that he heard Seb's phone after Amber left the pub means she couldn't have taken it with her, and the phone was still in Seb's possession.

"No," Trevor replies. "Either he was too drunk to realize it was ringing, or he didn't care."

"What happened after Seb came to the door looking for Amber?" April asks.

"He kept going. No one else seemed to notice when he made it outside, but I knew he was in trouble. He could've fallen, or got hit by a car, or something. I followed him and tried to lead him back inside the pub."

"Tried?" I ask.

"He was fine until I touched him. When I put my hand on his shoulder to guide him, he shook me off and told me to leave him alone, so I did." Trevor shrugs. "I went back inside to finish my beer and left him on the sidewalk."

"Why did you help him?" I ask. "Didn't you hate Seb?"

"I couldn't stand him," Trevor confirms. "But Seb was beyond drunk. He was incapacitated. He was vulnerable, and I didn't need it on my conscience if something happened to him. When he told me to leave him alone, I walked away, knowing I'd done everything I could. My conscience was clear. It still is."

"What time was this?" April asks.

"Around eleven," Trevor replies.

"I'm sure someone can place you inside the pub after Seb left," I suggest. "You must have spoken to someone."

"I don't think so," Trevor says. "The crowd thinned out by then. I downed the rest of my beer and headed out."

"You must have at least made eye contact with someone," April urges.

"Not inside the pub. But I saw a couple of people when I went to my car. The pub parking lot was full, so I had to park on the street."

"Who did you see?" I ask.

"Let's see," Trevor says, sighing and looking up at the ceiling. "The florist."

"Phillip?" I ask.

"The other one," Trevor clarifies. "Rose. She was driving and stopped at the crosswalk in front of the pub when I crossed the street. We made eye contact. I waved to her, and she nodded."

Didn't Rose tell Eric she stayed in her motel room after she ran into Seb at the pub? I've lost count of how many lies Rose has told since she arrived in Harmony Lake.

"Who else?" April asks.

"I had to wait for Doyle Bigg's car to pass before I could pull onto Water Street. I don't know if Doyle recognized me though, or if he'd even remember a random car waiting to pull onto the road. We didn't make eye contact, and he was going faster than the speed limit when he drove past."

April and I share a sneaky glance, both recalling the tasting when Doyle told us he drove his parents home just before eleven p.m. and went straight to bed.

"But you're sure it was him?"

"Positive," Trevor insists. "I saw Rose and Doyle."

Water Street was a hub of activity the night Seb died. Full of people who claim they weren't there.

"I'm sure if you tell this to Eric, he'll confirm everything and eliminate you as a suspect," April assures him.

"Suspect?!" Trevor's eyes dart back and forth between us. "I'm a suspect? Why? I tried to help Seb! I didn't kill him. I wouldn't hurt anyone. Especially not Seb Gillespie! Killing him wouldn't be worth the prison sentence. If anyone should be a suspect, it's Doyle Bigg. Eric should ask Doyle where he was when Seb was murdered!"

"Why would Doyle be a suspect?" April asks.

"Because Seb ruined his life. He took Doyle's business, his fiancée, heck, he even bragged about taking Doyle's cat!"

"Wait," I say, dropping into a nearby bistro chair to collect myself. "Seb was Doyle's business partner?"

Trevor nods.

"The same business partner who ruined his life?"

Trevor nods.

"But Doyle's business partner's name was Bash," April says.

"Bash is short for Sebastian," Trevor says, like it's common knowledge.

"It is?" April and I ask, looking at each other.

"Trevor, when you talk to Eric, tell him this part first."

# CHAPTER 15

ON OUR MIDDAY WALK, I pester Sophie for information about the top-secret honeymoon destination. She's a tough nut to crack. No matter how hard I beg, or how much steak I bribe her with, she says nothing. Not even a hint.

When we get home, Sophie keeps me company while I pillage Eric's home office. First, I remove the large whiteboard from his wall and rummage through his drawers until I find the dry erase markers. Then I gather sticky notes in a variety of colours, a ruler, and a pack of felt-tip pens.

In the family room, I prop up the whiteboard on the mantel and write Seb's name in the centre, circling it in red. Then, I surround Seb's circle with the names of each suspect and person of interest, forming a circle of names around him. I circle each name with a different marker, assigning each suspect a unique colour. Using the ruler, I draw a line connecting each suspect's circle to Seb's circle. On one side of the line, I write Seb's relationship to the suspect. On the other side, I note the suspect's motive for murder. I stand back to admire my chart so far.

"What do you think, Soph?"

Sophie responds by sighing and not lifting her chin off the armrest.

My chart resembles a spoked wheel. Seb's circle is the hub and the straight lines are the spokes. To complete my murder wheel, I draw lines connecting the suspects who know each other, noting on each line the nature of their relationship.

Now it looks less like a wheel and more like an evidence board from a television detective show. It's a schematic overview of Seb's murder, and the chaos he created when he was alive.

In the upper right corner of the whiteboard, I draw a circle, two triangle ears, two dot eyes, an upside-down triangle nose, and a round $w$ mouth.

I stand back to assess my drawing. There's no risk I'll win an art award, that's for sure. Hannah drew better cats when she was in kindergarten. I realize it's missing an important feature and draw three whiskers on either side of the cat's face and a question mark underneath.

In the upper left corner, I draw a piece of rope to represent the murder weapon. I'm much more satisfied with the rope drawing because rope is just thick yarn, and I'm pretty skilled at drawing yarn, if I say so myself. I draw a question mark under it.

I make notes of alibis, lies, and other information the suspects have revealed on sticky notes in each suspect's assigned colour, sticking them to the board near the people they apply to.

The doorbell startles me and sends Sophie into a frenzy of skittering paws and high-pitched yelps as she scurries for the door, trying to get traction on the wood floor.

"Rose!" I smile. "Hi!"

"I have your December floral arrangement," she says,

hoisting the bouquet in front of her face, then lowering it again.

When Eric and I started dating, we went to a fundraiser with a silent auction. One of the silent auction items was a year of monthly floral arrangements courtesy of Wilde Flowers. Eric won, and I received a beautiful, seasonal bouquet every month for a year. Eric renewed the subscription for our first anniversary. Today's floral arrangement is the final one for the second year. I'll miss having fresh flowers to look forward to, but I'm thankful to have had them for two years.

"Phillip wanted to bring it himself, but he's busy arguing with the poinsettia woman. They have differing opinions of what colour Ice Punch poinsettias should be."

"I don't envy the poinsettia woman," I joke, moving aside and gesturing for Rose to come in.

"Me neither," Rose chuckles.

I take the floral arrangement from her and invite her to join me for a cup of coffee. Now is as good a time as any to make a fresh start with Rose.

She accepts my invitation and shrugs off her gorgeous oversize, belted, waterfall, floor-length wool coat and reveals today's jaw-dropping designer outfit: a cream-coloured, belted, long-sleeved jumpsuit with a deep V-neck. The contrast of the cream silk against her long dark hair is stunning. Every time I see her, I'm overcome with wardrobe-envy. April would love this outfit! April and I have developed such a crush on Rose Thorne's wardrobe that we text each other about her daily outfits. And coats. From what we can tell, Rose has an entire wardrobe of just winter coats. She's worn four different coats in the five days she's been here. And she has a penchant for belts. So far, Rose's outfits and coats have all featured wide, trendy belts.

Belts.

Belts?

BELTS!

"Ahem." *Cough, cough.*

I clear my throat to stop myself from gasping, and use the large floral arrangement to hide my face in case my expression reveals my shock.

Rose's belt could strangle a person and not break. I bet one of those wide fabric belts could leave friction burns too! Did I just find the murder weapon?

Pretending I didn't just have an epiphany that Rose's killer wardrobe might actually be a killer's wardrobe, I flatter the heck out of her outfit and coat. She tells me her sister is a publicist for a popular fashion magazine and gets a lot of samples and gifts. She says most of her wardrobe is courtesy of her sister's designer hand-me-downs.

"I notice most of your coats and outfits have belts," I comment nonchalantly. "It's a flattering look for you. Are belts your favourite accessory?"

"I like them," she says, flicking the long tail of the belt tied at her waist. "But I don't love them. My sister just gives me a lot of belted outfits, I guess." She shrugs. "I'd never really noticed until you mentioned it."

"They look great on you," I reiterate. "Super flattering."

"Thank you, Megan." She smiles.

Still holding the floral arrangement, I spin in a confused circle.

"This is embarrassing," I admit. "I'm not sure where to put it. Phillip always decides, and I always let him."

"Phillip likes to have the final say on all things floral, doesn't he?" she asks, laughing.

"Yes, he does," I agree. "To be fair, he's always right."

"Yes, he is," Rose concurs, relieving me of the aromatic blooms and carrying them to the table under the living room window. "This one needs full light," she explains, setting them down.

While Rose fusses over the bouquet, I make coffee and plate a selection of cookies from Artsy Tartsy. When your best friend and her wife own a bakery, there's never a shortage of fresh cookies.

Lifting the tray to take it to the living room, the evidence board catches my attention from the corner of my eye. I wouldn't want Rose to see it, especially since I named her as a suspect. I sneak into the family room, turn the board so it's facing the wall, bring my finger to my lips, and make a silent *shhh* motion to Sophie, who's watching me, then join Rose in the living room.

"Is Eric close to finding Seb's killer?" Rose asks casually between sips as though she were inquiring about our weekend.

"He's confident he'll make an arrest."

"I hope he does. Soon," Rose says. "I've told him if I can answer any more questions, I'm happy to help in any way I can."

"You could help by telling Eric *everything* you did and *everywhere* you went on Thursday night," I suggest.

"I did," Rose insists. "I went back to my motel room. Just like I told Eric when he questioned me."

"Did you leave out the part where you saw Trevor Chipperfield later that night?" I ask. "Or did you forget you left your motel room, returned to Water Street, and saw Trevor?"

Without deviating from her perfect posture, she lowers her coffee cup to the coaster on the table in front of her and clasps her hands in her lap. She meets my gaze, her neck appearing even longer than usual.

"I don't recall encountering Trevor that night." She tilts her head and offers me a small smile.

"You stopped for him at the crosswalk in front of the pub," I remind her.

"Right!" She nods, her eyes fixed on the corner of the coffee table. "I'd gone to the pub for dinner but lost my appetite when I ran into Seb. But after returning to my room and calming down, my hunger returned. I drove to Water Street in search of something to eat. Trevor was at the crosswalk in front of the pub. I stopped so he could cross."

"Did you find something to eat?"

"The only thing open that late, aside from the pub, was Deliclassy. I picked up a chicken salad sandwich and took it back to my room."

This should be easy to verify. I remind myself to create a chicken-salad sandwich sticky note for the evidence board.

"Did you see anyone else?" I ask.

"Did someone else say they saw me?"

Why is she being cagey? What is she hiding?

"Look, Rose. I don't care who you saw or what you did," I say, hoping if I'm direct and honest with her, she'll be honest with me in return. "I just want to help Eric solve Seb's murder before we get married, so he can enjoy the wedding and relax on our honeymoon without being haunted by an unsolved murder case. The quicker we find Seb's killer, the quicker *everyone* can get on with their lives, including you."

Rose inhales and exhales.

"When I left Deliclassy, Doyle Bigg's car was in front of me on Water Street,"

"Was Doyle's car moving or parked? Are you sure it was Doyle's car?"

"Moving," Rose replies. "I'm sure *now* that it was Doyle's car. I didn't realize it that night, but I've since met

Doyle and have seen his car. I'm certain it was his car in front of me on Water Street the night of Seb's murder."

"How long did you follow him?"

"Until he pulled into the parking lot behind Knitorious."

She picks up her cup and sips her coffee.

Why didn't Rose mention this before? She knows we found Seb's body behind Knitorious, therefore she must know this is important information.

"Rose, why didn't you mention this on Friday, when you saw Seb's body?"

"I had already lied to you, Phillip, and the police," Rose explains. "I lied about when I arrived in Harmony Lake, and I lied about knowing Seb. If I'd admitted that I saw a car pull into the parking lot the previous night, it would've contradicted my alibi and exposed my lies." She sips her coffee and sets the mug on the coaster. "Also, I'd already lied twice, so I didn't think Eric would believe me, anyway. It would come across as an attempt to redirect his investigative focus to someone other than me, making me appear guilty."

She's not wrong, but it also would've given Eric another lead to follow, or at least another lead to eliminate.

Rose Thorne is a cunning and effortless liar who remains calm under pressure. I don't know if she's telling the truth or spinning another yarn.

# CHAPTER 16

"Hey, handsome." I smile, then turn my attention back to the evidence board.

I press a light blue sticky note near Trevor's suspect-circle with the information he told me about seeing Rose at the crosswalk the night Seb was murdered. I pick up the ruler and draw a line connecting the sticky note to both Rose and Trevor.

"Wow! Stunning," Eric says, grinning from ear to ear.

He lobs Sophie's stuffed squeaky squirrel down the hall. She runs after the toy and slides into the front door.

"It's an evidence board," I say, smiling.

"I was talking about you," he corrects me. "Somehow you're even more gorgeous than usual."

"Thank you," I say, my cheeks flushing with heat. "We went for our hair and makeup consultation this morning. The evidence board is stunning too, right?" I gesture to my creation with a flourish that would make a game show model proud.

"It's the most stunning evidence board I've ever seen." Eric chuckles and slides his hand under my hair, rubbing the back of my neck.

"Thank you." I stretch and kiss him.

"Did you leave any stationery supplies in my office?"

"You need more light green sticky notes."

I raise my eyebrows toward the impressive stack of light green sticky notes stuck to the evidence board. By far, the most popular sticky notes I've used today.

"Who's light green?" He gets closer to the board and follows the tangle of lines leading to and from the light green sticky notes. "Doyle Bigg. Hmm."

"And thank you for the flowers. They're beautiful." I kiss him again. "Rose Thorne delivered them. She stayed for a cup of coffee, and we had an informative chat. I might've discovered the murder weapon."

"Are you serious, babe?"

"As serious as a murder investigation five days before our wedding."

I tell him about Rose's enviable wardrobe and her flattering belts. Then I tell him how his description of whatever left the marks on Seb's neck match the characteristics of Rose's many belts.

"I need to get hold of the coat and clothes Rose wore on Thursday night," he says, typing on his phone.

Using the evidence board, we illustrate the events and their timeline on the night Seb died. I tell Eric about my chat with Rose and her disclosure that she saw Doyle Bigg's car pull into the parking lot behind Knitorious.

"As confirmed by Trevor"—I point to the blue sticky note near Trevor's suspect circle—"who made eye contact with Rose shortly before, at the crosswalk in front of the pub."

"What does the number on each sticky note mean?" he asks.

"It's the order the events occurred."

"Why doesn't Rose's pink sticky note about the chicken salad sandwich have a number?"

"It's coral," I correct him. "I haven't numbered it because I'm waiting for you to confirm whether she bought the sandwich and what time."

"Wow. I should hire you."

"No thank you." I smile. "One cop in the family is enough. Besides, I wouldn't want you to get sick of me."

"As if," Eric scoffs with a flirty grin. Then he sighs and opens his notebook to a fresh page. "So, Rose lied. Again. She had the opportunity. She was near the pub around the time Seb was last seen alive, and she might have worn the murder weapon around her waist."

"Don't forget motive," I remind him. "She was so angry when she saw Seb at the pub that she left. It was the first time she'd seen him since their one-night stand. And she refused to admit she'd ever met him until you confronted her with her lies."

"Aside from her belt, she might have had rope in her car," Eric suggests. "You know, that string florists tie around bouquets."

"Florist twine," I state. "Sometimes living and working next door to a florist comes in handy." I shrug. "And she lies," I remind him. "What's the saying? *People who have nothing to hide, hide nothing.*"

"We'll test the belts, and I'll ask the coroner if he thinks florist twine could have caused the burn marks on Seb's neck." He makes a note in his notebook. "But Amber was also angry at Seb, and she also had a motive."

"Amber had two motives," I point out. "She was told, but claims she didn't believe, that Seb was trying to sabotage her career and take her job. She admitted Doyle told her weeks ago, and her boss confirmed it after Seb died."

"And she had the opportunity because she turned off her phone when she left the pub," Eric discloses. "I can't track her movements. The last known sighting of her is when she walked in front of Adam's car. I can't account for her between then and when she turned on her phone in her hotel room and texted Seb."

"She never mentioned that when we spoke. Why would she turn off her phone late at night when she's alone?" I ask. "That's not safe."

"I asked her the same question, and she told me she turned it off to avoid Seb," Eric explains. "Amber said she was weak, and if Seb had called or texted her, she would've responded. She said she wanted to cool off before she dealt with him again." Eric pauses. "And Amber's text to Seb could be a red herring," he suggests. "To make herself appear innocent."

"How?" I ask. "By arguing that the text message proves she believed Seb was alive?"

"Yup." Eric nods.

"Amber is clever. If she killed Seb, she'd cover her tracks better than with a contrived text message. And if she used a lanyard to strangle him, she wouldn't have given me the box of lanyards. She's more logical than that."

"Murder isn't logical, babe, and Amber would have been emotional and stressed if she killed Seb. It's hard to make logical choices when you're emotional and stressed out."

"Fair enough," I agree.

"So," Eric says, using his pen as a pointer to follow the lines on the evidence board, "Trevor saw Amber on her way out of the pub, and Adam saw her just after she left the pub. The next time anyone saw her was the next morning. Trevor saw Rose at the crosswalk, and Rose confirms Trevor was alone. Where did Trevor go after he crossed Water Street?" Eric uses his finger to lift light blue sticky notes, reading Trevor's timeline. "Doyle Bigg passed him when he was pulling out of his parking spot?"

"Yup," I confirm. "That's two Doyle sightings." I point to a sticky note in Doyle's collection of light green sticky notes. "Rose saw him turn into Knitorious, and before that, he passed Trevor on Water Street. So much for driving his parents home and going straight to bed."

"Doyle's parents verified his alibi. They insist they locked up and went to bed when they got home from the pub."

"If Mr. and Mrs. Bigg went to bed, Doyle could have sneaked out without them noticing."

"Are there any light green sticky notes left?" Eric asks, standing up.

"A few," I say, handing him the pad.

In upper case letters, Eric writes LANCELOT and underlines it. He stands up, peels the sticky note from the pad and slaps it on the evidence board next to my kitty drawing. Then he uncaps the black dry erase marker and draws an arrow from the cat to Doyle Bigg's suspect circle.

"Are you serious?" I drop my butt onto the coffee table, flabbergasted. "Lancelot is the Chartreux you've been looking for?"

Eric nods, opens his phone, and hands it to me. It's a picture of a Chartreux. Not the stock photo he showed around town, but a photo he took himself in Mr. and Mrs. Bigg's kitchen.

"Doyle Bigg's cat is the source of the cat hair you found on Seb's body?"

He nods again, and I hand him his phone.

"I'm waiting for forensics to confirm the cat hair on Seb's body came from Lancelot, but initial examination indicates it did."

A knot of anxiety swells in my belly, and I'm overwhelmed by confused anxiety. Cognitive dissonance, but I prefer to call it instinct. The knot in my stomach and anxiety invade my body when there's a conflict between what I believe and the apparent reality. My instincts have always been right, even if it takes me a while to prove it sometimes.

Doyle Bigg is not a killer. Sure, he had good reason to hate Seb Gillespie, but Doyle didn't kill him. Did he? First, it's too obvious. Doyle would know that, given their history, he'd emerge as the prime suspect. Also, Doyle might appear rough and tough with his piercings and tattoos, but he's a calm, gentle soul who loves his kitty and makes sure his parents are home in time to take their medication. Isn't he?

"Babe, it's looking more and more like Doyle killed Seb." Eric sits on the sofa in front of me and takes my hands in his.

"Trevor told you Seb was Doyle's former business partner? The one who ruined his life."

"Yes," Eric replies. "And I confirmed it. Sebastian Gillespie was the Bash in Bigg Bash. You have to admit, it's suspicious that Doyle failed to mention it."

"He didn't just fail to mention it. Doyle outright lied to April and me when we asked him if he'd ever worked with Seb. He said something vague about them orbiting each other." I sigh. "But just because he lied doesn't mean he's a murderer. Rose lied about knowing Seb too," I argue. "Anyone who had a negative history with Seb would be tempted to lie about it after his murder. No one wants to admit they had a motive.

"Their history isn't the only evidence that suggests Doyle is the killer," Eric explains. "The cat hair evidence links Doyle to Seb's dead body and to the crime scene. And he lied about his alibi. Two witnesses place him near the crime scene, around the time of the murder." He inhales deeply and sighs. "I know it's difficult to believe."

"It's not difficult to believe. It's impossible." I pause,

searching for the right words. "It feels *wrong*. Like we're missing something. What are we missing?"

"The murder weapon," Eric responds. "It's the missing piece of the puzzle. The murder weapon is the key to untangling Seb's murder."

I shake my head in disbelief.

"It's too obvious. Doyle would've known he'd be the prime suspect if something happened to Seb. Why would he take that risk? It doesn't add up."

"I know." Eric strokes the tops of my hands with his thumbs. "Like I said, murder isn't logical. Sometimes the most obvious solution is the correct one. Occam's razor."

"Occam's razor states that the simplest explanation is usually the right one, *if one uses ONLY known facts and not anyone's testimony*," I point out. "The only proof we have that Doyle was at the crime scene and lied about his alibi is witness testimony. And one of those witnesses has lied at least three times."

"The cat hair isn't testimony," Eric reminds me. "It's tangible evidence."

"This will devastate Mr. and Mrs. Bigg," I say. "It will break their hearts. Mr. Bigg has a medical condition, and Mrs. Bigg's world revolves around her Doyle."

Doyle Bigg is a killer? I can't wrap my brain around it. How could my instincts have gotten it so wrong?

# CHAPTER 17

TUESDAY, December 21st

Doyle Bigg agreed to meet Eric at the police station first thing this morning. I haven't heard from Eric since he left the house before dawn.

In the meantime, I occupy myself by preparing and packing online orders, hoping if I stay busy, Connie won't notice I'm on pins and needles, waiting for an update from Eric.

When my phone dings, I almost jump out of my skin.

"Are you all right, my dear?" Connie asks, giving me the side eye. "You're a bundle of nerves today."

"I'm fine," I say. "Just distracted." I smile and crinkle my nose. "Wedding stuff."

Half-listening to Connie, I pick up my phone and open Eric's text message.

***Eric: He confessed.***

I gasp and cover my mouth with my hand.

"There's no need to panic, my dear. Everything will be fine…"

As I reply to Eric's text, I'm aware of Connie speaking

to me, but I'm only processing bits and pieces of what she says.

"It's understandable that you're nervous about getting married again," Connie assures me. "Everyone gets cold feet this close to their big day."

Wait! What? Cold feet? She thinks I'm having second thoughts? I hit send on my text to Eric and turn my attention to my surrogate mother.

"I'm not nervous about the wedding," I assure her. "There's been a break in the case. I've been on tenterhooks all morning waiting for an update."

"What kind of break?" Connie asks, watching for any context clues my body language or facial expression might divulge.

"Eric says the evidence leads to one suspect. He met with that person this morning."

"Who?"

I purse my lips and give her a small, tight-lipped smile.

"You can't tell me."

I shake my head, even though it was a statement and not a question.

"Well!" She rests her hands on her hips and looks past me in contemplation, then looks at me again and smiles. "This is great news! It means Eric will tie up this unpleasantness before Friday. Your future husband won't meet you at the altar, tangled up in knots about an unsolved case."

"Yes," I say with a massive sigh of relief that I don't have to hide my nervousness from Connie anymore. "*If* the suspect did it."

"You don't think…"

Connie's phone interrupts her before she can finish her thought.

"It's Marla," she says, reading the screen. "She's on her way to the Bigg residence."

"Why?" I ask.

"She says Eleanor Bigg is in a frenzy because the police showed up with a search warrant."

Connie looks at me for an answer.

"Oh," I say. "Tell Marla to let us know if she needs anything."

Connie types a reply to Marla, then sets her phone on the table.

"Doyle Bigg is Eric's suspect?"

Before I can confirm or deny her suspicion, both of our phones chime, ding, and vibrate.

Connie reads and replies to text messages, and I exchange texts with Eric as he gives me more updates about Doyle's confession and how it might affect our wedding.

"Pretty much everyone knows about Doyle and the police search at the Bigg residence," Connie says, scrolling her phone screen. "It's all over town."

"That must be a record," I say, walking to the door. "Doyle's been at the station for less than two hours."

I turn the sign from CLOSED to OPEN and unlock the door.

"Why don't you take Sophie for a walk, my dear?" Connie rubs my back, looking at me over her reading glasses. "You can leave your phone here and avoid the gossip for a while. The fresh air will do you good."

"Sophie's not here," I point out. "She's at home with Hannah today."

"Heavens!" Connie chuckles. "I forgot. I'm so used to her being here, I just assume she always is. She's part of the fixtures and fittings at Knitorious. The customers will miss her."

"What customers?" I ask. "There are no tourists

136

because Jules Janssen booked every bed in town, and the locals are in nesting-mode because it's four days before Christmas."

"And three days before your wedding," Connie sings, grinning from ear to ear.

As I walk around the store collecting items to fill the online orders, I break into a smile when I realize this is the last batch of online orders I'll send out before Christmas, and before Eric and I get married.

"Speaking of the wedding, my dear," Connie says. "Who will cater the wedding reception if Doyle is behind bars?"

"Would you believe Doyle still intends to cater it?" I ask. "Eric says they'll probably process and release Doyle pending a court date, and Doyle told him he still wants to cater the wedding."

"Oh my! That man certainly is dedicated to his work, isn't he?"

"Right?!" I drop an armful of yarn onto the counter. "Imagine catering a wedding for the cop who arrested you and his wife who helped him gather the evidence?!"

"It doesn't sound like a character trait of a cold-blooded killer."

"No, it doesn't," I concur. "Someone so selfless can't be a murderer, they just can't!" I stomp my foot in frustration.

"You don't believe Doyle Bigg killed Seb Gillespie, my dear?"

"Every instinct I have tells me Doyle is innocent," I admit. "But my instincts conflict with the evidence."

"It's not the first time."

"I know. But in murder investigations, evidence trumps instincts."

"Not always," Connie corrects me. "Eric has trusted your instincts over evidence before."

"In those cases, he used my instincts to guide him to evidence that proved my instincts were right. Here, the evidence always points at Doyle. The cat, the false alibi, the eyewitness seeing him enter the Knitorious parking lot, his acrimonious history with the victim." I sigh and sink into the sofa, defeated. "My gut feeling can't compete with tangible proof."

"Let's see what Eric finds out after he confronts Doyle with the evidence. You never know."

I FINISH packaging and addressing the online orders, then update the website to advise online shoppers that orders placed between today and January second won't ship until January third.

On January third, I'll be on my honeymoon... some-where... beachy... and accessible by plane. I can't stand not knowing where we're going. Hopefully, we won't spend our trip obsessing about Seb Gillespie's unsolved murder.

"Chief Sloane is in a meeting," says the youngish officer working the front desk at the police station.

"No worries," I say. "Can you make sure he gets this?" I hold up a bag of food. "It's his lunch."

After I delivered the online orders to the post office, I stopped at the pub and picked up lunch for Eric. He doesn't always eat properly or get enough sleep during a murder investigation. Today's lunch special was one of his favourites, Shepherd's pie served with salad.

"I'll let the Chief know you're here, Megan," another, older officer interjects.

"Thanks." I smile. "But if he's busy, don't disturb him..."

"He'd insist." The officer smiles.

"Thank you. I'll wait over here." I gesture to the nearby chairs.

"That's the chief's missus," the older officer hisses to the younger officer as I sit down.

Moments later, the secure door buzzes, and Eric opens it.

"Hey, babe," he says, gesturing for me to follow him into the epicentre of the police station.

"I'm sorry if I interrupted a meeting," I say as we navigate through the maze of hallways that lead to his office. "I brought you lunch." I hold up the bag.

We enter his office, and he closes the door behind us.

"It smells amazing. I'm starving," he admits, closing files and shuffling papers out of the way to make room to eat. "I've only had two large coffees and an apple fritter."

"I know you're busy, but you have to eat properly and get enough sleep," I lecture, placing the bag on his desk. "Unless you want our wedding photos to feature an exhausted, sick groom."

I open the bag and unpack the food containers.

"Thank you," he says, hugging me and kissing the top of my head. "Your timing is excellent. I needed to see you." We pull apart, and he gives me a kiss.

Eric sits at his desk and digs into his Shepherd's pie and salad. I sink into the leather sofa against the far wall, and we talk about the imminent arrival of our families tomorrow, the barber appointment he's rescheduled three times since Saturday, and our meeting tonight with the officiant to discuss our vows.

"I'll leave so you can get back to work," I say, standing up as he tosses the empty food containers into the bag on the floor.

"If you arrived a few minutes later, we would've missed each other. I was going to Knitorious. I need to talk to you."

"About what?" I sit back down.

"Doyle Bigg."

"He confessed, didn't he?"

"As soon as he sat down in the interrogation room," Eric replies.

"Really?"

"You're shocked," Eric says. "You're still convinced he didn't do it."

"If Doyle confessed, he must be the killer, and I must be wrong." I shrug, shaken because, for the first time in my life, my instincts have misled me.

"That's why I need to talk to you," Eric says. "I don't think you're wrong. I also suspect Doyle Bigg might be innocent."

"You do?" I ask, dubious. "Why?"

"He doesn't know any specifics about the crime scene or how Seb died," Eric explains. "Doyle said he strangled Seb with his bare hands, which conflicts with the coroner's findings and with the marks on Seb's neck."

"Maybe Doyle wore gloves or mittens?" I offer. "He's a muscular guy, and he has the physical strength to strangle someone."

"He insisted he did it with his bare hands until I told him about the marks on Seb's neck. Then he changed his story and said he wore gloves."

"Can you test his gloves?"

"They're leather," Eric replies. "The coroner says the burn marks aren't consistent with leather. He's adamant a rope-like fibre caused them. I took the gloves anyway. Maybe forensics will find Seb's DNA on them." He shrugs one shoulder. "But I doubt it."

"Why would Doyle confess to murder, then lie about the murder weapon?"

"Because he doesn't know what the murder weapon is," Eric theorizes. "Because Doyle Bigg wasn't at the crime scene. The best way to avoid admitting he doesn't know what the killer used to murder Seb is to pretend the weapon doesn't exist."

"What about the other holdback?" I ask. "Did he know about the damage to Seb's phone?"

"No." Eric shakes his head. "I asked him to tell me about Seb's phone, and he panicked. It was obvious he didn't know why I asked about the phone. He said he never heard or saw Seb's phone."

"Is it possible that Seb dropped his phone before Doyle killed him, and somehow, someone other than the killer—maybe an animal—damaged it and left it in the bushes behind Knitorious?"

Eric contemplates for a moment, stroking his chin with his thumb.

"What are the odds someone disposed of the phone so close to the crime scene?" he asks. "Without disturbing the bushes or the surrounding snow? No, I think the killer attempted to destroy and dispose of the phone, probably so the ringing and vibrating wouldn't draw attention to the crime scene."

"Why not just turn off the phone?"

"They could have," Eric agrees. "But the parking lot behind Knitorious isn't lit that late at night. I suspect that between the darkness and the killer's stress level, finding the button and waiting those few seconds for the phone to power-down required more patience than the killer had."

"What did Doyle say about Lancelot's fur on Seb's body?"

"I told him we're comparing Lancelot's DNA to the DNA from the cat fur we found on Seb's body. Doyle said the fur must have transferred from him when he strangled Seb. He didn't know Lancelot was a Chartreux."

Eric gets up from behind his desk and joins me on the sofa.

"Didn't you show the cat photo to Doyle a few days ago?" I ask. "The one you had on your phone before you found out about Lancelot?"

"Yeah," he replies, nodding. "On Saturday at Latte Da. He said the cat didn't look familiar. Today, he admitted he lied because he was scared the cat would somehow tie him to Seb's murder.

"So on Saturday, Doyle didn't want you to connect him to Seb's murder, or even admit Seb was his former business partner, but today out of nowhere, he confessed to Seb's murder. What changed his mind?"

"Remorse," Eric replies. "Doyle said he's sorry Seb died, and he wants Seb's family to have closure."

"I believe if Doyle killed someone, it would wrack him with guilt. Sometimes even killers get an attack of conscience, right?"

Somehow, Eric and I have switched sides. He's trying to convince me Doyle is innocent, and I'm making arguments for Doyle's guilt. I guess we both need to be sure of our positions.

"He wants me to believe he killed Seb. Why wouldn't he tell me what and where the murder weapon is? Or how Seb's phone ended up damaged and in the bushes?"

"Is there enough evidence for a jury to convict him?"

"A jury won't have to convict him if he pleads guilty."

# CHAPTER 18

"Do you want to taste some treats?" April asks, giving the large white confectionery box a gentle shake. "T and Trevor made them for the dessert table."

"Yes!" I declare, getting up from the harvest table. "I'm ready for a break. I've been sorting the donated yarn. It's mind-numbing."

"Where's Connie?"

"She left for lunch, and I gave her the rest of the day off," I call from the kitchenette as I gather plates, napkins, and two glasses of water. "We've only had a few customers today. I might close early."

In keeping with the wedding's winter-wonderland theme, everything in the confectionery box is snow-white or decorated to appear snow-covered. Vanilla cupcakes with white frosting sprinkled with coconut shavings, white meringue snowballs, shortbread snowflakes with powdered sugar, miniature powdered doughnuts, almond sugar cookie sandwiches with buttercream filling, and white cake pops with silver sprinkles.

"This is just what they've baked so far," April says, finishing a cake pop.

"There's more?"

"Lots more." She nods. "Are you finished? You only had one shortbread snowflake. Are you feeling OK, Megaroni?"

"I'm not hungry," I admit.

"It must be serious if you can resist T's baking," April teases. "Take these home for Eric." She closes the box and places it under the counter near my purse.

"It's the murder investigation," I say. "It's makes my stomach ache."

"Didn't Eric charge Doyle Bigg with Seb's murder? I thought it was a done deal."

"Eric thought it was a done deal too. Now he's not sure."

April follows me to the harvest table and helps sort the donated yarn.

"If Doyle didn't kill Seb, who did?" April asks.

"That's the big question."

"Well, I thought it was Doyle from the moment Trevor told us Seb was Doyle's former business partner. He had the biggest motive."

"Speaking of Trevor, he had a motive to kill Seb too."

"Trevor Chipperfield is not a murderer, Megapop! T and I have known Trevor forever, and he wouldn't hurt a fly."

"But would he hurt someone who almost ruined his career?"

"No, he wouldn't. I'd bet everything I own Trevor had nothing to do with Seb's murder."

"He doesn't have an alibi."

"He didn't do it. Trust me, if I had even a glimmer of doubt, I would tell you."

I know she would.

"I thought it was Rose Thorne," I admit. "She lied four times." I drop a partial ball of blue yarn into the worsted bin, then hold up four fingers. "Four!" I reach into the donation box and pull out a clear freezer bag with several skeins of red acrylic yarn. "She lied about when she arrived in Harmony Lake, she lied about her alibi, she lied about knowing Seb, and she lied by omission when she didn't tell Eric she saw Doyle's car near the murder scene that night." I drop the red skeins into the bulky bin, fold the freezer bag, and add it to the growing pile of bags on the chair next to me. "She's told so many lies, I don't know if Rose has been honest about anything."

"Why would Rose risk trading her awesome designer wardrobe for an orange jumpsuit just because Seb gave her a fake name and number after they hooked up nine months ago?" April picks up a yellow paper gift bag from the donation bin and sets it on the table in front of her. "Instead of killing him, she should have thanked Seb for ghosting her—pardon the pun." She giggles. "Rose had a lucky escape. Unlike Seb's girlfriend and Amber who were victims of his lies for months."

"Speaking of Amber," I say. "She has no alibi. She turned off her phone when she stormed out of the pub. She didn't turn it on again until later that night in her hotel room. And she had two powerful motives to want Seb dead. He used her to cheat on his girlfriend, and he tried to take her job by destroying her reputation."

"Seb didn't make very many friends, that's for sure," April says, tearing the decorative tape seal to open the gift bag, then pulling out several partial skeins of purple yarn. "What weight are these? There's no ball band or yarn tag."

I pick up a partial skein and inspect it.

"It's DK," I inform her. "Mrs. Bigg donated it. I remember this yarn. She made her niece a sweater with it about three years ago."

April drops the purple partial-skeins into the DK bin.

"Is this bag from Mrs. Bigg too?" she asks, plopping a larger yellow gift bag onto the table and tearing the decorative tape seal.

"Sure is," I confirm. "She's the only knitter who donated yarn in gift bags." I snap my fingers and stand up. "That reminds me, I promised Mrs. Bigg I'd order yarn for her to replace Doyle's scarf."

My planner lays open on the counter. I flip to the pocket at the front of the binder, pull out the yarn tag Mrs. Bigg gave me on Friday, then unplug the laptop, and take both items back to the harvest table.

"Why is this yarn so kinky?" April holds up a skein of cerulean blue yarn with beige tweed flecks.

"It's used," I say, reaching over the open laptop and taking the yarn from her. "Mrs. Bigg must have frogged it."

"Frogged?" April asks.

"Frogged." I nod. "Frogging is a knitterly term for ripping out your work."

April blinks at me.

"Unravelling your knitting."

"Why is it called frogging?"

I pinch the end dangling from the re-wound ball of yarn.

"Rip-it, rip-it, rip-it..." I repeat, pulling the end and unwinding the yarn.

"Oh! I get it!" April laughs. "Rip-it sounds like ribbit, the sound a frog makes."

"This is the exact yarn I'm trying to order for Mrs. Bigg right now," I say, tapping the laptop.

"Maybe I should steam this kinky ball," I think out loud. "Kink-free yarn is easier to work with. Steaming will only take a few minutes."

"If it only takes a few minutes to steam one ball of yarn, how long will it take to steam three?"

April removes two more identical balls of kinky yarn from the paper bag and places them on the table.

"Why would Mrs. Bigg ask me to order three skeins of this yarn when she already *had* three skeins?"

"Maybe she forgot she had them," April suggests. "Or she donated them by accident and was too embarrassed to ask for them back?"

This re-wound, kinky yarn seems significant. But why? What am I missing? I set the ball of yarn on the table with the utmost care, as if it's far more valuable and fragile than a merino-camel hair blend.

"If you steam it, will that remove the cat hair too?" April leans closer to the two skeins in front of her, furrowing her brow and inspecting them.

With careful precision she uses her manicured nails to pinch something I can't see and carefully slide it out of a yarn ball.

"Cat fur." She holds the short, fine fibre in front of her eyes.

"Are you sure?"

"Positive. I live with two cats, remember?"

"Maybe it fell off you and landed on the yarn."

"It didn't, Megaroon. It was embedded in this ball."

This could be Lancelot's fur. Eric linked the cat fur found on Seb's body to Lancelot, but he hasn't worked out how the cat hair made its way from the cat, to the killer, then to Seb's neck. I have a nagging suspicion this piece of cat fur is significant somehow. But how? Is it evidence? That's for Eric to decide. In the meantime, April and I should treat it like it is.

I glance around, looking for something to secure the strand of cat fur and settle on a plastic freezer bag from the chair next to me. I open the bag and check for any other fibres lurking inside. None. At least, none that I can see with my naked eye.

"Put the cat fur in here."

I hold the open bag under her hand, and she lowers her pinched thumb and index finger into it. Both of us watch through the plastic to make sure it doesn't stick to her fingers when she releases it. It doesn't. The fur floats downward, adhering itself to the plastic near the bottom of the bag.

"There," April says, slowly removing her hand so as not to disturb the piece of fur. "Be careful when you seal it."

I nod and pinch the seal, sliding my fingers slowly along the seam until it's secure. I hold the bag up and confirm the single hair is still there. It is. I close the laptop and place the empty-looking freezer bag on top.

"I'm certain this is the same yarn Mrs. Bigg used to knit Doyle's missing scarf."

"You already said it's the same yarn. And you said she asked you to order more of it."

"I mean, I think this is the *actual* yarn from Doyle's scarf. I don't think Doyle lost his scarf. I think he frogged it."

"Why would he do that? Did he hate the scarf so much that he unraveled it, re-wound the balls, and donated them to hide the evidence?"

"April, Doyle's missing scarf could be the murder weapon. What if he strangled Seb with the scarf, then frogged it to get rid of it?"

"If you're right, technically the murder weapon doesn't exist anymore. And he tried to camouflage the evidence in plain sight." She pauses for a moment, her eyes searching nowhere in particular. "Does that make him brilliant or arrogant?"

"It might have been brilliant, except he tried to hide

the yarn evidence in a yarn store and used his doting mother to drop it off, so I'll vote for arrogant."

"Megapop, there are seven more balls of yarn in this bag. All different colours and fibres. If Doyle sneaked the murder-yarn into the bag when she wasn't looking, Mrs. Bigg wouldn't have known her son used her to dispose of the murder weapon."

I gasp. "Doyle Bigg made his mother an accessory to murder."

How was I so wrong about him?

# CHAPTER 19

*ME: I have something for you*
   *Eric: A gift?*
   *Me: Kind of.*
   *Eric: Babe, you're the only gift I need.* Followed by
two heart emojis. *Every day with you is a gift.*

Eric is a hopeless romantic. He's prone to romantic
gestures and corny overtures. It's a side of him that no
one else sees. It took me by surprise at first, but I'm used
to it now and enjoy his schmaltzy declarations.

   *Me: In that case, you don't want the murder weapon?*
   *Eric: You have the murder weapon?*
   *Me: Yes.*
   *Eric: Where are you?*
   *Me: Lobby.*

Seconds later, the secure door buzzes and opens. Eric
raises his eyebrows and jerks his head for me to
follow him.

"Is that it?" He nods to the large white confectionery
box as we stride through the network of corridors. "Is the
murder weapon in the box?"

Before I can answer, a cop steps out of a nearby office, intercepting us, and bringing us to an abrupt halt.

"This just arrived," the cop says, handing Eric a file folder. "You said to interrupt you as soon as it got here."

Eric takes the folder and opens it, perusing the papers inside. The other cop stands by.

"I'll wait in your office," I say, smiling after exchanging pleasantries with Eric's waiting colleague.

"I'll be there in a minute." He nods without looking up.

"Megan!"

Who was that? Someone hissed my name. I stop and glance behind me at the empty hallway, cocking my ear into the silence.

"Megan, is that you?"

I knew I heard my name! I reverse around the corner and peek inside an open door on my left.

"Mrs. Bigg? What are you doing here?"

"The police asked me to give them a statement," she whispers. "They even sent a patrol car to pick me up." She cranes her neck and peers around me into the hall.

"There's no one out here," I assure her. "I'm alone."

"The officer taking my statement said he'd be right back. That was over ten minutes ago," she hisses. "What are you doing here?"

"Dropping off something for Eric." I hold up the white confectionery box. "Wedding stuff. Where's Mr. Bigg?"

"An officer is taking his statement at home. Because of his condition." She waves her hand in front of her torso. "I told them I needed to stay with him, but they said we had to give our statements separately. My Doyle is here somewhere. I hoped the police would reward my cooperation by letting me see him. Have you seen him?"

REAGAN DAVIS

"No," I reply. "You're the only other civilian I've run into."

"Megan, can you please do me a favour?"

"If I can," I reply, scared she might ask me to do something I either can't or shouldn't do.

"Can you use your influence with the police chief to speed up this process? My Doyle is innocent. You know he's not capable of murder. And he was at home with us when Seb died. He can't be the murderer. Our family has been through enough because of Seb Gillespie. We need to put this behind us."

"I wish I could help, but I don't have any influence here," I tell her. "None." I reaffirm. "Did you tell the police what you just told me?"

"Yes!" Mrs. Bigg snorts. "And I answered all their questions about Thursday night." She sighs. "Everything takes so long here. I didn't know the wheels of justice are so slow."

"They're very careful," I agree. "They don't want to make mistakes. Did you know Seb Gillespie was the other half of Bigg Bash?"

Mrs. Bigg shakes her head. "I was shocked when the officer told me. We never met him. He and Doyle met when Doyle was living in the city after culinary school. Doyle always called him Bash, not Seb. When we visited Doyle and his fiancée, Seb was never around. And he never accompanied my Doyle to visit us in Harmony Lake." She wipes a tear from her eye. "It must have been torture for my Doyle to have seen him in town and kept it to himself. I'm sure he didn't tell us because he didn't want to upset his father." She scrunches up her nose. "Because, you know"—she waves her hand in front of her torso again—"his condition."

Someday, I'm going to ask what specific condition Mr. Bigg has, but today is not the day.

"I'm sure your statement will help eliminate him," I say, trying to be reassuring under the stressful circumstances.

"Of course it will," Mrs. Bigg agrees. "Then the police can focus on finding the real killer."

"He's coming back," I say as a police officer turns the corner and walks toward us. I step back from the doorway. "By the way, did Doyle ever find that lovely blue scarf you made him?"

"No," Mrs. Bigg replies in her normal tone of voice. "Unfortunately not. Can you believe he lost it the same day I gave it to him?"

"Do you remember where you last saw it?" I stand aside so the officer can pass me and enter the small interrogation room.

"He wore it to the pub that night. Remember? You complimented it when you visited our booth. I went back to the pub the next day and searched for it, but it wasn't there."

"Shame," I say. "It was such a nice scarf. I'll see you later, Mrs. Bigg."

"I HEAR you ran into Mrs. Bigg," Eric says when he joins me in his office.

"She saw me walk by and called me," I explain, tucking my knitting into my large, vegan-leather, red tote bag. "I'm sorry if it was against the rules. It won't mess up her statement, will it?"

"No, it's fine. We record everything that happens in the interrogation rooms. She knows that, the officer explained it to her when she sat down." He closes his office door and tosses the file folder on his desk. "What did she want?"

"She wanted me to use my influence to speed up the wheels of justice, so she and Doyle can go home."

"Are you going to influence me?" Curling his mouth into a suggestive smirk, Eric narrows his eyes and probes me with his gaze. "I don't mind. I could use a bit of influence."

His intensity ruffles my composure, making my insides feel hectic. My quickening heartbeat sends a wave of warmth to the surface of my skin, and I bite my lip to resist the temptation that tugs at me from somewhere deep inside.

"*Ahem.*" I clear my throat and rearrange my hair so it cascades down one shoulder, easing the heat on my neck. "I told her that rumours of my influence in this establishment are greatly exaggerated."

Eric chuckles, skulking toward me like a predator challenging its prey. "You have more influence than you give yourself credit for, babe. You know I can't say no to you. Persuasion is your superpower."

I meet him halfway, giving myself a silent but stern reminder to remain focused on the reason for my visit.

"As much as I'm tempted to give you the influencing of a lifetime…" I kiss him. "It'll have to wait. Maybe later I'll influence you to tell me where we're going for our honeymoon. But for now, I'll settle for influencing you to keep Mrs. Bigg and Doyle here a little while longer. I suspect you're going to want to ask them a few more questions."

"Why?" Eric asks, correcting his posture. His gaze shifts from probing me temptingly to probing me professionally. "Does the murder weapon tie Doyle to Seb's murder?" He's back in cop-mode. Fantasies of me influencing him have been replaced by fantasies of solving Seb's murder. "I'll tell the officer who took her statement to stall and keep her here until I tell him otherwise."

He unlocks his cell phone and types a quick message, then picks up the white confectionery box off the coffee table.

"What was in the folder?" I ask, moving it aside so he can put the box on his desk. "Was it about the case?"

"Forensic reports," Eric says, opening a desk drawer and retrieving a latex glove. "The cat hair we found on Seb's neck came from Lancelot. A nylon lanyard is most likely *not* the murder weapon, but we'll continue checking each one for DNA, just in case. And the belt from Rose Thorne's coat can't be the murder weapon. It's attached to the coat and couldn't have left the marks on Seb's neck."

"What about her outfit?" I ask. "Or florist twine?"

"The outfit she wore under the coat didn't have a belt. She had no florist twine in her car or motel room." He opens the white confectionery box and knits his brows together, his face scrunched up with confusion. "The murder weapon is a bunch of white pastries?"

"No, those are samples of the selection T and Trevor are making for the dessert table," I reply. "April and I thought you'd want to taste them."

"Thank you." He takes a cake pop out of the box with his non-gloved hand and bites the ball off the stick while I reach into my tote bag and pull out the empty-looking freezer bag. "It's good!" he says with his mouth full.

"This is for you."

He takes the bag and inspects it, then holds it up to the light.

"Is the freezer bag the murder weapon?" Eric asks, swallowing the cake pop. "Or did the air inside it kill Seb?" He grins.

"There's a single cat hair in there," I explain. "April found it woven into the murder weapon and pulled it out before we realized it might be evidence. I wasn't sure what to do with it, so we bagged it. That's what you would've done, right?" I reach into my bag again and pull out the yellow gift bag containing the murder yarn. "If we contaminated the cat hair, there are plenty more on the murder weapon."

Eric places the empty-looking freezer bag on his desk and takes the gift bag with his gloved hand. He tosses the cake pop stick in the trash and slides the confectionery box out of the way. Then he sets the paper bag on his desk, opens it, and reaches in, pulling out three partial skeins of non-murder-yarn before choosing one of the kinky cerulean blue skeins with beige tweed flecks.

"There are two more," I say, then explain my theory that it's the yarn Mrs. Bigg used to knit Doyle's lost scarf. "When Mrs. Doyle called me into the interrogation room on my way to your office, I asked her if Doyle ever found his scarf, and she confirmed he hadn't. The scarf's last known sighting—still in scarf form—was at the pub. It was around Doyle's neck the night Seb was murdered."

Eric blurts out a curse word and lowers himself into the chair behind his desk, still holding the skein of murder-yarn.

"Can you test it to determine if it left the marks on Seb's neck?"

"Yes," he replies. "Forensics will figure it out." He looks at me, still holding up the yarn, still shocked. "Babe, this is incredible. You're amazing. I would never look at this yarn ball and connect it to Seb's murder or re-imagine it as a murder weapon."

Flattered by his kind words and his state of shock, I smile and look at the floor, my face flushing with heat.

"It was also luck," I say. "If Mrs. Bigg hadn't brought the bag to Knitorious, April and I wouldn't have found it. Doyle must not have known that he was hiding the unraveled murder weapon in a bag of yarn his mother planned to donate the very next day."

"You're positive Mrs. Bigg donated this yarn?" Eric asks.

"One hundred percent," I reply. "She's the only knitter who donated yarn in gift bags, and she handed me this specific bag on Friday. The day after Seb's murder." I point to the torn tape around the opening. "It was sealed until today, when April opened it. Also, Mrs. Bigg asked me to order the exact yarn so she could knit Doyle a replacement scarf."

"This explains why Doyle was so quick to confess to Seb's murder," Eric says, carefully placing the skein back inside the paper bag, closing it with his gloved hand, then removing the glove and tossing it into the trash. "He didn't want us to find the murder weapon. Finding it hidden amongst his mum's other yarn would implicate Mrs. Bigg as an accessory."

"He had me fooled," I say, shaking my head in disbelief. "I was so sure he was innocent. Even after he lied to April and me about his relationship with Seb."

"Doyle fooled me, too, babe." Eric says. "He was so convincing when he insisted he strangled Seb with his bare hands and when he panicked about Seb's cell phone. I was looking for evidence to prove his innocence. He fooled everyone."

"Thank goodness you're so evidence-driven and didn't trust my misguided hunch over tangible proof."

"Babe, you have incredible instincts." He reaches across the desk and takes my hand. "They led you to the murder weapon." He points to the bag of murder yarn on his desk. "That's the evidence that will put Seb's killer behind bars and close this case before we get married on Friday."

"But what about Doyle's alibi?" I ask. "Mrs. Bigg is adamant that Doyle was home with them."

"He could've sneaked out," Eric theorizes. "The Biggs all claim they went to bed as soon as they got home. Doyle's room is down the hall from Mr. and Mrs. Bigg's room. It would've been easy for him to sneak out and sneak back in without being heard."

"Can I go?" I ask, checking the time on my phone. "Or do you need a statement? I want to pick up groceries and finish wrapping Christmas gifts before our families arrive tomorrow."

Eric checks the time on his watch.

"We need you to provide a statement about how you got the yarn and how you concluded it could be evidence. We'll need a statement from April too. I'll find someone to take your statement so you can leave." He takes another latex glove from his desk drawer, puts it on, and stands up. "I need to log this evidence. I'd like to deliver it myself."

"OK," I say, standing up. "I need to use the washroom."

We kiss each other goodbye and leave his office together. I turn toward the washroom, and he goes the other way.

# CHAPTER 20

"MEGAN?" Mrs. Biggs hisses from the washroom door.

"You startled me," I say, flicking water from my hands into the sink.

"Are you alone in here?" She whispers, bent at the waist and scanning under the stall doors for feet as she steps closer to me.

"I think so." I nod.

"I saw you walk past and took a chance I'd find you here…" Mrs. Bigg continues to speak, but I can't hear her over the roar of the motion-activated hand dryer.

"I can't hear you," I mouth. "Just a minute."

"I SAID, SOMETHING IS WRONG," Mrs. Bigg shouts as the hand dryer shuts off. She clears her throat. "Oh my! I didn't mean to yell, Megan. I was trying to…"

"Don't worry, I understand," I say, interrupting her apology. "What do you mean something is wrong?"

"Well, for starters, I'm still here. And as far as I know, so is my Doyle," Mrs. Bigg replies. "And the officer who took my statement is acting strange suddenly."

"Strange how?"

"Shifty. He keeps coming up with excuses for why I

can't leave. Like there's no patrol car available to drive me home, or I have to sign out, but the person who runs the sign-out sheet is on their lunch break."

"Oh. That's unfortunate."

"And he's asking more questions. Different questions."

"About what?"

"About Friday. The day after Seb's murder," Mrs. Bigg replies. "What time was I at the pub? Where did I search for Doyle's scarf? What time did I visit Knitorious? What yarn did I donate at Knitorious?"

"Hmm. Why would he ask you about Friday?" I ask, feigning ignorance.

"I don't know. But I wonder if it's because of you. I mean, they cleared me to leave until you showed up. Is the timing a coincidence, Megan? Or did you say something to your fiancé that caused the police to ask more questions?"

"What could I have said that would make him curious about your schedule last Friday?"

"You tell me."

I shrug.

"What did you give to Eric? What was in the white box you were carrying?"

"Pastry samples for the dessert table at the reception," I reply. "Why? What do you think was in there?"

I sidestep to walk around her, but she mirrors my step, moving in sync with me and blocking my path.

"Has the charity knitting guild picked up the donation yarn yet?" she asks sweetly.

She knows! How shortsighted of me! Of course she knows. Mrs. Bigg would do anything for her Doyle. He didn't plant the yarn in her donation bag without her knowledge. She helped him dispose of it. They both fooled me. Like mother, like son.

"End of the month," I reply, maintaining my composure so as not to convey that I'm on to her.

I need to leave this washroom. I need to tell Eric that Mrs. Bigg knows.

"Have you sorted it yet?" Mrs. Bigg asks. "Marla mentioned something about you sorting the yarn before they pick it up."

The door opens and a uniformed police officer walks in. She smiles at us, and we smile back.

"Not yet," I reply, lying. "Busy with the wedding." I smile. "If I don't get to it, I'm sure Connie and Marla will take care of it while we're away."

"Perhaps I should stop by the shop and help them." Mrs. Bigg's mouth smiles, but the rest of her face is tense, and the tone of her voice is too sweet to be genuine, even for her. "It's the least I can do for a good cause."

I step around Mrs. Bigg and out of the washroom.

I hurry down the hall, slipping my phone out of my pocket and unlocking it without breaking my stride. I stop in view of the officer working at the front desk and type a quick text.

*Me: Mrs. Bigg knows about the yarn. She just confronted me in the washroom.*

*Eric: Where are you?*

*Me: On my way to your office.*

*Eric: I'll meet you there.*

"I SHOULD'VE KNOWN Mrs. Bigg wasn't an unwitting accomplice," I say. "Doyle isn't a knitter. He wouldn't think to unravel the scarf and camouflage it in a big box of random balls of yarn. I bet he doesn't even know where the scarf is."

"So, our latest theory is that Doyle killed Seb, then went home and told his parents—"

"His mother," I interrupt Eric's sentence. "He told Mrs. Bigg. There's no reason to suspect Mr. Bigg knows anything. In fact, I bet he knows nothing because Mrs. Bigg avoids subjecting him to anything stressful that could aggravate *his condition*." I wave my hand in front of my torso the way Mrs. Bigg does when she mentions her husband's health issues.

We're interrupted by a knock on the door.

"Come in," Eric bellows.

"You wanted this?" the officer says, extending his hand into the office without crossing the threshold. "It's the transcript of your interview with Doyle Bigg this morning."

"Thanks."

Eric takes the multi-page document, and the officer leaves, closing the door behind him. Eric tosses the papers, and they glide across his desk, sliding to a halt with the document dangling dangerously over the edge, flirting with a fall to the floor.

"Ok," Eric continues. "Doyle went home and told *his mother* that he murdered Seb by strangling him with the scarf she made, and she helped him cover his tracks by unraveling the scarf and disposing of the yarn."

I nod. "And corroborating his alibi."

"And she confessed this to you?"

"Not exactly."

"What did she say, exactly?"

I take a deep breath, sit on the sofa, and recount my conversation in the washroom with Mrs. Bigg.

"Which officer entered the washroom?" Eric asks.

"I didn't look at her name tag," I reply. "She went into a stall, and I left. She only heard the tail end of our conversation. The part where Mrs. Bigg offers to do something nice for charity."

"Babe." Eric sits down next to me on the sofa. "Mrs. Bigg didn't implicate herself. She didn't admit that the scarf was the murder weapon, or that she donated it knowing she was disposing of evidence."

"The literal meaning of her words doesn't implicate her, but how she said them does."

"The literal meaning is evidence. The hidden meaning isn't."

"Of course." I sigh.

"I believe you. I believe Mrs. Bigg knowingly disposed of the murder weapon at Knitorious. And Mrs. Bigg knows you figured it out too."

"She does?" I ask. "What did she say?"

"Nothing," Eric replies. "She asked for a lawyer and has said nothing since."

"I'm sorry," I say, shaking my head. "I messed up. If Doyle Bigg gets away with Seb's murder, it'll be my fault. I shouldn't have come here. I should've stayed at Knitorious and called you to pick up the yarn."

"If you hadn't come here, we wouldn't know Mrs. Bigg was a willing participant in covering up Seb's murder." Eric's cell phone chimes, and he checks the screen. "A text from the wedding officiant," he says. "She wants to know if we can reschedule tonight's meeting and meet tomorrow morning instead."

"Works for me." I shrug.

"She wants one of us to call her." Eric inhales, squeezing my knee, and stands up. "I'll call her and reschedule."

"OK," I say, nodding.

Eric reaches across his desk, picks up the landline, and dials the officiant's number. Then cradling the phone between his ear and shoulder, he leans against his desk, resting his butt on the desktop and crossing his arms and ankles. The breeze caused by his movements, combined with the desk shifting under the pressure of his body weight, sends the precariously perched pages of Doyle Bigg's transcript fluttering to the floor, where they scatter between my feet and Eric's desk.

While Eric speaks to the officiant, I gather the pages and shuffle them into the correct order. Something midway through page five catches my attention.

According to Doyle, before he left the house on Friday morning—the morning after he murdered Seb—he used the remote starter to start his car and warm it up, as he usually does when it's cold outside.

*Chief Sloane: What did you do while the car warmed up?*

*Doyle Bigg: I went into the kitchen and made a coffee in my insulated mug. My parents were having breakfast, and my dad told me a funny story about how much Lancelot loves the new scratching post they got him.*

*Chief Sloane: Did you leave the house after you made your coffee?*

*Doyle Bigg: I grabbed my coat from the closet and put on the blue toque my mum made me. I couldn't find the scarf though. I asked my parents if they'd seen my scarf. They helped me look for it, but we couldn't find it. My dad suggested I left it in the car. I had to leave, or I'd be late for work. I told him he was probably right. Then I left.*

*Chief Sloane: Was your scarf in the car?*

*Doyle Bigg: No. I laid my coat across the backseat, but my scarf wasn't there. I searched the car but no scarf.*

*Chief Sloane: You didn't wear your coat on Friday? It was below freezing.*

*Doyle Bigg: I hate driving in a coat. Same with gloves or a scarf. I don't like to wear anything that feels restrictive when I drive. I can wear a hat, though.*

*Chief Sloane: Then why did you bother to take your coat at all?*

*Doyle Bigg: I wear it when I brush snow off the car, or if I get stuck and have to shovel myself out, or something.*

*Chief Sloane: When was the last time you saw your missing scarf?*

*Doyle Bigg: I wore it at the pub the night before. I can't remember if I took it off when I drove home. I remember putting my coat in the back seat, but I can't remember if the scarf was with it.*

*Chief Sloane: Can you describe the scarf?*

*Doyle Bigg: It matches the hat I wore here today. It's about six feet long, a bit shorter than me.*

*Chief Sloane: What did you do when you realized your scarf wasn't in the car on Friday morning?*

*Doyle Bigg: I squeezed into the car, put my mug in the cup holder. I adjusted the seat, the rear-view mirror, and both side mirrors. Then I drove to work.*

*Chief Sloane: What time was this?*

Doyle goes on to state what time he left, the route he took, and what time he arrived.

I'm contemplating what I've just read and scanning the desktop for a loose paper clip to secure the document when Eric ends his call with the officiant and hangs up the phone.

"She forgot her son's school play is tonight," he says, tapping the screen of his cell phone. "I'll update the new date and time in the online calendar." He locks the screen and slips his phone into his pocket.

"Got it. Thanks," I say when my phone dings with a notification about the change he just made to our shared calendar.

"We need to find the officer who walked in on you and Mrs. Bigg in the washroom. Maybe she heard more than you think. Would you recognize her if you saw her again?"

"Before we do that," I reply, "I think we should talk to Mrs. Bigg. Does she know about Doyle's confession?"

"No," Eric replies. "We didn't tell her. The goal of a successful interrogation is to extract information, not give it. Besides, Mrs. Bigg's lawyer has advised her not to talk to the police anymore unless we go through him."

"I'm not the police," I remind him. "I think she'll talk to me. I don't care how many lawyers advise her otherwise, Mrs. Bigg will want to know what's going on with her Doyle."

# CHAPTER 21

"WE OFFERED to have a patrol car take her home, but her lawyer said he would drive her instead."

"Did she ask about Doyle?" I ask as we navigate our way through the labyrinth-like floor plan.

Eric nods. "She asked where and how he was. She asked if she could see him. When I told her a police officer would have to be present, her lawyer intervened and withdrew the request on her behalf."

"She wants to help her son," I say, trying to convince myself as much as him. "I'm sure her maternal urges will override her lawyer's advice."

"Babe, are you sure you want to put yourself in the middle? You don't have to do this. You can still change your mind."

"I'm sure."

"No pressure, but if this doesn't work, we'll have to release them."

"It'll work," I say, willing my voice to exude absolute confidence instead of the semi-confidence I feel. "And when it does, it'll be better than any wedding present I could've bought you." I smile.

We look at each other, our eyebrows arched, when a nearby door clicks open, followed by the indistinct murmur of voices.

"Good luck," Eric whispers, then kisses the top of my head. "I love you."

I take a deep breath, then stroll around the corner and down the hall toward Mrs. Bigg, her lawyer, and their police chaperone.

"Mrs. Bigg!"

They stop and turn around.

"Megan." She smiles. "My lawyer and I are just leaving."

Her voice is cheery, and her eyes are bright. A facade to cover up the scared, helpless mother underneath.

Her lawyer touches her back, guiding her to continue toward the lobby.

"I was hoping to talk to you."

She shakes off her lawyer's hand and turns to face me.

"About what?"

"Doyle."

Like her son's name is a punch in the gut, the fake smile disappears from her face. Now, a worried mother, scared for her son's future, is wringing her hands, and staring at me with wide, anxious eyes and concern etched across her forehead. She swallows hard, bracing herself in case I've come bearing bad news.

"Is he OK?"

"He's fine," I assure her.

She lets out a long breath.

"But he needs your help."

"Anything," she says, taking a step toward me. "What does Doyle need?"

Her lawyer reaches out and touches her shoulder.

"I advise against meeting with the police unless I'm present," he urges.

She shrugs him off again

"I don't work for the police," I offer.

"Megan is a family friend," Mrs. Bigg explains, taking my elbow. "Excuse us please, gentlemen." The chilliness of her trembling hand is palpable through my bulky, hand-knit sweater and betrays her composed demeanour. "I'd like to speak with Megan alone." She guides us just out of earshot and says, "Let's talk."

We continue down the hall and around the corner, Mrs. Bigg's trembling, icy hand still gripping my elbow.

"Where are we going?"

"Eric's office."

"Is my Doyle there?"

"No," I reply, stopping in front of the office door. "He's in the other interrogation room. They just brought him something to eat."

"What are they feeding him? He has a seafood allergy. Do they know about his seafood allergy?"

"He asked for pizza," I say. "Doyle chose the restaurant and the toppings. For all I know they even let him order it."

"Is Eric in there?" she asks, pointing at his name on the nameplate on the wall outside his office.

"No," I reply. "But he's around here somewhere if we need him." I crack open the door. "You can ask your lawyer to accompany you."

"No, thank you. My lawyer likes to remind me *I'm* his client, *not* Doyle. His priority is me, and my priority is my son. He's a capable lawyer, but we have incompatible priorities."

We enter Eric's office, and I close the door. Mrs. Bigg follows me to the sofa, and we sit on opposite ends.

"Would you like something to eat or drink?" I ask. "You've been here for hours. You must be hungry."

"They ordered me a sandwich from the deli for

lunch," Mrs. Bigg says. "But I wouldn't mind a cup of tea."

"Two milks, one sugar?" I confirm.

"Yes, please and thank you."

I unlock my phone.

"I'll ask if someone can deliver it."

"What's going on with Doyle?"

"Eric doesn't think Doyle killed Seb," I reply.

"I should think not!" Mrs. Doyle retorts. "I didn't raise a murderer!"

Maybe not, but she raised a liar at least.

"Eric wants to eliminate Doyle as a suspect and send him home, but Doyle won't cooperate."

"Oh?" Mrs. Bigg comments, furrowing her brow and wringing her hands in her lap. "What does his lawyer say about this?"

"Doyle waived his right to an attorney."

"What?!" She slams her fists into her lap. "Why would he do that? The last thing his father said to him was, *Say nothing without your lawyer*."

I shrug. "I just know he doesn't want a lawyer, and he confessed to Seb's murder but won't reveal any details."

"He confessed?!" she shouts, jumping up to a standing position. "Why would he confess? My Doyle is not a killer. He was at home when Seb was murdered, for goodness' sake."

"I know he was," I agree, trying to sound sympathetic. "Help me prove it."

Mrs. Bigg smooths her grey pencil skirt and sits down again.

"How?"

"Tell me why Doyle's car left your house again after he drove you and Mr. Bigg home from the pub."

"It didn't," Mrs. Bigg insists.

"Yes, it did."

A light knock at the door interrupts us, and we retreat to our proverbial corners.

"Come in," I say.

"Tea," Eric says, when he opens the door. "Two milks, one sugar." He places the mug on the end table next to Mrs. Bigg.

"Thank you, Chief Sloane," she says without looking up at him.

"You're welcome." He looks at me. "Anything else?"

I shake my head.

"Megan tells me you believe my Doyle is innocent."

"She's right," Eric confirms. "I think Doyle knows more than he admits, but I don't think he killed Seb Gillespie."

"How can you keep him here without proof?" she asks. "You must need evidence to back up a murder charge."

Eric drags a chair from in front of his desk and sits across from us, leaning forward and resting his elbows on his knees.

"He confessed, Mrs. Bigg. Doyle wants us to charge him with Seb's murder. And while there is enough evidence to support his confession, Doyle seems unaware of specific details about the crime. Details only the killer would know."

"What evidence? How can there be evidence? He didn't do it!"

"We found some of Lancelot's fur on Seb's body. Doyle lied about recognizing Lancelot when I showed him a photo of an identical cat. He also lied about his past relationship with the victim. We ha…"

"Victim!" she scoffs. "Seb Gillespie was not a victim. He was a *victimizer*. My Doyle was a victim. That florist, Rose, was a victim. Amber Windermere was a victim. I'm sure a complete list of that man's victims would stretch from one end of Water Street to the other. Seb Gillespie was a bully who amused himself by destroying people's lives."

"Nonetheless," Eric concedes, "someone murdered him, and your son wants to accept the consequences for the killer's actions."

"The cat hair could belong to any cat in Harmony Lake," Mrs. Bigg suggests with a sweep of her hand. "This town has hundreds, if not thousands, of cats. And just because my Doyle didn't want to admit he knew Seb and had a previous relationship with him, doesn't mean he's a murderer. You know what this town is like. Rumours about my Doyle would've spread like wildfire. He didn't want to relive that horrible time in his life."

"We compared Lancelot's DNA to the DNA from the cat fur we recovered from Seb's body. Both samples came from Lancelot."

"You can do DNA tests on cats?" she asks quietly, her shoulders slumped.

"Yes," Eric replies. "Cats have DNA too."

"The police have the murder weapon," I interject. "But I think you figured that out. At least, that's the impression I got in the ladies' room earlier."

"I don't know what you're talking about, Megan." She looks at her mug of tea, avoiding my gaze.

"No? Then why were you concerned about the contents of the confectionery box? And why did you ask if I'd sorted the donated yarn?"

"I was making small talk." She shrugs. "Showing an interest in your wedding and in a local good cause."

"Besides the evidence I've already shared with you," Eric continues, "two eyewitnesses saw Doyle driving near the crime scene around the time of Seb's murder."

"No, they didn't," she retorts, looking with conviction

into Eric's eyes. "They couldn't have seen my Doyle driving on Thursday night. It's not possible."

"Why not?" Eric asks.

Mrs. Bigg sits in composed silence, her posture perfect, and her hands folded on her lap.

"Because Mrs. Bigg was driving," I reply for her.

# CHAPTER 22

Mrs. Bigg gasps. "What? How?"

Eric raises his hand in a stop motion, and I pull myself up to my full-seated height.

"Mrs. Bigg, now might be a good time for your lawyer to join you," he suggests.

She locks her gaze with his. "I don't want a lawyer. But I want everything I tell you from this point forward to be official. How do we do that?"

Eric stands up and opens the office door. Then he walks over to his desk, picks up the landline, presses a few buttons, and issues instructions.

Moments later, a second officer joins us in the office, and a third sets up recording equipment, then leaves.

"Ready?" Eric asks Mrs. Bigg.

"Ready." She nods.

He starts recording and recites some official disclaimers. Mrs. Bigg obliges by giving verbal acknowledgement when prompted. Next, he asks formalities, like her name and address. She replies.

Eric opens his mouth to speak, but Mrs. Bigg beats him to it.

"How do you know I was driving Doyle's car last Thursday night?" she asks me.

"Doyle said he squeezed into his car on Friday morning. Why would he have to squeeze into a car he drove last? He also said he adjusted the seat and all the mirrors before he left the driveway. Again, why would he have to adjust everything if no one else had driven his car? Mr. Bigg doesn't drive anymore, and even if he did, he's close enough in size to drive the same car with minimal adjustments."

"Well played, Megan," Mrs. Bigg says. "You're the second person who picked up on that. It didn't occur to me to reposition the seat and mirrors when I got home."

Did she say I was the second person? Who was first?

"Also, I assumed if Doyle would take the blame for a murder he didn't commit, it would be for you or Mr. Bigg. The three of you are a tight-knit family."

"Mr. Bigg was not involved. At all. He knows nothing about it." She looks from the camera to Eric. "Was that recorded? I want to make sure you understand my husband was oblivious."

"We're recording everything, Mrs. Bigg," Eric assures her. "What happened on Thursday night? How did Seb die?"

"I killed Seb Gillespie," Mrs. Bigg confesses, looking into the camera. "I acted alone. I had no help before, during, or afterward." She takes a deep breath and lets it out. "While Sebastian Gillespie and I had never met, I recognized him from my Doyle's social media accounts and from the photos on their old business website." She looks at Eric. "Those photos are gone, by the way. If you look for them, you won't find them. My Doyle deleted every trace of his former fiancée and business partner from his social media accounts months ago. After they broke his heart and destroyed his life. The Bigg Bash website is long gone too."

"Did Seb know you recognized him?" Eric asks. "Did he recognize you?"

"No." Mrs. Bigg chuckles. "He was too self-absorbed to notice anyone other than himself. We'd never met. I'm sure he knew Doyle had parents but not what we looked like." She sighs. "My Doyle asked us to ignore Seb. He asked us to look the other way or change direction if we encountered him around town. He didn't want to have any interaction with Seb. This wedding was important to my Doyle. As assistant to the head wedding planner, Seb could ruin it, just like he ruined everything else in Doyle's life. Being the head chef at Jules Janssen's wedding would have reignited my Doyle's catering career and launched him into the upper echelons of private chefs. He would have been culinary royalty."

"But the service providers had to sign non-disclosure agreements," I point out. "How would Doyle's reputation benefit from the wedding if he couldn't brag about catering it?"

"These things leak all the time," Mrs. Bigg replies. "And the NDA would expire, eventually."

"It must have upset Doyle when Jules Janssen eloped to Italy and cancelled the Harmony Lake wedding," Eric urges.

"Yes, it did. At first," Mrs. Bigg admits. "But he got over it when you and Megan agreed to get married instead." She looks at me. "This will be the largest sit-down dinner my Doyle and his team have ever catered. He was happy there was still an event to cater."

"Tell me about Thursday night," Eric probes, "at the pub."

"We had a lovely time." Mrs. Bigg smiles. "It was nice to see everyone and enjoy the pub so close to Christmas without tourists occupying every table. We shared appetizers and visited with everyone who stopped by our booth to say hi."

"Did you see Seb at the pub?" Eric asks.

"We were aware he was there." She huffs. "How could anyone *not* be aware of Seb's presence? He was drunk as a skunk and made a spectacle of himself."

"Did you talk to him?"

"Of course not," Mrs. Bigg replies. "I promised my Doyle I would give Seb Gillespie a wide berth, and that's what I did."

"Was Seb inside the pub when you left?"

"Yes," she replies. "We left just before eleven p.m. My husband takes medication at breakfast and at bedtime"—her eyes dart back and forth between Eric and me as she waves her hand in front of her torso—"for his condition. Well, his medication is at home in our medicine cabinet, so we left. We walked to the car in the parking lot behind the pub. My Doyle laid his coat and scarf on the backseat like he always does, then he drove us home."

"What did you do when you got home?" Eric asks.

"My husband took his medication, brushed his teeth, and went to bed. Doyle also brushed his teeth and went to bed."

"What about you?" Eric asks. "What did you do?"

"I brushed my teeth and stayed up to knit for a while. We don't go out very often in the evening, especially not until eleven p.m., and I was still wide awake. My brain wasn't ready to go to sleep."

"How long did you knit?"

"I didn't," Mrs. Bigg replies. "Imagine my surprise when I went to get Doyle's hat out of my bag, and it wasn't there. It was gone!"

"You must have found it," I say. "You worked on it at

Knitorious on Friday, and I've seen Doyle wearing it. It's a lovely hat."

"Thank you, Megan," she says. "And you're right, I found it. It was at the pub."

"You went back to the pub?" Eric asks, sitting up straighter in his chair. "How did you get there?"

"I only went as far as the pub parking lot," Mrs. Bigg clarifies. "I drove Doyle's car because it was the last one to park in the driveway and was blocking my car. Also, his car was still warm from driving us home, so it made sense."

"Why did you stop at the parking lot?

"I thought for sure my knitting bag fell onto the floor under our booth when I tucked it into my purse. But it fell out in the parking lot when I reached into my purse for my mittens. I found the knitting bag—with my knitting still inside, thank goodness—on the ground between the parking lot and the pub."

"That was lucky," I comment.

"Yes, it was," Mrs. Bigg agrees. "If it had snowed, I might not have found it until spring."

"You didn't go inside the pub?" Eric asks, redirecting Mrs. Bigg's confession away from knitting and back to her movements on the night of Seb's murder.

"I did not go inside the pub," she confirms. "But I heard a kerfuffle outside the pub and peeked around the corner."

"What did you see?"

"Seb Gillespie and Trevor Chipperfield were having an altercation," Mrs. Bigg replies. "I think Trevor was trying to convince Seb to go inside the pub. Seb didn't want to. Trevor put a hand on Seb's shoulder and tried to lead him to the pub door, and Seb yelled and ranted, then pushed Trevor away."

"What did Trevor do when Seb pushed him?"

"Trevor threw his hands in the air and said, *If something bad happens, don't say I didn't try to help you,* then marched back inside the pub."

"What did Seb do?"

"He staggered in a clumsy circle until he chose a direction."

"Which direction did he choose?"

"He came toward me."

"And?" I urge.

"That was my moment." Her eyes narrow and the corner of her upper lip curls into a sneer. "I could tell Sebastian Gillespie exactly what I thought of him. The announcement earlier that day that Jules and her celebrity guests would not be coming to Harmony Lake meant Amber and Seb's services were no longer required. With Seb out of a job, he wasn't in a position to cause trouble for my Doyle. And he was so drunk, he probably wouldn't have remembered what I said the next day, anyway. When he was close enough to hear me, I stepped out from beside the building and let him have it."

"Have what?"

"I called him every name I could think of. I told him what kind of person I thought he was. And I said I hoped, one day, he'd get a taste of his own medicine. I had to yell, so he'd hear me over his phone. His phone rang non-stop the whole time I was telling him off."

"What did Seb say?"

"Nothing. He just stood there, swaying and laughing. He laughed so hard he almost fell over."

"That must have infuriated you," I say.

"It did," Mrs. Bigg acknowledges. "But I didn't want to break my promise any more than I already had. I got in the car and left. I was fuming and didn't want to go home. If my husband or son were awake, they would've known something had upset me and asked about it. I didn't want to admit that I broke my promise and confronted Seb."

"So, where did you go?"

"For a drive," she replies. "I cruised down Water Street, turned around, and came back. On the way back, I spotted Seb staggering along the sidewalk near Knitorious. He careened into the parking lot, and I followed him. I pulled into a spot, turned off the car, and watched him. First, he tried to open the door at Knitorious, then Wilde Flowers. They were locked. I think he spotted me in the car because he squinted at it and started staggering toward me. I rolled down the window and yelled at him."

"What did you say?"

"I said, *I saw you trying to break into those stores. I'll call the police. Why are you still in our town, anyway? No one wants you here! Go home.*"

It was freezing on Thursday night, and when Eric and I found him, Seb was underdressed. He had a jacket, but no hat, gloves, or scarf. He wore running shoes instead of boots. Drunk and alone in a strange town, I'd guess Seb pulled the doors, hoping one of them would open and lead him to warmth.

"What did Seb do when you yelled at him again?"

"He laughed and pointed at me," she recalls, "which made me furious. I was determined to make him apologize, no matter what it took. I didn't dress for the weather. Before I left the house, I only threw on a sweater and my leather driving gloves. I thought I'd be fine in the warm car, and I'd only be a few minutes. I looked around the car for something to keep me warm. Doyle's blue scarf was on the back seat. I wrapped it around my neck and got out of the car. Seb had wandered back to the building. He was pulling on the doors again. I kept calling his name and telling him to turn around and look at me. I don't know if he was ignoring me, or if he couldn't hear me over the never-ending ring of his blasted phone. I moved closer and yelled louder. He acted like I wasn't even there. I was so full of rage that I was hot, so I took off the scarf. Next thing I knew, it was around Seb's neck, and I was twisting it and pulling it as hard as I could." She looks at me with pleading eyes. "I'd never strangled anyone before. It's harder than it looks. It takes longer than you'd expect and every ounce of strength you have. If he weren't so inebriated, I don't think I could have done it."

"Were you trying to kill him?" I ask. "Was that your goal?"

"My goal was to make sure he could never hurt my son again," she replies. "It wasn't about killing him, it was about getting justice and making sure he knew not to mess with the Bigg family. First, he fell to his knees, then he struggled and tried to turn toward me. He was too uncoordinated to fight me off, and he was confused. Then he slumped over and stopped moving. But his phone rang and rang and rang. The annoying thing had fallen out of his pocket and onto the ground when he struggled. Her nasty, selfish face was flashing at me. Mocking me with her smug smile, and her name flashing across the screen in big letters. I hate her. Knowing that by hurting Seb, I was also hurting her, gave me the strength to twist and pull the scarf again with all my might."

"Whose face and name flashed on the screen?"

"My Doyle's former fiancée. Seb's girlfriend," she huffs, rolling her eyes. "I wanted to answer it and give her a piece of my mind too. I wanted to tell her what I thought of her and how she treated my son. But I didn't. I knew it was a bad idea."

"What did you do with the phone?" Eric asks.

"I stomped on it," Mrs. Bigg says, unconsciously

digging her heel into the floor as she speaks. "I stomped until it stopped ringing and until her stupid face disappeared. Then I tossed it across the parking lot. Goodness knows where it ended up. Somewhere near the shrubbery, I think."

There it is. The second holdback. With no prompting, Mrs. Bigg has mentioned both holdbacks, the rope-like murder weapon—the scarf—and how Seb's destroyed cell phone ended up in the bushes.

"Did you confirm whether Seb was dead or unconscious?" Eric asks.

"No." She shakes her head. "I didn't look at him again. I pulled the scarf off his neck, got back in the car, and drove home."

"Did you see either Doyle or Mr. Bigg when you returned home?"

"Lancelot was meowing outside Doyle's bedroom door, and I opened it to let him in. My son was sound asleep in bed. I saw Mr. Bigg when I went to bed. He was asleep and snoring on his side."

"What happened to the scarf you used to strangle Seb Gillespie?"

"Well, I couldn't let Doyle wear it, could I? Not after I used it to strangle the life out of someone. Before I went to bed, I unraveled it and wound the yarn into balls. Then I put them in the bag of yarn I had planned to donate at Knitorious."

"How does Doyle know you killed Seb?" I ask. "I mean, he must know, he confessed to protect you."

"He doesn't know for sure, but he suspects I did it," Mrs. Bigg explains. "The next morning, he couldn't find his scarf. My husband helped him look for it, and I helped too because I thought it would be suspicious if I didn't. We searched for a good ten minutes. My husband suggested the scarf might be in the car, and Doyle agreed.

I watched through the kitchen window while Doyle searched for his scarf. When he didn't find it, he got in the car. I looked away from the window and noticed he'd forgotten his coffee cup on the counter. I grabbed it, ran to the porch, and waved to get his attention. He came to the porch to collect his coffee and asked if I'd driven his car since last night. I asked why he thought that. He told me he had to readjust everything because someone smaller than him had driven the car."

Doyle must have included this in his statement by accident. He had to know it might tip off the police. I assume he was so caught up in his recollection of events that he said it before he realized it contradicted his confession.

"Did you admit you'd driven his car?"

"Yes," she confesses. "I hate lying, so I told him as much truth as possible. I told him I'd lost my knitting. I told him I drove to the pub and found my knitting bag in the parking lot. I didn't tell him anything else, I wanted him to have plausible deniability. I saw it once on a detective show on TV."

"Did he accept your answer?"

"Yes." Mrs. Bigg nods. "Why wouldn't he? Seb's death wasn't public knowledge yet. He asked me if I'd noticed his scarf when I borrowed his car. I lied and told him I didn't see it." She sighs. "I feel guilty for lying to him. He felt so bad for losing it. I visited the pub on Friday and asked about the scarf to keep up the appearance that Doyle had lost it."

"When Doyle heard about Seb's murder, did he suspect you knew more than you told him?"

"My Doyle is very perceptive," she explains, smiling at the camera. "After he heard about Seb's murder, he kept asking me if I saw anything when I went back to the pub for my knitting. I insisted I saw nothing, but I could tell he didn't believe me." She looks at Eric. "When he found out you recovered Lancelot's fur from the body, he must have confessed to protect me."

"Would you like to add anything else?"

"I have two regrets," Mrs. Bigg says. "I regret the grief this ordeal has caused my husband and son, and I regret not taking my car to the pub. Then the eyewitnesses would've identified my car, and you would have arrested me instead of my Doyle. If I had known he confessed, or that you had enough evidence to charge him, I would have come forward sooner."

# CHAPTER 23

TUESDAY, January 21st

"Welcome home, Mr. and Mrs. Sloane!" everyone chants in unison when Eric and I enter the store.

"Sophie!" The corgi bounces on her hind legs, scrabbling at my knees with her front paws. "I missed you!" I squat down and take Sophie's head in both hands, massaging her ears.

"How was your honeymoon?" April asks.

"Fabulous," I reply, standing up so Eric can take a turn greeting the excited corgi.

"Did you enjoy Saint Martin, my dear?"

"It was amazing," I reply to Connie. "A tropical paradise."

I hug Connie, Marla, April, and Tamara.

"It looks like you took separate honeymoons," Adam jokes. "And only one of you went somewhere sunny."

It's true. My alabaster skin's arch enemy is the sun. Fifteen unprotected minutes can earn me a week of playing a painful game I like to call, *Burn, Blister, Peel*. I stayed in the shade as much as possible, and when shade wasn't an option, I wore one of my wide-brimmed sun hats and enough SPF to cover a small country. Eric, however, looks like a bronzed sun god.

"Ha ha," I say, hugging him. "Thank you for dogsitting Sophie for us."

"Anything for my favourite ex-wife and husband-in-law," he says, then hugs Eric with one of those one-armed hug-handshake combos where they slap each other on the back.

Adam tells me about his adventures with Sophie—he's teaching her French, and she now responds to five commands in both languages—and assures me that Hannah made it back to university in time to start her next semester.

"Sophie might be the only bilingual dog in Harmony Lake," I brag.

Eric shows photos on his phone of the luxury villa we rented in Saint Martin.

Adam and I join the conversation, and soon everyone has their phone out and is showing each other photos they took at our Christmas Eve wedding.

"You chose the right shoes," April says.

"Yes," Connie agrees. "The mulberry satin, stiletto pumps matched the bridesmaid's dresses perfectly! It was like someone dyed them especially for the occasion."

"Just like the wedding socks," Eric says, pulling up his pant leg to reveal his dark red socks. "They couldn't have been a better match if we'd planned it."

I finished Eric's wedding socks the day before the wedding. Unbeknownst to me, Connie, Marla, Hannah, and even April—who'd never knitted socks before—made identical pairs for the rest of the groomsmen. It was a nice touch.

"I'll be sad to return the other five pairs of shoes," I admit with a sigh, "but I think I chose the right ones too." I touch Connie's shoulder. "That reminds me. Your mink stole is in the car. I'll return it to you as soon as I get it cleaned. Thank you again for lending it to me. It was the perfect *something borrowed.*" I hug her.

Connie surprised me on my wedding day with her mother's white mink stole. I *NEVER* wear fur, but this vintage mink stole was already made, and it's one of Connie's most cherished family heirlooms. Her mother got married in it, and Connie wore it when she married her late husband. I was so touched and honoured to wear it, that after she showed it to me, my eye makeup had to be reapplied. It was the perfect finishing touch to my wedding ensemble and made the outdoor photos much more bearable.

"I'm so pleased you wore it," Connie says, tearing up. "It was beautiful on you!" She leans in close to my ear. "I hope we get to see it around Hannah's shoulders one day."

Until Connie surprised me with her stole, the tradition of *something old, something new, something borrowed, and something blue* had completely slipped my mind. But it hadn't slipped my bridal party's collective mind. Connie's stole was my *something borrowed,* my dress and shoes were my *something new,* my late-mother's diamond earrings were my *something old,* and Phillip tucked a small blue flower into my white bridal bouquet as my *something blue.*

"Look," Phillip had whispered when he parted the flowers and pointed out the tiny blue bud hiding there. "I tuck one into every bridal bouquet, just in case." He winked and tapped his finger aside his nose.

I have the best friends and family in the world.

I'm gushing about how incredible the wedding and honeymoon were when we're interrupted by a knock at the door.

"Who could it be?" Connie asks, checking her watch. "We don't open for another half-hour."

"It's Phillip," Marla announces, unlocking the door to let him in.

"Welcome home, Mr. and Mrs. Sloane," he says from somewhere behind the large floral arrangement he's carrying. "I present to you"—he holds out the large bouquet—"your January floral arrangement."

He sets it on the counter, fusses with it, then stands back to appraise it before fussing some more.

"It's beautiful," I say, giving Phillip a tight hug. "But my year of monthly flower deliveries ended last month."

"These aren't from your husband," Phillip retorts.

"Oh?" I say, scanning the lush blooms for a card. "Who are they from?"

"Should I be jealous?" Eric teases with a chuckle.

"They're for both of you," Phillip replies. "Courtesy of Ms. Rose Thorne. She wanted to thank you for solving Seb's murder and clearing her name. She was worried she might take the fall for his murder."

"Tell her thank you," I say.

"And tell her she helped solve Seb's murder, too, by finally telling the truth about when she got here, how she knew him, and everything she saw that night," Eric adds.

The residents of Harmony Lake heaved a collective sigh of relief when they heard that Mrs. Bigg had confessed to Seb's murder. No one wanted the town's only murder investigator to leave for a three-week honeymoon with the murder unsolved and a killer still wandering the streets of our cozy, sweet town.

Since her confession, Mrs. Bigg has continued to cooperate fully with the authorities. She's determined to spare Mr. Bigg and Doyle the stress of testifying at a trial.

"This arrangement is from Rose," Phillip repeats, pointing at the bouquet. "The other eleven deliveries you'll receive this year will be from me." He touches his fingertips to his chest. "A third year of monthly floral arrangements is my wedding gift to you." He points at Eric and me.

"Thank you, Phillip! I was sad my flowers were over. I'm happy I get to enjoy them for another year." I hug him again. "How is Rose doing?"

"She's fine," Phillip replies. "She's gone back to her own florist shop in her own hometown. I don't think she'll rush back to Harmony Lake to help me with another wedding soon." He smiles and shrugs. "If another celebrity plans a fake Harmony Lake wedding, I'll be on my own."

"Fake Harmony Lake wedding?" I ask, confused.

"Yes, my dear. FAKE. Didn't you hear?"

I shake my head. "We took a vacation from news and social media while we were away. What did we miss?"

"Jules Janssen admitted to *Fame & Fortune Magazine* that she never intended to get married in Harmony Lake. The whole wedding was an elaborate ruse to lure the paparazzi away from Italy for the real wedding."

"Oh, I knew about that," I say, disappointed it wasn't a juicy bit of gossip I hadn't heard yet.

"How did you hear about it?" April asks. "The latest issue of *Fame and Fortune Magazine* with Jules's interview just came out yesterday."

"Jules texted me while we were away," I reply.

"She did?" April asks, agog. "What did she say?"

"She sent a thoughtful text congratulating us." I shrug. "I asked if she ever intended to get married here, and she said no. Jules admitted the Harmony Lake wedding was a red herring. She said she leaked the details to the press herself. She called it the bait-and-switch of the century."

"Did she say anything else?" Connie asks.

"She said she's glad we put the wedding to good use, and she thanked us for the generous donation to her non-profit organization."

Instead of gifts, Eric and I asked guests to donate to Jules Janssen's non-profit organization that provides scholarships to help struggling students pay for post-secondary education. Eric and I also donated our wedding budget to the worthy cause.

"That's more than just *Jules Janssen sent me a text*, Megastar!" April says, and I laugh at her impression of me. "That's, like, an entire conversation. She told you the wedding was fake before it was public knowledge. You're friends. You and Jules Janssen have a friendship. You're like besties with one of the biggest stars on the planet!"

"Let's not get carried away," I say. "It was a few texts."

April gasps and covers her mouth with her hands, looking at Tamara. "That means *we're* friends-of-a-friend of one of the biggest stars on the planet!"

"That means we're almost-almost famous!" Tamara reasons.

They clasp hands doing a double high-five and jump up and down, celebrating their newfound near fame.

"Can you imagine being rich enough to plan a fake wedding and rent every nearby hotel and motel room?" Marla asks, then she shakes her head and makes a *tsk, tsk, tsk* sound.

"No," we all reply, slightly out of sync and shaking our heads.

"Poor Doyle," I comment. "He was looking forward to adding Jules Janssen's wedding to his resume when the non-disclosure agreement expired. He said it would launch his career. Not only did he *not* get to cater the biggest celebrity wedding of the century, but he also almost took the blame for a murder he didn't commit, and lost his mother to a prison sentence."

"We exonerated Doyle Bigg, babe," Eric reminds me. "Everyone knows he didn't kill Seb."

Since the confession, forensics determined the three balls of cerulean blue merino-camel hair yarn with brown tweed flecks were indeed the weapon Mrs. Bigg used to strangle Seb Gillespie. Besides more strands of Lancelot's fur, they extracted Seb's DNA from the fibre. Also, forensics finished testing the leather gloves Doyle claimed to be wearing when he strangled Seb, and there was no evidence to support them ever touching Seb. Forensics also determined the gloves could not have left the marks on Seb's neck.

"The dinner Doyle made for your reception was fabulous!" Tamara adds. "It was the best Cornish hen I've ever had."

"And the prime rib," Adam adds with a chef's kiss. "Incredible. Melted like butter in my mouth."

"And Doyle's career plans have changed since his mother's confession," Marla interjects. "If Jules Janssen's wedding had made him a famous chef, Doyle would have had to spend most of his time in LA and New York, but now he wants to stay in Harmony Lake with his father. He said he realized he would've worried about his parents anyway, and the jet-set lifestyle of a celebrity chef wouldn't make him happy. He said if he moved away, he'd never stop worrying about his father's"—she waves her hand in front of her torso à la Mrs. Bigg— "condition."

I really must find out what condition Mr. Bigg has that involves his torso and keeps everyone so worried about him.

Scanning the store for the first time since getting back, I notice the yarn donation box is gone.

"The charity knitters picked it up on New Year's Eve," Connie says when she catches me staring at the spot where the box used to sit.

"Have they announced what their big yarn bombing project is?" I ask.

"They plan to yarn bomb the town hall and library in the spring," Marla answers instead. "It'll be a fundraiser. Residents can sponsor their favourite knitter for every yard of yarn they knit or crochet for the project."

"Brilliant," I say.

"On behalf of the Harmony Lake Town Council and Town Hall, we can't wait," Adam comments in the most unenthusiastic monotone voice he can muster.

"I hope you'll show more enthusiasm than that when they unveil the installation, Mayor Martel," Connie chides, arching her eyebrows and wagging her index finger at Adam. "And when the Charity Knitting Guild donates the proceeds to upgrade the fishing pier and pay for new playground equipment."

Connie has no patience for sarcasm when it's aimed at knitting.

"Of course," Adam concedes. "The local government is proud to support and promote the local arts." Put in his place, he grins and gives Connie a slight nod.

"Who won the gift card?" I ask.

"Amber Windermere," Connie replies.

"Good for her," I say. "Did you mail it to her?"

"Nope," Connie replies. "When I contacted her to tell her she won and get her mailing address, she told me to hang on to the card. She said she'll pick it up in the spring when she comes to Harmony Lake on vacation."

"Amber's coming back?"

"She said she's renting a lakeside cottage for two weeks."

"I can't wait to see her again!"

"Speaking of winning," Phillip interjects. "I have your award, Eric."

"What award?" Eric asks.

"The one you would have received if you'd attended the police fundraising gala last week," Phillip replies. "They couriered it to your house, but you were away so I signed for it. And opened it. Then I polished it and put it on my mantle. It's a beautiful award." He pulls out his phone. "It matches my decor. Here, I'll show you a picture."

"It's OK, Phillip," Eric says. "I'll swing by after work and pick it up."

"Well, Mr. and Mrs. Sloane? What's next for you?" Tamara asks.

Eric puts his arm around my shoulders and squeezes me into him.

"We're looking forward to settling into a nice, quiet married life."

"With no murders," April adds.

"Of course not," Eric agrees.

"Murder? In our little town?" Phillip asks, his voice oozing with sarcasm. "*Pshaw*. Never!" He flicks his wrist and chuckles.

A Knitorious Murder Mystery Book 11

# Bait &
# Stitch

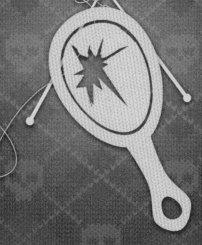

## REAGAN DAVIS

*For Marcelle. Thank you for raising an incredible man.*

# COPYRIGHT

ISBN: 978-1-990228-14-8 (ebook)

ISBN: 978-1-990228-13-1 (paperback)

ISBN: 978-1-990228-15-5 (hardcover)

ISBN: 978-1-990228-16-2 (large print paperback)

# FOREWORD

Dear Reader,

Despite several layers of editing and proofreading, occasionally a typo or grammar mistake is so stubborn that it manages to thwart my editing efforts and camouflage itself amongst the words in the book.

If you encounter one of these obstinate typos or errors in this book, please let me know by contacting me at Hello@ReaganDavis.com.

Hopefully, together we can exterminate the annoying pests.

Thank you!
Reagan Davis

# CHAPTER 1

FRIDAY, May 6th

I pop the trunk and unload the first suitcase, ignoring the warm, blustery wind as if refusing to acknowledge it, will stop it from blowing my hair in knots.

My hair is a tornado, and my face is the eye of the storm. Hannah points at my hair and covers her mouth, laughing at the Medusa-like curly chaos swirling around my head.

"Yours is just as bad," I say to my twenty-year-old daughter. "We have the same hair, remember?"

Hannah reaches up, still laughing, and tries in vain to tame her billowing brown curls.

I heave the last bag from the trunk and enjoy the satisfying crunch when it lands on the gravel parking lot. A fresh gust of warm wind rushes at me when I close the tailgate, blowing my wind-whipped hair swirls into a more frenzied vortex.

"Oh, goodness!" Connie giggles. "Look at your hair." She points just over our heads.

Mother Nature is kinder to Connie's sleek, chin-length bob. Her hair blows straight back, away from her face.

The sun highlights every subtle tone, like individual strands of glittery silver thread.

"The view is beautiful." Hannah spins in a slow circle as she takes in the storybook surroundings, recording it on her phone. "I only have one bar," she complains, repositioning her phone farther, then closer to her body, trying to improve the 5G data connection.

"We're halfway up a mountain," I remind her. "Service might be spotty up here."

"It looks like a storm is brewing." Connie nods toward the heavy clouds in the distance.

"According to Eric's last text, a storm is heading this way. He's glad we outpaced it."

Despite wearing sunglasses, I shade my eyes with my hand and appraise the approaching grey mass. The distant clouds are like a predator, creeping closer until it can overtake the perfect spring day. I'm not cold, but a blast of warm wind sends a shiver up my spine, leaving me with an unsettled, ominous feeling.

"You've only been apart for three hours, and he's already worried about you?" Connie tugs the handle of her rolling suitcase, extending it to its full length. "I guess the honeymoon isn't over yet."

My face flushes at the mention of my new husband. I try to suppress a sheepish grin and act like the mature, forty-two-year-old woman I am instead of the infatuated teenager I feel like when I think of him.

The official honeymoon ended three months ago. But the novelty of being married is stronger than ever. I still smile when I sign my new name. Sometimes, I write my new name in my fanciest handwriting and just stare at it, savouring the rush of happiness that surges through me.

"What a lovely way to spend Mother's Day weekend," Connie comments, as we pull our rolling suitcases toward the main building. "Why didn't we think of this years ago?"

She isn't my biological mother, but Connie has been my surrogate mother and Hannah's grandmother for exactly half my life. I was barely older than Hannah when Connie and I met. Shortly after my ex-husband and I moved to Harmony Lake, my mum died. I was grief-stricken, exhausted, and overwhelmed. I was knitting during Hannah's naps and after her bedtime to cope and had knit through every bit of yarn I owned. One day, I rolled Hannah's stroller into Knitorious, Connie's yarn store, searching for yarn to replenish my stash. Connie took us under her wing and into her heart. We've been family ever since.

Connie is seventy years young. She is mostly retired. I own Knitorious now, and she works there part-time.

Inside the spa, we're greeted by a friendly employee who offers to take our bags and places them on a luggage cart. The lobby is warm and inviting, despite being large and somewhat institutional. Not institutional like a school or government building, institutional like a medical office or laboratory.

The floors are dark wood, but everything else is white, smooth, and uncluttered. Clusters of cozy seating areas dot the lobby, creating an illusion of privacy for the guests occupying them. Two large, black massage chairs line one wall, occupied by two relaxed, perhaps even sleeping, guests.

"Welcome to SoulSpring Spa and Retreat," says the cheerful lady behind the counter. "How may I help you?" The tip of her blonde ponytail drapes over her shoulder.

She is centred below the FRONT DESK sign. Technically, the front desk is not a desk. It is a long white counter with white computer monitors in the centre and at either end.

"Hi, Maria," I say, smiling and reading her name tag, *Maria C.* Underneath in smaller letters are the words, *GENERAL MANAGER.* "We have a reservation."

Maria cuts a quick glance at my hair. Twice. I can tell she's trying not to look but can't stop herself.

"Name?" Maria asks, tapping a keyboard somewhere under the counter.

"Sloane," I say. "Megan Sloane."

Maria continues typing but sneaks a quick peek at Hannah's hair.

Hannah must notice because now she's petting herself, smoothing her long hair from root to tip.

Maria doesn't give Connie's hair a second glance because Connie's hair looks like she stepped away from a photo shoot for an *haute couture* magazine. Hannah and I look like we're wearing tumbleweed hats made of human hair.

"Is the wind picking up?" Maria asks, her blue eyes twinkling behind the black frames of her large, square glasses.

"Sure is," I confirm.

"We're expecting some active weather later."

"I heard."

"Is cell service reliable at the spa?" Hannah asks. "I've only had one bar since we've been here."

"Our Wi-Fi is great," Maria says, pointing to the Wi-Fi password posted behind the counter. "The spa is between two cell phone towers. We aren't close enough to either for consistent service. Your connection might cut in and out. It's worse today because of the approaching storm." She shakes her head. "Electrical storms always mess with internet and cell service."

"Great," Hannah says, rolling her eyes and tossing her hand in the air as if she gives up.

"This is an opportunity for a social media detox,"

Maria suggests. "A chance to unplug and unwind." I sense she's given this speech before. "To tune into your inner voice instead of tuning into the constant barrage of the information age. Your mind, body, and soul will thank you for the break."

Hannah nods, her expression blank. She's not buying whatever brand of analogue inner-peace Maria is trying to sell her. Maria might be young—I'd guess early thirties—but she's not twenty and doesn't appreciate the place of prominence cell phones have in the life of a twenty-year-old.

Maria tells our room number to the employee who took our luggage. She nods and disappears toward the elevator. Another employee joins Maria behind the front desk. All employees wear the same spa uniform: beige cotton, straight-leg trousers with a blue, short-sleeved, collared golf shirt with the spa logo on the upper right chest, and a silver name tag on the upper left chest with their first name and last initial etched in black, uppercase letters.

"Enjoy your stay." Maria issues us keys to our two-bedroom suite.

Actual metal keys. Not card keys like most hotels nowadays. Each key is attached to a blue silicone, coil keychain that guests can wear on their wrists.

"Thank you," we say, almost in sync.

Our room is on the top floor. There are only three floors. We decide to be healthy and take the stairs instead of the elevator.

"There's no room number on my key," Hannah observes, flipping the thing over in her palm. "What if it gets mixed up with someone else's? How will I tell them apart?"

A sudden gale-force gust hurtles a tree branch at the window just as we walk past.

"Heavens!" Connie declares, flinching and clutching her chest as we instinctively cower.

Other guests rush over to investigate the crash.

"It's just a spring storm," Maria announces over the chattering of the crowd gathered around the floor-to-ceiling window. "The weather service says the storm will be intense, but short."

Maria explains that intense weather is typical here and assures everyone that it will take more than a spring storm to topple the SoulSpring Spa and Retreat. Then she launches into the spa's history, explaining that it has stood on this land for almost one hundred years, weathering storms, floods, avalanches, and mud slides. We slip away from Maria's history lesson and into the stairwell.

# CHAPTER 2

My hair is a lost cause. Thanks to the wind tunnel in the parking lot, my tight, defined curls are bushy, frizzy clumps. I give up, gather it in a top knot, and put it out of my mind.

Connie and I spend a few minutes knitting while Hannah walks around the suite, pointing her cell phone in every nook and cranny like she's scanning for trace amounts of something.

"What are you doing, my lovely?" Connie asks her.

"Recording the suite for social media." Hannah sighs. "Not that I have enough bars to post anything right now."

"The Shaws have arrived," Connie announces when someone knocks on the door that connects us to the adjoining suite.

April Shaw is my best friend. Her wife, Tamara, is a close second—next to Connie—and their daughter, Rachel, is Hannah's bestie.

After everyone gets settled, Rachel and Tamara head to the nail lounge for a Mum and Me Mother's Day Mani-Pedi, Connie and Hannah leave for the Free Your

Mind Yoga and Guided Meditation class they booked, and April and I head to the acclaimed and award-winning spa restaurant, Epicurean Bistro.

Outside the bistro, we read Chef Nadira Patel's biography, which is posted inside a large frame just outside the door. Nadira is an award-winning chef specializing in vegan and Ayurvedic cuisine. As we read the long list of famous restaurants and spas where Nadira has worked as a celebrity chef, April nudges me.

"Listen," she whispers.

We hold our breath and focus on the silence.

"I don't hear anything," I whisper.

"Wait." She tucks a strand of long blonde hair behind her ear.

Then we hear it. Shouting. Then silence. More shouting. Still listening, we move closer to the source of the disturbance.

An irate guest is accusing Nadira of serving her chicken instead of tofu on purpose. The furious guest declares she is pescatarian and insists the chef sabotaged her meal. She uses words like "malicious intent" and "deliberate contamination."

"Why would someone deliberately serve chicken to a person who doesn't eat chicken?" April asks.

"Good question," I reply. "Nadira's grace and patience are impressive. I doubt I'd be as calm if someone was shouting, calling me horrible names, and tossing accusations at me."

The manager, Maria, appears and diffuses the situation. Whatever she says to the peeved piscivore has the desired effect. The outraged guest's voice quiets to a conversational tone. Heads turn away, and people return to whatever they were doing before the angry tirade distracted them.

April and I finish reading the chef's impressive biography, and highlights of her culinary career, then turn our attention to the posted menu.

"Oooh! Wanna split an order of Wagyu beef nachos?" I ask.

"Excuse me?" asks an unfamiliar voice.

A familiar woman leans close to me, giving me a good look at her face as she reads the Wagyu beef nachos description. It's the guest who just accused the chef of contaminating her tofu dish with chicken. And I just asked her to share a beef dish with me.

"Oh! I'm sorry," I declare, bringing my palm to my forehead. "My friend was right here. I thought you were her." I spin my head from side to side until I find April and point to her. She's perusing a menu posted on the other side of the doorway. "I-I wasn't suggesting you should eat meat," I stammer, hoping not to reignite the woman's anger.

My excuse is lame. April and the pescatarian guest bear no resemblance to each other. It would be impossible to confuse them. April is tall, and the woman is short, like me. April has long blonde hair, and the woman has shoulder-length dark hair.

"I recommend The Wagyu beef nachos. They're fantastic," the woman says, grinning. "I just ate." She shrugs her narrow shoulders. "But I'll share an order with you if you'd like."

I'm confused. Isn't this the same woman who just threatened to sue the chef for emotional pain and suffering for serving her meat? They have the same shoulder-length shag hairstyle, and the same piercing green eyes. They even have the same voice, though the woman next to me isn't yelling. I'm sure it's the same person. Did she undergo carnivorous conversion in the last five minutes? Whatever Maria said to calm her down was effective if it convinced her to become a meat eater.

"I thought you don't eat meat," I say, cautious of her potential reaction. "Didn't you just exchange words with the chef about a misunderstanding over chicken?"

April sidles up next to me, just as curious about the woman in front of us.

"I'm Summer," the woman says, thrusting her hand at me.

When she smiles, Summer's left upper lip curls more than the right, giving her a mischievous grin that makes me wonder if I said something funny without realizing.

"Megan," I say, shaking her hand. "It's nice to meet you, Summer."

"My twin sister, Autumn, is the angry pescatarian."

"I'm April, the hungry Presbyterian."

April and Autumn shake hands.

I nudge April's hip while stifling a laugh at her joke.

"This is Billie," Autumn says, gesturing to her ginger-haired friend.

"Don't feel bad," Billie says, shaking my hand. "I've known the twins since kindergarten, and sometimes I still mix them up for a minute or two." She chuckles. "We should ask Maria what her secret is."

"Secret?" I ask.

"Maria can always tell Autumn and Summer apart," Billie explains. "We got here on Wednesday, and she hasn't mixed them up once. It's incredible."

"Maybe spotting slight differences is Maria's superpower," I say, wondering what Maria noticed about the twins that helps her differentiate them.

If their best friend since kindergarten still confuses Autumn and Summer, how does a spa manager who just met them do it? Unless she's met them before. For all I know, they could be frequent guests.

"I assume you and Autumn are identical twins, and not the other kind?" April asks.

"Identical," Summer replies, "Right down to our voices."

"I'll say," I agree. "You even have similar hairstyles."

"Besides looking the same, my sister and I have similar taste," Summer explains, "which means our wardrobes are twice the size of everyone else's."

We laugh again. I like Summer. She's funny. And, at first glance, more laid back than her twin.

"It's easier to tell them apart when you know them," Billie interjects.

She and Summer recount a time when Billie couldn't tell them apart. It was Halloween. The twins dressed up as the twins from the movie The Shining.

"If we don't leave now, we'll be late for our appointment at the eyebrow bar," Autumn chides, checking her watch and interrupting Summer and Billie's Halloween story.

"Autumn, this is Megan." Summer gestures to me, and I offer my hand for Autumn to shake. "And April." She gestures to April, who extends her hand.

"Nice to meet you," Autumn says to both of us in a manner that is curt and efficient, but not rude. Then she gives us a small, tight-lipped smile.

"Likewise."

"Nice to meet you too."

April and I speak over each other.

"Let's go!" Autumn says, locking arms with her sister and Billie, dragging them away.

"Bye, Megan! Bye, April," Summer calls over her shoulder as she struggles to keep up with her sister.

"It was nice to meet you!" Billie adds with a smile as Autumn drags them around the corner.

My gaze lingers after the twins disappear around the corner. I know twins exist, and I've met identical twins before, but it still amazes me that there are people in the world who are physical clones of each other. I can't imagine looking into a face identical to mine or watching myself walk down the street.

INSIDE THE EPICUREAN BISTRO, the hostess seats us next to a window, and we flinch, making startled, gasping sounds when the wind whips an unsecured piece of nature toward us.

"The windows are reinforced glass," the server assures us as the wind rattles the floor-to-ceiling window. "But I can move you to an inside table if you'd be more comfortable."

We decide to trust her and stay at the table next to the window. Even with Mother Nature throwing a tantrum, the picturesque landscape is awe-inspiring, and I understand why there are so many floor-to-ceiling windows at the SoulSpring Spa and Retreat.

"Most of the twins I've met have the same features, but different senses of style. I can tell them apart by their hair or how they dress."

"Summer and Autumn appear identical at first glance, but there are some subtle differences," April says.

"Autumn is a pescatarian, and Summer isn't," I say.

"That's one difference," April agrees. "Summer was way more laid back than her twin. She was relaxed, chatty, and funny. Autumn was way more uptight. Everything about her is more tense than her sister. Even her smile was tense."

"Maybe that was because of the chicken incident," I suggest. "Maybe we just met her at a bad time." I shrug one shoulder. "Everyone has a bad day."

We're enjoying our order of Wagyu beef nachos and

Springtime Palmitate salad when the light above our table gets brighter.

"That's better," April says. "Now I can see what I'm eating." She stabs a black olive and a chunk of Buffalo mozzarella with her fork.

"What time is it?" I ask. "It's too early for sunset."

April glances at her watch.

"We have a few hours before the sun goes down."

"Wow, it's so dark," I say, separating a chip from the dwindling pile of nachos. "I was so focused on the pleasant conversation and amazing food, I didn't notice how dark the sky had become."

"It's like nighttime," April agrees.

A crack of thunder booms in the distance.

"How is everything?" a soft voice asks.

We look away from the window. Chef Nadira Patel is standing next to our table. How long has she been there?

"Wonderful," I reply.

"This honey-lime vinaigrette is to die for," April gushes.

"I'm glad you're enjoying it." Nadira smiles. "It's good to know some guests are happy with the food."

"We heard your exchange with Autumn earlier," I confess. "You handled it well."

"The occasional dissatisfied guest is part of the job." Nadira shrugs. "It was an honest mistake, but it shouldn't have happened. The cooked, cubed tofu and cooked, cubed chicken were next to each other in identical bowls. I mixed them up. I should have stored them in unique containers and used better labels."

"You redeemed yourself with these nachos," April reassures her.

We laugh.

"Mother Nature is putting on quite a show for you."

Nadira points at the large window, which is being pelted with loud, fat raindrops.

"We're hoping it will be one of her shorter productions," I joke.

"Without an encore," April adds, laughing at her own joke.

"I was here last spring too," Nadira says. "These spring storms are fast and furious. I'm sure it won't last long."

# CHAPTER 3

"Hey, sweetie! Where's Connie?" I ask when Hannah joins me in the change room. "Isn't she having this treatment with us?"

"She said to tell you she's fine, but tired," Hannah replies, opening the locker next to mine. "She went up upstairs to knit and relax."

"OK," I reply. "I'm sure she'll find us if she needs anything."

"Aunt April, Aunt T, and Rachel are soaking in a hydrotherapy salt spa."

"Oooh, I like the sound of that. Did we book a session in the hydrotherapy salt spa?"

"Tomorrow." Hannah nods with a smile, reaching for the fluffy white spa robe in her locker.

"What treatment are we getting?" I ask as I fold my clothes and place them in the locker. "I know it has a clever name, but I can't remember."

"We're about to have a Soul to Sole Hydrating Body Wrap," Hannah replies, gathering her long, thick curls in a messy bun and securing it with a scrunchie.

"Does it involve a massage? I could use a massage." I tighten the belt of my spa robe.

"First, they scrub away all the gross dead skin, then they massage us with hydrating lotions and potions from head to toe, then they wrap us up like burritos and leave us to marinate," she explains, tapping the screen of her phone.

"No phones in the change rooms, Hannah Banana!" I point to the large pictograph on the door—a cell phone with a red circle backslash.

"I'm turning it off," Hannah replies with a sigh. "I promised Lucas that I'd text him, but I can't get a good signal." She powers off her phone and sets it on top of her clothes in the locker. "The Wi-Fi isn't as good as Maria said. It's way slower than at home. It must be the storm."

Lucas is Hannah's boyfriend. She teases Eric and me, saying we are attached at the hip, but a wireless 5G connection attaches her and Lucas. Spotty cell phone service and slow Wi-Fi might give them withdrawal symptoms.

We close our lockers and pause mid-step, looking up at the ceiling when the lights dim, flicker back to full power, dim again, then return full power again.

"I hope we don't lose power," Hannah says.

We exchange skeptical sideways glances as we exit the change room.

SMOOTHER AND MORE HYDRATED than a pair of dolphins, Hannah and I return to the change room after our Soul to Sole Hydrating Body Wrap. We get dressed, accompanied by the booming soundtrack of thunder rumbling outside.

Each crack of thunder is quicker and louder than the one before it.

"Twins!" Hannah says under her breath as we head toward the change room door.

"Hi, Summer. Hi, Autumn," I say with my eyes shooting back and forth between them, hoping the correct name lands on the correct twin.

They're wearing identical white, fluffy spa robes, and their identical transparent plastic cups with identical white straws contain identical green contents.

"Hi, Megan!"

I recognize Summer's mischievous grin with the extra lip curl.

"Hi again," Autumn says, almost smiling.

April is right! Their demeanours and smiles are different.

"This is my daughter, Hannah."

"You're twins!"

Hannah's green eyes are bright and wide. Clearly, she inherited my fascination with twins.

"Yes, we are," Autumn says with a slight nod.

"This is so good," Summer says after she sips her green drink. "Have you visited the juice bar yet?"

"Not yet," I reply.

"Mmm." Summer nods. "I recommend the Green Powerhouse smoothie."

Autumn frowns at the spot on her wrist where her watch should be. I get the sense that Autumn struggles to relax more than her less-uptight sister.

"What's in it?" Hannah asks.

"I don't know, but it's incredible," Summer replies, rolling her eyes with bliss and savouring a long sip. "I've had one every day since we checked in. I'll miss Green Powerhouse smoothies when we go home."

"Maybe the spa will give you the recipe," I suggest.

"Yeah, maybe," Summer says. "The ingredients are listed on the menu. I could ask how much of each ingredient to include."

"We should go," Autumn urges, then sips her smoothie. "They won't extend our time in the sauna if we're late." She sips again.

As we approach the door, an employee walks in and calls, "Excuse me!" to the twins.

As the door closes behind us, the employee offers someone a hot stone massage, explaining that another guest cancelled at the last minute and the twins were on the waiting list. The door shuts before I hear whether her offer was accepted.

In the hall, Hannah's phone dings inside her pocket.

"Service! I have service?" She whips out her phone and unlocks the screen. "It's Connie." Her posture and face droop. "She forgot to pack a toothbrush and wants us to get one at the front desk. She tried to call the front desk, but the landline in our room keeps disconnecting." Holding her phone at arm's length, Hannah paces, searching frantically for a reliable signal. "How did Connie's text get through? I have no bars."

"Technology works in mysterious ways," I tease, pulling my phone from my pocket. "I don't have service either."

Determined to find a signal, Hannah continues to pace, holding her phone above her head, then as far from her body as her arm will stretch, then down low. I wait patiently while she repeats this ritual, without success, three more times. Defeated, she drops the hand holding her phone to her side.

"I'm craving one of those green smoothies the twins had," she says. "Do you want one?"

"No thanks," I reply. "Go to the juice bar. I'll get Connie's toothbrush, and we'll meet up after."

SUNSET ISN'T for another hour, but between lightning flashes, the sky is dark as night. Sheets of rain hammer the glass and blur the view outside the floor-to-ceiling windows lining the hall to the lobby.

A tearful woman wearing a spa uniform presses her cell phone against her ear as she rushes past. I turn to check on her, but a wind gust rattles the window next to me, making me recoil. A twig breaks free from the cyclone of debris swirling outside the window and flies into the frame. I rush past the series of giant windows. As I approach the front desk, Autumn is walking away from it. Her purposeful gait and stiff posture give her away. She returns my smile with a brief nod, then veers toward the stairwell.

"Mrs. Sloane." Maria smiles from behind her large, square, black frames. "What can I do for you?"

"Please call me Megan," I say. "Would you have a spare toothbrush? And I'm told the phone in our room isn't working."

"The storm knocked out our internet and landline," Maria explains, producing a basket from under the counter. She rummages through it, knocking a few bandages, alcohol wipes, and pregnancy tests onto the counter. "It happens sometimes. I'm sure normal service will resume shortly."

She smiles, sweeps the spilled items into the basket, returns it to wherever it came from, and pulls out another. "I know we have toothbrushes somewhere."

"There's no cell service either," I add, watching Maria ransack a basket of tampons, travel-size deodorant, and motion sickness medication.

The lights in the reception area flicker when a clap of thunder shakes the windows. The simultaneous flash of lightning floods the lobby with a brief pulse of harsh brightness.

"Hmm," Maria hums, shoving the second basket back under the counter and pulling out her phone. "You're right. No cell service." She looks at me. "It's because of the storm." She pushes her phone into her back pocket. "The toothbrushes must be in the office. I'll be right back."

As Maria disappears through the door behind the front desk, leaving me alone with the thunder and lightning, I convince myself that if Maria is unconcerned about the weather and the phones, I shouldn't worry either.

Maria and I have different definitions of *right back*. She's been gone for at least ten minutes when the entrance door swings open with the help of the wind. A police officer, holding her hat against her head, wrestles the door shut, then leans against it and inhales a sharp breath.

"Whoo! Windy enough for ya?" she asks, removing her campaign hat and smoothing her dark hair toward her tight bun as she scans the empty reception area. "Where's Maria?"

"Searching for a toothbrush," I reply. "She should be back any second."

"Twyla Proudfoot," the officer says, extending her hand. "Nice to meet you."

Sergeant Twyla Proudfoot, according to her name badge, is a tall woman with shiny dark hair, dark brown eyes, and a friendly smile. Her uniform is soaking wet, and water drops roll off the brim of her hat.

"Megan Sloane," I say, shaking her hand. "It's nice to meet you too. What brings you to the spa in this weather?"

"Phones are down. We couldn't reach the spa to check on everyone, so dispatch sent me to check in person."

I nod, smiling.

"I still don't have cell service, Mum," Hannah announces, coming down the hall with her cell phone in one hand and a Green Powerhouse smoothie in the other.

"Me neither," I confirm, checking my phone again to be sure. I look at Officer Twyla. "This is my daughter, Hannah." Twyla and Hannah exchange greetings. "Sweetie, would you mind going upstairs to check on Connie? I'll meet you up there as soon as Maria comes back with a toothbrush."

"Sure."

Without looking up from her phone, Hannah sips her smoothie and walks away.

A thunder boom shakes my insides, and lightning strobes in and out, creating temporary, exaggerated shadows on the walls.

"I don't have cell service either," Twyla mutters, checking her phone. "There's a satellite phone in my patrol car that I can leave with Maria until the work crews restore service. I'll go get it."

"I'll tell Maria you'll be right back," I offer.

Twyla nods, dons her hat, and pauses, staring down the door before opening it and venturing into the storm. Through the window, I watch Twyla's khaki uniform cling to the front of her body and billow behind her like a parachute. She presses her hat onto her head with her face aimed at the ground as she struggles against the wind.

After the longest toothbrush search in history, Maria returns empty-handed and shaking her head.

"I know they're here somewhere," she insists. "I remember unpacking them. We should have an entire box of unopened toothbrushes." She rubs her chin. "Where did I put them?"

"What are you looking for?" asks an employee, stepping behind the counter.

"The complimentary toothbrushes," Maria replies. "We have at least two dozen somewhere."

The employee walks to the other end of the long counter and pulls out a basket.

"Any particular colour?" she asks me.

"Any colour is fine."

"Soft, medium, or firm bristles?"

"Surprise me."

She hands me a blue toothbrush with soft bristles.

"Thank you," I say, taking the toothbrush.

"Floss?" she asks, holding up a travel-size package of dental floss.

"No, thanks." I smile, then look at Maria. "Officer Twyla Proudfoot is here," I say. "She went back to her car to get a satellite phone."

An ear-splitting explosion of thunder vibrates through my body. The simultaneous streak of lightning is so bright that I squint.

# CHAPTER 4

Silence. Darkness. Stillness.

No landline, no cell phone, and now, no electricity.

Who knew silence could be so loud?

The ringing in my ears replaces the incessant buzz of electricity that my brain has spent my lifetime training itself to tune out.

I swallow, but the ringing continues. I force myself to yawn, hoping if I pop them, my ears will stop ringing. They don't. Maybe they always ring, but I don't notice because the constant hum of electricity drowns it out.

The sudden silent darkness is unsettling.

My tinnitus is either fading, or I'm getting used to it.

"Megawatt?"

April likes to call me clever nicknames that are puns of my actual name. Her current choice, Megawatt, is fitting.

"April?" I call. "Over here." I use the flashlight on my cell phone as a beacon to guide her. "What are you doing here?"

"Hannah's smoothie gave me a craving. I was getting

223

off the elevator and heard the loudest boom ever. Then, the power went out."

Maria picks up the landline. "Great!" she huffs, remembering that it's not working, then slams down the receiver.

"Landline is down," her colleague reminds her.

"Thanks." Maria's voice is thick with sarcasm.

A breeze blows the stray hairs against the back of my neck. I spin around and a disheveled Officer Twyla is carrying her campaign hat and using her body to force the door shut.

In the confusion, I forgot about Officer Twyla. What took her so long? How far away did she park?

Twyla leans against the latched door, catching her breath and assessing her misshapen uniform hat. Her bun is still intact, but drippy strands of displaced hair hang around her head and face. Stained by the rain, her khaki uniform is several shades darker than it should be, and water drips from her cuffs.

"Are you OK?" I ask.

Twyla nods. "It's bad out there," she says.

"Did you get the satellite phone?" I ask, not seeing anything phone-like in her hands or attached to her duty belt.

"It's gone," she says.

"Your satellite phone is gone?"

"My patrol car is gone."

"Someone stole your patrol car?"

"Who would steal a police car in the middle of nowhere during a raging storm?" April asks.

"Mother Nature," Twyla responds. "She took my car when she washed away the road."

April and I rush to the window overlooking the parking lot.

It's too dark to make out the parking lot. Seconds

later, we let out audible sighs of relief when a flash of sheet lightning illuminates the gravel parking area. It's still intact, and our cars are still there. *Phew.*

"I parked on the opposite side," Twyla explains, jerking her thumb toward the opposite wall. "I only planned to be here for a few minutes." She shrugs. "A mudslide created a river that washed away my car."

"It also washed away the only road in and out of here." Maria sounds more inconvenienced than concerned.

Maria dispatches the employee who found the tooth-brushes to hunt down the maintenance person and start the generators. The employee retrieves a flashlight and disappears through the door behind the front desk.

"We're equipped for this," Maria explains. "We've only had municipal service for a few years. Before that The SoulSpring was off-grid. Between two huge genera-tors and solar panels with batteries to store solar power, we can function off-grid for several days."

"Good," Twyla interjects. "Because it will be days before anyone can come or go. The city won't even be able to dispatch crews until the storm passes."

"What if there's an emergency?" April asks. "What if someone needs medical help or something?"

"I'm a trained emergency medical technician and a law enforcement officer," Twyla assures us.

"And we have a well-equipped first aid station."

Hopefully, the well-equipped first aid station Maria refers to isn't the series of overflowing, disorganized baskets she pulled out from under the counter earlier. Some medical emergencies require more than bandages and pregnancy tests.

"Maria's right," Twyla adds. "The first aid station even has a defibrillator. We'll be fine."

A few minutes of anxious silence later, the generators

hum to life and artificial light once again illuminates the lobby.

"You're soaking wet, Twy," Maria says, now that there's enough light to assess the situation. "Let's get you dried off."

Without checking the computer, a book, or anything, Maria produces a key, hands it to Twyla, and mumbles under her breath.

"Thank you." The officer takes the key. "I'll be right back."

Spa uniforms trickle into the lobby. Maria explains that because the spa's intercom relies on the internet, she can't make announcements, and guests can't contact the front desk from their rooms. Maria informs her staff that she wants to do a headcount. She assigns employees to specific floors and sections of the resort, instructing them to gather every guest and employee and bring them to the Epicurean Bistro.

With their instructions issued, employees leave the lobby in pairs, heading to their assigned posts. April and I leave with them to collect Connie, Hannah, Tamara, and Rachel and bring them to the bistro. Worried about the possibility of another power failure, we forego the elevator and use the stairs to get to our third-floor rooms.

# CHAPTER 5

THE EPICUREAN BISTRO IS FULL. Extra chairs line the walls to accommodate everyone.

I'm knitting and listening as Maria reassures us that there is enough power, food, and supplies to run the spa for several days.

"What are you knitting?" Tamara whispers.

"Spa wash cloth," I whisper in reply.

"It's nice," Tamara says.

"Thanks," I say. "I'm making one for Eric's mum and each of my sisters-in-law. I'm going to purchase some artisanal soaps and stuff from the spa gift shop and make self-care gift packages for them."

"Good idea," Tamara whispers. "I wish I'd thought of that."

"I have more yarn and needles," I offer.

"Yeah?" she asks, her voice creeping above a whisper and causing a few nearby guests to give us *the look*. The disapproving, *please be quiet* look.

The worst of the storm has passed. The thunder is less frequent and more distant, and the wind hasn't wreaked any noticeable havoc since Maria approached the maître d' lectern to address us.

Craning my neck to look out a window, I glimpse Billie slinking in and taking a seat close to the door. We make eye contact. She smiles and gives me a small wave. I return the smile and wave with my knitting.

"And Officer Twyla is a trained medic in the unlikely event that anyone requires medical assistance," Maria announces.

Two guests, a registered nurse and a doctor, raise their hands and offer their professional expertise if necessary.

Officer Twyla must have borrowed clothes from someone because, instead of her wet uniform, she's wearing grey sweatpants, a white t-shirt, grey zip hoodie, and white sneakers. Her damp, dark hair is pulled into a high ponytail. It's much longer than the tight bun led me to believe.

"I'm sure we're all checking our phones regularly," Twyla says. "We're all eager for cell phone service to be restored so we can contact our loved ones. If anyone can make a call or send a text, please let me know right away." She smiles. "Thank you."

Maria takes over again, spinning a yarn about how this period of unintentional disconnection is *a wonderful opportunity for reflection and solitude,* and she hopes each of us *will take advantage of this mental space to embrace a digital detox* and *focus on introspection.* She's trying to reframe being stranded by a natural disaster as the universe providing us *a once-in-a-lifetime opportunity for growth and enlightenment.*

I would rather have cell service and a drivable road. Watching my digitally devoid daughter squirm in her seat and gnaw her lip as she makes yet another desperate attempt to find a signal by holding her phone up to the window, I'm guessing she'd rather have cell service, too, instead of *mental space to embrace a digital detox and focus on introspection.*

Instead of *reflection and solitude,* I'd rather contact my husband and let him know we're OK so he can relax and enjoy his weekend. And instead of *introspection,* I'd rather contact my ex-husband and assure him our daughter is fine, so he can stop pacing around his condo, trying to call her every thirty seconds.

Maria opens the floor to questions and hands pop into the air.

"Does anyone know we're stranded?" asks the guest. "I mean, if we can't contact anyone, how will they know we need help?"

"We don't need help," Maria reminds her. "We can function as normal for several days..." She repeats her spiel about generators, solar power, food, water, medical supplies... and ends with her speech about how this situation might be a blessing in disguise for those of us in need of a respite from the constant bombardment of online information.

Most people in this room have a loved one to worry about them. We live in the digital age, and people expect constant connection and instant—or almost instant—access to each other. By now, someone has figured out something is wrong at The SoulSpring Spa and Retreat. People know we're stranded, and they're trying to get to us. I know it. I feel it in my bones.

I have no doubt the local police force is wondering where Sergeant Twyla Proudfoot is and searching for the missing officer and patrol car.

Eric has texted me and is worried because I haven't responded. Lucas is worried because he hasn't heard from Hannah, and she hasn't posted on social media.

He'll ask Eric if he's heard from Hannah or me. I'm sure Adam is panicking because he can't contact our daughter, and his panic will increase when he finds out Eric and Lucas can't contact us either. Connie's partner, Archie, will ask them if they've heard anything, and April and Tamara's teenage son, Zach, will contact them because he can't reach his mothers or sister. I'm certain that by now, they've figured out we're incommunicado, and something is wrong.

My husband is a police chief. He'll contact the local authorities and ask why no one at the SoulSpring Spa and Retreat is reachable.

Maria and Twyla answer questions and allay concerns. Then Maria takes attendance. Sensing that this impromptu gathering is almost over, I stuff my knitting inside my bag and sit up straight, ready to shout, "Here," when she calls my name.

Maria is more than halfway through the roll call for the second-floor guests when a flustered twin swoops into the bistro, rushing to the maître d' lectern where Maria is calling attendance. Squinting, the twin scans the room, searching the crowd.

"Autumn or Summer?" April whispers.

"Autumn," I reply. "Her posture is rigid, and her face is tense."

"Agreed." April nods. "She's wound up tighter than a two-dollar watch."

"Did you want to say something, Autumn?" Maria asks, miffed by the interruption.

Maria uses Autumn's name with confidence. Summer and Billie were right, she has no problem differentiating the identical twins.

"Where's my sister?!" Autumn demands. "Summer?" she continues surveying the room. "Has anyone seen my sister?"

The crowd murmurs and shuffles, searching their immediate vicinities for the missing twin and asking their neighbours if they've seen her.

"When did you last see her?" Twyla asks, now on her feet.

"In the change room," Autumn replies. "We were going to the sauna. My plans changed. I left and Summer went to the sauna without me. We had planned to meet in our room, but she never showed up." She looks at Twyla with pleading eyes. "I've looked everywhere. I've tried texting and phoning her, but I don't have a signal."

"No one has a signal," says a random guest. "Phones down."

"There's no internet either," adds another disembodied voice.

This information further increases Autumn's apparent distress.

"She has to be here somewhere!" Autumn's breaths are quick, and her chest heaves. She might be on the verge of hyperventilating.

Billie threads her way through the room and joins Autumn at the lectern.

"I assumed you and Summer were together," Billie says.

"I thought she was with you," Autumn retorts. "I haven't seen her since I left the change room. I had a headache and went upstairs to lie down."

Maria turns her attention to a group of employees seated to her right.

"Who cleared the sauna after the blackout?"

Two employees exchange timid smiles and raise their hands.

"The sauna was empty," says the first employee.

"The doors were locked, and the lights were off," confirms the second.

"We'll mount a search," Twyla declares.

She steps in front of Maria and addresses the employees directly. I can't hear Twyla's words, but they pay attention and occasionally nod in unison.

The murmur of the crowd grows louder with concern and speculation about the missing guest.

"Excuse me," Twyla commands with an authoritative tone we haven't heard from her before. The room hushes, and everyone directs their attention to the officer standing at the lectern. "In an orderly fashion, please return to your rooms and stay there. Since phones are down and you can't call the front desk, we will position an attendant at either end of each floor. Please speak to them if you need assistance. We'll knock when we've cleared the premises, and you can leave your rooms."

"Won't it be faster if everyone searches for Summer?" a guest shouts from somewhere behind me.

"No," Twyla replies. "Too many volunteers will impede the search. The best way to help is to stay in your room until we tell you otherwise."

"Will you be searching our rooms in case she's in the wrong room?" another guest asks.

"It's possible," the police officer replies. "We'll search common areas first. If you find Summer in your room, please notify me or an employee immediately."

Maria resumes taking attendance, and Twyla continues instructing the spa employees in a volume that's inaudible to the curious guests. She dismisses them, and they file out of the bistro in a single, paired-off line.

Maria completes the roll call, thanks us for our collective patience and cooperation, and apologizes for the inconvenience. We leave the bistro amid the muffled mumbles of people hoping for a quick and happy resolution to the search for Summer, swift resumption of cell phone service, and conjecture about where Summer could be.

# CHAPTER 6

"Hannah mentioned she met the twins in the change room after your wrap session," Connie says as we inch our way toward the stairs. "She said it was the twins who encouraged her to try the juice bar."

"That's right," I say. "When Hannah and I left, they were talking to a spa employee about a hot stone massage."

"Do you think you should mention this to Officer Twyla, my dear?"

"Maybe," I reply with a shrug. "But not right now. Twyla's priority is locating Summer, and I don't want to slow down the search. Anyway, when they find Summer safe and sound, our encounter in the change room will be irrelevant."

"Mum!" Hannah weaves through the crowd until she's behind Connie and me. "Should we tell the police officer we saw Summer and Autumn in the change room?"

"I'll go with you," April jumps in.

"Fine," I relent. "If she can spare the time, I'll tell

Twyla about our conversation with Autumn and Summer."

"I'll go upstairs with Connie," Hannah offers, taking her surrogate grandmother's arm.

I step out of line and loiter in an out-of-the-way spot while April tells her wife and daughter that she's accompanying me to speak to the police officer.

"Don't either of you go missing!" Tamara cautions as she files past with the crowd, wagging her index finger.

April steps out of line, and we slip around the corner, out of sight of the employee monitoring the stairwell entrance.

"Now what?" April asks, rubbing her hands together. "Are we going to talk to Twyla? Or should we look for Summer?"

"Both."

We decide it makes sense to start the search in the change room since it's Summer's last known location. We expect Twyla and Maria are already there.

The hall leading to the change room is dark, and we use the flashlights on our phones to guide us. April and I surmise Maria turned off as many lights as possible to conserve energy since we're relying on generators and stored solar power to run the place. On the way, I tell April about the conversation Hannah and I had with the twins.

"We left before I could hear whether Summer or Autumn accepted the employee's offer."

"Which twin did she offer it to?" April asks, opening the change room door.

"I don't know," I reply as we enter the dark change room. "The employee didn't address anyone by name. She was probably trying to avoid mixing them up."

April gropes one wall, and I grope another. I find a panel of switches and flip them. The lights flicker to life.

"They're used to it," April reasons, checking the changing stalls. "They're identical. I'm sure people have mixed them up all their lives."

"Maybe neither twin took the hot stone massage," I suggest. "I saw Autumn walking away from the front desk before the blackout."

I check the showers while April checks the toilet stalls.

"How could Autumn be at the front desk and on a massage table?"

"I don't know," I admit. "But I saw Autumn walking away from the front desk when I was getting a tooth-brush for Connie. She was walking toward the stairwell. Then, Autumn rushed into the bistro searching for her sister. She told Twyla they were on their way to the sauna when her plans changed. She said Summer went to the sauna without her."

"You're sure the twin you saw leaving the front desk was Autumn?"

April pushes the door that leads to the hydrotherapy pools. It's locked.

"She had Autumn's intensity," I reason. "Her demeanour was uptight, and her smile seemed forced."

"Sounds like Autumn," April confirms. "If Summer was in the sauna, and you saw Autumn going toward their room, maybe neither twin went for a hot stone massage."

"Maybe," I concede. "When Autumn burst into the bistro searching for Summer, she said she was lying down in their room."

We scan the locker area. All the lockers except one are ajar. April approaches the closed locker and tugs the lock. It doesn't open.

"Summer and Autumn were standing near that locker when Hannah and I ran into them," I say.

"Do you think this could be Summer's locker?" April asks.

"I'm not sure," I reply. "But if it is, why didn't Summer return to her locker after the sauna?"

"It might not be Summer's locker." April dismisses my theory and drops the lock, letting it clang against the metal door. "It could belong to anyone," she reasons. "Guests probably leave stuff in lockers all the time, especially if they're coming back the next day for a treatment."

I point to the sign posted above the full-length mirror. PLEASE DO NOT LEAVE PERSONAL ITEMS IN LOCKERS OVERNIGHT. WE DISINFECT EACH LOCKER AND PROVIDE FRESH ROBES EACH EVENING. ABANDONED BELONGINGS WILL BE DISCARDED.

"Would Summer fit inside a locker?" I ask, standing sideways and sucking in my belly, wondering if I would fit inside a locker.

"That's morbid, Megnolia!" Horrified and amused, April gasps and smiles. "Summer isn't inside a locker."

The twins are taller but narrower than me. It wouldn't be an easy fit, especially with the hook and shelf configuration inside the lockers.

"She has to be somewhere," I reason. "If we don't find her anywhere else, someone will have to check the locker."

"Maybe Summer's stuff is in this locker," she concedes. "Maybe she never left the sauna."

We take cautious steps toward the door that leads to the sauna.

"You heard the employees in the bistro," I remind her. "Two of them told Maria the sauna was empty and locked."

"We should check anyway," April says.

I push the door that leads to the sauna. It opens. Success.

The lights are off, just like the employees said.

April feels along the wall next to the change-room door, and I fumble along the wall behind the reception desk. April finds the switch and lights up the room.

I lob my knitting bag onto the reception desk and take in my surroundings.

Across from the reception desk, four doors lead to four different saunas.

"That's a lot of saunas," I comment.

"According to this, each sauna is different and offers a unique experience and benefits," April says, studying a brochure she found on the reception desk. "The first sauna,"—she points to the first door—"is a traditional Finnish sauna. A low humidity sauna heated by a wood stove that heats stones to between 140 and 200 degrees Fahrenheit. Water poured over the stones creates steam."

I approach the first door and peer through the panel window.

"Empty," I say, then push and pull the door handle. "And locked."

I approach the second door.

"That's the infrared sauna," April informs me. "It's a high-tech option that heats the body instead of the room and creates no humidity."

"Empty," I confirm peering through the window. "And locked," I add, tugging the door handle. "What kind of sauna is this?" I ask, approaching the third door.

"Steam sauna," April replies. "Also known as a Turkish Sauna." She turns the page. "Boiling water releases steam into the sauna chamber. The temperature is about 110 degrees Fahrenheit. This type of sauna is especially beneficial for the respiratory system."

This panel window is higher than the others. I stand on my tippy toes to peek inside.

"Empty?" April asks.

I scan the room. The floors and walls are basic-white ceramic tile with matching ceramic benches built into the walls. In the middle of the room is a large pentagon bench covered in the same, plain-white ceramic tiles as the floors, walls, and benches. The pentagon centrepiece has an intricate mandala pattern on top made from ceramic tiles.

"What's that?" I whisper to myself.

Is there something on the floor? It's hard to tell if there is indeed something on the floor, or if the glare off the glossy tiles is playing tricks on me.

I squint and shade my eyes with my hand. The floor tiles to the left back of the pentagon differ from the rest of the plain white tiles. There's some sort of splatter pattern. I check the other side of the pentagon to see if the pattern is symmetrical. It isn't. The non-conforming design is green. I squint. Maybe it's not a design in the tile. Could it be a spill? A green spill?

I gasp.

"What is it, Megabot?"

"The twins had green smoothies! There's green on the floor."

"No food or drink permitted in the saunas." April points to the sign on the back of the sauna door.

I inspect the floor behind the pentagon again. A matte, white blotch interrupts the sheen of the polished floor tiles. Fluffy? A fluffy white blotch? Like a fluffy spa robe!

"It's her!" I shout, bouncing. "Summer is behind the pentagon."

I pull the handle, then ram my full body weight into the sauna door. Locked. I hurry to the reception desk. While I ransack the drawers searching for keys, April rushes to sauna three and takes my spot at the window. She doesn't have to stand on her tippy toes to look through the glass panel.

"I think you're right!" she declares, her eyes darting around the room in a frantic search.

"C'mon! Where are the keys?!" I open the next drawer and groan with relief. "Found them!"

I grip one of the dozen-or-so keys and shove it in the lock. It doesn't fit. I grab the next key. It doesn't fit either.

April tears the fire extinguisher off the wall and runs toward the sauna door, her guttural growl increasing in volume and intensity with each stride.

I duck and leap out of the way as April releases a primal shriek and heaves the red metal extinguisher into the window. Shattered glass crashes to the sauna floor as she tosses the heavy extinguisher aside.

It lands with a clamorous thump, shaking the floor beneath us.

She reaches her long willowy arm through the broken window and unlocks the sauna door from the inside.

Thank goodness April is here. My short arm would not have reached the lock.

She carefully pulls her arm back through the opening.

I yank the door and run, lunging to the floor behind the pentagon.

There on the floor, wrapped in a fluffy white spa robe, lies Summer. She's on her side. Her knees are bent toward her chest with her back pressed against the pentagon centrepiece. Her arm extends in front of her like she was grasping for something just out of reach. The other arm lays flat along her torso, her fingers resting on the curve of her bent hip.

Celery green splashes punctuated with intermittent dark green flecks create an abstract pattern on the floor. Summer's Green Powerhouse smoothie.

The cup isn't here, so I assume the smoothie originated from her intestines, as suggested by the strand of thick, green liquid stretching from the corner of her mouth to the floor and the stench of vomit lingering in the air.

"Is it her?" April asks from the door.

I look at her and nod.

"Is she?"

"Dead," I confirm.

# CHAPTER 7

"WHAT'S GOING ON HERE?" Twyla demands, rushing through the sauna door. "What are you doing?"

I shove my phone in my pocket just as Twyla spots the body and freezes on the spot. I hope she didn't catch me taking sneaky photos of the scene.

"Deceased?" Twyla nudges her chin toward the twin's plush clad body and looks at me.

I nod.

Our heads spin toward the door when Maria gasps. Her hand clutches her mouth and, as if she just remembered something urgent, she turns and runs away.

"The defibri..." she says, her voice growing fainter as she disappears.

"Are you sure?" Twyla asks me, squatting next to the body.

I slide backward toward the wall, out of her way. She reaches two fingers under Summer's fluffy white collar to check for a pulse.

I shake my head. "We're too late," I mumble.

"You did this?" Twyla asks, pointing at the shards of broken glass on the floor.

242

"I did," April replies, tapping her chest. "I broke the window with the fire extinguisher. The door was locked. There were too many keys..."

Standing up, Twyla nods and raises her hand in a stop motion, cutting off April's explanation.

"You did the right thing," Twyla assures her. "You couldn't tell from the panel window if she was..." Her voice trails off at the end of her sentence, and she looks at me. "What else did you touch?"

I run off a list of things April and I touched, starting with the light switches in the change room. I'm at the part where I rummaged through the reception desk and touched everything inside, when Maria returns, out of breath. She thrusts a small red bag toward Twyla.

"Defibrillator," she explains, her voice breathless. "And I sent someone to track down the guests who identified themselves as a doctor and a nurse."

"Did you find her?" Autumn bursts in. "Summer?" she shouts, trying to get past Twyla, who's using her body to block the doorway to sauna three. "What's going on?!" Autumn demands. "Why did Maria get the defibrillator? Is it for Summer?"

Twyla takes a step forward, forcing Autumn to take a step back.

"Answer me!" Autumn demands, stomping her foot and pinching her eyebrows together as she glowers at Twyla.

Twyla opens her mouth to speak, but Maria offers Twyla the defibrillator bag again.

"Take it," Maria says, jerking her head toward sauna three. "Hurry."

Twyla takes the bag, and Maria rests her hands on her knees and rounds her back, still catching her breath.

"It's too late," Twyla says, holding up the bag. "She's dead."

"Dead?" Maria asks, unfurling her spine until she is upright.

"Dead?" Autumn echoes, trying to look past Twyla. "No. You're wrong. Let me check."

"I'm not wrong." Twyla takes Autumn by the upper arm and walks her backwards to one of the two chairs in front of the reception desk. "I'm sorry for your loss."

The backs of Autumn's legs bump into the chair. She drops into it and slumps forward, resting her elbows on her thighs and staring at the floor. She rocks back-forth in a self-soothing manner, dissociating from the surrounding scene.

"How?" Maria's blue eyes probe Twyla's brown eyes for an answer. "We've never had a guest die at the spa. Maybe she's just unconscious."

Maria takes a step toward the body. Twyla steps in her path. Guiding Maria by the shoulder, Twyla sets the red, zippered, neoprene bag next to my knitting bag, while gently lowering Maria into the other armchair in front of the reception desk.

"You sit here," Twyla says to April as she rolls the ergonomic office chair from behind the reception desk toward a far wall. Then she looks at me. "And you sit there."

She points to a leather armchair against the wall between the first and second saunas. Away from April. I've seen Eric do this. Twyla is separating us so we can't get our stories straight—or influence each other's recollection of events, as my husband likes to say—until she questions us separately.

I do as I'm told and sit in the chair.

"Breathe," Maria says to Autumn, placing a gentle hand on her knee. "In through your nose. One... two... three... four." Maria takes in an exaggerated breath to show her the technique.

Autumn averts her gaze from the floor and stares blankly at Maria for a moment. She ignores the spa manager's breathing advice, returning her focus to the floor, crying silent tears, and resuming her gentle, back-and-forth rocking.

"And out through your mouth. One... two... three... four." Maria says, exhaling louder than necessary as she counts.

Unlike Autumn, I breathe along with Maria and repeat my mantra, *heavy shoulders, long. arms* in my head, trying to will the tension out of my neck and shoulders.

"I found the doctor," an employee says, holding the door for the guest who follows her inside. "But we can't find the nurse. She's not in her room."

"Where is she?" Maria asks. "We asked guests to stay in their assigned rooms."

"Lots of guests aren't in their rooms," the employee explains. "They're visiting each other and gathering in the halls with wine and snacks." She shrugs. "One lady is teaching people to knit on the floor outside her room."

"Is it Connie?" I ask, certain I already know the answer.

"Yes," the employee replies. "How did you know?"

"Lucky guess."

"We can't physically confine them," the employee continues her conversation with Maria. "So, we've switched tactics, and we're trying to at least keep everyone on their assigned floors."

I try to tune out the conversation between Maria and her employee and focus instead on the murmur of hushed voices between Twyla and the doctor. Twyla and the doctor slipped into sauna three while I was distracted by Connie's impromptu knitting class.

Despite my best attempts, I'm unable to decipher specific words. I assume they are assessing Summer's deceased body. I wonder if the doctor can tell how Summer died.

Maria finishes issuing instructions to the employee who delivered the doctor.

The employee agrees to whatever Maria said and leaves.

"Excuse me," April calls to her. "Would you mind telling our families that we're OK but we're delayed?"

"Of course," the employee replies, smiling. "Third floor, right? The guest giving knitting lessons?"

"Right," April confirms. "Thank you." She smiles.

The employee leaves, and Maria turns back toward the rest of the room. We exchange weak smiles. She looks away, directing her attention to sauna three, like she's trying to figure out what Twyla and the doctor are doing in there.

*Me too, Maria, me too.*

After their discussion, the doctor joins the rest of us in the reception area. She pats her cream-coloured linen culottes and matching tunic until she finds what she's looking for. She slides her cell phone out of the kangaroo pocket in her tunic.

The only unoccupied chair is next to me, so the doctor claims it and sits, crossing her ankles and typing into her phone. We exchange smiles, and as much as I'm dying to ask her about Summer, I dare not speak for fear of being labelled nosy or uncooperative.

With a hand gesture, Twyla beckons Maria into the corner. She whispers something in Maria's ear, after which Maria takes the key ring from the reception desk and unlocks sauna one. Twyla enters and, moments later, beckons Maria to join her.

It's easier to eavesdrop on sauna one. My assigned chair is right outside the door. Trying not to be obvious, I shift in my seat and cock my ear toward the murmur of their voices.

"The walk-in fridge is full of food, Twy! You *cannot* be serious!" Maria hisses.

"Shhhh," Twyla responds. "It's just an idea, Mare! We need to preserve the evidence but leave the scene as untouched as possible."

Evidence? Does Twyla think Summer's death was murder? Who would murder her? Why would they murder her?

I look at April, who's already looking at me. She opens her mouth, then taps on her lower jaw to close it. Picking up on her clue, I snap my jaw shut. I didn't realize it was agape.

"Excuse me?"

Autumn's weak voice takes us off guard. This is the first time she's spoken since Twyla sat her in the chair. She's looking at the doctor.

The doctor smiles at her.

"How did my sister die?"

"I don't know," the doctor replies. "The coroner will perform an autopsy to determine the cause of death."

"She was healthy," Autumn pleads. "She's had nothing worse than a cold. Was it an accident?"

"I don't know," the doctor replies. "I wish I could tell you more, but I can't. Sometimes people die suddenly. It's rare, but it can happen. I'm sorry for your loss."

Tears stream down Autumn's face, and her chin quivers. The doctor rises from her chair and hands Autumn a box of tissues from the reception desk. Autumn nods in acknowledgment, plucking a tissue from the box and sobbing silent tears.

Maria and Twyla emerge from sauna one. Maria retrieves two notebooks and two pens from the reception desk. She sets them on top of the desk, then leaves the sauna area through the change room. Twyla hands April and me a notebook and pen. She instructs us to write statements of everything that happened from the moment we left the bistro until she showed up.

"Got it," I say.

"No problem," April says.

"Eyes on your own papers," Twyla warns, pointing at us. "And no talking. No checking facts with each other. No reading each other's statements."

We nod.

Twyla and the doctor return to sauna three. April leans forward, trying to see what they're doing. According to the charades April uses to communicate with me, Twyla and the doctor are taking pictures of Summer's death scene with their cell phones.

Maria returns carrying a box of freezer bags, two rolls of decorative packing tape with a pink herringbone design, a box of tented place cards, and a box of felt-tipped markers. She spills the items onto the reception desk. Twyla comes out of sauna three to collect the odd assortment, then returns to the scene.

I'm re-reading my statement, and questioning my use of excessive commas, when Twyla and the doctor emerge from sauna three. The doctor leaves through the change room, and Twyla uses the keys to unlock sauna four.

"April."

My face jerks up from my notebook at the sound of April's name.

"Yes?" April says.

"Would you mind answering a few questions?" Twyla nods at the notebook on April's lap. "Bring your statement."

April rises from her seat and follows Twyla into sauna four. The police officer closes the door behind them.

After what feels like an eternity, the door to sauna four opens, and April emerges, followed by Twyla.

I scan April's facial expression for any hint about what happened in there, and whether she's OK. She takes her seat in the ergonomic office chair and gives me a reassuring smile.

"Ready, Megan?" Twyla asks.

I nod, standing up.

# CHAPTER 8

ON MY WAY to sauna four, I sneak a peek at sauna three. Twyla used the tented place cards as improvised evidence markers. She numbered each one and positioned it next to a shard of glass, or smoothie stain. She used the pink herringbone packing tape as crime scene tape, taping off the doorway in such a way that it would be impossible to enter or leave the room without disturbing it.

Inside sauna four, I hand Twyla my notebook. We sit on the cedar bleachers, and I wait while Twyla reads my two-page statement.

"Your statement is remarkably similar to April's," she comments.

Is Twyla suggesting April and I colluded to get our stories straight?

"Because we're telling the truth," I say.

"Why didn't you return to your room like Maria instructed?"

I explain how Connie and Hannah pressured me to tell her we saw Autumn and Summer in the change room shortly before the blackout.

"April offered to stay with me because,"—I shrug one shoulder—"that's what we do. We stay together."

"Why did you come here?" She points toward the floor, but I know she means here, the sauna area, not here, the SoulSpring Spa.

"April and I figured you would start searching at Summer's last known location. Autumn said she left the change room, and Summer continued to the sauna alone."

"Why did you break the window? Why didn't you report your suspicion to an employee?"

"Who?" I ask, gesturing around me. "April and I were alone. We would have had to go through the change room, and down the hall to find help. What if Summer was alive? What if she needed help? We didn't *want* to break the window. The first two keys didn't work..."

"I understand," Twyla says, interrupting my explanation. "But you must admit, it's weird that you found her so quickly. And by yourselves." She chuckles. "I mean, it's almost like you knew where Summer was."

"We didn't," I insist. "I told you, we assumed you would start searching here. We expected to find *you* here, not Summer. I'd never been in the sauna area before. We only checked in this afternoon."

"Did you touch Summer's body?"

"Yes." I nod. "I checked her wrist for a pulse. It's in my statement. I touched nothing else, I know better."

"What do you mean, you know better?"

"My husband is a murder investigator," I explain. "Actually, we met at a murder scene. I found a neighbour..."

"So, this isn't the first dead body you've found?"

Twyla's eyebrows disappear into her bangs and her pen dangles between her fingers.

"Not exactly," I admit with apprehension.

"How many dead bodies have you found?"

"By myself?" I ask, looking for a loophole. "One."

"And not by yourself?"

Uh oh. How do I explain this without coming across as a murder-scene groupie or serial killer? I look at the ceiling and take a mental inventory, counting bodies on my fingers.

My ex-husband's voice is in my head, telling me to refuse to answer more questions without an attorney. I would usually ignore Adam's voice, but he's a lawyer and his voice might be right. Twyla doesn't know April and me. She only knows that a few hours after we checked in, someone died under mysterious circumstances, and we found the body.

"More than one," I admit, refusing to be more specific for fear of incriminating myself.

"Have the police ever investigated you as a murder suspect?"

"You think Summer was murdered?"

"I asked first."

"Look, I've found multiple murder victims. But in every case, the police arrested someone other than me. In every case, the suspect they arrested was convicted."

I'm struck by the bizarreness of this conversation as the words pass my lips. Twyla must think I'm a pathological liar, or a serial killer who has mastered framing other people for my crimes.

"Your turn," I remind her. "Do you think Summer was murdered?"

"I can't rule it out," she admits, "until the coroner determines the cause of death..."

"You have to treat it like a crime scene and investigate accordingly," I interrupt, finishing her sentence.

"You've heard that one before?"

"I have," I admit, with a nod. "It's one of my husband's favourite lines."

"What do you think happened to Summer?" Twyla asks.

"At first, I thought it was a tragic accident. Like maybe she slipped on the slick ceramic floor and hit her head."

"But you don't think that anymore?"

"If Summer had hit her head, it would have been obvious at first glance. Instead of noticing green smoothie on the white floor, I would've noticed blood. Lots of it. And her body wasn't positioned naturally," I reason. "It was too tidy, like someone staged it."

"Almost like someone tucked her out of sight," Twyla suggests.

"Exactly," I say. "Then I thought Summer could have died because of an underlying health issue. Maybe she had a condition that was exasperated by the sauna. But Autumn told the doctor that Summer was healthy. She said Summer never suffered from anything worse than a cold." I take a deep breath and collect my thoughts. "Earlier, Summer was drinking a smoothie from the juice bar, but if she had died from an allergic reaction, wouldn't she have swelling? Or hives?"

"Not necessarily," Twyla replies. "The doctor says there are often obvious signs of anaphylaxis, but not always."

Twyla asks more questions, and I try to answer them in a way that doesn't make me sound like a person of interest or a true-crime fanatic.

When she finishes interrogating me, Twyla and I return to the reception area with April, Autumn, and Maria. In our absence, someone brought water bottles branded with labels bearing the spa logo. They're lined up on the reception desk, and April and Autumn each have a bottle. Either a thoughtful employee delivered them, or Maria fetched them while Twyla questioned me.

I join April, leaning against the wall next to her ergonomic office chair. Now that Twyla has questioned us, we can interact again.

"I want to see Summer." Autumn rises to her feet and gives Twyla a commanding stare. "Shouldn't I identify her? I'm her next of kin. How can you even be sure it's her if I don't identify her?"

Is she in denial? Or is Autumn desperate to see and touch her sister one last time?

"It's her," Twyla says. "Trust me. There's no trauma or damage that would make her difficult to identify. The doctor recognized her too. I'm sorry, but I can't let you see her."

"I recognized her too," I add. "I'm sorry."

"How did she die?" Autumn asks. "You must have an idea." She tosses her hands in frustration. "I need to see my sister," she pleads, her eyes welling up with fresh tears.

"It's not possible," Twyla reiterates, shaking her head. She positions herself so her body blocks the view inside sauna three. "Why don't you wait for me in sauna one, Autumn. I'll be there in a minute, and we can discuss this further."

Autumn opens her mouth as if to protest, but closes it again, and lets out a sigh of utter defeat.

"Fine," she mumbles, then shuffles toward sauna one, not even looking up when she passes the room where her twin sister's dead body lies.

Twyla closes the door behind her and turns her attention to Maria, April, and me.

"You can leave," she says to April and me. She opens a bottle of water and takes a long swig. "But please don't discuss this with any other guests or staff." She takes another sip and recaps the bottle, then picks up the roll of pink herringbone packing tape. "In fact, if anyone seems *too* interested in what you saw or obsessed with Summer's death, let me know immediately."

"Twy, won't *everyone* be interested in what happened?" Maria asks. "The staff are already discussing it amongst themselves, and I'm sure the guests are too."

"It's human nature," April adds. "People need to make sense of death. They look to one another for answers and reassurance."

"That's normal," Twyla says, tearing a strip of tape with her teeth and stretching it across the space where the glass window panel used to be. "If someone seems more interested than everyone else, or won't talk about anything else, I need to know."

She tears another piece of tape with her teeth. "You'll know if someone is too interested. Their interest will be noticeable and might make you uncomfortable."

April and I share a glance that says *we better be careful.*

My husband likes to say I'm made of questions. He worries that one day, I'll ask the wrong question to the wrong person and get myself in trouble.

"What am I supposed to say when guests and staff ask questions?" Maria asks. "I can't deny that someone died in the sauna."

"Admit that someone died. Admit it was Summer—after I talk to Autumn and get her agreement to disclose Summer's identity. But say nothing that will fuel speculation."

"Speculation about what?"

"How she died." Twyla stretches another piece of tape across the window. "We wouldn't want anyone to think Summer was murdered."

"Murdered?" Maria demands.

"I can't say for certain yet. But we should disclose as little information as possible."

"So the guests and staff don't panic?" Maria asks.

"So the murderer doesn't panic," Twyla clarifies.

# CHAPTER 9

"Twyla thinks someone murdered Summer!" April declares as we leave the saunas and make our way through the change room. "Did you see her face when she asked us not to speculate about Summer's death?"

"Yes," I nod. "It's the same look Eric has when he's waiting for the coroner to declare someone's death was murder. He knows in his gut it was murder, but he won't say it out loud until it's official."

"Exactly," April says, pulling open the change room door.

We step into the dark hall and pause while we remind ourselves which way to go.

"This way," I say, turning left. "How's your arm? And your hand?"

"Fine," she replies, wiggling her fingers. "Why?"

"I thought you might have hurt yourself when you Hulk-smashed the fire extinguisher through the window."

"I'm fine," she says, examining her hands in the dark. "Anyway, if I pulled something, I'll book a hand massage with a massage therapist tomorrow."

"If they clear the road tomorrow, do you want to leave?" I ask.

April opens her mouth to answer, but confusion clouds her face.

"Didn't you have your knitting bag when we went in there?" she asks, jerking her head behind us.

"Mothballs!" I mutter. "I left it on the reception desk."

We retrace our steps through the change room.

"Sorry!" I say to Maria and Twyla.

Pink herringbone packing tape covers the panel window in the door to sauna three. The door is closed, and more pink herringbone tape seals the crack where the door and the doorframe meet. Twyla stands guard as Maria goes through the keys on the key ring, one at a time, trying to lock the door.

"You forgot something." Twyla nods at my knitting bag on the desk, next to the defibrillator bag.

"My knitting," I explain.

"I know." She grins. "I searched it."

I pick up the bag.

"Sorry for the interruption," April says, pulling open the change room door.

"Summer?" Billie shouts, charging through the open door. She scans the room, her eyes darting from person to person, before landing on Twyla. "Is it true you found Summer?" Her eyes are wide and intense, and I think she's holding her breath.

Maria stops fidgeting with the key ring and looks from Billie to Twyla.

"Where did you hear that?" Twyla asks.

"The employees on our floor said so. To each other, not to me. I was eavesdropping. They said Summer is in the sauna. Autumn?" Billie stares at Autumn, who is now standing in the doorway to sauna one, her gaze fixed on the floor. "What's happening?"

Autumn remains silent. Billie inches toward her, trying without success to make eye contact. "Autumn?"

Autumn gives no indication that she hears Billie's voice.

"The employees said something is wrong with Summer," Billie says, directing her words at Twyla. "They said Maria got the defibrillator." Her eyes dart between us so fast it's like she's trying to make eye contact with all of us at once. "What happened?"

"She's dead," Autumn says, her voice thick with emotion. She looks up at Billie with red, swollen eyes. "My sister is dead."

"What?" Billie's eyes grow wider and glassier. "No." She furrows her brows together and sucks in a sharp breath. "Dead?"

"I'm sorry for your loss," Twyla interjects, confirming the truth without saying it.

Billie slaps her hand to her mouth, her panicked eyes searching the room. Just as her upper body heaves, her eyes narrow on something under the reception desk. She lurches, grabs the trash can, grips it like a steering wheel, and holds it near her face as she throws up. Billie's body shakes, and she retches loudly as the green, smoothie-coated contents of her stomach spew into the basket.

"ARE YOU OK?" April asks me as we climb the first flight of stairs toward our rooms.

"I'm fine," I reply, clutching my small knitting bag tight against my stomach. "Billie's reaction took me by surprise. I don't think I'll ever have another smoothie again."

"Some people have weak stomachs," April surmises. "They have a physical reaction to upsetting news."

I know April is right, but I can't shake the feeling there's more to Billie's reaction than meets the eye. She escalated from shock to disbelief to physical purging in a matter of seconds. Who processes information that fast? Eric says there is no such thing as a normal reaction to shocking news. But there must be a spectrum of normal reactions, right? I wonder where Billie's reaction would be on the shock spectrum.

APRIL and I enter our respective rooms and use the adjoining door between the suites to gather everyone in one room. Together, we detail to our modern family everything that happened after Maria's update.

"My goodness!" Connie gasps. "That poor girl!" She shakes her head and makes a clicking sound with her tongue. "She was so young. Summer had her entire life ahead of her. Such a tragedy."

"Did Twyla say Summer was, without a doubt, murdered?" Tamara asks, wrapping her kinky hair in the silk hair-wrap she wears to bed. "Or is she speculating? People don't get murdered at the spa on Mother's Day weekend!"

"She seemed pretty convinced that Summer's death wasn't an accident or underlying medical issue," April replies.

"I hope someone is fixing the cell towers or whatever the storm knocked out. We need to call for help," Hannah interjects.

"Speaking of cell phones," Rachel adds, "on our way upstairs, we stopped at the kitchen and asked for some aluminum foil."

"We made antennae," Hannah adds, holding up a long rolled-up piece of aluminum foil.

More configurations of aluminum foil antennae are piled on the writing desk.

"For what?" April asks.

"For cell phone reception," Rachel replies. "If we don't have cell service by morning, Hannah and I will hike up the mountain and use the antennae to find a signal."

"And we'll call for help," Hannah concludes.

"Is that a good idea?" I ask. "What if you get lost? How will we call for help to find you? What if you get hurt? What if the ground is muddy from the storm and you slide away?"

"Relax, Mum," Hannah says, rolling her eyes so far back in her head her irises disappear. "We're not kids. We'll be careful, and we won't go far. I am capable of good judgment, you know."

I take a deep breath and remind myself that Hannah is my adult daughter, not a child. I don't have veto power anymore.

"Sweetie, I know you'll be careful, but I still worry. I can't help it. I'm proud of you and Rachel for coming up with a plan, and I know you'll be careful."

"But in the interest of safety," Connie interjects, "I think it would be best to stick together until Twyla solves this mystery or we can return to civilization, whichever comes first."

"Connie is right," Tamara agrees. "There's safety in numbers. Let's agree we won't go anywhere alone."

We nod and mumble our agreement.

"And let's keep our eyes and ears open for anything that might be related to Summer's death," I add.

"Of course."

"Obviously."

"For sure."

"Absolutely."

"You don't have to ask me twice."

# CHAPTER 10

The Epicurean Bistro's dining room is almost empty.

Connie and I linger over a second cup of coffee, sitting on opposite sides of a table that's far too big for two people.

"Looks like it's just us, my dear," Connie says, then sips her coffee.

"Here's to quality time," I respond, then take a long sip of hazelnut-maple latte.

April and Tamara have already left for a morning of reiki treatments and acupuncture. Hannah and Rachel barely finished their bagels and yogurt parfaits before rushing upstairs to collect their homemade antennae and heading for higher ground in search of a connection to the outside world.

I hoped cell phone service would be restored by the time we woke up this morning, rendering Hannah and Rachel's trek into the wilderness unnecessary. I convinced myself the repaired 5G network would flood our phones with a flurry of unread text messages, emails, and social media updates. I was sure the accompanying cacophony of chimes and dings would wake us. It didn't happen.

There's still no cell service, no landline, and no internet. And, if it weren't for solar power and generators, we wouldn't have electricity either.

I'm exhausted and thankful that the spa makes a decent cup of coffee. Instead of being lulled to sleep by the peace and tranquility of our soundless surroundings, I tossed and turned all night, kept awake by the blaring silence. It's amazing how loud the world is when there's no sound.

"I miss the fridge," Connie muses, starting a new row on the shawl she's knitting and interrupting my introspection as if she can read my mind. "I never realized how the constant drone of the fridge helped me sleep." She fixes her gaze on something in the distance and smiles. "I think I use the fridge to tune out Archie's snoring." She laughs.

"For me it's the ceiling fan," I commiserate, knitting stitch after stitch on my washcloth without looking.

Eric insists on using the ceiling fan at night. It annoyed me at first, but the reliable hum of its motor has become my unchosen lullaby. I even turn it on when he's not there because the motor and light breeze lull me to sleep.

Last night, spa employees went room-to-room to check on everyone and do another informal headcount. They asked guests to conserve as much energy as possible overnight and not waste the precious stored solar power and generators.

Connie, Hannah, and I complied. We turned off and unplugged everything in our suite. The silence was deafening. We even unplugged the motion-sensitive night-light in the bathroom because we weren't sure if it sucked up electricity just being plugged in, or if it only uses electricity when it senses motion and turns on. Hannah offered to solve the mystery by searching the internet until she remembered we have no internet.

My brain kept tricking me into believing our connection to the outside world had been restored. Every time I was on the cusp of drifting off, my eyes would burst open, and I would raise my head, certain I heard my phone. I forced my bleary eyes to focus on the phone on the nightstand until realizing my restless brain was playing a cruel joke on my exhausted body. The phantom dinging and buzzing jolted me out of near-sleep until just before dawn.

When I wasn't listening for signs that the outside world still existed, I obsessed over Summer's death. I pictured her lifeless body in vivid detail, even recalling the chill of the cold floor tiles on my knees through my leggings, and how the dark green flecks in Summer's regurgitated smoothie contrasted against the light-green splatters. My mind's eye recreated the anguish on Autumn's face when Twyla told her that her twin had died, and the horrible retching sound that came out of Billie when she vomited in the trash can. It was an eventful night inside my head.

"Can I get you ladies anything else?" the server asks, collecting dirty dishes from our table.

"No, thank you," Connie replies. "We'll just finish our coffee, then we'll get out of your hair."

"No hurry," the server says, balancing a tower of dirty plates on her forearm. "Take all the time you need."

"Actually," I pipe in, "I read Nadira's impressive biography yesterday, and I'd love to try her famous crispy tofu with maple-soy glaze served over jasmine rice. Do you know if it will be on today's lunch or dinner menu? Or what other tofu dishes might be on today's menu?"

Sipping her coffee, Connie glares at me over the rim like I'm sprouting a second head.

"I'm afraid not," the server replies, bending her knees and leaning back to offset the tower of dishes balanced on her forearm. "Our tofu shipment didn't arrive. We are fresh out of tofu."

"Fresh?" I clarify. "As in, if I'd ordered it yesterday it would have been available?"

"No," she shakes her head. "We haven't had tofu all week." She nods toward the floor-to-ceiling window. "Our next grocery delivery is Tuesday. If the road is fixed by then."

She smiles. We smile. Then she walks toward the kitchen surprisingly fast, considering the swaying tower of dishes she's carrying.

"Since when do you eat tofu?" Connie demands, picking up her knitting from her lap. "In twenty years, I've never seen you raise a forkful of tofu to your mouth. I don't think I've seen you within arm's reach of a piece of tofu."

"You're right," I confirm. "I can't stand tofu. I was testing a theory."

"A tofu theory?"

"A lying theory."

"Whose lie?"

"Chef Nadira Patel."

"Did our server prove or disprove your theory, my dear?"

"She proved it," I reply, finishing a row of knit stitches. "I think Nadira lied to me."

I explain to Connie how April and I saw Autumn and Nadira arguing yesterday because Autumn accused the chef of intentionally serving her chicken instead of tofu.

"Later, Nadira visited our table. She told us it was an honest mistake. She said she mixed them up because the chicken and tofu were both cubed and in similar bowls."

"How could she confuse chicken with tofu if there's no tofu?" Connie asks.

"Exactly," I reply. "Her remorse seemed genuine, but something didn't feel right about her admission."

"It's hard to fathom a chef of her calibre making such a mistake," Connie agrees.

"And when Autumn shouted at her, and threatened to ruin her reputation, Nadira didn't flinch. She didn't argue or even defend herself. She just stood there and took it. No smile or frown. She was composed and patient. At the time, I thought her reaction reflected her professionalism. But, considering what happened after the blackout, I wonder if I misinterpreted her stoicism for smugness."

"You think Nadira served chicken to Autumn on purpose?" Connie asks. "To what end? Why would she serve chicken to someone who didn't want it?"

"That's what I'd like to find out," I reply, shoving my knitting inside my bag.

Connie leans across the table, and I lean toward her, meeting her halfway.

"Do you think the chicken scandal has something to do with Summer's death?" Connie whispers.

"I'm not sure," I admit. "Maybe it's a coincidence, or maybe Nadira took revenge on the wrong twin."

Connie straightens her back and returns to her side of the table, folding her knitting and packing it into her bag.

"If you give a baby a hammer, the entire world becomes a nail," she says.

"What?" I ask, confused and mildly concerned about Connie's mental state. "What do babies and hammers have to do with tofu or Summer's death?"

"You're the baby, my dear. When you hear about a

267

murder, you second-guess everyone. You re-analyze what they say and how they say it. Everyone becomes a suspect."

"I can't help myself," I confess. "Is it too much?"

"Not at all, my dear." Connie lifts her coffee mug. "The world needs more babies with hammers." She pauses her mug halfway to her mouth. "Metaphorically, of course."

And with that weird, yet logical comparison, Connie sips the rest of the coffee from her mug.

# CHAPTER 11

CONNIE, Hannah, and I had booked time in the hydrotherapy pools and saunas this morning. But the hydrotherapy pools are closed because of the power failure—filtering the water and maintaining the temperature would drain the spa's power reserves—and the saunas are off limits because of Summer's untimely demise. They offered us a variety of alternatives. Hannah went hiking with Rachel, and Connie and I chose a yoga class followed by guided meditation. The yoga class and guided meditation don't take as much time as the hydrotherapy pools and saunas. Between breakfast and lunch, we find ourselves with time on our hands and walk to the parking lot.

I want to make sure my car didn't suffer any storm damage. Also, we hope to tune into a local radio station for a news update about last night's storm and the road situation.

There are no local satellite stations. The only local station we can pick up is an AM station that plays non-stop country music hits from the eighties and nineties. We sit in the car with our knitting and listen, but the top of the hour comes and goes with no weather or news updates. When the opening bars of Achy Breaky Heart start for the third time, we give up and head back to the main building.

We take our time and explore the grounds, taking full advantage of the beautiful spring day. The sun is bright, and birds serenade us. A gentle breeze wafts through the budding trees and long wild grasses that line the perimeter of the property. Tulips and daffodils reach for the blue, cloudless sky from the cultivated beds that punctuate the well-groomed grounds and created walking path. Besides a few downed branches and snapped stems, there's no evidence that Mother Nature ripped through here last night in a vicious rage, stealing a police cruiser and leaving chaos, a lack of modern amenities, and death in her wake.

On the west side of the main building, we discover a large deck with lounge chairs and cozy sitting areas overlooking the breathtaking view.

"We must come out here at sunset," Connie comments. "It would be beautiful!"

"It's beautiful now," I respond.

The vast deck extends the entire length of the building and features chamfered deck boards that create the illusion the deck winds and undulates like the natural scenery that surrounds it.

Several doors exit onto the deck. The door that says, *Sauna* gets my attention. I squint to read the sign on the next door. *Ladies Change Room*. The next door reads, *Massage Therapy*. Inside, the sauna and massage therapy area are separated by the change room. Outside, their emergency exits are only a few feet apart.

Architecture is a mystery to me, but if Autumn got a hot stone massage while Summer was in the sauna, she would have been seconds away when Summer died.

Did Autumn use the emergency exits to sneak in and out of the sauna and kill her sister? The thought sends a shiver up my spine. Until now, it never occurred to me that Autumn might be a suspect in her twin's death. But, as Eric says, everyone is a suspect until they're eliminated.

"Where shall we sit, my dear?" Connie asks, bringing me back to the here and now. "Sun or shade?"

Guests dot the chairs and tables. Some chat in small groups, some sit alone with a book, and some relax with their faces aimed at the sun.

We scope out the seating situation, and spot two empty loungers, side-by-side.

"Over there," I reply, pointing to the loungers on the far side of the deck.

We weave through the chairs and tables, and I keep my stare affixed on our destination until a delicate sneeze distracts me.

"Bless you," I say, stopping to look down at the source of the sneeze. Her face is obscured by a wide-brimmed sun hat, but I recognize the woman and am surprised to find her sitting here by herself. "Autumn?"

She lifts the floppy brim of her hat to see who said her name.

"Hello," she says. "Megan, right?"

"Right," I reply. "And this is Connie." I gesture next to me.

Connie extends her hand and offers Autumn her condolences.

It's difficult to assess how Autumn is coping the day after her twin sister's death. Between the wide brim hat and large sunglasses, I can't make out her expression. But if her slumped shoulders, dipped chin, and deflated demeanour are any indication, she's not doing well. And who can blame her?

"Are you alone?" I ask. "Where is Billie?"

Is it presumptuous to assume that Billie would be with her? Using my relationship with April as a standard for comparison, I can't imagine leaving April alone for even one second after such a loss.

"She's here," Autumn replies, gesturing around her. "Somewhere. She's not feeling well this morning and rushed inside. Again. She'll be back any minute."

"Billie wasn't feeling well last night, either," I remark, having graphic flashbacks of Billie's physical reaction after she learned about Summer's death.

"She's struggling with Summer's death," Autumn remarks. "The three of us have a long, complicated relationship. It can't be easy for her to be best friends with twins. Sometimes Billie would get jealous of the bond my sister and I shared. She doesn't like to admit it, but I know she felt like a third wheel sometimes. Especially lately."

I'm about to ask Autumn what she means by *especially lately* when Connie changes the subject.

"Well, why don't we join you until your friend returns, hmm?"

"Unless, of course, you want to be alone," I add. "We'd love to sit with you but we don't want to impose."

"And you won't offend us if you say no," Connie says.

Autumn hesitates before she answers, glancing around her. I assume she's sizing up her options or searching for an excuse to decline our offer.

"That would be great," she responds, a hint of a smile on her pursed lips.

Connie and I claim the lounge chair next to Autumn's. We sit on it sideways as if it were a backless sofa. We pull out our knitting and start stitching.

"You're a suspect, you know," Autumn says curtly and out of nowhere.

"Excuse me?"

I place my knitting in my lap and give Autumn my undivided attention.

"Megan is a suspect in your sister's death?" Connie asks in a whisper, checking our immediate surroundings for eavesdroppers.

Autumn nods and turns toward me. I assume she's looking at me but can't tell for sure because I can't see her eyes behind her dark glasses.

"You and your tall blonde friend are suspects," she says like it's no big deal.

"April?" I ask, dumbfounded.

"If that's your tall blonde friend's name," Autumn replies.

Twyla thinks April and I killed Summer?

# CHAPTER 12

"Did Twyla tell you April and I are suspects?

Waiting for her answer, my body freezes. I hold my breath, and I swear, even my heart stops beating for fear that any bodily function will interfere with my ability to hear her response.

"She didn't say you *aren't* suspects, if you know what I mean."

"I know exactly what you mean." I nod, after untangling her double negative.

Twyla seemed skeptical about my responses to every question she asked me. Sensing her misgivings, I tried extra hard to appear honest and forthcoming. My aggressive efforts to convince her might have led Twyla to believe I have something to hide.

I add a visit with Twyla to my mental do list.

"Don't worry," Autumn continues. "I know you and your friend had nothing to do with my sister's death."

"We didn't," I assure her. "But how do you know that? If you know it wasn't us, you must have a suspect in mind."

"Oh, I know who killed Summer," Autumn states,

sitting up straight and exhibiting the same outspoken confidence she had when she argued with Nadira about the chicken-tofu mix-up. "The chef did it."

"You believe Nadira killed your sister?" Connie asks.

"I don't believe she did," Autumn clarifies. "I know she did."

"How?" I ask.

"She tried to poison me yesterday," Autumn explains. "And I confronted her. Nadira knows I know she intended to kill me. Summer wasn't her target, I was. She killed the wrong twin."

I'm not sure if serving someone the wrong protein qualifies as attempted murder, but since I already suspect Nadira is lying about the chicken-tofu fiasco, I'm open to Autumn's theory.

"That's a big accusation, Autumn," I say.

"If she didn't do it, then where was she when my sister died?" Autumn asks, emotion catching the last word of her question. "No one will tell me where Nadira was when Summer died. She won't talk to me. Twyla won't tell me anything. If Nadira was innocent, wouldn't she shout her alibi from the rooftop of this place?"

She makes a good point. But just because Autumn can't verify Nadira's alibi, doesn't mean Nadira killed Summer. And just because Nadira served Autumn chicken instead of tofu doesn't mean she was trying to poison Autumn.

"My sister was a good person." Autumn's voice is thick with emotion. "I don't mean she was a good person the same way everyone says their deceased loved one was a good person. My sister really was a good person. She was brave. She made sacrifices other people would never make."

"Like what?" I ask, wondering if Summer donated an

organ, or devoted her life to a worthy cause, or something.

"When we were eighteen," Autumn begins, "Summer had a part-time job at a local bar. One night, she witnessed a murder in the parking lot. Instead of looking the other way, she did the right thing and cooperated with the police. Her testimony put a killer behind bars and got justice for the victim's family."

"That certainly was a selfless act," Connie agrees. "Your sister sounds like an upstanding person. Your family must be very proud of her."

"I am her family. Summer and I didn't have anyone else. Now that she's dead, I'm all alone. That's what makes her actions so selfless. The murder my sister witnessed was committed by a mob boss's son. My sister risked her life to testify against him. For her safety, and for ours, she went into witness protection. They relocated her. They gave her a new name and new identity. To keep us safe, Summer couldn't have any contact with me or our mum. She was all alone for over ten years."

"She must not be in witness protection anymore, if she was here with you," I surmise. "What happened? Why did she come back?"

"The killer she helped convict died last year. His father, the mob boss, died a few months later. Summer felt safe enough to come back. The authorities agreed that the threat to Summer's safety was minimal since the killer and his father had died. But it was too late. Our mother passed away three years ago." A single tear streams down Autumn's cheek, and she takes a moment to compose herself. "Summer did not know our mother had died. She gave up everything to keep us safe. She gave up her life for us twice. First when she went into hiding, and again when she abandoned her new life and came home."

"Autumn, could your sister's testimony against the killer have anything to do with her death?" I ask.

"No," Autumn replies shaking her head, tears streaming down her cheeks from behind her glasses. "She'd only been back for a few months, and she laid low. Not many people knew she had left witness protection. Since the killer and his father died, the organized crime family fell apart. There was no one alive who wanted Summer dead. Even the authorities agreed it was safe for Summer to come home. Anyway, no one knew we would be here this week, except me, Billie, and Summer. Billie booked it a few days before we checked in."

"Did you accept the hot stone massage they offered you two in the change room yesterday?" I ask, hoping to establish Autumn's alibi.

"No. I offered it to Summer," Autumn replies. "I had the early symptoms of a migraine. I went upstairs for an early night."

"Summer had the hot stone massage?" I ask, confused because Summer died in the sauna.

"No," Autumn replies. "She wanted to go to the saunas. Summer loved the saunas. We've visited them every day since we checked in. Billie took the hot stone massage."

"I see."

I glance at the emergency exit doors. If Autumn is telling the truth, Billie was near Summer around the time Summer died. Well, Billie's emergency exit was next to Summer's emergency exit.

I sit up straight and squeeze my shoulder blades together.

"Are you all right, my dear?" Connie asks.

"Nothing a hot stone massage won't help," I reply, then turn my attention back to Autumn.

"When Summer was in the sauna, and Billie got a massage, you were in your room?"

"That's right," Autumn confirms. "Fighting migraine symptoms caused by the chicken Nadira tried to poison me with."

"Why did you visit the front desk last night?" I ask.

"I stopped at the front desk and asked Maria for ibuprofen."

"Did she give you some?"

"Yes, but it didn't help."

"How is your head today?" Connie asks.

"A dull throb," Autumn responds. "My whole body is a dull, achy throb. It's the only thing I've felt since Summer died. Dull and achy."

"When did you realize Summer was missing?" I ask.

"When the power went out. Summer and Billie didn't come back to the room. I went downstairs to find them."

"Did you find them?" Connie asks.

"No," Autumn replies, shaking her head. "I went upstairs again in case they returned to the room, and we missed each other. Our room was empty. I tried to text them, but my cell phone wasn't working."

"Did you stay in the room and wait for them?" Connie asks.

"I couldn't sit around doing nothing when I didn't know where Summer and Billie were," Autumn explains, somewhat defensively. "I was on my way downstairs to search for them again when an employee asked me to join the rest of the guests and staff in the bistro for a storm update. She said spa treatments were cancelled, and everyone should proceed to the bistro."

"But you weren't in the bistro," I remind her. "You came in late, searching for Summer."

"I waited outside," Autumn explains. "You just didn't see me in the crowd. I watched the door for Summer and

Billie. I assumed they were together and on their way like everyone else."

"But Billie was late," I point out. "She arrived partway through Maria and Twyla's update."

"I know," Autumn agrees. "She didn't see me in the hall when she slipped into the bistro alone. I panicked when Summer wasn't with her." She grabs her gut. "I had a bad feeling. Summer and I used to call it twintuition. I knew something was wrong. I knew Summer was in trouble."

"What did you do?" Connie asked.

"I ran back upstairs to check the room. Empty. Then I went toward the change room, but it was dark and abandoned. I assumed no one was there and ran to the bistro. I had hoped Summer was there, and I had missed her."

"But you didn't," I say.

"I didn't," Autumn concurs. "Summer wasn't there. She wasn't anywhere."

"There you are!" Billie exclaims, approaching us from behind Autumn's lounge chair. "You moved while I was inside."

Billie climbs over the chair and joins Autumn in the generous lounger. Autumn wriggles over to accommodate her friend.

"Sorry," Autumn says to her friend. "A chair in the shade came available, so I jumped at it. I would have texted you, but you know…" She holds up her useless cell phone and shrugs.

"Well," I say, smiling and stuffing my knitting inside my knitting bag, "now that Billie is back, we'll get out of your way."

Connie and I stand up.

"Please don't leave on my account," Billie says. "I think I'm coming down with something. If I hurry inside again, it's a relief to know Autumn won't be alone."

Connie and I sit back down and pull out our knitting again.

Autumn stands and dusts nothing from the front of her navy Capri pants.

"I was about to head upstairs, anyway. My migraine is making a comeback."

"I'll come with you," Billie offers, jumping to her feet.

"It's OK, Billie," Autumn insists. "I'd like to be alone. I'm not very good company right now."

"If you're sure," Billie says. "I'll come upstairs and check on you in a while. In the meantime, there is an employee near the stairs. They have walkie-talkies now, so they can call the front desk if you need anything."

Autumn thanks her, then she thanks us. She hitches her canvas tote bag on her shoulder and drops her book and cell phone inside. She takes one step away from the lounge chair and collides head-on with another guest, also wearing a wide-brimmed sunhat and large sunglasses. Victims of their valiant attempts to avoid sun damage.

"*Ooof*," the guest says, flailing her arms to stay upright.

"Sorry," Autumn mutters, stumbling backward.

Billie catches Autumn by the arm and navigates a controlled fall onto the lounge chair, and with the reflexes of someone half her age, Connie grasps the other guest around the waist and holds her steady while she regains her balance.

Both women are uninjured, but amid the commotion, their bags slip off their respective shoulders, landing upside down on the lounge chair and deck. Connie and I abandon our knitting, and the five of us drop to the ground, scrabbling to collect their commingled belongings before they roll away.

Grabbing at the scattered items, the mystery woman's sunglasses fall off her face.

"Hi," I say to the doctor.

The doctor's beige linen culottes and linen tunic match her sunhat and her beige tote bag with leather handles.

"Oh! Hello, again," she replies, replacing her sunglasses.

"It's you," Autumn says when she realizes who the woman is.

"It's me," the doctor replies.

While Autumn and the doctor exchange awkward pleasantries, we take turns holding out the items we recovered from the ground. Each woman claims their belongings by plucking them from our open hands. A guest from a nearby table returns a lip balm that rolled all the way to her chair, and another guest returns a pharmacy receipt that blew into her lap.

"I think we're sorted!" says the doctor.

"Again, I'm sorry!" Autumn says, assessing the contents of her canvas tote bag. "I'm tired and distracted today."

They exchange more apologies, and when they're both satisfied that they're sufficiently sorry and sufficiently forgiven, the doctor continues on her way, and Autumn continues to her room.

As Autumn leaves, a glint of amber plastic under a nearby chair catches my eye. I lunge for it. A prescription bottle with Autumn's name on it. *Lasmiditan*, according to the label.

"Autumn!" I shout.

She turns, and I hold up the pill bottle, shaking it. She starts back toward me, and I walk toward her, meeting her partway.

"Thank you," she says, taking the bottle from me.

"These are my migraine meds. I don't know how I'd cope without them." She slips the bottle into her bag.

"If you have migraine medication, why did you ask for ibuprofen at the front desk?" I ask.

For a split second, she freezes, then nods.

"The migraine pills are great," she explains. "But they have side effects. I feel dizzy and drowsy for a day after I take them. I use over-the-counter medication or natural remedies first and rely on the prescription as a last resort." She lets out a long sigh. "Today might be a last resort day." Autumn pats the side of her bag.

# CHAPTER 13

BACK AT THE LOUNGE CHAIR, Connie and Billie are deep in conversation.

"Billie was just saying she's worried about how Autumn is coping with Summer's death," Connie says. "Apparently Autumn is not herself."

"It's true," Billie admits, her eyes searching mine for something. Sympathy? Compassion? Understanding? "Autumn has hardly said a word since Summer died. I've never seen her like this, not even after their mum died."

"Twins share a special connection the rest of us can't understand," Connie reminds her.

"It's more than that." Billie bites her lip, her eyes darting in random directions, like she's struggling to find the right words. "You don't understand," she says, bouncing her knee and tapping the lounge chair cushion. "She's too... too... quiet."

"Can you give us an example?" I ask, trying to help her express herself.

Billie takes a deep breath, counting to four on her fingers. Then she holds it while she counts to four on her other hand.

"One... two... three... four..." Billie counts as she exhales. She looks me in the eye. "Autumn is not a quiet woman. I've known her since kindergarten. Autumn doesn't turn her emotions inward, she works through her feelings out loud. If she's sad, she cries and talks about why she's sad. When she's happy, she laughs and tells everyone why she's happy. If she's angry, she shouts and complains until she figures out how to fix it."

"Like she shouted and complained to Nadira about the chicken?" I ask.

"Yes!" Billie agrees, letting out a sigh of relief. "What if Summer's death is too much for her? What if Autumn is quiet because she's having a breakdown?"

"Maybe Autumn isn't processing her feelings out loud because she can't," Connie suggests, squeezing Billie's knee. "It's been less than twenty-four hours since Summer died. Autumn might still be in shock. Summer's death blindsided her."

"Connie's right," I add. "It's possible Autumn doesn't know how she feels yet. Or she's denying her feelings, so she can function until it's safe to get out of here."

"You're probably right," Billie concedes. "Autumn must feel like part of herself died, and that's gotta be hard to process."

"I can't imagine what she's going through," Connie sympathizes.

"How do I help her?" Billie asks. "Usually, I listen and sympathize. But how can I listen if Autumn won't talk?"

"Just be here," I reply. "She knows you're here to listen when she's ready."

"How are you coping with Summer's death?" Connie asks. "Autumn told us the three of you were a tight unit. This must be hard for you too."

"It is," Billie admits. "I have so many feelings. Sadness, shock, guilt, disbelief."

"Which emotion is causing your tummy trouble?" I ask, wondering why Billie feels guilty.

"Megan said you weren't well when you found out about Summer, and Autumn said you've been sick again today," Connie adds.

"I'm not sure the nausea has anything to do with Summer's death. I felt like this before she died. It started when we got here." Billie looks around for anyone listening nearby, then leans in closer to Connie and me. "I think it's the food," she whispers. "Nothing I've eaten here agrees with me. I know Nadira has won awards, and everyone raves about how talented she is, but her food doesn't agree with me."

"Oh," Connie says, rubbing her stomach in sympathy, "That's unfortunate."

"Did you mention your issues to Nadira?" I ask.

"No," Billie replies, "Autumn did. She's the one who pointed out that I was fine until I started eating here."

"What did Autumn say to Nadira?" I ask.

"Which time?" Billie asks. "Autumn kicked up a fuss every time I had a bout of nausea. She kept a list of everything I'd eaten and looked for common foods that might cause it. She's convinced Nadira uses secret ingredients that make me sick. Autumn has suffered with migraines most of her life. She's a big believer that what we eat affects our bodies. She's so desperate to keep the migraines away that she's tried more elimination diets than I can count."

"Is that why she's pescatarian?" Connie asks.

"Yes," Billie confirms. "Through elimination diets, Autumn determined that red meat, poultry, and pork contribute to her migraines. She's been pescatarian for almost a year, and she's very diligent about it. She also avoids refined sugar and dairy."

"So, yesterday's altercation with Nadira about the

chicken-tofu confusion wasn't their first argument?" I ask.

"No," Billie replies. "But Autumn doesn't like to call it arguing. She prefers to call it *advocating*. Autumn is a dedicated advocate. She confronted Nadira after every meal that made me nauseous." She shrugs. "So pretty much after every meal I've had here. I asked her not to. I told her I don't want my stomach issues to interfere with our vacation, but Autumn insisted. She said I'm too sick to advocate for myself."

"How did Nadira respond when Autumn accused her of not disclosing ingredients?" Connie asks.

"She denied it," Billie replies. "At first she was offended because Autumn attacked her integrity. Nadira said withholding ingredient information would be unethical and dangerous. She said she accommodates every guest's dietary needs."

"At first?" I ask.

"I think she was fed up with Autumn's constant advocating. She stopped arguing and just stood there, nodding until Autumn finished."

"That must've frustrated Autumn," I suggest.

"It did," Billie confirms. "And it made her more determined. She threatened to warn people. She said she would leave bad reviews, warn food bloggers, and ruin Nadira's career."

Earlier, Autumn mentioned they checked in on Wednesday. If she advocated on behalf of Billie after every meal, that's at least nine confrontations. Nine times she accused Nadira of making a guest sick. Ten times if we include the tofu-chicken scandal. Did Autumn's constant complaints and accusations push Nadira over the edge? Could Autumn be on to something with her theory that Nadira killed the wrong twin?

"There you are!" April calls, weaving through the chairs with Tamara, Rachel, and Hannah in tow.

"Hi," Connie and I say in unison.

"You remember Billie, right?" I say to April as I gesture to Billie.

"Of course," April replies smiling. "I'm so sorry about Summer."

April joins Billie on her lounger. Rachel, having inherited April's impossibly long legs, steps over the lounger with the same effort it would take me to step over a sidewalk crack and sits next to April. Connie and I squeeze together to make room for Tamara and Hannah on our lounger. It's snug, but we make it work.

April introduces Billie to everyone.

"Rachel and I just saw Autumn," Hannah informs Billie. "We went upstairs to drop off our antennae, and Maria was letting Autumn into her room because Autumn lost her key."

"She did?" Connie asks, squeezing her eyebrows together and pausing her needles mid-stitch. "I distinctly remember picking up a room key when Autumn and the doctor collided. The doctor took the key out of my hand."

"Are you sure?" Billie asks. "Because I picked up a room key too, and the doctor insisted it was hers and took it."

"It sounds like the doctor accidentally took both keys," I conclude.

"At least we know who has it," Connie says. "I'm sure Maria will find the doctor and get Autumn's key back."

As Hannah and Rachel tell us about their fruitless search for 5G service, Billie's complexion blanches. The skin around her eyes darkens, and her eyes appear more sunken than a moment ago. I hope it's not because we went from three people to seven people crammed on two lounge chairs. Despite the generous size of the lounge chairs, it's a tight fit.

"I hear you had a hot stone massage last night," I say to Billie, hoping to verify her alibi and distract her from her obvious discomfort. "How was it? I'm thinking of booking one."

"I can't say," Billie answers, then swallows hard. "The massage therapist was just getting started when the power went out." She swipes the back of her hand across her forehead and wipes it on the thigh of her grey leggings. "It was too dark to finish the massage, and the stones need electricity to stay warm. I got dressed, and the massage therapist and I left."

"Did you leave through the emergency exit, or the main door?" I ask, pointing to the emergency exit.

"The main door." Billie struggles to swallow, flaring her nostrils. "The massage therapist turned off the lights and locked up behind us."

"Did anyone else see today's lunch menu?" Tamara asks. "Today's special is one of Nadira's specialties, Zucchini Roshti Yucca Burger with French Mustard Dressing."

As we *mmm* and discuss how yummy and intriguing it sounds, Billie clutches her book with trembling hands. Her knuckles are white. She stands up.

"I'm sorry," Billie says. "I don't feel well." She clasps a hand over her mouth and navigates away from the crowded lounge chairs.

"Is there anything we can do?" Connie asks.

"Mmm-mmm," Billie hums, her hand still covering her mouth. "No thank you," she mumbles, striding away.

"Is she OK?" Hannah asks.

"I hope it wasn't something we said," Tamara adds, taking advantage of the space freed up by Billie's departure and switching lounge chairs.

"She's had tummy trouble for the last few days," I explain.

"She certainly looked like she wasn't feeling well," Connie observes. "Did you notice how quickly the colour drained from her face?"

"And she had beads of sweat on her forehead and upper lip," April adds. "It's not hot enough to sweat that much."

"Especially since we're sitting in the shade." Connie points her knitting needle at the overhead awning.

If Billie was with the massage therapist when the power went out, and they left together like she claims, why was she late getting to the Epicurean Bistro last night? She crept in more than halfway through Maria's update. Where was Billie between leaving the massage and showing up at the bistro? Could she have gone back to her room? Autumn said their room was empty. But Autumn left twice to search for Summer and Billie. Is it possible they missed each other?

"What's this?" April asks, producing a sandwich-size freezer bag from the crack where the back and bottom lounge cushions meet. "Is it yours?"

She looks back and forth from me to Connie, dangling the clear plastic baggie between her fingers.

"It's not mine," I say, shoving my knitting inside my knitting bag.

"It's not mine either," Connie confirms.

I reach out to take the baggie.

Hannah and Connie lean in to inspect the baggie with me. It's a collection of leaf clippings. I smush them around between the plastic sides of the bag, spreading them out and inspecting them.

"It looks like someone chopped up leaves or grass," Connie says.

The angular, straight edges on the non-uniform clippings look like someone used scissors to chop the leaves, or grass, or whatever this is into small, random-sized pieces.

"Why would someone chop them up?" I ask, turning the bag to inspect the contents from the other side.

"To smoke it?" Tamara suggests, shrugging one shoulder.

"You think it's weed?" I ask, bringing the bag to my face for a closer look. "Maybe it fell out of Autumn's bag. I've heard of people using weed to treat migraines."

"It doesn't look like weed," Hannah comments over my shoulder.

"How would you know?" I ask, narrowing my eyes on my daughter and raising one eyebrow.

"From the drug awareness campaigns and anti-drug posters at school," she counters with a smug grin.

"Hannah's right," Connie says. "These don't look like marijuana leaves." She pulls herself upright. "These leaves are fresh." She gestures to the baggie on my lap. "Marijuana leaves are dried."

"I see." I redirect my narrowed gaze to Connie. "How do you know about drying out marijuana leaves?"

"That's what I've heard," she replies sheepishly, fidgeting with her knitting and mumbling something about common knowledge.

April reaches across and takes the baggie.

"This piece has scalloped edges," she says, sliding the plastic between her thumb and forefinger until she separates and traps a larger piece. "It looks like parsley."

Tamara leans over her wife's shoulder for a closer look at the mystery leaves.

"Wild parsley is pretty common where we live. Or maybe the spa has an herb garden, and a parsley enthusiast pinched off a few stalks," I suggest.

"It's too early for wild parsley," Connie insists. "Even

with the warm spring we've been having, I doubt there's much wild parsley in the mountains yet."

"Here"—I hold out my hand and April gives me the baggie—"Parsley smells like grass. I'll open the bag and sniff it."

"No!" Tamara shouts as I'm about to breach the plastic baggie's zipped seal. "Megan! Don't."

Tamara snatches the still-sealed baggie and brings it close to her face.

"I think this might be spotted water hemlock." She rolls a few pieces between the plastic. "These look like young leaves. From a young plant. And these white bits could be pieces of root." She looks up at us and blinks, refocussing her large brown eyes. "The root is the most toxic part."

"Why would someone carry around a baggie of poison?" Connie asks.

Our collective silence speaks volumes. The only reason a person would have a baggie of cut-up, poisonous leaves would be to poison someone. We all know it, but none of us wants to say it.

"I think we should give this to Twyla," I say, breaking the somber silence.

"If T is wrong, and this is just parsley, Twyla will think we're alarmists," April argues.

"T" is Tamara's nickname.

"If Mum is right, and we don't hand it in, we could be withholding evidence," Rachel counters.

"I need to visit Twyla anyway," I say standing up. "This gives me a good excuse."

"I'll come with you," Tamara offers. "I can explain why I suspect it's spotted water hemlock, and she'll see it's an educated guess and not hysterical speculation." She rubs her tummy. "Can we stop at the juice bar on the way? It's almost lunchtime, and I'm starving. I've been craving a Green Powerhouse smoothie since Hannah had one last night."

"Of course," I say.

Tamara points at April and me.

"We have to wash our hands," she instructs. "Do not touch your face or anything else until you've washed your hands with soap and water."

April nods.

I nod.

"Just having skin contact with this plant is deadly."

Hannah takes my knitting bag, so I don't touch it with my unwashed hands, then she, Connie, April, and Rachel follow us to the door.

Never in my life has my nose been as itchy as it is since Tamara ordered me not to touch my face.

# CHAPTER 14

"How do you know so much about spotted water hemlock?" I ask Tamara while the juice bar attendant makes her smoothie.

"My mother is a botanist," Tamara replies.

"Oh, I thought she worked in the food industry."

"She did," Tamara clarifies. "She researched genetically modified edible plants."

"Well, I'm glad your mother shared her botanical knowledge with you. You just saved my life. If it weren't for you, I would've sniffed those leaves and picked them up with my bare hands too."

"Before my mum worked for the food company, she worked in the agricultural industry. Spotted water hemlock was a problem for local farmers. The plant spread and grew faster than farmers could eradicate it. Livestock would eat it and die. That's why it's also known as *cowbane*. My mum was part of a team that tried to find a large-scale solution to the spotted water hemlock problem. That's why I know so much." She shrugs. "She would talk about her work, and there were photos of it lying around our house."

"Lucky for me, your mother brought her work home with her."

The juice bar attendant hands Tamara a Green Powerhouse smoothie and a straw. I offer to carry the wad of paper towels, so she has both hands free to enjoy her drink.

On our way to the juice bar, we stopped at the bathroom to wash our hands. The first thing I did with my clean hands was scratch the tip of my nose. It was the most satisfying nose scratch of my life. The next thing I did was take photos of the suspicious baggie with my cell phone. Then Tamara wrapped the baggie in a wad of paper towels to reduce the likelihood of oils or trace amounts of spotted water hemlock transferring to someone's hands from the outside of the baggie.

On our way to the front desk to ask for Twyla, I tell Tamara what Autumn said about April and me making Twyla's suspect list.

"That's ridiculous," Tamara says. "If you and April killed Summer, why would you lead the police to her body? And why would you kill Summer, anyway? You guys didn't know her, and you have no motive. April and you have alibis. You were at the front desk when Summer died. April was with me and Rachel, then she went downstairs for a smoothie and ran into you."

"I know," I say. "But Twyla has to assume everybody is a suspect until she proves otherwise."

"Then we'll help her prove otherwise," Tamara declares, then sips her smoothie.

"This weekend was supposed to be about spending quality time together, relaxing, and pampering ourselves. We weren't supposed to find a dead body in the aftermath of a storm and solve the murder to prove our innocence."

"It can be two things." Tamara shrugs and sips her smoothie again.

"I regret not getting one," I say, watching the green liquid travel through the white straw. "Is it good?"

"Mmm-hmm," Tamara says, nodding and sipping the green liquid through the straw. "Want to try?"

We stop walking and Tamara offers me the clear plastic cup. I take it and use the straw to stir the green contents. Thicker than water, but not as thick as a triple thick milkshake. I bring the straw to my lips and take a small sip.

"Yummy," I say, then take a bigger sip. "It tastes better than it looks." I hold the cup at my eye level. "Where are the dark green flecks?"

"What dark green flecks?" Tamara asks, taking back the cup. She holds it at her eye level and inspects the contents. "Is there supposed to be dark green flecks?"

"I think so," I reply. "Summer's Green Powerhouse smoothie was the same colour as yours, but with dark green flecks."

"Are you sure?" Tamara asks. "Hannah's smoothie didn't have dark green flecks. It looked like this one." She holds up her cup like she's making a toast. "She let me taste it, and I didn't see any dark green flecks or taste any chunks."

I unlock my phone and find the photos I took at the crime scene last night.

"See," I say, showing Tamara the photo of the regurgitated smoothie. I pinch the screen and zoom in. "Dark green flecks."

"Weird," Tamara says. "Those are probably bits of lettuce that were in Summer's stomach."

We resume walking, and I think back to last night and the dark-green flecks in Summer's smoothie. Did bits of salad come up with the smoothie when she threw up?

Did Summer customize her smoothie? Was it a Green Powerhouse smoothie, or something else from the juice bar menu? I'm certain she said it was a Green Powerhouse smoothie when Hannah and I talked to the twins in the change room. As I contemplate the scene in sauna three last night, and the green flecks in Summer's smoothie, I stare at the wad of paper towel in my hand.

Then it hits me.

I freeze on the spot and gasp.

"What is it?" Tamara asks. "What's wrong?" She brings the straw to her lips.

"Tamara, no!"

As she closes her lips around the tip of the straw, I slam the smoothie cup out of her hand. We both leap back as it crashes to the wood floor, splattering light green smoothie everywhere. No dark green flecks.

"What the heck, Megan?!" Tamara looks at her empty hand, then at the mess on the floor. "That was a good smoothie!"

"I'm sorry, T," I plead. "But I'm positive that Summer's smoothie had dark green flecks."

"And?" Tamara urges, unsatisfied with my justification for destroying her smoothie and making an enormous mess.

"It just occurred to me that if Summer's smoothie was the only Green Powerhouse smoothie with dark green flecks, maybe the dark green flecks didn't belong in the smoothie."

As if we choreographed it, our eyes shift from each other to the wad of paper towels in my hand.

"What if the murderer put spotted water hemlock in Summer's smoothie?" Tamara ruminates, arriving at the same conclusion I reached just before I smacked her drink away from her face. We look up and our eyes meet. "That means Summer's killer dropped the baggie."

"Or planted it when they snuck out of the emergency exit after they killed Summer," I suggest. "But we don't know for sure that the leaves are spotted water hemlock. We might be jumping to a lot of conclusions."

"I'm over ninety percent sure it's spotted water hemlock," Tamara admits with a sigh. "I'd know for certain from the smell, but I'm scared to sniff it because I can't remember if the smell is toxic."

"And we don't have internet access to check," I say, finishing her sentence. "What does spotted water hemlock smell like?"

"Carrots," Tamara replies. "Mum used to talk about the strong carrot smell."

"I'm sorry about your smoothie," I say. "I panicked and thought your smoothie might have dark green flecks that we couldn't see through the cup."

We squat and examine the splattered smoothie against the wood floor. Tamara drags the straw through the green liquid, searching for anything out of place. Neither of us spot anything.

"Everything all right, ladies?" asks the perky employee with the bouncy ponytail. "Uh oh... it looks like we had a little accident."

"It's my fault," I admit. "I'm sorry. Sometimes I swear my fingers are butter."

We laugh.

"Don't worry about it," the employee assures me. "These things happen." She plucks a two-way radio from the waistband of her wrinkle-free beige uniform pants and summons a mop and bucket. "Can I have someone replace your smoothie?" she asks.

"No, thank you," Tamara replies. "It was good, but we're having lunch soon, and I don't want to fill up on smoothie."

The lie rolls off Tamara's lips as though it was the

truth. But I guess the truth, that we're worried an unhinged psychopath is poisoning smoothies, would either freak out the employee or make us sound like over-reacting drama queens. Dealing with paranoid guests' ridiculous-sounding conspiracy theories is probably above her pay grade.

"OK." The employee flashes us a cheery smile and re-holsters the two-way radio in her waistband. "Have a great lunch! You're in for a treat if you order Chef Nadira's Zucchini Roshti Yucca Burger."

"I know," Tamara agrees. "I can't wait. Have you tried it? Was it good?"

The peppy employee's animated review of Nadira's signature dish makes my tummy grumble. It feels like breakfast was four days ago, not four hours.

As a second employee pushing a mop and bucket on wheels approaches us, I ask both employees if they know where we can find Twyla.

"She was with Maria a while ago," replies the perky employee. "Maria will know where to find her."

"Maria's on lunch," says the employee with the mop and bucket. "She usually has lunch in her room. She'll be back in about an hour."

"Thanks," I say, smiling as Tamara takes my arm and tugs me away.

"I know where the employee rooms are," Tamara whispers as we continue down the hall arm-in-arm.

"How?" I ask.

"Last night when you and April were in the sauna, Connie and I socialized in the hall with the other guests."

"When Connie gave impromptu knitting lessons?" I ask.

"That's right," Tamara says. "She taught garter stitch to about ten people, including two employees. Connie chatted with them. You know what she's like."

"I sure do," I respond.

Connie is the most extroverted extrovert I know. She has never met a stranger and can make friends in an empty room.

"She made friends with the employees and asked them about their jobs, their love lives, their families, all of it," Tamara explains. "In the course of the conversation, the employees mentioned the staff dorm and where it's located."

"Maria's room is in the dorm?"

"No," Tamara replies. "Maria sleeps in the main building with us. Her apartment is on the first floor behind the front desk."

"If Maria is in her home, having lunch, maybe we should wait an hour and talk to her when she's on the clock."

"We won't hijack her lunch. We'll just ask where Twyla is," Tamara argues. "Nadira only serves the lunch special for a two-hour window. If we wait to talk to Maria, then talk to Twyla, we won't get any Zucchini Roshti Yucca Burger with French Mustard Dressing."

"Fine," I agree, doubting we'll get past the person at the front desk, anyway.

# CHAPTER 15

THE FRONT DESK IS UNATTENDED. A guest enjoying a nearby massage chair informs us that Maria left for lunch about five minutes ago. According to the guest, the person covering the reception desk in Maria's absence was called away to deal with a spill.

"She got a call over the two-way radio about a spilled smoothie." The guest's voice warbles from the vibration of the massage chair. "She rolled out of here with the mop-and-bucket cart."

"Thanks," Tamara says, smirking at me.

The guest doesn't see Tamara's smirk because her eyes are closed. Her back arches, and she moans as the massage roller travels up her spine. I make a mental note to try the massage chairs before we check out.

"Come on," Tamara mouths, jerking her head toward the reception desk with her eyes wide.

"OK," I mouth, following her into forbidden territory.

The door behind the reception desk leads into Maria's office. Her office is neat and messy at the same time, like my house. The messy bits are confined to designated areas.

Two stacks of paper and files sit on Maria's desk. Notices about upcoming spa events and health and safety reminders are pinned to a large bulletin board behind the desk. A variety of jackets and sweaters hang from the coat rack in the corner, and the boot tray below it features a pair of winter boots, a pair of rain boots, and a pair of hiking boots arranged in order of height.

I suspect Maria created the hand-drawn chart on the whiteboard last night in a haste. It lists all the areas of the spa. Some areas, like the pool and sauna, have *x's* through them. The areas that are closed because of the storm or because of Summer's death. Other areas have employee names listed, like the ones stationed on each floor to attend to guest inquiries until the landline is fixed.

The black and gold nameplate on Maria's desk reads: *MARIA CLARK* and underneath in smaller letters, *GENERAL MANAGER*.

"So that's what the C on Maria's name tag stands for," I mutter.

Every spa employee wears a name tag on their golf-style uniform shirt. Each name tag features the employee's first name and last initial.

"Why do they bother putting last initials on the name tags?" Tamara asks as if she can read my mind. "Why not just the first name, or the first name and full last name?"

"I guess it's useful if two employees have the same name. In case there are two Marias and you need to tell them apart?" I venture a guess.

Straight ahead of us is a closed door.

"Maria's apartment must be through here." Tamara reaches for the doorknob.

"Wait." I place my hand on her arm. "We should knock. What if this door opens into Maria's personal space? What if we walk in on her watching TV in her underwear and eating cereal?"

"That's unlikely," Tamara replies with a chuckle. "We're still using generators. There's no way Maria would waste power to watch TV."

That's the biggest concern Tamara took from my hypothetical scenario? Tamara raps her knuckles against the door. We wait. She knocks again, louder. Nothing.

Tamara wraps her hand around the doorknob.

I squeeze my eyes shut in case we're about to commit a heinous violation of Maria's privacy.

"You can open your eyes," Tamara says, her hand still gripping the doorknob. "There's no cereal or underwear."

I open one eye and sneak a tentative peek before committing to open both eyes.

"Which door is Maria's?" I ask, looking down the long hallway lined on both sides with doors.

"There's only one way to find out."

Tamara opens the door enough to step through.

I follow her, and she leaves the door open a crack behind us.

The door on my left says, *Janitorial*. The door on my right says, *Supplies*. Next, we have *Electrical*, then a vague, *Employees Only*.

A rattling doorknob freaks us out. Tamara and I reach for each other and squeeze hands in silent yet dramatic mutual panic. It's like a scene from a 1920s silent movie where the characters can't speak so they overemote and over-gesture to get their point across.

A door at the end of the hall opens, and Twyla steps into the hall. She's wearing the police uniform that got soaked during last night's storm, and her dark hair is in a tight, low bun like it was when we met. Twyla's back is to us. Her left shoulder and hip rest against the doorframe. I can't see Maria, but I hear her voice, so I assume she is standing in front of Twyla or inside the apartment. Twyla's head moves forward. Hands—that I assume belong to Maria—wrap around her khaki uniform shirt. Maria rubs Twyla's back from her shirt collar to the waistband of her khaki police pants and back again, in a lazy up-and-down motion. Smooching noises and occasional giggles pierce the silent hallway.

I suspect we just discovered the real reason for Twyla's visit to the spa last night: Maria.

This is worse than walking in on Maria watching TV and eating cereal in her underwear. We aren't just invading one person's privacy, we're invading two. We're intruding on an intimate moment we weren't meant to witness.

Should I cough and alert them to our presence? We can pretend we're lost and don't know how we ended up in this off-limits hall. Should Tamara and I try to sneak out the way we snuck in? We must do something. We can't stand here in silence while Maria and Twyla canoodle, oblivious to our presence.

Wide-eyed and engulfed in silent hysteria, Tamara and I tip toe backwards toward Maria's office. I reach behind my back and find the doorknob.

"That was close," Tamara whispers after we escape into Maria's office. "Did you know Maria and Twyla were a couple?"

"No," I whisper in reply. "But I noticed they were familiar with each other last night. They called each other *Mare* and *Twy*."

We press our ears to the door that separates the lobby from Maria's office. Silence. If we're lucky, the front desk is still unattended, and we can sneak away without explaining ourselves.

The clomping of approaching boots alerts us to

303

Twyla's imminent arrival. In a rush to exit Maria's office before Twyla enters it, Tamara opens the door at the exact moment Twyla opens the door on the opposite wall.

I grab Tamara's arm and spin her around so we're facing inside the office as if, by coincidence, we're arriving at the same time as Twyla, not sneaking out before she catches us.

"Perfect timing," I say, smiling and pretending I'm just as surprised to see Twyla as she is to see us.

"Is everything OK, ladies?" Twyla asks, pinching her eyebrows together.

"Fine," I say, smiling.

"Are you looking for Maria?"

"We're looking for you," I reply. "Someone told us you were with Maria."

"Here I am," she says, resting her hands on her slender hips. "You found me."

Twyla gives Tamara and me a head-to-toe scan, and Tamara takes the wad of paper towels from me.

"What's that?" Twyla asks, nodding to the paper towels pressed against Tamara's chest.

"I believe it's spotted water hemlock," Tamara says. "We wrapped it in paper towels in case there are trace amounts of the toxin on the outside of the bag."

"Show me," Twyla says, gesturing to Maria's desk.

Tamara sets the paper towels on the desk and unwraps them, revealing the small baggie of clippings. Twyla inspects the baggie without touching it. Tamara and I sit in the two visitor chairs in front of Maria's desk, then Tamara explains to Twyla why she believes the baggie contains pieces of spotted water hemlock leaves and roots.

"*Cicuta maculata* is quite common around here. It could have come from anywhere," Twyla says. "I've seen clusters of it just outside the property line of the spa.

I assume *Cicuta maculata* is the proper name for spotted water hemlock. I make a mental note to research spotted water hemlock as soon as I have access to either the internet or cell service.

Using two paper towels to protect her hands, Twyla opens the baggie close to her face and inhales twice, flaring her nostrils.

"Carrots?" Tamara asks.

Twyla nods as she seals the baggie and examines the contents, narrowing her brown eyes as she focuses on specific leaves and clippings.

"I think you're right," Twyla confirms. "It smells and looks like spotted water hemlock." She looks at us. "You found this on a lounge chair?" We nod. "On the deck?" We nod again.

"I suspect there was *cicut*—spotted water hemlock in Summer's Green Powerhouse smoothie," I say, abandoning my attempt to refer to the noxious weed by its botanical nomenclature.

"Explain," Twyla says, crossing her arms in front of her chest and narrowing her eyes at me.

I tell Twyla about the dark green flecks mixed in with Summer's spilled smoothie, and how I assumed the flecks were part of the smoothie until Tamara ordered one, and her smoothie didn't have any.

"And the smoothie Hannah had last night didn't have any dark green flecks either," Tamara adds.

"I'll show you." I unlock my phone and hand it to Twyla with the zoomed-in picture of Summer's regurgitated smoothie on the screen.

"You took photos at the crime scene?" Twyla asks, her mouth agape.

"A few," I reply. "But none that would identify Summer."

"You shouldn't have done that," she chides.

"I did it to preserve evidence," I argue. "In case there was a difference of opinion about the scene."

"I forgot"—Twyla rolls her eyes—"you're the crime scene hobbyist." She thrusts my phone toward me. "Being married to a cop doesn't make you a qualified murder investigator."

"I never claimed to be a qualified murder investigator," I retort, swiping my phone from her.

I open my mouth to protest her labelling me a crime scene hobbyist when the door behind her opens, interrupting our conversation.

"Oh!" Maria says, her eyes flitting around the office, taking in the unexpected scene. "Hello, everyone."

"Does the Green Powerhouse smoothie have dark green flecks, Mare?" Twyla asks.

Maria shakes her head, closing the door behind her "No. It's a consistent minty green colour with a smooth texture. Why?" she asks, sitting at her desk. "What's that?" She points to the baggie topped pile of paper towels on her desk.

Ignoring Maria's question, Twyla tells Maria she needs to talk to everyone who had access to the juice bar yesterday. Maria whips out a pen and makes a few notes on the pad in front of her.

Using her cell phone, Twyla takes photos of the baggie and its suspicious contents. Still smarting from her crime scene hobbyist comment, I resist the urge to offer her—sarcastically—the photos I took of the baggie in the bathroom.

"I need you to show me where you found it," she says to us. We nod in agreement and stand up. "One at a time," Twyla says, pointing at my chair. "You wait here." I sit down. "First, Tamara will show me, and explain the circumstances around the discovery, then Megan can show me."

"In the meantime, I'll make a list of everyone who had access to the juice bar, and make sure they're available to talk to you," Maria says.

Twyla bundles the baggie into its paper towel nest and places it in a filing cabinet drawer next to Maria's desk. Maria locks the drawer, removes the key from the key ring, and gives it to Twyla.

# CHAPTER 16

IF I KNEW I would be sitting in Maria's office with nothing to do, I would have kept my knitting instead of asking Hannah to take it back to our room.

"What game are you playing?" Maria asks, nodding at my cell phone.

"I'm not playing a game," I reply. "I'm looking at photos of my husband and dog."

"You have a dog?"

"A corgi," I reply, nodding. "Her name is Sophie."

"Can I see?"

I hand Maria my phone.

"Awww. She's adorable," Maria says. "I wish I could have a dog, but the spa is a pet-free zone. Except for service animals, of course." Her smile is sad and hopeful at the same time. "Is this your husband?"

She turns the phone toward me, and I nod.

"Eric," I say.

"He looks familiar," she says, then scrunches up her mouth. "Have you guys stayed here before?"

"No," I shake my head. "Eric doesn't care for spas, and this is my first visit."

"I'm sure I've seen him somewhere," she says. "Same last name as you?"

I nod. "Sloane."

"Eric Sloane," Maria mutters. "It'll come to me as soon as you leave." She laughs and hands me my phone. "You must miss him and Sophie."

"I do," I admit. "More than I expected. We've only been married four-and-a-half months. Other than a two-day conference he attended last month, this is the longest we've been apart since the wedding. At least when he was at the conference, we could text and talk on the phone."

"It's hard to be away from the love of your life."

Her voice is heavy with experience. I'm tempted to pry but resist.

"Can I ask you a question, Maria?"

"Sure." She looks up from the list she's making. "Shoot."

"Where is Summer?" I ask. "I heard you and Twyla arguing about moving Summer's body to the walk-in fridge." I shift uncomfortably in my seat. "I assume there's only one walk-in fridge, and it's full of food."

"Summer is *not* in the walk-in fridge," Maria insists. "Can you imagine the fallout if Health and Safety found out we stored a corpse with the perishables? Or if the guests found out? I'd lose my job." She guffaws. "I can't justify storing a corpse in the fridge and moving the food somewhere else. Improperly stored food could make people sick." Her eyes widen, and she drops her pen on the desk. "And Nadira would freak out. There's no way she would share her kitchen with a corpse!"

She scoffs, "I told Twy the walk-in fridge is not a morgue, and the topic was closed. She wasn't impressed. She rolled over and turned out her light without even saying goodnight." Panic flashes across her face.

"She's my guest," Maria blurts out the explanation like the words are in a race to leave her mouth. "We're fully booked for Mother's Day," she explains at rapid-fire speed. "I invited Twyla to stay in my apartment." Maria clears her throat. "We're friends."

She fusses with the pencil cup and office supplies on her desk, organizing them by height and making everything face the same direction. "We go way back."

"I figured you were at least friends when I saw you kissing," I confess, not mentioning that Tamara saw it too.

"It's not a secret. It's private," Maria says, looking me in the eye. "Secrecy and privacy aren't the same. I spend all day and night here. It blurs the line between my professional and private life. I just want the same amount of privacy as everyone else."

"It can't be easy when you literally live at work," I sympathize.

"It's not," Maria admits. "I live and work at a remote mountain spa, and Twy lives and works in town. We try to synchronize our days off, but her job is unpredictable, and they call her in on her days off. It's hard on our relationship when we don't spend much time together."

"I get it," I say, my heart stinging with empathy. "My first marriage ended because we didn't prioritize our relationship. The emotional distance made us apathetic, and our connection fizzled."

Maria's eyes well with moisture, and sadness clouds her face. She wipes her eyes with the back of her hand.

"That won't happen to Twy and me." Her voice is light with fake optimism, and an exaggerated smile is plastered across her face. "We have a plan. We're saving for a house." She straightens the piles of paper on her desk. "Somewhere else. Where I can get a job that doesn't require me to live on site. A house with a yard so we can have a dog. Somewhere with a bigger police force where Twy won't be on call twenty-four hours a day, seven days a week."

"I'm rooting for you," I say. "It's not always easy to be with a cop. Especially when you're a person of interest in the case they're investigating."

"I'm not a person of interest in Summer's death." Maria knits her brows together and tilts her head. "Why would you think I'm a person of interest?"

"I heard we're all persons of interest," I reply. "Everyone at the death scene."

"I have an alibi." Maria scoffs and clutches the buttons on her white spa uniform shirt. "I was working the front desk. Remember? You asked me to get a toothbrush for your mother."

I don't correct her about my connection to Connie, focussing instead on her alibi.

"You disappeared for at least twenty minutes and came back empty-handed," I remind her. "Remember? Your colleague showed up and found the toothbrushes under the counter."

"You don't have an alibi either!" she counters. "You were alone in the lobby when I was searching for a toothbrush."

"We're in the same position," I say. "Our alibis aren't verifiable."

"Twy knows I didn't kill Summer," Maria says, taking off her glasses and cleaning the lenses with the fabric of her shirt. "I gave her a full statement, and I told her who I suspect killed Summer."

"Who?"

"I shouldn't say." She holds up her glasses and inspects the lenses before returning them to her face.

"Is it someone who works at the spa?" I ask, watching to gauge her reaction. She's looks at me like I suggested the Easter Bunny killed Summer. "I'm right, aren't I? You suspect one of your employees murdered Summer."

I do not know if I'm right but hope the suggestion provokes a response from Maria.

"Of course not!" Maria exclaims. "I think it's her sister, Autumn."

"Why?" I ask, shocked by Maria's choice of suspect.

"Two reasons," Maria replies. "First, Twy said murders are almost never random. She said they're almost always committed by someone close to the victim."

She stops talking.

"And?" I urge. "What's the second reason?"

"I heard the twins arguing. More than once. They had issues."

"What did they argue about?"

"Family stuff." Maria shrugs. "This is their first Mother's Day without their mother. Well, for one of them. Summer, was estranged from the family for several years, and their mother died while she was gone. Autumn took care of their mother and buried her. She blamed Summer for their mother's poor health and death. She said their mother's constant worry about Summer lead to her illness. And she resented being their mother's sole caregiver and having to make the final arrangements alone."

"That's unfortunate, but it doesn't mean Autumn killed her sister."

"There's more," Maria says. "Autumn and her mother had a business together. A courier company or something involved with international importing and exporting. When their mother died, Autumn became the sole owner of the business. Summer wanted half of the mother's share, and she wanted Autumn to hire her. Autumn refused."

"Oh," I say, shocked by the conflict and issues

between Autumn and Summer. "How did you overhear this?"

"Spa employees fade into the background," Maria explains. "At first, guests maintain their public personas in our presence, then they stop noticing us, and conduct themselves as though we aren't around."

"Fascinating," I say.

A knock at the door distracts us from our conversation.

"Come in," Maria calls.

"Where's T?" I ask, shifting to peer around Twyla.

"You can see her after I question you. I escorted her to the bistro. She's having lunch with her family. She was eager to make the lunch special. She made me promise to take you there after."

I nod.

"Am I a suspect?" Maria demands, looking at Twyla and drumming her fingers on the desktop.

"Mare, can we talk about this later?"

"So, I am a suspect!"

"That's not what I said."

"It's not what you *didn't* say either."

I sink farther into my chair and hunch my shoulders, hoping not to draw attention to my role as instigator of their domestic dispute.

"Can we discuss this when I'm not conducting interviews?" Twyla opens her palms in a pleading motion.

"Like we discussed the fridge?" Maria challenges, crossing one leg over the other and bouncing her foot in the air. "The kind of discussion where you ignore me, roll over, and go to sleep?"

"I need to use the bathroom," I announce, eager to remove myself from their domestic dispute.

"I'll meet you in the lobby in a few minutes," Twyla says.

"Take your time," I assure her. "I'll be in the massage chair when you're ready."

"I recommend the first setting if you have upper back problems, and the third setting if you have lower back issues." Maria smiles.

# CHAPTER 17

"MEGAN?"

How long have I been here? Five minutes? An hour? Who knows? Time stopped when the massage chair and I became one.

I open one eye just enough to make out my fuzzy surroundings. Twyla stands over me, her feet hip width apart, and her arms crossed in front of her chest. She releases one hand and wiggles her fingers at me when she sees my partially open eye.

"Ready, sleepyhead?" she asks.

I nod and turn off the massage chair.

Outside, I squint into the daylight and lower my sunglasses from the top of my head to my face. Twyla does the same, covering her face with large, mirrored aviators.

"Which chair was it?" she asks.

"Over here." Twyla follows me through the maze of tables and chairs. "Connie and I were walking through here when I heard a sneeze," I say, recounting how we came to occupy the lounge chair.

"And you never saw the baggie before April pulled it out from between the lounge chair cushions?" Twyla asks after I finish telling her the events that preceded her finding Tamara and me in Maria's office with the baggie.

I leave out the part where we witnessed her and Maria sharing an intimate moment outside Maria's apartment.

"None of us had seen it before," I reply. "Connie and I sat here." I point to the lounge chair next to the chair in question. "We never sat in the lounger where April found the baggie."

"It could have fallen between the cushions when Autumn and the doctor bumped into each other," Twyla thinks out loud. "Or it could belong to whoever occupied the lounger before Autumn."

"The killer's fingerprints might be on the plastic baggie," I suggest.

"Your fingerprints might be on the baggie too," Twyla adds. "And April's. And Tamara's."

"Well... yes..." I agree, searching for words to defend myself and my friends. "But we brought the baggie to you. If we killed Summer, why would we hand deliver evidence that implicates us?"

"Sometimes suspects do strange things, Megan," Twyla replies. "You wouldn't be the first perpetrator to deliver the murder weapon to the police and expect to get away with it."

"Murder weapon?" I ask. "Did the killer poison Summer with spotted water hemlock?"

"You said it, not me," Twyla says, raising her hands in surrender.

"I said, I *suspect* the spotted water hemlock *could* be the murder weapon," I clarify. "You said it *is* the murder weapon. And you sounded confident."

"I found Summer and Autumn's smoothie cups in the change room," Twyla admits. "Someone wrapped the cups in paper towels and buried them at the bottom of the garbage can. Would you know anything about that?"

"Of course not!"

"If the killer left their fingerprints on Summer's cup, I'll know who did it. Soon."

"Good!" I declare. "But how will you know which cup belonged to Summer? Don't identical twins have identical fingerprints?"

"No," Twyla replies. "That's a common misconception. Identical twins share DNA, and their fingerprints often appear identical to the naked eye, but under examination, they're not. No two people have the same fingerprints. Even if there are no fingerprints on the cup, only one cup had dark green flecks stuck to the inside."

"The same dark green flecks as the sauna floor and the clippings in the baggie?" I ask.

"It appears so." Twyla nods. "The doctor also found dark green flecks inside Summer's mouth. Listen, Megan, no one can know Summer was murdered, or the murderer laced her smoothie with poisonous leaves."

"They won't find out from us," I say, speaking for all six of us. "By doing the right thing, and handing in the evidence we found, I've made myself a stronger suspect, haven't I?"

"I can't eliminate you," Twyla says. "You don't have an alibi."

"I don't have a *verifiable* alibi," I correct her. "But neither does Maria. Or you."

"Me?!" Twyla scoffs. "Are you serious? You think *I* killed Summer? I'm a law enforcement officer. I uphold the law. I don't break it."

"But you don't have an alibi," I remind her. "You were

REAGAN DAVIS

gone for over twenty minutes to retrieve the satellite phone from your car. It took you twenty minutes to realize your car and the phone were missing?"

"No, it took five minutes to realize the storm washed away my patrol car with the road," Twyla explains. "When I saw the river of mud where the road used to be, I conducted a perimeter check, assessing for potential danger and imminent threats to the spa." She gestures around us. "The perimeter check took longer than expected because of the strong winds and torrential rain."

"Did you check the deck when you checked the perimeter?"

"Of course. That's what perimeter check means, Megan. The entire perimeter."

I hate how often Twyla says my name and the condescending tone with which she says it.

"So, you were right here"—I point to the deck beneath our feet—"around the time Summer died?"

"It's possible." Twyla shrugs. "I'd need the coroner to estimate Summer's time of death to know for sure. Why?"

I point to the door that says *Sauna*.

"You admit you were at the crime scene at the approximate time of Summer's death," I conclude.

"Give me a break. Why would I kill Summer?"

"Why would I?" I counter. "Summer and I met for the first time a few hours before she died. What possible motive could I have to kill her?"

"I don't know," Twyla says, "but if you have one, I'll uncover it."

"How could I have sneaked the spotted water hemlock into Summer's smoothie?"

"You and your daughter were in the change room with Autumn and Summer. You had access to their smoothies."

I hadn't thought of that.

"Twyla, if I killed Summer, why would I return to the scene of the crime to tell you about our encounter with the twins and their smoothies? Then bring you the baggie of poisonous leaves that killed her?"

"Like I said, some perpetrators insert themselves into the investigation so they can keep tabs on it."

"I wouldn't do that," I say, then something Twyla said hits me. "Wait. You said *Hannah and I* had access to Summer's smoothie in the change room. Is my daughter a suspect?"

"Like I said, Megan. Everyone is a sus—"

"No way! Uh-uh," I cut her off, shaking my head. "Hannah was upstairs with Connie when Summer died. My daughter is not a suspect."

"It's doesn't matter where she was when Summer died," Twyla explains. "If the killer poisoned Summer's smoothie, they did it before she died."

Hannah's status as murder suspect further fuels my determination to uncover the killer.

"What about Nadira?" I ask, searching for compelling suspects besides Hannah. "Autumn and Nadira had multiple confrontations. The smoothie bar is beside her kitchen."

"I'm aware of Autumn's history with Nadira, and I'm investigating all leads."

"And Billie?" I ask, making sure Twyla is aware there is an entire spa filled with suspects besides my daughter. "She's close to the twins. She had access to Summer. They shared a room for goodness' sake. Where was Billie between the blackout and when she showed up at the bistro? She showed up late, more than halfway through Maria's speech. Also, she hasn't stopped puking since we found Summer's body. Could the guilt of killing one of her best friends be making her sick? Or maybe her nausea is a symptom because she had contact with the spotted water hemlock when she cut it up and added it to Summer's smoothie."

"That's not how spotted water hemlock works, Megan," Twyla explains. "Summer's death would have been painful, violent, and fast. Chronic nausea isn't a symptom."

"My point is," I clarify, "there are plenty of suspects with motives and unverified alibis who actually *knew* Summer. Hannah and I only met her yesterday."

"I get your point, Megan. You're trying to prove how observant you are. But like I said, if the killer poisoned her, they didn't have to be anywhere near Summer when she died."

"But they returned to the scene of the crime to pose her body," I argue. "Summer didn't drop dead behind the pentagon bench with her legs bent and her body tucked conveniently out of sight."

"I'm investigating every possible angle and every possible suspect," Twyla reiterates. "I'm retracing Summer's last hours and talking to everyone who had access to her or her smoothie prior to her death."

"Have you considered that Summer's killer might be someone from her past?" I ask, refusing to stop listing alternate suspects. "Summer's murder could have been a professional hit."

"What are you talking about?" Twyla asks, chuckling and dismissing my suggestion with a shake of her head.

"Are you aware that Summer was in witness protection?" I demand. "According to her sister, Summer witnessed a murder and her testimony helped convict a mob boss's son. Her testimony put her life in danger. Serious danger. Danger that made her give up her family, her life, and her identity. Summer's killer could have been exacting revenge."

"Shhh!" Twyla takes my upper arm and leads me off the deck to a secluded corner of the garden. "Autumn told you this?" she hisses. "What else did Autumn tell you?"

"Not much," I reply. "She said Summer's testimony and life in witness protection was a selfless act of courage, and they lost ten years together that they'll never get back. She wasn't gossiping, she was trying to portray what kind of person Summer was."

"This isn't public knowledge," Twyla whispers. "I'm shocked Autumn mentioned it to you."

"You already knew," I allege. "You're not surprised by Summer's past, you're surprised I *know* about it."

"Of course, I already knew," Twyla snaps.

"Is that the real reason you drove to the spa in such dangerous weather? Were you assigned to check on her?"

"Something like that," Twyla says, grinding her jaw and fixating on a random daffodil. "Who else knows about Summer's past? Who was there when Autumn told you?"

"Connie," I reply.

"Megan, you're in over your head. You have no idea what you're talking about, and I won't allow you to compromise this case." Twyla removes her sunglasses and locks eyes with me. She takes a single step forward. A step that, combined with her fierce, unblinking glare, intimidates me. Is that her intention? Is Twyla threatening me? "Do not interfere in this investigation, Megan," she warns. "Do you understand? Being an investigator's wife doesn't qualify you to solve a murder."

I swallow hard and defy my body's instinct to step back in retreat. Aware that my body is leaning away from her, and refusing to let Twyla see she intimidates me, I pull myself up to my full five feet, two-and-three-quarter inches and take a half step forward, meeting her gaze.

"Actually, I'm a police chief's wife," I correct her, overemphasizing my *f's*. "And you should get used to me asking questions because if solving this murder is the only way to eliminate Hannah and me as suspects, I intend to find Summer's killer."

# CHAPTER 18

WE FINISH INTERROGATING EACH OTHER, and Twyla escorts me to the bistro.

"Where are Hannah and Rachel?" I ask, joining them at the table.

"They went to the eyebrow and lash bar," Connie replies.

"Then they're having an effleurage scalp massage with aromatherapy," Tamara adds.

"Was the Zucchini Roshti Yucca Burger with French Mustard Dressing yummy?" I ask, gesturing to the empty plate in front of Tamara.

"Very," she replies, smiling and rubbing circles on her tummy.

"I guess I'm too late to order it." I check the time on my cell phone, and the lunch special ended ten minutes ago.

"We've got your back, Megabyte." April nods, looking behind me.

Nadira approaches our table, smiling and carrying a tray.

"Your friends asked me to save you a plate," she says, setting the dish in front of me.

"Thank you," I say, smiling up at her, then turning to my three friends. "And thank you. I'm starving."

"Thanks for breaking the rule and serving this outside of the two-hour window," Tamara says.

"It's my rule," Nadira says. "If I can't break it, who can?" She chuckles.

"Join us, Chef," Tamara insists.

"I shouldn't." Nadira scans the almost-empty room.

"C'mon," April urges. "The lunch rush is over. Take a break."

"OK, but just for a moment," Nadira says, pulling out the chair between me and Connie.

While I savour Nadira's vegan masterpiece, we make small talk and pepper the chef with compliments on her gastronomic genius.

April and Tamara excuse themselves to attend an appointment for lymphatic drainage massage, which somehow sounds relaxing and unappealing at the same time.

Nadira, Connie, and I are alone in the bistro dining room.

I nod, pretending to listen to Connie and Nadira's friendly chitchat, while brainstorming how to bring up Summer's death without bringing down Nadira's relaxed, chatty mood. This could be my only opportunity to ask her about her and Autumn's confrontational history. Next thing I know, Connie steers the conversation for me.

"Megan and I ran into Autumn earlier," Connie says, changing the subject like some kind of mind-reading fairy godmother. "She seems to still be in shock. Poor thing. I hope she's eating. She needs to keep up her strength. With Billie's tummy trouble, I doubt she'll make sure Autumn eats enough and stays hydrated. Have you seen Autumn? Did she come downstairs for breakfast or lunch?"

Well done, Connie! I'm tempted to give her a standing ovation but settle for turning my full attention to Nadira, awaiting her response.

"We've delivered Autumn's meals to her room," Nadira replies. "Her dishes came back to the kitchen with less food than when we delivered them." She shrugs one shoulder. "I assume she's eating."

"That's good." Connie smiles sadly.

"Did Autumn say anything else when you ran into her?" Nadira asks. "Anything about me?"

Connie nods, looking at me to chime in.

"She said the chicken you served her triggered the migraine symptoms that caused her to leave Summer alone before she died."

Nadira huffs, accompanied by a head shake and eye roll.

"She didn't even eat the chicken," Nadira argues. "How could it have triggered a migraine?"

Connie and I look at each other, then at Nadira.

"I know you said confusing the chicken with the tofu was an honest mistake, but Autumn insists you did it on purpose."

"Why?" Nadira demands. "What satisfaction would I get from feeding chicken to a pescatarian? Why would I provoke another verbal attack from Autumn?"

"Yes," Connie sympathizes. "Billie told us about Autumn's aggressive form of advocating."

"I don't know why Billie is nauseous all the time," Nadira defends. "And I know she and Autumn claim the nausea started when she came to the spa and started eating food I'd prepared, but I assure you, it's not my cooking. Contrary to what Autumn claims, I don't use secret ingredients. I disclose every ingredient in every dish. Whatever is wrong with Billie has nothing to do with me."

"Yesterday, I tried to order tofu," I say, "but the server told me the spa hasn't had tofu all week."

"It's true," Nadira admits. "Our tofu order wasn't on the delivery truck. I told the staff to tell guests that tofu is off the menu. But there is a small amount left in the kitchen. I put it aside for guests who have special dietary needs or allergies."

"So, you rationed the remaining tofu?" I clarify.

"Yes."

"And you intended to use some of it in Autumn's order yesterday?"

"Yes," Nadira replies. "I wanted to avoid another confrontation with her. If I didn't accommodate Autumn's tofu request, she would have made a big deal about it. I got distracted. The cubed chicken and cubed tofu were next to each other in identical bowls. I picked up the cubed chicken instead of the tofu by accident." She brings her hand to the top button of her chef's jacket. "It was an honest mistake. I would never intentionally contaminate food. No matter how much I dislike the guest who ordered it."

She admits she doesn't like Autumn, and she knows Autumn is spreading rumours about undisclosed ingredients and Nadira's food causing Billie's stomach issues.

"Has Autumn confronted you about anything since Summer died?"

"No," Nadira replies. "I haven't seen Autumn since dinner last night. Except for when she ran in here searching for Summer."

"It must infuriate you that Autumn questioned your professional integrity," Connie comments.

"I was infuriated at first," Nadira admits. "Then I

realized this is how Autumn is. Arguing encourages her. So, I stopped arguing. When she would yell and try to goad me into an altercation, I nodded until she finished, then I thanked her for her feedback and walked away. But yesterday morning she threatened to make it a bigger issue. She threatened to contact food bloggers and leave negative reviews at restaurants where I've worked."

"How did you react when she threatened your livelihood?" I ask.

"I counter-threatened her," Nadira admits. Connie lets out a small gasp, and Nadira turns to her. "With my lawyer," she clarifies. "I threatened to sue her for slander. Or libel. Or whatever they call it when someone spreads lies to ruin a person's reputation."

"I bet Autumn didn't like that," I say.

"Not at all," Nadira confirms. "She said it wasn't slander because it was true." She raises her hands in a conciliatory gesture and looks back and forth between Connie and me. "It's not. None of Autumn's accusations against me are true."

We stop talking when the server removes the last of the dirty dishes and offers to refill our drinks.

After watching the server walk toward the kitchen with an armful of plates and cutlery, Nadira leans toward me.

"Did Autumn tell you I killed Summer?" she asks.

"Why would you ask that?" I ask.

"The questions Twyla asked me earlier made me think Autumn accused me of killing her sister."

"She told us she thinks you did it," Connie admits.

"Why would I kill Summer? I had barely said two words to her since they checked in."

"Autumn believes she was the intended victim," I explain. "She thinks you planned to kill her to stop her from ruining your career, but you accidentally killed the wrong twin."

"I didn't kill anyone," Nadira insists. "Autumn should look closer to home if she wants to find her sister's killer."

"What does that mean?" I ask, squishing my brows toward each other.

"It means, why isn't Billie a suspect?" Nadira asks. "I overheard Billie and Autumn talking one day when they were eating alone. Billie warned Autumn not to trust Summer. If I recall, her exact words were, *I know she's your sister, but you know what Summer is like. Don't trust her too much, too soon.* Then Billie warned Autumn that *Summer might be up to her old tricks*, whatever that means."

"How did Autumn respond?" I ask. "Did she defend her sister?"

"Autumn told Billie not to worry because, in her words, *I know Summer better than anyone and can tell when she's lying.* Then Autumn told Billie she would *be careful and let Summer in slowly.*"

"Let Summer into what slowly?" Connie asks.

"I don't know," Nadira replies. "I only heard a snippet of their conversation."

Were Autumn and Billie talking about letting Summer into the family business? According to Maria, Summer wanted Autumn to hire her and give her half of their mother's share. Or maybe Autumn meant she would let Summer into her heart slowly? After years of no contact, the sisters could have had some issues to work through. I need to speak to Billie and Autumn again and find out the context of the conversation Nadira overheard.

"Who worked at the juice bar last night after dinner?" I ask, trying to figure out who else I should add to my to-be-questioned list.

"Me," Nadira replies. "I filled in as a last-minute favour for Maria."

"Why would a world-renowned chef fill in at a juice bar?" I ask.

"Maria was desperate," Nadira replies. "I was in the middle of today's meal prep, but she begged me. She covered the juice bar until I finished cleaning the kitchen and took over. She said she double-booked the staff member who was scheduled to work. She said the schedule was a mess. I agreed to fill in for thirty minutes while Maria sorted out the schedule and found someone to take over for me. But I ended up working there until the blackout."

"That means you made Hannah's smoothie last night," Connie concludes, clapping her hands once in front of her chest. "I had a sip. It was delicious." She smiles and crinkles her nose.

"Thank you," Nadira says. "Yes, I made Hannah's Green Powerhouse smoothie, but I can't take credit. I didn't create the smoothie menu, they established it before I started working here."

"Did you make Autumn and Summer's smoothies too?" I ask, intentionally not mentioning the specific smoothies they ordered.

Nadira shakes her head. "Billie visited the smoothie bar. I don't remember the exact time, but she was there before Hannah."

"What did Billie order?" I ask.

"Three Green Powerhouse smoothies," Nadira replies. "It's by far the most popular item on the smoothie menu."

"Did Billie customize any of the smoothies?" I ask, in case she requested an additional dark green, leafy ingredient.

"Nope. She just ordered three Green Powerhouse smoothies."

"Was Billie alone?" I ask.

"She approached the juice bar alone," Nadira replies. "But a twin was waiting for her several feet away."

"Which twin?" I ask.

"Beats me," Nadira admits, shrugging. "I can't tell them apart. I spend most of my time in the kitchen. I have very little interaction with guests. Except Autumn. I've had more than enough interaction with Autumn."

# CHAPTER 19

"How did you get in?" I ask. "It's the most popular treatment at the resort. Hot Stone massages are booked months in advance."

Earlier, when Connie and I spoke with Autumn, I made a flippant remark about getting a hot stone massage. Connie picked up on it, cancelled the afternoon treatments we had already booked, and scheduled hot-stone massages instead.

"I can be persuasive when the situation warrants it," Connie replies, her chin held high. "Also, the receptionist said they've had a few cancellations today. Apparently, some guests have lost their appetite for spa treatments since Summer's death."

With time to kill until our massages, we take a stroll through the gardens and enjoy the warm, spring air. Like most people who live with long, cold winters, we don't take spring for granted. We use any excuse to soak up the sunshine and mild temperatures.

"What's your opinion of Nadira, my dear?" Connie asks, as we wander through the herb garden, stopping to read the small information placards about each sprouting herb.

"She's a talented chef," I reply.

"That's not what I mean"—Connie swats my arm playfully—"Do you think she killed Summer?"

"We can't rule her out," I say. "She admits she didn't like Autumn, and she admits Autumn threatened to slander her and ruin her career. That's motive. She also admits she couldn't tell Summer and Autumn apart. Autumn could be right about Summer's murder being a case of mistaken identity."

"And let's not forget, Nadira had access to the smoothie ingredients," Connie reminds me.

"But if she made three identical smoothies, how could she ensure her intended victim would get the poisoned one?" I ask. "Unless Billie told her two of the smoothies were for the twins, how could Nadira have known two smoothies were for Autumn and Summer?"

"Maybe Nadira and Billie were in on it together," Connie suggests.

"If Billie and Nadira worked together to kill Summer, that would imply they knew each other before Billie and the twins checked into the spa," I surmise.

"Committing murder together is a commitment," Connie advises. "Murder is a big secret to trust with someone you don't know well."

We stop while Connie photographs the tulips.

"Maria had access to the smoothie ingredients too," I say. "She worked at the smoothie bar until Nadira relieved her."

"Maybe Maria murdered Summer and planted the chef at the smoothie bar to implicate Nadira as the killer."

"What motive would Maria have?" I ask. "Why would she want Summer dead?"

"Not Summer, my dear, Autumn," Connie clarifies. "If

Autumn follows through on her threat to slander Nadira and leave negative reviews online, those reviews and accusations would stain the spa's reputation too."

"You're right," I agree. "Earlier, Maria mentioned that she's saving to buy a house. She wants to move and find a job that doesn't require her to live on site. Bad reviews, accusations about contaminated food, and sick guests wouldn't look good on her resume," I speculate.

If Maria killed Summer, would Twyla help her cover up the crime? Love is a powerful motive, and from what I witnessed outside Maria's apartment this morning, Twyla and Maria love each other. Twyla is in the perfect position to manipulate the investigation. She could point the evidence away from Maria or even destroy evidence that implicates her.

She's the only law enforcement officer here. Twyla oversees the collection and preservation of all the evidence. What if, when Tamara and I gave the baggie of spotted water hemlock to Twyla, we pointed the finger of suspicion at Maria, foiling Twyla's plan to pin Summer's murder on someone else? What if Maria's fingerprints are on the baggie? This would explain Twyla's intimidation tactic when she warned me to stop asking questions. She was protecting Maria.

Or was Twyla protecting herself?

Did Twyla kill Summer? Is she a crooked cop? Does she work for the family of the man Summer testified against? Autumn said the man who Summer testified against, and his father, are dead, so their vendetta against Summer died with them. But what if that's not true? What if other family members kept the grudge alive? Biding their time, patiently and quietly waiting for Summer to reveal herself by resuming her old life and identity so they could kill her.

Maybe Maria helped Twyla by giving her access to the

spa. I wonder if Maria is aware of Summer's history with the police and the witness protection program? Twyla admitted she knew about Summer's past. Maybe she confided in Maria. Goodness knows, Eric confides in me and discloses things we both know he shouldn't. Twyla and Maria could have a similar dynamic.

"We should make our way inside," Connie says, distracting me from my thoughts. "If we start now, we'll be fashionably punctual for our massage appointments."

We circle the cluster of yet-to-bloom rose bushes in the centre of the garden that act as a roundabout, and veer toward the main building. As we meander past the hummingbird garden, I can't stop thinking about Twyla's coincidental arrival at the spa just before Summer died. She said she was checking on the spa because of the storm, but her trip to SoulSpring Spa and Retreat is suspicious. Her arrival coincided with a murder, and she made the drive in treacherous conditions. Twyla has no verifiable alibi. She's unaccounted for from just before the blackout until after the generators kicked in.

Maria was also unaccounted for much of that time. Was that a coincidence, or part of their premeditated plan? Maria knew Summer was in the sauna. She has access to the appointments for each spa treatment, and because Autumn visited the front desk to ask for pain medication, Maria knew Summer was alone.

Why did Twyla really come to the spa last night? Did her boss dispatch her to check on the remote location? After finding out about Twyla and Maria's personal relationship, I assumed the real reason for Twyla's visit on a dark and stormy night was to make sure Maria was safe. But maybe Twyla's motivation was neither direct orders, nor her love for Maria. Maybe she came here to kill Summer, and the power failure and storm damage were unplanned coincidences. I'm lost in my own thoughts, contemplating whether Maria and Twyla acted together or if one of them killed Summer alone, when Connie hooks her arm through mine and speaks.

"I have one more surprise for you, my dear," she teases. "I arranged for you to have the same massage therapist as Billie."

"You did?" I ask, wide-eyed. "Maybe I can confirm Billie's story about leaving with the massage therapist when the power went out. Wherever she went after the power failure, it wasn't the Epicurean Bistro."

"Billie's grief and shock about Summer's death seem genuine," Connie observes. "But it can't be easy being best friends with twin sisters. Billie must have felt left out sometimes. Summer left for a decade, and Billie was used to having Autumn to herself."

"I've had the same thought," I confess. "I'm sure at least a small part of Billie was jealous when Summer returned. I'd also like to know more about the snippet of conversation Nadira overheard between Billie and Autumn. Did Billie warn Autumn to be careful trusting her sister because she had a reason to question Summer's intentions, or was she jealous of Autumn and Summer's reconnection?"

"I don't know," Connie replies. "But if we noticed Billie's late arrival, Twyla noticed, too, and has already asked her about it." We slow our already leisurely pace and lower our voices as we get closer to the massage area. "Billie had access to the smoothies," Connie points out. "In fact, one could argue Billie *controlled* the smoothies. She ordered them, carried them away from the juice bar, and she could have chosen which smoothie to give to each twin."

"But if Nadira was at the Smoothie bar, and one twin was a few feet away, Billie couldn't have poisoned the smoothie without Nadira or the twin seeing her."

"What if the twin waiting near the smoothie bar was Autumn?" Connie suggests. "What if Autumn and Billie went to the smoothie bar together?"

"Why would Autumn and Billie conspire to kill Summer?"

"We already know Billie's motive, my dear. Jealousy. Maybe Billie convinced Autumn to help."

"Autumn doesn't strike me as someone who would be easy to manipulate," I reply. "If you'd seen her shouting at Nadira yesterday, you'd know what I mean. But you could be on to something. When the twins' mother died, Autumn became the sole owner of the family business. Summer wanted Autumn to hire her and give her half of their mother's shares."

"Maybe Autumn didn't want to share," Connie suggests.

"They also argued about their mother. Autumn blamed Summer for their mother's declining health and eventual death. She said the stress of Summer's testimony and losing contact when she went into witness protection, triggered the decline in her health and, ultimately, her death. Autumn also resented being their mother's sole caregiver."

"Did Autumn and Summer resolve these issues before Summer died?" Connie asks.

"I don't know," I reply.

"If Autumn is innocent of her sister's murder, the weight of her mother's death and her sister's murder are heavy enough without the added burden of unresolved issues."

"I know," I agree. "My heart breaks for Autumn and everything she's endured."

"But?" Connie asks. "I sense a *but*."

"But something Autumn did last night still bothers me." We stop outside the door. "Why did she visit the front desk for pain medication?" I ask in a whisper. "She suffers with chronic migraines and carries prescription medication with her. She even brought it to the deck today. She said the prescription medication is a last resort because of the side effects. If that's true, why does she carry the prescription medication but not ibuprofen, or acetaminophen, or whatever? It doesn't make sense."

"Why did I pack two tubes of toothpaste and forget my toothbrush?" Connie asks. "Whatever the reason, it sounds like you still have more questions than answers, my dear."

I intend to find the answers.

# CHAPTER 20

I SIT on the massage table in the centre of the dimly lit room and smooth the white cotton sheets around me. I'm sure this is ambient lighting and not an energy-saving tactic. Shelves of folded, white linens line one wall, and shelves displaying crystals, self-care books, and other accessories that promote relaxation line another. The third wall features a sink and cabinet with a hotel land-line phone. The emergency exit takes up most of the fourth wall. Soft guitar music plays from strategically mounted speakers that someone painted to camouflage with the walls. A familiar guitar chord catches my ear. It's from the chorus of a popular song, rearranged and slowed down. I hum along to the familiar tune, trying to place it. The exact moment the song title and artist pops into my head—*In My Life* by The Beatles—the massage room door opens and a smiley, short-haired, petite young woman in wire-framed, round glasses greets me.

"Namaste." She brings her hands together under her chin, averting her gaze downward for an instant.

"Namaste," I return, giving a slight nod, but skipping the prayer hands.

The massage therapist's name tag reads, *Logan S.*

On tippy toes, Logan reaches for the top shelf and feels around. When she lowers her heels to the floor, she's holding a red barbecue lighter and a box of incense. She slides an incense stick from the box, positions it in the wooden incense burner, and ignites it. Logan blows out the flame, leaving a tiny orange ember tip. A thin line of smoke dances toward the ceiling.

"We have the same last name," Logan informs me pointing to her name tag. "Except I spell it S-L-O-N-E."

"We were one letter away from running into each other at a family reunion," I joke.

Logan discovers more similarities. Besides our surnames being homonyms, our first names are two syllables, five letters, have a hard *g* in the middle, and end with *an*. The similarities intrigue the massage therapist, and she wonders out loud if there could be a universal significance. As Logan ruminates over the coincidences of our names, searching for a deeper meaning behind us meeting and a message from the universe, I hope the bond we've forged over our similar names increases the likelihood that Logan will be comfortable talking to me about Billie's massage last night.

The aroma from the incense stick hits my nose.

"Citrus?" I ask, inhaling and changing the subject.

"Yes," Logan replies, returning the incense and lighter to the top shelf. "It's a blend of frankincense, orange, and vetiver. This combination of aromas promotes relaxation and relieves stress. If you like it, you can buy it in the gift shop near the main entrance." Panic flashes across her face. "Is it OK?" she blurts, her eyes bulging. "I should've asked first. I'm sorry."

Logan motions to extinguish the incense stick.

"No," I say, stopping her before she covers the burning ember. "It's fine. It's a lovely scent."

"Are you sure?" she confirms.

"Positive." I smile. "Don't worry. If I didn't like it, I would tell you."

Logan sucks in a deep breath and lets it out slowly.

"Last night a client reacted to the incense," Logan admits. "I think it made her sick, but she was too polite to admit it. She turned a weird shade of green and broke out in a sweat."

Though not a description of her appearance, Logan's description of her client's nausea matches Billie to a tee.

"I think that was my friend, Billie," I say, exaggerating our relationship status.

"Right," Logan confirms. "It was Billie. Is she feeling better today?"

"She's fine," I assure the worried massage therapist. "I don't think the incense caused Billie's nausea. She's had a tummy bug for a couple of days."

"Well, regardless," Logan announces. "I learned a valuable lesson. I shouldn't introduce aromas without asking first."

Logan asks me a series of health questions, then explains how the hot stone massage will work. I fill out a brief questionnaire, sign a liability waiver, then Logan leaves the room while I undress.

"Come in," I say when she taps on the door.

"Ready?" she asks.

"Ready," I reply.

While Logan washes her hands, I shift one last time, ensuring I'm comfy, and hope I don't get a hard-to-ignore itchy nose partway through the massage.

"So, what made you decide to book a hot stone massage?" Logan asks, placing a small, warm stone between my eyebrows.

"My friend, Billie, suggested it," I reply, moving my

mouth as little as possible as Logan places a small stone on each of my cheeks.

"Hmmm," Logan mutters, balancing a small stone on my chin. "I'm surprised she had such a positive experience. The power went out right after I started her massage. I had to stop."

"She told me," I mumble, trying to not disturb the stones.

"I feel terrible about that," Logan says. "First her massage started late, then it ended early."

"Started late?" I mumble, trying to make eye contact with Logan without moving my head.

"Palms up," Logan says, ignoring my question.

I turn my palms toward the sky.

"Why did Billie's massage start late?" I ask again, hoping that Logan's experience administering hot stone massages has helped her to develop the dentist-like ability to understand the mumbles of people who can't move their mouth.

"It was partly my fault, and partly Billie's," Logan explains, pressing a warm stone onto each of my palms. "When I left the room while Billie undressed, I found my friend crying in the hall."

"Oh, no!" I respond. "Why?"

"She had a huge fight with her boyfriend on the phone. She accused him of cheating. They almost broke up! I consoled my friend and left Billie longer than I should. When my friend's cell phone rang—it was her boyfriend—I excused myself to check on Billie, but she wasn't here."

"What?" I open my mouth too wide, and the stone on my chin slides onto the massage table beside my head. "Where was she?"

"Careful," Logan says replacing the fallen stone. "I

don't know where she went. I knocked, but Billie didn't answer. I opened the door to check on her, and she was gone. She must have left through the back door"—Logan points to the emergency exit—"because my friend and I were in the hall, and there's no way Billie could have slipped past without us noticing."

"Wouldn't an alarm go off if Billie left through the emergency exit?"

"No," Logan replies. "The emergency exits don't have alarms, and they're only locked at night. Employees use them all the time to get from one part of the spa to another. It's quicker than navigating through the building."

"What did you do when Billie disappeared?"

"I went back to my friend in the hall," Logan replies, placing a warm stone on my right collarbone. "She was still talking to her boyfriend, and their conversation was kind of loud. I had to ask her to keep it down."

She places a warm stone on my left collarbone.

"Then what?"

"My friend went back to the sauna reception desk, and I knocked on Billie's door again."

Excuse me?! Logan's friend left the reception desk in the spa area? This explains why the sauna attendant didn't see the killer return to the sauna to pose Summer's body.

"Your friend worked at the sauna reception desk last night?" I confirm as Logan lays two larger, warm stones along my breast bone.

"Yup." Logan nods. "Where that guest turned up dead. She never saw the body though."

I gasp, but get it under control when the stones on my face wiggle. Luckily, they don't fall.

"How is your friend doing today?" I ask.

"She's OK," Logan replies, using a large, warm, oily stone to massage my arm. "It was a misunderstanding. She made up with her boyfriend before we lost cell service and the power went out."

I wasn't asking about her friend's love life. I'm curious how Logan's friend is holding up after having a guest die in the sauna during her shift. But I'm also kind of curious about the boyfriend situation, so I probe further.

"What kind of misunderstanding?"

"A guest told my friend that a massage therapist was bragging about stealing my friend's boyfriend. My friend asked the guest which therapist, but the guest didn't know her name. She gave my friend a vague description and told her she could catch them together in a massage therapy room, at that moment."

"Did she catch them?"

"Nope. The massage rooms were full of guests having legitimate massages. When she didn't find him, she called him on her cell phone. They were arguing when the call was dropped because cell service was unreliable during the storm. That's when I found her in the hall."

"Your friend must've been away from the sauna for quite a while," I surmise.

"I guess," Logan says, rubbing an oil-infused hot stone into my leg muscles.

"Which guest told your friend her boyfriend was cheating?"

"An anonymous guest," Logan replies. "The woman called from an internal line. She didn't give her name, and the landline went down before my friend could ask anything."

Did the landline cut out, or did the guest hang up before the sauna attendant figured out their identity? If I was a betting woman, I bet the killer called the sauna attendant with a made-up story to lure her away from her post. Then the killer returned to the sauna, confirmed Summer was dead, and positioned her body to delay the discovery.

But how did the killer know what would enrage her enough to leave her post? How did the killer know about the attendant's boyfriend? Or that she would believe he was cheating?

Billie could've used the landline in this room to call the sauna, convince the attendant to abandon her post, then use the emergency exits to sneak to the sauna area and sneak back again before Logan returned. Nerves could have caused the nausea that Logan witnessed. If Billie was about to commit murder, she was bound to be anxious and sick to her stomach.

"Did you and Billie leave together after the power went out?" I ask.

"Yup. We were the last two people here," Logan replies. "I was the key holder last night. It was my job to turn off everything and lock up. I continued Billie's massage as long as possible after the power failure because I felt bad that we had just gotten started. But the stones cool down fast without the heater, and I couldn't see in the dark. We left together, but my friend was waiting for me. I turned to say goodnight to Billie and apologize again for her interrupted massage, but she was gone." Logan shrugs. "Ready to flip over so I can do your back?"

She removes the stones from my body and I turn onto my stomach under the white sheet.

"Besides the many physical benefits, hot stone massage also has mental health benefits," Logan informs me. "It promotes stress reduction and better sleep quality, which results in improved mental clarity. The benefits will be more obvious to you tomorrow, after a good night's sleep."

"I already feel them," I say. "You've given me more mental clarity than I've had since I checked in."

# CHAPTER 21

"It sounds like your hot stone massage was very informative," Connie comments.

"Thank you again," I say, thanking her for at least the fifth time since our massages ended. "If you hadn't arranged for Logan to do my massage, we wouldn't know about Billie's disappearing act from the massage room or the coincidental disappearance of the sauna attendant."

"Hey, did you guys hear the helicopter?" April asks, power-walking toward us.

Connie and I halt at the stairwell entrance, shaking our heads.

"There was a helicopter!" Tamara announces, jogging to catch up.

"Did it land?" Connie asks, pushing open the stairwell door.

"No," Tamara replies. "It flew around in circles." She makes circles in the air with her index finger. "It only hovered for a couple of minutes."

"It was a police helicopter," April says as we climb the

first flight of stairs. "Maria said they're checking on the spa and making sure we're OK after last night's storm and power failure and everything.

"Did they drop off a satellite phone?" I ask.

"No one said anything about a satellite phone," April replies. "But at least they know we're stranded, and they're trying to get to us."

"Maria said the helicopter can't land near the spa or fly too low because of the mountains or something," Tamara adds.

We climb the stairs, each of us summarizing and reviewing the spa treatments we received this afternoon. When we reach the third floor, I hold the door while Connie, Tamara, then April file into the hall. We greet the spa employee who's stationed on our floor. She's sitting cross-legged on the floor near the elevator. She picks up a magazine from the pile on the floor next to her and leafs through it.

Connie and Tamara are several paces ahead of April and me when we pass Autumn and Billie's room.

"I'm glad they're eating," Connie comments, looking back at me and pointing to the cart of empty dishes outside Autumn and Billie's room.

I glance at the empty dinner plates on the food cart. One plate is smeared with remnants of a white sauce, and the other plate is empty except for a lamb chop bone picked clean of meat.

"Hopefully those empty dishes are a sign that Autumn is keeping her strength up, and Billie's nausea is improving," Connie observes.

April and Tamara stop at their door, and Connie and I stop at ours. We agree on a time to meet for dinner, then unlock our respective doors and step inside.

"Finally! You're back!" Hannah rushes toward Connie

and me with her cell phone in her hand and grips my arm, tugging me forward.

"What's wrong?" I follow my daughter's urgent gaze and find Twyla at the other end. "Why are you here?"

"I wanted to find you, Mum, but I didn't want to leave her here alone. She was already inside the room when Rachel and I got back from having our ears candled." She holds up her phone and scans each of our faces. "I'm recording audio and video footage of everyone and everything in Room 308 at the SoulSpring Spa and Retreat. Today's date is Saturday May, 7th, and the time is 3:27p.m." She points at me and nods, like a director cuing my line.

"Well?" I ask, glaring at Twyla.

"I'm searching for something." She gestures to the open suitcase on the bed next to her.

"In my belongings?" I ask. "Without a warrant?"

Hannah raises her phone and points it at Twyla, waiting for an answer. In my peripheral vision, I see the red dot on Hannah's screen that indicates she's recording.

"I don't need a warrant because I believe this search is necessary to prevent evidence of a crime from being contaminated, lost, or destroyed."

"What evidence?" Connie asks.

Twyla says nothing.

"You have to tell us what you're searching for," Hannah pipes in. "I study law and my dad is an attorney."

Twyla squints at me. "You told me your husband is a cop."

"Hannah's dad isn't my husband," I explain. "What are you searching for?"

"A key," Twyla says. "The key to sauna three is missing. No one has seen it since last night."

"Why would I have it?"

"According to your statement, the keyring was in your possession last night," Twyla states.

"There were at least a dozen keys on the keyring," I recall. "I tried a few, but they didn't fit. April broke the window with the fire extinguisher and unlocked the door from the inside."

"Where did you put the key ring?" Twyla asks.

"This is in my statement," I remind her. "I tossed it onto the reception desk. I didn't touch it again."

"Did you remove any keys from the keyring?"

"No."

"Did you see April remove any keys from the keyring?"

"No."

"Did you see anyone touch the keyring last night?"

"Yes," I reply. "Maria. Remember? She used the keys to unlock the sauna where you questioned us. I also saw her trying to fit different keys into the sauna three lock when you taped the broken window. And you had the key ring when you unlocked the door to sauna four."

Twyla's jaw clenches, and the muscles around her eyes tense. My insinuation that her or Maria could have taken the key will probably make Twyla hate me more than she does already, but she asked me a question and I gave her an honest answer. It's not my fault she doesn't like it.

"Anyone else?"

"No," I reply. "The sauna attendant would have used it to lock the door before she left. Did you ask her?"

"She said sauna three was already locked."

"If she didn't lock it, who did?" Hannah asks.

"You know she left her post, right?" I ask. "The sauna attendant visited the massage area because an anonymous caller tipped her off about her boyfriend having a secret tryst in a massage room. She was gone for a while.

Long enough for the killer to return to the sauna, stage Summer's body, and steal the key you're looking for."

Twyla blinks. "And?"

Her expression and tone give nothing away. I can't tell if this is new information to Twyla. If the police academy teaches a course on giving the perfect poker face, Twyla aced it.

"Listen, Megan"—Twyla inhales an exasperated breath and blows it out—"I'm not here to brainstorm potential scenarios with you. We aren't partners. You aren't even an investigator. If you don't have the missing key, consent to the search."

"You're going to search with or without my consent," I cede. "Do whatever you need to do, Twyla, but I'm not letting you out of my sight, and Hannah is recording every move you make."

"This is too much conflict for me," Connie announces. "If anyone needs me, I'll be next door making a cocktail with whatever alcohol I find in April and Tamara's mini-bar." She slides a strap off her shoulder and opens her tote bag, looking at Twyla. "Would you like to search it before I leave, Officer?"

"No thank you, ma'am." Twyla nods and gives Connie a slight smile. "That won't be necessary."

"Are you searching every guest or just me?" I ask as Twyla inspects the contents of my toiletries bag.

"Everyone who was at the scene last night," she replies, shoving my toiletries back inside the bag, then opening the cabinet under the sink and using her flash-light to search inside.

"How did you find out the sauna was unattended?" Twyla asks as we leave the bathroom. "Were you snooping again?"

Did she just roll her eyes? I make a mental note to

check Hannah's footage later to see if the eye roll was real or if I imagined it.

"I found out by coincidence during an unrelated conversation." Calling it a coincidence might be an exaggeration, but I don't want to give Twyla the satisfaction of being right about my snooping. "I know you think I'm a bored busybody who inserts herself in other people's business, but that's not entirely true."

Twyla's hands freeze, and she looks at me.

"Not *entirely* true?" She smirks, amused at her own observation. "You admit you're a bored busybody, and it's at least part of your motivation." She chuckles, picking up my tote bag and dumps the contents onto the bed. "Who needs this many knitting needles?" she asks under her breath. "Two hands should mean two knitting needles... right?" She holds up the two-point-two-five-millimetre, thirty-two-inch circular needles. "What the?" she mutters. "And so much yarn. Why?" she whispers, creasing her forehead and appraising the small yarn collection scattered across the bed.

"I like to have multiple projects to choose from," I say, defensive of my excessive knitting accessories. "Please don't drop any stitches."

Twyla glares at me like I'm speaking a foreign language.

"The needles in your hand are for knitting in the round."

She looks at me and blinks twice.

"For knitting tubes," I explain. She scans the yarn and knitting notions again. "I own a knitting store. Of course I have a lot of knitting stuff," I say, as a last attempt to justify the contents of my bag.

Ignoring my comment, Twyla feels around inside the empty bag, then inspects it with her flashlight before examining the contents one at a time and returning them to the bag.

"I disagree with the *bored* part of your assessment," I clarify as Twyla abandons my tote bag and steps toward me on her way to the minibar. I step backward out of her way and step on Hannah's foot as she films over my shoulder. I mutter an apology to my daughter, then chase Twyla to the minibar with Hannah limping behind me, aiming her phone at the police officer. "I am a bit of a busybody," I confess. "It's a small-town quirk. That's how we are in Harmony Lake." I shrug. "Everybody knows everybody. We care about each other and look out for one another. We stick our noses in each other's business. Small towns have boundary issues. At least my small town does."

"I knew you were from a small town as soon as I met you. You give off small-town, middle-class, and meddlesome vibes," she says. "You don't have to tell me about small towns and boundary issues, Megan." Twyla slams the minibar shut and moves on to the closet, pulling the spare linens and pillows off the high shelf, shaking each one in case I've hidden the key inside the perfectly folded sheets or between the down pillow and cotton pillowcase. "I grew up in a small town. I'm an expert on the small-town mentality."

Does Twyla hate me because I remind her of the small-town people she grew up with? Did her experience growing up in a small town leave her wounded and now she's bleeding—metaphorically—on me?

"I'm sorry if I represent everything you hate about small towns," I say. "My goal isn't to antagonize you, Twyla. I want to solve Summer's murder so you can cross Hannah and me off the suspect list. You and I have the same goal. We both want you to solve Summer's murder and arrest her killer. If I find out something useful, isn't that a good thing? I'm trying to help, not be a nuisance."

"Yet you are a nuisance."

Shaking my head, I turn to Hannah's phone and throw my hands in the air with a huff.

"You tried," Hannah mouths, then gives me a sympathetic smile before re-focussing her phone on Twyla as she removes the rod from the closet and shines her flashlight inside, searching for the key she thinks I hid there.

# CHAPTER 22

"SHE'S TURNING over the room next door now," Connie says when she returns from April and Tamara's room.

Twyla finished searching our hotel room and, satisfied that I'm not hiding the key to sauna three, moved along to her next search.

Hannah opens her mouth to say something, but Connie interrupts before she utters a syllable.

"Don't worry," Connie reassures Hannah, "I told Rachel to record every move Twyla makes. I even told her to say what you did at the beginning, where you name all the people who are present, record their faces, and advise us you're filming."

"Thank you." Hannah smiles, and her shoulders drop.

Twyla put everything back *where* she found it, but not *how* she found it. I go through my belongings, checking and adjusting each item.

"Are you all right, my dear?" Connie asks.

"I think so." I nod with a light sigh. "I didn't expect to feel violated by a police search. Twyla touched every-thing. Even my underwear and the emergency tampons in my purse."

"She was doing her job," Connie reminds me. "I'm sure she didn't enjoy it either. Though she could have been more pleasant. Touching strangers' personal effects must be uncomfortable, even if it is her job."

I'm sure Connie is right. Twyla might dislike me, but I don't feel like she harasses me. Whenever she's nearby, I get the sense Twyla would rather be anywhere other than in my presence.

"I wish I could talk to Eric," I say.

"It must be hard not to have contact with him," Connie sympathizes. "You are newlyweds, after all. I'm sure he misses you just as much as you miss him."

"Yeah," I agree. "I miss him a lot. Right now, I miss his access to the police database. He could make inquiries about Summer's history in the witness protection program. It's too coincidental that someone murdered her almost as soon as she resurfaced, using her old identity and reclaiming her old life. Also, Eric could help me with Twyla. How should I approach her? I don't care if she likes me. I just want her to be less hostile and not write off everything I say as the blathering of a bored busybody."

"Nooooo!" a woman's voice shouts from somewhere down the hall.

"What was that?" I look back and forth between Connie and Hannah, who both shrug.

"It's not mine! I've never seen it before!"

"That's the same voice," Hannah hisses.

"It's coming from the hall," Connie says.

Hannah heads for the door with her phone poised to record.

Curious faces and craned necks line both sides of the third-floor hallway.

"I swear I've never seen it before," Billie pleads, her eyes wide and her hands trembling.

"Then how did it get inside the lining of your suitcase?" Twyla asks, holding a shiny silver key between her gloved thumb and forefinger.

"How can I explain how the key got there if I didn't put it there?" Billie asks. "You're the cop. Aren't you supposed to figure out how it got there?"

"I assume Twyla found the key for sauna three," April whispers as we creep toward each other along the wall between our rooms, meeting in the middle.

"In Billie's stuff?" I ask.

"Looks like it," April replies.

"Anyone could've…"

"I'm sorry, Megan." Twyla glowers at me. "Is my investigation interrupting your conversation?" she barks, calling me out in front of everyone. "Do you have something you'd like to add? I'm sure everyone would love to hear it!" She gestures at the onlookers.

Maria taps Twyla's shoulder, and Twyla turns to look at her. Maria shakes her head. With her customer-service focussed attitude, I'm sure Maria won't tolerate Twyla's rudeness to guests.

I clear my throat.

"Someone else could have planted the key," I say. "Didn't Autumn lose her room key earlier?"

"That's right," Connie says. "Autumn and another guest bumped into each other and spilled their bags, commingling their belongings. The other guest accidentally left with Autumn's room key. Maria had to let Autumn into her room."

"This wouldn't happen if you put room numbers on the keys," Hannah adds.

"Thank you for the observation, ladies," Twyla says with an exaggerated, artificial smile. "Very helpful."

I roll my eyes and shake my head at her sarcastic comment.

"I don't have the key anymore," the doctor calls from down the hall. "I returned it to Maria when she found me and explained the confusion."

That's at least four people, aside from Billie, who could have planted the key: Autumn, Maria, the doctor, and Twyla.

"Key?" asks a curious guest.

"What key?" asks another guest.

"There's a missing key?"

"Whose key?"

"Key for what?"

The chatter of the guests grows louder as they migrate away from their doors and gather in small groups. The employee by the elevator seems unaffected, still cross-legged, still leafing through magazines. I wonder if she saw anyone other than Billie and Autumn enter their room?

"Excuse me!" Twyla shouts over the din of the crowd. "We need to keep the hall clear. Please return to your rooms, continue downstairs for dinner, or go somewhere else. Until further notice, this hallway is for walking through, not standing in. Do your socializing and gossiping elsewhere."

The chatter increases in volume again as guests make hasty arrangements to meet elsewhere. Then at least a dozen doors bang and thud as guests do as they're told and return to their rooms.

"Well, this should make for interesting dinner conversation!" Connie declares.

# CHAPTER 23

SUNDAY, May 8th

As my eyes adjust to the darkness, I remember I'm not at home. This isn't my bed. I'm at the SoulSpring Spa and Retreat.

"Hannah?" I whisper, wiping the sleep from my eyes. "I just had the strangest dream."

I stretch my arm in search of Hannah but find her empty pillow instead.

Where is she?

A *hiss* from my right. Pipes? I prop myself up on my elbows and scan the darkness for clues. The door to Connie's room is closed and dark. The bathroom door is closed, and a strip of light shines through the bottom. Hannah!

I fumble for the lamp on the nightstand, then remember that we unplugged it to save electricity. We weren't sure how much electricity a bedside lamp consumes when it's plugged in, and we couldn't ask the internet, so we erred on the side of caution and unplugged even the most useful modern conveniences.

As I feel my way through the unfamiliar room, the hissing gets louder.

"Dad! I hope you get this!" Hannah whispers as I'm about to tap on the door.

Dad? Adam lives and works in Harmony Lake. He's not in there with Hannah, which can only mean one thing…

"Service!" I declare. "You're talking to Dad?" I gasp as Hannah throws open the bathroom door. "You have service?" I stare at the phone pressed against her ear.

With the glow from the vanity lights around the mirror lighting my way, I rush to the nightstand where my phone is charging.

"I got a text," Hannah explains, following me with her phone still pressed to her ear. "It was from Dad." She pulls the phone away from her ear and looks at the screen. "No service again." She releases a heavy sigh and drops her phone on the bed. "I couldn't sleep," Hannah explains. "I was tossing and turning when the screen lit up. At first, I thought I imagined it. Like, people lost in the desert imagining a Starbucks, or a waterfall, or whatever."

"A mirage?" I ask. "You thought your flashing phone was a mirage?"

"I think she means hallucination," Connie interjects, tying the belt of her bathrobe.

"Right," Hannah says. "I thought I was hallucinating. Hallucinations are a symptom of cell phone withdrawal, right?" She looks back and forth from me to Connie. "I don't know for sure because I can't check the internet. But since we lost cell service, Rachel and I keep hearing our cell phones ring or feeling them vibrate in our pockets. But it's just our imaginations. But this time it was real. It wasn't a hallucination. I got a text from Dad." She picks up her phone from the bed and unlocks it, turning it toward me. "See?"

**Dad: Help is coming. Call me as soon as you have cell service. I love you, Princess.** Followed by a heart emoji, a crown emoji, and a happy face emoji.

The time stamp is today at 2:14 a.m.

Below Adam's message to Hannah is her response.

**Hannah: Hi Dad! I love you too.** Followed by a heart emoji and a smiley face emoji.

Time stamp is today at 2:16 a.m.

Under Hannah's response is a small red triangle with a red exclamation point inside.

"Does this mean your reply didn't go through?" I ask, pointing at the foreboding little icon.

Hannah nods.

"I lost service again before it got through." She smiles sadly. "I didn't want to wake you, so I took my phone into the bathroom and stared at it, hoping it would work again."

"Did it?" I ask.

"A few minutes after my failed text to Dad, my phone rang. It was him. I lost service again before I could say hello. He must've tried to call me because he saw I had read his text message."

"But I heard you talking to him," I say.

"I called him back. It went straight to voicemail. I talked fast because I didn't know how much time I would have. I told him about the storm, Summer's murder, the poison we found, and about Twyla treating us like suspects."

She shakes her head and looks at her phone like it's the most disappointing cell phone in existence. "My phone says, *No Service* again. I don't know when I lost the call. Maybe he'll get the entire message, maybe only a bit." She shrugs. "Maybe none."

"Let's hope he gets it," I say, pulling my daughter into a hug. "As soon as the road is safe enough, we're out of here," I assure her, rubbing her back. "I don't care what time of day it is." I pick up my phone. 2:42 a.m. and I have a text notification from Eric.

"I have a missed text!" I unlock my phone. The words *No Service* span the top right corner of the screen where the signal strength should be.

**Eric: Hey babe! Help will arrive soon. Call me as soon as you get service. Day or night. I love you.** Followed by multiple heart emojis in multiple colours.

"They must be close to restoring our cellular service," Connie says. "I'll be right back. I want to check my phone."

Connie turns and disappears into her dark bedroom. I plug in the lamp on the nightstand and turn it on.

TERRIFIED OF MISSING a fleeting window of precious 5G data, we don't go back to bed. Instead, we knock on the door that connects our adjoining rooms and wake up April, Tamara, and Rachel. They discover missed texts from their son Zach and don't go back to bed either. We sit together in exhausted anticipation, constantly monitoring our phones for signs of life and checking the battery strength.

When I comment on how fast my phone battery drains, despite not using it, Hannah and Rachel explain that the lack of cell service and Wi-Fi doesn't mean our phones aren't using any battery. In fact, according to them, the opposite is true. The phone's constant search for an available signal drains the battery faster than normal use with a stable signal. This is the same logic behind our decision to unplug everything in our rooms.

"Happy Mother's Day, ladies," Connie announces as the light of dawn casts a soft glow in the room.

"Happy Mother's Day," we respond with the same enthusiasm as five exhausted sloths.

We pass the next few minutes hugging and exchanging cards. Hannah gives cards to Connie and me, then she gives me a card from Adam. Rachel gives cards to April, Tamara, and Connie. Then, April, Tamara, and I give cards to Connie.

I forgot today is Mother's Day. The entire point of this weekend was to spend time together, celebrating the special women in our lives and the deep connections we share. Instead, we're stranded in luxury accommodation, halfway up a mountain, with a murderer, fighting to prove our innocence and hoping Twyla arrests Summer's killer before they claim another victim.

# CHAPTER 24

TAMARA AND CONNIE went to the Epicurean Bistro to claim a rare and coveted window seat.

"All the best tables will be taken," Connie lamented to encourage Tamara to hurry and get dressed. "I want to enjoy the view while we eat. I refuse to sit by the buffet again. Did you notice people walk faster toward the food than away from it?"

Motivated by our brief contact with the outside world, Hannah and Rachel gathered their homemade antennae and went for a pre-breakfast trek farther up the mountain—again—in search of a signal.

April and I retreat to our respective rooms to shower and get dressed before we join everyone for breakfast.

My cell phone is on the counter, screen up, plugged into the outlet near the sink. Every so often, I glance at it, in case we get another surprise surge of 5G service.

I work the conditioner through my hair, twist it, and pile the long, wet mound on top of my head. I rinse the conditioner from my hands and wipe a circle on the shower door, clearing it enough to peek at my phone.

It's moving.

The screen is flashing and the phone spins in slow circles on the marble countertop.

Don't hang up, Eric!

I step out of the shower, and Eric's face flashes on the screen. Dripping wet, I unlock the phone, leaving it on the counter.

"Eric?!" Water drips from my face onto the screen.

I dry my hand on a nearby towel and put the phone on speaker so I don't have to hold it against my wet head. "Hello?!"

"It's so good to hear your voice!" Eric exhales like he held his breath too long. "Are you OK, babe? Gawd, I miss you! How about Hannah and everyone else? Is everyone OK?"

"We're fine," I say. "How are you? How's Zach? April and T are so worried..."

"Zach's fine," Eric interrupts me. "He's with me. I invited him to stay here when we lost touch with you guys."

"Thank you," I say. "Tell him his mums and sister are fine."

"They can tell him themselves," Eric says. "Zach's right here."

While I wrap myself in a towel and barge into the adjoining suite through the connecting door, Eric tells me Adam was worried about Hannah, and Archie was worried about Connie, so he invited them to stay at our house too.

"It made sense to wait together," Eric says. "If one of us heard anything or contacted you, we would all be here."

"Where did everyone sleep?" I ask.

"Sophie and I were in our room, Adam slept in Hannah's room, and Archie and Zach shared the spare room."

"Sounds like quite the slumber party," I tease.

April emerges from the bedroom, and I hand her my phone.

While April enjoys the best Mother's Day gift possible, hearing her seventeen-year-old son's voice after being unable to reach him for almost thirty-six hours, I rush back to the shower and rinse the conditioner out of my hair.

Worried the data connection won't last, I set a new speed record drying off and getting dressed.

Clothed but with my hair wrapped in a towel, I emerge from the bathroom. April holds the phone out to me.

"Eric?"

"Happy Mother's Day, Meg!"

"Oh. Adam. Hi," I say, hoping my voice doesn't betray my shock. "Hannah's fine. She's not with me now, but I promise she's healthy and unharmed," I assure him. "Except for the emotional pain and inconvenience of not having a cell phone. I'm so sorry. I can't imagine how worried you've been."

As much as I'd prefer not to be stranded with limited modern conveniences in forced proximity to a killer, I wouldn't switch places with my ex-husband for anything. At least I know where Hannah is. I know she's safe, and I can keep an eye on her. I can't imagine not knowing and not being able to contact her. The past day-and-a-half must have been torture for Adam.

"I spoke with her," he says. "She called me from somewhere outside the spa. We spoke until her phone cut out," he says. "We figured you were all right. A helicopter flew over the spa yesterday, and the pilot reported that everything appeared fine. Also, Eric got hold of a satellite image of the spa after the storm."

"You know more than us," I say.

"I'm glad you're OK, Meg. I'm glad everyone is OK."

"Thanks."

"I'll hand the phone back to Eric," he says.

"Hey, babe."

I can hear the smile in Eric's voice.

"Hi!" I gush.

"Are you alone, babe?"

April uses hand motions to tell me she's going back to her room to finish getting ready. I nod in response.

"I am now," I reply after April closes the connecting door.

"Tell me about this murder."

"You know about Summer's murder?"

Adam received part of the voicemail Hannah left for him at 2:41 a.m. He played the partial message for Eric. The message ended mid-sentence, but after Hannah mentioned the storm, the power failure, the cell phone service failure, and Summer's murder.

"What's Twyla's last name?" Eric asks after I tell him about the baggie of spotted water hemlock, Twyla's investigation, and Hannah and I featuring on Twyla's suspect list.

"Proudfoot," I reply.

Eric repeats the name, drawing out each syllable like he's writing it down.

"Twyla hates me, honey," I say. "She thinks I'm an interfering busy body."

"You're a helpful, interfering busy body with good instincts," Eric assures me.

"She has a personal relationship with a suspect," I disclose. "And I can't verify her alibi."

"You can't verify whose alibi?"

"Twyla's," I clarify. "Actually, no one's. I can't verify any alibis."

"Why would the investigator need an alibi?" he asks with a chuckle.

I explain to Eric about Twyla's sudden arrival just before the power went out. I tell him how Twyla and Maria were unaccounted for when the killer lured the sauna attendant away while they sneaked into sauna three, moved Summer's body, locked the door, and stole the key.

"She searched our room for the missing key," I say. "Can she do that without a warrant?"

Eric says it sounds like Twyla's search was legal, but he wants to view Hannah's video footage.

"Be careful, babe."

"Always."

"Stay together. Don't eat or drink anything that looks or smells weird or you aren't familiar with. Try to stick with pre-packaged food and drinks."

"OK."

This would be a bad time to mention Nadira's culinary accomplishments and all the new foods I've tried this weekend.

"Adam is in contact with the mayor up there, and I'm in contact with the local police chief," Eric says. "They assure us the road will be clear sometime tomorrow. Crews have been working on it since yesterday morning."

"Honey, what do you know about the witness protection program?" I ask, changing the subject.

"Federal or provincial?"

"There are multiple witness protection programs?" I ask. "I'm not sure."

I tell him about Autumn's disclosure, that her sister's testimony helped convict a killer.

"I can't promise anything, but I'll look into it," Eric says.

"Thank you," I say. "I miss you and Sophie. Tell me all the news from Harmony Lake."

Eric distracts me with tales of how much Sophie loves having a house full of guests. He says she's convinced they're there to provide laps for her to sit on, give her treats, and take her for walks. Then he tells me that one of his officers is retiring next month after forty years of service.

"I have less than a month to plan his retirement party and hire his replacement," Eric says with a sigh.

"I can help with the retirement party," I offer. "Everyone in town knows him and will want to help. I'll put it on project status when I get home."

"Thank you," he says. "If you can also send out a job posting, sort through the applications, arrange interviews, conduct interviews, choose an applicant, then make them an offer, that would be great too."

"Ummm, I can help with the retirement party." We laugh. "But I'll keep my eyes and ears open for potential candidates."

WITHIN SECONDS of taking our seats, a server carrying a tray of mango mimosas wishes April and me Happy Mother's Day and places a champagne flute in front of each of us.

"Some guests have intermittent cellular service, and some have no cellular service," Connie updates us after we raise our glasses and toast each other.

April and I tell everyone about our conversation with Zach, Eric, and Adam. Tamara also had a brief conversation with their son, and Rachel tells us that she exchanged texts with Zack while she and Hannah wandered nearby hiking trails. Connie had a brief conversation with her partner, Archie, but the signal dropped, and she hasn't had service since. Hannah spoke with Adam, then her boyfriend, but her signal only lasts about two minutes at a time, with long gaps in between.

April and I join the buffet line and look at the other guests' full plates as they walk back to their tables. We deliberate about what to sample first. Someone's cell phone dings, and the rest of us whip out our phones.

"No service," I say, checking my phone.

"Me neither," April says.

"I haven't had service since Eric phoned earlier. We got disconnected right after he told me one of his officers is retiring next month."

"Who?"

I tell her the retiring officer's name—she knows him and his family because everyone knows everyone else in Harmony Lake—and we brainstorm ideas for his retirement party while we inch forward in line.

"Artsy Tartsy will do the cake, of course," she offers, referring to her and Tamara's bakery. "I'll call his wife when we get home and work out the details."

A server hands me a warm plate. I thank her and scan the long table of food in front of me.

"There's so much to choose from," I comment. "What should we try first?"

"This place goes all out for Mother's Day brunch," April concurs.

We agree to divide and conquer, choosing different items so we can share when we get back to the table. I load my plate with maple glazed breakfast sausage, banana bread pancakes, and bite-size spinach and ham egg tarts. As I make my way from dish to dish, Nadira emerges from the kitchen and, smiling, takes a visual inventory of the buffet. Her pride is well deserved. We make eye contact, and she gives me a thumbs-up.

"Amazing," I mouth to her, then make a chef's kiss.

April chooses a ham and cheese croissant with honey mustard glaze, smoked salmon puff pastry nests, and eggs Benedict with avocado spread and tomato slices.

"Nadira has outdone herself," Tamara comments, then sips her strawberry and sparkling wine punch.

"Who else is ready for another trip to the buffet?" Connie asks, laying her napkin on the table and standing up.

"This will be my third trip," I say, finishing the last bite of crepe with strawberries and lemon curd. "But I need to try the ham biscuits with apricot mustard."

I dab my mouth with my napkin and join Connie at the end of the buffet line.

"Oh, look! There's Billie," Connie says, pointing her chin toward the end of the buffet.

Billie's back is toward us, but her ginger hair makes her easy to recognize. I catch occasional glimpses of her face as she slides her empty plate along the buffet.

"I wonder what happened yesterday after Twyla evicted everyone from the third-floor hallway?"

"There's only one way to find out, my dear," Connie replies.

"I don't see Autumn," I say, scanning the tables. "Do you think Billie is alone? Maybe we should invite her to join us."

# CHAPTER 25

"Billie!"

She stops and looks around.

I speed up, closing the distance between us before she walks away.

"Oh. Hi, Megan," Billie says with a small smile.

"Hi," I say, closing the last few feet between us. "How are you? I've been thinking about you since Twyla found the key in your room yesterday."

"I'm fine," Billie assures me. "I don't know how it got there. I swear, I had never even seen the key before. Twyla made it clear she thinks I killed Summer."

"There are several suspects in Summer's murder," I say, hoping to ease her mind. "Myself included."

"At least I'm in good company," she says with a weak smile. "I can't stand being stranded with Summer's murderer. What if they get away with it? What if the police don't figure out who killed her?" Billie glances at her plate, then looks away as though it offended her. "It makes my stomach turn. I'm sure it's part of the reason I feel like this."

Her plate is empty except for a small slice of quiche Lorraine.

"Summer's killer won't get away," I say with more confidence than I feel.

"Happy Mother's Day."

"Thank you," I say, surprised by the sentiment.

I realize I don't know if Billie or the twins are mothers. None of them have mentioned kids, but that doesn't mean they don't have any.

"Do you or the twins have kids?" I ask.

"No," Billie replies, shaking her head. "Not yet. My husband and I hope to start our family this year. For the first half of the year, we're focussing on our physical and mental health. That's why we came here. Autumn and Summer thought it would be a good way to keep me motivated."

"Good for you," I congratulate her.

"My husband and I are working on making healthier food choices and learning to manage our stress better."

"It sounds like you're making positive changes," I say.

"I'm trying," Billie says. "It's difficult to make healthy food choices when I can't keep anything down and have trouble staying awake until sunset. It's hard to manage stress when one of my best friends gets murdered."

"Would you like to join us?" I ask, gesturing behind me. "We have a huge table by the window, and we'd love to have brunch with you."

Billie looks at the slice of quiche on her plate and crinkles her nose.

"I don't think so," she says. "Thank you for asking, though. I'm not sure I'll finish this piece of quiche, and the smell of food makes my nausea worse."

"Is that why you were late for roll call on Friday night?" I ask. "Were you sick?"

Billie nods. "After my massage, dinner made a reappearance. I went upstairs to lie down. When Autumn and Summer didn't come back, I looked for them. An employee asked me to join everyone in the bistro."

Autumn told me she was lying in their hotel room because of her migraine symptoms. How did Autumn and Billie miss each other? Is Billie lying? Is Autumn lying? Are they both lying?

"Wasn't Autumn in your room too? Resting because she had a migraine?"

"We figure we missed each other," Billie explains. "I must have gone upstairs after Autumn left to search for me and Summer. Then, she must have come back to check the room after I left to look for her and Summer."

"You didn't hear the knock at your door when Maria dispatched employees to herd the guests for roll call?"

"No one knocked at our door while I was there."

Billie turns up her nose and straightens her arms, maximizing the distance between her nose and the quiche.

"It's too bad you're so sick," I say, recalling Logan, the massage therapist's observation that the aroma of the incense also made Billie nauseous. "Have you always had a physical reaction to scents and aromas?"

"No," Billie replies. "I think it's a side effect of this stomach bug. It makes me sleepy all the time and certain smells make the nausea worse."

"I can relate," I sympathize. "I had a similar bug years ago. Same symptoms. Rolling nausea, hypersensitive sense of smell, chronic fatigue…"

"How long did it last?" Billie asks, interrupting my inventory of symptoms.

Before I can reply, Nadira approaches us, smiling and carrying a tray.

"Hi, Billie. I'm glad I caught you," she says.

"You're looking for me?" Billie asks after Nadira and I greet each other.

"I saw you in the buffet line. You seemed uncomfortable. I assume you were searching for something that would be easy on your stomach."

Billie nods and glances at her quiche Lorraine which is starting to look cold and dry.

"I thought this might help." Nadira holds up the tray and nods toward the thermos. "Chamomile tea to help with indigestion and nausea," she explains, then nods toward the white ceramic ramekin. "Ginger lozenges to help relieve nausea." She nods at the bowl next to it. "Applesauce to help settle your stomach." She nods at the plate. "And soda crackers and a banana."

"That's so thoughtful," Billie says, her eyes welling with moisture. "Thank you."

A bit of an emotional response on Billie's part, but she's going through a lot of emotional upheaval right now. Nadira holds out the tray, and Billie looks at the plate she's carrying, figuring out how to carry everything.

"Give me the quiche," I say, relieving Billie of the tray.

"You guys are amazing." A single tear rolls down Billie's cheek. "I don't know what to say. This weekend has been so overwhelming."

Nadira softens at Billie's emotional reaction to her thoughtful gesture. "Why don't we sit for a minute."

Nadira places a hand on Billie's shoulder and leads us to a nearby door, ushering us through, ahead of her. This must be Nadira's office. Like Maria's office, it has two doors. I assume the other door leads to the kitchen.

Nadira takes the tray from Billie and sets it on the desk, easing Billie into an armchair. Then, she takes the plate of quiche Lorraine from me and places it on a table behind the desk and gestures for me to sit in the armchair next to Billie's.

"I'm sorry," Billie says, sniffling. "I'm just so sad and tired and sick. Feeling lousy is exhausting."

"No need to apologize," Nadira assures her. "Do what you need to do. If you need to cry"—she shrugs—"you cry. Suppressing it does more harm than good. Crying relieves anxiety. Tears contain stress hormones. You're helping your body eliminate stress when you cry. Crying also causes fatigue, which may be why you're so tired."

"You know a lot about crying," Billie says with a sniffle.

"I am an Ayurvedic practitioner," Nadira explains, "and in the Ayurvedic tradition, we believe that suppressing tears leads to physical and mental symptoms."

I suspect something else is behind Billie's physical symptoms, but I don't mention it because Nadira's explanation makes sense and her calm, reassuring words help Billie relax.

"The foods on this tray are gentle for your stomach," Nadira explains. "And they don't require refrigeration or special storage. You can nibble at them throughout the day."

"I'll try," Billie smiles. "Thank you."

"Maybe the lamb chop you ordered yesterday was too rich for your stomach right now," Nadira suggests.

"I didn't order the lamb chop," Billie says. "Autumn ordered it for me. I couldn't eat very much. I ate most of the rice and broccoli that you served with it, though. It was delicious, I just couldn't stomach it."

Billie's comment gives me pause, and judging by the momentary confusion on Nadira's face, it gives her pause too. While Nadira shakes off the dissonance and explains to Billie reasons to consider avoiding animal products until her stomach feels better, I recall the meatless lamb chop bone outside Billie's room.

The door to the kitchen swings open.

"Nadira, can we go over next week's food order?" Maria asks, then looks up from the clipboard in her hand. "Oh. Hello, Billie. Hello, Megan." She smiles, nudging the bridge of her glasses with her spare hand. "How is everyone today?"

Pots and pans clanging in the kitchen make it difficult to hear her.

"Fine," we mumble almost in sync.

"Megan, I'm glad I bumped into you. Twyla would like to speak with you. Are you available after brunch?"

"Sure," I reply. "I was going to visit you later, anyway, and ask you for something. I'm scheduled to have a petrissage scalp massage after brunch, but…"

"Don't worry about that," Maria says, smiling and flicking her wrist. "I'll let them know you'll be late." She smiles again, this time showing all her teeth. "After brunch, in my office?"

"Sure," I say, trying to match her smile.

"I should get going," Billie announces, standing up and collecting the tray from Nadira's desk. "I don't like to leave Autumn alone longer than necessary." She hoists the tray to shoulder height. "Thank you again, Chef." She smiles. "And thanks for checking in with me, Megan."

"I should leave too," I say, standing up. "My family will wonder where I've disappeared to." I open the office door for Billie, and she steps past me and into the hall.

"Megan, can you hang back?" Nadira asks. "I'd like to ask you something."

"Sure." I sit down again.

"You two talk," Maria says. "Nadira, we can go over the food order later. Megan, I saw your family having breakfast. I'll let them know where you are, so they won't worry."

"Thanks," I say before Maria disappears into the kitchen. "What's up?" I ask Nadira.

"Be careful when you talk to Twyla and Maria," she warns in a whisper. "Take someone with you." She arches a perfectly shaped eyebrow. "A witness."

"Why?" I ask. "Do you know why Twyla wants to talk to me?"

"I don't know why they want to talk to you," Nadira whispers, leaning across the desk and shooting a quick glance at the kitchen door. "But something is going on. Maria and Twyla are more uptight than usual."

"Summer's murder is stressing out everyone."

"It's more than that." She narrows her gaze and shakes her head slowly. "I can't put my finger on it." She sighs. "Twyla hardly ever visits Maria at work. But she was here Wednesday, Thursday, and Friday."

"Interesting," I say. "Why?"

"I don't know," Nadira replies. "But something else weird is going on." She moves her index finger in a come-hither motion, so I lean toward the desk. "Maria and Summer had two intense discussions between the time Summer checked in on Wednesday and her death on Friday night."

"Intense?" I ask. "Did you overhear anything?"

"I couldn't get close enough to eavesdrop, but they were huddled together in a corner near the yoga studio on Wednesday afternoon, and on Friday morning, they were talking near the front desk. When Maria caught me watching them on Friday, she took Summer into her office."

"Are you sure Maria was talking with Summer?" I ask. "You admitted you couldn't tell Autumn and Summer apart."

"Trust me, it was Summer," Nadira insists. "I'm sure it was Summer because when I saw them outside the yoga studio, I watched Maria and Summer over Autumn's shoulder. Autumn was accusing me of poisoning Billie. And on Friday, Autumn and Billie were having breakfast when Maria and Summer had their heads together at the front desk. I was looking for Maria. I wanted to warn her about the accusations Autumn was slinging at me and tell her that Autumn threatened to take the accusations public."

"Did Maria and Summer appear friendly?" I ask. "Did they laugh and act familiar with each other?"

"The opposite," Nadira replies. "Summer cried during both conversations, and Maria cried outside the yoga studio. It wasn't angry crying. It was more like sad crying. Like they were sharing sad stories or something."

"What could Maria and Summer have discussed that made them emotional?" I wonder out loud.

"I don't know," Nadira replies. "But I saw Twyla give you the stink-eye on the back deck yesterday near the lounge chairs, and I heard how she chastised you in the third-floor hallway yesterday evening. I thought I should give you a heads-up."

"Thanks for the warning," I say.

The gossip network at the SoulSpring Spa and Retreat rivals the Harmony Lake gossip network.

# CHAPTER 26

"Thanks for coming with me," I say.

"Of course, I came with you!" April declares. "I'm dying to know why they want to talk to you."

"Please don't joke about dying," I say, forcing my face to stay serious.

We burst out laughing.

"Do you think the baggie is still there?" April asks, pointing to the filing cabinet where Twyla locked up the potential poison.

"I hope so," I say, just as Maria's office door opens.

"Thanks for coming, Megan." Maria smiles, then greets April with the same optimism and bright smile.

Twyla follows Maria into the office.

"Hello, ladies," she mutters, nodding and making brief eye contact with us before looking away.

"Hello," April and I respond.

Twyla leans against the back of the door, her shoulders stooped. She picks at the skin around her thumb. Physically, she looks the same as yesterday, but her energy and mood are different. Somehow, Twyla takes up less space than last time the four of us were assembled in

Maria's office. Her presence is less imposing, and the atmosphere is lighter than it usually is when Twyla is around.

"Megan," Maria says, wheeling her chair toward her desk and straightening her spine. "Twyla has something she'd like to say to you." She laces her fingers together on the desk and looks at the law enforcement officer. "Don't you, Twyla?"

"I'm sorry for yelling at you in the hallway yesterday in front of the other guests," Twyla mumbles, looking at me.

"I'd like to apologize too, Megan," Maria says. "We strive to treat every guest and employee at the Soul-Spring Spa and Retreat with the utmost respect and courtesy."

"Thank you," I say, taken aback by the apologies. "I'm sorry if my whispering interfered with your investigation."

"This... situation is stressful for all of us, but it's especially stressful for Twyla—"

"Because I'm the only law enforcement officer here," Twyla says, cutting off Maria mid-sentence.

"I understand," I say, smiling. "Do you mind if we go to our petrissage scalp massage now?"

April and I rise to our feet.

"I remembered where I'd seen your husband before!" Maria announces.

April and I sit back down.

"I told you it would come to me as soon as you left my office, and that's what happened."

"Oh?" I ask.

"He was a keynote speaker at the police conference Twyla attended last month." Maria opens her desk drawer. "I found the itinerary Twyla brought home from the conference. It includes a photo and biography of each speaker." She hands me the brochure. "Your husband's photo is the same photo you showed me on your phone yesterday. Him and your dog, Sophie."

"So, it is." I smile and pass the brochure to April.

"Twyla said his speech was her favourite part of the conference," Maria gushes.

"That's quite a compliment," I respond.

"I learned a lot from his talk about how social media impacts policing in small communities," Twyla adds. "It was really informative."

"I will tell him." I smile.

"I realized you were Chief Sloane's wife when I interviewed you in the sauna," Twyla adds, swallowing. "I panicked because I knew you had helped him solve a few cases. Chief Sloane has a stellar reputation as a murder investigator. I would hate if he based his first impression of my investigative skills on this case, under these circumstances."

Twyla inhales and fidgets with her fingers, shifting her weight from one foot to the other. "I freaked out. I was sure you could tell this was my first murder investigation. Summer's murder was the first murder scene I'd ever attended, and I didn't want it to be obvious. You've attended more murder scenes than me, and you're a civilian. I worried you would tell Chief Sloane that I'm inexperienced and incompetent. Then he would tell my chief, and I'd never get promoted or get hired somewhere else."

"Yesterday when I remembered where I'd seen your husband, I told Twyla, and she admitted she had already figured it out. Then she told me why she was avoiding you," Maria adds.

"I see," I say. "Twyla, I couldn't tell this was your first murder. You exude so much confidence and authority, that I assumed you were a seasoned investigator."

"Maybe I'm a better actor than cop." Twyla laughs

and her facial muscles soften. She straightens her spine, pulling herself up a little taller. "This is a small town. We've never had a murder here. Until this weekend, the biggest crime I had ever investigated was a string of bicycle thefts from the local high school." She laughs. "I don't want to sound cold, but Summer's murder is an opportunity for me. This is my chance to prove I can preserve a crime scene, collect evidence, interview witnesses... to prove I would be a good detective."

"I keep telling her she's doing a great job"—Maria shakes her head—"but she won't listen."

"I'm sure your boss, and everyone else, will be impressed. You're very professional," April adds.

"I bet if your boss shows up tomorrow and you hand him a short list of suspects, or better yet, a cuffed suspect, it would impress him," I comment.

"Yes, it would," Twyla confirms. "It would look great on my resume too." Something buzzes, and Twyla grabs the cell phone on her hip. "Excuse me, I have to take this."

April, Maria, and I grab our phones and check for service. Nothing. We sigh and put our phones down, frustrated by the fickle data connection.

"Thank you again for coming," Maria says after Twyla leaves the office. "And thank you for understanding."

"No problem," I say. "Can I ask you something?"

"Sure," Maria says.

"What did you and Summer discuss in private?"

"What are you talking about?" Maria squeezes her eyebrows together under the rim of her black frames.

"Someone mentioned that you had at least two private conversations with Summer. Conversations that included *sad crying*, to quote my source." I put air quotes around *sad crying*.

"Is Nadira your source?" Maria asks, crossing her

arms in front of her chest and shaking her head. "That interfering woman starts most of the gossip in this place. Why can't she stay in the kitchen where she belongs?" She huffs. "If it weren't for all her culinary awards and large following, I would've gotten rid of her ages ago."

April and I exchange subtle, shocked glances. These are the harshest words Maria has said in our presence.

"It doesn't matter who the source is," I say. "What matters is that you had multiple emotional discussions with Summer before her death."

"We talked about Mother's Day brunch," Maria declares. "This was the twins first Mother's Day together without their mother. It was an emotional conversation, and Summer cried, which made me cry. I'm a sympathetic crier. I can't control it." Maria cocks an eyebrow. "Summer wanted to surprise Autumn with the same Mother's Day breakfast they used to make for their mother. She asked if it would be possible to arrange a special, off-menu meal and have room service deliver it."

"What was the meal?" I ask.

"I don't know," Maria replies. "I told her I would discuss her request with the chef and if we could accommodate it, Nadira would reach out to Summer for the details."

"Did you discuss it with Nadira?" April asks.

"I forgot," Maria admits, scrunching up her face in shame. "She asked me the night they checked in, but it slipped my mind until Summer asked me again on Friday. I felt horrible for forgetting. I didn't have time to talk to Nadira about it before Summer died."

"So sad," April says.

"I know," Maria agrees.

"Can I ask you something else?" I ask, changing the subject.

"Of course," Maria says, dabbing the corner of her eye with her thumb.

"Why has Twyla visited you so often since Billie and the twins checked in? I heard she's visited you every day since they arrived, but before that, she rarely visited the spa."

"Twyla's visits have nothing to do with any spa guest," Maria replies. "Remember when I told you Twyla was job hunting?"

I nod.

"She found a few opportunities, and I was helping her with her resume."

"Good luck to her. I hope she gets an interview," I say. "Also, would you have any pregnancy tests?"

"Excuse me?" April and Maria ask, like I asked Maria to give me a grenade.

"A pregnancy test," I reiterate. "They were in the basket with the bandages on Friday night. May I have one please?"

"Of course." Maria stands up and blinks several times in quick succession. "I'll be right back."

"Are you pregnant?" April demands, when Maria leaves.

"I hope not," I reply.

"Does Eric know?"

Before I can answer, Maria returns carrying the basket of toiletries.

"Good luck?" She hands me a long, thin, shrink-wrapped box.

"Thanks." I smile, tucking the test inside my knitting bag.

"IF SUMMER WANTED to surprise her sister with a special breakfast, why didn't she ask Nadira? Why did she ask Maria?" April asks on the way to our petrissage scalp massage.

"I wondered the same thing," I admit. "And where was Maria's uncontrollable sympathetic crying response on Friday night when Autumn was sobbing over her sister's death?"

"This doesn't feel right," April concurs. "The key appearing out of nowhere in Billie's suitcase, Maria's secret conversations with the murder victim, Summer's past in the witness protection program, Billie's constant nausea, the baggie of spotted water hemlock stuck between the lounge chair cushions. I feel like it's just a matter of putting the clues in the right order, but no matter how I rearrange them, they don't make sense."

"It's like untangling yarn," I say. "Just when I think I've undone the last knot, and the yarn is tangle-free, I encounter an even bigger knot a few yards later." I sigh. "I never expected Twyla to apologize or admit that she was irritable because she's insecure about her investigative skills."

"Me neither," April agrees. "Is Twyla insecure, or does she think displaying emotional vulnerability will convince you that her behaviour wasn't because she was manipulating evidence?"

"Maybe she hopes I'll forget that she has no verifiable alibi for the time window when the killer likely moved Summer's body."

"Who drives halfway up a mountain three days in a row for resume help?" April asks, pulling the door to the scalp massage area. "Geesh! Just email the resume like a normal person."

So many questions, so few answers.

# CHAPTER 27

"Red Herring?" I ask Hannah, holding up the bottle of matte vermillion nail polish.

"Good choice," she agrees.

"What shade did you choose?" I ask as we settle into side-by-side pedicure chairs for our Mother's Day Mother-Daughter Mani-Pedi.

"It's called Kiss my A's." She holds up the bottle of neon-pink polish.

"Hi, Megan," a small voice says from the pedicure chair on my other side.

"Autumn!" I force myself to rein in my shock for fear of frightening her away. "It's nice to see you," I say in the same gentle voice I would use to convince a baby animal to leave the safety of its hiding place.

Autumn leans forward and looks around me, greeting Hannah. Hannah returns the greeting and smiles.

"Do you and Hannah visit a spa every Mother's Day?" Autumn asks.

"This is our first time," I reply. "Hannah's dad usually makes brunch for us."

"That's nice," Autumn says. "Tradition is important. My mother loved daisies. Every Mother's Day I would take her for lunch at her favourite restaurant and give her a bouquet of daisies. I always signed Summer's name, even though she wasn't there." Autumn's smile is sad and nostalgic.

"I'm sorry," I say. "Today must be hard. My mum died when Hannah was a baby. Mother's Day is still bittersweet."

"Since my mum died, I still buy daisies on Mother's Day, but now I put them in a vase in my kitchen and let them remind me of her," Autumn says.

"Did you have any Mother's Day traditions before Summer left?" I probe. "Like a handmade card, or a special breakfast, or something?"

"Sure," Autumn replies. "We made Mother's Day cards in school when we were little. But as teenagers, we were too cool for handmade cards, so we bought a card together and both signed it. As for breakfast"—she shakes her head—"Mum never ate breakfast. She had coffee in the morning but didn't eat until lunch."

Why would Maria tell me Summer wanted to arrange a special Mother's Day breakfast just like the one she and Autumn used to make for their mother? Who's lying, Maria or Autumn? Why would Autumn lie? She has nothing to risk by telling me about her family's Mother's Day traditions. Why would Maria lie? Because she doesn't want me to know the truth about what she and Summer discussed during their secret, tearful conversations. What secret is Maria lying to protect?

"How's your migraine?" I ask, aiming for a less emotional topic of conversation.

"I've kept it away so far," Autumn replies, lifting a foot out of the water at the nail technician's prompting.

"That's good," I say.

"It's temporary," Autumn corrects me. "I might have won the battle, but I haven't won the war. I've had migraines since I was eleven years old, and I expect to have them for the rest of my life."

"Did Summer suffer with chronic migraines too?" I ask, wondering if identical twins also share identical chronic health conditions.

"No," Autumn replies, shaking her head. "She had occasional sinus headaches before it would rain, but never migraines."

"Autumn," I say, thinking how sad she must be about marking Mother's Day so soon after her sister's death. "If you want to be alone and would rather not talk, I'll do my best to be quiet," I half joke.

"It's kind of you to offer," Autumn snickers. "I wanted to do something normal today. Getting a pedicure when you're staying at a spa is normal. Later, I might take a normal walk in the garden."

The nail technician taps her leg, and by instinct, Autumn lifts her foot out of the water and rests it on the ledge. "The spa has an extensive herb garden. I'd like to check it out."

"Do you garden?" I ask.

"I wish," Autumn replies. "I used to have a small herb garden, but I don't have time anymore."

"How's Billie feeling?" I ask.

"She's napping," Autumn replies. "These days, she either naps or throws up. She came back to our room with a tray of food prepared by Nadira." Autumn rolls her eyes. "I warned her not to eat it, but she won't listen to me. I don't know what Nadira does to Billie's food, but it's making her sick."

"Speaking of Billie," I say. "I hear she worried about

you when Summer came back from the Witness Protection Program."

"Who told you that?" Autumn asks.

"Someone overheard your conversation. She said Billie warned you to be careful trusting Summer again. Why did Billie say that?"

"Your gossipy friend only heard part of the conversation," Autumn says, then inhales a deep breath and lets it out. "My sister was gone for over ten years. A lot happens in a decade. Our mother's constant worry made her sick. Our mother's health got worse, and I took care of her by myself. I made every decision and the final arrangements. Billie supported me, but it's not the same as having a sister to share the burden and share the pain.

"When Mum got too sick, I took over the business. I had to teach myself how to be the boss. It terrified me. We have dozens of employees who rely on the business to take care of their families. Between caring for Mum and running the business, I didn't have time to hang out with friends, date, or start a family. I feel guilty for admitting it, but I resented Summer for leaving. For over ten years, she didn't have any responsibility. She lived her own life and didn't have to consider anyone else. I can't even imagine what that would feel like."

"It's understandable," I say. "You dealt with a lot by yourself. You handled your mum's illness when she was alive, her affairs after she died, and kept the business successful. It must've been hard when Summer came back and expected half of your mum's share of the business."

"Did your source tell you that too?" Autumn asks.

"I have multiple sources," I admit.

"I was hesitant," Autumn admits. "But Summer and I talked about it. We yelled and cried and worked it out. It turns out Summer felt bad too. She resented me. Summer was jealous that I spent those last years with our mum and she couldn't. She resented me for living in our hometown. She had to build a new life with new people. Her new life was a lie. Summer said every friendship she had in witness protection started with a lie—her name." The nail technician interrupts us to show Autumn her first painted nail, a lovely shade of pale lilac.

Autumn approves the colour, the nail technician continues polishing, and Autumn returns to our conversation.

"Summer's time away made both of us resentful. We were both hurt. Mum would have hated that. She would have wanted Summer to own part of the business. I instructed my lawyer to draw up the paperwork. I planned to surprise Summer with the paperwork next week when we got home."

I guess Summer's death means Autumn will continue to be the sole owner of the family business.

"How did Billie feel about Summer's return?" I ask, grimacing because the nail technician is filing my nails, and it tickles. "Was she jealous about sharing your attention with Summer again?"

"Billie was cautious," Autumn admits. "We hadn't seen or spoken to Summer since we were teenagers. What if she had changed? What if we had changed? I could tell Billie had reservations at first. But when she saw Summer hadn't changed, she was fine. They were both hesitant. Without Summer, Billie and I had each other, but Summer didn't have anyone. I think Summer resented that. Sometimes Billie and I would refer to something or make an inside joke that Summer didn't understand. I could tell she felt sad and left out."

Autumn's nail technician moves her across the salon to a chair with a dryer.

"Is Nadira your source, Mum?" Hannah asks, leaning toward me.

"She's one source," I reply.

"For someone who claims she's always in the kitchen, Nadira sees and hears a lot of stuff."

My daughter makes a good point.

# CHAPTER 28

Monday, May 9th

The road crew's progress brought them within earshot of the spa just before sunset last night. Buoyed by the prospect of a clear, safe escape route and cell phone service more stable than it has been since before the storm, the collective mood at breakfast is relaxed and optimistic. Smiles are brighter, conversations revolve less around speculation about when we'll be able to leave, and more about planning and packing for the trip home.

"Who are you looking for, my dear?" Connie asks between bites of yogurt-granola-berry parfait. "Are you waiting for someone specific to walk in?"

"Something like that," I admit, sipping my second cup of coffee. "I was hoping Billie would make another appearance today."

"Autumn said Billie is having breakfast in their room," Connie says. "I bumped into her at the buffet. She said Billie was a sickly shade of green when she woke up."

"Where's Autumn now?" I ask, scanning the tables

without missing a stitch on the spa washcloth I'm knitting.

"On the deck," Connie replies. "She fancied eating outside and taking in the view before they leave today. I invited her to join us, but she was in a hurry. She has a hot stone massage right after breakfast."

We have no scheduled spa treatments this morning, so after breakfast we return to our room to pack in anticipation of sleeping in our own beds in Harmony Lake tonight.

"Don't forget, my dear, you wanted to visit the gift shop and pick up some soaps and such to go with the washcloths you knitted," Connie says as we climb the stairs to the third floor.

"Right," I respond. "Thank you for reminding me." As we pass Billie and Autumn's room, I grip my knitting bag and feel the hard corners of the box Maria gave me yesterday. "I think I'll check on Billie," I say, stopping just past their door.

"I'll come with you," Connie offers.

"Thank you, but it's unnecessary. I'll only be a few minutes. You can pack, I'll be fine."

"Are you sure?" Connie narrows her gaze. "We promised to watch each other until Twyla arrests Summer's killer, or we leave this place."

"I'll be right here," I assure her, pointing to Billie and Autumn's room. "If something happens, I'll scream so loud the road crews will hear me."

"Fine," Connie agrees. "But if you aren't inside our room in fifteen minutes, I'm coming to check on you."

"Deal," I say, watching Connie let herself into our room and lock the door.

I'm about to knock on Billie's door when my phone vibrates and rings inside my knitting bag. It's Eric.

"Hello?" I say, striding down the hall toward the stairwell and out of earshot of the employee loitering near the elevator door.

"Good morning, babe," says my handsome husband. "The road is almost clear. You should be able to leave in a few hours."

"We heard the same thing," I say.

I step inside the stairwell and look down the stairs, making sure I'm alone.

"I can't wait to see you," Eric says. "I'm gonna cuddle you so hard!"

"I could use a good, hard cuddle."

"I did some digging," Eric says. "What do you want to hear first, what I learned about Summer and the witness protection program, or what I learned about Officer Twyla Proudfoot?"

"Summer, please."

"Babe, are you sure about the details? You said Summer was an innocent bystander who risked her safety to testify against a murder suspect, right?"

"That's right," I confirm. "That's what her sister told me. She called Summer's testimony *a selfless sacrifice*."

"Autumn's version of events doesn't match the information I have," Eric says. "According to my sources, Summer was a hostile witness."

"What does that mean?"

"It means her testimony was evasive. The prosecuting attorney alleged that Summer changed parts of her testimony from what she said in her original statement. Changes that would've helped the defendant."

"Are you saying Summer was reluctant to testify against the murder suspect?"

"That's what I'm saying," Eric replies. "According to my source, Summer wasn't an innocent bystander. She faced charges related to her involvement in the murder. The prosecutor believed Summer helped the killer dispose of the victim's body and gave the killer a fake alibi. If it weren't for the deal, Summer would have gone to prison."

"Deal?" I ask. "Why would the prosecution give her a deal if they believed she took part in a murder?"

"The prosecution needed Summer's testimony to convict the suspect. They wanted to prosecute him more than they wanted to prosecute Summer, so they offered her a deal. In exchange for her testimony, they granted Summer immunity, and because the prosecutor agreed that Summer's life would be at risk..." Eric's voice crackles and his words break up as the connection struggles to stay strong. "They offered..." more static and missing syllables. "...ness protec..." one last choppy sentence fragment, and the call ends.

I look at my phone. *No Service*.

"Shoot!" I grumble, stomping my foot.

The call failed before I could ask Eric the name of the killer Summer helped convict and the name of the victim.

What did he find out about Twyla?

With the clock ticking on Connie's fifteen-minute countdown, I emerge from the stairwell and knock on Billie's door.

"Oh, hey, Megan," says Billie, mid-yawn. She's wearing a long blue sleep shirt with the word, *Sleepyhead*, in cursive across the chest. Her eyes are heavy with sleep, and her mussed ginger hair looks like its last contact was with a pillow. "How are you?"

"I'm fine," I reply. "How are you? Autumn said you weren't feeling well this morning."

"I feel lousy," Billie admits. "But better than the first time I woke up." She runs her hands through her hair, taming her tousled tresses. "I'm glad you're here. I want to ask you something."

"Ask me anything." I smile.

"Yesterday, before Nadira showed up, you said you had experienced the same symptoms."

"I remember." I nod, recalling the weeks of exhausted nausea. "I felt awful."

"How long did it last?" Billie asks.

"Weeks," I reply. "Some days were worse than others."

"How did you make it stop?"

"It sorted itself out."

"Did you see a doctor?"

"Yup." I nod.

"What was the diagnosis?" Billie asks. "Was it a viral infection? What caused it?"

"Hannah."

"Hannah?" Comprehension sweeps across Billie's face. "Oh my," she gasps, gripping the door for support. "You were pregnant with Hannah?"

I nod.

"I'm not pregnant." Billie shakes her head. "I can't be pregnant." She laughs like it's the most absurd thing she's heard today. "Not yet." Billie's chest heaves with shallow breaths. "Can I?"

She does some mental math, counting on her fingers. "It's not part of the plan," she explains, her words quick and short as she paces back and forth in front of the open door. "We aren't scheduled to start trying until July," she exclaims. "It's only May." She combs her fingers through her hair. "We have a twelve-month plan. There's a spreadsheet." She throws her hands in the air. "Getting pregnant is in the July through December columns. Not the May column. A May pregnancy isn't on the schedule, Megan."

"Babies don't care about schedules."

I slide the pregnancy test out of my knitting bag.

"Here." I hand Billie the box. "If you want to know for sure."

"Come in." Billie jerks her head toward the interior of the hotel room. "Can I take this anytime? Or do I have to wait until tomorrow morning?" she asks, reading the back of the box.

"I think you can take it anytime," I say. "But I haven't used one in years. You should do whatever the box says."

"I want to take it now," Billie says. "I need to know."

"Do you want to wait for Autumn?" I ask.

Billie sighs and drops her butt onto the bed.

"I don't want to pressure Autumn," she says. "She's dealing with too much already. It's unfair to ask her to deal with this too."

"She's your best friend," I say. "She might want to be here."

"I'm not sure about that," Billie says. "I feel like Autumn has been avoiding me since Summer died. When I'm in the room, she finds a reason to leave. When I join her at the spa, she finds an excuse to come back to the room." Billie looks at me with wide eyes. "What if Autumn is avoiding me because she thinks I killed Summer?"

"I'm sure she doesn't think that," I reassure her. "Do you think Autumn would continue to share a room with you if she believed you killed her sister?"

"I guess not," Billie agrees.

"Maybe Autumn just needs space to process her feelings."

"Will you stay while I do the test?"

"Sure," I reply, just as someone knocks on the door.

Billie gets up.

"I'll get it. It's Connie. I'm supposed to pack, and she's trying to keep me on task." I chuckle.

"While you talk to Connie, I'll pee on this stick."

REAGAN DAVIS

"Are you OK, my dear?" Connie asks, craning her neck to look into the hotel room.

"I'm fine," I whisper. "But I need more time. Billie asked me to help her with something."

"Are you sure?" Connie asks. "You have that look in your eye. What are you up to?"

"I need to ask Billie some questions, but she's preoccupied."

"Her stomach issues?" Connie asks, rubbing her tummy in sympathy.

"Yes," I say. "She's in the bathroom right now."

"Fifteen more minutes," Connie says. "I'll be back in fifteen minutes if I don't see you packing in our room."

"Thank you."

I watch Connie return to our room across the hall and close the door.

"The box says the result takes three minutes," Billie says when she returns from the bathroom empty-handed. "I left the test on the edge of the tub so I won't check it every five seconds."

"Can I ask you something, Billie?" I ask, checking to proceed before I ask some personal questions about her relationship with Autumn and Summer.

"Sure," Billie says. "It'll help distract me for the next two minutes and fifty seconds."

"Why did you warn Autumn to be careful around Summer and be careful about trusting her?"

"Where did you hear that?"

"Someone mentioned it." I flick my wrist like I'm asking out of casual interest.

"It surprised me when Summer left witness protection and came home," Billie confides. "She had a fresh start where no one knew what she did, but she came back. I worried she had an agenda. I thought she came back for their mother's estate and would disappear again when she got it. Summer leaving again would have broken Autumn's heart."

Did Billie kill Summer to prevent her from breaking Autumn's heart?

"What do you mean, *no one knew what she did*?"

"Summer was a good person, for the most part," Billie explains. "But she made some poor decisions."

"For example?"

"Her choice of boyfriends, for a start," Billie replies. "Summer liked bad boys. She liked good-looking trouble-makers. Complicated, rebellious guys."

"Was Summer's attraction to good-looking trouble-makers the reason she witnessed a murder?"

"She didn't just witness the murder, she helped cover it up," Billie explains. "Summer's boyfriend committed the murder. She let him put the victim's body in her trunk. Then she drove the car to an abandoned lot where her boyfriend poured gas inside and set it on fire."

"That's not how Autumn explained it," I say. "She said Summer was an innocent bystander. She said the person Summer testified against was from an organized crime family, and his father threatened to kill Summer if she testified against his son."

"Except for the part about Summer being an innocent bystander, Autumn told you the truth," Billie confirms. "She didn't want you to judge Summer. Autumn believed that Summer's involvement in the murder case was an isolated incident."

"Do you believe it was an isolated incident?" I ask.

"I don't know." Billie shrugs. "We were so young when everything happened. We were barely adults. Who knows if Summer's involvement in the murder was a one-off or her first step toward a lifetime of bad choices? That's why I warned Autumn to be careful."

"Autumn must have believed it was one-off," I

suggest. "Otherwise, she wouldn't have instructed her lawyer to transfer part ownership of the business to Summer."

"Autumn didn't transfer part ownership of the business to Summer," Billie insists.

"Yesterday, in the nail salon, Autumn told me she instructed her lawyer to transfer part ownership of the business to Summer. She said it would be a surprise."

"There's no way Autumn would do that without telling me," Billie scoffs. "I can prove it. I have access to her email."

Billie retrieves a laptop from the desk and cracks it open.

"You have access to Autumn's email?"

"Pretty much," Billie replies, typing in the password that unlocks the computer. "I know her computer password, which means I can access her email. Her lawyer would have wanted Autumn to make the request in writing. If she made the request, it'll be in her email. In the sent folder. I should be able to find it even without internet access."

I get the sense Billie has accessed Autumn's email before. She's too comfortable violating her best friend's online space for this to be the first time.

"Would Autumn be angry if she knew you checked her email?"

"Here!" Billie exclaims, ignoring my question. "Autumn emailed her lawyer on Friday before the storm hit." She beckons me to look at the laptop screen with her. "You're right," Billie utters, staring into the distance. "I can't believe it. But there it is." She blinks and looks at me with big, hurt eyes. "Why didn't Autumn tell me?"

"Maybe she didn't want you to worry," I reply. "May I read it?"

It's difficult to read the small font over Billie's shoulder.

"Sure." Billie hands me the laptop, then her phone dings. "The test!" She declares, silencing the alarm on her phone. "I forgot about the pregnancy test."

"Are you ready?" I ask.

"I think so."

"Do you want me to go with you?"

"No," Billie replies. "But can you wait here? Regardless of the result, I'm not sure how I'll feel about it."

"Take your time," I say. "You don't have to look at it this second."

Billie nods and swallows hard. She sits on the edge of the bed, grappling with the possibility that she's pregnant with a baby who doesn't care about schedules and spreadsheets.

Billie is right; the email's timestamp is a few hours before Friday's storm and Summer's murder. Could this email be part of Autumn's premeditated defence? Did she instruct her lawyer to transfer part of the family business to Summer so that, if the police accuse her of murdering her sister, Autumn can claim that if she was planning to kill her sister, she wouldn't have made her a business partner? Unless Autumn had second thoughts after she emailed her lawyer and killed Summer to stop the transfer. No, that doesn't make sense. Sending another email to her lawyer instructing him to cancel the transfer would be easier than committing murder.

Wait! What?

In the email's second paragraph, Autumn instructed her lawyer to change her will. According to the email, Billie is the sole beneficiary in Autumn's current will, but Autumn instructed her lawyer to add Summer as co-beneficiary, with each beneficiary inheriting fifty percent of Autumn's estate.

I bite my lips to hide my reaction.

Does Billie know about this? Should I ask her? I have a feeling she only read the first paragraph of the email, the part about transferring shares of the business from Autumn to Summer. The shock of Autumn not telling her about the business transaction and her potential pregnancy probably distracted her from reading the entire email.

I guess it makes sense Autumn named Billie as her beneficiary. When Summer was away, Billie was Autumn's closest friend. Her mother had died, and she had no one else to leave everything to. But Summer's return cuts Billie's future inheritance in half.

Jealousy wasn't Billie's only motive to kill Summer. Money and greed are excellent motives for murder too. Summer can't steal Billie's inheritance if she's dead. Does this mean Billie is planning to kill Autumn too? Am I alone in a hotel room with a murderer?

"Earth to Megan! Did you hear me?"

Billie's voice brings me back to the here and now.

"I'm sorry?"

I casually shield the laptop screen from Billie's view.

"I said, I'll be right back. I'm going to check the pregnancy test result."

"Good luck," I say. As soon as Billie turns her back, I snap a photo of the email with my cell phone, close Autumn's email, then close the laptop, and return it to the desk where Billie found it.

"One more question," I say as Billie approaches the bathroom door. "What was his last name? The guy whose family threatened to kill Summer if she testified."

"Clark," Billie replies as she disappears into the bathroom. "If you search the internet, you'll find lots of articles about the case."

Clark! The name makes my belly clench, but before I

can contemplate my anxious response to Summer's ex-boyfriend's surname, Billie squeals.

"It's positive!" She skips out of the bathroom, waving the positive test in front of her and grinning from ear to ear. "I'm having a baby!" Billie throws her arms around my neck and bounces on the balls of her feet. "I'm not sick! I'm pregnant!"

"Happy Mother's Day."

# CHAPTER 29

BILLIE'S CELEBRATORY bouncing comes to an abrupt halt when she slaps her hand over her mouth and runs to the bathroom to throw up.

Connie arrives for her next fifteen-minute check-in and, upon seeing Billie's ashen, shiny face, goes into mum-mode.

"Billie!" Connie swoops past me. "You need medical attention." She places a hand on Billie's clammy forehead. "I'm going down the hall to knock on the doctor's door."

"I'm pregnant!" Billie bursts. "See?" Grinning and with a slight bop, she holds up the test stick and gives it a triumphant wave. "But please don't tell anyone. I want to tell Autumn myself, and I don't want anyone else to find out until I tell my husband." She picks up her phone and rolls her eyes. "I'll phone him as soon as we get another wave of data connection."

"Congratulations!" Connie says, hugging Billie around the shoulders. "What a wonderful story when you tell your future child how they made themselves known to you on Mother's Day!"

A subtle greenish tint washes across Billie's face and she gulps.

"Maybe you're right." Billie reaches for the ramekin of ginger lozenges that Nadira gave her yesterday, popping one in her mouth. "Maybe I should visit the doctor. Just to ask her a few questions."

Connie and I wait while Billie gets dressed, then walk her down the hall to the doctor's hotel room. The doctor is in, and she welcomes Billie into her room to talk and answer the expectant-mum's questions.

"Something happy came out of an unhappy weekend!" Connie claps her hands in front of her chest.

"So far," I say.

"So far, my dear?"

We take our time, dawdling toward our room, whispering with our heads together as I tell Connie about the email Autumn sent to her lawyer and, if Summer was still alive, how Billie's status would have changed from sole beneficiary to co-beneficiary.

"With Summer out of the way," Connie whispers, "not only would Billie get one-hundred percent .of Autumn's estate, she would reclaim one-hundred percent of Autumn's time and attention."

"I hate the thought of Billie giving birth behind bars," I admit.

"Would you rather let a killer roam free?" Connie asks as we approach our door. "She can prowl around society"—Connie waves her limp hands with dramatic flair—"killing people willy-nilly because she doesn't want to share them with their siblings."

"We should knock on the connecting door and ask April, Tamara, and Rachel what they think about the fresh evidence against Billie."

"They aren't there, my dear," Connie advises.

"They're on the hiking trails taking photos to post on social media."

The name and its significance hit me as soon as I grip the door handle.

"Clark!" I gasp, entering our hotel room.

"Who the heck is Clark?" asks Hannah, folding a sweatshirt and laying it in her suitcase.

"Clark is the lovely gentleman who washes windows on Water Street," Connie replies, then looks at me with her brow furrowed. "What does Clark have to do with anything?"

"Clark is the name of the family that threatened Summer for testifying," I explain. "It's also Maria's last name."

"Maria the spa manager?" Hannah asks.

I nod, lowering myself onto the bed and dropping my knitting bag to the floor.

"Let me get this straight," Hannah says, joining me on the bed and tucking her feet under her. "You think Summer testified against Maria's brother and helped convict him of murder?"

"It's possible." I nod. "I assumed it was her brother too, but maybe he was Maria's uncle or cousin."

"That's a pretty big leap, Mum," Hannah advises. "Just because they have the same last name doesn't mean Maria is related to the man Summer testified against."

"Hannah is right," Connie adds. "Clark is a common surname. Do we even know if Maria and the crime family share the same spelling? Some Clarks have an e at the end, some don't."

"Let's consider the evidence," I say, summoning my most cerebral voice. "Summer just returned from the witness protection plan." I raise my pinky finger. "She was in witness protection because the father of the man she testified against threatened to kill her."

I raise the finger next to it. "The family's last name is Clark." I raise a third finger. "Summer and Maria had at least two private, emotional conversations between Summer's arrival and her death. I can't confirm the details of those conversations because the only person who can corroborate is Summer, and she is dead."

I raise my index finger. "Maria's whereabouts during the blackout are unknown. This is also when someone lured the spa attendant away from the sauna, repositioned Summer's body, and stole the key."

I stick out my thumb and ball my other hand into a fist. "Before that, Maria had access to the smoothie ingredients because she worked at the juice bar before Nadira made Summer's Green Powerhouse smoothie."

I raise my pinky. "Also, Maria had access to spotted water hemlock. It grows right outside the perimeter of the spa gardens."

I raise my ring finger. "Even though Twyla hardly ever visits her at work, since Summer checked in, she drove up the mountain every day to visit Maria."

"If Maria is the killer, my dear, where does that leave Billie?" Connie asks, gesturing toward the door as if she expects Billie to appear there. "Five minutes ago, you gave me a list of evidence proving Billie murdered Summer."

"You have evidence that Billie killed Summer?" Hannah demands. "What evidence?"

"The Billie theory was *before* I made the Clark connection," I explain, looking at Connie. "The evidence against Maria makes a much more compelling case." I focus my attention on Hannah. "Just before Summer's murder, Autumn instructed her lawyer to transfer part of the family business into Summer's name and add Summer as co-beneficiary in her will."

"Co-beneficiary?" Hannah asks, picking up on the significance. "How many beneficiaries besides Summer?"

I hold up my index finger.

"Billie," I say.

Hannah makes a tiny *o* with her mouth and raises her eyebrows.

"Mum, the evidence against Billie is more compelling than the evidence against Maria."

"You're on Team Billie?" I ask.

"I wouldn't say *Team Billie*," Hannah objects. "It sounds like I'm cheering for her. That being said, in my opinion, based on the evidence you presented, Billie is the most likely suspect in Summer's murder."

Somewhere in Harmony Lake right now, Adam is grinning and puffing out his chest, unsure why he is suddenly bursting with pride.

"You sounded *exactly* like your father when you said that last sentence."

"You'll be a wonderful lawyer, Hannah!" Connie declares. "I can't wait to watch you in court."

"I'm on Team Maria," I say, bringing the conversation back to Summer's murder. "Hannah is on Team Billie. Connie, who do you think killed Summer?"

"Twyla."

"Twyla?" Hannah and I ask in stereo.

Given the events of the past hour, I'd forgotten Twyla was still in contention as Summer's killer.

"I think Twyla's motive was Maria," Connie suggests. "Imagine this." She clears her throat. "When Summer checked in, Maria recognized her as the witness whose testimony sealed the incarcerated-fate of her loved one. Powerful emotions consumed Maria. Anger." Connie makes an angry face. "Sadness." She frowns. "Hatred." Connie narrows her eyes until they're small slits and quirks her eyebrows.

"She confided in the person she trusts most in the world, Twyla. Maria told Twyla that she planned to exact revenge on her late-father's behalf and keep her family's promise to kill Summer. Twyla would never let Maria commit murder. She did it herself, convinced her police training meant she was clever enough to get away with it."

Connie waggles her index finger. "She planned to help investigate Summer's murder too. To position herself to manipulate any evidence that might point the finger of suspicion at herself or Maria. But she got stuck here when her patrol car floated away." She makes waves in the air with her hands. "Twyla arrived earlier than when Megan saw her walk in. She parked somewhere discreet, snuck the spotted water hemlock into the juice bar while the guests were having dinner, then snuck out using the dozens of back doors this place has. She dropped the baggie of spotted water hemlock on the deck chair when she made her escape, and either didn't notice, or couldn't risk coming back to search for it.

"Twyla lured the sauna attendant away from the saunas and met Maria there. Maria kept watch for the sauna attendant's return and ran interference with any guests who showed up while Twyla staged the crime scene. Twyla stole the key hoping it would delay the discovery of Summer's body and give her a vital piece of evidence should she need to frame someone else. Twyla planned to get far away from here before someone discovered Summer's body. Then, she could show up with her colleagues as if she hadn't been here at all."

"You're good," I acknowledge. "Whether your explanation is correct, they should make it into a movie."

"Question?" Hannah raises her hand, and Connie nods. "How did Twyla know to take the poison to the juice bar? I mean, how would she know to leave the spotted water hemlock at the juice bar? How would anyone know Summer would have a smoothie later? Twyla could have supplied the poison and delivered it, but someone else still had to add it to Summer's smoothie."

"Who?" I wonder out loud.

"The most obvious answer is Maria," Connie says. "She and Twyla are close. I'm sure they would trust each other with a massive secret. And Maria has a motive. It's unlikely they would have involved a third person. It's hard enough for two people to keep a secret, never mind three."

"Unless the third person was an unknowing accomplice," I suggest. "Nadira admitted she made Summer's smoothie. She wouldn't admit that if she had knowingly laced it with poison. Maybe, somehow, Maria knew Summer would have a smoothie. Summer had said she had a smoothie every day since she checked in," I suggest, grasping for a reasonable explanation for the killer's foresight.

"Nadira has been accused of poisoning a guest," Connie says, reminding me of the chicken-tofu scandal. "Maybe her involvement in Summer's murder isn't as farfetched as we think."

"Connie, may I borrow your phone?" Hannah asks.

"Of course, my lovely." Connie smiles and hands Hannah her phone.

Connie and I debate the suspects, their motives, their alibis, and opportunities.

After talking ourselves into circles, we conclude that while there's enough evidence to implicate each suspect, there's not enough evidence to eliminate anyone. We agree this is beyond our scope, and we've come as far as we can without the benefit of police resources and forensics.

"Are you sure it's safe?" Connie asks. "You can't confide in a murder suspect. What if Twyla killed Summer and comes unhinged because we've figured it out? Best-case scenario, she uses our intelligence to frame an innocent person for Summer's murder. Worst-case scenario, we end up on a sauna floor."

"She's the only law enforcement officer here," I plead. "Judging by the noise, the road crew will arrive any minute. When the road is clear, the killer will use it to get away with murder."

"What do you think, Hannah?" Connie asks.

Hannah's thumbs remind me of hummingbirds. They fly across the keyboard so fast, they're a blur hovering over the screen.

"Do you have service?" I ask, assuming she's typing a text.

"No." Hannah shakes her head without looking up or slowing down her thumbs. "I'm typing our theories into Connie's phone. If something happens to us, there's a written record of what we know." She stops typing and looks at Connie. "Don't give your phone to anyone. Next time we get a blip of service, the note will back up to the cloud. When it's backed up to the cloud, no one can destroy it, even if they destroy your phone."

"Whatever you say, my lovely." Connie smiles, taking the phone from Hannah.

"Mum, let's find Twyla."

As much as I admire my daughter's determination, I hesitate.

What if one of our theories is correct? What if we rattle the killer? They could panic and do something drastic. Summer's killer has nothing to lose and is growing more desperate by the minute.

The road crew won't be alone when they get here.

Police cars, the coroner, and a forensics team will be right behind them.

"We have to stay with Connie," I say. "We agreed to stay together until we're safe from Summer's killer or get away from this mountain."

"I'll be fine," Connie insists. "I'll finish packing our things. I promise to lock the door and not open it for anyone." She gestures to the connecting door between the adjoining rooms. "I'll lock the connecting door too." She flicks her wrist. "Besides, the Shaws will be here any minute. They still have to pack."

Phone in hand, Hannah wraps her hand around the doorknob and looks at me.

"Well?"

Connie gives me an encouraging nod.

"Fine," I concede with a sigh and an anxious knot swelling in my stomach. "Let's go."

# CHAPTER 30

THE LOBBY IS a hub of activity. Both massage chairs are occupied, and groups of chatty guests dot the sofas and chairs. There are two people ahead of me at the front desk.

"Hi," I say, when the desk attendant summons me with a smile. "Do you know where Twyla is?"

"No," she replies, shaking her head. "I haven't seen her this morning." She picks up the two-way radio in front of her. "I'll hunt her down for you. It might take a few minutes to locate her."

"Thank you," I respond.

"I'll broadcast a message." She fidgets with the dials. "If someone is near Twyla, they'll tell me where she is."

"Thanks," I say again. "In the meantime, I'll loiter around the massage chairs, waiting for a turn." I smile and turn to walk away.

"Samosas," Nadira sings, blocking my path with the food cart she's pushing. "I'm trying out some new variations." She brings the cart to a stop. "I'd love everyone's opinion!" Nadira pinches the centre of an unfolded cloth napkin and snaps her wrist, flicking the napkin off the food cart to reveal a platter of samosas.

"Curry vegetable." She flicks another cloth napkin. "Spicy pork." With extra flourish, Nadira flicks the third cloth napkin and reveals the third steamy platter. "And last but not least, beef." She smiles.

A table top sign with the flavour handwritten in red ink pokes through the centre of each platter.

The samosas tease me with their appetizing aroma. I'm tempted but refuse to let the yummy, fresh, steamy food distract me from my mission to find Twyla.

"Would you like a samosa, Megan?" asks Nadira.

"No thank you," I smile. "I'm still full from the wonderful breakfast you made."

I want to tell Nadira that Billie's tummy troubles had nothing to do with the food at the spa but resist the urge for fear that I might divulge Billie's secret.

Scanning the crowded lobby for Hannah, I catch my daughter settling into a massage chair. The other chair is still occupied.

"The lady at the desk is trying to track down Twyla," I say. "I'm going to the gift shop to pick up some soaps and lotions."

"OK," Hannah says, futzing with the massage settings.

"Do you want anything?"

"No, thank you." She rests the back of her head on the chair and closes her eyes.

"Megan!"

I stop in the gift shop doorway and snap my head left then right, searching for the source of my name.

"Over here," Maria says, smiling and waving as she comes toward me. "Hi."

"Hi, Maria."

"I hear you're looking for Twyla."

"That's right," I say. "Do you know where she is?"

"She's helping an injured hiker," Maria explains. "April's daughter…" Maria hesitates, searching for her name.

"Rachel," I say, filling in the blank. "Are my friends OK?"

"Your friends are fine," Maria assures me.

"Good."

I sigh with relief.

"Rachel ran back alone about fifteen minutes ago. She and her parents found an injured guest on the hiking trail. They think she broke her ankle. April and Tamara stayed with the hiker, and Rachel ran back for help. She's leading Twyla to the hiker's location."

"It sounds like Twyla won't get back for a while," I comment.

"I'm glad I bumped into you." Maria looks around, assessing the crowded lobby. "Can we talk?" She inches closer to me. "In private? We can talk in my office."

"OK," I reply. "I'll meet you there in two minutes."

Maria steps behind the front desk, helping herself to a few samosas on the way, and I lure a reluctant Hannah away from the massage chair.

"Come in," Maria calls when I knock on her office door.

"Hi," I say.

"Hi," Hannah says, following me into the small office.

"Hannah!" Maria widens her eyes and blinks like Hannah might be an illusion. "I didn't know you were joining us."

"Here I am!" Hannah chuckles and makes jazz hands, once again reminding me that she is her father's personality in a twenty-year-old woman's body.

"What do you want to talk about?" I ask.

"The *thing* I gave you earlier."

Maria says, *thing* like I should know its hidden meaning.

"Thing?" I ask, feigning ignorance, but knowing she's inquiring about the pregnancy test she gave me.

"You know. *The THING*." Maria draws out the last word and nods slowly. "The thing you asked me for."

"What thing?" Hannah asks.

"Right," I say. "I remember. What about it?"

"I'm just following up to make sure it worked, and you're happy with the result."

She's following up because she's nosy. She wants to know if I used the test and what the result was.

"Worked?" Hannah asks. "What did she give you?"

I squeeze Hannah's hand to acknowledge her question and let her know we'll talk about it later.

"It worked as expected." I smile. "Thank you for your concern."

"You used it?" Maria confirms.

"It was used, yes." I nod.

"If you want to talk about it, I'm here." Maria smiles and squeezes her shoulders toward her ears. "I'm a superb listener," she adds.

"I'll keep your offer in my back pocket in case I need it," I say. "Can I ask you something?"

"Anything!" Maria sits up straight, giving me her full attention.

"Why did Twyla park so far from the spa on Friday during the storm?"

"Who said she parked far from the spa?" Maria asks, answering my question with a question.

"She must have," I reply, thinking back to Connie's detailed theory about Summer's murder. "The storm washed away the road below us but the parking lot was undamaged. The storm could only have washed away

Twyla's car if she had parked at least a quarter-mile down the road."

"You're right," Maria admits. "Twyla parked down the road. Like she always does."

"Why?" I ask.

"I asked her to," Maria explains. "Whenever Twyla visits me at work while she's on duty, her patrol car draws attention and distracts guests. When they see a police car, guests assume something bad happened. They get anxious and ask why the police are here. When I tell them the police aren't here on official business, they think I'm lying. Guests who didn't see the car, hear about it, and next thing I know, rumours and speculation are rampant. SoulSpring Spa and Retreat is a haven for relaxation and rejuvenation, not an epicentre for stress and speculation."

"She must love you a lot to walk a quarter-mile up the road during a violent spring storm."

Maria smiles.

"Your last name is Clark?" Hannah asks, pointing to the nameplate on Maria's desk.

"That's right."

"Are you related to the organized crime family with the same name?"

If Hannah is using the element of surprise to gauge Maria's reaction, goal achieved. Maria's eyes widen. She pulls herself to her full-seated height and clears her throat.

"Clark is a popular surname." Maria smiles.

"Was the man who went to prison your brother?" Hannah asks. "Mum and I assumed he was your brother. Then we realized he might be your cousin or uncle."

"You know," Maria says, acknowledging the truth.

"We suspect," I say. "Are we right?"

"Yes," Maria confirms. "Summer was my brother's

girlfriend. She testified against him, and he went to prison for murder. He passed away late last year from a brain aneurysm. He died alone on the cold cement floor of his cell. A guard found him."

Maria's brother died on the floor of a locked cell. Summer died on the floor of a locked sauna. Coincidence or calculated revenge?

"I'm sorry for your loss," I say.

"Sorry," Hannah says.

"Listen," Maria pleads, spreading her fingers on the desk. "No one else at the spa knows I'm a Clark." She stumbles over her words and takes a breath, then blows it out. "I mean, they know my last name is Clark, but they don't know my father orchestrated international art heists and brokered black-market deals for priceless, smuggled artifacts. Or that my brother worked for him and took care of their less glamorous, more violent tasks."

"They won't find out from us," I assure her.

"Does Twyla know about your family?" Hannah asks.

"Of course," Maria replies. "We grew up in the same town. We're younger than them, but Twyla and I went to school with Billie and the twins."

"Did you tell Twyla that Summer was staying here?"

Maria nods. "Twy worried that seeing Summer was too much for me. She thought I might have a breakdown. I lost my father and brother within a few months of each other. They both died unexpectedly, and their deaths hit me hard. Summer walking into the spa on Wednesday shocked me. I'm sure when I called Twy to tell her, I sounded unstable."

"That's why Twyla visited you every day," I say. "Not because you were helping with her resume or because they dispatched her during the storm. She was worried about you."

Maria nods. "I recognized Summer the moment I laid eyes on her. The reservation was in Billie's married name. I didn't know Billie's married name and didn't realize she was the same Billie who was best friends with Autumn and Summer. The last person I expected to see was Summer. When the twins walked in, my heart pounded, and I couldn't breathe. I got someone else to serve them. I lied about an emergency in the mud baths. Then I locked myself in my office and phoned Twyla."

"Did Summer recognize you?"

"Yes." Maria nods. "We both look different now. We're older. My hair is longer, Summer's was shorter, but we recognized each other. She hid the shock better than me, but I saw the recognition in her eyes. I knew Summer better than I knew Autumn because Summer used to hang out at my house with my brother."

"You could tell the twins apart?" I ask.

"Always," Maria says. "They had identical features, similar taste in clothes, and even wore their hair the same, but there were subtle differences. Autumn is uptight. She walks fast, is socially awkward, and she smiles like she saw it in a movie once but isn't sure she's doing right. She's a typical type-A personality. Autumn is a good person, and she has kind eyes.

"Summer was laid back, chronically late, and had horrible posture. She loved small talk and got bored easily. Her smile was a lopsided grin. Like she knew something but wouldn't tell you. Her eyes appeared kind, but if you watched long enough, you'd get a glimpse of the dark, soulless place behind them. I could always tell Summer and Autumn apart."

I believe her. If Maria dislikes Summer, there isn't a hint of anger or contempt in her voice or her demeanour. She's just stating the facts as she knows them.

"What did you and Summer talk about during those huddled, emotional conversations?" I ask.

"Hours after they checked in, Summer came looking for me," Maria explains. "I was still in shock after seeing her earlier that day. I had hoped we could avoid each other for the duration of her stay, but she insisted that we talk."

"About what?"

"She wanted me to know that they didn't know I worked here when they booked their stay. Summer said she didn't want to upset me. She offered to leave if I wanted her to."

"Did you want her to?" I ask.

"Yes," Maria replies. "But I told Summer that she, Autumn, and Billie were welcome guests. She also told me she had heard about my brother and father. She gave me her condolences. Summer said she was sorry about everything that happened between her and my brother. She tried to justify her decision to take the deal and testify against him. She asked for my forgiveness and tried to convince me she was a different person now."

"Did you forgive her?" Hannah asks.

"I forgave Summer a long time ago," Maria replies. "Forgiveness is for the forgiver, not the forgiven. I didn't want to live the rest of my life tethered to my past by anger."

"Did you believe Summer when she told you she was a different person?" I ask.

"No," Maria replies without hesitation. "When I opened my mouth to tell her I forgave her, I saw something familiar in her eyes. Her voice and the rest of her face matched her repentant words, but Summer's eyes were empty. Not a hint of genuine emotion. I couldn't say the words. Instead, I burst into tears and excused myself from the conversation."

"Was that your last conversation with Summer?"

"No." Maria shakes her head. "After our first conversation, I journaled about my feelings. I meditated on the situation and realized I didn't want to be Summer's excuse for not living up to her potential. I didn't want her to use my lack of forgiveness to justify falling back into her old ways."

"That's a very mature and insightful attitude," I comment.

"On Friday morning, while most guests were having breakfast, I encountered Summer alone in the lobby. It was a message from the universe. I approached her, forgave her, and wished her well. I told her I hoped she lives her best life."

"What did Summer say?"

"She thanked me. She said my forgiveness meant a lot to her. Then she asked me something kind of odd and off-topic."

"What did Summer ask you?"

"She pointed out that I had approached her and forgiven her without making sure I was talking to the right twin. She asked how I could always tell her apart from Autumn," Maria says with a chuckle. "Summer said I was the only person the twins could never fool. She said they could even fool their mother if they set their minds to it. It amazed her that after all these years, I could still tell them apart."

The timing is odd. But if I had a twin, and only one person could tell us apart, I'd want to know how they do it.

"What did you say?" Hannah asks.

"The same thing I told you." Maria shrugs one shoulder. "Except the part about Autumn having kind eyes and Summer's eyes being void of emotion. I left that out for obvious reasons." Maria clears her throat. "Now that

I've answered your questions and bared my soul, I'd like you to answer a question for me."

"Shoot," I say.

"It's about *the thing*," Maria says. "What was the outcome?"

I can't believe she's still thinking about the pregnancy test.

"Positive," I say with a wink.

"Are we happy or sad?"

"Happy."

# CHAPTER 31

"Do you still think Maria killed Summer?" Hannah whispers as we linger within sight of the massage chairs, hoping they'll become available before Twyla returns from her rescue mission.

"We can't eliminate her," I reply. "Maria had motive, and she had opportunity. She also had access to spotted water hemlock and Summer's smoothie ingredients. Summer checked in on Wednesday morning, giving Maria two days to plan the murder."

"But Maria is spiritual and grounded. She's at peace with her family's past. She wouldn't kill anyone in case Karma punished her for it."

"I know what you mean," I admit. "But maybe she acts more at peace than she is. Maybe she's serene and Zen because she killed Summer and justifies it because the universe sent her a sign or something."

"Mine!" Hannah blurts, then jumps into the massage chair when the current occupant vacates it.

"I'm going to the gift shop again," I say.

"I'll be here," Hannah says, her voice wobbling from the vibration of the mechanical massage hands.

"Hı, Megan."

"Hi, Billie." I turn to face her without disturbing the precarious pile in my arms. "How are you feeling?"

"Not bad," she replies. "The sickness is more bearable now that I know why it's happening." Billie points in front of me. "It's your turn."

"Is that all you're buying?" I ask, pointing my chin at the bottle of ginger ale she holds in one hand and the sports drink she holds in the other.

"Yeah," she says. "Doctor's orders. She said the sports drink will help replace some electrolytes." She holds up the other bottle. "And my mother always gave me ginger ale when I had an upset tummy."

"Go ahead of me," I insist, stepping aside. "It'll take forever for me to cash out. You only have two items."

"Thanks."

Billie smiles and steps up to the counter.

"How was your visit with the doctor?" I ask.

"It was good," Billie replies. "She said nausea is a normal pregnancy symptom. But she wants me to see a doctor tomorrow. She said there's a chance I might have hyperemesis gravidarum, and my doctor will want to monitor me."

"Is that as serious as it sounds?"

"It's the medical name for relentless nausea," Billie explains, "Anyway, Twyla cut our conversation short when she banged on the door. She needed the doctor's help with an injured hiker or something."

Between Summer's death, Billie's pregnancy, and an injured hiker, the doctor's spa weekend is more like a business trip than a relaxing getaway. I know how she must feel. If I wanted to find a dead body, I would've stayed home. Goodness knows, I've found more than my share in Harmony Lake.

"Speaking of Twyla," I say. "Is it true that you grew up with Twyla and Maria?"

"Yes," Billie says, paying the cashier for her purchase. "We didn't hang out with Maria and Twyla, but we knew each other." She smiles and takes the small bag from the cashier. "I'll see you later, Megan. I'm going upstairs to pack, then lie down for a while."

I unload my armful of artisanal soaps, travel-size organic lotions, and scented candles on to the counter.

"Did you find everything you were looking for?" asks the sales clerk as she organizes my self-care haul and returns the toppled bottles to their upright positions.

"Yes." I smile. "Thank you."

The clerk is about to scan my first item when her face lights up.

"Are those the samosas everyone is talking about?" asks the eager cashier as she slides my items aside and leans across the counter.

"A fresh batch!" Nadira rolls up with her food cart, stopping next to me. Again. I swear these samosas are conspiring to force me to eat them.

The scrumptious samosa aroma, and Nadira's repeat performance of her dramatic three-platter reveal, attracts a crowd of spa guests and employees.

Not being someone who would come between hungry people and a fresh batch of gourmet samosas, I pluck one from the vegetable curry platter and step away from the counter.

"I'll browse the mud masks until you're ready."

The cashier nods and gives me a thumbs-up because her mouth is full.

Moments later, I'm wishing I'd grabbed two samosas

and comparing the ingredients of a kaolin clay mask against the ingredients of a red clay mask.

Movement in the corner of my eye distracts me from the labels. Autumn slips into the gift shop and takes a bottle of water from the refrigerator. The hood is up on her unseasonable, fluffy, fleece, hooded sweatshirt. She makes her way to the shelves of snack food near the counter. She picks up a pack of sugar-free gum and a bag of nuts as she inches closer to the food cart and infiltrates the crowd of enthusiastic snackers around the samosa platters.

A drip of excitement tickles my belly, and I'm struck by a sense of captivated awe. The same feeling I get when I'm sitting in the backyard, minding my business, and a squirrel or bird approaches me, suspending its fear of humans and granting us a rare, close-up encounter with each other.

I stay so still I even hold my breath in case an exhale spooks Autumn and she takes off.

I'm not proud of watching someone who doesn't know they're being watched, but I can't make myself look away. I bend my knees slightly to reduce the amount of me that's visible above the shelf. Is this what stalkers do? Am I stalking Autumn? Why am I so intrigued by her?

Autumn squeezes her way to the front of the crowd. She assesses the platters of samosas. She arranges the water bottle, nuts, and gum so they're in the same hand. Then, with her free hand, Autumn reaches for the first platter, vegetable curry samosas. She reads the sign and retracts her hand, moving it to the next platter. In one quick motion, Autumn takes a samosa from the spicy chicken platter and a second samosa from the beef platter. Who are they for? They can't be for Autumn because she's a pescatarian. A loud, dedicated pescatarian.

Clutching the samosas in her hand, Autumn backs out of the crowd and retreats to the magazine racks where I can't see her.

I return the clay masks to the shelf and creep through the store toward the magazine racks.

Autumn is chewing fast. Her eyes dart this way and that, furtively checking her surroundings. Just as she raises the second triangle pastry to her mouth and bites into it, our eyes meet.

"Megan," Autumn mumbles with her mouth full.

I gasp and stare into her wide, empty eyes.

I rush out of the gift shop with one thing on my mind.

"Hannah!" I grab her forearm and yank her out of the massage chair.

"I have to turn it off." She reaches for the chair's controller, but we're already out of arm's reach. "Mum, I should reset it for the next person."

"No time," I say, pulling her along behind me like a defiant toddler.

"Where are we going?"

"Upstairs," I say. "We're locking ourselves in our room until help gets here."

"What happened?" Hannah jerks her arm from my grasp and stops. "Why are we rushing?"

"I saw her," I say. "And she knows I saw her. We're not safe."

I grab Hannah's hand and tug my reluctant daughter toward the stairwell.

"Who did you see?" She stops again, reclaims her hand, and crosses her arms in front of her chest.

Why does she have to choose now to ask questions? Why did she have to get too big to carry? Why won't she let me drag her to safety?

"Sweetie." I summon my most composed and rational voice. "I know who the killer is. I know why she did it.

427

She knows I know. She's unstable and psychotic and has nothing to lose. We aren't safe. She'll do anything to keep her secret. I need you to cooperate." I take a calming breath to maintain my composed and rational facade. "Now, please let me take you upstairs and lock you in our hotel room," I say, sounding far less composed and much more irrational than I intend.

Hannah squints. An unsuccessful attempt to conceal the confusion and concern in her eyes as she considers my words.

"Twyla and the Shaws are miles away helping an injured hiker, which means Connie is all alone," I say, hoping to appeal to my daughter's affection for Connie.

Hannah nods, lurches past me, and opens the stairwell door.

"Who killed Summer?" she asks as I rush past her.

"It's not that easy," I say, leaning against the closed door so *she* can't follow us. "Nothing is how it seems."

"You're not making sense, Mum."

"I'll explain everything as soon as we're safe."

"Connie!" Hannah declares, remembering why she agreed to listen to me.

She grabs the handrail and conquers the first flight of stairs two-at-a-time, disappearing around the corner before I start my ascent. The thumping of her feet bounding up the stairs is the only evidence Hannah is still ahead of me.

"Hannah!" I shout, more breathless than I care to admit. "Wait!" I stop on the landing between the first and second floors. "Hannah?"

I tilt my ear into the silence, forcing myself to tune out the heartbeat pounding in my ears and listen for the thumping of Hannah's feet. Nothing. She must have stopped on the second-floor landing.

"Mu—"

Who muffled her voice?

"Hannah?"

A rush of adrenaline cures my breathlessness. I launch myself to the third step and take the rest of the stairs two at a time. Each leap reveals a bit more of the second-floor landing. As I search every new inch of the landing for a sign of Hannah, she slides into view. The backs of her hands are against her shoulders and her eyes are wide. She is trembling.

She is terrified.

Hannah gives me an almost indiscernible head shake.

A silent warning to stay back.

"Why?" I demand. "What's wrong?"

Hannah shuffles sideways, and the trigger of her fear comes into view. Someone is pressing a gun into my daughter's back.

# CHAPTER 32

"How did you find us?" I freeze on the spot, looking up at them from the second last step.

I control my breathing, taking measured breaths, and forcing my heaving lungs into submission.

I can't let her see my fear.

I've never been more afraid in my life.

"When you and your daughter stopped to have a pair of hissy fits in the lobby, I snuck past you and ran up the stairs." She grins. "I knew you'd take the stairs. You *always* take the stairs." She scoffs. "You're not the only one who's observant, you know."

"Well done."

Despite my sarcastic tone, she interprets it as a genuine compliment and smiles. I want to punch the arrogant, lop-sided smile off her stupid, smug face.

"You should have seen yourself. You looked like you saw a ghost." She laughs.

"I kind of did," I point out.

"Was it the samosas?" she asks. "Is that how you figured out it was me?"

I shake my head.

"It was the eyes."

"I was sure it was the samosas." She sighs. "If I never see another piece of fish again, it'll be too soon." She chuckles. "The samosas were a lazy mistake, but I was desperate for something meaty. Getting away with eating the lamb chop made me overconfident."

"The lamb chop you ate after you planted the missing sauna key in Billie's luggage?"

Summer nods.

"Twyla was asking too many questions," she explains. "I think she was starting to suspect something. She visited our room yesterday and spent too long searching our belongings. Then she came back today before breakfast and searched again. I'm sure she thinks I killed my sister."

"Summer, please let Hannah go," I plead. "I'll switch places with her. You can hold the gun against my back."

She grimaces. "It's still strange to hear my name," she says, ignoring my plea. "I just can't get used to it. I got used to my witness protection name, and Autumn's name, right away." She shakes her head. "But my name doesn't sound like it belongs to me anymore."

Summer clears her throat.

Hannah flinches.

Summer panics and raises the barrel of the gun from between Hannah's shoulder blades to the back of her head.

Hannah whimpers.

"It's OK, sweetie!" I move my foot to the last step before the landing, bringing me within arm's reach of them. I reach toward Hannah but don't allow myself to touch her. "It's OK. Shhhh."

I settle for muttering comforting *shhh* sounds instead of telling Hannah: stay calm. We can't freak out Summer.

We can't fluster her. Let's keep her relaxed. Distract her while we figure out how to get away.

"Why do you have a gun?" I ask, wondering why she killed her sister with a toxic plant when she clearly has a gun.

"The gun was Plan B," Summer replies. "In hindsight, Plan B would've been easier."

"What was plan A?" I ask.

"Plan A was for my sister to die in her sleep. It was supposed to look like she died of something undiagnosed."

"Why did you choose spotted water hemlock?" I ask.

"It's less obvious than a gunshot wound. It would've been impossible for the police to declare my sister died of natural causes if there was a bullet in her. Spotted water hemlock grows everywhere around here," Summer explains. "If the police discovered she had died from ingesting spotted water hemlock, I would've convinced them she confused it with parsley or some other herb. They would have believed me because I'm Autumn now. Everyone believes Autumn. Autumn doesn't lie. Autumn is a good person, She's an honest, productive, and respected member of society. She has no criminal record."

"You added the spotted water hemlock to your own smoothie, then when Autumn wasn't looking, you switched smoothies with her?"

"Yes." Summer nods. "Only a small amount. It only takes a small amount. I didn't mix it in very much, so the dark green leaf pieces weren't visible through the cup." She squints at me. "How did you know it was spotted water hemlock?"

"We found your baggie," I reply. "It fell out of your bag when you bumped into the doctor."

"I didn't realize I'd lost it until I went looking for it." Summer shakes her head. "I figured it fell out on the deck. I had breakfast there this morning so I could look for it. After Autumn died, I made sure to put her finger-prints all over the bag so the police would believe that she added it to her smoothie herself."

"Why did you try to frame Billie?" I ask.

"I always planned to pin it on Billie if the police discovered Autumn was murdered and wouldn't believe my parsley story."

"That's why you planted the key in her luggage?"

Summer nods.

"You said Autumn was supposed to die in her sleep, but she died in the sauna," I point out.

"Between fifteen minutes and three hours is a big window of time, Megan," Summer explains, rolling her eyes and prolonging the *n* in my name. "Autumn decided she wanted a smoothie *before* the sauna instead of *after*. I knew it was my last chance of the day to poison her. She wouldn't have ingested anything else until the next morning."

"Why did you steal her identity?"

The irony! Summer left the new identity and new life she'd built in witness protection, so she could reclaim her old identity and old life, then killed her sister to assume her identity.

"I killed her to reclaim my life," Summer clarifies. "While I lived a made-up life as a made-up person, Autumn lived my life. The life that should have been mine. The life I wanted. I wanted to live in our home-town with our friends and family. I wanted to learn the family business so I could take over one day. I wanted to take care of my sick mother. I wanted to go to her funeral. No one understands I gave up everything when I went into witness protection, then I gave up everything again to come back."

Ten years ago, she became a different person to avoid

a prison sentence for her role in killing someone, and now she'll serve a prison sentence for killing someone to become a different person. The prison psychiatrist will have a field day untangling this.

"But you came back," I say. "Most people in witness protection never see their loved ones again. You got a second chance to be Summer."

"No, I didn't," Summer insists through gritted teeth. "No one gave me a second chance. I gave up a secure future with guaranteed income, and everyone treated me like a criminal. I'm tired of being defined by one unfortunate decision I made over a dozen years ago."

Now she'll be defined for two unfortunate decisions.

"Maybe people just need more time," I suggest, hoping sympathy will keep her talking and keep my daughter alive until help arrives. "Maybe they're scared you'll leave again."

"My sister wouldn't give me a job or my fair share of our mother's estate," she hisses.

"But she did, Summer," I say, attempting to make her less agitated. "Autumn instructed her lawyer to add you to her will and to transfer part of the family business to you. I read the email."

"It was me, Megan." Summer shakes her head and clucks her tongue, pitying my gullibility. "I sent the email. I sent it before I killed Autumn. It was risky to leave it in her sent folder. She could've found it by accident. But I needed to ensure the police would find it if necessary. The email was part of my plan to frame Billie."

"Of course, it was," I say with a sigh. "You're clever. You lured the sauna attendant away from her desk while you staged Autumn's body and stole the key, and before you went public with your sister's assumed identity, you tested your Autumn impersonation on Maria, the only person who could always tell you apart. That's why you visited the front desk on Friday night. You didn't ask Maria for pain killers because you had a headache, you were testing her to make sure you could pass as Autumn. After you passed the test, you put the second part of your plan into action, delaying the discovery of Autumn's body as long as possible."

"Nice deduction, Miss Marple." Summer sneers. "If there's one thing I learned in witness protection, it was how to lie. My whole life was a lie. I practiced being Autumn for weeks. Her walk, her bossy voice, her tense smile, and her rigid posture. It's not as easy as you'd think." Summer shakes her head. "We might look identical, but I'm nothing like my sister."

"How did you know the sauna attendant would believe you when you lied about her boyfriend cheating in a massage room?"

"It's called paying attention, Megan. You should try it." Summer's words ooze smugness. "I listen to conversations around me. Autumn loved the sauna. We were there every day. The sauna worker was always on the phone. She went on and on about her suspicions that her boyfriend was doing the nasty with a massage therapist called Logan."

"I'm surprised Billie didn't figure out you were Summer pretending to be Autumn," I say, bringing us back to her sister's murder.

"If she wasn't so distracted by puking and sleeping, she would have," Summer says.

"That's why you've avoided her since you killed your sister," I theorize. "We thought you were in shock, but you were avoiding detection."

"I was planning to end Autumn and Billie's friendship," Summer confesses. "Otherwise, it was only a matter of time before Billie realized something wasn't right with Autumn and started putting it together."

"You've thought of everything," I commend her.

"Don't be glib," Summer says, shifting her weight from foot-to-foot with increasing frequency. "You think you're better than me, but you're not. We're the same except you got away with your bad decisions. Everybody is bad, Megan. Some people, like you, believe they're good because they don't get caught."

"I'm not better than you," I say. "I'm not a good person or a bad person. Neither are you. There's an entire spectrum between good and bad, Summer, and most of us fall somewhere in the middle."

"Why does everything you say sound so preachy?" She rolls her eyes. I assume her question is rhetorical. "Self-righteous people like you need bad people like me. I give you someone to feel superior to."

"Just because you've made a bad decision, or two, doesn't mean you're a bad person."

Summer uses the back of her gun-holding hand to wipe beads of sweat from her brow.

I give Hannah a reassuring nod and a small smile. She returns the tiniest nod.

"I am a bad person," Summer says. "I killed my sister. Before that, I stood by and watched someone else get murdered. Then I helped dispose of their body. I'm the bad twin. Autumn was the good twin. And look where that got her…"

A cough echoes through the stairwell, interrupting Summer's disturbing rant. We all look up at the ceiling, certain the sound originated from above us.

Is someone on the next landing? Who? How much did they hear? If they come down here, will Summer kill them? Will she kill Hannah?

I need a plan. Now.

"The gun isn't loaded."

Twyla?

"One step closer and I'll shoot the girl," Summer threatens.

I release the handrail, my fingers and knuckles stiff from the death grip I had on it. I shake my hands and wipe my sweaty palms on my thighs, leaving a dark streak on the thighs of my yoga pants.

"With what?" Twyla asks. "The gun is empty. I found it tucked into a secret compartment in Summer's suitcase when I searched your room. I took the ammo. All of it. There are no bullets in that gun."

"You're lying," Summer exclaims, moving the gun away from Hannah and pointing it up the stairs toward the landing between the second and third floors. She looks at me. "Twyla's lying."

Summer inspects the gun like she just caught it lying to her.

A bead of sweat streams down the side of Summer's forehead and past her temple.

Hannah glares at me, recalibrating her attitude and her body. She balls her hand into a fist and narrows her gaze on me. Her jaw clenches and unclenches. She bends her arm and cocks her elbow, raising her shoulder. Her forearm is rigid and tense.

Lucky for us, her bullet situation distracts Summer, and she doesn't notice the subtle changes to Hannah's posture.

Sensing that Hannah has a plan and is waiting for the right moment to execute it, I stealthily switch feet so my dominant, right foot is on the step above me, and grip the handrail with my less dominant, left hand. I'm prepared to launch myself, if necessary, and my dominant hand is free to help Hannah with whatever she plans to do.

A loud clink reverberates through the stairwell. Metal hitting concrete. A bullet dropping to the floor above us.

"That wasn't a bullet," Summer shouts, glowering at

me. "She dropped a key or a coin. She's trying to psych me out." Summer nods fast and swallows. "This gun is loaded." She shakes the butt of the gun. "I loaded it myself. If you don't believe me, I'll shoot your daughter to prove it."

"You can't shoot anyone with an empty gun, Summer," Twyla says. "Do yourself a favour and give up. You're surrounded and outnumbered."

Twyla used Summer's name. She knows who Summer is. Had she already figured it out, or was she standing there throughout Summer's confession?

"Shut up!" Summer screeches, stretching her arm to aim the gun up the stairs.

This is the farthest the gun has been from Hannah's body since Summer took her hostage.

This is our opportunity.

I nod at Hannah.

She nods back.

"Now!" Hannah shouts, scrunching her face and ramming her elbow into Summer's stomach and ribs.

The blow takes Summer by surprise. Winded and knocked off balance, she collapses at the waist, bending forward as she draws her arms protectively toward her torso.

Hannah grabs Summer's wrist and squeezes, digging her fingertips into the tendons and ligaments below Summer's palm.

Summer howls in agony, fighting the involuntary loosening of her grip on the gun. Her hand opens, her fingers contorted with pain and resistance.

The gun lands on the floor with a resounding clamour.

I launch myself toward the landing, gripping the handrail for balance, squeeze my hand around Summer's forearm and wrench her toward me as hard as I can, letting out a loud grunt.

Summer tumbles down the stairs, and I use the handrail to pull myself out of her way.

I leap to the landing and push Hannah against the wall, trapping her behind me where she is safe.

I'm a panting, sweaty mess.

Summer's gun is on the floor only feet away from me. Calling me. It would take less than one second to grab it.

Summer's crumpled body lies on the landing at the bottom of the stairs. Her eyelids flutter, and she moans.

My eyes flit back and forth between Summer and the gun. The gun she insisted has bullets in it.

Thirteen steps separate me from Summer. A clear shot.

The ball of rage and fear roiling in my gut pull me toward the gun like a magnet.

I want to do it so bad.

Summer could never hurt my daughter again. She could never hurt anyone. Ever. The world would be safer.

I could say I grabbed the gun to secure it, and it went off by accident. Oops! How did that happen? I've never used a gun; I didn't know what I was doing. My hands were sweaty and shaky. My finger must have slipped.

I want to destroy the person who threatened my daughter's life. But I refuse to take a step forward and leave Hannah unprotected.

"Mum." She taps my shoulder. "I can't breathe." She gasps. "Stop backing up." She wheezes. "You're squeezing me against the wall."

I take a half-step forward. Closer to the gun.

"Sorry," I say without taking my eyes off Summer or the gun.

Hannah takes a deep breath against my back.

Momentum surges through my body, and with my gaze fixed on the gun, my body twitches.

Just as I lunge, the clomping of boots diminishes my lunge to a dramatic wince. Twyla lands with a thud in front of me. She secures the gun, taking the choice out of my hands.

"Everyone all right?" Twyla asks, scanning Hannah and I from head to toe.

"Yes."

"Uh-huh."

Hannah and I nod.

"You did good," Twyla says. "Both of you." She looks at me. "I underestimated you."

"Ditto," I say.

Twyla rushes down the stairs, blocking my view of Summer.

"Are you OK, Mum?" Hannah steps out from behind me.

"I'm fine," I say, checking her for marks and injuries. "How about you?"

I grab her and squeeze tight.

"You're trembling," I say. "You need to sit down and drink water."

"I don't know why I'm shaking," Hannah says watching her shuddering hands. "I'm not scared." She looks at me. "At first, I was scared, but now I'm hyped. It's a rush. I feel like I can do anything."

"It's adrenalin." I guide her toward the stairs to the third floor. "It'll stop in a couple of hours," I say from experience.

"We were awesome!" Hannah brags as we climb the stairs side-by-side. "I wish we had recorded it. We were like superheroes. Who knew we could fight like that?" she huffs, amazed. "We disarmed a murderer!" Her chest heaves and her breaths are fast. "I feel unstoppable, like I'm capable of anything!"

"Me too," I agree, horrified of what I might be capable of.

"We kicked butt." Hannah lets out a half chuckle.

"You get that from me."

# CHAPTER 33

I lock my phone screen and shove the phone in my back pocket, then comb my fingers through my curls with a long, heavy sigh. I sink into the booth at the pub, processing Eric's text.

"What is it, my dear?" Connie asks, handing me a bouquet of balloons. "Bad news?"

The text was neither good nor bad. The information he gave me was neither good nor bad.

"No," I reply, tying the police-car shaped mylar balloon to the back of the guest-of-honour's chair. "I asked Eric to find out if there were bullets in the gun. He just texted me the answer."

"The gun that Summer pointed at Hannah?" Connie asks, horrified by the mere mention of the event. "What good comes from knowing, my dear? It's time to stop tormenting yourself and move on. Summer was arrested, and you and Hannah weren't injured. In fact, the experience empowered Hannah. She has a newfound, mature confidence that she didn't have before."

"I'd still rather she never had the experience, but there's no point in wishing the past was different."

"Was it loaded?" April asks, placing a square glass vase at the centre of the table.

"No," I say, tying a gold balloon to the chair. "Twyla was right. It wasn't loaded."

"This doesn't invalidate the fear you felt," Connie reminds me, dropping golf balls and fishing lures—hooks removed—into the glass vase. "As far as you and Hannah knew, the gun was loaded. You were at the mercy of a murderer." She pokes a blue daisy into the jar, then a yellow daisy.

"I still don't understand why Twyla took the ammunition but left Summer's gun behind," April says.

"Apparently, she was authorized to have it," I reply, recalling Twyla's explanation, but most of it is a blur because I was still in shock when she explained it to me. "It's complicated, but it had something to do with the original threat to her life. Anyway, because everyone believed Summer was dead, and the gun was part of her belongings, and not part of the murder investigation, Twyla didn't have the authority to seize the weapon. However, she had the authority to seize the ammunition."

"Thank goodness she did," Connie comments.

"She saved a life," I say.

April and Connie will assume I'm referring to Hannah's life, but I'm recalling my urge to end Summer's life with her own gun.

"What else is bothering you, Megnificent?" April asks, poking more yellow and blue daisies into the centrepiece.

"Am I a bad person?" I ask, untangling the balloon ribbons and separating a gold balloon from the bouquet.

"Bad people don't wonder if they're bad people," April replies. She sets a hat, sash, and giant pin-on badge at the guest of honour's seat. The badge reads, *I'm retired, not expired,* and features a border of flashing blue lights. "Also, I only hang out with good people, and you're my best friend, making you, by definition, a good person."

"You didn't kill her, my dear. You didn't even pick up the gun."

"But I wanted to," I admit. "And I was mid-lunge when Twyla stopped me."

Connie lays down the party accessories and hugs me.

"You aren't a bad person, and you mustn't pay attention to the inane ramblings of an unstable mind." She pulls away and starts assembling the next centrepiece. "Summer's speech about good and bad people was to justify her own actions. It was nonsense. Don't let her get in your head."

"Connie's right," April says. She grins. "Any parent would have the same urge. Heck, lots of parents would have reached for the gun without a second thought. You aren't a bad person, Megadoodle, you're a mother. It's how we're wired."

"Megan!"

Just as I place the familiar voice, its owner appears in front of me.

"Maria? Why are you in Harmony Lake?"

"I have something for you."

Maria pulls two envelopes from her bag and hands one to me and one to April.

"Thanks," I say.

"What is it?" April asks.

"Gift certificates for a weekend at SoulSpring Spa and Retreat," Maria replies. "Before I resign, I want to compensate you for the inconveniences during your last visit."

"You already refunded us for our stay," April reminds her.

"The refund didn't seem adequate to compensate for everything that happened."

"Thank you," I say, doubting I'll use my gift certificate because the last place I want to visit is the scene of Summer's crimes.

April and Connie also thank Maria, with as much as enthusiasm as one can muster when they're given a gift that they know they won't use.

"Wait a few weeks before you use them," Maria warns. "Nadira is away and a guest chef is filling in for her." She uses her hands like a verbal eraser. "The guest chef is great, but most people want Nadira's food."

"Did Nadira go somewhere exciting?" Connie asks.

"Northern Ireland," Maria replies. "She won another World Luxury Spa and Restaurant Award. She's attending the gala award ceremony in Belfast."

"Good for her!" April chimes in.

"Every guest who was at the spa that weekend will get gift certificates before I leave," Maria announces. "I won't be able to hand-deliver them, but I wanted to deliver yours and Billie's."

"You saw Billie?" I ask. "How is she?"

"I see Billie all the time," Maria says. "We've spent a lot of time together since…" Maria shakes her head and refocuses. "She's doing much better than last time you saw her," Maria replies. "Her morning sickness is better than it was." She taps her cell phone then hands it to me. "This is her first ultrasound."

"Awww," Connie, April, and I swoon over the grainy image.

"It was nice of you to visit her," Connie comments. "Billie lost her two best friends in three days."

"Billie is amazing," Maria says. "She has such a great attitude, despite everything that happened. And we have so much in common. We grew up in the same town and know the same people, and Summer changed our lives. We've become close since Mother's Day. Billie promises to visit Harmony Lake and bring the baby to meet everyone."

"When is her baby due?" I ask.

"December," Maria replies. "After Summer's sentencing hearing."

I nod.

Summer's confession makes it difficult for her to plead not guilty to killing her sister. In exchange for a guilty plea, the prosecution agreed to give her a say in which penitentiary she'll serve her sentence and accommodate her request for certain creature comforts that are scarce in prison.

"At least she's sparing us the stress of a trial," Connie says, looking for a silver lining.

"You drove all the way to Harmony Lake to deliver gift certificates?" I ask.

"Twyla is signing her offer today, and I tagged along so we could look at houses," she replies. "I went to Knitorious first. The lady said I'd find you at the pub."

"Congratulations to Twyla," Connie says. "We're proud to have her join the ranks of Harmony Lake's finest."

"Thank you," Maria says. "I'll tell her." She looks at me. "Thanks again, Megan, for putting in a kind word with Eric."

"I didn't," I say. "He inquired about her when I told him about Summer's murder. Everyone gave her glowing reviews. I mentioned she might be looking for a new opportunity. Twyla did the rest. She impressed him during the interview. If we're thanking each other, thank you again for alerting Twyla that Hannah and I were in the stairwell with Summer. You might have saved my daughter's life."

Maria witnessed Hannah and I arguing in the lobby when I tried to drag Hannah to our room. She also noticed the person she believed was Autumn sneak past us into the stairwell. Maria admitted it hadn't occurred to her that she sneaked into the stairwell to intercept us. She worried that something had upset her and caused her to rush out of the lobby. And she worried about Hannah and I because she had seen us arguing. She used her two-way radio to contact the attendant stationed on the third floor and asked her to check on Autumn and to check on us. The attendant contacted her when none of us were in our rooms. Maria then asked the second-floor attendant if we had emerged on the second floor and became worried when she learned we hadn't.

Twyla had just returned from rescuing the injured hiker. Maria told her that Autumn—who she didn't yet know was Summer—Hannah, and I went into the stairwell and never came out. Twyla cordoned off the stairs, took the elevator to the third floor, and snuck into the stairwell to search for us. She heard voices and realized something was wrong on the second-floor landing.

Twyla knew Summer's gun was not loaded, but knew Hannah and I believed it was. She tried to lure Summer upstairs so Hannah and I could get away. It didn't work, but she provoked Summer to point the gun away from Hannah, giving us the chance we needed to escape.

Twyla later told me that she considered ambushing Summer but worried that Hannah or I would end up badly injured, or worse, if we toppled down the cement stairs.

"Her predecessor's retirement party starts in a couple of hours." April flicks the police-car shaped mylar balloon. "We're just setting up."

"I see that," Maria says, adjusting a centrepiece so it is precisely in the centre of the table. "May I help?"

"You don't need to help," I say. "Thank you, though."

"No, I want to help," Maria insists. "I'll be a Harmony Lake resident soon, and I plan to immerse myself in the community."

"In that case"—I hand her a roll of crime scene tape—"this is for the guest of honour's table."

"Have you found somewhere to live?" April asks.

"I don't want to jinx it," Maria says, crossing her fingers. "But we loved one house we viewed today. As soon as Twyla finishes signing paperwork at the police station, we're meeting with our agent to make an offer."

"Good luck!" Connie says.

"Thanks," Maria says, wrapping the table with yellow tape. "Everything is coming together. It's like the universe wants us to move here. I have a second interview next week at a local spa. I have a good feeling about it. I'm pretty sure they're going to offer me the manager job."

"Which spa?" Connie asks, lowering her reading glasses to her eyes.

Before Maria finishes telling Connie which of Harmony Lake's two spas might hire her, Connie is tapping her phone screen.

"Who are you texting?" I ask.

"Everyone, my dear." Connie sends her text and looks at Maria. "We'll flood the spa with recommendations to hire you." She winks.

"People are so nice here," Maria comments, wrapping the back of the guest-of-honour's chair with crime scene tape. "Everyone is welcoming and friendly. Harmony Lake is nothing like the small town where Twyla and I grew up. In our town, everyone knew everyone else's business, and the town's collective pastime was gossip. I'm glad Harmony Lake isn't like that."

Connie, April, and I look at each other, eyes wide with raised eyebrows.

"Who wants to tell her?" April asks.

"Not me!" I blurt, beating Connie.

"Me neither." Connie flicks her wrist and continues assembling centrepieces with her back to us.

"Tell me what?" Maria asks.

"Nothing," we say, smiling.

A Knitorious Murder Mystery Book 12

# Murder, It Seams

# REAGAN DAVIS

*For those who survived, and especially for those who didn't.*

# COPYRIGHT

# FOREWORD

Dear Reader,

Despite several layers of editing and proofreading, occasionally a typo or grammar mistake is so stubborn that it manages to thwart my editing efforts and camouflage itself amongst the words in the book.

If you encounter one of these obstinate typos or errors in this book, please let me know by contacting me at Hello@ReaganDavis.com.

Hopefully, together we can exterminate the annoying pests.

Thank you!
Reagan Davis

# CHAPTER 1

The little dog at the top of the driveway pulls against his leash, bouncing on his hind legs, whimpering and yelping at me to hurry as I get out of my car.

Dogs are less tricky than people. You can know someone for a lifetime without ever *really knowing* them. But a dog will show you their soul and love you unconditionally from the moment they meet you.

The pooch's wiry tan and cream coat is scraggly but clean and healthy. Judging by the designer logo on his gem-studded collar and leash, someone loves this dog and spoils him.

"Hi, Rita. When did you get a dog?" I ask, stooping to pet the adorable bundle of energy before he explodes from anticipation.

"Hi, Megan. Gucci's not my dog," Rita explains. "I'm babysitting. He's Karla's dog."

"Karla Bell?" I ask, scratching Gucci's neck.

The small dog's impossibly long tongue hangs over the side of his mouth as he pants. He's unkempt and

457

hyper in that charming, endearing way only pets and children can get away with.

"That's right," Rita replies. "He dug a hole under the fence and burrowed into Karla's backyard. She found him scratching at the back door, wanting to come inside. He marched straight upstairs and took a four-hour nap on her king-size bed. Then he woke up and demanded dinner. Karla said Gucci acted like he'd always lived there, and she should've expected him."

"Where did he come from?" I ask, getting lost in Gucci's dark brown eyes.

"It's a mystery." Rita shrugs. "He had a tag, but the phone number was illegible. Karla took him to the vet, but Gucci didn't have a microchip. She put notices around the neighbourhood, posted his photo in online pet groups, and registered his description with the animal shelter." Rita shakes her head. "No one claimed him."

She taps her knee.

"Gooch!" She smiles and steadies the obedient pooch when he jumps onto her lap. "Gucci and Karla have been together for three months."

She makes Karla and Gucci sound like a new couple who are taking it slow and avoiding labels.

I glance at Karla Bell's house across the street.

Oh, my!

I snap my head toward Rita when I see the SOLD sign on Karla's manicured lawn.

"Karla's moving?"

"In three weeks," Rita says, stroking Gucci's button ears. "She's moving back to her hometown to take care of her sick grandmother."

It never occurred to me that Karla has a family. I *know* everyone has people, but the Karla Bell I know is so impersonal and impeccable that I can't imagine her as a doting granddaughter. I'd be just as likely to believe Rita if she said Karla had hatched from an egg as a fully formed adult, complete with designer heels, an expensive handbag, and a sarcastic-verging-on-offensive sense of humour.

"Too bad about her grandmother," I say. "What about the business? Karla loves her job. Just Task Me! is her baby."

Just Task Me! is a *hotel-style concierge service for your business and life,* according to the website. The website also says that Just Task Me! *prides itself with providing world-class service with small-town care.* They'll do everything from picking up your dry cleaning to planning your six-hundred-guest wedding.

Rita explains how Karla still owns Just Task Me! but has sold a piece to an employee. Her new partner will oversee the daily operations in Harmony Hills, and Karla will manage the strategic direction of the company. She might open an east-coast branch of the concierge business.

"Thanks for coming by to pick up the yarn order, Megan," Rita says, placing Gucci beside her lawn chair.

She stands up and stretches to her full height of less than five-feet, lacing her hands above her head and letting out a sigh that morphs into a yawn.

"No worries," I reply. "I visit Harmony Hills every Monday to run errands, anyway"—I shrug—"may as well pick it up while I'm here."

Rita approaches the keypad on the wall next to the garage door, rises to her tippy toes, and lifts her reading glasses to her face from where they dangle on a macrame necklace. She presses a code into the keypad, then lowers herself to her natural height. She raises the reading glasses from her eyes to her head, resting the lenses atop her salt-and-pepper pixie cut. Her red muumuu with large orange and yellow orchids wafts in the warm breeze as we watch the garage door inch open, its motor grinding and moaning in protest.

"Those two are yours." Rita points to the grey plastic tubs that have KNITORIOUS scrawled across the side in black marker.

"Are you moving too, Rita?" I ask, taking in the columns of boxes that line the wall.

"Heavens no!" Rita chuckles. "The only way I'm leaving this house is in a body bag."

I laugh, then stop, forcing myself to frown instead.

"That's not funny!" I chide. "Don't say that. You'll tempt fate."

"I'm not superstitious." Rita dismisses my comment with an eye roll. "It'll take more than an old wives' tale to finish me off!"

"I hope so."

Rita McConnell is one of the strongest women I know. Besides being a two-time cancer survivor, she suffered a tragic loss two years ago when her friend Meaghan died. Meaghan was the most important person in Rita's and Karla's lives. She was like a daughter to Rita, and she was Karla's best friend and business partner. Since her death, Rita and Karla have bonded over their shared love and grief.

"These boxes are Karla's donations," Rita explains. "She's downsizing before she moves. I offered to donate her cast-offs." She points to the farthest column of boxes. "These are clothes. They're destined for the women's shelter." She gestures at the rest of the boxes. "These are housewares and such. We'll auction the non-clothing and donate the proceeds to cancer patients." She makes a fist and raps her knuckles on a random box. "Good quality," Rita says, nodding. "Karla has expensive taste and likes luxury items. These boxes will help so many people."

I thank Rita for the yarn and pick up the grey plastic tubs from the cement floor. Yarn doesn't weigh much, so I lift them with ease.

Rita is a yarn dyer. My yarn store, Knitorious, carries her yarn. The quality and colours of her yarn are scrumptious and popular with local knitters and crocheters. Rita and I visit often when I replenish my inventory.

"You'll stay for a visit, right?" Rita uses her right hand to trap the watch face on her left wrist. The delicate, silver watchband is too big for her frail wrist. "It's still early." She crinkles her nose and smiles with her eyes. "I have fresh lemonade!" She raises an index finger. "I'll be right back!" She tugs on Gucci's leash and gives a low whistle before disappearing into the house with the little dog in tow.

I load the bins into the trunk and return to the top of the driveway as Rita and Gucci emerge from the house with lemonade and brownies.

Rita sets the tray on the plastic table between our chairs. Gucci laps water from the bowl under the table, then curls up under Rita's chair, resting his chin on his front paws.

We drink lemonade and chat. Rita tells me about the fall yarn colours she's creating. We ask after each other's families, and she asks about our mutual acquaintances in Harmony Lake.

I live in Harmony Lake, a cozy town nestled between the Harmony Hills mountains and Harmony Lake. My tiny town doesn't have big-box stores, chain restaurants, or corporate franchises, so the residents make regular trips to the larger, more suburban Harmony Hills to shop and access amenities we don't have.

"Brownie?" Rita nudges the plate of brownies toward me. "They're my secret recipe…" She prolongs the *e*'s in *secret recipe* as though the elongated vowels will tempt me. "They have pecans." Another elongated *e* in pecans.

"No, thank you," I say, smiling. "I'm driving."

"I should've made a batch without nuts."

It's not the nuts. I can drive while under the influence of pecans and chocolate. I can't drive while under the influence of Rita's secret recipe. It includes an extra ingredient—a dash of homegrown marijuana. It's medicinal, she says. For pain management and to encourage her appetite.

We talk about the beautiful late-summer weather and how the days are already shorter than a month ago. I sip lemonade while Rita eats one-and-a-half pot brownies.

We pause our conversation when Gucci steps out from under Rita's chair. Walking to the end of his leash, he trains his attention on Karla's house. On high alert, his button ears perk up, and his sickle-shaped tail forms a graceful curve in the air above his back.

Across the street, Karla's garage door creaks open. The slow, loud rise reveals unfamiliar body parts. Feet wearing bright white sneakers, denim-clad legs, a grey, short-sleeved t-shirt, and a large topknot of traffic-cone-orange hair; a shade found more often at the drug store than in nature.

The orange-haired woman smiles and waves at Rita.

Who is she and why is she in Karla's garage?

Rita returns the smile and the wave.

The woman turns away, disappearing into the depths of the dark garage, then reappears a moment later, pushing a red hand truck loaded with moving boxes.

Grinning over the tower of boxes, the orange-haired woman pushes the hand truck across the street toward Rita's driveway. The closer she gets, the more excited Gucci becomes about her imminent arrival. By the time she's within voice range, he's whining and tippy tapping his front paws, desperate for her attention.

"Hey, Gooch-the-pooch," the woman says, bringing the hand truck to a stop and standing it upright. "Are you happy to see me or my pockets?" she asks, reaching into her front pocket and pulling out a few small dog treats. "Sit." She uses a firm tone and raises her eyebrows at the small, eager dog.

Gucci complies. He sits without taking his eyes off the woman's hand, licking his chops, and fanning his tail back and forth on the driveway like a windshield wiper.

"Good boy," says the woman. She bends down and places the treats in front of him. "OK!" She smiles with a twinkle in her brown eyes, and Gucci lunges for the treats.

"Chelle Temple, this is my friend Megan Sloane," Rita says, gesturing to me.

Chelle and I shake hands, saying, "It's nice to meet you" at the same time.

She's older than my forty-two years, but younger than Rita's seventy-two. Too young to be Karla's mother, and too old to be her sister.

"Chelle works for Karla," Rita explains.

"Oh." I smile at Chelle. "Are you a concierge?" I ask, assuming Chelle works at Just Task Me!

"I'm more like Karla's personal concierge." Chelle grins. "I help Karla with her personal life, not her professional one."

"Chelle is Karla's PA," Rita explains. "That means personal assistant," she adds, grinning.

"I'll put these with the rest of 'em?" Chelle pats the top box on the hand cart.

"Yes, please," Rita confirms. "Clothing on the right. The rest against the wall."

Chelle nods in acknowledgement and pushes the hand truck around us and into Rita's open garage.

Chelle returns moments later with the empty hand truck. Rita offers her a glass of lemonade. Chelle declines. Rita offers her a pot brownie—with the same elongated-vowel technique she employed when she tried to tempt me with. Again, Chelle declines.

"Can I get you anything before I leave for the day?" she asks Rita.

"No, thank you, Chelle. I think I have everything I need." Rita traps her watch face again and checks the time. "Have you heard from Karla?" she asks, letting the watch face drop to the underside of her pale, bony wrist. "She said she'd be back by lunchtime." She raises her face toward Chelle, squinting into the sun. "Lunchtime was two hours ago."

"You know what Karla's like," Chelle reassures her. "She probably went to the mall after her Pilates class, found a sale, and lost track of time."

"I'm sure you're right," Rita agrees with a laugh and a dismissive flick of her hand.

Personal shopping is one of the many services Karla offers to her clients. She is also a shopping hobbyist.

"I'll be here tomorrow to meet the roofer," Chelle says, bending down to scratch Gucci under his chin.

"Oh! I forgot about that!" Rita laments. "Karla said I didn't have to worry about the roofer."

"You don't," Chelle confirms. "I'll be here to talk to him and answer his questions for you."

Chelle, Rita, and I say goodbye, then Chelle and I exchange, "It was nice meeting you," at the same time.

As Chelle pushes the hand cart across the street toward Karla's house, Rita tells me that Karla arranged for her roof shingles to be replaced. According to Rita,

Karla took care of the estimates, choosing a roofer, and scheduling the work.

Though I don't say it to Rita, I'm relieved that Karla has stepped into the role that Meaghan used to have in her life. But I'm worried how Karla's cross-country move will affect Rita. Who will look after her? Who will take care of things like roof repairs? Who will care for Gucci while Karla goes to Pilates?

We watch as Chelle opens her trunk, puttering between her blue hatchback and Karla's garage.

"I didn't know Karla had a PA," I comment as we watch Chelle close the garage door and get into her car.

"She hired Chelle over a year ago," Rita says as Chelle pulls out of the driveway and waves to us.

"I guess Chelle will be out of a job in a few weeks when Karla moves," I say, watching Chelle's car disappear around the corner.

Rita opens her mouth to say something, but a loud vibrating buzz sends her into a tizzy. In a panic, she searches her immediate surroundings. Groping the chair under her butt, lifting the plate of brownies on the table next to her, then standing up to pat down her red orchid-print muumuu. With obvious relief, she reaches into a pocket hidden in the voluminous garment and pulls out a cell phone. Panic returns when she jabs at the thing, trying to answer it.

"I hate these blasted things," Rita grumbles as she races to answer before it stops vibrating. "It was Karla's idea," she says, lowering her reading glasses from the top of her head. I hold out my hand for the phone. "Cell phones are a curse on society." She hands me the phone. "We don't own them, they own us."

I press the green *accept* button on the screen and hand the phone to her.

"Hello?" Rita squints, then gasps and opens her eyes so wide her eyebrows almost touch her hairline. "How?" She stares at a random spot on the driveway. "Are you OK?"

Is who OK?

Rita returns her reading glasses to her silver pixie cut.

"What did the doctor say?" She nods as though the caller can see her. "Is the doctor still there?" Brief pause. "Let me talk to them."

Doctor? Why is the caller with a doctor?

Rita cradles the phone between her shoulder and cheek, then traps her watch.

"Gucci's fine, Karla! He's right here, staring at me."

Karla! Why is Karla with a doctor? What happened?

Rita squints at her watch, then drops her arm with a silent huff when she can't make out the time without her glasses.

"Are you still in the ER?" More nodding. "Don't be silly. I'll come in and get you."

"What happened?" I ask when Rita ends the call. "Is Karla OK?"

"She says she's fine," Rita assures me. "But I'll believe it when I hear it from the doctor."

"What happened?" I ask.

"She was leaving Pilates and somehow found herself between an airborne medicine ball and its intended destination. The exercise ball hit her in the head and knocked her out. The doctor says she might have a concussion."

"That's awful," I sympathize. "Can I do anything?"

"Yes! Thank you, Megan!" Rita squeezes my hand with her smooth, cool-to-the-touch, pale hand. "Would you pick up Karla at the hospital and speak with the doctor?" She smiles.

My offer to help was sincere. It wasn't an empty promise or a socially appropriate platitude. But considering how Karla and I tend to clash like oil and water, it didn't occur to me that Rita would ask me to pick her up.

"Me?" I ask, pointing at myself. "Don't you want to go so you can speak with her doctor yourself?"

"Yes," Rita replies, "but I can't drive right now." She shifts her gaze to the plate of pot brownies on the table, then back to me. "And because she might have a concussion, the doctor won't discharge Karla without someone to accompany her home."

"I'll drive you," I offer.

"I can't leave the Gooch," Rita implores. "He hates to be alone."

The precocious pup tilts his head, causing his ear to flip inside out in the most adorable way possible.

"Of course." I sigh, then smile to distract from the sigh. "I'll pick up Karla, get discharge instructions from her doctor, and bring her home."

"Thank you, Megan!"

"No problem." I hitch my bag over my shoulder and dig out my keys, resigned to carry out my unpleasant assignment with all the speed and efficiency I can muster.

"I know Karla rubs you the wrong way sometimes," Rita says, rubbing my upper arm.

"Sometimes?" I mutter.

"She doesn't do it on purpose." Rita smiles. "I never understood why you aren't friends. You have so much in common."

"We have nothing in common."

"You and Karla are more alike than you want to believe. You just show it differently. Karla is hard on the outside and soft on the inside. You're soft on the outside and hard on the inside. She's fond of you. I can tell because she doesn't roll her eyes when she hears your name."

"Well from Karla Bell, that's practically a bear hug," I say, then flash a sarcastic grin.

"Aha!" Rita points at me and nods. "See! You and Karla are more alike than you think. You're both fluent in sarcasm." She tugs on Gucci's leash. "You both have big hearts, and you're both too clever for your own good."

I walk to my car, giving myself a pep talk about not letting Karla's backhanded compliments and sarcastic jabs bother me. I instruct myself to rise above her petty attempts to goad me.

# CHAPTER 2

"Down the hall, past the nurses' station, fourth curtain on the right."

"Thank you," I say to the auxiliary volunteer at the information desk.

As I approach the nurses' station, there's no need to count the curtains because Karla's throaty laugh, like a beacon, guides me to her cubicle.

"Knock, knock," I say to announce my presence.

"Hello!" The doctor sweeps aside the light blue curtain and smiles. "Are you here for Ms. Bell?"

"Yes," I reply to the doctor while peering around him at Karla. "How is the patient doing?"

Karla sits upright on the hospital bed with her sculpted legs stretched in front of her, ankles crossed, feet tapping against each other nonstop. There isn't a hair out of place on her chic blonde bob. Her hair is longer now. It used to be a sharp, angular line along her jaw, but today it dusts her shoulders. Her designer, black tank top and leggings coordinate with her black, brand-name athletic shoes. A teal bolero shrug covers her arms and ties in a loose knot under her chest. Even with a head injury,

Karla looks perfect. She grins at me and waves. Then behind the doctor's back, she looks at him, widens her eyes, then looks at me, panting and fanning her face with her hand.

I narrow my gaze at her and give my head a slight shake, disappointed but not shocked at her objectifying the handsome young doctor.

"... and you'll stay with Ms. Bell overnight?"

The doctor's question distracts me from Karla's silent shenanigans. I missed whatever he said before he asked me about Karla's overnight plans.

"No," I reply, "someone else will stay with her. I'm here to drive her home."

He hands me a faded photocopy titled *Adult Head Injury Protocol* and uses his pen to highlight the main points. Just when I think we're done, the doctor flips the page, revealing an equally faded list of symptoms and side effects that, should they occur, warrant a return trip to the emergency room or a call to the paramedics.

"I think I've got it," I say when the doctor asks if I have questions about his instructions.

"If you have questions"—he circles a number at the bottom of the page—"phone this number twenty-four-seven."

"Thank you." I smile.

The doctor gives Karla some parting words of encouragement, reminds me she can have another dose of acetaminophen in four hours, and warns us she should avoid ibuprofen until tomorrow. He wishes me luck, instructs Karla to take her time standing, then sweeps out of the small cubicle with his white coat billowing behind him.

"Where's Rita?" Karla asks.

"She couldn't drive, and she didn't want to leave Gucci," I explain.

"Brownies?"

"One-and-a-half."

We nod.

So far, so good. Karla is less abrasive than usual. Maybe the exercise ball broke the part of her brain that makes her say mean things.

"Well, thank you for coming to get me."

Did Karla just thank me? Am I on one of those shows that prank people and records their reaction?

"No problem," I say. "I was picking up a yarn order from Rita when you called."

She looks me up and down as she stands and rubs the back of her neck.

"Well, I appreciate you dropping everything to rush over here without stopping to worry about how you look."

There she is! The Karla Bell I know and don't love is back! Her head will be fine.

I look down at my black, loose, off-the-shoulder, jersey-knit dress and rose gold sandals.

"I look fine," I defend, petting my long brown curls and tucking a few stray coils behind my ear.

"Of course you do," Karla says, tilting her head with a pitiful smile. "Your eyes look extra hazel with that lipstick."

On the way to the lobby, Karla tells me about her collision with the exercise ball. She says it knocked her off her feet but didn't render her unconscious, though she admits it left her dazed for a while afterward. She says the gym manager insisted on driving her to the emergency room, and she was unable to argue in her stunned state. Her wits returned as the triage nurse strapped a blood pressure cuff to her arm, and Karla insisted to the gym manager that she would be fine and he should leave.

Ahead of us, an elderly patient gripping his IV pole with one hand and holding his hospital gown closed with the other tries to press the elevator button. Karla jogs ahead, presses the button for him, then smiling, waits until the elevator arrives. She blocks the sensor to stop the door from closing as he shuffles across the threshold. Next, she asks him what floor he wants and presses the button for him.

Do head injuries cause random acts of kindness? Is this a one-off, or have I misjudged Karla Bell's capacity for sympathy?

"How is your head now?" I ask when we resume walking.

"The pain meds helped," she replies. "But I'm glad I have my sunglasses. The world is too bright right now."

I use my keychain to unlock the car.

"Congratulations," Karla says as she reaches for the door handle. "I heard you and Detective Hottie got married."

"Thanks," I reply, rolling my eyes behind my dark lenses when she refers to Eric by the crude nickname she gave him when he investigated her best friend's murder.

"Rita showed me some photos from your wedding," Karla continues, opening the door. "You were a beautiful bride." She smiles. "I hardly recognized you."

Karla drops into the passenger seat and closes the door.

I close my eyes and take a deep breath, bracing myself for what I expect will be the longest fifteen-minute car ride of my life.

"I hear you're moving in a few weeks," I say, steering us out of the hospital parking lot.

"That's right," Karla confirms. "Will you miss me?" She grins.

"As much as possible," I reply, also grinning.

"YOUR HOME IS LOVELY," I compliment.

This is my first time inside Karla's house. Like the exterior, the interior is clean, stylish, and beautiful. Even amid the chaos of packing and moving, Karla's sophisticated taste is obvious.

Nothing screams confidence like white furniture. I don't have the mental fortitude to own white furniture. My love of non-white foods and drinks is greater than my love of white furniture.

"It's usually more organized," she replies, fussing with piles of bubble wrap and tissue paper.

"Don't be silly," I say. "This is the most organized packing assembly line I've ever seen." I smile. "Sit down. I'll get you a glass of water and text Rita to tell her you're home."

I return moments later with a crystal tumbler of water.

"That sculpture is beautiful." I lift my chin toward the lone sculpture on the bookshelf. "It reminds me of an iceberg." I set the water on the round glass coffee table in front of the white tuxedo sofa where Karla sits.

"Thank you," she says, picking up the glass and taking a small sip. "It's not a statue, it's a bookend." She lowers the water glass to the table. "The other one must be here somewhere." Karla rises and scans the room, taking a mental inventory of her scattered belongings. "It's a limited edition. There are only twenty-five pairs in existence."

She squints, eyeing the boxes stacked against the wall and reading the bullet list of contents written on the side of each box. "The artist is one of my favourites. The bookends are white cast stone," she explains. "They were expensive, but their sentimental value is priceless." She looks at me. "They were the first expensive piece of art I bought for myself." She picks up a clipboard from the sleek marble mantle and scans the pages.

"I'm sure the other bookend is here somewhere," I assure her. "You're supposed to rest. Why don't you sit and let me find it?"

Karla shakes her head. "It's fine," she says. "I'm sure Chelle packed it and forgot to write the box number on the inventory sheet." She sighs and returns the clipboard to the mantle. "I'll have to search every box until I find it." She rests her hands on her hips and bites her bottom lip. "I hope she didn't pack it inside one of the donation boxes in Rita's garage."

As if on cue, Rita and Gucci walk through the front door. Rita has a saucepan in one hand, and Gucci's leash in the other.

"Look, Gooch! There's Mummy!" Rita drops the dog's bejewelled leash so he can run to Karla. "I brought you some soup," she says, holding up the saucepan as proof. "I'll warm it up."

Rita disappears into the kitchen, and Karla and Gucci reunite like they've been apart for years, not hours.

"How's my wittle Gucci poochie," Karla says with her lips puckered.

It's strange to watch someone who I know as emotionless and indifferent to people behave with such affection and tenderness toward an animal. Has Gucci melted Karla's icy heart?

"Why do you call him Gucci?" I ask.

"What do you mean?" Karla asks, scratching the dog's back just above the base of his tail. "That's his name."

"Rita said his nametag was illegible," I say. "How did you teach him to answer to Gucci?"

"I didn't." Karla shrugs. "He looks like a Gucci." She unlatches the designer leash from Gucci's designer collar.

"I called him Gucci, and he responded. He's been Gucci since."

"Look what I found in the kitchen," Rita says, appearing around the corner and waving a cell phone.

"That explains why Chelle didn't answer when I called her from the hospital," Karla comments with a sigh. "That woman is forever leaving her cell phone behind."

"I'll make sure she gets it when she comes to my house tomorrow to meet the roofer," Rita says, dropping the cell phone into the folds of her muumuu.

While Karla eats a bowl of minestrone soup, I give Rita the head injury information sheet the doctor gave me. I reiterate what time the doctor said Karla can have more acetaminophen and to avoid ibuprofen until twenty-four hours have passed since the accident.

"Thanks again, Megan. I appreciate it," Karla says as I position myself near the door, ready to leave. "Try not to miss me too much." She winks.

"Good luck with your move," I say with my hand on the doorknob. "And good luck to your new friends and neighbours." I smile.

Rita shakes her head at us.

# CHAPTER 3

Tuesday, August 30th

As I sink into the sofa with my knitting, Sophie's corgi ears prick to attention at the muffled squeak under my butt. The rest of her follows. She sits at my feet in alert watchfulness as I reach between my backside and the sofa cushion and pull out her plush, squeaky chipmunk.

"What's this, Soph?"

I shake the plush dog toy between my thumb and forefinger.

Sophie's eyes dart back and forth, following the replica rodent's spastic movements.

"Want it?" I squeeze the squeaker in the end of the chipmunk's tail. "Want the chipmunk?" I squeak it again. "Here you go!" I toss it across the store. "Get it!"

Sophie scampers after it and slides to a halt under the harvest table.

We enjoy the rare moment of quietude; me making one stitch after another and Sophie chewing her chipmunk.

A familiar jingle pierces our comfortable silence.

Sophie abandons her plush prey and rushes to the

door. I drop my half-finished sock in my lap, prepared to greet the first customer of the day.

"Hey, handsome." Eric stoops and I stretch to kiss him. "Thank you." I grin and accept the coffee cup he offers. "How did you know I was craving caffeine?" I crack the lid and inhale the glorious scent of cinnamon-maple latte.

"I didn't," he admits, joining me on the sofa. "The coffee is just my excuse to visit the most amazing woman in Harmony Lake."

"It must flatter the barista that you think so highly of her," I tease, then savour a sip of coffee.

"Ha! Ha!" Eric says with a sarcastic head-shake-eye-roll. "You know I mean my beautiful wife." He rubs my back and plants a soft kiss on my forehead.

Eric and I are newlyweds. We celebrated our eight-month anniversary last week. Yes, we celebrate our anniversary every month. Eric assigns the same level of sentimental value to every milestone and treats them all with equal significance. I don't mind being married to a hopeless romantic, but it means remembering dozens of special dates, including the day we met, our first date, our first kiss, and on and on. My post-Eric calendar is much fuller than my pre-Eric calendar.

"How's your day?" I ask.

I listen while he tells me about his morning so far and admire my handsome, muscular husband. His deep laugh and charismatic smile distract me from his story about the missing vacuum at the Harmony Lake Police Station. There's a glint in his eye when he laughs at the absurdity of an entire police department being unable to solve the mystery of a missing upright vacuum. His large, powerful hands gesticulate as he speaks, and he strokes his chiselled chin at the end of his story.

Standing on her hind legs. Sophie rests her front paws on Eric's knee so he can rub her.

"Did you find the vacuum?" I ask.

"Yes," he replies with a chuckle.

"Where was it?"

"In the closet."

"Where was it supposed to be?"

"In the closet." He shrugs his broad shoulders. "No one checked because everyone assumed someone already did."

"So, it wasn't actually missing," I conclude.

"I guess not," he agrees, flashing me a wide smile. "Where's Connie?" He scans the empty store, looking for my part-time employee.

"She has a late start today," I reply. "I should give her the day off. We've been open an hour and haven't had a customer yet."

"We're alone?" he asks.

He cocks one eyebrow, and the familiar twinkle in his eye makes me squirm.

"Sophie's here," I tease, watching the corgi perk up when she hears her name.

"Sophie doesn't count," Eric's low voice vibrates through me. "I can't remember the last time we were alone on a Tuesday morning."

I swallow hard.

He narrows his gaze.

I bite my lower lip.

The short sleeve of his black Harmony Lake Police Department golf shirt strains across his bicep as he wraps his arm around my waist and slides me into him like I weigh nothing.

I run my hand through his short dark hair and trail my fingers down his neck, shoulder, and arm, resting it on his muscular forearm.

He picks up my knitting and tosses it on the coffee table.

I take a deep breath and enjoy his subtle, warm scent. This is what temptation smells like. I'm addicted, and he knows it. I inhale again, letting the intoxicant flood my mind with impure thoughts.

"Shouldn't you get back to work, Chief Sloane?" I ask, looking up at him through my lashes.

He shakes his head slowly without blinking. His pupils dilate, engulfing the honey-coloured flecks in his brown eyes.

He inches closer until I can feel his breath.

The butterflies in my belly flutter out of control.

Sophie yelps.

I flinch.

Eric's demeanour tenses, and he spins his upper body toward the door.

The bell jingles.

We jump up and apart, fussing, smoothing, composing ourselves.

I haven't jumped off a sofa this fast since I was sixteen years old, and my mother came home two hours early while I was *watching a movie* with my boyfriend.

"Hi, Megan. Hi, Chief Sloane." Mason smiles.

"Hey, Mason," we say in our most casual voices.

"Are you OK, Megan?" Mason asks. "You're flushed." He touches his cheeks while looking at mine.

"I'm fine," I reply with a nervous laugh. "Warm." I fan myself by tugging the collar of my yellow, button-down, sleeveless shirt. "It's hard to keep these old buildings the right temperature."

"It's warmer than usual," Eric agrees, clearing his throat and nodding.

"What can I do for you, Mason?" I ask, relieved to change the subject.

"Would you mind if I go downstairs and search through my mum's boxes?" Mason jerks his thumb and rolls his brown eyes toward the basement door in the back room.

"Of course," I reply.

Mason pets Sophie and tosses a nearby squeaky bone for her.

"I'm sorry I'm here so often. I'm looking for paperwork to settle my mum's estate," Mason explains. "Between my regular hours at the Town Hall and the extra hours getting ready for the grand opening, I only have a few minutes here and there to go through her stuff."

Mason is Harmony Lake's Building and Facilities Maintenance Manager. He keeps town facilities clean and in good repair, including the new pool.

The lightning bolt between the *AC* and the *DC* on Mason's vintage concert t-shirt is peeling, and I resist the urge to smooth the loose piece of red vinyl hanging over his round belly.

"Come by whenever you'd like." I smile. "I'll get the key," I say, already behind the counter.

Mason cleaned out his mother's apartment after she passed away two months ago. I offered him the basement at Knitorious to store whatever wouldn't fit in his small apartment.

It's more like a dungeon than a basement. It's too cold, too damp, and too dark. There are no windows. The low ceiling makes it a crawl space for anyone over five feet, ten inches. A single, dim bulb in the ceiling creates an eerie, swaying spotlight in the centre of the room. It's the basement of horror movies and nightmares. We don't use it. Ever. For any reason. I don't go down there unless I have no choice.

"Everything ready for the grand opening this afternoon?" Eric asks Mason.

"Ready," Mason replies with a thumbs-up.

Harmony Lake has a new indoor pool. After years of fundraising and construction, the addition to the community centre is complete and ready for its unveiling at this afternoon's huge—for our small town—grand opening ceremony.

"Found it," I declare with victory when my fingers recognize the fuzzy, faux-fur gnome beard. "Here you go." I hand him the red and blue, white-bearded gnome with the basement key attached to the pointy tip of his red gnome hat.

Because the dungeon is creepy and I like to pretend it doesn't exist, I keep it locked with a double-sided deadbolt. I wouldn't want a customer to confuse the basement and restroom doors and tumble down the stairs.

"Thanks, Megan." Mason sticks out his lower lip and blows his sandy-blond bangs out of his eyes as he takes the key. "I promise to bring it back this time."

Last time Mason visited the dungeon, he left with the key. He walked halfway across town before Mrs. Bianchi asked him who his little friend was, and he realized he was still holding the knitted gnome.

"It's not a big deal if you leave with the key," I assure him. "I have a spare at home. I have a key rack in the laundry room just for spare keys."

"Are they all attached to gnomes?" he asks.

"No," I laugh. "I don't have a spare gnome, but I can make one if necessary."

"I'll see you in a few minutes," he says, turning toward the back room.

"Listen, Mason, the store is dead, and Connie will be here soon. Do you want help?"

"I can't ask you to do that," Mason says, smiling and

shaking his head. "You hate the basement. You shudder whenever I go down there."

"Two searchers are better than one," I reason, relieved that he didn't take me up on my offer. "I feel bad that you're down there all alone, fumbling around in the dark." I snap my fingers. "You'll need the flashlight." I reach under the counter and produce the large black rubber flashlight. "The bulb in the ceiling is still burnt," I explain. "I picked up light bulbs when I was in Harmony Hills yesterday, but I forgot them at home."

The lone bulb that illuminates the dungeon burnt out last week, and I haven't replaced it yet.

"This is brighter than the bulb anyway," Mason says, taking the flashlight. "Besides, my mum was organized, so it's pretty easy to find what I need."

"You don't have any family who can help you?" I ask. "What about your aunt? The one who used to visit Harmony Lake every summer."

"She's in a home now," Mason says. "My other aunt lives far away." He shrugs. "My dad is dead, and I don't know anyone on his side of the family."

"I knew your dad died before you were born." I nod. "But why don't you know his family?"

"They don't know about me," Mason explains. "Before I was born, my mum lived in Los Angeles, where she met my dad. He was from Australia but worked in LA. Mum got pregnant with me before they got married. She said my dad's family was traditional and deeply religious. He had planned to go home for a visit to tell them about me before I was born." Mason shakes his head. "He died before his trip to Australia. Car accident. My dad had warned my mum that he expected his family to reject me and disown him because they conceived me out of wedlock, so she never contacted them about me. After he died, Mum quit her job and moved home to be near my grandparents and aunts."

"I never knew your mum lived in Los Angeles," I say. "All the times I'd met her, she never mentioned it."

Mason's grandparents used to have a cottage in Harmony Lake. He grew up spending summers and Christmases here. They weren't year-round residents, but the Shillings were part of our community. Mason moved here full time when he finished school, and his family sold the cottage a few years ago.

"She worked in the music industry," Mason says. "That's how she met my dad. He was a musician, a studio drummer."

"So, you come by it naturally," Eric adds.

"I guess I do," Mason chuckles.

Mason is a music enthusiast. His extensive mental catalogue of music trivia is impressive and guarantees his choice of team at pub quiz nights. He plays drums and electric guitar, and he boasts an extensive collection of vintage records and concert t-shirts.

"I'll drop this on the counter if you're with a customer when I'm done." He holds up the gnome.

"Great." I smile. "Leave the door open," I call as he walks toward the back room with Sophie guiding his way. "The upstairs light will help guide you."

Without turning, Mason nods and gives me a thumbs-up.

"I should head out," Eric says with a sigh. He leans across the counter and kisses me. "I have to visit my least favourite resident before the grand opening this afternoon."

"Right," I say, remembering that it's Tuesday, Eric's least favourite day of the week. "Why don't you delegate it? You're the chief of police. Can't you dispatch a uniformed officer this week? You've gone every week and deserve a week off."

"No one wants to deal with him, babe," Eric says with a shrug. "And I don't blame them. Besides, how can I justify exposing someone else to him when I don't even want to go?" he adds under his breath.

Eric is dreading his weekly visit with Clarence Fawkes, the town's most reviled, unpopular resident. Before relocating to Harmony Lake, Clarence Fawkes was serving an eighty-eight-year prison sentence for crimes against dozens of young women under his influence.

Fawkes wrote and produced the biggest musical hits of the 1990s and 2000s. Young, female, ingenue singers performed his toe-tapping, chart-topping pop anthems. Until fifteen years ago, when a once-promising songstress who found fame with Clarence Fawkes songs accused him of deplorable improprieties. Within days, dozens more women came forward, telling their truth about Clarence Fawkes and the depraved demands he made of the pop starlets he abused under the guise of nurturing their careers. Witness accounts followed the accusations. If a victim declined his advances, Fawkes would blacklist her, destroying her career, and relegating her to musical history.

In days, Clarence Fawkes went from being the defining voice of a generation to the world's most casti-gated celebrity. There was a boycott of his songs and videos. It became unacceptable to reference his name in pop culture. I haven't heard a Clarence Fawkes song on the radio in years.

Justice was served. Then it wasn't. A few months ago, the world reverberated in shock when news broke that Fawkes's legal team's last-ditch, desperate attempt to overturn his convictions based on an administrative tech-nicality was successful. A judge granted him a new trial and release from prison—subject to many restrictions and conditions—until his next court date, whenever that is.

"I became a cop to put bad guys away, babe, not to watch them live their best lives in my town."

"I hope he's not living his best life," I say. "No one wants him here, and he knows it. He's still a prisoner but in an upgraded cell. He's a recluse."

"Only because he has no choice," Eric retorts. "The judge put so many conditions on Fawkes's release, he can barely step onto the driveway without risking going back to prison."

"Let's hope he steps onto the driveway."

To secure his release, Fawkes had to find living accommodations that wouldn't involve him living with other people or within a certain proximity to anyone younger than eighteen. One of his family members owns a rental cottage on Harmony Lake that meets the requirements. Fawkes cannot go outside before dawn or after sunset. He must get approval from his parole officer to attend appointments or go on outings. He must not possess, borrow, or use a cell phone or any internet-enabled device. His home must not have access to Wi-Fi. He can't go any place where people younger than eighteen might gather. Harmony Lake is a family tourist town, so everywhere outside his cottage is pretty much off limits.

The cottage is remote enough that the media lost interest in trying to get photos or video footage of him, and they left town.

"Honey, I'm sorry," I say. "I know you hate the situation." I squeeze his hand. "But everyone in town feels safer knowing you're keeping a close eye on him."

Eric forces a weak smile.

Among Fawkes's many parole conditions are twice daily check-ins with the local police department. An officer phones the landline at Fawkes's cottage twice each day at random times, and he must answer to comply with his parole. At least once each week, Fawkes must present himself at the local police station. No one wants Clarence Fawkes coming to town, mingling with the locals and tourists, on his way to and from the police station, so Eric drives out there every Tuesday to lay eyes on the felon and ensure he's complying with his plethora of conditions and restrictions.

"I'll see you at the grand opening?" Eric asks, perking himself up.

"I'll save you a seat."

"I can't wait." He kisses my forehead. "This week's visit will be over. I won't have to go there again for seven days." He smiles.

Eric gives Sophie a quick ear-scratch, says goodbye, and leaves.

I deliberate hollering downstairs to offer Mason a beverage or snack but decide against it because I don't want to deliver them to the dungeon if he accepts.

Instead, I return to the sofa and pick up my knitting while Sophie remembers she left the plush chipmunk waiting for her under the harvest table.

I'm thinking about the dungeon and shuddering when the front door slams into the wall, startling Sophie and me.

"What's wrong?" I say, jumping off the sofa. "What happened?"

# CHAPTER 4

"Hannah's fine," Adam says, breathless, as if reading my mind.

"Thank goodness." I exhale.

Hannah is our twenty-one-year-old daughter. She's a third-year university student in Toronto.

"Is Mason here?" he asks, scanning the store.

I nod.

We're divorced, but Adam and I are still family. We've forged a strong friendship from the ruins of our marriage. We still love each other, but not the romantic way spouses should. Our relationship has evolved, but our commitment to Hannah and to our chosen family is as strong as ever.

"There's a flood at the library," Adam explains. "Mason isn't answering his cell phone. Someone saw him come into Knitorious."

"He's in the dungeon with his mum's belongings. There's no cell service down there."

We rush to the basement door.

"Mason!" Adam bellows in the volume he reserves for yelling at politicians on television.

Mason appears at the bottom of the stairs carrying the flashlight and a blue floral notebook. When he sees the mayor, he rushes up the stairs two at a time.

Adam brings Mason up to speed about the leak as they hurry toward the door. Mason comes to an abrupt halt at the counter and leaves the flashlight. He turns to me, and I nod, waving him toward the door with my hand. I'm about to offer to take the blue floral notebook from him, but before I open my mouth, Mason and Adam disappear onto Water Street. The door jangles closed behind them.

"That was exciting, wasn't it, Soph?" I ask the confused corgi as she stares at the closed door, wondering why her friends left in such a hurry.

I return to the basement door and lock it with the gnome key Mason left in the lock.

Sophie and I are strolling through the park across the street from the store when my phone dings. While Sophie sniffs the leg of a bench, I pull out my phone and unlock the screen.

*April: Karla Bell is here.* Followed by an eye-roll emoji.

April and I have been best friends since I moved to Harmony Lake twenty years ago.

*Me: Karla is in Harmony Lake?*

*April: She's in Artsy Tartsy. She came to say goodbye.*

Artsy Tartsy is the bakery April and her wife own. Sometimes, Karla commissions Artsy Tartsy to provide baked goods for her clients and their events.

*Me: Karla and I said goodbye yesterday. I doubt she'll visit me, but thanks for the warning.*

April knows firsthand how unpleasant Karla can be.

As Sophie and I meander to the next tree, I glance toward Artsy Tartsy. If Karla leaves the bakery right now, she might see me. What if she spots me and seizes the opportunity to squeeze in a few more verbal jabs before she moves?

"Let's go, Soph," I say, turning around and tugging Sophie's leash toward Knitorious.

"Did you hear about the leak, my dear?" Connie asks when Sophie and I return from our walk.

"Yes," I reply. "Mason was in the dungeon when Adam told us. Is it fixed? Will they have to reschedule the pool's grand opening?"

Harmony Lake is a small town. Our town hall, library, and community centre are in the same building. A problem in one affects all of them.

"The ceremony will go ahead as scheduled," Connie says, detaching Sophie's leash and scratching the corgi's chest.

"That's good," I say.

"Mason turned off the water," Connie adds. "The firefighters evacuated the building to confirm it was safe. A small thingamajig needs to be replaced, but Mason is confident he can fix it before the ceremony."

"Business is slow today," I say. "I almost called to offer you the day off, since we're closing early anyway for the pool ceremony."

"It's been steady since I arrived," Connie counters, tucking a piece of her sleek, chin-length silver hair behind her ear. "I rang up three sales while you were out with Sophie."

"You're good for business." I smile.

Connie is like a mother to me, and she's also Knitorious's original owner. We met twenty years ago when Adam, Hannah, and I moved to Harmony Lake. I was a young mum, married to a workaholic lawyer, and building a life in a new town. My mum passed away just before we moved here. Overwhelmed and grieving her sudden death, I would knit through my grief during Hannah's naps and after her bedtime. My mum had taught me to knit and knitting helped me to feel close to her. It still does.

One day, after I had grief-knitted through every inch of yarn I owned, I rolled Hannah's stroller into Knitorious to replenish my stash. Connie welcomed us. She took Hannah and me under her wing, filling the mother and grandmother-shaped holes in our hearts. We've been family ever since.

I began working part-time at Knitorious seven years ago. Connie passed the store on to me almost three years ago, when she semi-retired. Now, I own Knitorious, and Connie works here part-time. We've switched roles.

"How was your day off, my dear?" Connie asks, straightening the button display and tidying the rack of knitting notions next to it.

I tell Connie about my visit to Rita's house and show her the new yarn, which I've already shelved. Then I tell her about the SOLD sign on Karla's lawn, her adorable dog, Gucci, and my trip to the hospital to pick up Karla from the emergency room.

"Rita was grateful you were there yesterday," Connie says. "She told me she doesn't know what she would have done if you hadn't offered to pick up Karla."

"If you spoke to Rita and know what happened, why are you asking me?"

"I wanted to hear your version of events," Connie says with a smile. "Rita will miss Karla. I worry about her."

"You worry about Karla?" I ask.

"I worry about my friend, Rita," Connie clarifies, organizing the shelves of knitting books. "First, she lost Meaghan, and now she's on the verge of losing Karla." She looks at me with wide blue eyes. "I can't imagine you and Hannah moving across the country. It's hard enough with Hannah away at university most of the year."

"I can't speak for Hannah," I assure her. "But I'm not going anywhere."

Connie gives me a small smile.

"You and Rita talk almost every day," I say. "Between the two of us, we'll watch over her and make sure she is OK."

My phone dings again.

*April: Karla's on her way to you. This is your two-minute warning.*

I utter a mild curse word under my breath and shove my phone in the back pocket of my denim capris.

"What's wrong, my dear?" Concern corrugates Connie's forehead.

"Karla is on her way here," I whisper, as if Karla might hear me.

"How nice," Connie says, doing her best impersonation of being surprised.

"Uh-uh," I retort, shaking my head. "We said goodbye to each other yesterday. Why is she here today?"

"Rita said Karla is visiting clients and suppliers to say goodbye and thank them before she moves."

"I'm neither Karla's client nor supplier," I remind her as I walk toward the back room. "I have to take care of something. Can you please tell Ka—"

The ominous jingle alerts me that my attempted escape is seconds too late.

Karla, looking as if a medicine ball never touched her head, steps into my store.

"Karla." I summon my widest smile. "What a surprise."

"Hello, Megan!" She takes both my shoulders, and we exchange a double air kiss.

"You remember Connie, right?" I say, gesturing to Connie.

"Of course, we remember each other. It's so nice to see you again, Karla!" Connie hugs Karla, pressing their cheeks together. "Rita talks about you all the time."

"Good things, I hope," Karla says, beaming.

"She's very fond of you." Connie grins.

"Such a quaint, winsome store," Karla comments, soaking in her surroundings and stepping farther into my inner sanctum. "It must be nice to devote so much time to your little hobby, Megan."

I inhale and bite the inside of my lower lip so hard it hurts.

It's true that knitting is my hobby, but Knitorious is a business. A successful one. Karla's backhanded compliment isn't just an insult to me, it's an insult to Connie, who established Knitorious and made it a hub of Harmony Lake's fibre arts community. Just because I enjoy my job doesn't mean it's less of a job than running a concierge company.

"As my mother used to say, *do what you love, and you won't work a day in your life*." Connie smiles.

Connie has far more grace and patience than me.

"What can I do for you, Karla?" I ask, eager to help her fulfill her mission so she can leave.

"I'd like to take you out for lunch," Karla replies. "To thank you for your help yesterday."

"That's sweet," I say, thinking up an excuse and watching Sophie sniff Karla's designer stiletto sandals. "I'd love to, but we're closing early today for a town function."

"Not for two hours," Connie pipes in. "That's plenty of time for lunch."

"I don't want to leave you alone," I say to Connie, my eyes pleading for her support.

"Don't be silly." She waves away my comment. "I managed this store alone for decades. I'll be fine for two hours."

"Wonderful." Karla grins and raises her eyebrows. "How about the pub down the street?" Karla's phone rings, distracting her and giving me time to think up another excuse. "I have to take this." She looks from Connie to me. "I'll be outside when you're ready, Megan."

Karla answers the call and disappears onto the side-walk in front of the store.

"What does she *really* want?" I wonder aloud, watching through the window as Karla lowers her Dita black and gold sunglasses to her eyes. Her crispin-green, petal-sleeved, form-fitting sheath dress complements her sun-kissed skin.

"There's only one way to find out," Connie replies, nodding toward Karla on the sidewalk. "Rita says Karla is wonderful once you get to know her."

"That's a polite way of saying, *she's a bitch but you'll get used to it.*"

"Rita thinks Karla has trust issues," Connie continues her pro-Karla campaign. "She says Karla's brusque demeanour is a defence mechanism to prevent people from getting close enough to hurt her. Rita says it's gotten worse since Meaghan died."

Meaghan was Karla's best friend and business part-ner. She seemed to be one of the only people Karla trusted and loved.

"Wait," I say when I realize. "You knew Karla was

coming here, didn't you? You knew she was going to ask me to lunch."

Connie shrugs, staring sheepishly at the floor. "Rita may have mentioned it."

"Why didn't you warn me?"

"You would have come up with an excuse," Connie reasons. "Rita thinks Karla wants to make amends with you. This is a big step for her. She doesn't make friends easily. Especially women friends."

"I can't imagine why." I roll my eyes. "Maybe it's because she's about as pleasant as a wet cat."

"It's just lunch," Connie argues. "Aren't you curious to find out what she wants?"

"She wants to thank me for driving her home yesterday," I remind her. "She said so."

"I suspect there's more to Karla's agenda than lunch, my dear."

I inhale and expel a loud breath.

"Fine," I say, reaching for my purse under the counter. "I'll go."

# CHAPTER 5

"THANK you again for picking me up yesterday, Megan," Karla says as the server drops off our menus. "Rita always enjoys your visits."

"No problem." I smile and peruse the menu, despite knowing it by heart. "I'm sure you would have done the same in my shoes."

"Perhaps," Karla says. "But I'd never wear your shoes. I prefer style over function."

She knows I was speaking metaphorically but can't resist an opportunity to make a dig. *Don't fall for it, Megan.*

I sneak a peek at my feet. My black wedge-heel sandals might be more practical than Karla's strappy stilettos, but they're cute, no matter what she says.

"Rita will miss you when you move," I say, ignoring her passive-aggressive insult about my footwear.

"I don't want to move, but my grandmother needs me," Karla explains. "I'm the only one who can save her."

Save her? I'm sure Rita said Karla's grandmother is ill, not in danger.

"Save her from what?" I ask.

"My mother," Karla replies. "If I don't intervene, my mother will put my grandmother in a nursing home." Karla shakes her head and chuckles, squinting. "My grandmother will go to a nursing home over my dead body."

"Where is your hometown?"

Karla tells me about her hometown on the East Coast. She tells me why she left—limited career opportunities— and why she's ready to go back—to care for her grandmother and, maybe, open an east-coast branch of Just Task Me! She hopes to return to Harmony Hills in the future. I sense she's omitting details but don't probe.

The server takes our lunch order. We both choose the Black & Bleu salad with grilled sirloin tips on top of mixed greens, cucumber, tomato, red onion, and creamy bleu cheese dressing.

"How's Gucci?" I ask.

"More adorable every day," Karla replies, then sips her water. "Chelle and Rita are taking care of him until I get home."

"Rita says he hates to be alone."

"Gucci's fine with being alone," Karla confesses. "That's just a white lie I tell Rita."

"Why?"

"Picking up and dropping off Gucci gives me an excuse to visit Rita every day without being obvious about checking on her."

"You're a clever and thoughtful friend," I say, watching Karla blush at the compliment. "I'm sure Rita would be happy to see you regardless of Gucci."

"Rita likes to help," Karla explains. "Taking care of Gucci makes her feel helpful."

"Rita is lucky to have you and Gucci."

It sounds like Karla and Rita use Gucci as an excuse to

dote on each other. Regardless of my opinion about Karla, I must admit that using her dog as a covert operative to help Rita and make her feel useful is clever.

"Megan," Karla says, "will you do me a favour?" She takes a breath and steels herself. "I know we're not friends, and I don't have the right to ask…"

"Just ask."

At last! The *real* reason Karla invited me to lunch.

"Will you look after Rita when I'm gone?"

"Of course," I reply. "Connie and I have already discussed increasing our visits and phoning Rita more often."

Karla's tanned shoulders drop when she releases a sigh of obvious relief.

"Thank you." She smiles. "I've arranged for Chelle to continue helping Rita around the house and with errands and appointments, but I'd feel better knowing someone who isn't getting paid, and cares about Rita, is watching over her."

"Connie and I are already on it," I assure her. "If anything happens to Rita, we'll contact you right away."

"Thank you."

Karla's cracking voice, and the moisture she blinks from her eyes, are the biggest displays of emotion I've ever witnessed from her. I'm not used to this compassionate and caring version of Karla Bell. I'm used to getting frustrated at the thinly veiled insults from her icy and indifferent alter ego.

"If I were moving away from Connie, I'd feel the same," I assure her.

Karla sniffles and shakes her head.

"I'm not usually emotional," she says with a half-laugh. "That medicine ball must have hit me harder than I thought."

"You're human. We're emotional creatures," I say.

"Rita says you're hard on the outside and soft on the inside."

"She gave you that spiel too?" Karla rolls her eyes and chortles, then glowers at my shoulder.

I follow her gaze and pick a long, curly hair from my blouse, dropping it onto the dark wood floor.

Even without words, Karla is the queen of criticism.

The server delivers our lunch and, as I unroll my napkin to place it in my lap, Karla reaches across the table and grabs my left hand. She squeezes, digging her manicured nails into my skin as she examines my ring finger.

"Beautiful rings," she compliments, letting go of my hand. "Who chose them, you or him?"

"Thank you," I say, stretching my fingers and admiring my engagement and wedding rings. "We chose them together."

"I can't believe you married Detective Hottie," she says, stabbing her salad with her fork. "I wonder if I'll be ready to settle when I'm your age."

"We're only three years apart, Karla," I remind her, smoothing the napkin across my lap. "We're almost the same age."

"Really?" She waves a forkful of lettuce over her plate. "You seem so much older and more mature than me."

I rest my fork on the edge of the plate, looking her straight in the eye.

"And I didn't *settle* for Eric. He's the most amazing man I've ever met."

Her face softens, and she smiles. "I meant *settle down*, not settle." She shakes her head. "You misheard me."

*No, I didn't,* I scream on the inside, forcing myself to remain composed on the outside.

Wishing I hadn't accepted her lunch invitation, I remind myself it would be rude to leave. Getting into a verbal sparring match with Karla will only make me more frustrated. I take a deep breath. *Heavy Shoulders, long arms.* I repeat my mental mantra, trying to release the tension that I accumulate in Karla's presence.

"You have a type." She shovels a forkful of food into her mouth.

"Eric and Adam are nothing alike," I say.

"Law-abiding," Karla says as she swallows. "One's a lawyer, the other's a cop. You like tall, law-abiding men."

"What's your type?" I ask, hoping to divert her scrutiny.

"Speak of the devil," Karla purrs, narrowing her gaze on someone behind me as she dabs the corners of her mouth with her napkin. "Adam!" She summons him with a coy grin, penetrative eye contact, and a come-hither motion with her manicured fingers.

*… walk into my parlour said the spider to the fly…*

"Karla?" Adam asks from behind me as he approaches our table.

"Long time no see."

Adam takes Karla's outstretched, limp hand, shakes it, and releases it.

"Twice in one day," Adam says, smiling and giving my shoulder a gentle squeeze.

"Three times if we include the grand opening, Mayor Martel." I smile.

"Mayor?" Karla asks. "You're the mayor of Harmony Lake?" Karla feigns annoyance, quirking her brows and wagging her index finger at him. "How have I not heard about this?"

Ugh! I forgot how aggressively flirtatious she is.

Still resting his hand on my shoulder, Adam tells Karla about his law practice in Harmony Lake and becoming mayor eighteen months ago.

I pick at my salad, dipping cucumber chunks into the bleu cheese dressing.

They recall a funny moment at a corporate event Karla organized for Adam's former law firm.

As they reminisce, I remember that Adam and Karla haven't seen each other since Adam left the firm three years ago. Karla's company, Just Task Me! was on retainer with them. She organized their corporate events and functions.

Adam chuckles, crinkling the corners of his blue eyes.

Karla laughs and tosses her head back, smoothing her glossy blonde hair behind her shoulder to reveal her neck.

I smile and nod, feigning interest and feeling like a third wheel.

"Join us!" Karla insists, sliding sideways to make room for him.

"I'd love to," Adam says, "but unfortunately, lunch with two beautiful women isn't on today's busy mayoral itinerary. I almost didn't have time to eat lunch today."

"No rest for the wicked," Karla coos.

The pub owner waves at Adam.

"It appears my order is ready, ladies," Adam says.

"Philly cheesesteak?" I ask.

"You know me too well, Meg," he jokes, then looks at Karla. "It was great running into you, Karla." Once again, she extends her limp hand and once again, he squeezes it. "Good luck with your move." He looks at me. "I'll see you at the ceremony later." He winks and squeezes my shoulder.

"See you around, Your Worship," Karla croons, gazing up at him through her lashes.

She turns her head and watches Adam stroll away.

"I'd forgotten how handsome your ex-husband is," Karla comments, stabbing a piece of steak. "Well-dressed men are a particular weakness of mine." She looks at me. "Is Adam seeing anyone special?" She pops the sirloin into her mouth.

"No," I say, nervous that my answer will encourage her. "He was with someone. They broke up a few months ago."

"Oh?" Karla picks up her water. "Why did they break up?" She sips.

"I'm not sure," I reply. "Adam doesn't like to talk about it. He'll only confirm that their split was amicable." I shrug.

Even if I knew the intimate details of their break-up, I wouldn't tell Karla.

"He gives off an unavailable vibe," Karla comments. "Single and available aren't the same. He might be single, but he's not looking."

I assume she means he wasn't as flirty with her as she was with him, therefore he must be unavailable.

"Eric thinks they grew apart because Adam's law practice and mayoral duties take all his time."

"Eric?" Karla asks, screwing up her face. "How would Eric know?"

"They're besties," I admit, then brace myself for a snide retort.

"Are you serious?"

I nod.

"You know it's weird, right?" Karla squeezes her eyebrows together and bites down on a forkful of baby spinach.

"Not for us," I reply.

"Raise your hands and stick out your tongue," she instructs.

"Why?"

"I want to make sure you're not having a stroke." She glares at me like I said something shocking. "Your former husband and current husband are BFFs, and you're acting like it's normal."

I close my eyes and take a breath, willing myself not to give Karla the dramatic reaction I'm certain she's after.

"What did you mean when you said Adam *gives off an unavailable vibe*?" I probe, once again changing the subject.

"He's not interested in dating," Karla clarifies, half-shrugging one shoulder.

"How can you tell?"

"The same way I can tell the melancholy man's wife or whatever left him."

Karla nods behind me, her gaze fixes on the end of the bar. I turn and find Mark Hillman propping up one end of the bar, lost in his thoughts and hypnotically tracing his index finger around the rim of a pint glass.

"His wife moved out last week," I confirm, amazed. "How did you know?"

Karla must have overheard it. The Hillman's split is the biggest news in town right now. Everybody is talking about it.

"The server brought his lunch without taking his order," Karla explains. "Then she took his plastic shopping bag of frozen pizza, ice cream, and beer into the kitchen with her. Probably to store it for him. I'm guessing he eats here every day and always orders the same thing. When the server brought his lunch, she asked how he was doing. Her eyes were full of pity, and her smile was sad instead of uplifting." Karla shrugs. "I figure either he got dumped or his cat died." She gestures toward the glum man with her fork. "Judging by the cat fur on his t-shirt, his cat is fine."

"Both of your hunches are right," I confirm. "His wife moved out last week, but she came back yesterday to collect the cat." I shake my head. "You deduced all of that from watching a simple interaction between him and the server?"

Impressive! Karla figured out Mark Hillman's sad situation without missing a beat in our conversation or appearing distracted. She was so discreet that I didn't notice she was paying attention to our surroundings.

"It's not a big deal," Karla says, pushing salad around the plate with her fork. "I notice stuff, like the contents of someone's shopping bag, the sympathy behind their hopeful smile, or the longing when they touch their ex-wife's shoulder. Sometimes, like today, it's hard to ignore."

"You prefer to ignore the things you notice about other people?"

Karla nods. "It can get pretty exhausting. Once I work out how someone feels, I feel it too."

"It's called empathy."

"I don't care what it's called," she responds. "It's awful. I don't like feeling my own emotions, never mind other people's."

"This must be why you're so good at your job," I say as my brain links the two otherwise unrelated traits.

After Adam and I separated, I learned—from Karla, no less—that Adam had hired her to buy gifts for me during our marriage.

"What do you mean?"

"Think about it. When Adam hired you to buy gifts for me, you always chose the perfect thing. We'd never met, yet you knew what I would like. The gifts you selected are some of my favourite things. From talking to him, and the photos he showed you, somehow you gleaned enough about me to choose just the right thing. Every time."

"Nah," she dismisses me. "I'm great at my job because I have amazing taste. Don't overcomplicate it."

"Is that so?" I challenge. "Would the last client you shopped for like the Chanel bag you picked out for my fifteenth anniversary? Or the gold necklace you chose for my thirty-third birthday?"

"Doubtful." Karla drops her fork on her plate and lays her napkin on top. "The last gift I bought was for a CEO's husband. He was a minimalist, well-travelled, eco-warrior. His wife wanted to wow him on their twenty-fifth wedding anniversary."

"What did you get him?"

"A month volunteering at an elephant sanctuary in Cambodia." Karla's eyes light up. "He loved it."

"See?" I drop my napkin on my empty plate. "I would not love that gift as much as your client. Picking up on subtle clues is your superpower. Empathy is a gift, Karla. Embrace it."

"My therapist says empathy is a trauma response."

At a loss for words, I'm saved by the bell when my phone dings, giving me an excuse to abandon the conversation.

*Eric: I won't make it to the pool's grand opening. Fawkes is missing.*

Clarence Fawkes is missing? I blink and re-read the text.

*Me: Good luck with the search. Let me know if you need anything.*

*Eric: I love you.* Followed by three heart emojis.

"Everything OK?" Karla asks, hailing the server and drawing a check mark in the air to let her know we're ready for the bill.

"Fine," I say, returning my phone to my purse. "Eric is running late. He's searching for a missing person."

A missing parolee, but there's no need to bore Karla with the details.

"Never a dull day in Harmony Lake," she remarks.

OUTSIDE THE PUB, I thank Karla for lunch and wish her well with her move and her grandmother's health. She thanks me for checking on Rita, and I assure her that Connie and I are happy to do it. We love Rita.

Karla hugs me, which seems to startle her as much as it startles me.

I stiffen at the unexpected embrace and hope she doesn't notice.

"I have to go," I say, pulling away.

"Don't worry"—Karla scans me from head to toe—"you look fine."

She says it like I'm worried I don't look fine. I scan myself and pat my curls. What's wrong with how I look? I run my tongue over my teeth, searching for a stuck piece of lettuce or steak.

Great, I'm internalizing her mean comments.

Regardless of how I look, if I don't get my butt to the community centre in the next few minutes, I'll miss the grand-opening ceremony.

A passerby pushing a stroller drops a twenty-dollar bill. Karla steps on the bill, trapping it between the sidewalk and the pointed toe of her stiletto sandal. She picks it up and, waving it over her head, chases the stroller, yelling, "Excuuuse meee!"

Her ability to run in six-inch heels is impressive. I'd roll my ankle if I tried it.

SHUFFLING sideways toward Connie and April, I spy Mason on the pool deck, staring at his phone. He looks up, and we make eye contact, wave and smile.

The stench of chlorine and pool chemicals hangs in the air, burning my eyes.

"I assume Mason fixed the leak?" I ask, squeezing myself onto the metal bleacher between April and Connie as they wiggle apart, making space for me.

"Yes!" Connie says, bringing her hands together in front of her chest. "Isn't he wonderful? I swear that young man can fix anything."

"I don't know how Harmony Lake would function without him," April adds, pulling her long, blonde hair into a ponytail. "It's humid in here."

"It is," I agree, fanning myself with the collar of my shirt.

"Where's Eric?" Connie asks.

I curl my index finger toward me. Connie and April lean in and lower their heads.

"Clarence Fawkes is missing," I whisper.

They gasp in unison.

"If he left the cottage without permission, he's in breach of his parole conditions," Connie hisses.

"He'll go back to prison," April adds, her eyes wide with hope.

"Eric has to find him first," I say. "Please don't say anything. It's not public knowledge."

My friends nod in acknowledgment.

Connie and April return to their upright positions, and I glance around the crowded spectator's gallery. Most of the businesses on Water Street closed early so everyone could attend the major event. We're crammed into the bleachers like sardines packed in a tin, and some people are standing along the walls. I scan the crowd, exchanging smiles and waves with friends and neighbours.

Curtains made from strips of blue and brown crepe paper block the new pool from view of the overheated spectators. Long pieces of gold ribbon suspend the cheap and cheerful curtains from the high ceiling.

"I guess we're starting late," April observes, checking her watch.

"How was your lunch with Karla, my dear?" Connie asks.

"The food was great," I reply.

I tell Connie and April about lunch with Karla, mentioning every backhanded compliment and insult she hurled at me.

Connie insists we misunderstand Karla and her struggle to connect with people. Connie likes to see the best in everyone.

One day, I aspire to reach the same level of enlightenment as Connie.

"Letting Karla goad you into an argument will only confirm her belief that she should continue to push people away," says my surrogate mother. "Deep down, Karla is afraid people won't like her, so she acts like she doesn't care if they don't like her."

"But people *don't* like her," April chimes in. "Are you suggesting that Karla pushes people to their limit, then when they snap, she's shocked?"

"Yes," Connie replies. "Rita suspects Karla's behaviour stems from abandonment issues."

"Just because someone cut her once, doesn't give Karla the right to bleed all over everyone else," April says.

I fist bump April, agreeing with her metaphor.

"Armchair psychology aside, it doesn't matter why Karla is a bully," I say with a smug smirk. "She's moving far away, and I won't have to deal with her again."

Adam and the deputy mayor appear on the pool deck. The crowd quiets amid murmurs of *shhh*.

Mason hands Adam a microphone, and the crowd

groans in protest when it lets out a brief, ear-splitting screech. Mason adjusts the speaker, then Adam makes a brief speech, thanking everyone for attending, for their fundraising support, their input into the project, and their patience throughout the long process.

Then, using comically giant ceremonial scissors that require both hands to maneuver, Adam cuts a piece of gold ribbon, causing the blue curtains to drop from the ceiling, billowing to the pool deck and landing in a soft heap around the perimeter of the pool.

Two balloon archways stretch from opposite corners of the pool, intersecting several metres above the centre. The blue and brown balloons are an homage to the official town colours: blue for the lake and brown for the mountains.

Gasps and screams draw my attention to the still water.

A body floats in the corner of the deep end. The unmoving body is facedown with outstretched limbs, like a starfish. Grey hair around the head drifts on the surface of the otherwise undisturbed surface.

"Oh, my!" Connie clutches her chest with one hand and grasps my hand with the other.

"Is that?" April points to the body with one hand and covers her open mouth with the other.

I pull out my cell phone, unlock the screen, and use my free hand to call Eric.

"I think we found Clarence Fawkes."

# CHAPTER 6

SATURDAY, September 3rd

Clarence Fawkes's surprise appearance at the grand opening ceremony dominates local gossip. It has eclipsed the new pool, and the Hillman's ongoing marital drama —Mr. Hillman is pursuing joint custody of the cat, but I digress.

The town is abuzz with speculation about how Clarence Fawkes's corpse wound up in the deep end of our community's brand-new indoor pool.

"Have you read the statement Fawkes's family released this morning?" asks Mrs. Roblin, before counting her stitches.

I shake my head and reach for my phone. "What did it say?"

Conveniently, Mrs. Vogel saved a copy of the statement on her phone.

*Effective immediately, all proceeds from Clarence Fawkes's music will benefit his victims via a trust fund set up by the Fawkes family. Details to follow as they become available.*

"Interesting," I say, after Mrs. Vogel finishes reading. "His family believes he was guilty."

"The entire world believes he was guilty," Mrs. Roblin adds with a small snort. "Because he *was* guilty. They convicted him for heaven's sake." She waves away the air in front of her face. "An insignificant technicality might have won him a new trial, but it didn't make him less guilty!"

"It's too bad his family didn't speak up to support his victims when he was alive," Mrs. Vogel says, depositing her phone into her knitting bag and picking up her needles.

"We don't know for certain that anyone killed him," Mrs. Roblin reminds her knitterly friend. "Fawkes's death isn't officially a homicide." She flips over her knitting and starts a new row. "*Yet.*"

"*Yet* being the operative word since everyone knows it was murder," Mrs. Vogel yanks her strand of working yarn, causing the ball to roll off the sofa onto the floor. "What other explanation could there be?" she asks, staring at me.

"Who knows?" I shrug.

"You must know something," Mrs. Vogel insists.

From the corner of my eye, I catch Mrs. Roblin sliding her fist out of her pocket. She checks to make sure I'm not watching, then slips an unforbidden treat to Sophie who's waiting at her feet for the sneaky cookie. For whatever reason, the Charity Knitters insist on smuggling dog treats into Knitorious. I don't know why they're so covert about it. We don't have a DO NOT FEED THE DOG sign, and I've never asked them *not* to spoil Sophie. In fact, whenever someone asks if they can give Sophie a treat, I gladly accept on her behalf.

The smugglers are easy to spot because either Sophie remembers them as a cookie-source, or she smells the unsanctioned snacks in their pockets and follows them around, giving them her undivided attention until she gets her fix.

"I know the same as you about Fawkes's death." I sit in the overstuffed chair and pick up my knitting.

Cookie-in-mouth, Sophie trots past me on the way to her dog bed.

"But you always have the inside scoop," Mrs. Roblin says.

"Not this time."

Truth is, I've hardly seen my husband since Fawkes died. With more than half of Harmony Lake present for the dead man's unveiling, Eric's witness list is long. He's been working day and night.

"But you found the body," Mrs. Vogel implores. "Whenever you find a body, you get to the bottom of what happened."

We ignore the obvious crunching and chewing coming from Sophie's corner of the store.

"Technically, half of Harmony Lake found the body." I gesture around me. "And I'm quite happy to be a bystander this time. It's a pleasant change."

"Not for us," Mrs. Roblin protests, placing her knitting in her lap. "Megan, we need you to take an active interest in Fawkes's death."

"Yes," Mrs. Vogel agrees, staring at me without missing a stitch in her rhythmic knitting. "Harmony Lake needs to move on from this ghastly incident, and that means figuring out who killed Fawkes."

"If Fawkes's death was murder, Eric will figure out who did it," I assure them, working a cable without a cable needle. "I have no doubt."

"He'll solve it faster with your help," Mrs. Roblin implores in a more complimentary tone of voice than usual.

She looks at Mrs. Vogel, and the two women nod in agreement.

"The Charity Knitters are here for you, Megan." Mrs. Vogel gives me an exaggerated wink. "We will provide whatever support you need to pursue your *hobby, won't we?*" Mrs. Vogel glares at her friend.

My *hobby* is how the Charity Knitters refer to my tendency to help Eric with his investigations.

"Yes, we will," Mrs. Roblin agrees. "We have freed up our schedules. Should your hobby take you away from Knitorious, we'll be here to help. All day. Every day. Until Eric arrests Fawkes's killer."

"Connie would cover the store," I remind them.

My other part-time employee, Marla, is golfing in Myrtle Beach. So, it's just Connie and I holding down the fort until next weekend.

"Well, now you have Connie and a network of helpful fibre enthusiasts," Mrs. Vogel says.

"You'll have all the time you need for your *hobby*." Mrs. Roblin accompanies her dramatic wink with a dipped chin.

The Harmony Lake Charity Knitting Guild is more than a group of kind, community-focussed knitters who support worthy causes. The Charity Knitters—as they're known affectionately by us locals—are not stereotypical knitters. They are a well-organized centre of local influence. They perpetuate the wholesome-and-harmless knitter stereotype so they can stay under the radar, invisibly and stealthily pursuing their true agenda of protecting Harmony Lake's friendly, small-town ambience and way of life.

The Charity Knitters boast an extensive network of strategically recruited members who represent the group's interests in every issue and decision affecting our cozy community. More than once, they've mobilized their resources to protect our cozy town from attempts by big-box corporations and property developers to profit from our beautiful location and throngs of tourists.

The Charity Knitters were instrumental in Adam's mayoral campaign and Eric's installation as police chief.

They meet every week at Knitorious to discuss Guild business and plan their charitable projects. I'm not a member, but Connie is, and she attempts to recruit me. My presence in the background of their regular meetings has given me some insight into their mysterious inner workings.

They have a matriarchal organizational structure, with the top positions held only by women. The older, more experienced members occupy the highest-ranking positions and mentor the younger members to carry on the organization's mission.

They are the sweetest, scariest, most maternal, most mysterious group of women I have ever encountered. They love Harmony Lake and do whatever necessary to ensure it remains... harmonious.

Either Mrs. Roblin or Mrs. Vogel—or both—are the de facto commanders-in-chief of the entire operation.

"Has The Charity Knitting Guild chosen their next project?" I ask, guiding the conversation away from Clarence Fawkes's death.

"Considering Fawkes's death, and his family's state-ment, our next project will benefit victims of violence and harassment."

"Fabulous," I say. "As usual, you have my support." I gesture to the rest of the store. "Knitorious is at your disposal."

Mrs. Vogel and Mrs. Roblin explain that The Charity Knitters will make stuffed animals and lap blankets and donate them to a local shelter for women and children. This is a sponsored project. Residents can sponsor their favourite knitters and crocheters, making a cash donation for every animal or blanket their knitters and crocheters complete. The donated money will benefit a local organization that supports survivors of sexual assault and violence.

Besides promoting their campaign in the store and on the Knitorious website, I offer to host extra knitting events and donate a year's supply of yarn to the crafter who completes the most animals and blankets. Most local businesses will contribute something toward the community project.

"Good morning, ladies," Eric bellows from behind me.

I turn just as he crouches to scratch Sophie between the ears.

"Hello, Chief Sloane," Mrs. Roblin says sweetly. "I made those Chunky Drop Cookies you love." She smiles. "Megan put them in the kitchenette for you."

I resist the urge to roll my eyes. Eric is a forty-year-old adult. He's capable of feeding himself, but The Charity Knitters act like he's on the brink of starvation and their constant catering is the only thing keeping him alive. I suspect they do it for the personal visit when he drops off their empty dishes and containers.

"Thank you, Mrs. Roblin," Eric says. "Your cookies always hit the spot."

Mrs. Roblin blushes and gushes modestly in her corner of the sofa.

"Eric!" Mrs. Vogel beams, giving him a wiggly finger wave. "I made you some of my special cabbage rolls. I know how much you love them, and you're working so hard. We want to make sure you're eating properly."

"Mmm," Eric says. "Thank you, Mrs. Vogel." He rubs his flat stomach. "I can't wait." He smiles.

Eric hates cabbage rolls. And I suspect Mrs. Vogel

hates making them. But somehow, at the beginning of their relationship, Eric left her with the impression that he *loves* them. Especially hers. He feels guilty for letting the lie continue. Dozens of cabbage rolls later, he's too embarrassed to admit the truth and forces himself to eat them. She hates making them and he hates eating them, yet neither will stop.

Eric hands me a takeout coffee cup.

"Ladies, may I borrow Megan for a minute?" he asks as I crack the lid and inhale the glorious, cinnamon-maple aroma emanating from the coffee cup.

"Of course!" Mrs. Roblin straightens her spine, sitting at attention and ready to serve. "Is this about the case?"

He winks at her with a coy grin, which makes all of us swoon.

"Take all the time you need," Mrs. Vogel adds. "We'll watch the store as long as necessary."

Why would Eric need to talk to me about Clarence Fawkes's death?

# CHAPTER 7

"What's going on?" I close the door behind us.

"I miss you." Eric pulls me into a hug and presses a gentle kiss on my temple.

"I miss you too." I bend my neck backward and look him in the eye.

His exhaustion is obvious. His chin is scruffy with yesterday's five o'clock shadow—out of character for my clean-shaven husband. The skin around his eyes is heavier than normal, and red veins marble the whites of his eyes. His short, brown, usually tidy hair spikes in every direction like he's been running his fingers through it in frustration.

"You need a good night's sleep," I say, reaching up to tame his mussed hair. "Since Tuesday, you haven't gotten home until after I'm asleep, and you've left for work before I wake up." I run my hand over his bristly cheek. "I bet I can count on one hand how many hours you slept last night."

"You can count on one hand how many hours I've slept all week," he says, stifling a yawn.

"Are you eating enough?" It's a rhetorical question; I

already know the answer. "There's a container of pasta salad in the fridge." I gesture to the nearby refrigerator. "And a slice of rhubarb-strawberry pie. I was going to bring it to the station on my lunch break."

"Thanks." He kisses my forehead. "Speaking of lunch, do you remember what you did for lunch on Tuesday? Before the grand opening?"

"Umm, yes!" I say, recalling the yummy Black and Bleu salad. "I had lunch at the pub with Karla Bell."

Eric's face clouds with confusion, like this isn't the response he expected.

"Why do you ask?" I sip my cinnamon-maple latte.

"You never mentioned it," he says, his brows pressing toward each other. "Lunch with someone you dislike would have been worth mentioning."

"I would have mentioned it, but my lunch plans seemed pretty insignificant after Fawkes's body showed up at the community centre," I justify. "And we've hardly seen each other since."

"I thought you and Karla didn't like each other. Why did you have lunch with her? And why on Tuesday?"

The authoritative tone of Eric's voice, and the urgency of his questions, puts me on the defensive.

"She invited me."

"When did Karla invite you to lunch?"

"Just before we arrived at the pub."

"Did you notice where she parked?"

"No."

"How would you describe her demeanour? Was there anything *off* about her?"

"Now that you mention it, she was nicer than I'm used to and showed more emotional depth than usual."

"Can you give me an example?"

"She cried when she talked about moving away from Rita," I explain. "And after lunch, she hugged me,

517

which has never happened before. She seemed kind of sad."

"Sad in a remorseful way?"

I hold up my hand in a stop gesture and set my coffee cup on the nearby counter.

"Are you questioning me?" I cross my arms in front of my chest. "Why are you using your cop voice?"

Tucking a rogue curl behind my ear, Eric takes a deep breath. His facial muscles soften, and he places his hands on my shoulders.

"Babe, we found Karla's fingerprints at the crime scene," he says in his familiar, calm, deep voice.

"What?" I ask, dumbfounded. "Are you sure?"

"Her prints were everywhere."

"Karla's fingerprints were all over the pool?" I ask, confused.

"Fawkes's cottage," Eric clarifies.

"But Fawkes drowned in the pool," I say, trying to stitch together this new information.

"No, babe, Fawkes drowned at his cottage. In the bathtub. The killer moved his body to the pool."

"How do you know Fawkes drowned in the bathtub?"

"The coroner found bath water in Fawkes's alveoli, and we tested it against the water from the full bathtub at The Fawkes Den."

The Fawkes Den is the name of the Fawkes family cottage. Many cottages in Harmony Lake have names.

"Alveoli?" I ask, pronouncing the new-to-me word one syllable at a time. "How did the coroner distinguish bath water from pool water?"

"Alveoli are the smallest, farthest branches of the lungs. The water in Fawkes's alveoli contained bath oils and body wash, but the water found in the larger branches of his lungs was a combination of bath water and pool water. The pool water could enter his lungs because when Fawkes died, his muscles relaxed. The pool water didn't reach the alveoli because he wasn't breathing."

"He was dead when his body went into the pool," I conclude.

"Yup," Eric agrees. "Babe, the bathtub is a holdback, OK?"

He looks at me for acknowledgement, and I nod. "Of course. I won't say anything."

A holdback is evidence that the police keep to themselves. Something only the killer or someone at the crime scene would know. The police use the holdback evidence to eliminate or implicate suspects. If a suspect mentions the holdback, it's a pretty good sign that they were present when the crime occurred. If a suspect is unaware of the holdback, it's a good sign that they weren't there. Why would someone claim responsibility for a crime they didn't commit? I don't know, but according to Eric, it happens.

"Why would Karla be inside the Fawkes's Den?" I ask, still stunned by his earlier revelation. "What link could she have to Clarence Fawkes?"

I rub the knot forming in my stomach. Most of the time, my knot is dormant. It only awakens to draw my attention to cognitive dissonance. When something I know, at my core, to be true doesn't match the facts in front of me, my knot reminds me to trust my core belief and follow the truth. In the forty years my knot and I have been together, it's never been wrong. Not once.

"That's what I'm trying to figure out," he replies. "We found Karla's fingerprints in every room. We also found hair that matches her hair colour and length. Forensics is running tests to see if it belongs to Karla. Someone, likely the killer, tossed the cottage."

"Tossed?"

"It was a mess. Torn apart. Every drawer and cupboard ransacked. Every piece of furniture overturned," Eric explains. "Someone was searching for something or staged the scene to look like a robbery." He pauses while I process his words. "I think Fawkes's killer staged the robbery to mislead the investigation."

"Why?"

"To distract us from the murder scene," he theorizes. "They hoped the chaos would distract us from the fact that a murder occurred there. Or they wanted it to look like a robbery, instead of a targeted attack."

"How do you know they're Karla's fingerprints? What did you test them against?"

"Karla's prints are on file because she volunteers for a women's shelter," Eric explains. "Regular police checks are a condition for volunteers who work with vulnerable people."

"Are you sure it's the same Karla Bell?" I ask, dubious. "The Karla I know isn't very altruistic."

"It's her." He nods.

The knot in my stomach grows two sizes larger.

This feels... wrong. I can't imagine Karla, self-absorbed and superficial, sacrificing her time to help others. Sure, I can imagine her donating money, or her business services, but not her time and energy.

Have I misjudged her? Did I allow her pointed remarks and mean comments to distract me from seeing the real Karla? Is her outward demeanour a carefully crafted facade? Has she manufactured a hard outer shell to convince the world that she's more hardened and indifferent than she truly is?

"Maybe Rita was right," I mumble to myself, recalling Rita's claim that Karla is hard on the outside and soft on the inside.

Would a cold-hearted killer fuss over Rita and Gucci

with such genuine affection? Would a hardened, self-absorbed narcissist go out of her way—when she has a head injury—to help an elderly hospital patient struggling to use the elevator? How many indifferent people would run down the street—in stilettos—to return a twenty-dollar-bill that fell from a passing stroller?

Karla did not kill Fawkes.

The knot in my stomach shrinks. I'm on the right track.

"Karla isn't strong enough to move a soaking-wet, dead body by herself," I argue. "She's a smidge taller than me, and she weighs less. I couldn't schlep a water-logged corpse from Fawkes's cottage to the pool and dump him in the water. How could she do it with no one seeing her and without getting wet? If Fawkes struggled, how could Karla hold his head under water? He would have overtaken her. If she had managed to do it, they would both show signs of a struggle."

"It takes less than one minute to drown someone," Eric informs me. "We have physical evidence Karla was in the cottage."

"But not *when* she was in the cottage," I specify.

"It's true. We can't use fingerprints to determine a timeline," Eric admits. "You don't even like Karla. Why are you defending her?"

"I don't dislike her," I attest, stopping short of liking her because I don't. Just because she's kinder than she lets on, doesn't mean she's likeable. "It's complicated. She's complicated." I shake my head. "Regardless of my feelings about her, it doesn't make sense. How did she move the body by herself? She didn't have one hair out of place. Everything about her appearance was perfect and put together when I saw her on Tuesday."

I poke his broad chest. "You need to speak to April. She saw Karla before me, and she'll tell you how flawless

Karla looked on Tuesday." He stares at me, unconvinced. "She wore stilettos, Eric." I scoff and rest my hand on my hip. "Do you know how difficult it would be to move a dead, wet corpse while wearing stilettos?"

"Maybe she had a change of clothes and shoes in the car."

"Does Karla even know Clarence Fawkes?"

"I'll tell you in a few hours when I've finished interviewing her," he replies. "I left her at the station while I came here to verify her story about having lunch with you."

"Did I answer all your questions?" I ask.

Eric produces a clear plastic evidence bag with a single earring. A large, metal, heart-shaped hoop with a key dangling in the centre.

"Have you seen this before?"

"Never," I reply. "Where did you find it?"

"Outside The Fawkes Den," Eric replies. "Have you seen Karla wear earrings like this?"

"Never."

I chuckle at the thought of Karla wearing something so opposite to her usual elegant accessories. Unless... could this earring be part of a disguise? No. Karla's not a killer. I can imagine her *hiring* a killer, but not doing it herself. I chuckle again at the idea of Just Task Me! offering a murder-for-hire service to their clients.

Oh, Karla. What have you done? Why were you inside The Fawkes Den?

# CHAPTER 8

"HE DIDN'T TELL you anything about Fawkes's death?" Mrs. Roblin asks for the gazillionth time since Eric left.

"I already told you. He said the coroner classified Fawkes's death as a homicide," I remind her again, leaving out the bombshells about the murder scene being the bathtub at The Fawkes Den and my lunch companion's fingerprints all over the cottage.

"Did you ask him for details? Does he have a suspect? Why did the killer choose our new pool?" Mrs. Vogel's rapid-fire questions give me déjà vu to the last time she asked me. Three minutes ago.

"If Eric needs my help, he'll ask," I say. "I'm happy to cheer him on from the sidelines this time."

Mrs. Roblin opens her mouth to speak, but the bell jingling over the door interrupts her before she utters a word.

Connie? She should be here any minute. Then I can use my lunch break to escape from this repeating loop of questions.

Two people enter the store. Neither person is Connie. I'm sure they aren't locals. I've never met them, but there's something familiar about the woman. The arrival of tourists puts us on our best behaviour.

Mrs. Roblin and Mrs. Vogel resume knitting in the cozy sitting area, flashing the newcomers their sweetest, most grandmotherly smiles. Sophie rushes to greet them, panting and wagging her charming corgi butt.

"Hi." I smile. "Welcome to Harmony Lake. Are you visiting for Labour Day weekend?"

"Yes," says the woman. "We've been here since last week. We're renting a cottage on the water." She smiles, chewing and popping her gum. "It's gorgeous here."

Do I detect a New York accent?

"Thank you," I say in response to the compliment. "Where are you from?"

"Boston, originally," the man replies. "But New York for the past couple of decades."

"Two of my favourite cities," I say, forcing myself not to stare at the man's neck tattoos.

He's taller than me, but shorter than Eric. His dark hair is slicked back, and his thick eyebrows are well-groomed. Either he hasn't shaved today, or his five o'clock shadow grows in before noon. His short-sleeved, button-down shirt is open just enough to show off the gold chains nesting in his thick mat of dark chest hair.

"My name is Megan." I extend my hand.

"Trevor Howe," says the man, extending a tattooed hand. "This is my wife, Mel." He steps aside, allowing Mel to step forward and shake my hand.

"It's nice to meet you," she says.

Her wide smile reveals ultra-white, straight teeth. Except for the occasional popping sound, the only evidence that she's chewing gum is the almost indiscernible motion of her jaw. Her dark, wavy hair is pinned up at the front, with the back cascading over her denim-clad shoulders and back. She favours bright makeup colours and an abundance of noisy jewelry. I count three holes in one earlobe and at least four in the other.

There is something familiar about her, but I can't place it. I'm certain we've never met before. Assuming I must have seen her around town, I shake off the nagging sense of familiarity.

"You know about the guy who died in the pool?" Trevor asks, the chains around his neck jangling as he jerks his thumb over his shoulder, toward the sidewalk.

"No," I reply. "But I can assure you it was an isolated incident. Harmony Lake is the safest, friendliest town ever."

I glance at Mrs. Roblin and Mrs. Vogel for support.

"Yes. Friendly and safe."

"It's lovely here. Very close-knit community."

They nod and smile.

"That's a relief," says Mel as she fidgets with her many rings and pops her chewing gum. "We heard it was that musician who got out on parole."

"Is that so?" I feign ignorance and tilt my head to one side like a dog hearing a strange sound. "How interesting."

Once again, I look to The Charity Knitters for backup.

"Like my mother used to say, *believe only half of what you see and nothing you hear*," Mrs. Vogel chirps.

"My mother used to say, *I refuse to repeat gossip, so listen carefully.*"

Mrs. Roblin grins, and I wonder if she understands the point Mrs. Vogel and I are trying to make.

"The police have been all over the dead guy's cottage since it happened," Trevor adds. "We couldn't believe it when we found out he was staying in the cottage across the lake from us."

"Had you ever seen him around the outside of his cottage?" I ask.

"No," Mel replies. "But we weren't looking either, you know?" She pops her gum. "Anyway, we can only see the back of his cottage. The part that backs on to the lake."

"The police questioned us though," Trevor offers. "Wish we could have told them something helpful, but" —he shrugs—"we didn't see or hear anything."

I picture the area surrounding The Fawkes Den. It makes sense for the police to question his neighbours across the lake. That section of the lake is narrow. The cottages across the water have a decent view of Fawkes's dock and back door. Depending on the lapse rate, sounds coming from the direction of Fawkes's cottage may have been amplified on the day he died. It's possible that the Howes could have heard something significant.

I shudder at the thought.

"I'm sure your cooperation was helpful," I assure him.

"They kept asking us if we'd ever been to the dead guy's cottage." He looks at Mel, who nods in agreement. "They must have asked us at least three times. Why would they keep asking?"

"*Had* you ever been to Fawkes's cottage?" Mrs. Roblin asks.

Both ladies pause mid-stitch, waiting for Trevor's answer.

"Of course not." He chuckles. "We didn't even know the guy. Anyway, I drive a classic car and avoid gravel roads and driveways. Chips in the custom paint job are a real pain in the arse."

If the Howes haven't visited The Fawkes Den, how would Trevor know whether the driveway is gravel?

"I hope this awful incident hasn't disrupted your vacation," I say.

"It's not a big deal," Trevor says with another shrug. "It's just not something you expect to happen in a small town."

"Are you knitters or crocheters?" I ask, changing the subject.

Trevor waves away my comment and steps away from the counter.

"I crochet." Mel raises her hand in front of her shoulder, causing her many bangles to clang like armour.

Is this why she's familiar? Could we have crossed paths at a knitting retreat or yarn festival?

"Have you visited Knitorious before?" I ask, trying to narrow down potential past encounters.

"No," she replies. "This is our first trip to Harmony Lake." She smiles. "Your store is charming."

"Thank you," I say. "Can I help you find something particular?"

"A mindless crochet pattern, some yarn, and a hook, please," Mel replies, smiling and popping her gum.

"How long have you been crocheting?" I ask, gathering a few books of crochet patterns.

"Since my early twenties," Mel replies. "My therapist taught me. Crocheting is one of my coping strategies. Having a real-life murder nearby has triggered my anxiety symptoms. I didn't bring my crochet supplies on vacation because we had limited space in the car." She shoots Trevor a side-eyed sneer.

"Oh," I say, "I'm sorry to hear that." I walk over to the community bulletin board near the door and tear off a card. "A confidential hotline you can call if you need to talk to someone." I hand her the card. "Twenty-four-seven."

"Thank you," Mel says, tucking the card into the upper chest pocket of her jean jacket.

"What's your favourite thing to crochet?"

"Amigurumi!" Mel grins. "They're quick, and I like to give them to my friends' kids."

Amigurumi is the art of knitting or crocheting—

mostly crocheting—small animals, or objects like fruit, fantasy creatures, insects, or even people.

"I have just the project for you."

I explain to Mel about the Charity Knitting Guild's latest campaign, and she'd love to make a few animals to donate. Mel chooses patterns for a sloth, unicorn, and bumblebee, then I gather the hook, stuffing, and a portable notions kit for her while she chooses yarn colours.

"I love your phone case," I say as Mel hovers the phone over the card reader to pay for her purchase.

Mel's phone case is a rhinestone mosaic in various shades of pink. The glitter factor is off the charts.

"Thanks," she replies. "I made it at one of those work-shops where you make stuff and drink wine with your friends. The craft store supplies everything and cleans up the mess."

"We have a knit and crochet night every week at Knitorious," I say, placing her receipt in the bag. "You're welcome to join us." I slide the bag toward her. "And we love drop-ins whenever we're open." I nod toward Mrs. Roblin and Mrs. Vogel, knitting and eavesdropping.

"We'll be here all day, every day, until further notice," Mrs. Vogel confirms. "We'd love to have you join us."

"Maybe I'll take you up on it before we go home," Mel says.

Trevor and Mel turn to leave, and the knitters and I wish them an uneventful end to their vacation.

As Trevor reaches for the door handle, the door swings open.

Whoever opened it must have waved them through because they nod and mumble thank you as they cross the threshold to the sidewalk.

"Why didn't you text me, Megastar!?" April

demands, closing the door behind her and rushing to peer through the display window.

April likes to come up with nicknames that are puns of my name. Today, I'm Megastar.

"About what?" I ask.

"The celebrity that just left Knitorious!" Her eyes are wide like she can't believe I didn't recognize the celebrity she's referring to. "It's her," she mumbles, squinting through the window and craning her neck to follow someone up the street.

"Who?" I point to the door. "Trevor and Mel? The couple you held the door for?"

"Mel?" April says, in a tone that implies she isn't asking me a question but pointing out something so obvious it shouldn't require pointing it out.

My blank stare conveys my cluelessness.

"Mel-o-dy." April annunciates each syllable in Melody's name.

She rests her hands on her hips and taps her foot, waiting for me to catch up.

I gasp and slap my hand across my mouth when it hits me.

"Melody!" I say, lowering my hand enough for April to hear me. "The singer."

April nods.

"I can't believe I didn't recognize her."

I rush to the window and search the street, but Melody is nowhere.

Hindsight reveals the clues to Mel's identity that I missed. The New York accent. The smile. Snapping her chewing gum. The abundance of loud jewelry. Even her hairstyle is the same. I bring my palm to my forehead in disbelief and disappointment.

"To be fair, I only recognized her because I was one of

her biggest fans," April says. "She'd only been spotted in public a handful of times since... her last performance."

"Mel, the crocheter, is the young singer from the awards show?" Mrs. Roblin asks, just as shocked as me.

April and I nod.

"Which young singer?" Mrs. Vogel asks, confusion etched between her eyes. "Which awards show?"

I listen as Mrs. Roblin reminds Mrs. Vogel of Melody's last public appearance almost fifteen years ago.

Melody was a famous young popstar known for her chart-topping dance hits and soulful ballads about first love and first heartbreak. She was the voice of a generation. Was.

The awards show host introduced her and announced that she would perform her latest number-one hit song, "Playing with Fire." The camera panned across the crowd as the celebrity audience cheered. Her band played the first bars as Melody rose to the stage from a hidden platform underneath, amid plumes of pyrotechnic smoke—a metaphorical phoenix rising from the ashes.

The beat dropped, and Melody began belting out lyrics. But instead of the upbeat, lighthearted first verse the world expected, she sang different lyrics. Her voice was loud and emotional. She sang about abuse of power. About a young girl taken advantage of by someone she trusted to protect her. About being trapped and victimized and ignored.

Viewers at home only heard the first verse before the network cut to commercials.

The world later learned from people who attended the event that Melody kept singing after the cameras stopped. She kept singing when the director ordered her band to stop playing and cut the power to their instruments and her microphone. She kept singing as her own security people dragged her from the stage, trying to clamp their hands over her mouth.

After the commercial break, the awards show continued as planned, without a word about the confusing pre-commercial performance.

After the show, the host referred to Melody's strange, interrupted performance as *an unsanctioned change to the evening's agenda*. He said he could not comment further. No one commented further. At least, no one official.

However, gossip magazines and entertainment websites speculated about Melody's lyrics. What did they mean? Who were they about? Attendees had recorded the performance on their cell phones—uncommon technology back then. The lyrics went viral. Melody had titled the new version of her song, *Sacrificial Lamb*.

News channels interviewed supposed experts, attempting to decipher the controversial lyrics.

Meanwhile, Melody disappeared. A few days after the awards show, the world began whispering about the missing pop star. Her closest friends came forward, scared because they hadn't seen or heard from her since her forcible removal from the stage.

Melody's management team issued a statement on her behalf, claiming the singer had suffered an emotional breakdown. They claimed her exhausting performance schedule, pressure to be perfect, and an ongoing, secret drug addiction triggered Melody's *episode*—as they called it—at the awards show.

As worldwide sentiment shifted from confusion to concern for Melody's health and well-being, we heard rumblings. A handful of young female singers and their older, more experienced counterparts disputed the claims about Melody's mental health, insisting that she was being silenced and intimidated by lawyers working on behalf of the music industry.

Some media outlets tried to discredit the women who disputed Melody's situation, accusing them of exploiting poor, sick Melody to extend their fifteen-minutes of fame.

The bad press didn't discourage Melody's supporters. They kept talking to whoever would listen, insisting that Melody's performance was her truth. And they grew. Every day, more women came forward and joined Melody's supporters.

They claimed that the powers-that-be in the music industry had silenced Melody, and now they were undermining her credibility by portraying her as unstable and untrustworthy. They revealed incidents of the abuse Melody sang about at the awards show.

The women claimed to suffer the same abuse by the same man, Clarence Fawkes. The man who wrote and produced their hit songs. The man with the power to decide who would become famous and who would be blacklisted.

Melody Howe was the first Clarence Fawkes victim who came forward. Her brave act of defiance started the avalanche of accusations that resulted in Fawkes being sentenced to eighty-eight years in prison.

"Aside from one statement, several weeks after the awards show, Melody never spoke publicly again," Mrs. Roblin says, ending her explanation to Mrs. Vogel.

"Who can blame her for hiding?" April asks rhetorically. "So many people didn't believe her. She received death threats, and people blamed her for the boycott on Fawkes's music and the music industry losing money."

Could it be a coincidence that the Howe's Harmony Lake vacation coincides with Clarence Fawkes's murder? Or that they happened to rent a neighbouring cottage?

I make my way to the cozy sitting area and sink into an overstuffed armchair.

"What is it, Megan?" Mrs. Vogel asks.

"Trevor said they didn't know Clarence Fawkes," I reply. "You heard him, right?" I ask looking at the knitters to confirm my recollection. "When Mrs. Roblin asked him if they'd ever visited The Fawkes Den, he said they *didn't even know him.*"

"I heard him loud and clear," Mrs. Roblin confirms.

"Me too," adds Mrs. Vogel.

"Melody was in Harmony Lake when Fawkes died," I say, thinking out loud. "She had motive."

"She had opportunity," Mrs. Roblin adds. "The Howes are renting the cottage across the lake."

I nod.

"He knew about the gravel," I add, distracted by my thoughts.

"What gravel?" April asks.

"When Trevor said they'd never visited Fawkes, he said he avoids gravel roads and driveways because of the custom paint job on his vintage car," I explain. "How did he know the Fawkes cottage has a long gravel driveway?"

April shrugs with her hands. "Maybe he assumed? Tons of cottages have gravel driveways."

"Melody is a suspect." I look over at April.

"Why would she still be here if she killed Fawkes?" April counters. "She would have left Harmony Lake days ago if she did it."

"Maybe she stayed because leaving town right after a murder would look suspicious," Mrs. Roblin suggests.

"I wish I had an excuse to visit her," I mutter. "I'd love to talk to her again."

"Leave it with us, Megan." Mrs. Vogel winks, already typing into her phone. "We'll take care of everything."

I flash the knitters a small smile and resist the urge to ask what they're planning. The less I know, the better.

# CHAPTER 9

WALKING to the car after work, something catches Sophie's ear. Her body moves toward the car, but her head is turned toward something behind us. It could be a leaf blowing across the pavement or a squirrel mocking her from a safe distance. By the time I'm within arm's reach of the car door, the rhythmic clicking is loud enough to catch my ear too, and I turn toward it.

"Thank goodness I caught you!"

Karla's heels click with increasing urgency as she closes the final distance between us.

"Karla!" She's the last person I'd expect to see in the parking lot behind Knitorious. "What are you doing here?"

I tug Sophie's leash to prevent her from pawing at Karla's knees. Karla bends and gives Sophie a quick rub.

"You'll never guess where I spent most of the day!"

"The Harmony Lake Police Station?" I venture an educated guess.

"Of course, you know!" She tosses her hands, and they land hard against her hips. "Mrs. Chief of Police," she mumbles. "Your husband questioned me for hours.

Then he had someone else question me. They didn't release me until a few minutes ago." She takes a deep breath and releases it. "But I'm sure he already told you everything."

"Eric hasn't told me anything," I fib. "But he asked me about our lunch on Tuesday."

"He thinks I did it, Megan." Karla's green eyes bulge, and her brows arch toward each other. "Eric thinks *I* killed Clarence Fawkes."

"Did you?" I ask.

"Are you kidding?!" she demands, screwing up her face. "Of course not!" She opens her mouth to speak but lets out a loud huff instead. "I didn't even know him. I'd never met him. But your husband insists I was inside the dead man's cottage. He said he found my fingerprints and hair. I know it's impossible, but he said he has proof!"

"How could your fingerprints be there if you weren't?" I ask.

Karla opens her hands in front of her like she's prepared to catch a beach ball. "I do not know." Then she covers her face with her hands like she can't believe her eyes. "This doesn't make sense," her voice is pleading and desperate. "Nothing makes sense." Her shoulders heave.

Is Karla crying?

"I believe you," I say.

"You believe I was never inside the dead man's cottage?" she asks, lowering her hands to reveal her eyes.

"I believe you didn't kill him," I clarify. "But if the police found your fingerprints and hair inside his cottage, they got there somehow, Karla. If you *ever went* there, even for a minute, tell Eric. He can verify your explanation and eliminate you as a suspect."

Karla rests her hand on my forearm, her eyes probing me.

"Megan, I swear on Gucci's life that I have *never* been inside Clarence Fawkes's cottage. Or outside. I'm not even sure *where* his cottage is. I've never met the man."

"I believe you." I place my hand on top of hers and give it a reassuring squeeze.

"Help me prove it," Karla pleads. "Please?" Her breaths quicken and become shallower. "Please?" she implores. "What if I'm charged with murder? What if the fingerprints are enough proof to send me to prison?" She touches her fingertips to her chest. "I didn't kill anyone. I could never kill anyone." She shakes her head. "This could destroy my reputation."

She's pacing now. "It could destroy my business! Do you know how many employees rely on me?" She paces faster. "What would happen to my grandmother if I went to prison? I'd never see her again." She fans her face with her hand. "What would happen to Rita? She won't survive losing another friend." She combs her hand through her blonde hair, biting her lower lip. "Who would take care of Gucci?"

"Deep breath, Karla," I say, reaching out but not touching her. "Heavy shoulders, long arms." I take a deep breath, hoping to encourage her to do the same.

"Help me. Please?" Karla pleads. "You helped solve Meaghan's murder, remember?"

I nod, acknowledging my role in uncovering her best friend's killer.

"Thank you!" Karla gushes, letting out a rush of relieved breath. "Oh, thank you, Megan."

Thank you? I didn't agree to help clear Karla's name; I acknowledged helping to solve her friend's murder.

Karla's demeanour relaxes. Her shoulders drop, and her breath slows. Her face relaxes into an expression of cautious hopefulness. There's no way I can refuse her request and send her back to the scared, desperate place she occupied a minute ago.

Besides, I'm certain Karla didn't murder Fawkes, and she's right about the devastating effect this situation could have on her grandmother, Rita, Gucci, and Just Task Me!

"It's Sophie's dinnertime. I need to take her home and feed her," I say. "Come home with me until you're calm enough to drive home."

"No, thank you," Karla replies. "The police have my car. I missed a ton of messages and emails while they questioned me." She glances at her phone. "I don't want Rita to see me like this." She swipes her thumb under one eye, then the other, smooths her hair, and takes a deep breath. "I'll go to the pub where we had lunch. I'll have something to eat and sort through my emails. I hope when I'm done, the police will have contacted me to pick up my car. Then, I'll go home and explain this situation to Rita. She'll know something is wrong. I'm not ready to explain it to her."

"Are you sure?" I ask. "I can feed Sophie, then meet you at the pub. If it would help, I can be there when you talk to Rita."

"No, thanks." She forces a smile. "I'll be fine."

"There's another suspect in Fawkes's murder," I say. "Someone who visited the store today."

"There is?"

"I'll stay up late to tell Eric about it," I reply, nodding. "You and I can talk about it tomorrow."

"Tomorrow." Her smile is now genuine and not forced. "Tomorrow will be a better day."

"Get some rest," I advise. "You'll feel better after a good night's sleep."

"I will." Karla nods. "Thanks, Megan."

She walks away, and as her rhythmic clicks fade into the distance, I realize that Karla and I had an entire conversation without her insulting or criticizing me. Granted, she wants my help, but it's a start, right?

# CHAPTER 10

I PULL into the driveway next to Eric's car. Is he home or just his car? Sometimes Eric uses a patrol car for work and leaves his car at home, or if he's working with a partner, they'll ride together and his colleague drives.

Sophie rockets into the house, tearing down the hall and disappearing into the kitchen.

His shoes by the door, and his keys and wallet in their usual spots, confirm my suspicion that Eric is here. Somewhere. The house is silent.

I follow Sophie to the kitchen. Her dinner is waiting for her, but instead of eating, she's scratching the glass pane in the back door and whimpering.

Someone has set the table with two plates, cutlery, glasses, and a bottle of wine. The back door opens, and Sophie lets out an excited yelp.

"Hey, Soph," Eric says, rubbing her head. "Are you hungry? Your dinner is over there."

"Hey handsome," I say. "I thought you were working late."

He smiles at me with tired eyes, places the barbecue tongs on the table, then kisses and hugs me.

"I needed to come home," he says, pouring two glasses of wine and handing one to me.

"Why?" I ask. "Are you sick?"

I worry about Eric's health when he investigates a big case. The pressure to solve the case, combined with the lack of sleep and healthy food, must wreak havoc on his immune system.

"Sick of the Fawkes murder case," he mutters, then clinks his glass against mine. He takes a swig of pinot grigio, which seems to perk him up, and smiles. "We haven't had a meal together all week. I miss you, babe." He moves his hand up and down my back in long, lazy strokes. "I was hoping we could spend some time together tonight. We can take Sophie to the park after dinner, then snuggle up with a movie?"

He looks at me like he just remembered something. "Unless you have plans!" He shakes his head. "I should have asked you first. I didn't think. Did you make plans because I was working late? If you're busy, we can do this another…"

"I don't have plans," I say, interrupting him. "Your plan is perfect."

On tippy toes, I stretch to kiss him.

"Dinner is almost ready." He gestures toward the backyard with his wine glass. "Grilled honey garlic shrimp with grilled garlic-basil vegetables. Zucchini, bell pepper, onions, asparagus, and mushrooms."

"My favourite veggies," I say, then sip my wine. "I'm starving."

He sets the wineglass on the table, picks up the barbecue tongs, and returns to the back deck.

We enjoy a delicious dinner and clean up with no mention of work or Clarence Fawkes.

During dinner, and on our walk to the dog park, Eric is talkative but distant. I attribute his mood to distraction and fatigue. It's easier for him to leave work physically than mentally.

"Do you want to talk about it?" I ask, watching Eric scoop up Sophie's ball with the throwing stick.

"Talk about what?" he asks, bringing the stick behind his shoulder.

He hurls the tennis ball into the distance.

Sophie launches herself after it, zooming across the open field as fast as her short corgi legs will carry her.

"Whatever is on your mind."

He sighs, looking at me, then sits next to me on the bench.

"I don't know how to put it into words." He leans forward, resting his elbows on his thighs and dropping his chin to his chest.

I rub the back of his neck and watch Sophie in the distance. She lifts her head with pride, prancing in circles and showing off the tennis ball in her mouth.

"I hate this case, babe," Eric says, shaking his head. "For the first time in my career, I'm unmotivated to solve a murder." He sits up straight and squeezes my knee. "My job is to protect society from bad people. I make sure criminals face the consequences of their actions. I represent a system that is supposed to be transparent and trustworthy. In exchange for trusting us to investigate, arrest, and prosecute criminals, people agree not to resort to vigilante justice."

"But?" I ask, sensing his implied but.

Sophie has returned from her victory lap around the dog park. She is lying at our feet, panting, and admiring the orange tennis ball in front of her.

"Fawkes was an easy target," Eric continues. "He was alone, with no internet or cell phone, in an isolated cabin on a secluded lake in a remote town." He shakes his head. "I tried to tell his parole officer that Fawkes would be safer in a halfway house, somewhere more populated." He sighs. "But no one listened. His parole officer said Fawkes was intent on staying at the family cottage in Harmony Lake. Fawkes believed if he went to a halfway house, or somewhere more visible, someone would hurt him."

"His fear was legitimate," I acknowledge. "Someone hurt him."

Sophie jumps to her feet. She stares at the ball, signalling that she's ready for another throw.

"The system failed Fawkes's victims, babe. We let him out. Despite being guilty, he won a new trial because of a minor administrative glitch. Why should his victims, or anyone else, trust the system to make it right after the system failed them?"

Eric stabs the ball with the stick and stands up. He cocks his arm and flings the orange ball farther than last time. Sophie sprints in pursuit, her ears flat against her head for maximum aerodynamics.

"Are you saying that you suspect one of Fawkes's victims killed him?"

"I think it's probable." He shields his eyes against the setting sun and watches Sophie reach the ball in the distance. "If it *is* one of Fawkes's victims, I'm not sure I want to be the cop who investigates and arrests them." He turns away from Sophie and returns to the bench. "His killer wouldn't have had access to kill him if Fawkes was still in his cage where he belonged."

"Oh, honey." I squeeze his hand. "I'm sorry you're in such a difficult situation."

If only I could do or say something that would help my idealistic, principled husband. Morally ambiguous situations are a no-win for him. If he doesn't find and arrest Fawkes's killer, he'll have to live with letting a murderer get away. If he finds and arrests Fawkes's killer, it could condemn a Fawkes victim to the life sentence Fawkes died trying to avoid.

Either outcome would torment Eric for the rest of his life.

Sophie appears in front of us. She sits at attention and reveals her victory by letting the orange ball fall dramatically from her mouth. We praise her fetching skills, and the tired corgi laps water from her portable water bowl, then lies in the grass, tired and content.

"Fawkes's killer might not be one of his victims," I remind him. "But if *it* was, the prosecutors can take it into consideration, right?"

"Maybe." Eric shrugs one shoulder. "Maybe not. I only have control over the investigation, not what happens after I press charges."

"Can you assign the case to another investigator?"

"Who, babe?" he answers my question with a question. "I'm the only experienced murder investigator in Harmony Lake. Borrowing an investigator from another police force would destroy our budget, and I don't want to put anyone else in this situation."

"You'll figure it out," I assure him. "Sometimes doing the right thing feels wrong, and sometimes doing the wrong thing feels right."

"Would either outcome make you think less of me?" he asks.

"No!" I insist. "Never. I love you, and I know you are a compassionate, fair person. Choose the option you can live with. I'll support whatever you decide."

"I love you." He wraps his arm around my shoulder and pulls me toward him.

"I love you too." I nuzzle into the crook of his neck.

Eric's phone vibrates in his pocket, and I back away so he can reach it. He reads the screen with narrowed eyes, sighs, and slides the phone back inside his pocket.

"Is it urgent?" I ask.

"No," Eric says. "It's Fawkes's sister. I asked her for some information, and she just sent it to me."

"He had a sister?" I ask, remembering that besides being a horrible human being, Clarence Fawkes also had a family. "Were they close?"

The dynamics of Fawkes's relationship with his family suddenly fascinates me.

"Fawkes's sister owns The Fawkes Den," he replies. "She said they weren't close, but she felt obligated to help him because their parents pressured her. The parents are elderly, and they worried about their son, to the detriment of their own health. She's relieved they won't have to deal with the stress of Fawkes's retrial. She said she won't miss him."

"It sounds like Fawkes's sister had a motive," I comment. "She didn't want to look after him, she didn't want her parents to worry about him, and she wanted to spare her family the media circus that would come with her brother's retrial. She had opportunity too. As the owner, she would have a key to The Fawkes Den."

"She has an alibi," Eric says. "An officer is verifying it as we speak. She claims that aside from visits to drop off provisions, she hasn't stepped foot in the cottage since Fawkes moved in. Her parents live in an expensive care home, and she said if her brother hadn't moved in, she would have sold The Fawkes Den this summer and used the money to help cover their expenses."

"Even more motive," I say. "Her cottage is on a premium location on the lake. She would have gotten top dollar for it, especially if she'd sold it in the summer, during peak cottage season."

"We found her fingerprints and DNA at the scene, but we expected them to be there because it's her cottage."

"Unlike Karla, whose fingerprints and hair had no business being at The Fawkes Den." I finish his thought.

"Exactly."

"Speaking of Karla," I say, "I agreed to help clear her name."

"Why?"

"She asked," I reply.

"Are you sure, babe? You and Karla don't always get along."

"She's not my favourite person," I agree. "But I believe Karla is a kind person who, for whatever reason, hides it well. Rita's health is frail enough without stressing about Karla going to prison. If this investigation damages Karla's reputation and affects her business, it could impact the Just Task Me! employees who need their jobs. I don't believe Karla killed Fawkes. I can't explain why Karla's fingerprints and hair were at the crime scene, but I'll find out."

"Other than the fingerprints and hair, there's no evidence to suggest Karla Bell and Clarence Fawkes ever crossed paths," Eric says. "I've combed through their histories." He lets out a frustrated breath. "We have her car, but so far there's no evidence that Fawkes's body was ever inside. But until Karla admits when and why she was inside the cottage, I can't eliminate her. Her alibi is flimsy."

"Leave it with me," I say. "If Karla is hiding something, I'll find out."

"I know you will." Eric winks.

"Have you heard who's visiting Harmony Lake?"

"Who?"

"Melody."

"Melody..." Eric pulls away enough to look me in the eye. "Your friend from high school whose locker was next to yours?" he asks, unsure.

I shake my head and open my mouth to speak.

"Don't tell me," Erics says, holding up his index finger. "The cousin on your mum's side that you went to camp with for ten summers?"

I shake my head again.

"Give up?" I ask.

"Yes," he says with a chuckle. "Who is Melody?"

Eric has heard of Melody because of her infamous awards-show performance, but he doesn't know what she looks like because bubble-gum pop was not teenage-Eric's preferred music genre.

I pull out my trusty cell phone and find images of her on the internet.

"Her current style is similar to when she was famous," I say, scrolling through photos and showing him. "Her hair is shorter, but the denim and the gum and the jewelry haven't changed."

"Why was she at Knitorious?" he asks.

"Melody crochets!" I declare. "Have you noticed how only the coolest people knit and crochet?"

"I have noticed," he replies, laughing. "And I see proof every day."

That compliment earns him a kiss.

We attach Sophie's leash, gather her toys and water dish, then walk home.

"Melody was the first Fawkes victim to come forward," Eric says.

"I know," I say, then tell him about the conversation The Charity Knitters and I had with Trevor and Melody about Fawkes's murder and their proximity to his cottage.

"They denied knowing Fawkes?" Eric asks.

I nod.

"I'll contact the officer who canvassed the neighbours and ask him a few questions," Eric says.

We stop walking while Eric unlocks his phone and sends a quick message.

"What was the husband like?" Eric asks when we resume walking.

"His name is Trevor. He has a lot of tattoos and a New York accent." I unlock my phone. "I'll search for a picture of him on the internet."

When I open the browser on my phone, the last photo we looked at of Melody fills the screen. An album cover featuring a headshot. She's blowing a huge, pink bubble. Her eyes are wide, like she can't believe the bubble hasn't burst yet. Her hair is in a bushy, teased ponytail and her bangs are a perfect, straight line across her forehead. Next to the giant bubble, her ear with a plethora of trendy earrings. One earring catches my eye. I pinch the screen and zoom in.

"Honey." I poke Eric's bicep. "Look at this."

We stop walking again, and I hand him my phone.

"Whose ear is this?" he asks, the muscles around his eyes tense.

"Melody's," I reply. "It's from the cover of an album she released fifteen years ago."

"Mind if I send this to myself?" he asks, examining the heart-shaped hoop earring with a key dangling in the centre.

# CHAPTER 11

I have an earworm. A Melody song has wiggled its way into my brain and gotten stuck there. Not the entire song, just part of the catchy chorus. I've been replaying it on a mental loop all morning. Since Fawkes's family announced his future royalties will benefit his victims, radio stations have ended the boycott and are playing his songs nonstop. Songs I haven't heard in years, yet somehow, still remember every word. This is a good thing. The other artists and people who contributed to Fawkes's extensive music catalogue will also earn royalties again, including his victims.

I'm still humming the snappy tune when I knock on Adam's door.

Adam and I have brunch with our daughter every Sunday. We alternate between my house and his condo, but Adam always cooks. Today, brunch is at his condo. Hannah is away at university and joins us by video chat.

Adam doesn't answer, so I knock again, louder.

The door swings open.

"Sorry! Adam is in the kitchen and didn't hear the door."

"Karla!" I can't believe my eyes. "Why are you here?"

"I slept over."

"You said you were going home to talk to Rita," I remind her. "Who's looking after Gucci?"

"Change of plans," Karla coos. "Gucci slept over at Rita's house. They watched Breaking Bad and ate popcorn."

She sneers and gathers the collar of the plush purple bathrobe.

"Is that?" I point at her. "Are you wearing my daughter's robe?" I'm pinching my eyebrows together so hard my forehead hurts.

"Adam said it was OK," she says, smiling.

"Did he…" I inhale hard.

"Are you all right, Megan?" Karla asks. "Cat got your tongue?"

"Get dressed," I instruct through gritted teeth. "Then bring me Hannah's robe, and whatever else you borrowed from my daughter so I can wash it."

"If you say so." Karla spins and sashays down the hall toward the bedrooms.

Speechless, I stand in Adam's kitchen doorway, hands on hips, tapping my foot, reeling from the shock of Karla Bell—wearing our daughter's robe—answering his door.

"Oh! Hey, Meg!" Adam stands in front of the stove, unaware of the interaction his houseguest and I just had. "Been standing there long?"

"No," I reply with intentional snark, tapping my foot faster. "Karla let me in."

"I can't hear the door when the range hood is on." He

taps the stainless-steel device over the stove, oblivious to my snark, then turns his attention back to cooking.

"Smells delicious!" Karla appears next to me wearing yesterday's clothes. "What's for breakfast?" she chirps over the hum of the range hood, rubbing her hands together and licking her chops.

"Huevos Rancheros Breakfast Casserole," Adam replies, turning off the loud range hood. "Crispy tostadas topped with enchilada sauce, beans, cheese, and queso, then topped with fried eggs, avocado, sour cream, and cilantro." He slides a spatula into the frying pan and transfers two fried eggs to the casserole dish.

"Yummy," Karla purrs. "Almost makes me wish I ate breakfast."

"I can pack up a serving," Adam offers. "Take it with you and eat later."

"That's sweet, Adam, but I won't be home to heat it up. You keep it and enjoy the leftovers."

She thanks Adam for his hospitality and kisses his cheek. Kind of formal after spending the night together, but what do I know?

"I'll walk you out," I offer, following her to the door.

"Hannah's robe," Karla says, pointing to the folded robe resting on top of my purse.

"Thanks."

"What's wrong, Megan?"

I shake my head. "Nothing."

"You aren't jealous, are you?" she asks, crinkling her nose.

"No," I reply, opening the door. "Drive safe."

"We're supposed to get together today, remember? To discuss the suspect you found."

"I remember." I smile and gesture toward the open door.

"What time shall we meet?" Karla asks. "Should I

come back to Harmony Lake this afternoon?"

"I'll come to you," I reply. "I have to drop off Rita's empty yarn bins."

We agree on a time, and Karla leaves.

Maybe Eric was right. Maybe helping clear Karla's name is a bad idea. She insists on using my last nerve as a scratching post, and I'm not sure how long I can ignore her barbed remarks without biting back.

*I'm not helping Karla. I'm helping Rita,* I remind myself. *I'm doing it for the employees at Just Task Me!, for Gucci, and for Karla's grandmother. After we clear her name, I never have to speak to Karla again.*

I suspect this will be my new mantra until we eliminate Karla as a suspect.

"WHAT'S WRONG, MEG?" asks my ex-husband for the second time since we ended our weekly call with Hannah.

"Why do you think something is wrong?"

"Because if looks could kill I would be face down in my huevos rancheros."

I sit back, crossing my arms and legs.

"I don't think you should invite your overnight guests to wear Hannah's bathrobe."

"Overnight guests?" Adam chuckles. "Plural?" He squints at me. "How many *overnight guests* do you think I have?"

"I don't care." I shake my head. "It's none of my business."

"I don't have *any* overnight guests, Meg." He rolls his eyes and sips his coffee.

"Then Karla must be special." I add foot bouncing to my crossed arms and legs situation.

"Nothing happened between me and Karla. She slept in Hannah's room," Adam says. "I didn't think it would be a problem if she borrowed Hannah's robe." He removes the napkin from his lap and drops it on his empty plate. "I'll wash it before Hannah comes home for Thanksgiving."

"I'll wash it," I retort, tipping my head toward my purse. "It's already with my stuff."

"Fine. You wash it." Adam raises his hands in a conciliatory gesture.

"Why didn't Karla go home?" I ask. "She only lives thirty minutes away."

"I ran into Karla at the pub," Adam explains. "I was picking up a takeout order—the fish and chips special—for dinner. Karla was there. She was alone in a booth. When I said hi, I could tell she wasn't OK. She was shaky, her eyes were red and swollen, and there were three empty martini glasses in front of her. I offered to join her and changed my takeout order to dine in."

"Did she tell you what upset her?" I ask.

Adam nods. "Karla told me she's a suspect in Fawkes's murder. She told me about the fingerprints and hair. She told me about her grandmother and Rita. And she told me you agreed to help her, even though she didn't deserve it."

"You invited her to come home with you because she was too drunk to drive?"

"Yes," Adam confirms. "She was drunk and emotional. I couldn't drive her home"—he pokes himself in the chest—"I had two beers while we talked. I wasn't comfortable waving her off in a cab with a stranger. It made sense to bring her here."

"You're a good man," I say.

Why am I relieved that Adam and Karla's sleepover was platonic? Is it because I don't like her, and if they get together, I can't stand the idea of seeing her at family functions? Because she's a man-eater who will break Adam's heart? Because she's a murder suspect? How certain am I that Karla isn't capable of murder?

"Can I ask you something, Meg?"

"Sure."

"Would it have bothered you if Karla didn't sleep in Hannah's room?"

I shift in my seat and swallow.

"Of course not," I say, looking him in the eye. "But I would've preferred if she'd left before I arrived."

Adam pours us a second cup of coffee, and we make small talk between sips, ignoring the lingering tension in the air.

"Eric said the killer dumped Fawkes's body in the pool after the sprinkler system forced us to evacuate and before the grand opening ceremony," Adam says when the conversation turns to Fawkes's murder.

"How did he determine that?"

"When the pool committee finished putting up the balloon arches and paper curtains, Fawkes's body wasn't in the pool," Adam explains. "When the leak in the library activated the sprinkler system, it also activated the fire alarm, which summoned the fire department," Adam discloses. "The fire captain insisted on inspecting the building before anyone re-entered. Eric said the fire-fighters would have noticed Fawkes's body floating in the pool."

"Who had access to the pool after the evacuation ended?" I ask.

"It would be quicker to tell you who *didn't* have access," Adam replies with a chuckle. "It was all-hands on deck, Meg. We had to mop up the water, salvage the books, and fix the leak so we could turn on the water. The floors were filthy with boot prints from the firefighters."

He sighs. "Everyone chipped in. We were thankful for all the help we could get."

"Sounds chaotic," I comment.

"It was," Adam agrees. "We ran around like headless chickens trying to finish before the grand-opening ceremony."

Did the killer camouflage their covert mission in the surrounding chaos and drag Fawkes's body through the commotion without being seen? Maybe the killer's decision to dump Fawkes's corpse in the pool was impulsive. Maybe the killer was searching for somewhere to dump the body, and the flurry of activity at the community centre/town hall/library gave them the opportunity they needed.

"Did the library lose many books?" I ask.

"No," Adam replies. "Mason shut off the water, which minimized the damage."

"How is Mason doing?" I ask.

"Mason insisted he was fine, but Eric and I could tell it rattled him. It's only been two months since his mum passed away. Other than her, Mason had never seen a dead body, much less a surprise corpse floating a few feet from him."

"Mason and his mother were very close," I say. "He spends a lot of time in the dungeon with his mum's boxes." I smile. "He says he's looking for paperwork for her estate or bank statements, but I suspect those are excuses so he can find comfort being near her belongings."

"I suspect you're right," Adam says. "I haven't asked Mason for anything related to his mum's estate. She was super-organized and made sure I had everything before she died. It will be an easy estate to execute."

"It's too bad Fawkes's death isn't as straightforward," I comment.

# CHAPTER 12

"COME IN," Karla shouts when I knock on the door.

"Just me," I say, stepping into the house.

Gucci bounces in front of me, swishing his quill-like tail.

"I thought you might have changed your mind," Karla comments, then seals a box with a loud strip of packing tape.

"Why would I change my mind?" I ask, not admitting that I had pondered it. "If I had changed my mind, I would have mentioned it when we bumped into each other this morning."

"Are you still angry about that?" She heaves the sealed box onto a stack of similar boxes and wipes her hands on her faded skinny jeans.

"I wasn't angry," I correct her. "Surprised, but not angry. I understand you do things for shock value. To get a reaction. I've met your type before."

"Oh." Karla's face brightens. "So, I'm the second super-cool person you've met."

She smirks.

I don't.

She inhales, and her smirk disappears.

"Nothing happened between Adam and me," she says. "Your ex-husband was a perfect gentleman."

She makes a few notes on the clipboard in front of her.

"It's none of my business," I say, raising my hand in a stop gesture and shaking my head. "But it would've been considerate if you'd left before I arrived."

"And miss your expression when I opened the door? No way!" Karla laughs. "You should have seen your face when you recognized Hannah's robe." She laughs again and claps her hands, remembering the hilarious moment. "Your reaction made the hangover and restless night in a strange bed worthwhile."

I shake my head.

"But seriously," Karla adds, gathering the tape gun, marker, and clipboard in front of her, "Adam was a great listener." She caps the pen and adds it to her collection of packing accessories. "He also gave me contact information for a few criminal lawyers." She shrugs one shoulder. "But I hope I won't need to call a criminal lawyer."

Karla moves her armful of packing accessories to the fireplace mantle, and I find an opportunity to change the subject.

"Did you find the missing bookend?" I ask, pointing to the lone piece of art resting on the mantle.

"No," she replies, tightening her low ponytail. "It's inside one of these boxes." She gestures to the piles of boxes lining the walls of the large room. "Or it's in Rita's garage." She shakes her head. "I've instructed Chelle not to move any boxes or donate anything until I find it, which could take hours."

Karla releases a long, hopeless sigh, and I wonder if she is hopeless about finding the missing bookend or about having multiple hours at her disposal to search for it.

"Hi, Gooch-the-pooch," Chelle says, as if Karla mentioning her name was her cue to join the conversation.

"Karla!" Chelle says, surprised to find her employer at home. "I thought you were packing up your office today?"

"Change of plans," Karla replies. "Why are you here?" She gives Chelle a dubious full-body scan. "Don't you spend Sundays with your parents?"

"We have family visiting from out of town," Chelle replies. "My parents find too many visitors tiring, so I left. I thought I'd continue packing until I meet everyone for dinner later."

"You didn't mention family visiting from out of town. You usually ramble about the details of your life," Karla comments, her doubt obvious. She narrows her eyes. "Was it an unexpected visit? Is something wrong with your parents?"

If Karla thinks Chelle is lying or not telling the entire truth, she does not bother hiding her suspicions.

"My parents are fine," Chelle replies with a dismissive wave. "Well, fine for them. At their age they have so many health issues, their medical files are thicker than two bricks."

Chelle chuckles, and we chuckle with her, but Karla's chuckle includes a skeptical side glance.

Karla reminds Chelle about the extensive cataloguing and cross-checking system she devised to ensure she doesn't lose or mispack her belongings. She also tells Chelle not to move any boxes, sealed or open, from Karla's house or Rita's garage. Karla then points to the single bookend displayed on the mantle, reminding Chelle that if she finds its missing partner to place it on the mantle with its mate.

"Call or text me if you have questions," Karla

instructs, removing Gucci's designer collar and replacing it with a different designer collar from a nearby drawer.

"If you want to leave Gucci here, I'll walk him and feed him for you," Chelle offers.

"Thank you, Chelle, but no need." Karla smiles and attaches the matching designer leash to Gucci's collar. "Rita already offered."

Across the street, I return Rita's empty yarn bins to her garage, while Karla hands over Gucci's fashionable reins to Rita, casually asking her if Chelle mentioned anything about out-of-town family members coming for a visit.

"She said nothing to me," Rita replies. "I hope her parents are OK. They're quite old, you know." She giggles. "Even by my standards."

"She says they're fine," Karla assures her. "I'm sure Chelle wouldn't be at my house today if one of them was ill. I was just shocked to see her because she always spends Sunday with her parents."

"You don't believe Chelle is telling the truth about family visiting from out of town?" I ask, as we drive away from Rita's house in my car.

Karla is eager to pick up her car from the police station, and I offered to drive her there.

"She's not herself," Karla replies. "Today is the first time I've seen Chelle in person since last Monday. I think she is avoiding me. Did you notice how shocked she was that I was home?"

"I noticed she seemed shocked, but I've only met Chelle once," I remind her. "I don't know if her behaviour was out of character." We wait while another car goes through the four-way stop. "To be fair, I wasn't sure you were home, either," I admit. "Your car wasn't in the driveway. For a moment, I forgot the police still had it."

"I got the distinct impression Chelle wouldn't have shown up if she knew I was home."

"Why would she avoid you?"

"That's a good question."

"I don't want to offend you," I say with caution, "but do you make snide remarks at Chelle? Do you make sarcastic comments about her appearance or flatter her with backhanded compliments? Because that might explain why she's avoiding you."

"Of course not, Megan." Karla huffs and glares at me. "Chelle Temple is my employee. I treat her with the same respect as every employee." She waves her hand in front of her face like she's waving away a foul smell. "I don't have time to obsess over a fifty-year-old woman's moods. I need my mental energy to prove I didn't kill Fawkes."

We stop at the last traffic light before the highway.

"Where were you on Tuesday morning?" I ask. "According to the coroner, Fawkes died before noon."

"I woke up at 7 a.m.," Karla recalls. "I showered, dressed, and took Gucci for a walk. Then, I dropped off Gucci with Rita and went to the office. I was at the office until I drove to Harmony Lake. I visited Artsy Tartsy, then went to Knitorious to invite you to lunch. After lunch, I returned to the office, then came home for dinner."

"If Eric could verify your alibi, he would have eliminated you as a suspect," I say, merging onto the highway toward Harmony Lake.

"Your husband said I had enough time between leaving the office and showing up at Artsy Tartsy to kill Fawkes." Karla slaps her denim thigh. "How would I have convinced Fawkes to get in my car, let me drive him to a community centre, and allow me to drown him in the pool? Does Eric think I rendered Fawkes unconscious at his cottage, touched everything to make sure my fingerprints were there, dragged the unconscious body to my car, then from my car to the pool, drowned him, and left with no one noticing that I dragged a body around town?"

Either Karla doesn't know that Fawkes died in the bathtub at his cottage, or she's pretending not to know to further convince me she's innocent.

"Did you stop anywhere between the office and Harmony Lake?" I ask.

"Nowhere," Karla admits. "There was an accident on the highway, so I took side streets instead."

"It takes over an hour to take side streets to Harmony Lake from your house. You'd have to drive around the mountains," I point out. "Wasn't Tuesday's accident in the opposite lanes? It wouldn't have slowed you down."

"You sound like Eric," she says, shaking her head. "I guess I misheard the traffic report. I was certain the reporter said the accident caused the lanes toward Harmony Lake to back up. It made sense at the time."

"Your cell phone would have placed you on the side streets. It would prove you were weaving through the mountains when Fawkes took his last breath."

"If it was on," Karla adds.

"You turned off your cell phone?" I ask, incredulous. "I've never seen you go longer than a few minutes without checking your phone."

"I didn't know it was off," she laments. "I didn't turn it off on purpose. It was an accident. Something in my purse must have pressed the button." She shrugs. "I didn't realize it was off until I parked at Artsy Tartsy and picked it up to check my messages. The screen was black. I thought I was lucky it wasn't broken." She shakes her head. "Boy, was I wrong."

"We have to prove you weren't in Harmony Lake when Fawkes died," I mutter.

"Even if my phone was on and tracked my journey from the office to Artsy Tartsy, it wouldn't be good enough," Karla says. "Eric said it would only prove my phone wasn't in Harmony Lake when Fawkes died, not that *I* wasn't."

My phone dings, and I press the button on the steering wheel that makes the automated voice inside my car read the message.

*Mrs. Roblin: We have something for your hobby. Please meet us in the parking lot behind Knitorious ASAP. Thank you.*

"We'll worry about your alibi later," I say, pressing on the accelerator. "Right now, we need to meet the Charity Knitters."

"We're going knitting?" Karla asks, confused. "I thought you found a suspect? How will meeting with a bunch of do-good knitters clear my name?"

"First of all, I wouldn't call them that to their faces."

# CHAPTER 13

WE PULL into the parking lot behind Knitorious, and I cut the engine. Knitorious is closed on Sundays, so the parking lot is dead. Pardon the pun.

"Is that them?" Karla asks, unbuckling her seatbelt and nodding toward the only other car in the lot.

"No," I reply. "That's an upstairs tenant. Hannah's boyfriend and Eric's nephew share the apartment above Knitorious."

"Maybe you should text your charity knitters and let them know we're here."

"They already know," I say, forgetting that Karla isn't familiar with the inner workings of Harmony Lake and how well informed The Charity Knitters are about every movement in town.

"How?"

"Here they are," I say, sitting up straight when Mrs. Vogel's four-door sedan pulls into the lot and parks across from us.

"How did they know…"

"I'll be right back." I unbuckle my seatbelt, ignoring her question.

"Why so serious?" Karla asks. "You're meeting a couple of elderly knitters, not mafia kingpins."

"They prefer *queenpins*," I joke, opening the car door.

Mrs. Roblin, Mrs. Vogel, and I meet halfway between our vehicles. A car door shuts behind me, followed by the rapid clickety-clack of Karla's open-toed stiletto mules as she joins us in the middle of the parking lot.

"Ladies," I say to Mrs. Vogel and Mrs. Roblin. "This is Karla Bell." I gesture to Karla.

"Hello, ladies," Karla schmoozes, extending her hand. "I'm—"

"We know who you are," Mrs. Roblin says, interrupting Karla's sentence and shaking her hand.

"And we know where you spent the night," Mrs. Vogel adds with arched eyebrows.

Karla blinks at the two elderly ladies, her jaw lax.

"You're Karla Bell of the Bellbrook Bells," Mrs. Roblin advises, mentioning the hometown Karla left twenty years ago.

"And you took a cab home from Mayor Martel's house this morning because the police have your car." Mrs. Vogel removes her fist from her pocket. "You left this in the cab." She opens her hand to reveal a tube of lipstick.

"Oh!" Karla blinks at the tube with the pink lid. "It must have fallen out of my purse. How did you...?" She abandons her sentence and plucks the cosmetic from Mrs. Vogel's hand. "Someone did their homework," she chirps. "I'm impressed, ladies."

"You don't seem as unpleasant as people say." Mrs. Roblin's saccharine smile could melt a polar ice cap.

"They were right about your expensive taste, though," Mrs. Vogel adds, nodding to the lipstick in Karla's hand.

"I hide my unpleasantness well," Karla muses

without missing a beat, patting her low ponytail, "I styled my hair to hide my horns, and I tucked my tail into my jeans today." She gives the Charity Knitters a crooked grin and a devilish wink.

"Is this what you wanted to give me, ladies?" I nod toward the pink lipstick tube. "Or is there something else?" I ask, steering the conversation to the reason we're standing in the middle of an empty parking lot.

Mrs. Roblin hands me a glass food storage container with a red lid.

"Plastic bags are bad for the environment," Mrs. Vogel says, tapping the lid. "Reusable containers are much more eco-friendly."

"Eric will drop it off when we're finished with it," I assure Mrs. Roblin.

She grins. "No rush, Megan."

I inspect the contents through the glass and recognize the glittery pink-mosaic rhinestone case.

"Ladies!" I summon my sternest voice and purse my lips to hide my grin. "You *stole* her phone?" I admonish.

With humble pride, The Charity Knitters flash each other, then me, a smug smirk, pleased with themselves and their contribution to *my hobby*.

Karla's expression is equal parts confusion and concern.

"We spread the word that you needed an excuse to visit the young lady," says Mrs. Roblin, full of sweetness and light. "And it just so happened that she *forgot* her phone at another establishment."

"An amazing coincidence," I agree.

"The proprietor turned off the phone—to preserve the battery, of course, not to prevent the owner from tracking its whereabouts," adds Mrs. Vogel, her eyes innocent and wide.

"Of course not," I agree. "It was very thoughtful of them to consider the battery life."

"Yes, it was," the ladies mumble in agreement.

"We thought you might return the phone to its owner since you've already met her and have established a rapport."

"Thank you." I smile and touch their arms. "We'll make sure she gets it," I assure them. "We won't tell anyone where we got it."

"You weren't kidding about the mafia-thing," Karla mutters as we return to my car and the pleased-with-themselves Charity Knitters return to theirs.

"Listen, Karla," I say when we're ensconced in the car, away from prying ears and eyes, "whatever The Charity Knitters know about you, they didn't find out from me."

"Then how did they find out?"

I shrug. "They have their ways."

"What ways?" Karla pushes her brows together and narrows her eyes at me.

"It's best if we don't know."

"Harmony Lake isn't as sweet and cozy as it looks from the outside, is it?"

"Yes," I reply, "and no."

Karla opens the glass storage container on her lap.

"It's Melody's phone," I inform her.

"Melody who?"

It doesn't take much prompting to remind Karla who Melody is and why she disappeared. It turns out, back in the day, Karla was a huge Melody fan. She had every album and even attended her concerts.

"Melody is your alternate suspect?" Karla asks.

I nod. "She was in town when Fawkes died. Her rental cottage backs onto The Fawkes Den. She was the first Fawkes victim to come forward."

"I remember." Karla nods solemnly. "The media

called her *ground zero*." She shakes her head. "It was awful." She stares at the glittery phone. "Should we poke around her phone? Read her texts and emails? Check her internet search history?"

I nod, hesitant about breaching someone's privacy in such an obvious way. I remind myself that the Howes made themselves suspects when they lied about knowing Clarence Fawkes.

Karla presses the power button, and we wait in silence while the screen comes to life.

We try to unlock the phone, but it requires either facial recognition or a password. We decide against trying to guess the password because we have no clue what it might be, and we aren't sure if Melody will notice the failed password attempts and know we tried to snoop. Instead, we turn off the phone and return it to the glass container.

For the rest of the drive to Melody and Trevor's rental cottage, Karla shuffles through a playlist of Melody's songs and bounces in her seat with anticipatory glee about meeting her pop idol.

"Now that the boycott is over, maybe Melody will go on tour or release a new album!"

"Maybe," I agree.

I don't believe Karla killed Fawkes, but if she did, perhaps her motive wasn't a personal grudge against him, but a desire to repopulate the music charts with the bubble-gum pop songs she loves.

We turn onto the long, single-lane driveway that leads to the secluded cottage. As we round the first bend, a car creeps toward us. I pull over as much as one can on a narrow, tree-lined driveway and give the oncoming car space to pass. The driver waves his thanks as he rolls past, and the backseat passenger locks eyes with me. Expressionless and unblinking, we maintain eye contact until we can no longer turn our heads enough to continue the connection.

"Who was in the back of the police car?" Karla asks, turning down the music.

"Trevor Howe," I reply. "Melody's husband." I check my mirrors and continue up the driveway.

"Oh my," she whispers.

# CHAPTER 14

AT THE TOP of the driveway, there's a paved parking pad large enough to park at least six cars. But there's nowhere to park my small SUV because a tow truck, a mid-1980s, blue and silver two-tone Camaro, a police cruiser, and a late model Charger are scattered across the black asphalt surface.

"Do you think the police arrested Melody's husband for Fawkes's murder?" Karla asks, removing Melody's cell phone from the glass storage container and tossing the empty container onto the back seat.

"I don't know," I reply, pulling over to the side of the narrow driveway and positioning halfway on the dirt shoulder and halfway on the driveway. "But if they did, your name would be clear. Aside from returning Melody's phone, there would be no reason for us to be here."

"As much as I don't want to be a murder suspect, I hope Melody's husband isn't the killer," Karla admits.

"Why?"

"She's lost enough because of Fawkes." Karla shrugs

one shoulder. "She lost her career, her fame and fortune, and if her husband is a murderer, she'll lose him too."

"You're right, it would be another tragic outcome for Melody," I say with a sigh. "I don't see her outside. She must be in the cottage."

"Unless the police arrested her too," Karla suggests, wide-eyed. "What if the police car we saw was the second car? What if they arrested Melody earlier, and she's already at the police station?"

"There's only one way to find out." I unbuckle my seatbelt and open the door.

"I'll catch up," Karla says, unlocking her phone. "I need to reply to a message."

"Hey, babe!" Eric smiles, striding toward me from the parking pad. "Watch your step." He extends his hand and breaks into a jog as if he foresees a fall in my immediate future.

"Hey, handsome!"

I take his hand, and he kisses my forehead.

He asks about brunch and how Hannah is doing.

I give him the abridged version of Karla's unexpected presence at Adam's condo.

"I'll tell you more later," I say, quirking my eyebrows at the tow truck driver and uniformed police officer hovering nearby. "We drove past Trevor Howe in the back of a police cruiser."

"He's helping us with our inquiries," replies my husband with a chuckle. "I spoke with Trevor and Melody this morning. Based on our discussion, I got a warrant to seize Trevor's car." He turns toward the vintage, blue two-tone Camaro being hoisted onto the back of the flatbed tow truck. "He agreed to answer more questions if we agreed to tow his car on a flatbed instead of a wheel-lift tow truck. The car is pristine, and he wants it to stay that way."

"Does this mean you've decided to solve Fawkes's murder?"

"Yes," Eric replies.

I nod. "Are you sure?"

"I'm fine," Eric insists. "It's my job to investigate crimes and apprehend criminals. I'm a professional. Professionals don't allow their personal opinions to interfere with their professional obligations."

"As long as you're comfortable," I say, still unconvinced.

"I am," Eric says, rubbing my shoulder, "for the most part." He sweeps my hair behind my shoulder and rubs the back of my neck. "If I still feel conflicted after we figure out who killed Fawkes, I'll deal with it then." He squeezes my hand.

"Did he do it?" Karla shouts, closing the car door. "Did Trevor kill Fawkes?"

Eric mutters a curse word under his breath.

I gently swat his arm and stifle a giggle.

"She messaged me all night and all morning asking when she can pick up her car," he mutters under his breath, watching Karla from behind his sunglasses. "And she wants the department to reimburse her for the cab ride, even though I offered to have an officer drive her home."

Heels clicking, Karla stalks toward us like a stealthy cat that forgot to retract its claws before sneaking across a hardwood floor.

Eric gives Karla the same explanation he gave me; he has a warrant to seize the car, and Trevor is helping the police with their inquiries.

"Does this mean you didn't find any evidence in my car?" Karla asks.

"I haven't received the completed forensi…"

"It's a rhetorical question, Chief Sloane," Karla interrupts him. "There *can't* be evidence because I. Didn't. Do. Anything."

"We've finished processing your car. I sent you a text. You can pick it up at your convenience."

"*Hmph*," she huffs. "I'll pick it up today when I drop off the cab receipt."

"Why are you here?" Eric directs his question at me.

"We're returning something Melody left in town yesterday." I smile.

From the corner of my eye, I notice Karla clutching the glittery pink phone as she crosses her arms in front of her chest, tucking the phone out of Eric's sight.

"Are you returning something I should know about?" he probes, lifting his sunglasses and eyeing us with suspicion.

"Does your search warrant include anything besides the car?" Karla asks, nodding at the car as the driver secures the tires to the flatbed.

Eric shakes his head.

"Then, no," Karla concludes. "We aren't returning anything you need to know about."

The tow truck driver shouts that he's ready to go, and Eric waves in acknowledgement.

I make Eric wait while I run back to the car, retrieve Mrs. Roblin's glass container, and give it to him with instructions to drop it off at her house. We say goodbye. He jogs back to his car, then follows the tow truck as it inches toward the narrow driveway.

Karla watches with a cheeky grin as the vintage Camaro passes us.

"Have you ever been in one?" She nods toward the sports car's disappearing taillights.

"No," I reply. "Have you?"

"I dated a guy who drove a red one with black racing stripes down the hood," she replies. "It was a great car."

Still gazing into the distance where the car disappeared, she bites her bottom lip. "The back seat was huge." She grins. "Very accommodating."

"Nice ride?" I ask as we stroll toward the front door of the cottage.

"The Camaro or its owner?" she asks, cheekily.

I roll my eyes and shake my head. "What are you, twelve?"

"Only on a scale of one to ten," she retorts.

I can't help but laugh. When she's not using her sharp tongue to cut me, Karla has a wicked sense of humour.

We knock, and Melody opens the door so fast, I wonder if she was standing on the other side, waiting for us.

"Hi, Mel." I smile. "Do you remember me? We met yesterday at Knitorious."

"Megan, right?" she asks, glancing over my shoulder at the empty parking pad.

"Right," I confirm. "And this is... my... friend, Karla Bell."

I hope the hesitance at referring to Karla as my friend isn't obvious to Mel or Karla.

"It's wonderful to meet you," Karla says, extending her hand. "I'm a huge fan."

"Thank you." Melody shakes Karla's hand but looks at me. "Is this why you're here? Did you bring your friend to meet me?"

"No," I insist. "We found something, and we think belongs to you."

"*Ta-daaa!*" Karla sings as she whips out the bejewelled pink phone with a flourish that would make Vanna White blush.

"My phone!" Mel gives Karla an open-mouth smile. "Where did you find it?"

I should have prepared myself for this question, but I didn't.

"Thank goodness you have such a distinct case," I say, ignoring her question. "I noticed it at Knitorious yesterday, and when I saw it again today, I knew right away it was yours," I continue, hoping my inane rambling will make her forget the question. "Trevor mentioned which cottage you're renting. That's how I figured out how to return it to you."

"Where was it?" she asks, powering up the pink, sparkly device.

"At a store," I improvise. "The owner found it and put it aside. He said he turned it off because the battery was low."

"What store?" Mel asks, pausing her phone inspection to glare at us.

Judging by the dubious undertone in her voice, and her increasingly defensive body language, she is asking to prove to herself that her instinct not to trust us is correct.

"Ummm..."

"I found the phone," Karla interjects. "On the sidewalk. I picked it up and handed it in at the closest store, hoping you would retrace your steps and find it."

"Right," I agree. "Today, when Karla went to see if you had claimed it, I was with her. I recognized it, and here we are!"

We smile.

Mel smiles.

I think she bought it.

"Which store?" she asks.

Ughhh! Why won't she let this go and just be happy she got her phone back?

"That charming store," replies Karla, making use of

her quick wittedness. "The cute one... small... quaint." She nudges me. "What was it called again, Megan?"

"It's on the tip of my tongue," I reply, feigning a momentary lapse of memory, despite knowing, without hesitation and in order of location, every store and business in town.

Karla flicks her wrist at Mel. "You know the one." She half-laughs and crinkles her nose. "The name is a whimsical pun about something..." She rolls her hand as if her vague description of every store in Harmony Lake should cue Mel's memory.

"Right!" Mel snaps her fingers and recognition sweeps across her face. "I bought flowers there." A brief pause while she recalls the name. "Wilde Flowers!" She blurts out the name of the florist next door to Knitorious.

Karla and I nod and, continuing to play along, exchange exaggerated expressions that say, *of course.*

"Well, thank you for returning my phone." Mel waves at us with the phone as she steps backward, retreating into the cottage, ready to close the door. "I have to go now." She smiles.

"We saw Trevor," I say, employing the metaphorical foot-in-the-door technique that salesmen use to build rapport with prospective customers.

"He was leaving as we got here," Karla adds, helping our cause.

It works. Mel releases her grip on the door and steps toward the threshold.

"They took the car too," she says.

"We saw," I sympathize.

"They have my car too," Karla says, pointing to herself. "The police seized it yesterday, and they're already done with it. I'm sure they'll process your car quickly too, and your husband will drive up that freakish, long, narrow driveway sooner than you think."

In awe of Karla's sympathetic demeanour, I remove myself from the conversation and observe as Karla uses her powers of persuasion for good—charming and disarming Melody Howe's hesitation to trust us.

"Why do the police have your car?" Mel asks Karla.

"Same reason they have yours," she replies. "I'm trying to clear my name. I'm sure you want to clear Trevor's name. Maybe if we share what we know, we can clear both names."

Mel deliberates, biting the corner of her lower lip and drumming her fingers on the door frame. I hold my breath, fearful that my thumping heart will startle her to close the door and retreat inside the cottage.

After a few seconds that feel like more time than it takes to knit a lace-weight sweater, Mel smiles.

"Would you like to come in, ladies?" she asks, stepping aside and gesturing inside the cottage.

"We'd love to," Karla and I reply in unison.

# CHAPTER 15

"TREVOR WILL BE SO WORRIED," Mel says softly, closing the door behind us. "He loves his car. He treats it like a person." She laughs sadly.

Would someone as committed to their car as Trevor use it to move a dead body? Or is his extreme devotion to the vintage Camaro an act? If Trevor used his car to transport Fawkes from the cottage to the community centre, there would be evidence. Minute microscopic evidence that he couldn't bleach or wash away. Trevor and Mel could have contrived his intense attachment to the car to manipulate the police. They could be hoping the police reach the same conclusion as I have—Trevor adores his car too much to defile it with a corpse—and not bother to investigate him since he had no other means to transport the body.

"The police will be careful with it," I say. "I have it on good authority that several of our local officers are vintage car enthusiasts." I spot a half-finished sloth on the kitchen counter. "Your sloth is coming along nicely," I comment.

"I finished the bumble bee last night," she says,

digging into her project bag and pulling out a chubby yellow and black bumble bee with small white wings.

"It's adorable!" I admire the bee, then set it on the counter beside the sloth-in-progress.

"Lovely flowers!" Karla declares, admiring the simple but stunning arrangement of black-eyed Susans in a round, cobalt-blue crystal vase. "The contrast between the yellow petals and the blue vase is striking."

"These are the flowers I bought at Wilde Flowers when I lost my phone," Mel says.

"Are they for a special occasion?" I ask. "Or an impulsive gift for yourself?"

"I love the flowers," Mel says in a tone that suggests a *but* is forthcoming. "They're beautiful. But I bought them because of the vase." She nods toward the floral arrangement. "I collect blue crystal. The vase is beautiful, and I already know where I'm going to display it when we get home." She smiles sadly.

Mel offers us a beverage.

We politely decline.

Mel invites us to have a seat while she makes herself a coffee.

The main floor of the cottage is an expansive, open concept space. Without walls to distinguish one living area from another, furniture and accessories are arranged to create the illusion of distinct spaces.

Mel is in the kitchen space, and Karla and I walk past the dining space to the lounging space. I call it a lounging space because whoever designed it clearly intended it for lounging. Instead of sofas and chairs arranged around a television or fireplace, the lounging space has an oversized, overstuffed four-seat chaise lounge facing a glass wall. The glass wall overlooks the lake, with the Harmony Hills mountains in the distance.

"It's breathtaking," I whisper, choked up at beauty of this cozy, little piece of the world that I get to call home.

"The view was the reason we rented the cottage," Mel says. "We loved it so much that Trevor agreed to rent it, despite the cracks and potholes in the driveway that could mess with Dorian's suspension."

"Dorian?" Karla asks on behalf of both of us.

"Dorian Gray," Mel explains. "The name Trevor gave to the Camaro. It was grey when he bought it, and no matter how old it gets, Trevor makes sure it still looks brand new, like it just rolled off the lot."

Maybe Trevor's affection for his vintage car isn't a contrived hoax.

"We sit here every evening and watch the sunset." Mel sighs and her sad smile makes another appearance. "Have a seat." She sits in the centre of the grand chaise and taps the cushion next to her.

Karla and I sink into the inviting upholstery on either side of her.

The three of us cross our elevated ankles and let out a weary sigh as if we'd choreographed it.

Mel and Trevor sit here daily, enjoying an unobstructed view of The Fawkes Den. I stare at the small, red cottage across the lake. It's set closer to the water than the surrounding cottages, making it even closer to Mel and Trevor's cottage. The lake is narrower here than I remembered. I can make out enough detail to tell that Fawkes's blinds are closed.

"Did you ever see—" His name gets stuck in my throat. Uncomfortable, like an unexpected surge of acid reflux. It feels wrong to speak his name in Mel's presence —"him?"

"We wouldn't have chosen this place if we had known Fawkes was there," she explains, staring across the lake. "I swear. We did not know. His location was a secret. The judge who released him issued a media ban. The press can't report anything about Fawkes's location or details about his life outside of prison." She shakes her head and rolls her eyes. "What are the odds that we chose the same random, tiny town where Fawkes lived?"

"When did you realize he was across the lake?" I ask.

"A couple of weeks ago," Mel admits after swallowing a mouthful of coffee. "It was a Tuesday. Trevor spotted Fawkes on his morning run. At least, he suspected it was Fawkes."

"Fawkes was a runner?" Karla asks, dubious.

"No," Mel clarifies with a chuckle. "Trevor is a runner. He's been running since before we met. He runs five mornings a week."

"So does my husband," I say. "Are you a runner too?"

"No," Mel replies. "I have an elliptical machine at home, and we live in Manhattan most of the year, so walking everywhere is my exercise." She turns to me. "How about you? Do you run?"

"Not even in my nightmares," I admit.

"Megan's exercise is walking her dog and jumping to conclusions," Karla adds.

Mel giggles.

"Trevor ran all the way around the lake to The Fawkes Den, then back again?" Karla asks.

"He could run that far," says Mel. "But he runs half of that distance. He runs around the lake to The Fawkes Den, cuts through the trees between Fawkes's cottage and the neighbouring cottage,"—she points to the thicket of evergreens dividing the two properties—"then jumps off Fawkes's dock and swims across to our dock." She points down, toward the tip of the wooden dock that juts into the lake below the glass wall.

"Where did he spot Fawkes?" I ask, ignoring the

nausea when his name passes my lips. "His conditions didn't allow him to wander beyond his front porch."

"Trevor said when he ran up the driveway to cut through the trees, a man was banging on the door. Fawkes answered the door, and that's when Trevor spotted him. But only for a few seconds. He said the visitor blocked his view. Trevor swam home. He said nothing at first, but I knew something had happened that shook him. When I finally pried it out of him, he tried to convince me we should pack and leave town that day."

"Why didn't you?"

"We would have lost the money we paid for this place." She gestures around us. "And Trevor wasn't certain the man he saw was Fawkes."

"Did Trevor recognize the man who was knocking on Fawkes's door?" I ask, wondering if the unknown man could shed some light on Fawkes's murder. "Fawkes didn't have many visitors."

"Trevor only saw the man's back," Mel says. "Tall, broad shoulders, dark hair." She shrugs. "My husband is a talented man, but remembering names and faces is not among his many talents."

"I bet he remembers cars, though, doesn't he?" Karla asks.

"He does," Mel replies with a flash of *aha!* In her eyes. "Trevor never forgets a car. He might not remember what clothes he wore yesterday, but he can describe every car he's ever seen down to the smallest paint chip and licence plate number." She nods vigorously. "As soon as the police release him, I'll ask Trevor if he saw the man's car. This means there's another suspect, right?"

"It's possible."

"Let's hope."

Karla and I reply, speaking over each other.

"How did you confirm Trevor's suspicion that he saw

Fawkes?" I ask, steering the conversation back to the Howe's interactions with the murder victim.

"At first, we agreed it wasn't him," Mel explains. "Trevor only glimpsed him, and neither of us had seen Fawkes for years. We even avoided the news when he got out of prison to avoid hearing his name or seeing his face. We convinced ourselves the odds were one in a million that we travelled seven hundred miles to spend two weeks at an isolated lake front cottage that would be a fifteen-minute swim from a monster. My monster."

"It still niggled at you, didn't it?" Karla asks. "You felt unsafe. Jumpy. You sat here in the evening, admiring the sunset, and wondering if he could see your cottage as clearly as you saw his."

Mel's nod is slow and almost imperceptible. Her chin quivers, and she gazes across the water with glassy eyes.

"That's exactly what happened," she confirms, her voice shaky. "How could you know that?"

"It's written all over your face," Karla replies.

"Did you know him?" Mel asks, eyeing Karla with an expression somewhere between fear and dread. "Were you one of his victims?"

"No," Karla replies. "I'd never met him. And I didn't know he was living in a cottage in Harmony Lake until the police showed up at my office a couple of days ago."

"If you'd never met him, how can the police suspect you murdered him?" Mel asks, sharing our confusion.

Karla explains how the police inexplicably found her fingerprints and hair inside The Fawkes Den and how they can't verify her alibi.

"Speaking of alibis," I say, knowing how to take advantage of an opening. "Where were you and Trevor the morning of Fawkes's murder?"

"I was here," Mel says. "I spoke to my mum on the phone for two hours that morning. She's taking care of our cats, and I called to check on them. She had family gossip to tell me. Next thing I knew, we were on the phone for two hours. Trevor was on his morning run."

The route that takes him straight to the murder scene? No wonder Eric wanted to question Trevor again.

"Did he run his usual route?" I ask.

Mel hesitates, then nods, admitting that her husband was at Fawkes's cottage the morning of the murder.

# CHAPTER 16

"DID TREVOR'S run start and end at the usual times?" I ask.

Mel nods. "It was a normal day." She inhales and exhales. "Until it wasn't."

"How did you find out about Fawkes's murder?" Karla asks.

"We knew something had happened, but we didn't know what," Mel attests. "Trevor and I went down to the dock just before lunch. There were police officers all over Fawkes's property. They peered in windows, searched outside the cottage, and a cop in a wet suit swam around and under his dock. We came back inside, and within a few minutes, the police knocked on our door. They said our neighbour was missing. They didn't say he was dead. And they didn't tell us his name."

"But you knew it was him," Karla surmises. "You and Trevor had already confirmed that Fawkes was staying there, hadn't you?"

Mel sighs, and her next breaths are deeper. Her relief at being able to talk about it is palpable.

"I had to know if it was him," Mel explains. "I became obsessed with finding out."

"How did you find out?"

"Trevor ordered a pizza and had it delivered to Fawkes's cottage," Mel explains. "He hid in the trees next to the cottage until it arrived."

"He confirmed Fawkes's identity when Fawkes opened the door for the delivery person," I deduce.

"Not quite," Mel corrects me. "Fawkes didn't answer, and the delivery person left with the pizza. Trevor chased the car and waved him down. He gave the delivery guy an extra tip and instructed him to knock as loud as he could, shout *pizza* as loud as he could, set the pizza on the porch a few feet from the door, and leave."

"And?" Karla asks.

"About ten minutes after the delivery guy left, Fawkes opened the door and stepped onto the porch to collect the pizza. That's when Trevor saw him."

Pastabilities is the only local restaurant that delivers pizza. This should be easy to verify.

"Did you hide in the trees with Trevor?" I ask.

"No way." Mel shakes her head. "Uh-uh. If it was Fawkes, I didn't want to see him."

"Then how did your earring end up outside Fawkes's cottage?"

"It wasn't my earring," Mel replies.

"Yes, it was," Karla challenges.

How would Karla know? I didn't show her a photo of the earring or of the album cover I found online, with Mel wearing a similar one.

"They can always check the earring for DNA," I suggest, not knowing if it's true.

"Fine." Mel sits up straighter. "I was at Fawkes's cottage. But not when Trevor ordered the pizza, and not the day he died. I went the day before he died."

"Why?"

"I wrote him a letter. It was my victim impact statement," Mel reveals. "Trevor tried to talk me out of hand-delivering it, but I wanted to confront him and make him hear how his actions impacted my life."

"Wow," I mutter.

"It would have been my only opportunity to confront him," Mel justifies.

"*Would have*?" I ask. "You didn't get the opportunity?"

"Fawkes didn't answer the door." Melody shrugs. "We went there on Monday morning. Fawkes died on Tuesday. We didn't kill him," she implores, desperate for us to believe her.

"Did you drive to Fawkes's cottage in Trevor's car?"

"No," Mel replies. "Trevor doesn't like gravel roads. Loose bits of gravel can chip Dorian's paint. We took the boat." She points downward toward the dock below. "Our rental agreement includes use of the boats."

"Where's the letter you wrote?" I ask.

"I closed the letter in the screen door. At eye level, so Fawkes would find it next time he opened the door." Mel slides out of the chaise and opens the drawer of a nearby writing desk. She holds up a blue floral envelope and matching sheet of blue floral stationery. "The letter was inside an envelope identical to this one." She waves the blue floral stationery, then closes it in the drawer, and returns to her spot on the chaise. "We left and never went back. I swear!" Mel turns her head from side to side, her eyes pleading with us. "Please believe me. As soon as we left, I realized it was a bad idea."

"Why was visiting Fawkes a bad idea?" Karla probes.

"When Fawkes didn't answer the door, I felt like I'd dodged a bullet. The relief made me realize I wasn't mentally and emotionally prepared to confront him, and I might never be, and that's OK. I expected Trevor to be relieved too because until I knocked on the door, he tried to talk me out of it. But I was determined to confront Fawkes with or without him, so Trevor went with me. When Fawkes didn't answer the door, I could tell Trevor wasn't relieved."

"What was he?" I ask.

"Disappointed," Melody admits. "He denied it, but I think Trevor planned to confront Fawkes too."

"Confront how?" Karla asks, giving us the side-eye.

"If Fawkes had answered the door, I think Trevor might have hurt him."

What if Trevor hurt him? What if Trevor returned to The Fawkes Den alone, seeking the confrontation Mel suspects her husband was hoping for?

Maybe Trevor ran to the driveway on his usual morning run, but instead of cutting through the trees, he took a detour to the cottage and drowned his wife's abuser in the bathtub. If Fawkes struggled and soaked Trevor with bath water, his dive off the dock and brief swim across the lake would camouflage the evidence. Trevor could have drowned Fawkes, swum home for the sake of his alibi, changed his clothes, then returned to the cottage to move Fawkes's body.

"Did either you or Trevor leave the cottage the day Fawkes died?" I ask.

"No." Mel shakes her head. "Aside from Trevor's morning run, of course."

Either Mel is lying for her husband, or Trevor didn't have any opportunity to remove Fawkes's body from the cottage and dump it in the pool. And why would he? What motivation would Trevor have to move the body, especially across town, which would have increased his chances of getting caught? Whoever left Fawkes's body in the pool wasn't trying to hide it. They wanted his body found fast and by as many people as possible. It would have made more sense for Trevor to dump or bury Fawkes's body in the woods next to the cottage, or weigh him down and dump him in the lake. Unless Mel was the reason he moved the body. Maybe Mel is unaware that Trevor killed Fawkes, and Trevor hoped by making it appear as though Fawkes died at the community centre, she wouldn't suspect him. The police would focus on the community centre as the crime scene, sparing Mel from police questions and disclosing her history with the dead man.

"If Fawkes hadn't died, your attempt to confront him and give him the letter could have jeopardized his re-trial," I comment.

"I gave up hoping for justice a long time ago," Mel responds, cackling. "This retrial was just another opportunity for Fawkes to torment his victims. I'm glad his killer denied him the satisfaction. I'm happy he's dead. Now, I never have to think about him again. I can get on with my life. My music is on the radio again, and every time they play one of my songs, Fawkes's share of the royalties benefits the women he hurt. He would've hated that. I don't know who killed Fawkes, but I feel sorry for her. She shouldn't face any consequences for ridding the world of a parasitic psychopath. She did the world a favour."

She? Melody used the feminine pronoun to describe the killer. Three times. Does Mel know who killed Fawkes? Or is she referring to herself in third person?

"Did you tell the police about Trevor's pizza stunt and your visit to confront Fawkes?" Karla asks.

Mel shakes her head. "Trevor told me to tell the police we didn't know Fawkes was across the lake until we overheard it in town after he died." She looks at me. "You're going to tell them, aren't you?"

"Excuse me?" I ask.

"I saw the police chief kiss you when you got here," Mel says. "And somehow, you knew about my missing earring. You're going to tell them about us luring Fawkes out of his cottage with a pizza and about my victim impact statement, aren't you?"

"I don't know." I give Mel a small, closed smile. "Harmony Lake is a small town. The restaurant or the delivery guy might have already told the police about the delivery. And the police probably found your letter at The Fawkes Den. If you left it wedged in the screen door, it must be somewhere. It's not like Fawkes ever went anywhere to dispose of it."

"I never thought of that," Mel admits. "I didn't sign it, but the stationery would lead the police to this cottage."

"Chances are, the police know at least part of what you've told us. That might be the reason they wanted to question Trevor again," I suggest.

"That's not why the police took Trevor for questioning," Mel admits.

"Oh?" Karla asks, her interest piqued. "*Why did* they want to question him again?"

"The first time they questioned him, Trevor *forgot* to tell the police about his previous incarceration. Their computer was down earlier, and they couldn't access our criminal histories. When Chief Sloane asked Trevor if he was ever charged with or convicted of a crime, Trevor lied."

"What crime was he convicted of?" I ask.

"He got into a bar fight," Mel replies. "When the police intervened to break it up, Trevor punched a cop. He broke the cop's nose. The cop required surgery to repair a deviated septum. Trevor served eight months."

"Oh," I say, shocked and hoping, for the sake of my husband's nose, that Trevor's cop-punch was an isolated incident.

# CHAPTER 17

AFTER LEAVING Mel and Trevor's cottage, I drop off Karla at the police impound lot to collect her car. Before I drive away, we agree to reconvene at my house to compare notes about the revelations Mel disclosed during our visit.

While Karla reclaims her car and visits the police station to drop off the receipt for her cab ride home this morning—and argue her case for reimbursement—I go home to walk Sophie and work on a pair of amigurumi guinea pigs I'm hooking for the charity knitting project.

"What do you think, Soph?" I hold up the half-finished guinea pig and inspect the safety eyes I just installed. "Are the eyes even?"

Being the type of dog who prefers to keep her opinions to herself, Sophie glances up, says nothing, then resumes gnawing on a chew toy.

As I shape the nubs that will become the guinea pig's front paws, my phone dings.

*Mason: Hi Megan! If you are at Knitorious today, could I stop by to get something from my mum's boxes?*

I check the time, not that I have any time-sensitive

appointments today. Karla and I can plot our next move at Knitorious just as easily as my house. I can crochet stuffed toys at either location, so I may as well go to Knitorious and let Mason do whatever he needs to do in the dungeon.

**Me: Hi Mason! No problem. Give me about twenty minutes.**

Mason replies with a thumbs-up emoji.

I send Karla a text, letting her know about the change of location. She replies with an animated GIF of a dog riding a Vespa. The caption reads, *On My Way!*

"Wanna to go to the store, Soph?"

Before I finish asking, Sophie is halfway to the door with her toy.

KARLA and I get to work at the wooden harvest table, making visual sense of what we've learned so far about Fawkes's murder. Stickie notes and novelty mugs with funny knitting puns depict people, locations, and clues. We use yarn to make connections between them.

I scrawl *Mel's earring* across a blue stickie note and slap it to the table above the "It Takes Balls To Knit" mug that represents Melody Howe. Then, I cut a length of yarn to connect the earring to Mel, and the "Knit Happens" mug that symbolizes The Fawkes Den.

"Mel's earring caught me off guard," Karla says. "You didn't tell me about it before we spoke to her."

"Sorry about that," I say. "I meant to tell you, but between the Charity Knitters giving us Mel's cell phone, passing Trevor in the backseat of a patrol car, and watching them tow the Camaro, I forgot."

I tell Karla about the earring Eric found outside the

Fawkes cottage and how I found an old album cover with Mel wearing a similar earring.

"Why did you confront Mel about the earring?" I ask. "You couldn't have known she was lying."

"Mel has a tell when she lies," Karla divulges.

"A tell?" I ask, intrigued.

"A quirk," Karla explains. "A small tic when she lies. I picked up on it when she told us she and Trevor were unaware that Fawkes's cottage was across the lake when they came here for vacation."

"That was a lie?" I ask, feeling gullible.

"I think so," Karla says. "When she denied owning the earring, she did it again. I challenged her to test my theory."

"What's her tell?"

"When Mel lies, she raises her eyebrows, but she raises the left one a smidge higher."

Karla tries to show with her eyebrows but looks more like she's fighting off a sneezing than lying.

"That tiny inconsistency stood out to you?"

Karla nods. "You didn't notice?"

I shake my head.

"Most people have a tell," Karla explains. "It's just a matter of figuring it out. I don't trust anyone until I figure out their tell."

"What's my tell?" I ask.

Sophie yelps when someone raps on the display window, distracting and startling Karla and me.

"It's Mason," I say, using my phone to snap a photo of our improvised murder board in case the items shift when I cover them. "He's wants to go into the dungeon."

I grab the inexpensive plastic tablecloth we use when we serve food and drinks on the harvest table, and Karla helps me cover our secret project.

"You have a dungeon, Megan?" Karla raises her

eyebrows. "I'd never have guessed that dungeons are your thing. You sly little minx."

Smirking, she winks at me and emits a click from the corner of her mouth like she's telling a horse to giddy up, leading me to suspect that we have different definitions of *dungeon*.

"The basement," I clarify with an eye roll. "Mason's storing some of his deceased mother's belongings downstairs."

"That makes more sense." Karla tilts her head to one side like Sophie does when she hears a strange sound. "For a second, I thought you had a secret, interesting side." She half-chuckles. "Silly me."

Forming an emotional callous to Karla's frequent snarky comments, and not wanting to make Mason wait any longer, I ignore her and huff on the inside as I stride to the door.

"Hi, Mason!" I smile, closing and locking the door behind him.

"Thanks for letting me in, Megan. I promise I only need a few minutes."

"No problem," I say. "Karla and I are just hanging out." I smile with pursed lips and gesture at her. "Mason, this is Karla." I gesture to him. "Karla, this is Mason."

"Nice to meet you," Mason says, walking toward her.

He wipes his hand on his blue Grateful Dead t-shirt, then extends it toward her.

"Likewise," Karla says, shaking his hand and pressing her brows together. "Have we met before?" She squints. "You're familiar."

"I don't think so," Mason replies. "I'm sure I'd remember."

"I'm sure you would too," Karla says, still eyeing him.

Is she flirting with him? Mason is at least fifteen years

younger than her. He's shy. He's bereaved, for goodness' sake.

"Do you ever visit the library or community centre?" Mason asks. "Or the town hall? That's where I work."

"What do you do?" Karla inquires.

"I'm the town's Maintenance and Facility Manager," he replies. "It's a fancy title for fixing stuff and cleaning the new pool."

"Mason, the pool boy," Karla coos.

"Don't forget the flashlight." I reach under the counter. "I forgot to bring the replacement bulb for the dungeon. Again. I'll try to remember on Tuesday." I hand him the flashlight. "Watch your step. Those stairs are steep." I give him the gnome keychain and sweep my hands toward the back room, encouraging him to move along, safely out of Karla's orbit.

"Thanks," he says, flicking the flashlight on and off to test it. "I won't be long. I just want to grab some banking information." He smiles with flared nostrils.

"Adam can do that for you," I say. "It's his job as the executor of the estate."

"I know." Mason shrugs one shoulder. "But I respond quicker than the bank. Adam didn't ask me to help, but I want to. Anyway, I enjoy sorting through her things."

Mason goes to the dungeon, and I glare at Karla.

"What?" Karla asks. "Stop staring at me like that?"

"Do you flirt with every man you meet?" I ask.

"You think I flirted with him?" She jabs her thumb over her shoulder in the direction Mason left. "I wasn't flirting. He looks familiar. I'm sure we haven't met, but I've seen him somewhere."

I wish I knew Karla's tell, but I don't, so I have to assume she's telling the truth.

"Fine," I agree. "I'm sorry for assuming you were flirting with Mason. I didn't mean to offend you. He's young and just lost his mum. I was in the same situation once. He has no other family nearby, and I guess I'm protective of him."

"Can I ask you a personal question?" she asks, ignoring my apology.

"Why not." I inhale and brace myself.

"Are you still in love with your ex-husband?"

"No!" I declare. "Of course not! I'm in love with Eric. I haven't been in love with Adam for years. Why would you ask that?"

"Before Mason arrived, you asked me about your tell," Karla reminds me.

"I remember," I say.

"I just figured it out," she explains. "Right after you tell a lie, you smile for a second. A small, tight-lipped smile."

"I'm not lying," I insist. "The only man I'm in love with is Eric."

"I know," Karla confirms. "You lied to Mason when you told him we were just hanging out. You also lied to Mel earlier when she asked you if you were going to tell the police about Trevor's pizza ploy and her letter to Fawkes." She points at my mouth and traces a small circle with her index finger. "You followed both lies with the same smile. The question about Adam was a control question to test my theory. I asked you something you weren't expecting, and I was confident I knew the answer."

"My lack of smile confirmed for you that the smile is my tell," I surmise.

"Yes."

"Now that I know my tell, I can change it, right?"

"I suppose," Karla replies. "But it's subconscious, so it won't be easy. You'll replace it with something else."

"What if I don't replace it?" I ask.

"You will," she says with confidence. "Unless someone is a psychopath, lying causes stress. Even minor lies are stressful. To release the stress, the body increases the heart rate, sweats, fidgets, and creates small quirks and tics to take the pressure off."

"Fascinating," I say. "How did you learn to be a human lie detector?"

"It's a by-product of having trust issues," she says with a half-shrug. "If I can't figure out someone's tell, I assume either they always lie to me, or they don't have a tell because they're a psychopath. I keep a safe distance from those people so they can't hurt me."

"Let me guess," I say. "You push them away with backhanded compliments and passive-aggressive insults?"

"Sometimes."

"Is it possible that when you can't figure out a tell it's because the person is honest?"

"It's easier to trust the truth if you know when someone is lying," Karla says with a poignancy that suggests she speaks from experience.

"Now that you know my tell, will you stop with the snide, backhanded compliments?"

"I'll try."

She gives me a small, tight-lipped smile, and we both laugh.

As far as visual aids go, we agree that our mug-and-stickie-note creation is less than ideal, so I remove the notices from the community bulletin board and repurpose it as a murder board.

Karla finds online photos of the relevant people and locations and prints them. I cut them out and stick them to the board. She uses yarn to connect suspects to the victim and to connect clues to relevant people and places.

Then we jot down the how and why on a stickie note beside each yarn connection.

"There's something I don't understand," Karla says as she stretches a length of yarn between the victim and the community centre. "If Trevor and Mel killed Fawkes, why did they do it at the pool?" She shakes her head. "It makes no sense. The Fawkes Den is more isolated than the community centre. They could have drowned him in the lake and walked away. It would've looked like an accident." She looks at me. "Why risk taking him somewhere public?"

"I've wondered the same thing," I admit, without disclosing to Karla that Fawkes drowned at the cottage before his killer, for unknown reasons, dumped him in the pool. "The only explanation I've come up with is the killer was trying to distance Fawkes's murder from Melody."

"Also, If Mel and Trevor killed him, why didn't they leave town?" Karla asks.

"I don't know." I shrug. "Mel and Trevor are still a mystery to me."

"What if no one killed Fawkes?" Karla suggests. "What if he fell in the pool by accident or fell in on purpose?"

"He didn't."

"It's possible," she argues. "His retrial was just a formality. He would've been behind bars again. Maybe he didn't want to go back to prison. Or maybe he read Mel's letter, grew a conscience, and took himself for a last swim."

She pinches her nose and wiggles her hips, pretending to sink underwater.

I chew the inside of my cheek, thinking up a way to tell Karla that Fawkes was murdered without divulging Eric's holdback.

"Fawkes was murdered. The police have evidence."

"What evidence?" Karla asks. "Why are you keeping it from me? I thought we were working together."

"We are," I assure her. "This is the only thing I can't share with you. I want to, but Eric asked me not to. It could compromise his case. Fawkes was, without a doubt, murdered. The evidence that proves it does not implicate a specific suspect."

"I see," Karla says, miffed about being left out of the loop.

"I'm sorry I can't tell you."

"This blue flower represents Mel's letter to Fawkes," Karla says, ignoring my apology. "I'll put it near Mel and connect it to both cottages."

"Eric didn't mention Mel's letter," I contemplate out loud. "She said she didn't sign it, but I'm surprised he didn't mention it."

"Maybe the police didn't find it," Karla suggests.

"You could be right," I agree. "He said Fawkes's place was a mess."

"I mean, maybe the letter wasn't there," Karla clarifies. "Think about it. If the letter wasn't there when the police searched Fawkes's cottage, the killer must've taken it when they forced Fawkes to go to the community centre. Two people had reason to take the letter. Mel and Trevor."

"Only one person had a reason to take the letter," I correct her. "Mel wouldn't have told us about the letter if she'd taken it back. But she would if she believed it was still in Fawkes's cottage. If the letter is missing, Trevor must've taken it."

"And he didn't tell Mel," Karla continues where I left off. "Otherwise, she would never have told us about it."

"Which means if Trevor killed Fawkes, he acted alone."

597

# CHAPTER 18

My THUMBS FLY across the keyboard on my phone.

*Me: Did you find a handwritten letter at Fawkes's cottage? Blue floral stationery. Unsigned.*

Within seconds of sending the text, three dots appear, indicating that Eric is typing a reply.

*Eric: Letter? I haven't heard about a letter. Do we need to talk?*

*Me: Yes. In the meantime, can you look in to the letter?*

*Eric: Leave it with me. I love you.* Followed by a heart emoji and a heart-eyes smiley face.

"Eric hasn't seen the letter, but he's looking into it," I say.

"He replied to you already?"

I nod. "He always does."

"Must be nice," Karla mutters. "I waited twenty minutes for the desk sergeant to tell me Eric was unavailable to discuss my cab fare reimbursement."

"So if Mel's letter isn't at Fawkes's cottage, either the killer took it or Mel made it up," I speculate.

"Why would she make up a fake letter that incriminates her husband?" Karla's eyes bulge with comprehension as she finishes asking the question. "Do you think Mel used us to implicate Trevor?"

"Anything is possible." I sigh.

Karla snips a length of red yarn long enough to connect the letter to Trevor. I press a stickie note with a question mark next to it.

"This orange stickie note represents Fawkes's sister," Karla informs me, as she writes *Michelle A. Fawkes* on the yellow stickie note. "It's a popular name, and there were too many photos. I tried searching for *Clarence Fawkes sister*, but the internet doesn't seem to know he had a sister."

"Interesting," I say, cutting a snippet of yarn for Michelle A. Fawkes's stickie note. "She's connected to the victim and the family cottage is in her name."

The clomping of heavy feet reminds me that Mason is still here. Racing against his increasingly loud footsteps, I lift the murder board from the wall and lean it against the back of the counter, facing away from prying eyes.

"Who's that?" Mason asks, setting the gnome keychain on the counter and lifting his chin toward the photo of Trevor that Karla is trimming for the murder board.

"His name is Trevor," I reply. "He and his wife are renting a cottage on the lake. Why? Do you recognize him?"

"No." Mason shakes his head and hands me the flashlight. "Well, I might've seen him around. He's kind of familiar."

"Now, Mason," Karla purrs. "Tell the truth. You recognize Trevor, don't you?"

"I'm not lying." Mason locks eyes with Karla, tightening his grip on the blue floral notebook in his hand. "Why would I lie?" His nostrils flare in rhythm with his awkward chuckle.

"I don't know," Karla says, circling Mason like a predator circling its prey. "You tell me."

"I don't know him," Mason insists.

"But you have seen him before," I state, finishing his incomplete sentence. "Karla's right, isn't she?"

"Does he drive a vintage mid-eighties Camaro?" Mason asks. "Blue?"

"Yes," Karla and I reply, nodding.

"I've seen it around. Nice car. He's the driver."

"Where and when did you last see it?" Karla asks.

"Tuesday morning," Mason replies. "There was a leak at the library. The local hardware store didn't have the part I needed, so I drove to Harmony Hills. I stopped at the four-way stop by Temple Road, and the Camaro stopped across from me. I waved him through so I could admire the car."

"Are you sure this man was driving?" I ask as Karla thrusts Trevor's photo toward Mason.

"We made eye contact and waved," Mason reasons. "He looked like this guy." Mason nods at Trevor's photo. "He had slicked-back hair. When he waved, there were tattoos on the back of his hand and fingers."

"Was he alone?" I ask.

"Or was there someone else in the car with him?" Karla specifies, in case Mason doesn't understand what *alone* means.

"I didn't see anyone," Mason replies. "I'm pretty sure he was by himself."

We thank Mason for his honesty and apologize for the onslaught of questions.

"Is this about the Fawkes murder?" Mason asks.

"It could be," I say, making a conscious effort not to flash my telltale small, tight-lipped smile.

"I didn't mean to lie," he says. "I just didn't want to risk getting anyone in trouble unless I was a hundred percent certain."

"You didn't get anyone in trouble," Karla assures him.

Satisfied that we won't make a citizen's arrest based on his uncertain identification, Mason and his notebook leave.

"Does Trevor have tattoos on his hand and fingers?" Karla asks after I lock the door behind Mason.

"He sure does." I nod. "And Temple Road is the private road that leads to The Fawkes Den."

"Trevor was there," Karla says. "We've got him."

"How did you know Mason lied about recognizing Trevor?"

Karla points to her nose and flares her nostrils.

"He did it when he said he was sorry he lied, and earlier when he told you he was looking for his mother's banking information."

"Adam and I already figured out that Mason lies about searching for paperwork as an excuse..."

Sudden, loud banging rattles the windows and walls when someone pounds on the door.

Sophie jumps off the sofa, emitting a low, long growl. She fixates on the door, inching toward it with her hackles up.

"It's Trevor!" Karla declares, comparing the angry face glaring in the window with the photo in her hand. "I thought Eric arrested him?"

Trevor thumps on the door with the side of his fist.

Sophie yelps, then lets out a warning bark.

"I guess there wasn't enough evidence to keep him," I venture a guess, bending over to give Sophie a reassuring head rub. "Melody must have told him we were asking questions."

He bangs on the window with the heel of his hand.

More warning barks.

"Should I let him in?" I wouldn't consider it if I were alone.

"Unless you want him to smash his way in," Karla replies. "I'll keep my finger near the emergency button on my phone."

"Where do you get off upsetting my wife?" Trevor demands before he is inside the store.

Sophie positions herself between us and Trevor, staring at him and growling. No wagging tail, no enthusiastic welcome for our uninvited guest.

"We didn't intend to upset her," I explain, changing locations to ensure neither Sophie nor I are within reach of the fuming man. "We returned her phone. She lost it in town yesterday. Mel was fine when we left." I look to Karla for support.

"If you didn't want to upset Mel, maybe you shouldn't have rented a cottage next to the man who destroyed her career."

What is she doing? Why is Karla poking the proverbial bear?

While Trevor and Karla have a staring contest, I lean against the counter and pick up my phone, slipping it behind my back. Just in case.

"Mel is confused. For obvious reasons, this situation is stressful for her. Whatever she told you isn't admissible in court," Trevor advises us.

"Says who?" Karla asks, crossing her arms in front of her chest and tilting her head. "Did you study law during your eight-month prison stint?"

Is she trying to push him over the edge?

"You work for the police," Trevor accuses. "But you didn't read her rights or offer her a lawyer."

Stoic, Sophie continues to sit with her attention focussed on Trevor but has stopped growling. I interpret her less aggressive stance to mean she senses a de-escalation in his behaviour.

"We aren't cops," I clarify, standing next to Karla. "I run a yarn store, and Karla owns a concierge business." I inhale and hope for the best. "Listen, Trevor. We're trying to eliminate Karla as a suspect. Mel wants to eliminate you as a suspect. We thought it would benefit everyone if we shared information. It's not our fault your wife shared things with us you withheld from the police."

"Because of you"—he jabs his angry, tattooed finger toward us—"I'll probably get arrested again as soon as I go back to Mel."

"Then don't go back to Mel," Karla says with a *duh! You're such a loser* tone in her voice and a condescending headshake. "Go back to the police station. Tell them the whole truth. Stop asking your wife to lie for you."

"Karla's right," I agree. "Tell Eric about the pizza delivery to The Fawkes Den and about Mel's letter. Tell them how you accompanied her to confront him on Tuesday morning."

"Tuesday?" he asks, surprised. "You mean Monday. We dropped it off on Monday. If Mel said Tuesday, she was wrong. It was Monday."

He's right. Mel claimed they delivered the letter on Monday. I was testing Trevor's recollection.

"Are you sure?" Karla challenges.

"She wanted to read the letter to him," Trevor says. "I knew it was a bad idea, but she had made up her mind. When Mel decides something, there's no stopping her, so I agreed to go with her. In exchange, she agreed we could leave town on Tuesday. That's how I know we were there on Monday. She wasn't anywhere near that cottage on Tuesday."

Karla and I glance at each other. Mel never mentioned leaving town on Tuesday.

"Did you devise a plan to kill Fawkes before leaving town?" I ask.

"Yes." Trevor nods, hands on hips. "I drugged him, threw him over my shoulder and ran through the centre of town, all the way to the pool. I ran so fast that not a single person saw us." He waves his hand in front of his face. "I was a blur." He chuckles and shakes his head. "Then I drowned him in the pool and ran back to Mel. And I did it without being one second late because I'm a superhero, and my superpower is running at the speed of light while carrying a grown man."

"Don't be glib, Trevor." Karla rolls her eyes.

"Believe it or not, we're trying to help," I say. "Don't you want the police to eliminate Mel as a suspect?"

"Of course, I do." He softens and smooths his shiny hair.

"Why didn't you leave on Tuesday?" Karla asks. "You said Mel agreed to leave on Tuesday if you accompanied her to confront Fawkes."

Karla shifts her weight, shielding most of her behind me.

"We went down to the dock for our last swim. Cops were crawling all over Fawkes's place. We went back to the cottage to finish packing and leave town, but the police showed up, asking questions. The cop who canvassed the neighbourhood was too young to recognize Mel or know about her history with Fawkes, and we didn't mention it. We thought it would be suspicious if we left early." He shrugs. "We figured leaving would draw attention. So, we stayed in Harmony Lake and tried to fly under the police radar."

A soft *whoosh* behind my back. Karla steps forward, once again standing next to me.

"A witness saw you near The Fawkes Den on Tuesday morning," I say.

"On my usual run."

"In your car."

"They're mistaken."

"Are they?" I challenge. "They were quite certain."

Could Mason be mistaken? Did he see Trevor driving his Camaro on Monday morning? I might not be a human lie detector, but the knot in my stomach believes Mason. He claims he encountered Trevor on his way to the hardware store to fix the leak at the library. The leak was on Tuesday. I suspect it's more likely that Trevor and Mel are lying. I bet they spoke and got their stories straight before he came here.

"Mel said the first time you spotted Fawkes, someone was knocking on his door," I say.

"That's right," Trevor confirms. "Two Tuesdays ago."

"Mel said it was a tall man with broad shoulders and dark hair. Did you recognize him?"

"No. Not right away," Trevor replies. "But since I've spent so much quality time with Harmony Lake's finest, I now recognize the knocker and the car he drove. It was a late model, black Charger."

"Eric?" I ask.

Trevor nods.

*Sigh.* A dead-end. Trevor's description of the knocker matches my husband, and Eric drives a newer, black Charger. He saw the mystery knocker on a Tuesday, the day Eric made weekly pilgrimages to check on the felon.

"Trevor, don't make Mel watch the police arrest you again," Karla pleads. "Go back to the police station voluntarily. Tell the truth and help eliminate her as a suspect."

"Fine. I love my wife, and I'll do whatever it takes to protect her from this mess." Trevor clears his throat. "But the police have my car. I don't know my way around Harmony Lake. Can one of you call me a cab?"

"No need," Karla says. "The police are already on their way to pick you up."

"They are?" Trevor's bewildered expression reflects the shock we both feel.

"You should wait outside," I say, reaching for the door.

"I did you a favour," Karla adds. "The police in this town are horrible about reimbursing cab fare."

Confused but calm, Trevor walks through the open door, and I lock it behind him. Sophie jumps onto the floor of the display window and continues to monitor him, prepared to alert us if he returns.

My phone rings. It's Eric.

Karla sent him a cryptic text: *Pick up Trevor at Knitorious. NOW.*

He's calling to make sure we're OK.

I assure him we're fine, and he tells me he's almost here to collect Trevor.

I give him the highlights of Trevor's visit, and we end the call, then I join Karla by the window.

Trevor paces on the sidewalk.

A car pulls up.

Eric gets out and opens the rear passenger door.

Trevor gets in.

Eric closes the car door, turns to the window, and waves.

We wave back.

Our eyes meet, and he winks.

He returns to the driver's side of the car.

"Did Trevor lie?" I ask as Eric's car pulls away from the curb and disappears down the street.

"I'm not sure," she shakes her head. "I couldn't figure out his tell."

"So, either Trevor was honest with us…"

"Or he's a psychopath," Karla says, finishing my sentence.

# CHAPTER 19

"Why are you still here?" I ask, standing on tippy toes and pressing the back of my hand against his forehead. "Do you feel OK?"

"I'm fine." Eric chuckles, takes my hand off his forehead, and kisses it. "I'm working from home this morning." He hands me a cup of coffee.

"Thank you," I say, then blow on the surface of the steaming, caffeinated goodness. "What time did you get home?"

"Late," Eric admits. "Trevor was talkative. Thanks to you."

"Thanks to me and Karla," I clarify.

"Are you still convinced she's innocent?" Eric asks.

I nod. "Even more convinced."

"Why?" He sinks into the corner of the sofa and rests his ankle on his knee.

Sophie sits at the back door, supervising the squirrel activity in the backyard.

I sit sideways, facing Eric with my legs crossed and my feet tucked under my butt.

"Twice"—I make a peace sign for emphasis—"Karla has questioned why Fawkes's killer drowned him in the pool at the community centre and how the killer convinced Fawkes to go there. She doesn't know he died in the bathtub at the cottage. You said not knowing about the hold back is a good sign the suspect didn't commit the crime."

"Karla is clever, babe. It's possible she's being careful only to mention the details that we made public."

"She has no history with Fawkes. She's not strong enough to drown a struggling man, then drag his dead body around town, and dump it in a pool," I say, reiterating my original argument. "You didn't find any evidence that Fawkes had been in Karla's car. How did she transport his body to the pool?"

"Her car was clean," Eric confirms. "The cadaver dog didn't signal on it either. We brought in a second cadaver dog to be sure, and neither dog picked up decomp."

"Because she didn't do it."

"Then why won't Karla tell me why her fingerprints and hair were at the murder scene?"

"She swears she doesn't know. I believe her. Maybe someone set her up," I suggest.

"Who?"

"I don't know," I admit. "A disgruntled former employee? An ex-boyfriend? An angry client? Who knows?"

"We're exploring the possibility that Karla is involved with a group of radicalized women's rights advocates," Eric says.

"Are you serious?" I ask, wondering why Eric's statement offends me. "You've met Karla, right? She's one of the most headstrong people I know. I can't imagine she would be easy to radicalize."

"Karla donates a lot of time and large amounts of

money to organizations that provide services to female victims of violence and abuse and advocate for tighter laws and stricter sentencing for perpetrators of crimes against women."

"Good for her," I declare. "It's a cause I support."

"It's a noble cause," Eric agrees. "But groups devoted to advocacy and change can attract extremists. Fawkes represents everything those organizations fight against. It's possible a few fringe members conspired to dole out vigilante justice. She could have had accomplices."

"Karla has been honest and cooperative with you from the start," I say, summoning my calmest, most rational voice. "Aside from fingerprints and a few hairs, which can't prove *when* she was in the cottage, you have no evidence linking her to Fawkes and no realistic theories about how she did it," I argue. "Trevor and Melody Howe had a motive and opportunity to kill Fawkes, lied to the police every time they answered a question, and Trevor has a documented history of violence."

"Trevor is my prime suspect." Eric places his hand on my knee. "Babe, I don't believe Karla killed Fawkes," he says quietly with intense eye contact. "But I have to investigate her and explain her fingerprints and DNA. Otherwise, the fingerprints and hair, combined with Karla's weak alibi that she took the scenic route and accidentally turned off her phone, could create enough reasonable doubt for the murderer to avoid conviction."

"That makes sense," I say, remembering that, unlike mine, Eric's investigation goes beyond eliminating one suspect. He must ensure the evidence is admissible, investigate and eliminate alternate possibilities, and investigate within the law. "Can I tell Karla she's no longer a suspect?"

"You can tell her she is an unlikely suspect." Eric smiles.

"Did you find Melody's letter to Fawkes?" I ask.

"It was in the trash at The Fawkes Den," Eric replies, nodding. "Someone ripped the letter to shreds. We had to piece it together like a jigsaw puzzle."

"Was it signed or dated?" I ask.

Eric shakes his head.

"But we have evidence that suggests Fawkes received the letter on Tuesday, the day he died, not Monday like Trevor and Mel claim."

"What kind of evidence?"

"Despite the clutter and mess, there was very little actual garbage at Fawkes's cottage. When we interviewed his sister, she mentioned she visited Fawkes the evening before he died. She picked up his garbage and took it to the dump."

"So, the garbage you collected was from the day Fawkes died or the night before," I conclude.

"She also said the cottage was tidy when she was there," Eric adds. "She said she often showed up unannounced, and the place was always neat."

"Maybe Fawkes's sister found Mel's letter wedged in the screen door," I hypothesize. "He might not have read it until after she'd left with the garbage."

"Great minds think alike, babe!" He squeezes my knee. "I've already left a message for her. When she calls back, I'll ask about the letter."

"Mason Shilling saw Trevor Howe driving his Camaro on Tuesday morning," I say.

"Trevor and Mel insist neither of them left their cottage on Tuesday, aside from Trevor's morning run."

I nod.

Eric produces his handy-dandy notebook and pen from his pocket. He opens the small notebook to a blank page, rests it on the arm of the sofa, and clicks open his pen.

"Was Mason certain he saw Trevor? Was he sure of the date?"

"Mason is a vintage car enthusiast," I remind him. "He was on his way to get a part for the leaky pipe at the library."

"The leak was last Tuesday," Eric ponders as he writes. "Did he tell you where he saw Trevor?"

"The four-way stop at Temple Road."

Eric pauses mid-word and turns to me.

"Temple Road is The Fawkes Den driveway."

I nod. "I know."

Eric emerges from his state of shock and resumes writing.

"Here's a theory," I say, about to suggest a complicated scenario. "What if Mel returned to The Fawkes Den by herself to confront Fawkes, and she killed him? Maybe he had just finished drawing a bath for himself when she showed up. Somehow, she overpowered him and drowned him in the bath water. Then, she confessed to Trevor, who moved the body to make it look like Fawkes died elsewhere, and therefore, Mel couldn't have done it. In the meantime, she kept her mum on the phone to create an alibi."

"Why didn't Mel or Trevor take the letter?" Eric asks. "Why would they leave it at The Fawkes Den?"

"Good question," I admit. "It could have been a mistake. Mel, freaked out that she'd killed him, ran away in a panic, and forgot about the letter. Trevor could have been too shocked or distracted to remember. You always say perpetrators make mistakes when they're stressed. Maybe Mel and Trevor were stressed and made a mistake."

"It's possible," Eric concedes. "But Trevor would never let Mel take the blame. He would take full blame for the murder himself before he'd allow her to be

MURDER IT SEAMS

charged. The only way to prove that Mel killed him is if Mel confesses. She wouldn't confess to losing her earring outside The Fawkes Den, even when I showed it to her, so I doubt she'd confess to murder."

"How did Trevor enter the country?" I ask. "They live in New York. Mel said he served eight months in prison. Wouldn't he need a special visa or something to cross the border?"

"Trevor's a dual citizen," Eric replies. "He has a right to be here." He clicks his pen and closes his notebook. "Mel and Trevor divide their time between the US and Canada. Trevor was on our side of the border when he assaulted the police officer."

"Mel didn't mention that," I comment.

"Did she mention Trevor served his sentence in the same facility as Clarence Fawkes?"

"What?!"

My gasp distracts Sophie from squirrel-watching. She trots over and noses our hands, urging us to rub her. Then, satisfied all is well, returns to the back door.

"The Howes are coincidence-prone," I muse sarcastically. "First, they unknowingly rent the only cottage within spitting distance of Clarence Fawkes, then we learn that, by happenstance, Trevor served eight months in prison with him."

"I don't think the prison sentence was a coincidence," Eric reveals.

"Why not?"

"Trevor negotiated the terms of his guilty plea," Eric explains. "He didn't ask for the shortest potential sentence or reduced charges. Trevor was a first-time offender, babe. He could have gotten a non-custodial sentence if he'd asked. Instead, he negotiated where he would serve his sentence."

"That's weird, right?"

"Very," Eric confirms. "Until he broke the cop's nose, Trevor had no history of police involvement. No criminal record. The man has never had a speeding ticket, never mind started a bar fight and punched a cop."

"Okaaay…" I say, not sure of the point he's trying to make.

"I read the police reports, babe. I think Trevor started the fight to get himself charged. He hit the cop because he knew it would be a more serious charge. He did whatever necessary to get inside the same facility as Clarence Fawkes."

"Do you think Trevor tried to get close enough to Fawkes to kill him?"

"Trevor denied it, but I suspect that was his plan."

I shake my head, speechless.

"Did Trevor and Fawkes cross paths in prison?" I ask.

"No," Eric shakes his head. "It's an enormous facility. They housed Fawkes in the maximum-security wing, and they housed Trevor in the medium-security wing. They didn't share any common amenities. They never laid eyes on each other."

"So, Trevor sacrificed himself for nothing," I comment. "Have you received the forensics report for Trevor's car?"

"Not yet," Eric says. "I'll check my email right now."

He leans toward the coffee table, resting his elbows on his knees and rubbing small, fast circles on the track pad, urging the screen to wake up.

"In the meantime, I'll update the murder board to reflect that Mel's letter was at The Fawkes Den." I stand up, scribble on a stickie note, and stick the note next to the blue flower on the murder board.

I brought the murder board home from Knitorious yesterday. It would have been impossible to hide from The Charity Knitters when the store opens tomorrow.

"Nice murder board," Eric comments. "At work, we call it a *big board*. We use a large white board and dry-erase markers."

"Karla and I went for a pleasing aesthetic. Something with diverse textures," I jest.

"You're missing a photo," he comments, nodding to the board leaning against the wall on the fireplace mantle. "I might be able to help." He opens the file folder beside his laptop and flips through the pages, pulling out a single sheet of paper. "My contribution to your board." He hands it to me. "It's a driver's licence photo."

If, heaven forbid, someone should ever ask my loved ones to choose an image of me to disseminate to the masses, I pray they don't choose my driver's licence photo. The unsmiling pose and harsh fluorescent lighting at the licencing office makes even the kindest, most emotionally stable person look like a deranged, homicidal maniac.

"Thank you." I take the page.

I stare at the poor-quality, grainy headshot, wondering why Eric has this photo and why he would think it belongs on our murder board. I flip over the page, assuming the photo for the murder board is on the other side.

The other side is blank.

"Chelle Temple?" I ask, my face screwed up in confusion. "Why do you have a photo of Karla's personal assistant?"

"Karla's personal assistant?" Eric asks, matching my confusion. "This is Michelle Fawkes, Clarence Fawkes's sister. She owns The Fawkes Den."

I drop my stunned self onto the sofa beside him. "I know this woman as Chelle Temple." I gasp and cover my mouth when my brain connects the dots. "Chelle is short for Michelle. Temple is the name of the road that leads to The Fawkes Den." I hold the grainy printout of Chelle's face at eye level. "Michelle Fawkes *is* Chelle Temple."

"Temple was their mother's maiden name," Eric adds. "Michelle and Clarence's maternal grandparents, the Temples, were the original owners of The Fawkes Den. Michelle and Clarence's parents changed the name of the cottage when they inherited it, but they didn't change the name of the private road."

"Is Chelle a suspect?"

"She wasn't," Eric replies. "But she's looking mighty suspicious right now, so yes. She's a suspect."

"Does she have an alibi?"

"She was at work when her brother died. She said she was a housekeeper with multiple clients in Harmony Hills. She provided us with a bunch of addresses for the homes she cleans, but her clients aren't home when she cleans, so we couldn't confirm what time she showed up or left. We had to rely on her cell phone to verify her alibi. She didn't tell me she works for Karla. Her phone pinged off a location in Harmony Hills."

"Karla lives in Harmony Hills," I remind him. "Chelle left her phone at Karla's house last Monday," I explain. "It was there when I drove Karla home from the hospital. Karla said it wasn't a big deal. She said Chelle is forgetful and leaves her phone all the time. She said Chelle would pick it up on Tuesday. How convenient that she forgot it when it could give her an alibi."

Eric sucks in a breath and takes to his feet, pacing in front of the coffee table and rubbing the back of his neck.

"I asked Michelle... Chelle... whoever she is... if she knew Karla. I had hoped she might explain why Karla's fingerprints and hair were inside The Fawkes Den." He stops pacing. "She told me she'd never heard of Karla Bell."

"She lied," I tell him. "This woman works for Karla. She has access to Karla, Rita, and The Fawkes Den."

"She had access to the murder victim too," he adds.

"May I see the crime scene photos?" I ask.

"Which crime scene?" Eric asks, waking up his laptop again.

"Fawkes Den, please."

He opens a digital photo album and hands me the laptop.

I sit back with the computer on my lap and examine the first photo.

Eric wasn't exaggerating when he said The Fawkes Den was a mess. It looks like a tornado tore through the place and upended everything in its path. Whoever caused this chaos made it impossible to find *anything* by camouflaging *everything*. It reminds me of those hidden object games where the goal is to find specific, hidden objects in a cluttered room.

I pinch the track pad and zoom in on the upper left corner of the photo, inspecting it before moving to the next zoomed-in section.

About halfway through my grid search, I spy something that doesn't belong at Clarence Fawkes's murder scene.

I zoom out and scrutinize the entire jumbled-up scene from a new perspective, strengthening my suspicion.

"Honey, did you find Karla's fingerprints on anything permanent?"

"Permanent?" he asks. "You mean on the structure itself?"

"Yeah," I reply without taking my eyes off the photo. "A doorknob, faucet, wall?"

"I can check."

He leans over and closes the digital photo, then opens

something else. I turn the laptop toward him while he scans a document.

"Now that you mention it, we only found her prints on items, nothing attached to the building," he confirms, continuing to scroll through the document.

"I think I figured out why Karla's fingerprints and hair are at the murder scene," I say. "Michelle Fawkes, aka Chelle Temple, planted them there."

With Eric's permission, I take a screenshot of the zoomed-in grid where I found Karla's missing, limited-edition bookend, and send it to myself.

I text the photo to Karla, and she texts back, confirming that as far as she can tell without inspecting it, her missing bookend is in the photo.

"She says the bookend is signed and numbered," I tell Eric. "If you find out the number, she can confirm it's hers."

"Her fingerprints are on it," he responds. "That's enough proof for me."

*Karla: Where was it?*

*Me: The Fawkes Den.*

*Karla: WTF?! How did it get there?*

"She wants to know why her bookend is at The Fawkes Den. Should I tell her about Chelle or wait and tell her in person?"

"That's a tough one," Eric replies.

"I'll tell her now," I decide. "It miffed her when I couldn't tell her the holdback, and she was surprised when I forgot to tell her about Mel's earring. I don't want her to think I'm keeping it from her."

*Me: Chelle Temple is Fawkes's sister.*

Three dots appear as Karla types a message. They disappear. I wait. Should I phone her? Is she in shock? Three dots appear again. I wait. They disappear. I wait. Is she OK? If she isn't OK, I hope someone is with her.

*Gasp!*

"Babe, what's wrong?"

"What if Chelle is with her?"

"Call Karla," Eric instructs.

I nod, tapping Karla's name at the top of our text thread.

Her contact information appears, and I'm about to touch her phone number when my phone dings and a text message appears at the top of the screen.

***Karla: How fast can you get here?***

# CHAPTER 20

I VIDEO CHAT with Karla to confirm she is safe. She is flabbergasted by the revelation that Chelle Temple and Michelle Fawkes are the same person. She tells me how she started to type a reply several times but was at a loss for words, which explains why the three dots kept appearing and disappearing. Then she panicked when she remembered Chelle is due at her house in under an hour.

Hence her last text: *How fast can you get here?*

I grab my purse and run out of the house during our video chat. Before we disconnect, Karla promises not to let Chelle inside the house or be alone with her. Then she panics about Rita. Karla is about to phone her and instruct her to lock her doors and windows, but I remind her that Rita and Connie went to a Labour Day concert in the park and won't be home for hours.

Turning onto Karla's street, I spot Chelle's car on the road outside Karla's house. She's early. Such a diligent and trustworthy personal assistant.

"Ha!" I grunt to myself at the irony.

Karla stands on her driveway, tapping her left foot

like her designer sandals are angry at the pavement, and crosses her arms in front of her chest.

Chelle stands in front of her, gesticulating and bobbing her head as she speaks.

Gucci is on the lawn, rolling in the grass, tethered to Karla by a long, gold, sparkling designer leash.

I slam my car into park in front of Rita's house and lurch forward from the force of the sudden stop.

"I never said I *wasn't* Michelle Fawkes," Chelle insists as I run across the street and up Karla's driveway.

Gucci bounces on his hind legs, wagging his tail to welcome me.

"I changed my name years ago," Chelle continues. "Temple is my mother's maiden name."

I come to a stop next to Gucci and squat down to give him the greeting he deserves.

"I changed my name to distance myself from my brother and his disgraceful behaviour. My parents and I used to get threats. Journalists and paparazzi would follow us. The stress was too much for them. It's the reason I moved them to the care home. It's easier to protect their anonymity in a small, closed community."

"You believe the accusations against your brother," Karla says as a fact, not as a question.

"Of course I do," Chelle acknowledges. "Clarence was an arrogant, narcissistic psychopath. I know he preyed on those girls."

"Is that why you're donating his royalties to a fund to help his victims?" I interject.

"Yes. His victims deserve compensation," Chelle says. "And my brother deserved what he got."

"Did you kill Clarence Fawkes?" Karla asks, her eyes probing Chelle like she has transparent skin.

"No," Chelle replies. "I would never harm a soul. But I'm glad he's gone. I'm relieved there won't be another trial, and I'm happy he can't harm anyone ever again."

I don't have Karla's gift for lie detection, but I'm inclined to believe Chelle.

"If you hated him, why did you look after him?" I ask.

"For my parents," she explains. "They're old and frail. They don't fully comprehend what my brother did and struggle to accept their son is a monster. My parents cling to the hope that the accusations against him were a big misunderstanding." She shakes her head. "Clarence was an awful son. He never wrote to our parents and only called them from prison when he needed something. He refused their visits. They worried about him.

"When that stupid judge gave him a get-out-of-jail-free card, Clarence was broke. He'd spent all his money on legal fees and hadn't earned significant income since the world boycotted his music. He needed a place to stay that met his parole requirements. My parents begged me to let him stay at The Fawkes Den. I offered him a deal. He could stay at The Fawkes Den—rent free—and I would look after him. In exchange, he would have a phone conversation with our parents every week. He had to call them every Sunday evening and talk to them for at least thirty minutes, or I wouldn't drop off groceries that week."

"When you visited your brother on Tuesday morning, did you see anyone else near The Fawkes Den?"

"I wasn't there on Tuesday morning."

"I don't believe you," Karla says, her foot tapping harder and faster than ever.

"Fine!" Chelle rolls her eyes. "I was only there for a minute."

"Was your brother alive when you arrived?"

"Yes. He was still alive when I left."

"Did you find a blue floral envelope by the door?"

Chelle shakes her head. "I found nothing near the door."

"Again, *Chelle*," Karla says her name like it's fake, which I guess it is, "did you see anyone else near The Fawkes Den the morning your brother died?"

Chelle stares into the distance, the muscles around her mouth tense.

"I didn't see anyone," she replies. "But there was a weird vehicle."

"Keep talking," Karla urges, glowering at her personal assistant.

"A Town of Harmony Lake van sped through the stop sign at the bottom of the driveway."

"A Harmony Lake van?" I ask.

Chelle nods. "It was a white hybrid van with the blue and brown Harmony Lake logo."

"Where did you see it?" Karla asks.

"At the bottom of Temple Road, the road that leads to the cottage."

"You mean the four-way stop?" I clarify.

"That's the one," Chelle replies. "When I drove down the driveway, the van was at the four-way stop. The driver was signalling to turn into The Fawkes Den. I thought it was odd since I knew Clarence wasn't expecting anyone. When I approached the intersection, they turned off the indicator and sped away. I assumed they realized they were about to turn onto the wrong road. The van was gone before I came to a full stop."

"How could you see the van model, the town logo, and the indicator before the van sped off?" Karla asks.

"There's a traffic mirror mounted on a tree on Temple Road," she says. "The road is narrow and twisty, with trees blocking the view. I installed the mirror years ago after I collided with my aunt's car because we couldn't see each other."

"Mason," I mutter to Karla, hoping she'll remember that Mason drives a Town of Harmony Lake van and already told us he drove past Temple Road last Tuesday morning.

"Mason?" Chelle asks. "Mason who?"

"Mason, the pool boy?" Karla asks me.

"Harmony Lake's Building and Facilities Maintenance Manager," I correct her.

"Didn't he see Trevor's car at the four-way stop?" Karla asks, then looks at Chelle. "Were there other vehicles at the four-way stop?"

"Not that I noticed," Chelle replies.

"Mason could've seen Trevor on his way to the hardware store, and Chelle could've seen him on his way back? Or vice versa?" Karla suggests.

"Now that I think about it, I could be wrong about the white van," Chelle backtracks. "I visited my brother several times a week. I might have seen the van on a different day."

"Yet you were so confident about the details," Karla challenges.

"But the more I listen to you and Megan talk, the less sure I am," Chelle explains. "I'm not even sure it was a van." She shrugs. "Could've been one of those boxy SUVs."

Clearly, the van is a dead-end. The more questions we ask, the less certain Chelle becomes about every aspect of the morning her brother died.

I watch Gucci jump, startled when the grasshopper he was sniffing hops away.

"Why did you lie to the police about knowing Karla?" I ask, hoping to salvage the conversation.

Chelle turns to me and jabs her fists into her hips.

"How would you know about my police interview?"

"Lucky guess," I reply.

"Chelle, did you find my missing bookend while you were packing yesterday?" Karla asks, setting up her personal assistant to get caught in a lie.

"No, I didn't," Chelle replies. "But I'll keep searching today."

Does Chelle seriously think Karla will continue to employ her after this?

"How about an Hermés permabrass belt buckle?" I ask. "Or a pair of Fendi black-patent, stiletto Mary Janes? Did you find those, by chance?"

"What?!" Karla shrieks, stomping her foot. "You stole my Hermés belt and Fendi Mary Janes?" she shouts, tossing her hands. "In addition to my bookend?"

"And more," I say under my breath.

"No!" Chelle shouts. "Karla, I would never steal from you." She presses her hand against her chest. "I'm not a thief."

"I looked everywhere for those shoes last week!" Karla exclaims.

"No, you didn't," Chelle argues with a dismissive chuckle. "You only wear Mary Janes in the winter." She rolls her eyes. "You wouldn't have noticed those shoes were missing until at least the end of October."

"Is that a confession?" I ask. "Karla, does that sound like a confession to you?"

"It sure does."

"Fine," Chelle groans. "I took a few insignificant items I thought you wouldn't miss." She lowers her voice. "I'm sorry. It was a terrible mistake. Please believe me." Her eyes plead with Karla. "This isn't who I am. As soon as the police release the cottage, I'll return everything I took. I promise."

"Did you steal anything from Rita?" Karla asks, her green eyes full of anger.

"Never," Chelle replies. "I swear." She traces an X over her heart.

"Why did you do it?"

"I was desperate," Chelle replies, her chin quivering and her eyes wide and glassy. "I planned to sell them because I needed the money. I couldn't sell the cottage or rent it out with Clarence living there, but I still had to pay the expenses. Clarence had no money, so I was financing his necessities too. Care homes are expensive. My parents have outlived their money, and it's up to me to pay their expenses now. They don't know how bad their financial situation is. When they begged me to let Clarence stay at the cottage, I couldn't bring myself to tell them we needed to sell the cottage this summer to keep our family finances afloat." A single tear streams down her cheek. "It would have been the final nail in their coffin."

Unfortunate choice of metaphor given the situation.

Eric's car pulls up and parks behind Chelle's car.

The patrol car following him passes Chelle's car and parks in front of it, blocking her vehicle on both sides.

"You called the cops?!" Chelle shouts, her face almost as bright as her hair and her eyes bulging.

"They were here the whole time," I admit. "Parked up the street." I point to the end of the street where Eric sat in his car, watching our interaction. I asked him for a head start when we left the house at the same time. "He knows everything."

Gucci barks and, balancing on his hind legs, paws the air to welcome Eric and the uniformed officer striding up the driveway.

"You'll be sorry," Chelle hisses, pointing at Karla and me. "You'll be sorry when the truth comes out. I shouldn't have taken your stuff, Karla, but it wasn't my fault. It was Clarence's fault. Everything was his fault."

# CHAPTER 21

"OF COURSE, YOU'RE SHAKEN," I assure Karla. "Anyone in your position would be."

So far today, Karla has discovered her personal assistant—whom she trusted with her home, Gucci, and Rita—isn't who she claimed, stole from her, and might be a murderer.

It's not even noon.

"Does Chelle have a tell?" I ask, picking up my cinnamon-maple latte and taking a small sip to test the temperature. "Do you know when she's lying?"

"In hindsight, yes," Karla reveals. "When her lips move, she's lying."

I laugh, and Karla smiles for the first time—that I've seen—today.

"I thought I knew when Chelle was lying, but she must've had another tell I didn't notice," Karla admits, then cracks the lid on her honey almond milk cold brew.

"Are you saying she had different tells for different lies?" I ask. "A tell for a white lie, and a different tell for bigger lies?"

"That's one theory," Karla agrees. "It's possible that,

because I could tell when she told me an insignificant fib, I got lazy and didn't look for other signs she was lying." She shrugs one shoulder. "I can only figure out someone's tells if I look for them."

"She fooled the police too," I remind her. "Don't blame yourself. You're a victim. Chelle lied and stole from you."

"What if I had moved?" Karla asks, her eyes full of fear. "If Clarence Fawkes didn't die, we wouldn't have caught Chelle's lies. She would've gotten away with lying about her identity and stealing from me. I would have moved and left Rita at her mercy."

"Have you met Rita?" I ask. "She is not at anyone's mercy. Rita is a force of nature." I smile. "Connie and I will look out for her. So will her sister and her nieces and nephews. Rita is surrounded by people who love her. She'll miss you like crazy, but she'll be well loved regardless of where you live."

"I trust you, and Connie, and Eric to look out for her," Karla says.

"I'm honoured," I say, shocked. "That's the biggest compliment you've ever given me."

"Don't get used to it," she teases. "I'm having an *off* day."

"Got it."

We sip our coffees in silence at Knitorious while I wind a skein of yarn into a ball.

"I should have realized Chelle was a fraud," Karla laments, refusing to stop punishing herself. "It's what I do. I see people for who they are. I assume the worst and never let my guard down for anyone." She shakes her head. "But somehow, Chelle fooled me."

"This isn't your fault, Karla," I reiterate. "Chelle learned to fool everyone. For her, lying is a survival skill. She's spent the past fifteen years running from her identity so people wouldn't judge her by her brother's notorious reputation. You met your match with her. She's as good at telling lies as you are at detecting them."

"This is why I don't trust anyone until I know I can beat them at their own game."

"You're still in shock, so I won't argue with you," I say, pulling the ball of Savannah Goldenrod yarn off the ball winder. "But waiting around, expecting people to hurt you sounds like an exhausting and lonely life."

"Listen, Megan," Karla says. "I owe you an apology. I've been mean to you since the first time we met, and I'm sorry."

"Why?" I ask. "Did I offend you when we first met?"

"No," Karla replies. "I have a few toxic traits, like assuming the worst of people. I assumed you were an entitled busybody who entertains herself with other people's problems."

"Ouch," I say. "Is that still your opinion?"

"No," she replies. "How could it be? You helped me clear my name even though I didn't deserve it."

"I don't know what to say." Stunned speechless by Karla's unexpected apology, I make three unsuccessful attempts to tie a slip knot while I process her words.

"C'mon," Karla urges, "Isn't is satisfying to hear me admit I'm a horrible person?"

"No," I admit. "It's not as satisfying as I imagined it would be."

There's a brief pause before we burst into laughter.

"Why are we here again?" Karla asks when we stop giggling.

"Eric asked you to identify the bookend the police found at The Fawkes Den," I remind her. "I insisted on driving you to the police station because you were too upset to drive. After you identified your bookend, we swung by Knitorious so I could pick up a skein of yarn for the lion I want to crochet for the Charity Knitters project. Next, we're going back to my place to update the murder board."

"Right." She nods. "It was good of Eric to let us talk to Chelle before he arrested her. I can't remember if I thanked him. I'll send him a text later, in case I didn't."

"He's a good guy." I smile, hooking a magic ring to start my lion.

"Why did you get married again?" Karla asks. "It didn't work with Adam. Why would you expect it to work with Eric? Aren't you scared you'll get hurt again?"

Karla's words touch my soul like emotional sandpaper, but I know she's asking from a place of genuine curiosity, not judgement.

"You're right. In the end, my first marriage didn't work," I acknowledge. "But it worked for a long time. Our marriage lasted for twenty years. Most of those years were happy until we drifted apart because Adam was obsessed with his career, and I was focussed on raising our daughter. Our marriage produced Hannah. I could never regret marrying Adam."

I drop my crochet hook in my lap. "As for Eric," I take a deep breath and let it out, "the idea of another relationship terrified me. But he was persuasive and very patient. Eric was married once. His marriage ended because his job caused stress in their relationship too. He understood how I felt. He convinced me that we had both learned from our previous marriages and wouldn't make the same mistakes again. He offered to take our relationship slower than molasses in January, and I trusted my instincts. It was the best leap of faith I've ever made."

I pick up my hook and resume stitching the lion's butt.

"What if he hurts you?" Karla asks.

"It's a risk," I acknowledge, without hesitation.

"What's scarier, the possibility that someone *might* hurt you or never allowing yourself to love or be loved?"

"Now that I've spent time here, I understand why Knitorious is a community hub," Karla remarks, changing the subject and abandoning our deeper conversation.

"I wouldn't call it a community hub," I say with equal parts pride and humility. "But Knitorious is my second home, and I hope the people who come here feel the same."

A gentle rap on the display window interrupts us.

Phillip waves and makes exaggerated faces at me through the window.

Phillip Wilde is my next-door neighbour at home and work. He owns Wilde Flowers, the florist next door to Knitorious. We share a wall and a parking lot.

I set my knitting on the coffee table and unlock the door for him.

After introductions and small talk, Phillip and Karla *ooh* and *ahh* over each other's fabulousness.

"You both look spectacular in vertical stripes," I say when they each insist the other looks better in vertical stripes and put me in the impossible position of casting the tie-breaking vote. "It's impossible to choose."

Phillip and Karla are wearing similar short-sleeved, button-down shirts with blue and white vertical stripes.

"Oh, please!" Phillip flicks his hand at me. "I look like a referee next to this navy-striped goddess." Phillip points to Karla's feet, and she giggles. "Matching blue and white striped Manolos? She's so hot she's practically on fire!"

"You do not look like a referee," I retort, even though since he made the comparison, I can't unsee the similarity.

"Staaahp!" Karla says to Phillip, giggling. "Let's take a selfie."

They take somewhere between four and fifteen selfies before getting one they agree on.

Karla sends the pic to Phillip. They post the photo to their social media accounts, tagging each other and using the hashtag, #twinning.

"Do you need something in particular?" I ask.

"I have your monthly floral arrangement," he says.

I glance at his empty hands.

"It's much smaller than usual," I joke.

"Ha! Ha!" he says, unamused. "It's in the back of my delivery van. If it's all right with you, I'd like to deliver it to your house, let myself in, and use your dryer."

"Is your dryer broken?" I ask, already rifling through my purse in search of my keys.

"No, it's old," Phillip replies. "Your newfangled appliances have all the bells and whistles. Your dryer has a steam feature. I'm doing flowers for a photo shoot, and the photographer wants a draped floral backdrop. I need to steam the draperies."

"You know the alarm code, right?" I ask, removing the house key from my key ring.

"Sophie's birthday?"

"That's it!" I hand him the house key.

"Thank you, sweetie." He pockets the house key. "I'll take Sophie for a quick walk while I'm there."

"Thank you, Phillip. Sophie and I appreciate it."

We exchange a double-cheek kiss; Phillip and Karla exchange air-kisses and toss a few more compliments at each other before he leaves.

I lock the door behind him.

"Your next-door neighbour brings you flowers every month?" Karla asks.

"It's a long story," I reply. "The short version is,

Phillip gifted us a year of monthly floral arrangements as a wedding gift."

"He has the code to your security system?"

"Phillip is my friend. I've known him for over twenty years. We look after each other's dogs sometimes. It's all good."

My phone dings.

"Is it Eric?" Karla asks. "Did he charge Chelle with Fawkes's murder?"

"It's Connie," I reply, shaking my head. "She's asking if I need anything from Harmony Hills. After the concert, they're going for a bite to eat before Connie drops off Rita at home." I reply to Connie and lock the screen. "Earlier, I texted her and asked her to let me know when they would be home. I didn't want them to show up during your confrontation with Chelle," I explain.

"Good thinking," Karla says with a sigh. "I'd like to be home when Rita gets there. I don't want her to hear what happened from the neighbours."

"If Eric releases Chelle, I'll text you right away," I say. "After Trevor shocked us yesterday by showing up when we thought he was still in custody, Eric said he'll text me if he releases Chelle."

"Let's hope he doesn't release her." Karla sets her coffee on the table in front of her. "Let's make a list of updates for the murder board," she says, starting a list on her phone.

"First, we need to remove you as a suspect," I say.

"I haven't been told I'm no longer a suspect," Karla says.

"We explained why your fingerprints and hair were at the murder scene," I say.

"But my alibi is still weak," Karla says. "And Chelle is a pathological liar. What if she changes her story, or the police don't believe her? Think about it, Megan. What

633

would you believe, Chelle Temple a.k.a. Michelle Fawkes or forensic evidence?"

"The forensic evidence doesn't implicate you in Fawkes's murder, Karla. It proves that Chelle stole your belongings and was storing them at The Fawkes Den until she could sell them."

"Let's leave me on the board until Eric tells me I'm off the suspect list," Karla says. "I don't want to jinx it or tempt fate."

"Since when are you superstitious?" I ask, pausing my hook to check the size of the lion's butt.

"I'm not," Karla confirms. "But I'll take all the help I can get."

I drop my hook on my lap and sigh at her.

"The police would have to explain why and how you murdered Fawkes," I assure her. "What motive could you have?"

"I like his music," she says, grasping.

"Your motivation for killing Fawkes was to end the boycott on his music?"

"I hated him as much as every woman on the planet," Karla admits.

"Do the organizations you volunteer with have members with extreme views about Fawkes's parole and retrial?"

"I don't think so," Karla replies. "But I'm not involved in policy or social justice work."

"What do you do?"

"I work with people we help," Karla explains. "I help women re-enter the workforce and gain independence. I prepare them for job interviews, style them with an interview outfit, and give them makeovers to boost their confidence."

The pride in Karla's voice isn't her usual smug, self-satisfied pride. Her face is bright and open, and her excited voice has undertones of empathy and admiration. She's proud of someone else—the women she helps. "I teach seminars on budgeting and money management. Sometimes I accompany them to court for moral support."

"You are so different from the image you project to the world," I say, awestruck and humbled by Karla's passion and devotion to her cause.

"So are you," she says, smiling. "You've taken a community of small-town busybodies and whipped up a network of supportive family and friends who take care of one another."

"I can't take credit for that," I say, choosing to focus on the compliment instead of the *small-town busybodies* insult. "Our community is a group effort. We need each other. We're stronger together than each of us are alone."

"People steal cell phones for you and give you flowers every month. I'm surrounded by paid employees who put up with me for a pay cheque and mimic me when they think I'm not watching."

Karla finishes her coffee and gets up to dispose of the cup, taking a leisurely lap around the store.

"Another reason to remove you from the murder board," I say. "There's no way you could have killed Fawkes without an accomplice."

"Even my best employee doesn't earn enough to help me get away with murder," Karla jokes. "Anyway, if I was going to kill someone, I'd hire a hitman. I wouldn't do it myself."

"Don't say that in front of Eric," I tease. "He might interpret it as a confession."

"You're right, I couldn't have moved Fawkes from his cottage to the community centre. I'm not strong enough," Karla admits, returning to her seat. "But if I'm not strong enough, neither is Chelle. We're close to the same height and weight, and she's at least ten years older than me."

"What if Fawkes didn't struggle," I suggest, hoping to give Karla a better idea of Fawkes's inanimate state when he left The Fawkes Den for the last time, without disclosing that he was already dead. "What if he obeyed his killer under duress or was unconscious?"

"If he was unconscious, I still wouldn't be strong enough to move him and neither would Chelle," Karla insists. "Not without leaving evidence or being seen."

"Last Monday, Chelle moved a bunch of boxes from your house to Rita's garage. She used a red hand truck. Was it still at your house the morning Fawkes died?"

"I don't own a hand truck," Karla replies.

# CHAPTER 22

"The hand truck belongs to Chelle," Karla explains. "It folds up and she stores it in the trunk of her car."

"Maybe she used the hand truck to move her brother's body."

"Someone would have noticed a woman pushing an unconscious man strapped to a hand truck"—she holds up her index finger—"wearing his pajamas and house-coat, according to the news reports." She lowers her finger. "Even if Chelle threw a blanket over him and pretended she was moving a rug, it would have been suspicious enough for someone to notice."

"Maybe not," I counter. "There was a leak at the library that morning. The community centre was evacu-ated. When the emergency was over, everyone was busy saving the books. Apparently, it was chaos. Chelle could have used the commotion to her advantage."

"She had access to him," Karla says, considering this new-to-her information. "She admitted she visited The Fawkes Den the morning he died, and she had a hand truck to move him. Her hatchback is large enough to accommodate a body."

"Chelle had multiple motives," I add. "She hated her brother and resented helping him. She admitted she couldn't sell the cottage with Fawkes living there, and his death eliminated that obstacle." Struck with an adjacent idea, I snap my fingers. "I bet that's why she moved him to the pool! She didn't want the murder scene to interfere with selling the cottage. If Fawkes died elsewhere, she wouldn't have to deal with prospective buyers who don't want to live in a murder house, or who use the murder to negotiate a lower price."

"I thought she killed him at the pool so the police wouldn't find out she was a thief," Karla adds. "If he didn't die there, the police wouldn't be interested in the cottage or notice my stolen property."

"So, Chelle has multiple motives to kill her brother, and multiple motives to do it elsewhere."

"She had opportunity too," Karla adds. "She admits she visited him, but no one can verify the time. Her cell phone was at my house where it couldn't ping off the cell tower near The Fawkes Den."

"And she lied to the police about knowing you," I remind her.

"Hang on," Karla says, unlocking her phone. "Let me update the notes."

While Karla types into her phone, I finish my coffee and toss the cup in the recycling bin.

"Does this mean we can eliminate Trevor and Mel as suspects?" she asks when she finishes updating the murder board notes.

"They're still suspects," I reply. "They had motive and opportunity. Mel hated Fawkes because of what he did to her, and Trevor hated him for hurting Mel. Trevor hated Fawkes enough to trick his way into prison. He wanted to get close enough to Fawkes to get revenge."

"What?!"

"I found out this morning," I say. "Just before I found out about Chelle's true identity."

I tell Karla about Eric's suspicion about Trevor's ill-fated scheme to kill Fawkes in prison.

"Wow," Karla says, processing the bombshell. "Do you think Mel knew about Trevor's plan to kill Fawkes in prison?"

"I don't know," I admit. "I can't figure out if Trevor killed Fawkes alone, if they did it together, or if Mel was the brains behind the murder and Trevor was the muscle."

"Mel couldn't have acted alone," Karla surmises. "She would have the same physical limitations as me. She's not strong enough to overpower him or move him."

"Trevor's alibi is about as solid as quicksand, and Mel's alibi is weak," I add. "She could have talked to her mum on the phone from The Fawkes Den. Her phone could have pinged off the same cell tower as her cottage. If her mum is chatty, Mel could've muted herself while they dragged Fawkes out of the cottage, and her mum would have been oblivious."

"It's true," Karla agrees. "And Trevor insists he and Mel didn't leave their cottage the day Fawkes died, aside from his run, but Mason said he saw Trevor's Camaro at the four-way stop in front of The Fawkes Den."

"The Howes have told multiple lies to the police," I point out. "People with nothing to hide don't lie. Trevor is strong enough to hold Fawkes underwater, even if there was a struggle."

"And strong enough to move Fawkes—either by coercion or by carrying him," Karla concludes.

"But the Camaro was clean," I remind her. "The police didn't find evidence Fawkes was ever in the car."

"Could the Howes have transported him by boat?" Karla asks.

"Maybe," I admit, embarrassed. I live on a lake. It should have occurred to me that a boat is a viable method for moving a body.

"Mel said their rental included use of the boats," Karla reminds me.

"They would have had to moor it at the pier and move him to the community centre without witnesses."

We wonder if Mel and Trevor could have used a rental car to move their victim.

Then we remind ourselves that Clarence Fawkes was universally hated, and the pool of suspects extends way beyond the borders of Harmony Lake. Any of his victims, their families, a rogue activist, or anyone else could have murdered him.

Our conversation has come full circle. We have the same suspects, more motives, more opportunities, and more shaky alibis than one murder requires. With some reluctance, Karla agrees to allow me to change her murder-board status from suspect to person of interest.

While Karla catches up her notes again, I text Eric and ask him about the possibility that Mel and Trevor used a rental car to move Fawkes from the cottage to the pool. He replies that there was no evidence of a rental car in Mel and Trevor's financial records. Another dead-end.

"Another thing," Karla says, placing her phone face down on the table. "Why did the killer toss the cottage? What were they searching for?"

"Eric suspects the killer wanted to make it look like a robbery-gone-bad. A random act of violence instead of a targeted attack."

"That implies Fawkes's killer is someone close to him."

My phone rings, and I set my lion-in-progress aside.

"Hello?"

"Megan? It's Phillip."

"I know. I have call display," I smile, assuming he's calling with a question about using the dryer. "Is everything OK?"

"No. You need to come home. Now."

# CHAPTER 23

MY FEET ARE SOAKED. The cold water almost covers the cork soles of my Birkenstocks. Sophie mills around my feet, lapping at the water and occasionally lifting a paw to shake it off.

I catch my breath and have a moment of silence for my water-covered hardwood floors.

After Phillip called, Karla and I devised a plan as we ran to the back door.

Karla didn't have her car because I insisted on driving her to identify her bookend and stitch up Chelle for stealing it.

I lobbed my keys to her as soon as I locked the back door behind us.

Already running toward the car—in heels—Karla turned and caught the keys in mid-air with a fluid elegance that would make an NFL wide receiver blush with pride.

She dropped me off at home, then drove to her house in Harmony Hills so she would get there before Rita. We don't want Rita to hear about today's events from the neighbours that gathered on their lawns for a front-row seat to Karla and Chelle's confrontation and Chelle's subsequent arrest.

As I sprinted from the car toward the house, Karla shouted something about coming back later to drop off my car and make the updates to the murder board.

Phillip opened the front door and stood back as I ran inside without assessing the situation. Which is why my feet and rose gold Birkenstocks are soaking wet.

"I turned off the water," Phillip says. "The washer and dryer have a separate shut-off valve, so you have running water in the rest of the house, just not in the laundry room."

He rings the sopping wet mop into the bucket.

"Thank you for turning off the water," I say, taking in the scene. "Do you know what happened?"

"I think your washing machine has a leak, sweetie." He pauses his mop. "I found it like this. Just like you, I walked into a puddle of water." He sticks out one dripping bare foot. "I followed the evidence, and it led me to the washing machine." He gestures to the short hall that leads to the laundry room.

Unfamiliar sheets cover the laundry room and hall floors. They're saturated with water and bunched up in some areas and stretched flat in others as if someone smooshed them around the floor with their feet. Then I realize why I don't recognize them.

"Oh, Phillip!" I gasp and bring my hand to my mouth. "Your backdrop!" I gesture to the sopping swaths of fabric. "I'm sorry."

"You're sorry?!" Phillip glares at me like I'm sprouting a unicorn horn. "Sweetie, your floors are drowning." He shakes his head. "The backdrop is the least of our issues right now. Don't worry about the fabric, I can get it dry and wrinkle-free in an hour."

I reach into Sophie's Stash—the collection of treats

and toys we save for special occasions—and find a brand-new, unopened version of her favourite chew toy. She follows me, bouncing and panting, to the back door. I toss the treat into the yard, and she races after it, scoops it into her mouth, and curls up under her favourite tree to chew it.

Next, I gather every towel, rag, and absorbent linen I can find and get to work soaking up water.

Phillip runs next door to grab his mop because, according to him, "Two mops are better than one."

I soak up water, and Phillip mops each section of floor after me.

"I called your husband before I called you because he's handy with plumbing," Phillip says as we wring out towels and such on the front lawn. "Since Eric's snake cleaned my pipes, I haven't had one clog."

"Drain," I correct him. "He snaked your drain."

"All I know is, my sink empties faster than ever," Phillip says. "Anyway, I called Eric first, but I got his voice mail and left a message."

"It's for the best," I assure him. "He's busy with the murder investigation. I'll take care of this without him." I sigh. "Thank goodness you discovered the leak before it got worse." I shake my head, imagining how bad the damage could have been. "I'm sorry about your back-drop. With the water turned off, the steam setting on the dryer won't work."

"Don't worry about it," Phillip says. "Connie has a steam dryer too. I already texted her. She invited me for dinner while I dry and de-wrinkle the fabric." He smiles. "We're going to make an evening of it. We're calling it Margarita Monday: Laundry Edition."

"Sounds fun," I say.

"You didn't have to come home. I've got this under control."

"I know you do, babe," Eric says from the laundry room floor where he's assessing the source of our plumbing predicament. "But I'd already listened to Phillip's message and was on my way home when you called." He rolls from his stomach to his side and cranes his neck as he reaches for something out of sight. Sophie is next to him, poking her muzzle toward him and sniffing the air. "Aha!" he declares, holding up a section of blue flexible pipe.

He explains the problem: a cracked PEX pipe. Whatever that is.

I know better than to ask unless I want a plumbing lesson.

"We're lucky Phillip arrived when he did," I say.

"I could fix this in ten minutes if I had a piece of pipe." Eric drops the blue, damaged pipe on the table near the door. "I'll take the rest of the day off and fix it. The hardest part will be finding a hardware store that's open on Labour Day and has the pipe I need."

"Let the plumber take care of this," I suggest. "I've already left him a message. You're busy enough without adding plumbing to your list."

"Babe." He wraps his arms around my waist. "It's Labour Day. It will cost a fortune to get someone out here today. You know I hate paying for something I can do myself." He squeezes me. "I want to fix it. I don't want some stranger's hands and tools all over our pipes."

"How about a compromise?"

"I'm listening," he says, in the same cop-voice he uses when he says it to a witness.

"We still have running water in the rest of the house," I start. "We can live without the laundry room for a few days. In the meantime, send me a list of what you need, and I'll go to the hardware store tomorrow."

With that settled, Eric helps me carry the wrung-out linens to the backyard so I can hang them on the clothesline.

"Thank you," I say when he delivers the last armload of rags. "Are you going back to work today?"

"Yes," he replies, handing me a rag. "I have to finish interviewing Chelle."

"You left her in an interview room while you came home?"

"Chelle's fine." Sophie drops a ball at Eric's feet, and he throws it across the yard. "We ordered lunch for her, and another officer is questioning her about her timeline the day Fawkes died."

"Did she admit to stealing from Karla?" I ask.

"Chelle's version of events differs from what she told you and Karla," Eric reveals.

"How?"

"According to Chelle, Karla *asked* her to store items in The Fawkes Den."

"What?" I ask, not sure I believe my ears.

"Chelle said she didn't know why Karla wanted her to store the stuff. She said the items were random and expensive. Chelle suspects Karla was planning an insurance scam. She would claim the moving company lost or stole items during her cross-country move and file an insurance claim. Then, after the insurance company paid her claim, Karla could collect her missing items. Chelle insisted she didn't want to store the items, but she was afraid to say no in case Karla fired her. She needed the money. She said Karla has an intimidating presence."

"That's an oddly specific accusation," I say. "Do you believe her?"

"I don't believe a word Chelle says," Eric admits. "She

tells so many lies, I'm not sure she knows the difference between her lies and the truth."

"Maybe that's her strategy," I suggest, "To create a knot of lies so big that you'll never untangle it."

"Some suspects think they're smarter than the police," Eric says. "Chelle is one of them. She suggests plausible but improbable scenarios to influence the investigation."

"What other plausible but improbable scenarios has Chelle suggested?" I ask.

"She tried to convince me that Karla killed Fawkes and is using her charm and intelligence to insert herself into the investigation so she can manipulate me," Eric says. "Chelle also claimed that Karla borrowed her keys and accessed The Fawkes Den by herself on multiple occasions."

"Why is Chelle so determined to implicate Karla in Fawkes's murder?" I ask.

"She hopes Karla will be too busy defending herself against a murder accusation to charge her with theft?" Eric suggests. "Because of the value of the stolen items, we would charge Chelle with Theft Over Five Thousand Dollars, which carries a maximum sentence of ten years. It wouldn't surprise me if Chelle offered to revoke her multiple statements and un-implicate Karla in exchange for Karla agreeing not to pursue a theft conviction."

"I hadn't thought of that," I admit. "I was going to suggest that Chelle is framing Karla to deflect suspicion from herself or someone she loves."

"Do you think if Chelle didn't murder her brother, she knows who did?" Eric asks.

"Yes," I say. "It wouldn't make sense to frame Karla unless she already knows who the murderer is. Assume Chelle is innocent, and she knows Karla is too. If Chelle's plan works and they convict Karla of murdering Fawkes, the case would be closed. Chelle would know the actual killer was still free. The only way she could be at peace with that is if the killer is herself or someone she loves."

"We have evidence that Fawkes was in Chelle's car," Eric reveals. "The problem is, his DNA *should* be in her car because she was his caregiver. She drove him to appointments."

"Just like her fingerprints are all over the murder scene, but it's her cottage, and she spends time there," I say. "Did the cadaver dog sniff Chelle's car?"

He nods. "Two dogs. Neither dog signalled a corpse had been there."

How the heck did Fawkes get from The Fawkes Den to the community centre?

# CHAPTER 24

TUESDAY, September 6th

"It's lovely, my dear!" Connie says, admiring the murder board like a mother gushing over her child's science fair project.

"Using a blue flower to represent the blue floral stationery is a nice touch," April adds, looking over Connie's shoulder at the murder board photo on my phone.

"That was Karla's idea," I say, taking my phone from Connie. "The colour coding was my idea."

"Congratulations, Megabomb! You did it," April says, plucking a blueberry-cream cheese kolache from the white confectionery box on the coffee table. "You and Karla solved the mystery of why her fingerprints and DNA were at The Fawkes Den." She pops the breakfast pastry into her mouth.

"And you made a new friend along the way," Connie points out.

"I'm not sure if Karla and I are friends," I say, setting my cinnamon-maple latte on the table and picking up the crochet hook in my lap. "But we understand each other better, and I have a newfound respect for her." I create a slip knot and chain two stitches to start the lion's first ear. "Karla keeps people at arm's length until she trusts them. She's very caring and generous but doesn't let the world see that side of her."

"Karla made a similar observation about you," Connie says. "She told Rita that underneath your whole-some, mild-mannered exterior, you are cunning and clever.

"Wow?" April and I ask in unison.

"Karla also told Rita that Megan is a natural leader."

"How many homemade brownies had Rita eaten when Karla said these nice things?" April asks.

April and I laugh, but Connie does not.

"The Karla Bell I know doesn't hand out compli-ments," April adds. "Maybe her new complimentary personality is a symptom of her head injury."

"She insists she's fine," I say. "Karla said she hasn't even had a headache since the exercise ball hit her."

"Rita says Karla doesn't seem to have any ill afteref-fects from the unfortunate incident," Connie confirms. "Thank goodness because she has enough stress with her upcoming move, being a murder suspect, and finding out that Chelle had lied since the day they met."

"That's a lot for anyone to deal with," April sympa-thizes. "At least she can cross murder suspect off her list, thanks to a little help."

"Chelle betrayed both of them," Connie reveals. "Rita liked and trusted Chelle too. Chelle had agreed to continue helping Rita after Karla's move. It's jarring to think that someone you know and trust could be entirely different from the person you believe they are."

April and I agree, then she and Connie update me on topics that have fallen off my radar since Fawkes's murder, like the Hillman's marital issues—they've agreed to a shared custody arrangement for the cat but are still negotiating Christmas and the cat's birthday—and sign-ups for the Charity Knitters latest endeavour.

We chat, sip coffee, and eat kolaches until it's time to open the store.

April leaves to work behind the counter at Artsy Tartsy. I tidy coffee and pastry remnants from the coffee table, and Connie turns the sign from CLOSED to OPEN and unlocks the door.

"Good morning, ladies." Connie holds the door for Mrs. Roblin and Mrs. Vogel. "How long were you waiting? You should have knocked."

"We just got here," Mrs. Vogel says.

"It's a lovely morning to spend a few minutes outside," Mrs. Roblin adds.

"Tea or coffee, ladies?" I ask.

"Tea."

"Coffee."

Mrs. Vogel and Mrs. Roblin settle into the cozy sitting area, and I excuse myself to the kitchenette.

Emerging a few minutes later, Connie and the knitters are discussing the community's enthusiastic reaction to the new charity knitting project.

I set the tray of coffee, tea, and shortbread biscuits topped with lemon curd and raspberries on the coffee table.

"Thank you, Megan," the ladies say, pausing their knitting to claim their beverages and plate a few biscuits.

"We heard Eric arrested Fawkes's sister yesterday," Mrs. Vogel says.

"Did she murder her brother?" Mrs. Roblin asks.

"Is she in solitary confinement at the Harmony Lake Police Station?" asks Mrs. Vogel.

"Eric hasn't laid charges in Fawkes's murder yet, but he's confident that he'll press charges soon," I reply to

Mrs. Roblin, then look at Mrs. Vogel. "He released Fawkes's sister last night, and I'm not sure the HLPD has solitary confinement."

"I have faith that an arrest is imminent," Mrs. Vogel declares with such certainty that I wonder if she knows something I don't.

"Ladies," I say, "I appreciate your help and support, but you don't need to sit at Knitorious all day, every day."

"We don't mind." Mrs. Roblin smiles, dunking her shortbread biscuit into her tea.

"You never know when our unique skill set might come in handy," Mrs. Vogel says.

"Unless your unique skill set includes finding PEX pipe, you might get bored," I say with a sigh, remembering my promise to swing by the hardware store today so Eric can fix the washing machine.

"How could we ever get bored?" Mrs. Roblin asks. "We have our knitting and an unlimited supply of refreshments."

"Besides," Mrs. Vogel adds, "Knitorious is where the action is!"

"It's like watching a mystery show or Agatha Christie novel in real life." Mrs. Roblin sips her tea with raised eyebrows.

"If you can't beat them, my dear, join them," Connie adds, sinking into the sofa next to Mrs. Vogel and picking up the lap blanket she's knitting for the charity project.

I follow Connie's lead, join the ladies in the cozy seating area, and make some progress on my almost-finished lion. Connie and I take turns greeting and serving customers.

"How many brothers does she have?" Mrs. Vogel asks after I cash out a customer who bought almost every skein of red and green Aran weight yarn in the store.

"Three," I reply, making a note in my planner to order more Christmas-coloured yarn. "She's making them matching Christmas sweaters for a family portrait."

"Where's Karla today?" Mrs. Roblin asks.

"At work," I reply, pretending not to notice as Mrs. Vogel slips Sophie another dog treat under the coffee table. "She's tying up loose ends before she moves."

My phone dings.

"Here she is," I say when a message from Karla appears on the screen.

*Karla: Chelle is coming to pick up some items she left. Do you want to join us? This might be our last chance to wring the truth out of her.*

As I contemplate Karla's text, another text appears.

*Karla: Metaphorically, of course. I'm not suggesting we literally wring her.*

My phone vibrates in my hand. Another text from Karla.

*Karla: But I'm not against the idea, especially her neck.* Followed by a winky-face emoji.

I laugh out loud at her blunt humour.

I want to be there and hear what Chelle has to say, but I'd planned to spend my lunch break in the plumbing section of the local hardware store.

*Me: When?*

*Karla: One hour.*

I let out a long sigh, torn between optimism that Chelle might provide the clue we need to solve Fawkes's murder and frustrated by the more likely outcome that she will spin another yarn of lies to protect the killer.

"What's wrong, my dear?" Connie asks. "You're making your on-the-fence face."

"I have an on-the-fence face?" I ask, wondering if she also knows about the small, tight-lipped smile when I tell a fib.

According to Connie, Mrs. Roblin, and Mrs. Vogel, I have a distinct on-the-fence face, which is news to me.

I read Karla's text out loud, and they encourage me to go.

"You must go," Mrs. Vogel insists.

"I agree, my dear," Connie adds.

"We'll take care of Knitorious and Sophie," Mrs. Roblin offers. "We promise to do whatever Connie says, and we'll see that Sophie gets to the park at lunchtime."

"Thank you," I say, typing a reply to Karla's text.

*Me: I'll be there!*

# CHAPTER 25

THE LOCKSMITH'S van is leaving just as I arrive.

Instead of driving away like I expect, the van backs out of Karla's driveway, stays in reverse, and backs into Rita's driveway across the street.

"I don't trust her," Karla says in response to my obvious but unspoken confusion about the locksmith. "I'm having the locks changed on my house and Rita's. Even if Chelle returns our house keys, I don't trust her. She could have made copies."

Karla places a cardboard box on the hood of her car.

It's bigger than a shoe box but smaller than a moving box. The ease with which Karla handles the thing implies it's almost empty or the contents are light.

"What's this?" I ask, pointing my car key at the box.

"Chelle's stuff," Karla replies, then holds up each item. "Phone charger, insulated travel mug, hair scrunchie, ceramic mug, sweatshirt."

"Did Chelle contact you to pick up her stuff, or did you reach out to her?"

"She contacted me," Karla replies. "I couldn't care less about her junk. I would've added it to my donation pile."

I peer inside the box, and the ceramic mug catches my eye. "Who's kid?" I ask, holding up the white ceramic mug with a photo of a toothless, grinning young boy posing with a fish he had just caught.

"Her godson," Karla replies. "Chelle's best friend's son. She hasn't seen the boy since her bestie's family emigrated overseas. He's fifteen now."

I return the mug to the box.

"Everything in here is inexpensive and replaceable," I comment.

"So?"

"So, isn't it strange that picking up this random assortment of everyday items is Chelle's biggest priority after she spent yesterday, and most of last night, being questioned by the police for her brother's murder?"

"It didn't occur to me," Karla admits, re-examining the contents of the box. "Do you think she's eager to get it because there's a clue in here?"

"Or she has another reason, and her stuff is just an excuse," I suggest. "Maybe we should photograph everything in the box, just in case."

"Good idea," Karla says, already sliding her phone from behind the wide belt of her black, belted mini skirt.

Chelle arrives, parking on the street outside Karla's house and blocking the driveway.

Before she gets out of the car, Karla marches the box to the halfway point between Chelle's car and where I stand, drops the box on the lawn, and backs away until she's standing next to me. She crosses her arms in front of her chest, shifts her weight to one foot so her opposite hip juts out, and glares at Chelle walking toward the box.

Chelle squats to examine the contents. The direct sun makes her orange topknot appear brassy and faded. She removes the insulated travel mug from the box and places it on the grass. Then she picks up the box and backs away.

"That's not my mug," Chelle shouts across the lawn to Karla. "Mine is in my car." She jerks her head toward her car.

"We have identical mugs," Karla reveals, uncrossing her arms. "Rita gave them to us."

Karla approaches the mug and picks it up. When she turns and starts walking toward me, she blinks and flinches as though the mug sent an electric shock through her. She pauses, fidgeting with the nondescript drinking vessel as clarity sweeps across her face. She shakes her head, composes herself and resumes walking.

"You have some nerve, lady!" Rita shouts, crossing the street with Gucci in tow. "How dare you show your face again after what you did!"

I smile and wave to the cluster of neighbours gathering on the sidewalk across the street, to watch the latest dramatic installment.

They look to each other for guidance on how to react. A few of them nod, smiling weakly and returning a discreet wave.

I recognize many of the faces from yesterday's confrontation and arrest. At least they'll get closure.

"Why did you lie to the police about knowing Karla?" Rita demands, stretching to her full height and yelling as close to Chelle's face as her less-than-five-feet stature will allow. "Why would you implicate Karla as a suspect in your brother's murder when she didn't even know him?"

Rita tugs Gucci's black and white, houndstooth, bowtie collar and leash to stop him from greeting the enemy.

"Rita, I did everything in my power to keep Karla out of this," Chelle lies.

"Bull—!"

Taken aback by Karla's profane blurt, the sidewalk neighbours expel a collective gasp.

Gucci makes another attempt to get Chelle's attention by whimpering and pawing in her direction. Rita picks up the dog and holds him over her shoulder like a baby, so he can't see the object of his attention.

Gucci spots Karla and me. I wave. He doesn't wave back but pants a little harder, which is close enough.

"You've had plenty of opportunities to tell the truth, Chelle," I say. "Instead, you doubled down and told more lies. Ridiculous lies."

Chelle turns to me and shakes her head. "How would you know? Were you hiding in the interrogation room?" Her sarcastic, annoyed tone and her eyes squinting into the harsh daylight give her a menacing impression.

"Obviously, I wasn't in the interrogation room," I say, rolling my eyes behind my sunglasses.

"The police told me your lies," Karla fibs. "How else could they verify the nonsense you spewed?"

"Can you speak up?" shouts a bystander from across the street.

Are they serious? Would they like us to use a bullhorn for their listening convenience?

"We missed whatever happened after the redhead accused the woman with curly hair of hiding in the interrogation room," shouts another.

The four of us glare at the growing group of onlookers.

"I thought nosy neighbours were a small-town phenomenon," I mutter.

"The suburbs are almost as bad," Karla mumbles in response.

"Sometimes the suburbs are worse," Rita adds, passing Gucci to Karla.

"I'm sorry," Chelle says in a conversational tone that

the nosy neighbours would need a lip reader to interpret. "After everything that led to Clarence going to prison, I'm terrified of the police. I was desperate to deflect their attention away from me. Karla was the easiest target." She looks at Karla. "I knew the police could never pin my brother's murder on you, Karla. I knew they would never charge you."

"How?" I ask.

"Excuse me?" Chelle asks.

"How do you know the police couldn't pin your brother's murder on Karla?" I ask.

Chelle shrugs. "Because she didn't do it."

"You could only be certain who *didn't* do it if you know who *did*," Karla clarifies.

Chelle shifts her weight and adjusts her grip on the box.

"I don't know who killed my brother, and I don't care. I believe it was karma, to be honest," she says.

Rita scoffs. "You wouldn't know honesty if it smacked you and said, *Hi, there! I'm honesty!*"

Chelle ignores Rita's rebuke.

"Your parents must want to know who murdered their son," I say.

"My parents understand Clarence had a lot of enemies," Chelle explains. "They're devastated by his murder but accept it was a consequence of his actions."

"I don't buy it," Karla turns her head and mumbles in my ear.

"Me neither," I whisper in reply, unable to fathom a reality where I could rest without finding the person or people who harmed my child.

"I'm sorry," Chelle says, her eyes darting between Karla and Rita. "I wish I could make it up to you."

"You can make it up to us by telling the truth," Rita offers.

"Do you even know the truth anymore?" Karla's tone is sarcastic and defeated.

"I left my cell phone at your house by accident, not to give myself an alibi. That part is true," Chelle explains. "The morning Clarence died, I visited The Fawkes Den. Twice. When I arrived the first time, my brother was already dead."

The sidewalk neighbours, unable to hear since we stopped shouting, whisper amongst themselves. No doubt speculating about what Chelle could have said that left the rest of us guffawed.

"But Fawkes died at the community centre," Karla reminds Chelle. "His killer drowned him in the pool." Karla looks me in the eye. "Right?"

I shrug.

"Do you mind?" Rita shouts at the sidewalk neighbours when their murmurs grow loud enough to distract us. "We can't hear ourselves think!"

"Sorry, Rita," shouts a random neighbour.

"He died at the cottage, or at least, I thought he did," Chelle replies. "He was in the bathtub. Well, part of him was. The tub was full of water. It looked like Clarence had run a bath. Water had spilled all over the bathroom floor. He was wearing his robe and slippers and kneeling next to the tub. His face and shoulders were submerged. His hair was floating on the surface."

Chelle knows about the holdback! Whether her latest retelling of the morning her brother died is true or not, she mentioned the holdback, which means she was there or spoke to someone who was.

"Did you confirm he was dead?" I ask.

"No," Chelle replies. "I was too spooked. But I knew he was dead. The cottage was too still. Too quiet. Void of life. It didn't occur to me someone murdered him. I assumed it was an accident. I was about to call the police, and that's when I remembered my phone was at Karla's house. I went to use the landline, but the phone wasn't where it belonged. Nothing was where it belonged. I was searching for the phone when I saw Karla's things and stopped myself.

"The décor at the cottage is outdated and shabby. Karla's belongings stood out like a sore thumb. I knew if the police saw them, they would ask questions and maybe arrest me for theft. I didn't have room in my car to remove all of Karla's belongings in one trip. Also, Clarence's weekly groceries were in my trunk. So, I took as many of Karla's items as I could and drove home to empty my car."

"There's more?" Karla asks. "You stole more than just my bookend, Hermés belt, and Fendis?"

Chelle nods.

"Did you empty your car and drive back to The Fawkes Den?" I ask, hoping this version of events is true, and she'll divulge enough information to verify it.

"Yes," Chelle replies. "I'd planned to move the remainder of Karla's things to my place. Then, I would have driven back to the cottage and pretended I had just arrived and found my brother's dead body."

"Your plan must have fallen apart," Karla comments. "Otherwise, the police wouldn't have found my bookend inside The Fawkes Den."

"When I arrived the second time, the cottage door was ajar," Chelle explains. "I was certain I had closed it when I'd left. The place looked like someone shook it like a snow globe. I stepped over the mess to check on Clarence. He was gone. First, I panicked. Then, I assumed he must not have been dead. I convinced myself he either had some sort of violent episode and ran away, or someone broke in and scared him, and he was hiding nearby."

"The first time you left, did you lock the door?" I ask.

"No, I'm certain I closed it, but I don't remember locking it." Chelle shrugs. "Force of habit. My brother always locked the door behind me when I left. He kept the doors and windows locked and the blinds closed. He was terrified for his safety."

Was Fawkes terrified for his safety because he was hated in general, or was he afraid of a specific threat or person?

If Chelle is telling the truth—a huge assumption at this point—about Fawkes always keeping the cottage locked, that means either his killer had a key, or Fawkes let them in. If he was terrified for his safety, he would only open the door for someone he knew or someone he was expecting.

"Did your brother have a planner or calendar?" Karla asks. "Maybe he was expecting a visitor or a delivery and wrote it in his calendar."

"My brother didn't have any friends to visit him," Chelle reminds us. "I'm the only person he trusted enough to let inside or bring him anything."

This lines up with Mel's story about Trevor hiding in the bushes, waiting for Fawkes to answer the door for the pizza delivery guy. She said Fawkes didn't open the door until ten minutes after the pizza guy left. Fawkes must've waited to make sure the coast was clear.

"Did your brother order pizza a couple of weeks ago?" I ask.

"No," Chelle replies. "But I remember a pizza box in his garbage. I asked him about it, and he said the restaurant must have delivered it to the wrong cottage. He said he left it outside in case the delivery guy came back for it, but no one came, so he ate it. He said it was pepperoni with double cheese."

"So, you assumed Fawkes was alive and either ran away or hid?" I ask. "Did you search for him?"

Why didn't it occur to Chelle that whoever ransacked the cottage also took her brother?

"I searched the outside but didn't find him. I didn't want to go inside the cottage again in case whoever looted the place was still there. I drove to Karla's house to get my phone. Rita was outside weeding her garden. The roofers were just getting started, and I stopped to talk to them."

"I remember," Rita confirms. "You said you were busier than a moth in a sweater closet."

"Right," Chelle acknowledges. "Rita and I had a nice natter, then I retrieved my cell phone. Next thing I knew, it rang and Clarence's parole officer informed me that Clarence died in a public pool."

"That must have confused you," Karla comments.

"It sure did."

"I understand why you were afraid to go inside and use the landline," I interject. "But why didn't you drive to a nearby cottage, or stop a passing motorist, or ask *anyone* to call nine-one-one? Why did you drive all the way to Karla's house, then stop and chat with Rita? Weren't you in a hurry to report what had happened?"

"I guess I was in shock." Chelle shrugs. "Part of me hoped Clarence would show up and explain everything. I dreaded the police and media attention that would follow if I reported it."

"If everything you just told us is the truth, thank you," Rita says to Chelle.

"You're welcome, Rita," Chelle responds. "I'm sorry you got dragged into this."

"*Ahem*," an unfamiliar man clears his throat.

The locksmith stands nearby, waiting for Karla or Rita to notice him.

We apologize for ignoring him, and he insists he didn't mind because Chelle's story gripped him, and he wanted to hear the end. He gives Rita the new key to her house and gives Karla an invoice for both jobs.

While Karla pays the locksmith, Chelle returns to her car and places her box of belongings in the back seat. She settles in the driver's seat and buckles her seatbelt. She pulls away from the curb, disappearing down the street with the sidewalk neighbours waving her off.

We've been standing in the midday sun for quite a while, and Rita is hot and tired. She assumes Gucci is also hot and tired and takes him across the street to her house for a fresh bowl of cold water and an air-conditioned nap. She offers to bring Karla and me lemon iced tea and homemade brownies.

We politely decline.

The locksmith leaves, the sidewalk neighbours disperse, and Karla invites me inside for a cold drink.

"Do you believe Chelle's story?" I ask.

"I don't know," Karla says. "Lying is innate for her. She lies as easily as she tells the truth."

"Who ransacked the cottage?" I ask. "And why? What were they looking for?"

"If Fawkes was dead the first time Chelle went to the cottage, why didn't the killer move his body right after they killed him?" Karla asks. "Why did the killer leave then return?"

"Why did the killer move Fawkes's body at all?" I add. "Why not leave him in the bathtub?"

"Maybe something or someone spooked the killer before they could move the body," Karla suggests.

"If Chelle spooked the killer when she arrived, they didn't have a car. She would have seen it."

"That would mean they either left by boat, swam, or hid nearby until Chelle left," Karla deduces. "If that's what happened, Chelle is lucky. If she had encountered the killer, they might have killed her too."

"Maybe the killer went to get help before Chelle got there because they couldn't move Fawkes alone."

"Maybe someone else showed up between Chelle's first and second visit, tossed the place, and moved Fawkes's body," Karla proposes.

"It makes little sense to move a dead body unless you killed it," I counter. "It would only make sense if you wanted to keep the police away from the cottage."

"The killer was searching for something and didn't find it," Karla speculates. "They moved the body to keep the authorities away so the police wouldn't find it either. Something inside The Fawkes Den points to the killer."

# CHAPTER 26

On the drive back to Harmony Lake, I call Eric and update him while the details of Chelle's latest version of events are fresh in my brain. Like me, he's floored that Chelle mentioned the holdback. He's also disappointed that Rita, Karla, a locksmith, and an assortment of sidewalk neighbours heard it too.

I pull into a parking spot outside Hammer Time and text Connie to make sure all is well at the store. She assures me they do not require my presence at Knitorious and encourages me to take all the time I need to finish my errand and indulge *my hobby*.

Hammer Time is Harmony Lake's local hardware store. It crossed my mind to stop at one of the big-box hardware stores in Harmony Hills since I was there anyway, but I try to support my fellow local small business owners whenever possible.

"Hi, Megan."

"Hi, Glenn." I smile. "How are you?"

Glenn Landry owns Hammer Time. His father established the business almost fifty years ago, and Glenn has been in charge since his dad retired.

We exchange pleasantries and make small talk.

"I can count on one hand the number of times you've been here," Glenn jokes. "And I've been to Knitorious even less."

"If I had any interest or home improvement skills, I'd be here all the time," I say.

"If I was crafty and could see colours, I'd be at Knitorious all the time."

"You're colour blind?" I ask. "I didn't know that."

Glenn explains he has achromatopsia. This means his eyes are sensitive to light, and he experiences our world in varying tones of grey.

"I'm the original *Fifty Shades of Grey* guy," he jokes, adjusting his tinted glasses.

"Is that why you wear tinted lenses indoors?" I ask.

"Yes!" Glen replies. "Tinted lenses indoors and very dark lenses outdoors."

"Fascinating," I say, which encourages Glenn to further educate me about his condition.

"Can I help you find something, or are you just browsing?" Glenn asks, after explaining the various forms of colour blindness.

"I need two metres of blue, half-inch PEX pipe."

He sucks in air through the corner of his mouth in a way that leads me to believe he might not be able to help me.

"Follow me," Glenn says, already several paces ahead of me.

I follow him up and down the plumbing aisles until we stop in front of a wall of red, blue, and white flexible piping. Far more options that I expected.

Each coiled pipe is secured with black nylon cable ties. The hoops are organized first by diameter, then length, then colour.

"Is ten feet all right?" Glenn asks. "I know you want

two metres, but we don't sell it in increments of less than ten feet."

Quick mental math helps me convert ten feet to three metres. Close enough.

Canada's official method of measurement is the metric system, but our unofficial method of measurement is a bizarre metric-imperial hybrid. Most people I know can reference and compare both methods of measurement interchangeably. Not me. I can compare metric to metric or imperial to imperial, but can't mix them without getting confused.

"I'm sure three metres will be fine."

Glenn runs his pointer finger up and down the wall, whispering, "one inch... three-quarter inch... two inch... three-eighths." He turns to me, shaking his head. "Sorry, Megan. We don't have any half-inch diameter in blue."

"What if I take a longer length?" I ask, scanning the price tags attached to the end of each display hook.

"Best I can do is end of the week."

"We'll need clean laundry before then."

"Most plumbing issues are urgent," Glenn sympathizes, nodding. "Sometimes electrical can wait, but not plumbing."

"Does the colour matter?" I shrug. "No one will see it after it's fixed, anyway."

Glenn laughs like I'm joking.

I'm not. I don't care what colour the pipes are. It's not like I plan to look at them.

He clears his throat and stops laughing when he realizes I'm serious.

"The colour matters," he explains. "Red pipes carry hot water and blue pipes carry cold water. You could get away with white for either hot or cold, but if Eric asked for blue pipe, he wants blue pipe."

"I'll take the white," I say. "If Eric wants blue pipe, we can paint it or wrap it in blue tape or something."

"PEX isn't very popular. We go months at a time without selling any, but you're the second customer in as many weeks to ask for that specific size and colour." Glenn comments, reaching for a hoop of the white pipe. "The other customer took white too. I've ordered more, but it takes weeks to arrive."

"Wait!" I say, spying a flash of blue mixed in a row of red. I slide a bunch of red coils off the display hook. "This one is misfiled." I slide a lone blue coil of flexible pipe off the hook and read the cardboard label: one-point-two-seven centimetres diameter, two metres long. "One-point-two-seven centimetres is half an inch, right?"

"It sure is," Glenn says. "Good eye."

"Thank you," I say. "It was mixed in with the red pipe."

"They all look the same to me." Glenn shrugs and walks toward the cash register.

While Glenn rings up my purchase, he asks if Eric is close to making an arrest for Fawkes's murder.

I reply with my standard response, "He's confident he will make an arrest soon."

As I push the door to leave, Mason Shilling pulls it from outside and holds it open.

"Hi, Mason."

"Hi, Megan," he says. "Are you doing some DIY?"

"Not me," I say. "We have a leaky laundry room." I hold up the bag. "Eric is planning to fix it tonight. Getting the pipe is my contribution to the DIY process."

"If we had run into each other a few minutes earlier, I could have saved you some money," Mason says. "I bought a hundred feet of the same pipe to fix the library leak."

"You needed one hundred feet of pipe to fix the leak at the library?"

My knowledge about plumbing might fit on the tip of a knitting needle with room to spare, but to my inexperienced ear, one hundred feet of pipe sounds like a lot.

"Glenn didn't have this diameter or length last Tuesday," Mason explains. "I had to drive to The Tool Box in Harmony Hills. The Tool Box is great, but they only sell in bulk, and one hundred feet was the shortest length they offered." Mason lets the door close with us standing on the sidewalk. "I only needed about a foot, so there's plenty left over. I could have given you some."

"That's a nice thought, but I've purchased it now," I say. "Keep the extra ninety-nine feet in case the library has another leak," I jest.

"I hope not," Mason replies. "It took way longer to clean up the mess than to fix the leak." Mason checks the time on his watch. "Can I come over later and fix your leak?"

"It's sweet of you to offer, but Eric likes to fix stuff," I say, trying to make out the faded prism and rainbow on Mason's vintage Pink Floyd t-shirt. "I already tried calling a plumber, but Eric shut it down."

"I'd like to fix it for you, Megan," he insists. "You've stored my mum's boxes in the dungeon for over two months. You make them accessible whenever I need something. Eric is busy working overtime because of the murder. Fixing your leak is the least I can do, and it's something I'm good at."

"How can I refuse?" I say, giving in. "This evening?"

"I'll text you with an exact time."

Grinning, Mason pulls the door open and disappears inside Hammer Time.

# CHAPTER 27

WHEN I GET BACK to Knitorious, there's an available parking spot in front of the store, so instead of driving around back, I opt for convenience and take it.

"How was your visit?" Mrs. Vogel asks.

"Informative," I say, smirking at them. "You were right, ladies." I pause, giving them a moment to enjoy their four favourite words. "Thank you for encouraging me to go."

Without mentioning the holdback, or most of the details of Chelle's latest story, I tell Connie, Mrs. Roblin, and Mrs. Vogel about our interaction with Chelle.

Connie is especially proud of Rita's up-close shouting at Chelle, which she'd already heard about firsthand because Rita phoned her as soon as she and Gucci hit the air conditioning.

The Charity Knitters are quite sympathetic toward their suburban counterparts, the sidewalk neighbours.

Connie and the Charity Knitters leave as soon as I turn the sign from OPEN to CLOSED. I hold the door for them on their way out and thank them for taking care of the store and Sophie in my absence. As the last lady crosses the threshold onto the sidewalk, Sophie releases a loud belch—a sign that she's had more than enough sneaky dog treats today.

I look at Mrs. Roblin.

"She drinks water much too fast," Mrs. Roblin observes. "Makes her gassy."

I look at Mrs. Vogel.

"Yes, I've also noticed Sophie's drinking problem," Mrs. Vogel adds.

"You must be right," I agree. "It can't be too many dog treats because I only give her two per day."

Mrs. Roblin and Mrs. Vogel nod and grunt sounds of agreement.

"Have a lovely evening, my dear!" Connie says, kissing my cheek.

"You too." I smile. "See you tomorrow."

I spend a few minutes sweeping the floors and turning on the dishwasher in the kitchenette before Sophie and I head home for dinner.

Sophie jumps onto the passenger-side floor, then the passenger seat.

I close the door, and she stands with her front paws perched on the armrest so she can look through the window.

With my hand on the driver's side door handle, I look both ways so I don't clothesline an oncoming cyclist or lose a car door to a passing motorist.

"Dorian Gray," I whisper to myself when I spot Trevor Howe's distinct, vintage, blue-on-silver Camaro parked a few stores away.

As I stare at Trevor's car, debating whether Sophie and I should procrastinate until the Howes return so we can run into them, someone taps my shoulder from behind, and I almost jump out of my skin.

"Sorry," Mel says, cracking her gum. "We didn't mean to scare you."

"We called your name, but you didn't hear us," Trevor adds.

"I was distracted," I say, pressing on my chest like it will help slow my heart rate. "It's been a long day." I smile.

Trevor is carrying a takeout bag from Thai-tanic, Harmony Lake's Thai and sushi restaurant.

"I recommend the Kao niew moo yang," I say, gesturing to the takeout bag.

"This is our second visit to Thai-tanic," Mel says. "Their food is incredible."

We discuss other local restaurants and agree that the variety and quality of our local cuisine makes Harmony Lake a food-lover's paradise.

"A friend of my mine likes your car," I say, nodding toward the Camaro.

"Oh, yeah?" Trevor gazes upon his vintage vehicle with pride and admiration. "I'd be happy to take your friend for a spin. It's always fun to meet a fellow car enthusiast."

"I'll let him know," I say. "He saw your car at a four-way stop on Tuesday morning. He had the right of way but waved you through so he could admire the Camaro as you drove past."

"Which four-way stop?" Trevor asks.

"The one at the foot of Temple Road," I say.

"Tuesday morning, you say?" Mel asks. "We didn't use the car on Tuesday. Your friend must be mistaken."

"My friend was certain about the date," I confirm. "He was also certain that Trevor was alone in the car. He noticed Trevor's hand tattoos when they exchanged waves."

"I was at that four-way stop the day before, on

Monday," Trevor says. "Mel was with me, but I don't remember anyone waving me through the intersection."

"I was on the floor." Mel nudges her husband's arm. "Remember? I lost an earring, and as you approached the stop sign, I unbuckled my seatbelt and bent over to search the floor and under my seat."

"The earring Eric found outside The Fawkes Den?" I ask.

"Do you think he'll give it back before we leave town?" she asks, touching each earring in her pierced ears and verifying their presence.

"I'm not sure," I reply. "You'd have to ask him. I can give you his number if you don't have it."

"You're awfully involved in this case for someone who claims she isn't a cop," Trevor says.

"I'm not a cop," I remind him. "But I have two reasons to be interested in Fawkes's murder investigation. I'm married to the lead investigator, and my friend was a suspect."

"Was?" Mel says, clinging to my use of the past tense. "Your friend who found my cell phone, Karla, is no longer a suspect?"

"That's right," I reply. "She's very relieved."

"How?" Trevor asks. "How did she prove she didn't kill Fawkes?"

"Karla was completely honest and cooperative. She told the police the truth. They verified her story and eliminated her."

I hope my oversimplified version of the truth will convince the Howes that honesty is the best way to get their names crossed off the suspect list.

Trevor opens his mouth to speak, but Mel touches his arm. He closes his mouth.

"Were you about to say something, Trevor?" I ask.

"Nothing," Mel replies on his behalf.

"OK." I smile and tug the door handle, cracking open the car door. "Well, I'll let you get back to the cottage before your food gets cold." I open the door. "Enjoy your dinner and that beautiful view of the sunset from your lounger."

"Mel…" Trevor moans under his breath.

"Not now," she ventriloquizes behind her toothy smile. "We'll discuss it later."

"No," Trevor says. "Enough. Let's tell the truth and get on with our lives."

"What truth?" I ask, glaring at Trevor.

"This is a bad idea," Mel utters, shaking her head. "We should just stick with the story."

"The story makes us look like liars. Lying makes us look guilty," Trevor says with a sense of finality.

"Whatever," Mel mumbles.

"Fine," Trevor declares. "We dropped off the letter on Tuesday morning. We lied because we knew that if we admitted to being at The Fawkes Den the morning Fawkes died, they would suspect us in his murder."

"What happened to the letter?" I ask. "Did you close it in the screen door, or did you give it to Fawkes and confront him?"

"We left it," Mel replies. "Fawkes didn't answer the door. I wedged it in the screen door, like I said."

"Did you hear anything from inside the cottage?" I ask. "A television, radio, footsteps?"

"Are you asking if we heard any signs of life?" Mel clarifies.

I nod.

She shakes her head. "I heard nothing, and Trevor was several feet behind me, so he wouldn't have heard anything either. Do you think Fawkes's killer had already taken him to the community centre? Was he already dead when I knocked on his door?"

"I don't think so," I reply. "They found your letter inside the cottage. Someone found it and took it inside."

"A cop could have found the letter. The place was crawling with cops after Fawkes died."

"You should ask Eric about the letter," I say, not wanting to reveal details that Eric might want kept quiet.

The police found the letter ripped-up in the trash. Aside from Fawkes, who else would rip up Mel's victim impact statement? Assuming Chelle told the truth about not finding the letter when she arrived at The Fawkes Den, Fawkes must have retrieved it, read it, then ripped it up and tossed the pieces before his killer drowned him in the bathtub. This means the killer was at The Fawkes Den after the Howes and before Chelle's first visit. The killer then returned to The Fawkes Den between Chelle's first and second visit that morning. Eric must have arrived for his weekly check-in after the killer left with Fawkes's corpse and before the entire town discovered his body floating in the pool.

With all the comings and goings at The Fawkes Den that morning, it's a miracle none of the visitors encountered each other.

"If we had killed the perverted creep, we wouldn't have used our car and left a handwritten note behind," Trevor reasons. "My car doesn't blend in. People notice it. The letter would implicate my wife. It's covered in her fingerprints and handwriting. I wouldn't have left anything that implicated Mel."

"We didn't kill Fawkes," Mel says. "I would never give up my freedom for him." She shakes her head. "I wouldn't give up anything for him. I wouldn't have spat on him if he was on fire."

"Mel doesn't have the physical strength to kill someone," Trevor argues. "How could she get him to the community centre and hold him underwater? If either of

us is a suspect, it should be me! I'm strong enough."
Trevor pounds on his chest with his closed hand. "But I
didn't do it, either. If I had killed Fawkes, I would have
made sure Mel was safe from suspicion. I would have
made sure she had a solid alibi, far away from here. I
would've either swum or rowed to Fawkes's cottage in
the middle of the night, killed him, and left him there to
rot."

"You've put a lot of thought into how you would kill
Fawkes," I comment.

"It's not premeditation if that's what you think," Mel
asserts, jumping to her husband's defence. "My
husband didn't kill Fawkes. He knows he would spend
the rest of his life in prison, and he would never
leave me."

"Yet he went to prison before," I accuse, then look at
Trevor. "Didn't you, Trevor? You punched a cop and
negotiated a plea deal to serve time in the same facility
that housed Fawkes. Were you trying to get close enough
to Fawkes to kill him?"

"That's not true," Trevor denies, sneering and shaking
his head. "It was a coincidence."

"Like how it was a coincidence that you rented the
closest possible cottage to The Fawkes Den?" I shake my
head. "You two have had more than your fair share of
coincidences."

"I'm sure I'm not the only person who wanted five
minutes alone with Fawkes," Trevor says, making an
indirect admission.

"But you're the only one who committed a crime to
get close to him."

"I realized it was a dumb plan when I got there,"
Trevor explains. "Prisons have cameras everywhere. They
keep everything locked. Inmates can't roam around the
place looking for someone. Real prison isn't like TV

prison. Each section is a self-contained smaller prison. I couldn't get near Fawkes."

"My husband didn't research his idea before he put it into action," Mel explains. "If he had told me what he was planning, I would have talked him out of it."

"I learned my lesson," Trevor adds. "Mel was furious when she found out. In hindsight, I'm glad it didn't work. It would have re-traumatized Mel, and we would have been apart for the rest of our lives. That's the last thing I wanted. It was an impulsive, desperate attempt to stop Fawkes from being released. The media had just broken the news that a judge would hear Fawkes's appeal. They said if the judge overturned the verdict on a technicality, they could release Fawkes pending the appeal. Mel was a mess. The thought of Fawkes being free terrified her. I wanted to spare her from that."

Was Trevor desperate enough to murder Fawkes?

If, as they claim, the proximity of their rental cottage to The Fawkes Den was a coincidence, it must have horrified them to realize who their neighbour was. Trevor's decision to kill Fawkes, and eliminate his wife's biggest fear, could have been another spur-of-the-moment, poorly planned decision he hasn't admitted to Mel.

# CHAPTER 28

STARING at the murder board over the fireplace, the crime scene photo with Karla's missing bookend distracts me. Why do I keep coming back to it? It's a small section of the overall photo. I should look at the entire picture again.

My phone dings, bringing me back to the here and now.

*Karla: Can I come over?*

*Me: Sure! Do you want to stay for dinner? We can order something.*

*Karla: Yes! You open a bottle of wine, and I'll bring pizza and evidence.*

Evidence? What evidence could Karla have? Has she found something that disproves one of Chelle's many lies?

*Me: Evidence? Should Eric be here?*

*Karla: I already texted him. He'll be there soon.*

When Karla arrives with pizza, Mason has sequestered himself in the laundry room to fix the leak.

Karla squats to greet Sophie, and I point to the laundry room with one hand and press my index finger to my lips with the other. Karla nods, acknowledging that we aren't alone and shouldn't say anything we wouldn't want to share with everyone in town.

We eat pizza, sip wine, and discuss the length of Karla's to-do list before she moves.

"The leak is fixed," Mason declares as he appears in the doorway.

"Wow! That was fast," I comment. "Thank you so much, Mason."

"No problem, Megan," he says, smiling and shaking his head. "I'm glad I could help."

"Hello, Mason," Karla says. "It's lovely to see you again." She smiles. "I still can't figure out why you're so familiar, but I'm working on it."

"I hope you figure it out. I'd love to know where we met." His awkward chuckle turns into clearing his throat. "I can't believe I could ever forget meeting you."

Is Mason flirting? His awkwardness is kind of charming.

"Would you like a slice of pizza, Mason?" I ask, gesturing to the pizza boxes.

"No, thank you," he replies. "I should get going."

"I ran into Trevor, the man who owns the vintage Camaro you admired last week," I say, as Sophie and I accompany Mason to the door. "He offered to take you for a ride if you're interested."

"Can I let you know tomorrow?" Mason asks. "Work is busy right now. I'm not sure when I'll have time."

"Sure," I say.

"How do you know Trevor?" Mason asks.

"He and his wife, Mel, are renting a local cottage for a

few weeks," I reply. "Mel is a crocheter. They visited Knitorious last week."

"*Ooof!*" Mason grunts when the front door bumps him in the back.

"Sorry, Mason," Eric says, slipping in through the ajar door. "I didn't know you were there."

"It's OK, Eric," Mason says. "I'm not hurt, just surprised."

I thank Mason again for fixing the leak and wish him a good night.

He leaves, and Eric closes the door behind him.

"Show us the evidence," I say, not giving Eric and Karla a chance to say hello.

"Watch this." Karla unlocks her phone, touches the screen a few times, and hands it to me. "Press play."

It's video footage of Karla making a purchase in a coffee shop. The camera is behind the cashier and shows a front view of Karla's face.

Karla pays, and the cashier disappears, leaving her alone at the counter. She's wearing the same form-fitted, Crispin-green dress she wore when we went to the pub for lunch. The back of the cashier's head reappears moments later, and she slides a travel mug across the counter. Karla picks up the travel mug and gestures with it as she says, "Thank you" to the cashier.

The video has no sound, but I can read Karla's lips, and I'm familiar with the smile of gratitude when someone hands over a much-needed dose of caffeine.

I rewind the video to the part where the cashier slides the travel mug across the counter.

"Is that the travel mug Rita gave you?" I ask Karla. "The one Chelle left on the lawn?"

"The timestamp," Eric says, pointing over my shoulder to the timestamp in the bottom right corner of the screen. He looks at Karla. "You couldn't have killed Fawkes."

He's right. I was so focussed on the details of the actual video, that I didn't notice the timestamp. Tuesday, August 30th, 10:11 a.m.

Karla explains that when she picked up the mug off the lawn this morning, she remembered purchasing coffee on her way to Harmony Lake the morning Fawkes died. This coffee shop offers a discount to customers who bring their own mugs. After everyone left, Karla searched her wallet for the receipt but couldn't find it.

"I went to the coffee shop and explained my situation," Karla says.

"You told the coffee shop manager you were a murder suspect and needed the receipt to prove your alibi?" I ask.

"Yes," she replies. "She was very sympathetic. Not only did she reprint my receipt, but she sent me the time-stamped video of my visit. She offered to send it to the police, so I gave her Eric's email address."

We look at Eric.

He pulls out his phone and scrolls through his inbox.

"It's here," he says. "I haven't opened it yet. I saw the coffee shop name in the email address and assumed it was spam."

"Here's a copy of the receipt for my purchase."

I examine the receipt. The timestamp on the bottom of the receipt matches the timestamp on the video.

"She remembered me as soon as I reminded her what I'd ordered." Karla grins.

No wonder they remembered Karla's order. High maintenance people are never easy to forget. How many people order a caramel macchiato, medium, skim, extra shot, extra-hot, extra-whip, sugar-free? I pass the receipt to Eric.

"Based on the time of your coffee purchase, the time April says you arrived at Artsy Tartsy, and the proximity of the coffee shop to Harmony Lake, there's no way you could have killed Fawkes," Eric concludes.

Karla makes a mic-drop motion with her hand. "I'd need a time machine or superpowers."

Her phone rings.

"It's one of my biggest clients," she says. "I need to take this. Do you mind if I step outside?"

Sophie doesn't mind. As soon as Karla asks, she races to the backdoor and waits for Karla to open it.

"Of course," I say. "It looks like Sophie wants to go with you."

Eric picks up a slice of pizza and folds it in half lengthwise before taking a bite. "I hate to eat and run." He grabs a second slice of pizza and stands up. "I have to get back to work. Chelle and her lawyer are coming to discuss the latest version of her story and her two visits to The Fawkes Den the morning her brother died."

"I bumped into the Howes on my way home," I say.

"You have a knack for bumping into people." He grins. "It's one of your best qualities."

"It's a blessing and a curse," I admit, joking. "They came clean about visiting The Fawkes Den the morning of the murder too."

"I'm starting to think the list of people who *weren't* at The Fawkes Den that morning would be shorter than the list of people who *were*." He sighs.

"They still insist Mel left the letter wedged in the screen door," I continue. "It doesn't make sense for the Howes to leave the letter behind if they killed him. Trevor swore he would never allow Mel to be implicated like that, and I believe him."

"Maybe this is what they want us to believe." Eric bites into his second slice of pizza while I try to unravel the riddle of his last sentence.

"I don't understand," I say.

"Because the letter is at the crime scene, it's evidence," he says.

"I understand that part," I say. "I don't understand how leaving it behind would help their defence."

"The letter would be evidence for both sides," he explains. "The prosecution could submit it as evidence that the Howes were at The Fawkes Den and killed Fawkes. The defence could submit it as evidence of the abuse Fawkes inflicted on Melody. It could make the Howes sympathetic to jurors and could help justify their actions."

"I hadn't thought of that," I admit. "One more thing before you go. Can you please send me the crime scene photo with Karla's bookend? The wide-angle photo that shows the mess at The Fawkes Den?"

"Sure, babe." He grips the remaining pizza slice between his teeth while he texts the photo to me.

"Thank you," I say when my phone dings with his text. "Good luck with Chelle."

He stoops to kiss me goodbye.

Soon after Eric leaves, Karla and Sophie come inside from the backyard.

"I'll be right back," I say, rushing to the printer in our home office.

I return with two copies of the crime scene photo Eric sent me and hand one to Karla.

"This would be an impossible jigsaw puzzle," she comments, squinting at the photo. "Rita would love it."

"This is the photo where I spotted your bookend."

Karla scans the photo.

I hand her a light-up magnifying glass from my knitting basket.

"I see it," she says, hovering the magnifying glass over her bookend.

"What's wrong with this picture?" I ask.

"I don't know," Karla replies, confused. "What's wrong with it?"

"I'm asking you," I clarify. "Something isn't right, but I can't put my finger on it. Is there something that doesn't belong, or is something missing? When I look at this photo, I get a knot in my stomach."

While Karla obsesses over the crime scene photo, I tidy up the pizza boxes and dishes.

"There's almost an entire pizza left. I'll package it up for you to take home."

"I don't want it," she says. "You and Eric keep it—" *Gasp!*

"What is it?" I ask, bounding in from the kitchen.

"I think I found something," Karla says, positioning the photo on the coffee table and handing me the magnifying glass.

"Where?" I ask, searching the photo.

"Aside from so much of my stuff being scattered throughout this mess, look at this." She points to a specific spot.

I search the area with the magnifying glass. When I see it, I let out a similar gasp to Karla's.

"A blue floral notebook."

"Where have you seen that notebook before?"

"Mason had one just like it," I say. "The morning Fawkes died, he went down to the dungeon to find something in his mum's boxes. When Adam raced in searching for him, Mason ran up the stairs and out of the store so fast, I don't think he realized he was still carrying the notebook."

REAGAN DAVIS

"He had another one on Sunday, remember?" Karla reminds me. "He went down to the dungeon and when he came upstairs, he saw Trevor's photo and told us about seeing the Camaro the morning Fawkes died."

"Mason was carrying a blue floral notebook," I recall. "Is it yours?"

"No, it's not mine," Karla responds with a small huff.

"I have to ask," I say. "Your stolen property is all over the photo."

"Well, it's not mine," she reiterates. "If Chelle planted it there, she didn't get it from me."

Until now, it never occurred to me that Chelle could have planted other stolen items at The Fawkes Den. She cleans and runs errands for multiple families. For all I know, Chelle has been stashing stolen property at The Fawkes Den for years.

"What are the odds the notebook belonged to Fawkes?" I ask.

"That would be quite a coincidence," Karla replies. "It's a unique notebook. This is the second time in my life that I've seen one. The first time was Mason's."

"How would you feel about snooping through a deceased person's possessions?"

"Would we even be snooping? The boxes are in your basement. It wouldn't be snooping if it's *your* basement," Karla justifies.

"Yes, it would," I argue. "It might be my basement, but it's not my stuff."

"It wouldn't be snooping if we heard a sound and went downstairs to check it out."

"If a box had fallen over and the contents spilled, we would have to clean it up," I add.

"Of course, we would," Karla agrees. "And we wouldn't be able to help but see the contents when

686

picking up the mess. We would be helping, not snooping."

"I think I heard a funny sound in the basement at Knitorious," I say from the comfort of my family room, ten minutes away.

"Let's go."

# CHAPTER 29

"Hello?"

"Hey, babe! Are you in the car?"

"Yes," I reply.

"Hi, Eric," Karla says from beside me.

"Hi, Karla," he responds. "Where are you going?"

"We're following a hunch," I reply.

"A hunch I should know about?"

"It might be nothing. I'll tell you if it turns into something," I assure him. "How was your meeting with Chelle and her lawyer?"

"I stepped out so they could speak in private," Eric says. "Adam wants to see me. He says it's urgent. We're getting together after my meeting with Chelle. I'll be later than usual."

"What does Adam want?" I ask.

"I'm not sure, but I don't think he wants to watch the Jays game and have a beer. He said he was contacting me in an official capacity."

"Official capacity as mayor or as a lawyer?"

"I don't know yet."

He reminds Karla and me to be careful following our

hunch, and I remind him not to work too hard.

"You and Eric have a genuine connection," Karla comments after we end the call. "That's rare."

"Less rare than risky," I say. "You have to risk being vulnerable to connect with people."

"Some risks aren't worth taking."

Using the broad beam setting on the flashlight, Karla and I find our way down the steep concrete stairs.

At the bottom, Karla changes the flashlight setting from broad to focussed, and trains it on the piles of boxes against the far wall.

Shoulder to shoulder, we creep through the dank darkness.

"*Aaah!*" I scream, flailing my arms like I'm being attacked.

"What?!" Karla aims the focussed beam of light at my face, blinding me and making me flail harder. "It's a string," she says, grabbing hold of the swaying cord.

"It feels like a giant spider web," I pant, catching my breath and reining in my fear. "It's the string for the light bulb." I'm too embarrassed to admit that I have the same fake-spiderweb experience every time I come down here.

Karla follows the string to the single bulb in the ceiling. She tugs the cord and the bulb wiggles and shakes. There's a click but no light.

"Don't," I advise as she's about to tug the string again. "The bulb is burnt. I keep forgetting to replace it. One of these days, a gentle tug will make it crash to the ground. It's not the most stable light fixture."

She nods and releases the string.

"You weren't exaggerating when you called it a dungeon," Karla observes, panning the flashlight around the basement. "This is the spookiest basement I've ever seen."

We take turns, one of us holding the flashlight while the other opens a box and rummages through it. The first few boxes are household items and knickknacks. Next, we come across a box of generations-old Christmas tree ornaments and decorations. We place each box aside as we open it, careful to ensure they stay in the same order we found them.

"Bingo," Karla says, after she lifts the lid off a banker's box.

I aim the flashlight at the box of blue floral notebooks.

"That's them," I confirm. "Same as the notebook in the crime scene photo, and the notebooks we've seen with Mason."

"Wait." Karla grabs my hand as I reach into the box. "They might be in alphabetical or chronological order or something," she says. "Let's be careful. We don't want Mason to know we snooped."

"Good thinking," I agree. "Mason said his mum arranged her stuff before she passed to make it easier for Mason and Adam to execute her estate."

With a little digging, we determine this entire stack of boxes is blue floral notebooks.

"These are her journals," Karla says. "They're in chronological order, but there are a few time gaps. The earliest ones predate Mason, and the most recent ones are from last year."

"Are we nosing through someone's innermost thoughts and feelings?" I ask with pangs of guilt and regret.

"Kind of," she replies. "There are occasional deep-thought entries, but it's mostly dated pages with to-do lists, appointments, notes about Mason's accomplish-ments, phone messages, notes about her job." Karla looks at me. "These were multi-purpose. It looks like she used them to record of the details of her life."

"And she kept them," I point out. "They're an archive of her day-to-day life."

"They're identical," Karla observes. "Where did she find so many identical notebooks?"

"Who knows?" I hand Karla the flashlight so I can have a turn exploring the notebooks.

"Mason said his mum was an executive assistant," I comment. "I assumed she worked in an office, but here's a phone number for Mick Jagger's assistant and a note to send Stevie Nicks her recipe for seven-layer nacho dip."

"No wonder she catalogued her life," Karla says. "Does Mason know his mother mingled with musical royalty?"

"I don't know." I shrug. "He's never mentioned it or name-dropped." I slot a notebook in the box.

"And there are gaps," Karla points out. "It took about three months to fill each notebook, but some are missing. Where are they?"

"Maybe she wasn't always diligent about maintaining them," I suggest. "Or maybe she lost a few, or Mason has them?"

"Maybe," Karla concedes.

After our unauthorized intrusion into Mason's mum's fascinating life, we move along to the next pile of boxes.

"I bet Mason discovered the notebooks after his mum died," I speculate. "Maybe that's why we've seen him bringing notebooks to and from the basement. Maybe he's using them to learn about his mother's life before he was born."

"Shall we bother with this one?" Karla asks, pointing the flashlight at a pile of nearby boxes with *For the Dump* scrawled across the lid in Mason's mum's handwriting.

"May as well," I say.

We switch again; I hold the flashlight steady while Karla explores the contents of the *For the Dump* box.

"Old kitchen linens," Karla announces, lifting folded tablecloths out of the box. "More notebooks!" She picks up a blue floral notebook and skims through the pages. "This one is full of poetry." She slides the notebook back where she found it. "This one is a missing notebook from the other box," she says. "Why would Mason's mum selectively discard certain notebooks?"

"I don't know," I say.

"It's full of references to CF," Karla says. "A schedule of studio times for CF. Notes from meetings between CF and other people. CF's itinerary for a trip to New York. A note to send Christmas gifts to CF's parents."

"CF must have been her boss," I venture a guess.

Karla picks up another notebook.

"More poetry," she says, flipping through the pages. "Hold up." She pauses and takes the flashlight from me. "Read this." She lays the open notebook on a nearby box and aims the light at the handwritten words. "Familiar?"

"The lyrics to one of Melody's hit songs," I say, bopping from side-to-side as I read the handwritten lyrics but hear Melody's voice singing them in my head. "Weird."

I flip through several pages until I come across more familiar lyrics.

"Why did Mason's mum handwrite song lyrics in her notebooks?" Karla asks.

"Maybe she was a fan?" I shrug one shoulder. "Before Mason was born, she lived in LA and worked in the music industry."

"CF," Karla says.

I aim the flashlight at the ceiling and place it on the box next to us, like a lamp.

"CF," I repeat.

Our eyes widen at the same time.

"CF," we shout at each other. "Clarence Fawkes!" we declare in stereo.

"Mason's mum worked for Clarence Fawkes," I deduce. "She discarded the notebooks that mentioned him so Mason wouldn't find out. Her illness progressed quickly near the end. She must have become too sick to throw away these boxes before she died."

Karla glances at the pile of boxes under the box we're nosing through. "Do you think all the *For the Dump* boxes contain notes from working with Fawkes?"

"I don't know," I admit. "Judging by the dates, she worked for Fawkes a decade before his scandal broke."

"Maybe she quit because she knew he was a creepy predator," Karla suggests. "She could have made notes about his behaviour or times and dates that confirm his crimes." She removes the lid from the next box. "There's no turning back now."

"Shoe boxes," I say, opening one. "Photos."

I pull out a handful of photos.

Karla does the same.

We hover around the flashlight beam and go through them.

"Is it me, or is the flashlight getting dimmer?" Karla asks.

I pick up the flashlight, turn it off, shake it, and turn it on again. It's brighter.

"Better?" I ask.

"For now," she says.

I flip through the photos until I come across a familiar photo of a young boy holding a fish he'd just caught. His toothless grin is full of pride. He's standing on a dock. I've seen this photo before. I hold it up where Karla can see it.

"Why is there a photo of Chelle's godson in Mason's

late mum's belongings?" Karla asks, confirming my suspicion.

"*Mason, age eight. First time reeling in all by himself,*" I say, reading the handwritten note on the back.

Karla snatches the photo from my hand and turns it over.

"This is Mason's mum's handwriting."

I nod in agreement.

"Chelle told me her godson is fifteen years old now. She said he was seven years old in this photo."

"She lied," I state matter-of-factly. "It's what she does."

"Mason, the pool boy, is Chelle Temple's godson?"

I glance down at the pile of photos in my hand. The next one is a photo of young Mason with two women. He's about five years old. I'm drawn to the bright orange updo on the woman next to him. I'd recognize that shade of orange anywhere.

I hold up the photo where Karla can see it.

"Chelle!" she confirms.

"*Mason, aged six, with me and Aunt Chelle.*" I overemphasize the word *aunt.*

"Whose aunt?" Karla asks.

"Chelle and Mason's mum were around the same age," I point out. "Chelle is too young to be Mason's great aunt."

"Maybe aunt is an honorary title," Karla theorizes. "I call my mum's best friend auntie. She's not my real aunt, but she's like my aunt."

"Or," I suggest, "Chelle is Mason's biological aunt."

"Let's keep searching."

I use my phone to take photos of the information we've found so far, then we finish going through the photos, and open the next shoe box.

Karla checks the time on her phone.

It's easy to lose track of time in a windowless dungeon.

She holds her phone above her head. Then toward the stairs.

"There's no signal down here," I remind her. "Something about the age of the building and the concrete."

"It's gets eerier down here by the second."

I nod in sympathy.

"Letters," Karla says, picking up a pile of folded papers and envelopes.

"Handwritten," I say, plucking a remaining letter from the box.

Aside from occasional letters from friends, postcards from exotic locales, and old birthday cards, this box is full of letters to Mason's mum from Clarence Fawkes and his sister, Chelle.

The letters that predate Mason's birth are love letters. Fawkes's poetic declarations of his undying love for Mason's mum. There are several letters where he asks her to reconsider his marriage proposal. I wonder if she felt the same about him? I wish we had the letters Mason's mum wrote to Fawkes.

Several handwritten letters later, there is no doubt about it: Mason Shilling is Clarence Fawkes's son. He references her pregnancy several times and begs her to stay in LA to have the baby.

"Imagine finding out your father is an infamous predatory misogynist," Karla mumbles.

"I don't think Mason knows," I say. "The other day, he told Eric and me his dad was a drummer from Australia. He said his dad died in a car accident before he was born."

"According to these letters, that's what his mum wanted him to believe," Karla says. "In the letters following Mason's birth, Fawkes promises to respect her wishes and keep Mason's paternity a secret."

"Chelle knows too," I say, holding up a letter as proof. "She praises Mason's mum for leaving LA and coming home to raise him. As far as Mason knows, Chelle and his mum are old school friends."

"Mason has a right to know the truth," Karla says. "He's entitled to Fawkes's future royalty payments."

"Chelle and her parents have already committed to donating Fawkes's royalties to benefit his victims."

"But if Mason is Fawkes's son, he's entitled to have an opinion," Karla argues.

"What a horrible legacy to inherit."

"Fawkes wrote to her for years," Karla observes. "He wrote to her from prison every week. Do you think she wrote back?"

"I don't know," I shake my head. "She received the last letter a few weeks before she died," I say. "Around the time she went into hospice, and they released Fawkes on parole."

The handwritten letters continue despite the age of email. I suppose Fawkes wasn't given the option to use email or text from prison, but Chelle could have. Although technology might have made their communications more susceptible to being discovered or intercepted.

"In this letter from Fawkes"—I hold up the letter—"he reminded Mason's mum that the lyrics he dictated to her when she was his assistant might be worth a lot of money someday. He advised her to store them somewhere safe, sell them should the opportunity arise, and give the money to Mason."

This explains why Mason's mum had Melody's handwritten lyrics in her notebooks. Her boss dictated them to her.

"According to this letter, Chelle transferred money

into Mason's mum's bank account every month to contribute to Mason's upbringing. It was a small amount, but all the family could afford, especially after the scandal ended Fawkes's career, and his income dried up." Karla flips the letter over. "There's no doubt this is Chelle's handwriting."

She holds up another letter. "Chelle and her parents appreciated the regular photos and updates Mason's mum sent to them." She produces another pile of letters. "In the last letter, just before Mason's mum died, she reiterates her support for the decision to keep his paternity a secret. Chelle assures Mason's mum that she'll protect Mason from the truth, no matter what."

No matter what.

A shiver runs up my spine.

Considering Fawkes's murder, Chelle's *no matter what* is ominous and kind of threatening. No matter what she must do? No matter what Fawkes wants? No matter what the consequences could be?

"Remember when Chelle told us she saw a Harmony Lake van at the four-way stop near The Fawkes Den?" I ask.

"I remember," Karla confirms. "Then she got confused and backtracked about everything."

"She backtracked when I mentioned Mason," I remind her. "She asked who Mason was, then got flustered and forgetful."

"Oh my—" Karla brings her hand to her mouth, muffling the last word. Panic fills her eyes. "She killed him. Megan, Chelle killed her brother."

"We don't know for sure," I say, trying to temper Karla's rising certainty.

"Think about it," Karla says. "Mason's mum was the driving force behind keeping her son's paternity a secret. Then she died, and Fawkes got released. There was nothing stopping him from contacting Mason and telling him he was Mason's father. Chelle promised to protect Mason from the truth. *No matter what.* She killed her brother to protect her nephew from discovering the truth."

"If she got caught, the truth would come out," I add. "That's why she tried to frame you for the murder. She was desperate."

"Killing her brother also solved her cash flow problems," Karla reminds me. "Without Fawkes around, Chelle can sell the cottage and use the money to help care for her parents and proceed with her plan to donate the future royalties."

"It makes sense," I agree.

"Chelle killed a lot of birds with one stone," Karla nods, grinning with pride at her deductive prowess.

Darkness.

Silence.

We gasp and reach for each other.

# CHAPTER 30

Just when I think the dungeon can't get creepier, we're plunged into a windowless, chilly darkness and silence when the batteries die in the flashlight.

Clinging to each other across an open box, we turn on the flashlights on our cell phones. We light each other up and make sure we're OK.

We're fine. Freaked out and scared but fine.

The flashlights on our phones aren't strong enough to illuminate our snooping mission.

"I'm going to the store to buy batteries and a light bulb. I'll also text Eric and tell him about the evidence we found against Chelle," I say. "You can come or stay here. It's up to you."

"I'll stay," Karla decides. "There are still a lot of unopened boxes. I'll use the flashlight on my phone and keep working until you get back."

"How's your phone battery?" I ask.

"Almost full," Karla says. And I have a portable charger in my purse if I need it."

"OK."

It's after 8 p.m. on a Tuesday night. Tourist season came to a screeching halt yesterday when the last tourists made a Labour Day mass exodus back to their normal lives. Most of the businesses on Water Street are closed.

I power walk toward the local pharmacy. The Pharmer's Market is open until midnight, seven days a week. They'll have light bulbs and batteries. Before I left, I removed the batteries from the flashlight and brought one, to be sure I'd get the right size.

As I walk, I unlock my phone and text Eric.

**Me: Call me. Urgent.**

At The Pharmer's market, I learn they don't carry the type of lightbulb the dungeon requires, but I find the batteries, grab more than I need—just in case—and join the line of customers waiting to complete their purchases.

Why hasn't Eric called me? He always calls seconds after I ask. I'm rearranging my armload of batteries so I can unlock my phone when someone taps my shoulder. Startled, I flinch.

"Didn't mean to scare you," Mason says.

"I was distracted," I say, smiling and noticing the latest issues of Motor Trend Magazine and Hot Rod in his hand. "I thought your generation prefers digital magazines," I tease.

"I prefer old-fashioned paper and ink," he says, chuckling. "I get it from my mother. She hated the digital revolution. She put pen to paper until she was too weak to write and insisted on reading paperback books and actual newspapers instead of the digital options. Mum even exchanged letters with her pen pals until just before she died."

"You don't say." I nod and try to hide how freaked

out I am by Mason's disclosure about his mum and the eerie timing.

"You OK, Megan?" Mason asks. "You seem jumpy."

"I'm fine," I insist with nervous laughter. "Too much caffeine. I treated myself to a late-day coffee. I guess I'll never learn." More nervous laughter.

I'm such a horrible liar. My heart is pounding, and I'm overheating. I stick out my bottom lip and blow, hoping to hide the beads of anxious perspiration on my upper lip and forehead.

"That's a lot of batteries you have there." He nods at the multipacks of batteries in my arms.

"Not really," I say, trying to sound calm and casual. "They're just big, so it looks like a lot."

Worst logic ever, but improvisation is hard when I'm nervous and overcome with guilt about rummaging through Mason's family secrets.

"What are they for?" he asks. "Most household items don't use batteries that size."

"They aren't for household use," I confirm. "They're for the store. I got a new ball winder, but it didn't come with batteries."

Huge lie. Electric ball winders plug into the wall. And the batteries I'm purchasing are almost as big as an actual ball winder. Hopefully, Mason doesn't know enough about electronic knitting accessories to catch my lie.

"They never include batteries," he laments. "You must be eager to try it if you're buying batteries this late, at the pharmacy. You'd save a few bucks if you bought them tomorrow at Hammer Time."

He picks up a long-barrelled barbecue lighter from the impulse-purchase display near the cash register.

"You're right," I blurt. "Eric's working late, and I had nothing else to do tonight, so..."

"Next!" calls the cashier.

Thank goodness! I'm next in line and ready to escape from this uncomfortable conversation. I've never told so many lies in a row. The anxiety is awful. How does Chelle do it?

"Megan," Mason calls as I walk toward the cashier. "I found a storage unit for my mum's stuff. I'll move the boxes out of your basement by the end of the week."

"OK," I say, smiling. "But there's no hurry."

"I know, but Adam says I should move them somewhere that only I have a key."

"Oh?"

"Next!" calls the cashier again, louder.

I don't have time to ask Mason why Adam cares where he stores his mother's boxes. Spilling my batteries onto the counter, I make a mental note to follow up with Mason or Adam later.

On the sidewalk outside The Pharmer's Market, I assume I must have somehow set my phone to silent and missed Eric's call. I unlock my screen, expecting to see a missed call from him. No missed call. I open our text thread. *Ugh!* I didn't hit send on the text. I hit send and keep my phone handy.

Trevor's Camaro drives past me and pulls into a spot in front of Knitorious. I pick up my pace until my phone rings.

"Hello?"

"What's up, babe? Are you OK?"

I tell Eric about the evidence Karla and I discovered that implicates Chelle in Fawkes's murder.

"Can you keep her in custody? I can send you photos of everything we found."

"It's too late," Eric says. "Chelle and her lawyer left the station half an hour ago. Adam is here. He was just telling me that Mason intends to sue Fawkes's estate."

"What?!" I stop dead in my tracks and drop the bag of batteries.

Eric puts me on speakerphone, and Adam confirms Mason intends to sue Fawkes's estate.

"Why?" I ask.

Adam gives me a brief, undetailed explanation.

"Plagiarism?" I ask, stunned. "Mason is accusing Fawkes of plagiarizing him?"

I pick up the bag of batteries and resume walking, albeit slowly, as Adam explains how Mason found hand-written song lyrics in his mother's notebooks. His mother was a bit of a poet, and Mason believes Fawkes used her poetry as inspiration for the lyrics to dozens of hit songs for which he took credit for writing and received royalty payments.

"Adam, there might be another explanation."

"It gets better, Meg," Adam continues. "Fawkes's family made regular monthly payments to Mason's mum for years. It turns out Mason's mum worked as Fawkes's assistant during his heyday. Mason's lawsuit will allege that the monthly payments were hush money for his mum not exposing Fawkes's plagiarism. Why else would Fawkes send her money every month?"

"I can think of at least one other explanation," I say, then tell them about the evidence Karla and I found that Clarence Fawkes was Mason's father.

"I've seen Mason's birth certificate, Meg," Adam says. "It does not list Clarence Fawkes as the father."

"Because she didn't want Mason to know," I say. "Mason's mother wouldn't be the first woman to leave the father's name blank or give someone else credit on her baby's birth certificate."

My argument is met with silence. I stand still, waiting for Adam to tell me I'm wrong.

Chelle Temple's four-door hatchback rolls past slowly. We make eye contact, and she speeds away.

"I'll look into it," Adam says. "Leave it with me."

"Chelle just drove past me," I say.

"Are you sure?" Eric asks. "Where are you?"

"Yes, I'm sure," I reply. "I'm on Water Street. Halfway between Knitorious and The Pharmer's Market."

"Is Karla with you?"

"No, she's at Knitorious. I left to get batteries."

"Listen to me, babe," Eric says. "Go to Knitorious. Lock the door. Stay with Karla until a patrol car locates Chelle and picks her up."

"Got it," I say.

"We'll stay on the phone with you until you're inside the store."

I increase my pace.

Approaching Knitorious, Dorian Gray is out front. I peer inside. Empty. Where are Trevor and Mel? I scan the immediate area. The streets are empty. Where did Chelle go and why was she cruising around Harmony Lake?

INSIDE KNITORIOUS, I lock the door.

Eric says he'll phone when Chelle is in police custody.

"There's no service in the dungeon," I remind him. "I won't get your call."

"Stay out of the dungeon," he instructs. "Get Karla and bring her upstairs. Stay together where it's well lit and your phones work."

We end our call and I rush to the dungeon as fast as one can down steep, dark, concrete stairs, guided by the glow of a cell phone, while carrying a bag of batteries.

"What took you so long?" Karla demands. "I was starting to worry."

"Chelle had already left the station when I called Eric," I say. "She drove past me a few minutes ago. She slowed down and stared at me."

"A threatening stare?" Karla asks.

"No." I shake my head. "More like a hesitant stare."

"She's worried that we've figured out she's a murderer."

"It was like she wanted to say something but changed her mind," I explain. "I told Eric we would wait upstairs where there's a phone signal and electricity until she's in police custody."

"OK," Karla agrees. "Let's put everything back where we found it." She pans her cell phone flashlight across the boxes and papers strewn about.

As I fumble with the blister packaging on the batteries, I tell Karla about Mason's plagiarism allegations against Fawkes and his plan to sue the estate.

"But it wasn't plagiarism!" she insists, training her flashlight on my hands while I try to insert the batteries into the larger, more useful flashlight. "The letters and notebooks don't mention plagiarism. She was taking notes for her boss."

"That's what I said," I agree. "I told them our theory about Fawkes being Mason's biological father and offered to send proof."

I close the battery compartment and switch on the flashlight. Nothing.

"*Grrr!*" I let out a frustrated groan and scold myself for removing the old batteries without noting how to insert them.

I remove the batteries and squint at the crude diagram that illustrates how to insert them, while cursing the battery industry's lack of a worldwide standard configuration for the stupid things.

I re-insert the four large batteries and close the battery compartment.

*Thud!*

We freeze.

"Did you hear that?" Karla whispers.

I nod. "What was it?" I hiss.

*Thud!*

We lock eyes in silent acknowledgement of the second thud.

It's coming from the stairs.

Silence, except for my heart pounding in my ears.

"A rat?" Karla whispers.

"No," I hiss. "We don't have rats!"

Please don't be a rat. Please don't be a rat. Please don't be a rat.

I'd hate to meet the rat large enough to make that thud.

*Thud!*

Karla redirects her phone toward the sound, leaving us in the dark.

"Why are you here?" Karla asks the intruder. "Who let you in?"

She shoves me backward, farther into the darkness, and points her flashlight at the intruder's face.

# CHAPTER 31

THE INTRUDER RAISES their hand to shield their eyes from the harsh brightness of Karla's cell phone flashlight.

"I have a key." Mason holds up the key he stole from my laundry room when he fixed our leaky washing machine, and I recall telling him about my rack of spare keys and where I keep them. "Why are you here?" he asks, squinting against the beam of light and scanning the darkness. "Where's Megan?"

"She went somewhere," Karla lies. "I snuck down here when she left. She doesn't know I'm snooping."

"Through my mother's things?"

"I suspect your mother and Clarence Fawkes shared a connection," Karla explains, cool as a cucumber. "I'm looking for proof. It could lead to a clue about his murder."

"They were connected," Mason confirms, nodding. "Fawkes killed my mother."

I bite my lip to stop myself from yelling, *WHAT!?*

"Megan said your mother died after a long illness."

"Fawkes caused my mother's illness," Mason alleges. "She got sick because of the stress *he* caused."

"Help me understand," Karla says, empathy oozing from every word. "Tell me what he did to her."

"My dad died before I was born," Mason begins. "She left her job and moved back home so we would be near family. My mother's family isn't wealthy. They did the best they could to help us, but my mother worked multiple jobs to support us. Hard jobs. Physical labour. She was always stressed about money and worried about paying the bills."

"I'm sorry you and your mother struggled," Karla says. "Your mother was a strong, determined woman."

"She was," Mason agrees. "But a person can only tolerate so much physical and mental stress before it affects their health. The stress won, and my mother got sick. She was sick for a long time before she died."

"I'm sorry you had to watch your mother's health deteriorate. It must have been awful." Karla tilts her head in sympathy. Her voice has a new, comforting, maternal quality. "But I don't understand how it was Clarence Fawkes's fault."

"Fawkes stole my mother's poetry and turned it into lyrics for his hit songs," Mason claims. "If he had given her proper credit, she would have earned royalties from those songs. Our life would have been very different. Mum wouldn't have had to work so hard. She would have worried less. She wouldn't have gotten sick, and she would still be here."

Oh, Mason! You poor, tormented, grief-stricken man. My heart aches for him. If I weren't hiding in the shadows, I'd give him a hug.

"You believe your mother wrote Fawkes's lyrics?"

"I *know* she did," Mason asserts. "I have proof. She wrote the lyrics in her notebooks, long before the songs were number-one hits."

Despite his mum's diligence about removing the notebooks that mention Clarence Fawkes and his music from her catalogue of notebooks, Mason's mum must have left a few in the wrong box.

"I understand your anger, Mason. Better than you think," Karla says. "But all the money in the world might not have spared your mother from her illness."

"How would you know?" Mason demands.

"I've spent my life building a successful business and chasing the almighty dollar," Karla admits. "I have lots of money, but it won't keep my sick grandmother on this earth a moment longer than her illness allows, and it didn't erase my bad childhood memories."

"It could have made her life easier while she was here," Mason comments.

He's right, except Fawkes did not plagiarize her.

"Wait." Karla holds up her index finger, then rummages through the photos piled on a nearby box. "Do you know this woman?"

Keeping her distance, she shows Mason the photo of him, his mum, and Chelle.

"That's my Aunt Chelle," he says. "She's not my real aunt. She was a friend of my mum's. Our families had cottages on Harmony Lake. We used to visit each other when I was little."

"When did you last visit Aunt Chelle?" Karla asks.

"Aunt Chelle and I talk on the phone all the time. It devastated her not to be able to come to mum's funeral."

"When did you last see her in person?"

Mason shrugs and shakes his head. "Years ago," he admits. "Aunt Chelle and her family moved overseas when I was ten. I haven't seen her since."

Aunt Chelle's pretend move coincides with Clarence Fawkes's sexual misconduct scandal. It can't be a coincidence. Chelle probably fabricated the move to protect Mason and not lead the press to him.

"Aunt Chelle's full name is Michelle Fawkes," Karla tells him. "She's Clarence Fawkes's sister."

"Lie!" Mason's shout reverberates off the concrete dungeon walls. "Why would you say that?"

I recoil in the darkness, clutching the large flashlight to my chest like a security blanket.

"It's not a lie," Karla replies, her voice level and calm. "She also uses the name Chelle Temple, but she is Michelle Fawkes."

"You're nuts!" Mason booms. "Do you have an over-active imagination or something? You think you're a good sleuth, like Megan, but you're wrong!"

We stand in silence while Mason composes himself, and Karla rifles through piles of handwritten letters.

What should I do? Should I show myself? Stay hidden in the shadows and let Karla continue this conversation by herself? She knows I'm here—she pushed me here. I need to trust her and trust that, if she needs my help, she'll let me know.

"Mason, read these." Karla steps forward and sets a few letters on the concrete floor. "They prove Aunt Chelle was more than your mother's friend."

She illuminates the letters with her cell phone as she backs away from them.

I wish I could call for help! I feel so useless. *Heavy shoulders, long arms.* I take a couple of deep breaths. *Think, Megan! Think!*

Mason steps forward and picks up the letters. He uses the flashlight on his cell phone to read them.

Mason's cell phone gives me an idea. The dungeon might be a dead zone for cell service, but lots of features on my phone don't need cell service or an internet connection. Like the voice record feature.

I turn away from Mason and Karla, then I slide the silencing button, so the phone won't make any sounds. I squat and using my body, hands, and shirt to shield the glow of my phone, I unlock the screen, open the voice memo app, start recording, and lock the screen. I don't use the voice memo feature enough to know if the app will record with a locked screen, but I hope for the best, and, without making a sound, set the phone on top of a nearby box.

The more he reads, the more Mason's hands tremble and the redder his face gets. The muscles around his eyes and mouth tighten and tense until they twitch.

Mason Shilling is coming unhinged.

"He was telling the truth," Mason mutters through clenched teeth as he turns off the flashlight on his phone and slips it into the front pocket of his baggy, faded jeans. "I thought he was lying to save himself."

"Who was telling the truth?" Karla asks. "Did Clarence Fawkes tell you he was your father?"

Mason's nod is so slight it's negligible.

"He knew my name, but we'd never met before," Mason says, staring into the darkness beyond Karla. "I thought that was strange."

"When did he know your name, Mason?" Karla asks, trying to keep him focussed.

"When I went to The Fawkes Den to confront him about stealing my mother's poems," he admits.

"Were you at The Fawkes Den the day Clarence Fawkes died?"

He nods, still staring into the darkness.

"Mason, did you kill Clarence Fawkes?" She asks.

He nods again.

# CHAPTER 32

I SWALLOW my gasp and force myself to remain in utter silence.

"A few weeks ago, I started reading my mum's notebooks," Mason recalls. "She always had a notebook with her. Every day she would start a fresh page with the day's date in the top right corner. She would make notes and lists and stuff throughout the day. I was only interested in her notebooks when I needed to find a phone number or remember a date." He looks at Karla. "I found out after she died that she'd kept them. All of them. Boxes of notebooks full of my mum's thoughts, and ideas, and reminders of the ordinary things that happened in our lives. Reading them helped me remember her. Sometimes, I could remember where we were and what we were doing when she wrote something. One time, she wrote the recipe for what she'd made for dinner, and I could smell it."

"That must have been comforting," Karla comments.

"It was," Mason agrees. "I came down here a few weeks ago to put away the notebook I'd just read and choose another one. It was from before I was born. It was full of notes about her job, to-do lists, stuff she had to do for her boss, and poetry." He grins. "My mum wrote poems sometimes. But these poems were different. I assumed she was experimenting with a different poetry style. One poem was familiar, but I couldn't place it, so I typed a verse into an internet search bar. It came back with the lyrics to a Clarence Fawkes song. I searched for another poem, then another. Every poem in the book was lyrics to a Clarence Fawkes song. But she wrote them long before they released the songs. He stole my mother's words. But how?" Mason glares at Karla as though he's waiting for her to respond.

"I don't know," she replies. "How did he steal her poetry?"

"She worked for him," Mason announces. "I re-read the notes between the poems. She kept referring to CF. *Pick up CF's dry cleaning. Confirm location for CF photo shoot. Book CF's hotel for Grammy awards.* It wasn't hard to figure out CF was Clarence Fawkes. If she worked for him, he would have had access to her notebooks and her poems."

"What did you do?" Karla probes.

"I wanted to confront him, but I wasn't sure how, and I didn't want anyone to find out," Mason replies. "I was afraid that if he called the police, I could get into trouble for talking to him. I did some research and found out he had a bunch of conditions and restrictions on his release. The police were watching him closely. I made a plan."

"A plan to kill Fawkes?" Karla asks.

"No," Mason replies. "A plan to confront him. But I knew I could kill him if necessary. He might have been old, but Clarence Fawkes was a dangerous man. I'd read the news articles and watched some of his victims' interviews. I had to be prepared in case my accusation made him snap."

"What was your plan?"

"First, I went to Hammer Time and scoped out their inventory. I made notes of items that were out of stock, and unlikely to be restocked soon. I purchased some white, half-inch, PEX pipe because they were out of blue. Then, I dug up an old receipt from The Tool Box in Harmony Hills. I chose The Tool Box because they email the receipt to you. Using photo manipulation software, I changed the details on the receipt so it would look like I'd bought one hundred feet of blue, half-inch PEX pipe on Tuesday, August 30th."

"Why Tuesday, August 30th?" Karla asks.

"Because that was the day of the pool's grand opening," Mason replies.

"You future-dated the receipt so you would have an alibi for the time that Fawkes died," Karla surmises.

"He wasn't supposed to die," Mason clarifies. "I future dated the receipt, so I would have an alibi for visiting him. In case he reported me to the police for harassing him or something."

"What happened on Tuesday, August 30th?" she asks.

"I went to work early to clean the new pool before the grand-opening ceremony. Everyone was busy getting ready for the event. No one noticed when I used a utility knife to slice open a piece of blue, half-inch PEX pipe near the library. Then I told a co-worker I was taking a break. I turned off my cell phone and drove to The Fawkes Den. I brought one of my mother's notebooks with me to show him proof I knew he was a fraud. I knocked on the door, then put on a pair of latex gloves so there would be no evidence I was there. Fawkes peered at me through a window. I didn't think he would open the door, so I was walking back to my van, about to pull off the latex gloves, when I heard the cottage door open behind me. When I turned around, he was standing there in pajamas, slippers, and a bathrobe. His grey, frizzy hair was sticking out in every direction, and he was grinning like the Cheshire cat. I remember thinking, *Why are you grinning? What gives you the right to be happy after what you did?*"

"What happened next?" Karla urges.

"He said, 'Mason! I knew you'd find me sooner or later. Sorry it took so long to answer the door. I was running a bath and had to turn off the water.' How did he know my name? He invited me inside. I told him I knew about him and my mother. He said he always wanted to tell me, but my mother wouldn't let him, and he deferred to her judgement. I didn't understand. Why would he want me to know he plagiarized my mother's poetry? I told him I had proof and showed him a page in her notebook."

"What did he say when you showed him your proof?"

"He praised her handwriting and her dictation skills. He said she was the fastest dictation-taker of any assistant he ever had who didn't use shorthand." Mason shakes his head. "I was confused. Couldn't he see that I'd discovered his secret? That I knew he wrote his hit songs with someone else's words?"

He clenches his hands into fists. "He just stood there, grinning at me with this stupid, proud look on his face. What kind of person is proud of their plagiarism? Then Fawkes said, 'Ask me anything. I'm sure you have a lot of questions, son.' When he called me son, something inside me snapped. I dropped the notebook and lunged for him."

Mason shakes his fists, screwing up his face. "I grabbed him around the neck. He tried to pry my hands off, but he was too weak. He was gasping something. I couldn't tell what he was trying to say, so I let go of his neck and held him by the collar of his pajama shirt. I put my face right up to his and said, 'What are you trying to say, old man?'"

"Did he answer you?" Karla demands.

Mason nods and makes eye contact with her. "He said, 'Why are you doing this, Mason? I'm your father.'"

Karla covers her mouth.

"I didn't believe him," Mason admits. "I assumed he made it up so I would stop choking him. But he said the wrong thing. I was angrier than I've ever been in my life. From the corner of my eye, I saw the bubbles from his bubble bath cascading over the edge of the tub and I thought, *How dare you enjoy a bubble bath with your stupid grin when my mother died because of you.* I dragged him in there and held his head under the water. After a few seconds, I fisted his hair and pulled his face out of the water. I said, 'Who are you?'

"Fawkes gasped and replied, 'I'm your father.' I pushed his head under again. We did this three times. Three times I pulled his head out and asked him who he was. Three times, he said he was my father. I would have kept going until he admitted the truth—he was a liar and a thief." Mason shakes his head. "But the fourth time…"

"What happened the fourth time?" Karla asks.

Mason shakes his head, his eyes red and his body trembling.

"What happened the fourth time you pulled Fawkes's head out of the water?" Karla asks again, more insistent.

"He didn't answer me," Mason whispers, then shrugs one shoulder. "He was dead."

"How did you feel?"

"Terrified," replies Mason, swallowing hard. "I freaked out. I'd never killed anyone. I wanted him to die but not because of me. I caught my breath and stuck to my original plan."

"Original plan?"

"The plan I was already following," Mason clarifies. "I would proceed as though the confrontation didn't turn violent, and Fawkes was still alive. I ran out of that cottage as fast as I could. I was about to drive away when I remembered mum's notebook and ran back inside the cottage to find it. But the cottage was a mess, and I couldn't see it. I guess between lunging at Fawkes and dragging him to the bathtub, stuff got tossed around."

"Did you find the notebook?" Karla asks.

Mason shakes his head. "The more I searched and couldn't find it, the more I panicked. I tore apart the sofa, the chairs, I flipped the furniture to check underneath." He waggles his index finger. "You know that feeling when something is right in front of you, but you can't see it?" he asks.

"I know what you mean." Karla nods.

"I ran out of time and had to stop searching. Someone would discover the leak any minute, and half the town would look for me. I had to leave without the notebook. As I drove to Knitorious, I devised a plan to come back for the notebook later."

"Why did you come to Knitorious?" Karla asks. "Why not go back to work?"

"Everyone in town knows all the local gossip and news finds its way to Knitorious first. News about the leak would get here before the water damage was too serious. Megan would know I was here, and I'd get to the library before the leak got out of control. I could use the dungeon as an excuse for not being reachable on my cell phone. Everyone would assume I was here the whole time unless someone asked Megan what time I arrived. Can you think of a better alibi witness than the police chief's wife?"

"No," Karla replies. "It was a good plan."

"Adam showed up looking for me. We rushed to the

library, and I turned off the water. I told Adam I needed to buy a part to fix the leak. On my way out of the building, I pulled the fire alarm and activated the sprinkler system. I knew everyone would have to evacuate until the fire department checked the building. I thought it might buy me more time."

"Is this when you returned to The Fawkes Den?" Karla asks.

"Yes," Mason nods. "I was about to turn into the driveway, but a car was leaving. I panicked, and sped away, did a u-turn, and came back."

"The car leaving The Fawkes Den was Chelle Temple," Karla says. "What happened when you went back?"

"I couldn't believe the mess I'd made searching for the notebook earlier. It was like searching for a needle in a haystack. A creepy haystack because, out of the corner of my eye, Fawkes's dead body was bent over the bathtub. I wasn't sure if the person I saw leaving The Fawkes Den had seen Fawkes's body and called the police. I couldn't waste time searching for the notebook. But I knew if the police found Fawkes's body there, they would find the notebook and link it to me. So, I moved Fawkes and hoped to come back for the notebook later."

"You moved him in the van?" Karla clarifies. "The Town of Harmony Lake van?"

Mason nods. "I drove back to work. I was going to leave Fawkes in the van and deal with him after the grand opening ceremony. When I got there, everyone was waiting for the fire department's permission to re-enter. I went inside and scoped out the situation." He laughs, a chilling, hollow laugh. "Finding out the firefighters cleared the pool area first was like winning the lottery. The new pool has an outside door. I moved Fawkes's body into the pool area without witnesses. I dumped him in the water and hoped everyone would assume he died there."

"Then what?"

"I went back to work like everything was normal," Mason states matter-of-factly. "I fixed the leak in the library, spoke to the firefighters, and started cleaning up the water. When everyone came back inside, they assumed I was fixing the leak and cleaning the whole time."

"Given the circumstances, and your mother's history with Fawkes, I'm sure the authorities will sympathize and give you the lowest charges possible," Karla says.

"The police won't find out," Mason retorts. "No one will. Do you think I want the world to know I'm Clarence Fawkes's son?"

"I won't tell a soul." Karla holds up her fingers like a boy scout. "I swear. No one will hear it from me."

"You're right," Mason agrees. "They won't."

I know a threat when I hear one. I also like to think I know a bluff when I hear one. Mason isn't bluffing.

"Why did you come here tonight?" Karla asks, shifting her weight and backing up.

"You and Megan were getting too close." He points at Karla and shakes his head. "The way you're always whispering and meeting at each other's houses. On Sunday, when you showed me the picture of the guy who drives the Camaro, I knew it was a matter of time. He saw me near The Fawkes Den after I killed Fawkes. That's why I asked about him. I figured he would look more guilty, and I would look innocent if I snitched on him before he snitched on me."

"How did you know we were here?"

"Didn't Megan tell you we ran into each other when she was buying batteries?"

"No," Karla lies. "I told you, Megan isn't here."

"She's here somewhere," Mason says. "I watched her come inside the store. I would've come with her, but she was on the phone with Eric."

What the fair isle?! Mason followed me? He's been spying on us?

"She left again," Karla maintains. "But she'll be back any second. You never know who might be with her."

"I'll take my chances."

"What about the upstairs tenants?" Karla asks. "Two strong young men live in the apartment above the store. I have a shockingly shrill scream. They'll hear me for sure."

"They aren't home," Mason counters.

"The police are on their way," she bluffs, backing toward me.

"How?" Mason asks. "Who called them? There's no cell service down here."

"What are you going to do?" Karla pleads.

Mason produces a barbecue lighter from his back pocket and pulls the trigger. The barbecue lighter I watched him pick up at The Pharmer's Market. He knew the batteries were for the flashlight. He planned this while he waited in line with me.

The dim, yellow glow of the single flame makes Mason's evil smirk more intimidating.

"I'm gonna start a fire," he says. "You and the evidence are gonna burn. I don't want to do this, but I don't have a choice, Karla." He grins. "At least my mother's paper hoard will come in handy."

Karla shuts off the flashlight on her phone, plunging us into total darkness.

Mason inches toward us, one hand holding the barbecue lighter and the other groping at the darkness in front of him. He squints into the void, the single useless flame guiding him.

Karla and I hold our breath each time he takes a step. We've backed ourselves against the wall. There's nowhere left for us to hide.

I take a deep breath and grip the flashlight with both hands.

"Get behind me," I whisper, stepping away from the wall.

Karla slips into the gap between me and the wall.

"Karlaaaaa?" Mason sings. "Where are youuuu?"

He steps forward.

"*Argh!*" He swings his arms like a windmill, and the lighter flies out of his hand into the darkness.

He walked into the cord for the light. He thinks it's a spiderweb.

"Run!" I yell at Karla as I lunge toward Mason.

I turn on the flashlight and aim it at his face as I run at him.

Thank goodness I got the battery configuration right this time!

Blinded by the sudden light and still fighting the cord, Mason flails harder and brings his hands to his face to shield his eyes.

Karla runs past him toward the stairs. She turns back.

"*Aaagh!*" she grunts as she hoofs the back of his knee.

Mason drops to one knee.

"Run," she shouts as she Tonya Hardings his other knee with her silver stiletto heel.

With both knees knocked out from under him, Mason kneels on the concrete, stunned and blinded by the focussed beam of light aimed at his eyes.

I nod at Karla.

She nods back.

I run toward Mason and butt him in the face with the handle of the flashlight, turn it off, and throw it into the darkness as I run to the stairs.

Upstairs, we slam the basement door and lean against it, catching our breath.

The back door swings open, and Eric rushes through. We jump aside and open the basement door for him. Followed by several uniformed officers carrying flashlights. Eric hurries down the concrete stairs.

# CHAPTER 33

MONDAY, September 25th

Rita and Connie sit at the top of Rita's driveway, in side-by-side lawn chairs, surveying their kingdom like two suburban queens perched on plastic thrones. They cross their legs in the same direction, lazily bouncing their feet in sync.

"Thank you for dyeing a batch of Christmas yarn for me," I say, stacking the plastic bins of yarn in my arms. "The Christmas rush started earlier than usual this year."

"I found comfort in the distraction," Rita says. "It helped keep my mind off the funeral." She shudders. "Oh, I hate funerals, and I hated this one more than usual."

"It was kind of you to attend," Connie says.

"Funerals are for the living, Connie, not the dead," Rita says.

"You're a good friend, Rita, even to people who don't deserve it."

The *people who don't deserve it* to whom Connie refers is Chelle Temple.

Despite Chelle lying about her name, stealing from

Karla, and trying to frame her for murder, Rita attended Clarence Fawkes's funeral last night. She went because she knew no one else would. She was adamant that Fawkes's parents should receive condolences from someone.

"He was their son," Rita reminded us when we asked if she was sure she wanted to attend. "They aren't grieving the loss of a horrible human being, they're grieving the loss of their baby boy, and the hopes and dreams they once had for him. They deserve to have their grief acknowledged."

Chelle invited all of us, but Rita was the only attendee. Well, Rita and Eric, but Eric attended out of professional duty.

Fawkes's funeral was held at an undisclosed location in the dead of night. The family couldn't find a funeral home willing to prepare his body or a cemetery willing to host his final resting place, even with an unmarked grave. They advised the family that a funeral might re-trigger the societal trauma Fawkes caused when he was alive, claiming some deaths were unmournable. They worried that even an unmarked grave would become a target of anger and hate, which they insisted wouldn't be fair to the families of the other residents trying to rest in peace.

So, Fawkes's family scattered his ashes at a secret location because a grave that doesn't exist can neither offend nor remind. To avoid being followed, the handful of family members who attended took a series of indirect routes to the location. They staggered their arrivals, parking far away from each other and the site so their midnight gathering wouldn't attract attention.

Eric was there to ensure the safety of the mourners if protestors discovered the secret plan and tried to disrupt the private service. He got home after 3 a.m., showered, and fell into bed. He's still asleep.

"Will you keep in touch with Chelle?" I ask.

"I don't think so," Rita replies, shaking her head. "I prefer the company of people I trust."

Chelle avoided charges for stealing from Karla. She returned Karla's stolen belongings with a written apology. Karla wanted to put the incident behind her. She told Eric she didn't want to pursue charges. The police found other people's stolen items at The Fawkes Den too. Chelle had been stealing for years from the families that employed her. She would sell their belongings to augment her income. I don't know if she'll face legal consequences for the other thefts.

I ran into Chelle Temple this morning. I was dropping off some misdelivered mail to Adam at his mayoral office and held the door for Chelle as she was leaving the Town Hall. She was carrying a box of personal belongings from Mason's desk. I didn't ask about her brother's funeral, but I asked how she's doing.

"I grieved the loss of my brother a long, long time ago, Megan," she said. "If not for my parents' longevity, I would never have claimed his body."

I suspect she's grieving the loss of her nephew most of all.

Mason's recorded confession was on my phone. It turns out the recording app works with a locked screen. According to Eric, Mason offered to cooperate with police and plead guilty to murdering Fawkes on one condition —that the identity of his biological father remain a secret. Since the documents that suggest Fawkes was Mason's father would be evidence at his murder trial, the condition is beyond Eric's bargaining power. It's up to the prosecutor and Mason's criminal defence attorney to negotiate.

Even if Mason tries to revoke his confession, Eric has

been busy gathering enough evidence to ensure a guilty verdict.

When Chelle drove past me on Water Street, she was following Mason and realized he was following me. She considered warning me but didn't think I would believe her, so she sped away and called Eric who was already on the phone with me. After I entered Knitorious and locked the door, Eric took Chelle's call.

She explained she was following Mason and admitted that she had followed him on occasion, since his mother's death, because she worried about him. Chelle told Eric that Mason was becoming unstable. She confessed to him she was Mason's aunt and Clarence Fawkes was his biological father. She told him Mason did not know his mother and Fawkes ever knew each other. In her last letter to Chelle, Mason's mum assured her that all evidence proving Fawkes was Mason's father was going to the dump that day. For whatever reason, the boxes didn't get to the dump and ended up in the dungeon instead.

Eric also spoke to Glenn Landry at Hammer Time. He confirmed Mason was the other customer who had been searching for PEX pipe two weeks before I came to his store. He gave Eric the receipt for the purchase Mason made that day: two metres of half-inch, white PEX pipe. Eric then went to the library and found the pipe that Mason fixed. He had replaced a blue section of pipe with the white pipe he purchased from Hammer Time, not the blue pipe he claimed to purchase from The Tool Box. In fact, The Tool Box had no receipt or security camera footage of Mason visiting their store on the date or time of the receipt he admitted he forged.

The police searched the van that Mason drove. They found Fawkes's hair and DNA in the back. Two cadaver dogs signalled they smelled decomp.

"I'm just going to put these bins of yarn in my trunk," I say, picking up the stacked bins.

"Wait!" Rita says, searching for something in the garage. "I made these for the charity project."

She hands me a reusable shopping bag, and I peek inside.

"Thank you, Rita!" I exclaim. "They're perfect." I rummage through the bag of knitted teddy bears, bunnies, and pigs. "These will bring comfort to a lot of kids."

"It's the least I could do," Rita says. "If I'm going to knit anyway, I may as well knit something useful. Your Charity Knitters quite impressed Karla. She said they're formidable women."

While Chelle was talking to Eric on the phone, she got distracted and lost sight of Mason. Lucky for Karla and me, the Charity Knitters never lose sight of anything or anyone.

One of their *members* was at The Pharmer's Market when I bought the batteries. She heard me tell Mason about the new ball winder that required a massive number of large batteries. Being a knitter, she knew it was a lie. She also noticed that I was jumpy, and Mason was following me. She alerted the other knitters. They took it upon themselves to spring into action. They dispatched nearby members to discreet locations and, using cell phones, kept each other apprised of his and my movements. When Chelle got distracted while talking to Eric, Mason slipped behind Knitorious and used the key he stole from my laundry room to unlock the back door.

Mrs. Roblin called Eric. She got his voicemail because he was on the phone with Chelle. She texted him, but he didn't reply, so she called the station. Unfortunately for the officer who answered the phone, Mrs. Roblin refused to take no for an answer when he told her he couldn't interrupt Eric's phone call.

Convinced it would be in his best interests, the officer interrupted Eric.

Mrs. Roblin told Eric to get to Knitorious and bring the cavalry with him. He listened.

A white pickup truck pulls up in front of Karla's empty house. Melody's voice blares from the truck's open windows.

Melody is everywhere. After years of unchosen obscurity, she's back with a vengeance. According to the news, Melody just signed a record deal with a big label, has a greatest hits album coming out soon, and she's planning a worldwide tour next year. Trevor is her manager now, and there are rumours he'll also manage other musicians who are making a comeback.

Since Fawkes's death and Chelle's plan to donate his royalties, many of his victims, and others who suffered because of their professional association with him, are seeing a resurgence in their careers and their incomes.

"It's hard to believe Karla doesn't live there anymore," Rita says with a sigh.

We watch in silence as the man removes the SOLD sign from Karla's old front lawn and tosses it on a pile of real estate signs in the back of his pickup truck.

"Have you met your new neighbours?" I ask.

"Not yet," Rita replies. "Karla said they're moving in on Friday."

"How is Karla doing?" Connie asks.

"She's halfway there," Rita replies. "She says Gucci loves road tripping." Rita looks at me and raises her sunglasses to her head. "Megan, Karla said to tell you she'll miss you as much as possible."

I laugh at the backhanded compliment and remember

telling her the same thing when I picked her up from the hospital after her head injury.

"Please tell her that each day I will miss her more than the next."

I've learned that snark is Karla's love language, so for the sake of our friendship, I'm becoming fluent.

"Karla and Gucci are stopping at a hotel tonight. They'll arrive in Bellbrook tomorrow," Rita says. "She'll arrive in plenty of time for the funeral."

Karla's grandmother passed away on Friday. She took an unexpected turn for the worse last week. Her death was sudden but peaceful. It devastated Karla that she wasn't there, but she enjoyed several long video chats with her grandmother in the days before her death.

Karla continued with the move anyway since she had already made the arrangements, and she is the executor and sole beneficiary of her grandmother's small estate.

"If I'm not there to stop her, my mother will try to take the little money my grandmother had," Karla told me. "The only way I'll let that happen is over my dead body."

Rita sniffles and wipes her eyes behind her sunglasses.

"She'll be fine, Rita," Connie assures, giving Rita's hand a squeeze. "Karla is an independent, capable woman."

"That's what she wants us to believe," Rita says. "But underneath, she's sensitive and scared. Karla left that place for a reason. She wasn't happy there."

"It will be good for her to reconnect with her roots and make peace with her past," Connie advises.

In my experience, Connie is never wrong about anything.

"Karla is a different person now. She's a mature,

successful woman, not the young, idealistic teenager who left," I add. "Karla knows what she's doing."

"It's hard to face your past, especially when it's painful," Rita says. "What if Karla can't handle whatever is waiting for her in Bellbrook?"

If you ask me, Bellbrook should worry about whether they can handle Karla.

CLICK HERE to be notified when the next Knitorious Murder Mystery is available for preorder.

CLICK HERE to read an exclusive Murder, It Seams bonus scene.

## ALSO BY REAGAN DAVIS

Knitorious Murder Mysteries Books 1 - 3: A Knitorious Murder Mysteries Collection

Knitorious Murder Mysteries Books 4 - 6: A Knitorious Murder Mysteries Collection

Knitorious Murder Mysteries Books 7 - 9: A Knitorious Murder Mysteries Collection

Knitorious Murder Mysteries Books 10 - 12: A Knitorious Murder Mysteries Collection

Neighbourhood Swatch: A Knitorious Cozy Mystery Short Story

Click here to sign up for Reagan Davis' email list to be notified of new releases and special offers.

Follow Reagan Davis on Amazon

Follow Reagan Davis on Facebook, Bookbub, Goodreads, and Instagram

# ABOUT THE AUTHOR

Reagan Davis is a pen name for the real author who lives in the suburbs of Toronto with her husband, two kids, and a menagerie of pets.

When she's not planning the perfect murder, she enjoys knitting, reading, eating too much chocolate, and drinking too much Diet Coke.

The author is an established knitwear designer who has contributed to many knitting books and magazines. I'd tell you her real name, but then I'd have to kill you. (Just kidding! Sort of.)

http://www.ReaganDavis.com/